Praise for
FALL; OR, DODGE IN HELL

"A one-of-a-kind synthesis of daring and originality, unafraid to venture into wild and unmapped conceptual territory."
—*The New York Times Book Review*

"Stephenson isn't just playing with words, he's playing with ideas, and he isn't joking either. He is sci-fi's great contrarian, and *Fall* deserves to be rated as one of the great novels of our time, prophetically and philosophically."
—*Wall Street Journal*

"Stephenson devotees with a taste for Tolkienesque fantasy will revel in the author's imaginative world building. . . . Still, there are enough futuristic, envelope-pushing ideas here, especially related to AI and digital consciousness, to keep even nonfans and science buffs intrigued."
—*Booklist* (starred review)

"*Fall* is at once science fiction and fantasy, with quantum computing enabling what amounts to magic, and while Stephenson spins out a pleasingly plausible vision of our near future, he carves out his most comfortable position in the uncertain nexus where that future becomes past and we rewrite our own apocrypha. Vintage Stephenson, which is to say it's like nothing he's ever written."
—*Wired*

"Those ready for an endlessly inventive and absorbing story are in for an adventure they won't soon forget. An audacious epic with more than enough heart to fill its many, many pages."
—*Kirkus Reviews* (starred review)

"A novel with genuine heft. It keeps you reading, it makes you think, and, by the end, it generates that sense of wonder that is the very lifeblood of science fiction and fantasy."
—*The Guardian*

"*Fall* is a stunning combination of science fiction and Tolkienesque epic fantasy. Neal Stephenson moves deftly between real and simulated worlds, following characters in both settings and the long-term consequences of their actions. *Fall* is biblical in theme and scope. At nearly 900 pages, Stephenson's bifurcated world is easy to get lost in."   —*Shelf Awareness*

"Neal Stephenson's *Fall* explores higher consciousness, the internet's future, and virtual worldbuilding in one mind-blowing adventure."   —Slate

"A rich and luxurious book."   —Vox

"Like Dodge, Stephenson is creating a new universe from scratch, fighting battles and wrestling with big ideas. Those of us in Meatspace can only sit mutely by and watch the spectacle in wonder.   —*Nature*

"Stephenson is not merely a fantasist of the future; he is a prophet of our present, a virtual architect of the ideas that define our world. . . a science fiction writer who is not only determined to entertain, but to make the world a better place—even if it means inventing that future himself."   —*Reason*

"[*Fall; or, Dodge in Hell*] will take the reader down the rabbit hole of technology to provide a mythological digital "Wonderland" that people are literally dying to see. It's pretty spooky, all the more so for being just close enough to reality to send a shiver down the spine."   —SeacoastOnline.com

FALL; OR, DODGE IN HELL

ALSO BY NEAL STEPHENSON

The Rise and Fall of D.O.D.O. (with Nicole Galland)

Seveneves

Some Remarks

Reamde

Anathem

The System of the World

The Confusion

Quicksilver

Cryptonomicon

The Diamond Age

Snow Crash

Zodiac

Neal Stephenson

FALL

or, Dodge in Hell

a novel

WILLIAM MORROW
An Imprint of HarperCollinsPublishers

FALL; OR, DODGE IN HELL. Copyright © 2019 by Neal Stephenson. All rights reserved. Printed in the United States of America. No part of this book may be used or reproduced in any manner whatsoever without written permission except in the case of brief quotations embodied in critical articles and reviews. For information, address HarperCollins Publishers, 195 Broadway, New York, NY 10007.

HarperCollins books may be purchased for educational, business, or sales promotional use. For information, please email the Special Markets Department at SPsales@harpercollins.com.

A hardcover edition of this book was published in 2019 by William Morrow, an imprint of HarperCollins Publishers.

FIRST WILLIAM MORROW PAPERBACK EDITION PUBLISHED 2020.

Designed by Fritz Metsch

Maps by Nick Springer/Springer Cartographics LLC

Title page and section opening art from Now Night Her Course Began by Gustave Doré (1832–33)/Central Saint Martins College of Art and Design/Bridgeman Images

Front cover seal from The New York Times. ©2019 The New York Times Company. All rights reserved. Used under license.

The Library of Congress has catalogued the hardcover edition of this book as follows:

Names: Stephenson, Neal, author.
Title: Fall; or, Dodge in hell : a novel / Neal Stephenson.
Description: First edition. | New York, NY : William Morrow, [2019]
Identifiers: LCCN 201900947| ISBN 9780062458711 (hardback) | ISBN 9780062458728 (paperback) | ISBN 9780062887467 (large print) | ISBN 9780062458735 (ebook)
Subjects: | BISAC: FICTION / Tecŷological. | FICTION / Action & Adventure. | GSAFD: Science fiction.
Classification: LCC PS3569.T3868 F35 2019 | DDC 813/.54—dc23 LC record available at https://lccn.loc.gov/2019002947

ISBN 978-0-06-245872-8 (pbk.)

20 21 22 23 24   LSC   10 9 8 7 6 5 4 3 2 1

to O. L.

B O O K   1

P A R T 1

1

odge became conscious. His phone was burbling on the bedside table. Without opening his eyes he found it with his hand, jerked it free of its charging cord, and drew it into bed with him. He tapped it once to invoke its snooze feature. It became silent. He rolled onto his side and slid the phone under his pillow so that, when the alarm resumed in nine minutes, he would be able to put it back into snooze mode with less trouble. It was a small miracle that his brain contained a sufficient 3-D model of his bed and its surroundings that he was able to do what he had just done without opening his eyes. But there was no reason to press his luck.

He felt no particular desire to go back to sleep, for he had been enduring a curiously boring dream whose central plot seemed to be the difficulty of finding coffee. In this dream, he was in the small town in Iowa where he had grown up. Its landscape and its cast of characters were commingled with places he had been and people he had encountered during the decades since he had left it in the rearview mirror of his pickup truck. But the grid street pattern of that town, covering just a few square blocks, and easily mastered by a boy on a bicycle, was, decades later, the spatial lattice on which virtually all of his dreams were constructed. It was the graph paper on which his mind seemed to need to plot things.

In the dream, he had set out to get some coffee, only to find himself thwarted at every turn by any number of incredibly prosaic obstacles. In the story-world of the dream, this was bizarrely frustrating; it was simply unreal how so many contingencies could get in the way of this simple task.

But from the point of view of the awake, or at least snoozing,

Dodge, it all had a clear explanation: it was, in fact, very difficult to obtain coffee while lying in bed with one's eyes closed.

During the next hour, he hit "snooze" several more times. In between, he slept. But it was a twilight sleep, semiconscious and mindful for a few minutes at a time, until his thoughts would lose coherence and stray into blurry wisps that were to real dreams as cobwebs are to spiderwebs.

He wondered whether the designers of the phone had performed clinical studies on snoozers in order to decide on the nine-minute interval. Why not eight minutes, or ten? The makers of the phone were famously particular about design. This had to have been data-driven. It was no coincidence that Dodge was being afforded just enough time to lose the thread of consciousness before the alarm went off again. If the interval had been much shorter, he would not have had time to drift off and so this feature could not have truly been called a snooze alarm. Much longer, and the snooze would have deepened into true sleep. He was able to maintain a rough count: *I have hit the snooze button three times. Five times. Enough times that I have overslept by about an hour.*

But no sense of guilt or urgency attended these makeshift calculations. He knew it didn't really matter, because during the interval of consciousness that had followed the third tap of the snooze button he had remembered that he was not expected in the office today. For he was scheduled to undergo a routine out-patient medical procedure at eleven in the morning, which was still hours away.

Other than the desire for coffee, the only thing that was making him feel any pressure to get out of bed was, curiously, a mild awareness that all of this extra sleeping was going to make it harder for him to have his afternoon nap. This happened every day at two or two thirty. He had been doing it religiously for about a decade. When he had taken up the practice, he had wondered if it was age related, since the oldsters in his family were known for nodding off in church pews, on porch swings, or even behind the wheel. But he could remember being eighteen years old, driving all over the western United States and Canada in various beat-up vehicles, and being overtaken every afternoon by a need for sleep so intense it was almost painful. He'd always tried to fight it off, or else simply avoided driving at that time of day. The only things that had really changed since then were that he was richer, so he could have a private office with a yoga mat and a pillow in the corner, and he was wiser, so he knew better than to fight the midafternoon lull. By closing the door, silencing his electronics, unrolling the mat, lying down, and letting sleep take him for twenty minutes, he was able to refresh himself to a degree that would then keep him working alertly for several hours more.

The amount of time spent asleep didn't really matter. He had decided that the key to it all—the one thing that determined whether the nap would actually refresh him—was the breaking of the thread of consciousness: that moment when he ceased to think in a coherent, sequential, self-aware way and went adrift. Often, this was connected with a jolt of an arm or a leg as he stepped over the threshold from conscious thinking into a dream where he was obliged to reach out and catch a ball or open a door or something. If the jolt didn't wake him up, then it meant he had snipped the thread of consciousness and that the nap had thereby achieved its only real purpose. Even if he woke up ten seconds later, he would be as refreshed—possibly more so—as if he'd slumbered deeply for an hour.

He had studied the jolt. On those increasingly rare occasions when he slept with a woman, he would sometimes will himself to stay awake as she fell into slumber, listening to her breathing and feeling her body go soft against his until, just at the moment when she drifted away, she would convulsively move a limb.

His business activities (he was the founder and chairman of a large video game company) sometimes involved flying in a private jet to the Isle of Man, eight time zones away, where a longtime business associate—an independently wealthy writer—dwelled in a renovated castle. The writer would put him up in a bedchamber in one of the towers: a round room decorated with medieval bric-a-brac and warmed by burning wood in a fireplace built into the wall. The bed was a four-poster with a heavy canopy. A couple of years ago, after climbing into that bed and lying there sleepless for a while, Richard—for that was Dodge's real name—had finally drifted off and fallen into a nightmare involving a very dangerous and unpleasant character he had tangled with some years earlier. He had awakened to the hallucinatory awareness that this man was standing next to his bed looking down at him. Which was impossible, since the man was dead—but Richard had been in a half-dreaming state where logic did not hold sway, and all he knew was what he saw. He tried to sit up. Nothing happened. He tried to raise his arms. They did not move even the tiniest amount. He tried to draw breath and scream, but his body did not respond to the command from his brain. He was perfectly helpless, lacking even a bound captive's power to struggle against his bonds. All he could do was experience the terror of it, and the horror of his complete lack of agency, until somehow he drowsed off again.

Moments later, he had awoken with a start, and sat up convulsively. His body worked again. He threw off the heavy duvet and swung his feet off the bed, turning to face the dying fire a few feet away. No one else was in the chamber. The massive fortress-style door was still bolted. The nightmare impression, which had been so convincing a minute ago, now seemed ridiculous. Lying back down experimentally, he looked up and saw that the lamp on his bedside table was casting a firelight shadow onto the canopy above him, and that the shadow moved about as the fire flickered and the logs settled. He must have half-opened his eyes while sleeping and interpreted this as the shadow of a man.

So the nightmare had an explanation. Still mysterious, though, was the absolute paralysis that had trapped him in that bad dream. Later, Richard had learned that this was a well-recognized and scientifically verified phenomenon known as sleep paralysis. Primitive cultures identified it as some form of enchantment, or made up stories about eldritch night-stalking creatures that would sit on your chest and pin you to your bed and suck the air from your lungs and the screams from your throat.

But there was a perfectly reasonable explanation for it. When you were awake, your brain could of course control your body. When you slept, however, you tended to dream. And in your dreams you could run, fight, and talk. But if the body continued to answer commands from the brain, you'd be thrashing all over the bed, vocalizing, and so on. So a mechanism had evolved whereby, at the moment that the thread of consciousness was severed, the link between brain and body was cut, like throwing a switch. And at the moment you woke up, the switch was thrown back to the "on" position and you went back to moving around as you always did. Normally the system worked with an amazing degree of perfection, so most people lived their whole lives not even knowing that it existed. But every system had glitches. The jolt you sometimes made while drifting off to sleep was one such—it happened when the switch was a fraction of a second late going off. Another, much more impressive and terrifying sort of glitch happened every so often, especially to people who—as in Richard's case on the Isle of Man—were sleeping off of their accustomed schedule. You would wake up, but the switch would not be thrown to "on" and so you would remain as perfectly paralyzed as you had been a moment ago while sound asleep. Just like a person who, while seeming to slumber and breathe peacefully, is in fact having a terrible nightmare, you would lie there with eyes open in perfect, inescapable repose, unable to do anything about the imaginary monster on your chest, the intruder next to your bed, the fire consuming your house.

In any case, the only lasting consequences for Dodge had been more desultory browsing about how sleep worked and further introspection about his own napping practices. This was how he had developed his theory—which was unsupported by any scientific evidence whatsoever—that the one and only key to a successful nap was to break the thread of consciousness just long enough for the switch to be thrown to "off." When it got thrown to "on" again, even if it was only a few minutes later, the brain–body system rebooted itself, like a fucked-up computer that just needs to be unplugged from the wall for ten seconds and restarted in order to come back to life in clean working order.

This notion around thread cutting was what finally brought him awake, since a connection had somehow been made in his mind, and now it was going to keep him awake. He had reached the point in his life where very few things could really compel him to get out of bed, but one of the calls to which he would readily answer was that of his own stray musings and thoughts, his mind's desire to make connections.

It did not, however, actually get him out of bed. Ringing in the ears did that. His tinnitus was especially annoying today—the world's way of telling him he needed to get up and make a little noise. He'd long suffered from a mild case, the result of too many guns fired and nails pounded in his youth, too many nights in British Columbia biker bars. Then, a few years ago, he had been exposed to a lot of close-up gunfire without appropriate hearing precautions. Without precautions of any kind whatsoever, for that matter. Ever since, he had rarely been without some amount of ringing in the ears—sometimes a high-pitched tone, sometimes a hiss. The cause of the condition was somewhat mysterious. It seemed to be some sort of well-meaning attempt by the brain to make sense of a loss of valid signals from ears that were no longer in perfect working order. Tending to confirm this idea was that it was at its worst when things were quiet; the environment wasn't giving his auditory system any good data to lock on to. The solution was to get up and make noise. Not necessarily a lot. Just the normal sounds of footsteps and faucet running that reassured his brain that there was a coherent world out there and gave it a few simple clues as to what was actually what.

He got up, pulled on pajama bottoms, urinated, took the pills he was supposed to take before breakfast, and went out to the so-called great room of his penthouse, which was on the top of a thirty-two-story building in downtown Seattle. It was a very expensive piece of real estate that, in the manner typical of Northwest tech industrialists, was built out and decorated in a manner so simple, bare-bones, and informal as to be actually kind of ostentatious. Glass doors made up much of its western exterior wall, and he had left these open all night, doubling the size of the living area by joining it to the terrace. The terrace had a glass roof with infrared heaters like the ones suspended above the cash registers at Home Depot to keep the Somalian and Filipino checkout clerks from succumbing to hypothermia. These made it comfortable even when it was fifty degrees Fahrenheit and raining, which was about half of the year. In late summer and (as now) early autumn, the heaters weren't needed, and so the terrace just served as an extension of the great room, which flowed into it without interruption. It faced toward Elliott Bay and the Olympic Mountains beyond.

Anomalous splashes of pink and purple flared against the wood, leather, and stone. Richard had a grandniece, Sophia, who for all intents and purposes was his granddaughter, and she came over frequently. Last weekend, her parents—Richard's niece Zula and her husband, Csongor—had left her with him for two nights so that they could enjoy a little getaway in Port Townsend, on the other side of Puget Sound. Richard's terrace had a direct view down onto the ferry terminal. He had a huge pair of Soviet military surplus binoculars mounted on a tripod at the railing. As their ferry had churned away from the terminal, Richard had perched Sophia on a stool and helped her get the lenses aimed down at the ferry, where Zula and Csongor, after parking their car belowdecks, had ascended to the topmost deck and stationed themselves at the stern to wave up at her. The whole affair had been coordinated via text message and had come off with the precision of a drone strike, all to the delight of little Sophia. Richard had been unaccountably depressed by it, or perhaps "ruminatively melancholy" was a better way of putting it.

Forty-eight hours of intensive grandniece/great-uncle bonding had ensued. In that short time Sophia's apparatus of modern kiddom had permeated Richard's apartment. Even if she never again set foot in this place, he would be finding Cheerios, glitter, sticky handprints, and barrettes for the next twenty years.

Sunday evening they had done the thing with the binoculars again as the parents had steamed back into port. Zula had explained what a good thing it was psychologically for a kid Sophia's age to see the parents go away, but then to see them come back again. During the stress of executing their withdrawal, they had left behind a Whole Foods grocery sack containing several of Sophia's books. Richard had placed it by the door so that it would be more difficult to overlook next time. But while his coffee machine was processing he retrieved it. He took it and his coffee to the low table on the terrace and pulled out two large-format picture books, which he had bought for Sophia on Saturday. Both of them featured the same style of colorful faux-naive artwork, for they were both by the same coauthors, Ingri and Edgar Parin d'Aulaire. One was entitled *D'Aulaires' Book of Greek Myths* and the other *D'Aulaires' Book of Norse Myths*. Richard had picked them up on impulse while he and Sophia had been hanging out in a bookstore. The cover art on *Greek*, perceived dimly in his peripheral vision, had jumped down his optic nerve to his brain and caused his body to freeze up almost as when he'd experienced sleep paralysis on the Isle of Man. Or, considering the context, as if he had beheld a Gorgon (and come to think of it, might it not be the case that ancient myths concerning Gorgons and basilisks were pre-scientific explanations of the phenomenon of sleep paralysis?).

The d'Aulaire books had been new when Richard had been young. He had worn out his boyhood copy, paging through it again and again, memorizing the lineages of the Titans, the gods, and whatnot, but mostly just staring at the pictures, letting them invade and shape his brain. In their general style they had a lot in common with little-kid art, which was probably what made them glom on to kid neurons like herpes. And like herpes, those pictures had remained silent and dormant in his central nervous system until adulthood. This had been triggered and made virulent by his having spied them in an unguarded moment. In the bookstore last weekend, he had approached the display like an ancient Hellene ascending the steps to the Temple of Zeus, and beheld the book, just like he remembered it, but brand new and unworn, with a new preface written by a famous modern novelist who had apparently had what Richard had had in the way of an infatuation with these books. Sophia, dragged along the whole way as she had been hugging his thigh and using his trouser leg as a handkerchief, had sensed something of the numinous in her uncle's reaction; she had looked up and been infected. Richard had bought *Greek* and its companion volume *Norse* and taken Sophia back to the penthouse for a day's total immersion, then handed her back to her parents an obsessed changeling, jabbering about Hydra remediation tactics and the house-sized mittens of Utgardsloki, reprimanding her elders for mixing up the Greek and Roman names of the gods. Great had been the wrath of Sophia when it had been discovered that the books had been left behind in the Whole Foods sack. Wide-famed would be Uncle Richard's deed this afternoon when, following his outpatient procedure, he would swing by the young family's condo with a d'Aulaire under each arm.

In the meantime, he needed to settle one small point of mythological confusion, lest Sophia find out that he was not perfectly clear on the matter, and take him to task. It had to do with Fates and Norns.

One of Richard's first acts upon picking up *Greek* in the bookstore had been to thumb to its index and look up "Furies." He had done so in a furtive, somewhat guilty frame of mind. A peculiarity of Richard's was that he lacked a conscience or superego in the normal senses of those terms. His was a soul lacking any built-in adult supervision. In the course of his life, however, he'd had ten or so girlfriends of consequence. All of those relationships had gradually gone sour as those girlfriends had got to know him more thoroughly and drawn up manifests of all that was wanting in Richard. Some of them had kept their opinions to themselves until a relationship-ending moment of cathartic outpouring. Others had registered frank objections in real time. But Richard remembered every word of it, decades after they had presumably forgotten about him. And more than that, his brain had somehow contrived fully autonomous simulacra of these ex-girlfriends, which lived on between his ears immortally, speaking to him at the strangest times, actually changing the way he thought and behaved; before firing an employee or overlooking someone's birthday he would pause to consider the consequences that would follow as one or more of the Furious Muses—as he called them—would coalesce from his brain vapors long enough to deliver a few choice remarks that would make him feel bad. This conflation of Furies and Muses was, of course, an invention of his own, and the sort of deviation from mythological purity for which Sophia (already turning into a sort of junior-league Furious Muse) would call him to account. He'd been carrying the idea around in his head for so long that the line between those two categories of subgoddesses had become blurry, and so he thought it would be illuminating, now that he had the ur-book in hand, to look them up.

The F section of the index was very short, having only two entries: "Fates" and "Furies." The latter being a mere cross-ref to the more correct "Erinyes." The former were glossed as "three old goddesses who determined the life span of man." Richard had merely scanned those words, since he was really interested in the Furies. Cross-reffing to "Erinyes" ("avenging spirits"), he turned to page 60, their first appearance in the book, and read of souls crossing the Styx (in a ferry no less) and drinking from the spring of Lethe under "dark poplars," causing them to forget who they were and what they had done during their mortal lives. Fine. But then it said "great sinners" were sentenced to suffer forever under the whips of the Furies. So, that part of it matched up pretty well with Richard's Furious Muses concept. It was troubling, however, to think that you could be whipped forever in punishment for sins that you had forgotten under the dark poplars. The sinners in the Christian version of hell could at least remember why they were burning in eternal fire, but these poor dumb Greeks could only suffer without knowing why; without, for that matter, even remembering what it was like to be alive and to not suffer. It wasn't even really clear to Richard that a post-Lethe soul could even be considered the same being, for weren't your memories a part of you?

And yet it all rang true on some level. He did feel sometimes that he was continuing to suffer guilt pangs for acts he had long ago forgotten—deeds done when he wasn't the same person. And who hasn't known a sad sack, a hard-luck case who seems to be undergoing eternal punishment for no particular reason?

The next Erinyes reference happened to occur just before a two-page spread featuring the more cheerful topic of the Muses, which was good stuff, way more Sophia-appropriate, as well as reminding Richard that his own Furious Muses were at least as creative as retributive, for some of his best work had emerged from imaginary dialogues with those estimable ladies. So "Furies" had been the text he was after, and "Fates" an accidental subtext— but this morning something about it was nagging at him.

It had to do with the threads. Lying in bed a minute ago he'd been thinking about the thread of consciousness, and how sever-ing it—breaking the brain–body link—was the key to a proper nap. And he knew that somewhere in d'Aulaire was a picture of the Fates spinning, measuring, and cutting thread. He looked all through *Greek* as he drank his coffee, and found it not.

The coffee was unutterably fantastic. The machine cost more than Richard's first car and there was nothing known to coffee technology that was not embodied in its hardware and its algo-rithms. The beans had come from an artisanal roaster a hundred yards away—a nimble coffee startup founded by java wizards who had been brought here to work for Starbucks and spun out the moment their stock options had vested. The taste of the coffee was not wonderful, however, merely because the machine and the roasters had done such good jobs, but in the categorical sense that Dodge was awake, he was alive, he was actually physically tasting this stuff with his body in a way that sleeping-Dodge-in-a-dream could never have done. In that sense awake Dodge was as superior to sleeping Dodge as a living person was to a ghost. Dreaming-of-coffee Dodge was to drinking-coffee Dodge as one of the shades in Hades—likened, in d'Aulaire, to dry leaves whirling about in a cold autumn wind—was to a living, flesh-and-blood person.

He exhausted the first cup while looking for the thread-cutting picture. He did find a textual description of the spinning, measur-ing, and cutting operations being carried out by Clotho, Lachesis, and Atropos, respectively, but not the illustration that he clearly remembered showing to Sophia just a couple of days ago.

On his second cup of coffee he had the idea of checking *Norse*. And there it was: a full-color half-pager of three blondes—here, they were called Norns—spinning the threads of life at the base of the world tree. Urd, Verdande, and Skuld. Names and hair color aside, they seemed to be a direct drop-in replacement for their Greek equivalents.

Now, Richard had run off to Canada before obtaining a higher education and had not set foot in a classroom since, but he had done enough reading to understand that mythology piled up in sedimentary layers. This had to be one of those cases where there had been some early culture predating the Greeks and the Norse alike that had featured the Norns/Fates and laid it down in a base layer on which their various descendants had then added more stuff. Consequently, they always read like an add-on to the more fleshed-out mythology. Or perhaps vice versa. They were too simple to mess with. Richard, who had grown wealthy in the tech industry, saw in the Norns or Fates or whatever you called them a basic feature of the operating system. Zeus had no power over them. They knew the past and the future. They only got invoked in these stories when something had gone drastically wrong on a metaphysical/cosmological level, or else to cover plot holes. In the Greek version, Clotho was the spinner—the creator of these threads. Lachesis was the measurer. So that would be your snooze button right there—she had her nine-minute tape measure out the whole time Dodge was lying in bed. And Atropos was the cutter. The Greek version of the Grim Reaper. Though, according to the theory that Dodge was developing, the loss of consciousness when you fell asleep was basically the same as dying except that you could wake up from it.

He did not eat breakfast because the medical assistant who had scheduled him for the procedure had said something about the desirability of showing up with an empty stomach. Instead he went and took a shower. When he emerged from the shower, he was fascinated to find the bathroom illuminated by a strange light, chilly and mottled, not artificial but not the light of the sun either. The effect was surreal, like entering a dream sequence in a movie made by a director who hasn't the wherewithal to produce anything truly dreamlike and so is faking it with simple lighting effects. The weird light was flooding in through a window that was aimed north. Was someone welding outside? Finally he worked out that the sun, rising over the Cascades in the east, was hitting him with a bank shot off the half-silvered windows of an office tower a few blocks away. Dodge had been living here for five years but was still occasionally surprised by the way sunlight would carom in from surrounding architecture. He supposed that an astronomer could have a field day calculating the angles: how they varied from hour to hour and season to season.

Because of the weird light, his reflection in the mirror took on a strange new aspect. He turned his head this way and that, checking for new moles. Richard, who was ruddy and freckle prone, had for decades been psyching himself up for a climactic battle with melanoma, which, according to dark prophecies uttered by multiple dermatologists, loomed as a near certainty in his future. Early on he had performed his monthly skin checks with anxiety bordering on clinical paranoia. But then years had flown by with no action. He was now actually beginning to feel somewhat crestfallen that this terrible foe, against whom he had so girded himself, looked to be passing him over.

Presently he fell to shaving, for he had noticed a few days' reddish growth. Medical personnel would soon be handling his body while he was unconscious. They would be able to stare at him all they wanted, to notice all the ways he wasn't looking after himself. He was semifamous and ought to be mindful of such things. Maybe it would affect his company's stock price or something.

He had assumed that the strange light would be a short-lived phenomenon, so was pleasantly surprised that it was getting stronger by the minute. The weird pallor was ripening into something warmer, like fire. A shaft of it was coming in through the window and illuminating the little sink and its backsplash. Richard had shaved, as was his habit, using a bar of soap—a specific type that he bought from a company in southern France. It had a pleasant fragrance, not perfumey and not too persistent. He had just put the soap back in its dish a moment ago and so it had bubbles on it. In a few minutes these would dry out and pop, but just now they were capturing the light being bounced off the windows of the office tower after its passage through ninety-three million miles of space from the vast thermonuclear inferno at the center of the solar system. Each bubble was producing an intensely brilliant spark of light, not white, but iridescent, as some kind of prismlike phenomenon inside the soap film (he was a little weak on the details) fractured the light into pure brilliant colors. A beautiful but perfectly commonplace phenomenon that would not have given him much food for thought were it not for the fact that his video game company had put a lot of money and engineer-years into the problem of trying to more perfectly depict an imaginary world using computer code, and this was exactly one of those things that was most difficult to capture. Oh, there were various ways of faking it; e.g., by applying special computational shaders to bars of soap during the sixty seconds after they had been used and were therefore covered with lather. But they were all just hacks. Actually simulating the physics of soap, bubbles, air, water, etc., was ludicrously expensive and would never be achieved in his lifetime.

It was hard even if you simplified matters by treating each bubble not as a small miracle of fluid dynamics, but as a simple reflecting sphere. At one point, some years previously, one of the engineers at Corporation 9592—a classic liberal-arts-major-turned-coder-so-he-could-make-a-decent-living—had identified this as the *Hand met Spiegelende Bol* Problem, and had discomfited many of the more hard-core engineers, during a meeting, by flashing up a graphic of the Escher lithograph of the same name. It was a self-portrait depicting the artist reflected in a mirrored sphere supported in his left hand. Escher's face was in the middle, but a geometrically distorted rendering of his office could be seen around it. In the background of that was a window. This, of course, was gathering in light from at least ninety-three million miles away. The point being that in order to make a faithful 3-D computer graphics rendering of an object as simple as a shiny ball, you would, in theory, have to take into account every object in the universe. The engineer—a new hire named Corvallis Kawasaki—had footnoted his own remarks by mentioning that the mirrored-ball problem reached at least as far back as the German genius and polymath G. W. Leibniz, who had written of it as a way of thinking about monads. At this point in the meeting, the more well-established engineers had shouted him down and Dodge had made a mental note to yank the boy out of whatever branch of the org chart he'd landed in and employ him in Weird Stuff, which was Dodge's personal department. In any case, the point, in this instance, was that every single bubble on the surface of the bar of soap was at least as complicated as Escher's ball. Rendering such a scene realistically was completely out of the question. Far from being a source of frustration, this comforted him, and made him happy—perhaps even a little smug—that he lived in a universe whose complexity defied algorithmic simulation.

He closed his eyes while splashing water on his face and then looked back up at the mirror. Now there was a little spot in the middle where he had been dazzled by the brilliant sparks of light from the bubbles. Soon enough the dazzled patch would shrink and be replaced by a correct view of what was really there.

Except that it did not in this case. When Richard closed his eyes again to towel his face, he could still see a little patch of nothing in his visual field. This was a different sort of nothing from the field of red-tinged black that his eyes were seeing simply by virtue of the fact that his lids had closed over them. He knew what this was. The flash of reflected sun, a minute ago, had triggered a thing in his brain called an optical migraine. It was painless and harmless. He got them a few times a year. It was a visual display—"Aura"—caused by a temporary disruption of blood flow to the visual cortex. It always started thus, with a tiny dazzled region that refused to go away. Over the next half hour it would get bigger, making it impossible for him to read. Then it would gradually migrate rightward and mess with his peripheral vision on that side for a little while before disappearing without a trace.

The affected region—the spot where he was absolutely blind— was not black, as you might imagine. This could be proved simply by closing his eyes so that he actually was seeing just black. The blind spot then showed up as a region of vaguely defined yellow and black stripes, like the patterns painted on factory floors to limn danger zones, except that these flashed and fluctuated like an old-time television with its vertical hold out of whack.

Even as he drew these connections he was erecting defenses against a likely flanking attack from Polycultia, one of the Furious Muses, who was always pointing out that everything Richard could possibly think of was culturally relative. In this instance she might expect tactical support from Cerebra, an unintentionally offensive FM who had a knack for pointing out that any idea Richard came up with that he thought was clever was, in fact, but an imperfect rendering of a smarter idea that had occurred to her a long time ago. The projected line of attack from the Polycultia–Cerebra axis went something like this: Okay, because part of Richard's visual cortex was on the blink, he was seeing "nothing" in that region. His brain was in the business of constructing, from moment to moment, the sort of three-dimensional model of the universe that, for example, enabled him to grab his phone from his bedside table without opening his eyes. As such, it couldn't tolerate seeing a patch of "nothing" in the middle of an otherwise coherent reality. So it tried to fill in the nothing with something. It was simply the visual equivalent of tinnitus.

But why this particular something? He construed it as black and yellow danger stripes, on-the-fritz TV sets, etc., but that was only because he was a white guy of a certain age from Iowa. A Maori midwife or a gay Roman centurion or an eleventh-century Shinto Buddhist, in the grip of the same underlying neurological phenomenon, would fill in the "nothing" with some other kind of hobgoblin derived from their own set of cultural referents—e.g., the wall of cold magical flames surrounding Gymir's realm in Jotunheim (according to *Norse*).

Being temporarily blind gave him an excuse to not expose himself to the Din. In an earlier decade he'd have said "not check his email," but of course email was actually the least intrusive of all the ways the Miasma—as Richard referred to the Internet—had devised to bay for your attention. Richard lumped all of them together under the general heading of the Din. He deemed it unlikely that there would be much that was important in this morning's Din, since he had caused his administrative assistant to weave a system of spells and wards: robotic "out of office" messages and whatnot.

He had, in consequence, time to kill before his appointment. He put the d'Aulaires back into their sack. As best as he could while half-blind, he made a sweep through the joint looking for any more of Sophia's stuff. Then he took the elevator down to the lobby of the building. There was a café and bakery between it and the sidewalk. He had it in mind to buy a copy of the *New York Times* and, once his vision had cleared, to do the crossword puzzle. Not that he was even really all that fond of crossword puzzles as such, but the mere fact of having time to spend on it was an indicator of being a free man, in a certain sense.

Vo, the proprietor of the bakery, came out to greet him by name. He was a Vietnamese man in his sixties or seventies who, Dodge inferred, had acquired world-class baking skills as some consequence of the French colonial presence in his home country. This operation was serious business: not just a toaster oven under a counter but a whole complex of expansive kneading boards and marble slabs, Evinrude-sized stand mixers, and walk-in ovens reaching deep into the building. Senior Asians and hairnetted hipsters could be viewed rolling out pastry dough and hand-shaping croissants. Vo would not deem the business to have succeeded until he had everyone in a half-kilometer radius walking home every evening with a baguette under his or her arm.

The front of the house sported half a dozen small tables and, where it fronted on the sidewalk, a window counter. A secondary entrance connected to the building's lobby. Richard came in that way and picked up another cup of coffee and a *New York Times*. Vo wanted him to understand that he had yesterday acquired a bushel of ripe Yakima Valley apples from a personal connection at the Pike Place Market—just enough to make a few tartes tatin, which he was keeping in reserve for special customers. Not that it was much of a secret, since the apple-y aroma had permeated the whole ground floor. He was wont to back up his verbal communications with physical demonstrations, perhaps a habit acquired during the decades when he had been learning English the hard way. Gently cupping one of Richard's elbows in the palm of his hand, he led him around behind the counter to display a cardboard box stashed there, half-full of apples. He bent down and pawed through them until he had found a worthy specimen, then pulled it out and held it up in front of Richard's face, perching it atop his fingertips in a pose that strongly called to mind Escher's *Hand met Spiegelende Bol*, save that in this case, of course, it was an apple. It was an apple from which earlier generations of American grocery shoppers would have recoiled in dismay, had they seen it in the produce section at their local Safeway. It was half the size of the brawny, cottony Red Delicious apples usually seen in such places, its color ranged from an almost purple shade of red to an almost yellow shade of green, it had a few minor spots and dimples, and a couple of actual leaves were still attached to its stem. But it was so round and taut that it looked ready to explode. Vo kept thrusting it higher and higher into the air, looking back and forth between it and Richard.

"Now, *that* is a real apple!" Richard finally said. It was not a particularly clever thing to say but he knew it was the only thing that would calm Vo down. Vo rewarded him by insisting that he take the apple "for lunch." Richard received it with due ceremony, like a Japanese businessman accepting a business card, running his fingers over its curves and turning it this way and that to admire its color, then placed it carefully into the bag slung over his shoulder. He soon found himself at his customary table with his coffee, his crossword puzzle, and his slice of tarte.

He was at least two-thirds finished with it when he remembered with a start that he was under doctor's orders not to eat any food before the medical procedure. He had obeyed earlier but forgot himself when confronted with the opportunity of tarte tatin fresh from the oven.

He looked at the remaining part—the best part, since it comprised the edge crust, and he had been raised to save the best for last—with a mixture of guilt and embarrassment. In the end he decided to eat it. He doubted that having food in the stomach was *really* a significant danger. It was just one of those general recommendations, like turning off your cell phone while pumping gas, that had been promoted to a hysterical warning by lawyers. And to the extent it might actually be dangerous, the die was already cast. Having three-thirds of a slice in his stomach couldn't be much worse than having two-thirds. And if he left the remainder on his plate, Vo would notice it and take it the wrong way and perhaps demote him from special-customer status.

More important than the possible medical complication was the question, which came quickly to mind, of whether this lapse was an early indicator of senility. The speed with which he had demolished the crossword puzzle seemed to argue against it. But that was all long-term memory, right? He wasn't sure. As a boy he had been oblivious to the existence of this thing called senility until an older cousin had clued him in to it during a family reunion and supplied a brief (and in retrospect hilariously imprecise) rundown of its symptoms while casting significant glances at Grandma. After that, young Richard had overcompensated for his earlier naivete by becoming hypervigilant to its onset in family members of even modest decrepitude.

2

The doctor's staff had been very firm on the point that, following the procedure, he would be unfit to drive because of the powerful drugs they were going to give him—that he would, for all practical purposes, be an ambulatory basket case, and that they wouldn't even begin the procedure unless he had a designated minder who would sign him out afterward and take responsibility for keeping him away from heavy machinery. Accordingly, Richard now walked two blocks to a transit stop, boarded a city bus that would take him to the medical complex on the hill above downtown, and made himself comfortable in a seat amidships.

He woke up his phone. Its home screen was chicken-poxed with little red dots with accusatory numbers in them, the consequences of having turned a deaf ear to the Din for twelve whole hours. He willed himself not to see those and instead brought up his address book. He scrolled to the K section and found five different entries for Corvallis Kawasaki. Some of them had little pictures attached to them, which helped Richard guess how out-of-date they were. Most had accumulated during the years that Corvallis had worked hand-in-glove with Richard at Corporation 9592, the game company that had made Richard a billionaire and Corvallis, in the lexicon of the tech business world, a decimillionaire. The pictures on those tended to show him hoisting pints in bars or in various funny/celebratory poses connected with the company's rise to prominence in the online gaming industry. One of them, however, was a very straight, formal head shot of Corvallis with his hair neatly trimmed and gelled, wearing a suit and tie. This card—which was only a few months old—identified him as the CTO of Nubilant Industries, a company that did cloud computing. It had been formed last year as part of a "roll-up," which was tech biz parlance for acquiring and combining several companies that were all operating in the same "space." Corvallis had been induced, by means of a hefty stock option grant, to leave his position at Corporation 9592 and join the new company. Richard had been sorry to see him go, but he had to admit that it was an excellent fit—Corvallis had overseen the shift of all Corporation 9592's operations from old-fashioned server racks to the cloud, and he hadn't been as lavishly compensated as others who had been luckier in their timing. Since Corvallis's departure to Nubilant—which was headquartered near downtown Seattle—he and Richard had exchanged texts on several occasions, trying to find time to meet up for a drink. So far, it had not come together. But when Dodge pulled up his Corvallis text message stream, he found, at its tail, a flurry of messages from over the preceding weekend, in which Corvallis agreed to take the afternoon off and serve as Richard's designated minder, collecting him from the clinic in his narcotic haze and taking him to lunch or something as he returned to his senses.

omw to clinic, Richard thumbed. Then he fetched a substantial pair of headphones from his bag and placed them over his ears. The sounds of the bus were muted. He plugged the cord into the phone and turned the headphones on. For these were electronic noise-canceling headphones. Directly they began to feed anti-noise into his ears, making everything quieter yet.

Corvallis texted back, *K.* The phone displayed the ellipsis indicating that he was still typing.

Dodge activated the music player app and began scrolling through his playlists, looking for the P section. His tinnitus was ramping up because of the unearthly quiet produced by the noise-canceling feature.

Corvallis added, *if u r feeling up to it I will take you by the office— would like to show you what we are up to—cool stuff!*

Richard decided not to respond to that one. As much as he liked Corvallis, he dreaded going on tours of high-tech companies. He tapped the words "Pompitus Bombasticus." The lavish tonalities of a full symphony orchestra, backed up by a choir and fortified by a driving modern percussion section, filled his ears. Pompitus

Bombasticus was Richard's favorite group. Apparently it was just one guy working alone in a studio in Germany; the philharmonic, the choir, and all the rest were faked with synthesizers. This guy had noticed, some years ago, that all inexpensive horror movies used the same piece of music—Carl Orff's *Carmina Burana*—in their soundtracks. That opus had become a cliché, more apt to induce groans or laughs than horror. This German, who had been living the starving-artist lifestyle while trying to establish a career as a DJ, had been struck by an insight that had transformed his career: the filmmakers of the world were manifesting an insatiable demand for a type of music of which *Carmina Burana* was the only existing specimen. The market (if the world of composers and musicians could be thought of as such) was failing to respond to that demand. Why not then begin to make original music that sounded like the soundtrack of the sort of movie scene in which *Carmina Burana* inevitably played? It didn't have to sound exactly like *Carmina Burana* but it needed to evoke the same feelings. The German gave himself a new name, which was Pompitus Bombasticus, and put out a self-titled album that was enthusiastically ripped, torrented, downloaded, and stolen by innumerable aspiring young filmmakers united by a common sentiment that if they heard *Carmina Burana* one more time they would shove pencils into their ears. Since then, Pompitus Bombasticus had come out with five more albums, all of which Richard had legally downloaded and merged into this one long playlist. The breathtaking sweep and emotional bandwidth of the music made unloading the dishwasher seem as momentous as the final scene of *2001: A Space Odyssey*. In this case, it cast a haze of fake poignancy over this text from C-plus (as Dodge called Corvallis). He did not wish to come out and say as much directly, for fear that C-plus would take it the wrong way, but, in the later phases of their professional relationship, C-plus's role had become less all-around tech expert and more general intellectual sidekick and helpmeet. When it came to all of the stuff that Richard had omitted to learn during his extremely colorful late teens and early twenties, Corvallis Kawasaki was Virgil to his Dante, Mr. Peabody to his Sherman.

As an example, when Richard had remarked, a few years ago,

on the fact that nearly all of his dreams were set in the landscape of the same small town in Iowa, C-plus had told him that this was related to a well-known insight by a German philosopher named Kant, who had posited that the mind simply was not capable of thinking about anything at all without mapping it onto space and time. The brain was just hooked up that way, nothing you could do about it. Young Richard had learned the basic properties of space-time by pedaling around a particular street grid on his bicycle, trick-or-treating on particular blocks, fleeing from big kids and vice principals through convenient backyards. It was burned into his neural "connectome" now; it was the Kantian substrate of all mental activity relating to space and movement. Perhaps worrying that Richard wasn't following his argument, C-plus had then wrapped it all up by likening it to the hexagonal graph paper that nerds used to plot out the landscapes on which war games were prosecuted. This final detail had planted a suspicion in Richard's mind that C-plus was just fucking with him. This had all happened, for no particular reason, minutes before a board meeting: the most important board meeting in the history of Corporation 9592, during which they announced that the company's annual revenues now exceeded those of the Roman Empire at the height of the Augustan Age. Richard had fobbed the task off on the CFO, who would revel in that kind of thing. While the CFO was running through his PowerPoint deck, Richard had pulled out his phone and, in a merely pro forma attempt to conceal what he was doing, had, under the conference table, Googled Kant. The results looked formidably hard to read but sufficed to prove that there had actually been a guy named Kant and that he had indeed concerned himself with such topics.

The music of Pompitus Bombasticus made Richard's fifteen-minute bus ride seem as inspiring and yet tragic as the Battle of Stalingrad. As the vehicle swung around a corner downtown, it was halted by a man holding up a stop sign as a long truck full of dirt pulled out into the street, bound for wherever excess dirt was dumped. The soundtrack in Richard's headphones made this labored but basically simple operation seem as much a technological miracle as the departure of a massive yet graceful starship from its orbiting dry dock. It was taking Dodge a few moments to get his bearings. He realized that an older skyscraper—a building that had helped to define the city's skyline since the 1960s—had been obliterated while Richard's attention had been elsewhere. A rendering on a sign depicted a much taller building that was going to replace it. Fogeyish as this was, he felt somehow let down and scandalized. You take your eye off the ball for a minute and a building's gone.

But in the very next block was a building that had been a celebrated architectural happening when it had gone up, what, five, no, ten years ago. Now it was just part of the landscape. It occurred to him to wonder whether he would still be alive when it was torn down. For that matter, he had been known to wonder whether his current car was going to be the last car he would ever buy, whether the leather jacket he was wearing now was going to outlive him. He was not being morbid. He was not depressed, not thinking about death overmuch. He just assumed that he was on a very long glide path leading to death in perhaps another thirty to fifty years and that he had plenty of leisure in the meantime to ponder it. He saw life as a trench in the First World War sense of that term, dug very deep at one end but becoming more shallow as you marched along, gradually ramping up to surface level. Early in your life you were so deep down in it that you didn't even know that shells were bursting and bullets zipping over its top. As time went on these became noticeable but not directly relevant. At a certain point you began to see people around you getting injured or even killed by stray bits of shrapnel, but even if they were good friends of yours, you knew, in your grief and shock, that they were statistical aberrations. The more you kept marching, however, the more difficult it became to ignore the fact that you were drawing close to the surface. People in front of you died singly, then in clusters, then in swathes. Eventually, when you were something like a hundred years old, you emerged from the trench onto open ground, where your life span was measured in minutes. Richard still had decades to go before it was like that, but he'd seen a few people around him buy the farm, and looking up that trench he could see in the great distance—but still close enough to see it—the brink above which the bullets flew in blazing streams. Or maybe it was just the music in his headphones making him think thus.

They passed a good restaurant—a favorite of Richard's when he needed to host a business lunch. A box truck pulled out of the adjoining alley and inserted itself into a gap in traffic in front of the bus. It was decorated with the logo of a company that evidently provided table linens to restaurants that were classy enough to make use of them. Off the little truck went, headed for the next restaurant where it would make a delivery. The bus driver was annoyed by the manner in which it had claimed the space. Richard, ahead of schedule and not responsible for anything, just zoned out on the flow of traffic. As they passed the alley, he saw a beer truck unloading kegs of microbrew. The purposes of linen and beer trucks were obvious, being printed right on their sheet metal, but of course every vehicle on the street and every pedestrian on the sidewalk had a purpose as well. It was the flowing-together and interaction of all those intentions that made a city. The early failure of Corporation 9592's game designers to capture that feeling had led to several months of Richard's doing what Richard generally did, which was to attack problems so weird that merely to cop to their existence would have been career suicide for anyone who wasn't the company founder. The name of the game, and of the imaginary world in which it was set, was T'Rain. The world's geology had been convincingly simulated by a man who went by the name of Pluto and who was very gifted at that sort of thing. The urban landscapes had turned out to be much less convincing, for reasons not immediately clear. It was one of those problems assumed to be trivial that had turned out to be really hard. What it boiled down to, once they had spent millions of dollars flying people in for seminars and simulating urban traffic flows on supercomputing clusters, was that, in a real city, everyone had something they were trying to do. Sometimes everyone had a different goal, other times (as just before a big sporting event) everyone had the same goal. The way that people and vehicles moved reflected their pursuit of those goals. When you had spent some time in a real-world city, your brain learned to read those behaviors and to process and understand them as citylike. When you visited a made-up city in a massively multiplayer online game, however, you generally saw group behaviors that failed to match those that convinced your brain that you were looking at something real, and the illusion failed.

"Pill Hill," which loomed above downtown, had long ago been seeded with several hospitals that had done nothing but grow and consolidate as the city had developed into a horn of plenty, morbidity-wise. The few spaces not claimed by the hospitals themselves had sprouted medical buildings, twenty and thirty stories high, all interconnected by skybridges and tunnels. That combined with mergers and consolidations had turned the hill into a fully interlocked, mile-wide, three-dimensional maze entirely devoted to health care. It was well served by mass transit. Richard could have taken the bus right to the entrance of the clinic. Instead he decided on the spur of the moment to get off several blocks early and enjoy a stroll down Cherry Street. The neighborhood was old by local standards, with mature maples that had presumably been imported by settlers who wanted it to look like the leafy towns of the northeastern and midwestern United States. The autumn color was peaking. His earlier musings had caused him to wonder, again just in an idle and non-gloomy way, how many more times in his life he would see the leaves turn. Twenty or thirty? Not a super-large number. One of the Furious Muses was pointing out to him that the smallness of this figure should drive him to appreciate the beauty more than he was doing. That didn't seem to work, but he had to admit that the glorious colors were made even more impressive by the current Pompitus Bombasticus selection.

What pathways in the brain, he wondered, connected these patterns of sound to pleasure? And were they intrinsic to the working of the mind or just an accident of evolution? Or to ask the same question another way, if there was an afterlife, either old-school analog or newfangled digital—if we lived on as spirits or were reconstituted as digital simulations of our own brains—would we still like music?

It hadn't exactly rained, but the walk was wet anyway, with moisture that had condensed from the atmosphere. Red leaves were plastered to it, as if the place had been overrun by patriotic

Canadians. The ones underfoot had gone a little dark, but when he gazed down the length of Cherry Street, the trees lining it had a Canadian-flag purity and intensity of redness no less than that of the traffic lights suspended above major intersections.

Corvallis Kawasaki had told him that there was a word for this: "quale." The subjective experience of (for example) redness. Or of music, or of a tarte tatin. Neurologists and philosophers both wrote of qualia, tried to puzzle out what they were exactly, how you got them, whether they were intrinsic to consciousness. Did the ants feeding on a puddle of spilled soda experience its sweetness? Or were they too simple for that and only responding programmatically? The infrared sensor on an elevator door did not experience qualia of people stepping through its beam; it was just a dumb switch. Where on the evolutionary ladder did the brain stop being a glorified elevator door sensor and begin to experience qualia? Before or after ants? Or was it the case that an individual ant was too simple to experience qualia but a whole swarm of them collectively *did*?

All of these lofty considerations aside, Richard enjoyed qualia to a degree that bordered on the sexual. He had ruined more than one first date by reacting to a swallow of wine or a bite of steak in a manner that the woman across the table seemed to find a little creepy. A few years earlier, he had passed through a sort of prolonged near-death experience during which he'd had way too much time to think about this. He had even drawn up a list of good ones, as if cataloging them would lead to mastery, or at least understanding:

The black sheen of an old cast-iron griddle, its oily smell when heated.

The pucker in the back of a man's powder-blue dress shirt.

The smell of a cedar plank fractured along a grain line.

Sparks of sunlight reflecting from waves.

The shape of the letter P.

Finding your exact location on a map.

Shortening your stride as you approached a curb.

Moving around in a house—walls you can't pass through, doors you can.

Remaining upright. Balance. Standing on one foot.

Bubbles on the bottom of a pan getting ready to boil.

Having an appetite.

Just having been hit on the nose.

The opening strains of "Comfortably Numb."

So much for the poet in him; the tech magnate idly wondered about all of the processing power that was being consumed by his brain, even in its most idle moments, simply taking in qualia and organizing them into a coherent story about the world and his place in it.

He snatched a particularly brilliant red maple leaf right out of the air and let it plaster its wet anatomy to the palm of his hand. He looked at it the way he might've as a kid looking at just such a leaf on a farm in Iowa. An observer at a distance would assume he was looking at his phone. There was something almost sinister about its symmetry, which was far from perfect and yet obvious and undeniable. Dark veins forked away from its spine. On its back surface, they stood out, like girders under a roof. On the front, each vein was a channel grooved into the red flesh, draining it like a system of rills and creeks and rivers, or feeding it like capillaries in an organ. It was a little triumph of spatial organization, like the state of Iowa, replicated millions of times along the length of Cherry Street and about to become mulch in the gutter. He decided to spare this one such an ignominious fate and slipped it into his bag. Later he would show it to Sophia.

He became aware of being looked at. A boy of perhaps twelve was walking up Cherry Street. He had recognized Richard and was approaching, to the mild consternation of his adult minder—presumably his father. On his left forearm he wore a newfangled plastic splint, the kind that made the wearer look like a bionic superwarrior instead of a damaged gimp. And indeed the music of Pompitus Bombasticus made his final approach to Richard seem like the triumphal entry of a hero into Valhalla. With his good hand the kid was fishing his phone out. He would want to take a selfie with Richard so that he could post it and achieve, at least for a few hours, the Miasma's equivalent of Valhalla-like glory. Richard obligingly pulled the phones from his head and let them encircle his neck. He shook the boy's hand—this was awkward because of the splint and the phone. Followed at a seemly interval by the adult, the two of them walked side by side for half a block. The boy was a heavy player of T'Rain. He was smart and appealing, with well-formed and completely reasonable ideas on how to make the game even better. They drew to a halt in front of the entrance to the clinic. The kid's monologue continued, Richard paying attention and nodding, until the father, sensing the nature of Richard's errand, intervened and directed the boy to wind it up. The boy had, while talking, got his phone configured to take a selfie, which he now did. He was narrating as he did so and Dodge understood that he was not taking a still photo but a snippet of video, more difficult to counterfeit and thus, when posted, more cred enhancing. He shook the kid's hand and exchanged nods with the dad: *Over to you.* The kid had got a mildly stricken look on his face; it had occurred to him that Richard Forthrast might be sick.

That's what medicine was to kids: an acute response to disease. When you got older you understood it was more like brushing your teeth: a system of highly evolved strategies for preempting bad things that could happen to you if you took no preventive measures. Part of him wanted to explain this to the kid, to assuage his little pang of anxiety, but the conversation had gone on long enough and was over now. He went into the building musing on the weird role that his society had picked out for him as a guy who had built, or caused to be built, an imaginary world.

No expense had been spared on the interior design front to make the building seem as little as possible like what it really was. They had even eschewed a traditional matter-based directory in favor of a touch screen. Dodge employed this to remind himself which floor his appointment was on. The thing read like an electronic compendium of maladies. To browse it was to be grateful for all of the things that had not yet gone wrong with his body and his mind. Almost as miraculous as life itself was the number of ways it could end, or at least turn into a living hell. And for each of those there was a different, exquisitely evolved medical sub-subspecialty. He almost felt that he was failing this stupendous industry by not being sick in any interesting way. For today's procedure was utterly routine, a thing done a thousand times a day. He found his destination on the screen and walked to the correct elevator bank, casting a glance toward the entrance to the parking garage just in case C-plus might happen to show up. But this did not happen and so he had the elevator to himself at first. His clinic was on a high floor. En route, people with various impairments got on and off. Either they were lost or else they were being transferred between cooperating sub-subspecialists. For the most part they were oddly cheerful. Beyond a certain point it was all just kicking through wreckage.

A prominent sign on the check-in counter at the clinic read, PATIENTS: DO NOT EAT OR DRINK ANYTHING BEFORE YOUR SURGERY. But it gave no instructions as to what you should do if it was already too late, and so Richard socked it away in the same round file as the cancer warning signs that were posted on every single flat surface in the state of California. The nurse who was checking him in asked whether he had anyone lined up to take him home. Richard pulled out his phone, shingled with texts from Corvallis Kawasaki complaining of traffic delays, and held it up as a sort of affidavit that his ride would be here long before he was needed. On went the inevitable plastic bracelet. They led him back and had him change into the obligatory gown. An unseemly fuss was made over his wallet, phone, and other valuables, for which they wanted it understood they could not be responsible. Dodge once again scented lawyers with too much time on their hands. He heard C-plus's voice outside, and thought of calling out a greeting, but didn't really want to be seen or communicated with in the bracelet and gown—these made him seem sick, which he wasn't. The pace of preparations was accelerating almost exponentially. Dodge got a clear sense of the proceduralist doctor as a cash cow of such fiscal immensity that his time and movements had to be scheduled and accounted for as carefully as an airline did with each 737. Dodge's slot was next. They invited him onto a gurney and wheeled him into the procedure environment. An IV was started and taped to his arm. Sensors were clamped to his fingertips and Velcroed around his bicep; machines came alive to him and began to display information about his vitals. He knew where this was going.

They were about to render him unconscious with amazing pharmaceuticals. In a minute, Atropos would snip the thread of his consciousness and he would, for all practical purposes, be dead. But when the procedure was finished Clotho would resume spinning his thread and he would come back to life as if it had never happened. It was weird stuff from that deeper and older stratum of myth, pre-*Greek*, pre-*Norse*, definitely nothing he would share with Sophia later, when he showed up at her house with the books.

A man came in, presumably the doctor since he didn't introduce himself and seemed to expect that Richard would know who he was. He mentioned that he had a character in T'Rain and began to ask questions about a certain technicality in the rules of the game. Richard was already getting a little foggy, but he understood that this wasn't a real conversation. The doctor just wanted to know when the patient had lost consciousness. They must have injected the drug into his IV line. New qualia: a mask over his nose, cold dry gas flooding his nostrils, a hiss. Atropos snipped his thread.

3

Corvallis Kawasaki had, in a funny way, been looking forward to the day's activities, or lack thereof. His job was to show up in the waiting room of a certain medical specialist, wait for Dodge to come out all groggy, get him into a car, and then take him to some combination of movie and lunch. Compared to what he normally did for a living, it was simple. It was also physical. Not as physical as skiing or welding, but much more physical than his job, which consisted of moving pixels around on screens in certain ways that were projected to be highly lucrative.

There was some professional guilt entailed in taking the day off. He assuaged it in the waiting room by opening up his laptop, connecting to the building's guest network, establishing a secure link to his company's network, and writing a number of emails. These were all more or less calculated to hurl tasks into colleagues' laps, which he reckoned might keep them off balance long enough that they wouldn't miss him while he was taking in some kind of stupid action movie with Dodge. As he always did while working, he went into a sort of flow state that must have lasted for about half an hour. At the beginning of it he was conscious of his surroundings: patients biding their time, receptionists checking people in, medical personnel in scrubs striding to and fro on their sensible shoes. And, just for a moment, Dodge's voice heard dimly from the back, making a crack as he was wheeled to the procedure room. Nothing that needed concern him at the moment. Into the universe of email he went, and abided for a time.

He was vaguely aware that people were, all of a sudden, distressed about something. This almost pulled him out of his reverie. But he knew that, whatever was going on, there was nothing he could do about it. People got stressed out at work all the time. It was not his problem.

He did raise his head and look when the front door of the office suite was punched open by a team of three firemen. Waiting for them was a woman in scrubs. She had made eye contact with the firemen before they even reached the door. As they burst in, she turned on her heel and ran into the back, and they understood that they should follow her. They were carrying not axes and hoses, but large boxes emblazoned with red crosses.

The initial reaction of Corvallis was, some would say, curiously detached and unemotional. Evidently, someone in the back of this medical practice had been taken ill. Perhaps an elderly doctor had suffered a heart attack, or something. One would think that a medical practice, sited in a building full, from top to bottom, of medical offices, in a neighborhood entirely given over to the medical industry, would have some special procedure to follow in such a case. But, if Corvallis Kawasaki understood correctly what he was seeing, this was not the case. When there was a problem, the people here dialed 911, just like anyone else. The call was routed to the nearest fire station and the EMTs were dispatched. This was mildly surprising, but the technology executive in him found it actually to be quite reasonable and, in a way, comforting. The EMTs in the fire stations were the best at what they did, the quickest to respond. The system was working.

Now that his focus on the screen of his laptop had been broken, he sat up straight and began to take in further details. A woman in pink scrubs was standing where he could see her, hands clasped together in front of pursed lips, staring down a hallway Her eyes began to glisten. The EMTs were firing off tight bursts of words. The receptionists had stopped doing their work entirely and were just sitting frozen at their workstations, gripping the edges of their desks, like officers on the bridge of a starship getting ready to be hit by photon torpedoes. The voices of the EMTs became louder and clearer. While continuing to do their work, they were, it seemed, wheeling the patient out of a room, down the hallway, toward the exit. The woman in pink scrubs sprang out of the way. One of the receptionists, who had a better angle than Corvallis, scrambled up, ran across the lobby to the door, and hauled it open.

The EMTs wheeled Richard Forthrast out on a gurney and maneuvered him at reckless speed out the door and in the direction of the elevator bank. He was only visible to Corvallis for one, perhaps two seconds, and so it took a little while for Corvallis to process what he had seen. Richard was shirtless, the open-back hospital gown stripped away from him, and electrodes had been stuck to his torso. A tube had been inserted between his teeth and, presumably, down into his windpipe. One of the EMTs was holding a sort of rubber bag, squeezing it in a slow steady rhythm to force air into Richard's chest.

Corvallis Kawasaki's first, absurd instinct was to pull his phone out of his pocket and dial Richard's number. Because what was going on here was obviously weird, obviously a crisis. On both of these counts it was very much a Richard sort of problem. For much of his postcollege life, Corvallis had been in the comfortable habit of knowing that any such matter could automatically be handed off to Dodge, who would be not merely willing but eager to take it on. Why, Dodge would be offended if weird crises were not instantly dumped into his lap. This was now at odds with the intellectual awareness that Dodge was dying or dead.

He closed his laptop, slid it into his bag, stood up, and followed a debris trail of medical wrappers to the elevator lobby, which he reached just in time to glimpse Richard's gray face and wired-up torso as a pair of doors glided shut on it. He punched the "down" button and waited for the next lift in a very odd state of mind. Nothing was certain yet. Word had not yet gone out on what Dodge referred to as the Miasma. Corporation 9592's stock had not begun to slide. Standing there alone in that lobby, he could convince himself that he had just imagined it, suffered a kind of waking nightmare. If Dodge was about to die, should the world not have been crumbling all about him? Should the streets not have been full of wailing gamers? And yet the elevator lobby was just an elevator lobby, changeless as the stars.

When he reached the ground floor he was able to follow a

trail of shocked bystanders—security guards, incoming patients, scrub-wearing medics waiting in line for their lattes—to an exit of the building just in time to see an ambulance peel out. A moment later it turned on its lights and its siren.

Corvallis broke into a run. He was able to keep pace with the ambulance for about a block as it negotiated some turns, slowing to honk in righteous fury at a dim-witted motorist, then cutting across six lanes of traffic. Presently it went around a corner and disappeared from view behind a vast hospital, but Corvallis was able to track it by sound, and compare those findings with red signs pointing the way to EMERGENCY. Dodge's ambulance ride had been all of about three blocks long. They could almost have rolled him there on the gurney.

Corvallis resisted an urge to just run out into traffic, the way characters did in movies. He whacked buttons and waited in law-abiding fashion for pedestrian signals, then ran when he could. He reached the emergency room perhaps sixty seconds after the ambulance had pulled in. Dodge had already been wheeled in past the reception barrier. Here the receptionists were shielded behind thick walls of glass, like inner-city liquor store clerks, and watched over by ceiling-mounted cameras in black glass bubbles, as well as an actual human security guard who seemed a little distracted by what had just blown by him. Corvallis found himself on the outside of the glass barricade, sharing a waiting room with a Hispanic construction worker who had damaged his left hand and a stocky black woman who was texting. The nurse behind the glass wall asked Corvallis whether she could help him. He sensed that she was sizing him up, putting her training to use as she evaluated him for signs of trauma or mental illness. He was wearing khaki trousers and an old T-shirt with a black raincoat. He approached the glass wall and explained that he was with the man who had just been wheeled in from the ambulance.

He didn't make it past the barrier. It was some kind of policy issue regarding Corvallis's actual relationship to the patient. He and Richard had not come in together. Richard had not formally designated Corvallis as his wingman. Corvallis could have been anyone. For all they knew, he was a mentally ill person who had just followed the ambulance in. Or perhaps Richard and Corvallis were lovers, and it was a domestic violence situation. The nurse at the front desk had no way of knowing. She had made some remark about "next of kin." This shut him up and sent him to the nearest waiting room chair. Partly because it was a disturbing turn of phrase and partly because, yes, of course, that was his highest responsibility at this moment: to get in touch with Zula Forthrast and let her know that she needed to come to the hospital.

She was there twenty minutes later, breathing hard. She had simply run from her condo, which was less than a mile away in the adjoining hilltop neighborhood. She worked part-time now, mostly from home, which was within walking distance of Sophia's preschool. The Forthrast family had adopted her, at the age of seven, from an orphanage in Eritrea, and raised her in a farm town in Iowa. Her adoptive mother had died in an accident and she had become a ward of the whole extended family. Corvallis wasn't certain who her parents were according to the letter of the law, but she'd become very close to her uncle Richard. Corvallis saw her running down the sidewalk, puffs of steam coming from her mouth. To have come here on foot was an unusual choice, but just the sort of calculation that Zula would make; the distance was such that she could cover it this way faster than it would take to summon an Uber. She slowed to a fast walk as she approached the building. The glass doors opened for her automatically. She was wearing a sweater and jeans and toting the knapsack she often used in lieu of a purse; she hadn't bothered with a hat or a raincoat. Her uncontained hair had drawn humidity from the air and was a bedewed, corkscrewy glory. As she came in she recognized Corvallis, who had stood up. She took a step in his direction before correcting her course to the nurses' station. "Zula Forthrast," she announced, reaching for her wallet. "Here to see my uncle Richard Forthrast." She slid her driver's license across the counter. "I was told he was here." And only then did she look up and meet Corvallis's eye. She looked alert and interested. After some of the things she had lived through, nothing much could make her distraught. Not that she didn't have feelings, but she'd learned how to wall them off. The events of a few years ago had thrust her into the public spotlight for a while, forced her to develop the knack that all famous people had of maintaining a certain persona while exposed to the gaze of strangers. It was serving her well now. She had a kind of distracted air about her, and Corvallis couldn't tell whether she was dazed by the news or being wry. How many things could go wrong in her life?

"Nothing is simple with my uncle, huh?" she said.

"Nope" was the best Corvallis could come up with.

"How bad is it?" she asked.

He didn't know what to say.

"It's pretty bad, huh?" she said. Giving him permission.

"I kinda got the sense that it was super bad," he admitted.

She nodded and blinked.

The nurse informed them that Richard had already been transferred to the ICU and gave them an idea of how to find it.

Corvallis and Zula went down the suggested hallway, found some elevators, and began to navigate the three-dimensional labyrinth of the hospital. Other patients or medical staff were always getting in between them, and so they didn't try to talk. Zula sent a couple of text messages, then tilted her head back to trap some tears in the pouches of her eyes.

Finally they got to the entrance of the intensive care unit. "Here we go," Zula said.

"Is there anything—" Corvallis began, but she strode ahead of him and approached the nurse at the front desk. "Zula Forthrast," she said. "Next of kin of Richard Forthrast, who I think was just brought up here. Is there anyone who can give us the rundown? We have no information whatsoever yet about his condition."

They found themselves sitting in a small office that, Corvallis guessed, had been placed here specifically for conversations of this type. Modern sofas formed a right-angled U around a coffee table with flowers in a vase. Kleenex boxes competed for space with Purell dispensers. Takeout menus for local restaurants were neatly arranged in a binder; the Wi-Fi password was handwritten on the inevitable Post-it note. A big window afforded a rain-spotted view down the hill to the central business district, white sky above it and gray sea below.

A perfunctory knock on the door preceded the entrance of a scrub-wearing man in his forties. Asian-American, heavy-framed eyeglasses chosen to fit a square face. He introduced himself as Dr. Trinh and invited everyone to make themselves comfortable on the available seating.

"He suffered an unusual complication during the procedure that caused him to stop breathing. The staff were unable to correct the situation. By the time the emergency medical technicians were able to arrive on the scene and insert a breathing tube, his heart had stopped. They had difficulty restarting it. Currently he is on a ventilator. That means that a machine is breathing for him."

"He's not capable of breathing for himself?" Zula asked.

"We don't think so."

"That means his brain is badly damaged, right?"

"We are observing a complete lack of brain function. In my estimation, he is not coming back. I'm sorry to have to give you this news. But I need to ask you whether your uncle had a living will. Did he ever make a statement as to how he wanted to be treated in the event he ended up on life support?"

Corvallis interrupted the long silence that followed by saying, "I can work on that."

He knew in his heart that he was taking the coward's way out. He suspected that Zula knew it too. Her task was a nightmare: to contact all of the other family members and to tell them what was going on while holding it all together for Sophia. And, possibly, to make an executive decision to pull the plug on the man who was the closest thing she had to a father. Merely being in proximity to someone going through all of that was enough to put Corvallis into a cold sweat.

Tracking down a legal document seemed light duty.

Zula nodded and spared him a little smile. "Thank you, C-plus." She looked at Dr. Trinh. "I would like to see him, if that is okay."

In the college town that was his namesake, Corvallis had been raised by a father who was clearly on the autism spectrum and a mother who was within spitting distance of it. He was an only child. The household was stable and drama-free. They read books and played board games. Emotional matters were outsourced to relatives, who were all rather far away. From time to time Mom or Dad would be called upon to offer support to a relative or a family member in distress, which they generally did by wiring money, solving a logistical problem, or making a donation to an apposite charity. They didn't go to church, which—never mind what you actually believed, or didn't—inoculated children with a steady low-level exposure to christenings, bar mitzvahs, weddings, and funerals. While in middle school Corvallis had started to become aware that he was not much good, compared to other people, at situations where he was called upon to express his emotions. Like the early warning signs of a dread disease, this had first surfaced when he had found himself at a party and discovered that he couldn't dance. Movement per se he was good at—he already had a brown belt in tae kwon do—but movement expressive of feelings was impossible for him. Since then the condition had only become more pronounced.

This lack of surefootedness extended to simple matters such as talking to strangers on the telephone and complimenting female friends on their new haircuts—two things, among many, that he would cross the street to avoid doing. The mere thought of all the telephone calls that Zula was about to have to make, the crying, the hugging, the writing of notes, tear-soaked airport pickups, long wrenching heart-to-hearts with third cousins twice removed—merely being in proximity to it, with no real expectations or responsibilities at all, was nearly enough to send Corvallis into a panic attack.

But there was always a way out. Corvallis's dad was the designated photographer at family reunions. He was not a hugger, but he did a dynamite job of taking pictures of people hugging; no hug could escape the sleepless gaze of his bleeding-edge Nikon. Corvallis was enormously relieved now to have a specific task in which expressing emotions was not merely unnecessary but actually somewhat counterproductive. He opened his laptop. He figured out how to get on the hospital's guest Wi-Fi network. He forced himself to ignore all of the email that had piled up during the hour or so since he had last checked it and went to the website for Argenbright Vail. This was a Seattle-based law firm with branches in San Jose and a few other centers of the tech economy. Formerly a small, white-shoe sort of practice, it had, during the decades since Microsoft had taken root in this area, grown to the point where it now had something like a thousand lawyers. Argenbright Vail had helped Dodge form Corporation 9592, accepting payment in the form of an envelope of twenty-dollar bills, and had represented both him personally and his company ever since. Corvallis didn't know whether Dodge even had a will, or, if he did, where it might be found, but this was an obvious place to start looking.

Argenbright Vail occupied ten floors of an office tower that was directly visible out the window of this very room. When Corvallis dialed the extension of Stan Peterson, the partner there whom he deemed most likely to know the answer to his question, he could almost imagine that Stan was visible through one of those windows, the white French cuff of his shirt flashing as he reached out to pick up his handset. For once, the telephone gods were smiling upon Corvallis, and he was able to get through on the second ring. It probably helped that he was the CTO of a hot startup, his name, title, and photograph enshrined in Argenbright Vail's awesome high-tech phone system and displayed on the screen of Stan's computer at the same time the phone rang.

"Corvallis Kawasaki, as I live and breathe!" Stan called cheerfully.

"Stan, are you in your office? Someplace private?"

"Yeah, let me just close the door." Corvallis heard Stan doing so. "What's up? Should I get Laura?" He was referring to another partner there who handled the account of Nubilant—the company Corvallis now worked for. Stan, on the other hand, was Dodge's personal lawyer. Perhaps he was assuming that Corvallis was confused and had dialed the wrong extension. Happened all the time.

"No, this is about Dodge."

"Is he in trouble again?" Stan asked with feigned exasperation that was meant to be humorous, and would have been, if Dodge hadn't been brain-dead.

Corvallis gave him an explanation of what was happening. Or *had happened* was truer, but more painful, as it captured the reality that it was not going to un-happen. Every so often, he paused in case Stan wanted to jump in with a question. But Stan was utterly silent, except for some breathing, which sounded a little faster and heavier than normal.

"Of course!" he blurted out, when Corvallis had finally got around to asking about the will. "I mean, yes! We drew up his will. Years ago. It's got the thing you're asking for."

"A living will?"

"Health care directive," Stan corrected him. "Same thing. But, C-plus, are you sure . . ."

"Sure of what?"

"That his condition is really at the point where—where we need to be reading that document?"

"You mean the document that states what Dodge wanted to happen in the case where he was brain-dead, and on life support?" Corvallis asked.

After a long pause, Stan said, "Yeah."

"The doctor didn't pull any punches. He's with Zula now. When he comes back I'll double-check. But in the meantime I think you had better get it over here."

Stan was slow to respond. Corvallis tried, "Worst case is that it's a false alarm and we have a laugh over it."

This was a lie, but it worked. "I'll do it," Stan said immediately.

Dodge's will arrived twenty minutes later, delivered by a bicycle messenger who pulled it out of a rain-washed bag slung over one shoulder. *Homo Seattleus,* Corvallis thought as he regarded this lanky young man, his dreadlocks, his long reddish beard, his Utilikilt, his blinding array of independently flashing bike safety lights, his stainless-steel water bottle. Somewhat contrary to his appearance, he was all business and insisted that Zula would have to sign for the receipt of the documents. She did so without interrupting a telephone conversation that she was having over her earbuds. Corvallis took the envelope back to the little private room that they had turned into their operations center and undid the string tie and pulled out a stack of documents. There were three of them: a fat one that was the actual last will and testament, and two shorter ones, the health care directive and the disposition of remains. He did so with a feeling of dread so powerful that it induced tingling in his fingertips. He was afraid that the voice of Dodge was about to speak to him from the health care directive, stating bluntly that if he ended up on a ventilator he was to be put to death forthwith. In which case it would happen now, before Corvallis had had time to even Google the five stages of grief. He was holding out some hope that Dodge might have gone soft—or, much more likely in the case of Dodge, that he had been so bored by the process of drawing up these documents that he had simply signed whatever they had put in front of him, and that it might afford some kind of loophole. An excuse to keep him on the machine for a few days at least—long enough for more family members to converge on the scene and shoulder Corvallis out of the way and make it not be his problem.

What he found was neither. The health care directive was curiously verbose. And it was a bit odd from a typographical standpoint. The introductory paragraph and some of the connective tissue was in the Palatino that was standard at Argenbright Vail. But big slabs of it were in Monaco, a sans-serif typeface that tended to be used by nerds to display computer code in terminal windows. This was, in other words, a document that had been assembled largely by copying and pasting material from something else— something that looked like it had been downloaded from the Internet back in the pre-web days. Probably straight text, as opposed to a word processing document. The quotation marks and other punctuation suggested that it had originally been composed in the nerd-friendly text processing program Emacs. No effort had been made by Stan, or whoever had drawn this thing up, to "select all" and tidy up the formatting.

Those sections of the document contained instructions. Detailed instructions. Weird ones. Technically precise instructions on how to kill Dodge in a controlled manner, should he ever wind up on a ventilator. The machine was not just supposed to be disconnected. Instead it was to be left on while Dodge's body was infused with a certain mixture of drugs and his core temperature was dropped using an ice bath. Only then was the ventilator to be removed. And then, at the moment that Dodge stopped being a living person at death's door and became legally dead, the reader was urged to set aside the health care directive and pick up its companion document, the disposition of remains. And this had exactly the same typographical peculiarities. It was a seamless continuation of the protocol begun in the health care directive. Once the ventilator had been disconnected, Dodge's body was supposed to be chilled down as quickly as possible with an ice-water IV, bath, and enema. Only then was it acceptable to move "the remains," and this was supposed to happen in a meticulously described way, taking the corpse directly to a particular facility in the high desert outside of Ephrata, Washington, where it was to be kept cryogenically preserved.

The nerd in Corvallis was fascinated by the level of technical detail embodied in these documents, and wanted to have a conversation with whatever team of doctors and neuroscientists had toiled over them. And the socially awkward geek was relieved, in a way, to have something to take his mind off of what was happening around him. As long as he was hunched over these protocols he was absolved of responsibilities on the emotional front. But there was a third aspect of his personality that slowly came to the fore, and wrestled the steering wheel, as it were, away from the others. That was the CTO, the responsible business executive who was at least passingly familiar with the world of lawyers. And the CTO was curious about the typography thing. Argenbright Vail was a sophisticated tech law firm. Richard Forthrast was one of their most important clients. Many thousands of dollars must have been spent poring over these documents before they had been sent to Dodge for his signature. To set them all in Palatino and clean up the formatting would have been the work of a few moments for an intern. Leaving them in this state, he suspected, had been a deliberate choice. A way for Argenbright Vail to put the protocol in scare quotes. To make it clear, to any future reader, that they had just been following instructions. Dodge's instructions, presumably.

Corvallis had an "oh shit" moment then. A clear memory and an understanding. He checked the signature date on the documents. They were nine years old. Richard had caused them to be drawn up when he had become wealthy. He had signed them, filed them away, and forgotten about them. He was the last man in the world who would have bothered to update and maintain his will.

"Is he wearing a bracelet?" Corvallis asked Zula during a rare moment when she wasn't on the phone to Iowa.

"A what?" she asked, not certain she'd quite heard him correctly. It was a weird question; Dodge was about as likely to wear a bishop's miter as a bracelet.

"I mean a medical alert kind of bracelet. You know, like people wear if they have drug allergies or something."

"For the doctor to read in the ER if you're found unconscious."

"Yeah."

"I don't know," she said, "but I don't think so. Want me to go check?"

"Hang on," Corvallis said, "I think I can spare you the trouble." He had brought up the photo application on his laptop. He had thousands of pictures archived on this thing. Organizing them into albums was one of those tasks he never seemed to have time for. But the application did have a built-in ability to recognize faces, and automatically to produce collections of pictures that included a particular face. During stretches of bored downtime on airplanes, Corvallis had taught it to recognize a few faces that were important to him, including that of Richard Forthrast. He clicked on "Dodge" in the interface. The application cogitated for a few moments and then populated the window with thumbnails of pictures featuring Dodge, or people who, according to its algorithm, resembled him. With another click Corvallis sorted them according to date, then began to page through them from the beginning. His earliest personal photograph of Dodge was from about eight years ago, but he had a few older photos, taken before he had even met the man, that had found their way onto his drive as the result of being attached to emails or what have you. Some of these showed a very young man: the long-haired 1970s draft-dodging edition of Richard Forthrast, hanging out in wild places along the Idaho–British Columbia border, and depicted in the flamboyant hues of scanned Kodachrome. No bracelets for him. Hitting the right-arrow key, he worked up through the years until he stumbled into a series of pictures taken around the time of Corporation 9592's initial public offering. In one of those, Dodge was gripping a magnum of champagne in both hands, bracing it against his penis, holding a thumb over the mouth of the bottle to make it spray foam at Pluto. The photo was harshly lit by a flash and it showed both of his arms clearly. On his left wrist, competing for space with a cheap digital wristwatch, was a medical alert bracelet: a metal plaque about the size of a large postage stamp, held on with a chain, blazoned with a red caduceus, otherwise covered with print too fine to read. Way more metallic real estate than what would have been needed for "I am allergic to penicillin."

Corvallis didn't need to read it because he knew exactly what it was. Just to be sure, he checked the date of the photo and verified that it had been taken within a couple of months of the signing of the will.

He opened up a new browser window and clicked in the search box. He turned his attention to the health care directive and skimmed through one of those Monaco-font sections until he found an unusual series of words. He typed those in and hit the Enter key and was immediately presented with a screen full of exact matches. The same text had been copied and pasted in many places on the Internet. For his purposes, most of them would be red herrings. Corvallis scanned through the search results until finally he saw the word that he had, this entire time, been trying to dredge up from his memory.

He went back to the search box and typed "Eutropians." A memory from the early days of the Internet, the 1990s tech boom.

The primary website had not been updated for more than ten years. The organization, if it even still existed, seemed to have gone dark in 2002, in the black years after the implosion of the tech bubble and 9/11.

The Wikipedia entry was bracketed in multiple layers of warnings; people had been fighting over it.

Some of the basic facts, however, seemed indisputable. The Eutropians were a movement that had taken shape during the early 1990s, when all things had seemed possible through technology. It was just an informal discussion group in Berkeley, with a branch around Stanford. They had adopted the World Wide Web early and created what at the time was an unusually sophisticated website. Now, of course, it was as dated as black-and-white TV. A nonprofit had been founded, later obtained 501(c)(3) status, and ceased to exist in 2004. More than one for-profit company had emerged from the movement. The Wikipedia entry was littered with question marks and complaints from various editors. Corvallis didn't have to check its history to know that it had been the battleground of many flame wars. The details didn't matter.

"If I can get Dr. Trinh in here," Corvallis said, "can I then have a few minutes of your time?"

Actually he didn't say it; he texted it to Zula, who was across the table from him, trying to calm someone down over the phone. She glanced at the screen of her phone, then looked up at him and nodded.

Corvallis had a bit of a hard time convincing the nurse at the front desk that what he had to tell Dr. Trinh was really more important than what he was doing at the moment, but when he used the words "health care directive" and "legal" it got her attention. A few minutes later, the doctor was in the room again with Corvallis and Zula.

"There was this group of geeks in the Bay Area in the 1990s who thought they saw a path to immortality through technology," Corvallis began. "They became known as Eutropians. It is a quasi-technical name. If entropy is the tendency of things to become disorganized over time, then eutropy is a statement of optimism. Not only can we defeat entropy, but the universe, in a way, wants us to use our powers as conscious beings to make things better. And part of that is defeating death."

"How'd that work out for them?" Zula asked, deadpan.

"These guys were smart," Corvallis said. "Not flakes. There was nothing they didn't know, or couldn't learn, about the science. They knew perfectly well that it was going to be a long time—decades at least—before practical life-extension technology became available. They knew that in the meantime they could die at any point in a car accident or whatever. So, they instituted a stopgap. Based on the best science at the time, they designed a protocol for preserving human remains and keeping them on ice indefinitely."

"So that, down the road—" Zula began.

"Down the road," Corvallis said, "when it did become technologically possible, they could be brought back to life."

"Like Walt Disney," said Dr. Trinh.

"Apparently that's an urban myth," Corvallis said, "but yeah, it's the same idea. Cryonics. It's a big long hairy story. The idea has been around since the 1960s and it's come and gone in waves. Well, what you both need to know is that Richard got caught up in one of those waves for a little while."

"It doesn't seem like him," Zula said.

"Yes and no. Sure, he is—was—skeptical. A fatalist. But he was also open-minded. Willing to take calculated risks."

"I'll give you that."

"Around the time that his company became a big deal, he was making a lot of contacts in the tech world, going to conferences, hanging out with VCs. One of the VCs who had backed Corporation 9592 also had some money in a startup that had been founded by an offshoot of the Eutropians. To make a long story short, it was a cryonics company. They constructed a facility in eastern Washington State. Electrical power is cheap there because of the Grand Coulee Dam."

"And that was their biggest expense," Dr. Trinh surmised. "Power to keep the freezers running."

"Exactly. They approached a lot of people who had new tech money and offered them a Pascal's Wager kind of deal."

"Pascal's Wager?" asked Dr. Trinh.

"Pascal once said that you should believe in God because, if you turned out to be wrong, you weren't losing anything, and if you turned out to be right, the reward was infinite," Corvallis said.

Zula nodded. "It was the same exact deal here."

"Exactly," Corvallis said. "If cryonics turned out to be worthless, and it was impossible to save your frozen body, who cares? You're dead anyway. But if it actually did work, you might be able to live forever."

"I can totally see Richard going for that," Zula said, nodding. "After a few drinks."

"He did go for it, and he followed all of their recommended procedures," Corvallis said. "For a little while, he wore a special medical bracelet giving instructions on how to freeze his body." He spun his laptop around and let them see the photograph. "Around the same time, he updated his will. And most of it, I'm guessing, is just an ordinary will." Corvallis rested his hand on the thickest of the three documents. "But the health care directive and the disposition of remains consist mostly of boilerplate instructions that had been developed by the Eutropians. And basically what it says is that after his body has been chilled down, it's supposed to be shipped to this facility out in eastern Washington, where a team of medical technicians will take over and prepare him for the full cryonic-preservation thing."

"I've never seen that bracelet on him," Zula remarked.

"Because he stopped wearing it before you came out to Seattle," Corvallis said. "He told me this story once, a long time ago. About the Eutropians and the VC and all the rest. I had kind of forgotten it. Dodge had a lot of stories and this wasn't the most interesting of them."

"No, it wasn't," Zula confirmed, with a slow shake of the head.

"It was pretty clear from the way he told the story that he had decided the whole thing was ridiculous. Like when he went out and bought that Escalade and then wrecked it."

"One of those silly things that boys do when they suddenly get a lot of money," Zula said.

"Exactly. It's long forgotten. But"—and Corvallis now rested his hand on the health care directive—"he never updated his will."

"That is still legally binding?" Zula asked sharply, nodding at the documents.

"I'm not a lawyer," Corvallis said.

They both looked at Dr. Trinh, who held his hands up as if under arrest and shook his head.

Stan Peterson—who *was*, in fact, a lawyer—was there half an hour later. He had canceled all of his appointments, he wanted it known. He did not announce this in a self-congratulatory manner.

He just wanted Zula to understand that the full resources of Argenbright Vail, up to and including drone strikes and private rocket ships, were at her and the family's disposal.

"Alice is on a plane," Zula told him. "She'll be here late tonight."

Stan looked a little nonplussed.

"Richard's sister-in-law," Zula explained.

"She'll be the executor?"

Zula shook her head no and glanced at the will. "She's just the most senior next of kin, I guess you would say. I don't know how it works. If we're going to do something—to pull the plug or whatever—she would want to be in on it." Her face screwed up and she went into a little cry.

"I'm sorry," Stan said. In addition to nonplussed, he seemed a bit of a mess emotionally. It was evident that he too had cried, and done it recently enough that he had a lingering case of the sniffles. He had probably looked at Richard on his way in. "Who *is* named as the executor?"

Zula looked up, sniffled, controlled it. Then her eyes turned to Corvallis.

"Sorry, I haven't read the will," Corvallis began.

Zula interrupted him. "I have. You're the executor, C-plus."

"Oh." Corvallis said. "Holy shit."

"You and I have a lot to talk about then," Stan said.

"But he's not technically dead yet, right?" Corvallis said. "So, the will doesn't kick in. Not until—"

"Not until there is a death certificate," Stan said with a nod. His eyes strayed toward the health care directive. He sniffled once more and nodded at it. "That was drawn up personally by Christopher Vail Jr.," he said. Seeing that this meant nothing to the others, he elaborated: "The cofounder of our firm. He took early retirement about five years ago. Early-onset Alzheimer's. He's in a special hospice now. He's feeling no pain. But he won't be able to help us with these documents."

"Have you read them?" Corvallis asked.

"In the Uber, on the way here." Stan raised his eyebrows in a mute commentary on what he had seen on those pages, and Corvallis was unable to hold back a faint smile.

"I took the liberty of running a diff," Corvallis said.

"I'll guess that is some kind of technical term?"

"I ran a text analysis program that compared these documents with the ones on the Internet that they were obviously adapted from."

"How did you obtain an electronic copy? These are paper," Stan pointed out.

"I took a picture of it with my phone and OCRed it," Corvallis said.

Stan seemed to find it all a bit irregular. "What did you learn from 'running a diff'?"

"Christopher Vail Jr. didn't just blindly copy the boilerplate language," Corvallis said. "He made changes."

"I would certainly hope so!" said Stan.

"Not to the technical instructions, of course—that's all the same, word for word. But in the language around it he added some other provisions."

"C-plus, you'll have to forgive me for being, frankly, a little unprepared for all this," Stan said, and sighed. "I will admit I hadn't looked at Richard's will or these other documents. If I had been aware of their unusual contents, I might have spoken to him, at some point, about refreshing them, doing a little routine maintenance. As it is, I am in all honesty running a little behind. Perhaps you could just tell me what it is that you think you have found and I can give you my word that by the time Alice arrives I will be fully on top of all of this."

"It looks to me like the original language from Ephrata was written by nerds."

"Ephrata? Sounds biblical."

"It is. But in this case I'm talking about Ephrata Cryonics Inc. The cold storage place in the town of the same name. It's in the desert east of the mountains. Or it was."

It took a moment for that last word to sink into Stan's brain. "Oh, shit."

"It's okay," Corvallis said. "See, this is where Christopher Vail earned his fee. The founders of Ephrata were true believers. They believed they had come up with the ideal way to preserve human remains. And they believed that Ephrata Cryonics Inc. was going to be around forever."

"Because so many people were going to sign up for the service . . . ," Zula said.

"That they'd have a fat bank account, economies of scale, the whole bit," said Corvallis.

"Well, as one who knew Chris Vail well when his faculties were intact, I'm guessing he took neither of those presumptions for granted," Stan said.

Corvallis nodded. "If you read this, I think what you'll see is him basically saying: look, if Ephrata Cryonics is actually still in business when Richard Forthrast dies, and if they are solvent, and if no better technology has been invented in the meantime to preserve the remains, then go ahead and follow these instructions and ship Dodge off to the big freezer in Ephrata."

"But if any of those is not true . . . ," Stan said.

"Well, then it gets complicated," Corvallis said.

"Like it was all so simple before," Zula muttered.

Corvallis pulled the disposition of remains over to him and flipped through to the last few pages, which were all in the standard-issue justified Palatino of Argenbright Vail. "Complicated in a way that makes my brain hurt—but I'll bet you can make sense of it."

"At your service, sir," Stan said.

Fortuitously, they were joined a moment later by a woman who introduced herself as the hospital's general counsel. It was easy enough to infer that she'd been alerted to the presence of a patient's attorney in the ICU department and was coming down to find out what was up. That the patient was a famous billionaire and the lawyer a senior partner at Argenbright Vail had presumably put some spring in her step. She was younger and less heavily groomed than might be expected; a Catholic feminist soccer mom with a Brown degree, according to the Miasma. Esme Hurlbut, believe it or not. Enjoyed knitting and free climbing. A few minutes were lost in making introductions and bringing Esme up to speed; Dr. Trinh repeated what the others already knew of Dodge's condition. Corvallis spent the time rifling the Miasma for more information about Ephrata Cryonics Inc.

When the conversation resumed, he was in a position to say more: "Ephrata took in a bunch of money from people like Dodge. They froze a few bodies almost immediately—which probably seemed like progress at the time—but it forced them to keep the freezers running forever after that. They got hit with a lawsuit from some pissed-off Eutropians that depleted their reserves. They never really hit their targets financially. The bottom fell out after the dot-com crash. In 2003 they did a reorg. Their first step was to cut the heads off and burn the bodies."

"I'm sorry, could you say that again?" Stan asked.

Esme Hurlbut, who had clearly been apprehensive when she had entered the room, was now more fascinated.

"They had eleven bodies in cryostorage at that point," Corvallis said, flicking his gaze down at his laptop to verify the stats. "The contract that all eleven of those people had signed, while they were alive, when they gave Ephrata Cryonics their money, contained an out. It said that the remains were to be preserved in cryogenic storage—or through whatever means, in the judgment of Ephrata Cryonics, were best suited to the desired goal of eventually bringing the deceased back to life."

Esme raised her hand like the smart girl in the front row. "Judgment? Or *sole* judgment?" she asked.

"Sole judgment," Corvallis answered after scanning the words on his screen. In his peripheral vision he saw Esme and Stan exchanging a fraught glance.

"And based on that," Corvallis continued, "the argument that Ephrata Cryonics now made was that the only thing that mattered was the head. Or, when you get right down to it, the brain. The body was basically disposable. Any future society that had enough technology to bring a frozen brain back to full conscious functioning would be able to grow a new body from DNA. So, to save money, Ephrata Cryonics decapitated the eleven frozen bodies and packed the heads into a much smaller freezer."

"Cut their operating expenses to the bone!" Stan proclaimed approvingly. Momentarily losing track, perhaps, of whose side he was on.

"What does this mean for us today?" Zula asked.

Stan pulled the health care directive over to himself and began scanning it. He seemed to be focusing on the part of it that had been contributed by his former colleague Christopher Vail. As he did so, he spoke in a somewhat distracted manner: "I think that is going to depend, Zula, on the questions we talked about a minute ago . . . whether the company is solvent . . . what the current state of the technology is. . . ."

"Depends on what you mean by 'solvent,'" Corvallis said. "According to the Internet—"

"Which as we know is never wrong," Esme put in.

"Yeah. According to the Internet, the decapitation gambit only bought them three more years. Then they reached a point—"

"Oh, my god, I remember this now. It was a news story, briefly," Esme said. "The power company was threatening to shut them off for nonpayment. The company insisted that letting the brains thaw out would be tantamount to murder. It was a standoff."

Stan literally slapped his forehead. "Jesus. I can't believe Dodge got into business with these people." Which merely drew quizzical looks from both Zula and Corvallis, wordlessly asking, *Do you have the first idea of the kinds of people he* did *get into business with?* Oblivious, Stan shook his head. "But at least we've answered the question of whether they are solvent."

"Depends on what you mean," Corvallis said. His Googling was still keeping pace with the conversation. "A deal was worked out. One of the original Eutropians swooped in. Elmo Shepherd."

"One of those pissed-off Eutropians who had sued them earlier?" Zula asked.

"You got it. Shepherd was the main instigator of that lawsuit. He claimed that Ephrata Cryonics had laid claim to some IP— some intellectual property—that ought to have been in the public domain—the open-source work of the original Eutropians."

"Hang on, I know who El Shepherd is. Hell, I've *met* him," Stan said. "I think he's one of our clients in the Silicon Valley office."

"He made some money on an IPO and became a venture capitalist," Corvallis said. "Mostly conventional tech VC stuff, it looks like—but he has maintained a side interest in life extension."

"So, what happened when he 'swooped in'?" Esme asked.

"He formed a new company called Ephrata Life Sciences and Health," Corvallis said. He had ceased to be an autonomous participant in the conversation and become a conduit for whatever was on the Miasma. "He funded it with his own money. And he worked out a deal—he acquired Ephrata Cryonics lock, stock, and barrel. Ephrata Cryonics is now a wholly owned subsidiary of ELSH, which is based out of the Presidio, San Francisco, California."

"So technically it *is* solvent?" Zula asked. She had been juggling text messages and ignoring phone calls for several minutes and was losing the battle against electronic distractions.

"As long as El Shepherd is pouring money into it, it's difficult to claim otherwise," Stan said. "But listen, that's not the only out in this document. Assuming you're looking for an out. There's also the question of whether the technology that ELSH is now using is really the best."

"In the *sole judgment* of ELSH?" Esme asked.

Stan permitted himself a look of mild satisfaction. "Nope. In the *boilerplate* contract that was signed by the Ephrata Eleven—the people whose heads ended up in the freezer—the word 'sole' is used, but Chris Vail, bless his heart, struck that word out in the one that was signed by Dodge."

"So we get some say over it," Zula said.

Esme looked like she wanted to say something, but thought better of it and crossed her arms.

"You get lots of say over it," Stan said, "and I'll bet we can make an argument that cutting Dodge's head off and throwing it in a freezer is no longer the best technology—if it ever was in the first place."

Zula nodded at this and Corvallis had to swallow a mild feeling of discomfort. Later, he would sit down with Zula and Alice Forthrast and remind them that Argenbright Vail stood to make a lot of money if that case went to court and they had to argue it against El Shepherd's lawyers. Anyway, his Googling had uncovered more facts that might make it irrelevant. "Turns out," he announced, "that it's no longer heads in a freezer. ELSH has moved on."

"I'm ready," Stan said. Again, Corvallis found his tone to be a little off. What really mattered was whether Zula was ready. But he could see where this was going. Stan was gradually asserting control over the situation. By the time Alice got off the plane, he'd be fully in command, ready to introduce himself as the Forthrast family lawyer.

Zula exchanged an unreadable look with Esme. A women-in-solidarity kind of thing, he guessed.

Corvallis waited until he had caught Zula's eye and she had given him the nod. "Now that we have cloud computing," he said, "storing bits is way cheaper than storing body parts in a freezer. A few years ago, ELSH, in its sole judgment, decided that the only thing that *really* mattered was the connectome—the pattern of connections among the neurons in the brain. They took each of those eleven brains and scanned them. Reduced them to data structures. Stored the data in the cloud."

"And where are those brains now?" Esme asked. Because that shoe was going to drop eventually.

"The scanning," Corvallis said, "is a destructive process." He was reading about it as he spoke. "Destructive" was putting it mildly but he saw no need to be heavy-handed. "By the time it is finished, there is nothing left that could be considered a brain. What *is* left is, they claim, disposed of in a respectful manner. Cremated. Ashes returned to the next of kin."

"And since ELSH went over to this process," Stan asked, "have there been any more?"

"Any more what?" Corvallis asked.

"Any more like Richard," Zula said.

Stan nodded. "People who had signed a contract with Ephrata Cryonics and then died after the company got into difficulty."

"If so," Corvallis said, "no one is talking about it on the Internet." He scrolled back. "One of these articles does say that ELSH refunded money to some clients, at their request, and canceled the contracts."

"But not Richard," Zula said.

"I would have no way of knowing," said Corvallis.

Zula was staring at him. "C-plus. Come on. This is Richard. Do you really think he would have bothered?"

"No," Corvallis said. "Dodge wouldn't have bothered. If he even remembered signing the contract."

"So, I have some action items," Stan announced. "If it's okay with the family, I can reach out to ELSH and find out whether that contract is still in force. Then it'll be up to you all to decide how you would like to proceed. My recommendation is that we do a little background research on this—what do you call it? The connection thing?"

"Connect—connectomics," Corvallis said, stumbling over the word in a way that drew puzzled looks from the others. Because some part of his brain had put up an *oh shit* flag while he was saying it.

"Everything okay, C-plus?" Zula asked. Giving him a mild feeling of shame that she, of all people, was concerned for his state of mind at such a moment.

"Umm, sorry. There's a weird connection. Pardon the pun."

"Connection to what?" Esme asked. Her primary reason for remaining in the room had long since become sheer intellectual curiosity.

"I should explain," Corvallis said, "that I work for—I am the CTO of—a cloud computing company here in Seattle. And one of our clients is—well—"

"Don't tell me," Zula said. "Ephrata Life Sciences and Health."

"Not quite. But Elmo Shepherd has a stable of companies that he runs out of the Presidio. Some for profit. Others are more like think tanks, research institutes, and the like. He's really interested in the Singularity, which is—"

"I know what it is," Zula said.

"I don't. Would you indulge me?" Esme said. She had, in some nonverbal way, bonded with Zula.

Zula nodded and said, "It's a kind of belief system that in the future we are going to upload our brains into computers and live forever digitally."

"How do you get 'Singularity' out of that?"

"You add in Moore's Law," Corvallis said.

"That's the one that says computers keep getting faster?"

"Exponentially. Extrapolate it out, and it suggests that the souls that have been uploaded to silicon will become super fast, super powerful, and render living, biological brains irrelevant."

"I still don't see how 'Singularity' describes that—isn't that a word for a black hole?"

"It'll happen in a flash, is the idea," Zula explained.

"And El Shepherd believes in this," Esme said.

Stan was just sitting there with his hands cupped around his eyes. *When is this day going to stop getting weirder?*

"Some of his other companies exist to support research on different aspects of phenomena relating to the Singularity. One of those is the connectome of the brain. There's a whole stable of them. Look, I'm on thin ice here because I can't breach the confidentiality of Nubilant's relationship with its customers."

"But it's obvious," Stan said, "from the look on your face that El Shepherd is storing the connectomes of the Ephrata Eleven on your company's servers."

"If you haven't gotten sick of everything being ironic yet," Corvallis said, "you might enjoy knowing that our biggest server farm is out in eastern Washington State. Not far from Ephrata."

"Where power is cheap, and cooling water is plentiful," Zula said. She had majored in geology.

"I feel like I'm losing the thread of this conversation," Esme admitted.

"This is either really good or really bad, in terms of my ability to be useful," Corvallis said. "I'll ask around and see if I can get through to some of Elmo Shepherd's people in the Presidio."

"Or El himself," Stan said. "This warrants his attention, I think."

4

T he conversation petered out as it became clear to them that they were not going to pull the plug on Dodge right away. Dr. Trinh left the room to attend to patients who weren't beyond helping. Esme distributed business cards and swapped cell phone numbers, then excused herself. Other patients' families needed to use the room and so Stan, Zula, and Corvallis shifted to the hospital cafeteria. From there they went their separate ways: Stan to his office to bone up on the documents, Zula to her home, Corvallis to his office.

The conversation paused for an afternoon. The pause grew to encompass the evening and the night that followed. Twenty-four hours elapsed before it resumed. Corvallis spent it in a kind of limbo. Until there was a death certificate, Dodge wasn't legally dead, and so there was no need for an executor. Executor—or, in the more modern gender-neutral usage, "personal representative"—was to be Corvallis's role. He devoted a little bit of effort to learning how the job worked, but it was mostly legalese of the sort that made his head hurt. He had responsibilities at work.

And at about ten in the evening, word somehow leaked to the Miasma that Richard Forthrast was in the ICU with serious medical problems. Then his world exploded for about six hours and ruled out getting very much sleep. The Miasma behaved, sometimes, as if it expected every man, woman, and child on earth to have a social media and PR staff on twenty-four-hour call. It would have been impossible even if Corvallis had been at liberty to say anything.

When next they got together, it was in a suite in an old but well-maintained luxury hotel a couple of blocks from the hospital. Corvallis knew Alice Forthrast a little—well enough to guess that she hadn't chosen this place. Zula had done it for her. Alice would have made a sort of performance of her frugality and her lack of interest in the ways of big coastal cities by staying in the cheapest available motel near the airport. Zula had preempted all of that by making other arrangements and simply driving her here and dropping her off last night. The place was within walking distance of where Zula, Csongor, and Sophia lived. The relatives back home would wonder why Alice didn't just sleep on Zula's couch, or in Richard's now-vacant apartment for that matter. But Corvallis followed Zula's thinking. The family would need a command center near the hospital, some neutral ground from which they could operate. A conference room at Argenbright Vail would have put them too much in the law firm's pocket. The kitchen table at Zula and Csongor's condo would have made certain conversations awkward, if Sophia were underfoot asking to have everything explained. So the hotel suite it was.

By the time Corvallis got there with Jake Forthrast—Richard's younger brother—in tow, Zula had already stocked its fridge with milk, yogurt, and a few other staples so that Alice wouldn't have to go on making outraged Facebook posts over the cost of room service. Csongor had taken a few days of leave and was at home on full-time Sophia duty so that Zula could focus everything on this. Corvallis had warned people at Nubilant that he would be out of pocket for a few days—almost unnecessary given that most people there had awakened this morning to gales of social media coverage of the Forthrast tragedy. Number one on Reddit was a brief video that some random kid had shot yesterday of himself standing next to Dodge outside of the medical building where, only a few minutes later, Dodge had been stricken. Corvallis had forcibly ignored it for a few times and then just broken down and watched the damned thing. Dodge was being reasonably cheerful about being waylaid by his young fanboy; he'd pulled his headphones down around his neck so that he could hear what the kid was saying, and tinny music could be heard from them when cars weren't shushing past on the wet street. Corvallis had expected that the video would wreck him, but instead he found it weirdly comforting, and watched it several times. Reminding himself of who Dodge was, and getting ready for the post-Dodge world.

Corvallis had, a few minutes ago, picked Jake Forthrast up at the train station downtown. He was in his late forties—a straggler, much younger than the other three Forthrast siblings. He lived in northern Idaho, in a remote community of like-minded people, which was to say extreme libertarians with a religious bent. He had a wife and a brood of kids there. Outside of his little area, he couldn't drive, because he didn't have a driver's license, because he did not believe that the government had the authority to issue them. Yesterday, upon hearing the news, he had somehow made his way to the train station in Coeur d'Alene and boarded a westbound Amtrak that was running seven hours late. He and Corvallis had crossed paths before and were more comfortable around each other than might have been expected based on the differences in their backgrounds and their political and religious thinking. The drive from the train station to the valet parking in front of the hotel had not lasted much more than five minutes and so Corvallis had not been able to tell him much, other than that Richard's condition was unchanged. Jake had a somewhat scruffy beard, auburn turning gray, and had gone mostly bald. He was wearing the sensible flannel-lined work clothes that he wore day in and day out at his job, which was building log cabins and rustic furniture. He gazed around at the lobby's opulent furnishings with an expression Corvallis did not know how to read. The elevator, which was paneled with finely wrought hardwood, gave him something to focus on.

Alice Forthrast was the widow of Richard's older brother, John, and the matriarch of the extended family, operating from a farmhouse in northwest Iowa. She was in her seventies but could have passed for younger. She hadn't bothered with trying to color her hair, which was thoroughly gray now, and cut short. When Corvallis first saw her she was smiling at Zula, showing real teeth, somewhat the worse for wear. They had been remembering something funny that Richard had done. But when Corvallis and Jake came in they sobered up, as if they'd been caught out misbehaving. Jake greeted Zula with a long, warm hug and Alice with a more perfunctory one; she did not fully rise out of her chair, but she did smile at him, lips pressed together, eyes slitted against tears.

Corvallis and Alice had met before, but Zula reintroduced them just in case Alice had forgotten his name. Maybe Alice's short-term memory was a little leaky, or maybe it was one of those all-Asians-look-the-same deals. Anyway Alice nodded and said, "Of course, I remember Dodge talking about you and your Rome activities." Referring to an eccentric hobby.

"But he's also—" Zula put in.

"Of course, I know that there's much more to C-plus than just that," Alice said, then turned to Corvallis. "Otherwise I don't think that Dodge would have entrusted you with being the executor of his will, would he?"

Good. So someone had laid that on her.

Alice continued, "I want you to know that Richard, whatever some people might say about him, was a fine judge of men, and if he trusted you, then we trust you. And I can see all kinds of intelligent reasons to have the executor be someone outside the family—an impartial person."

"Well, I'm just sorry that we are re-meeting under these circumstances," Corvallis said. This was a bit of dialogue he had concocted ahead of time, and it sounded that way. So he improvised, "Thanks for your statement that you just made." Zula and Alice kept looking at him as if they were expecting more. "It means a lot to me," he tried. Both women seemed to find this acceptable as a termination of whatever it was he'd been trying to gasp out. "I'll do my best," he tacked on, unable to stop himself, and they began to look a little unnerved.

He was saved by the timely arrival of Stan, who showed up with a younger lawyer in tow.

The summit conference had now attained a sort of quorum. Alice, Zula, and Jake were the closest Richard had to next of kin: to put it bluntly, enough critical mass to pull the plug on Richard's ventilator. Corvallis was there in his role as executor, which had not formally commenced yet, and the lawyers were in the house, and on the clock. Insensitive to the ways of lawyers and their hourly rates, Alice insisted on making coffee and small talk, racking up, in Corvallis's loose estimation, about a thousand dollars' worth of billable hours before allowing the conversation to spiral around to matters that might be considered business. Distracted by the meter running in his head, Corvallis sipped his coffee—which was terrible—and looked around at the room, which was finished like the abode of a wealthy old lady. Of course, Alice Forthrast *was*, in fact, a wealthy old lady, but he suspected that her house was finished in an altogether different style.

The younger lawyer was named Marcus, he was from Shaker Heights, he had attended Penn, where he had majored in philosophy and lettered in rowing. After a stint working in a rural Mississippi town with Teach for America, he had gone on to Stanford Law School. He had a lovely wife of Korean ancestry and a six-month-old baby and was just days away from closing on a Tudor Revival three-bedroom in the Queen Anne neighborhood—a bit of a fixer-upper but with good bones, a great family dwelling once they pulled the asbestos-covered heating ducts out of the basement, a job on which they were taking bids now. Alice extracted all of this from him and then, almost as an afterthought, got him to admit that his specialty was structuring transactions in the tech industry and that he didn't really know anything about family law and had never drawn up a will. Before Stan—who had spent most of the conversation checking his phone—was fully aware of the trap that his young associate had just stepped into, he made a similar confession. Now that it was too late, he assured Alice that Christopher Vail had been quite good at that kind of thing.

Alice shook her head like a disappointed mom. On the flight from Omaha last night, she had blown fifteen bucks on wireless Internet service and apparently spent the whole three hours researching Chris Vail's background and career and found no evidence at all that he knew anything about wills. "Yesterday I had Zula send a scanned copy of Richard's will to our family lawyer back home," she announced, "who may be a small-town lawyer but I can tell you that he has made out a lot of wills, as it is a major part of his practice, and he found three things wrong with it *on the first page*. Rookie mistakes, he called them." She shook her head.

Stan had put his phone away and was sitting there red faced. Marcus was agog.

"Do you know what it looks like to me? It looks like this Chris Vail character got a call from Dodge that Dodge wanted a last will and testament drawn up, and he said to himself, 'I don't want to lose my billionaire, I do believe I'm just going to take care of it myself. How hard could it be to draw up a will?' And he wrote the first and probably the last document of that type of his career, and I'm sure he was well-intentioned, but he botched it."

"Alice—" Stan began.

"Malpractice, is what some would call it," Alice said.

This woman was a cobra. Corvallis made a note of it.

Wishing he were elsewhere, he let his gaze stray to Zula, who was looking back at him deadpan. *Welcome to the family, C-plus.*

"Well, it's all water under the bridge," Alice sighed. "The will is written the way it's written and Dodge signed it because he was too busy to care and there is nothing we can do about it now. The man who did it has moved on to a different place and there is no sense in bedeviling him with recriminations and threats. But I am not Dodge. I am paying attention and I will hold Argenbright Vail to a higher standard as far as *competence* and *billing* are concerned."

"Yes, ma'am," Stan said. But the moment was ruined by the ringing of a phone: Corvallis's. Stan, perhaps feeling that he had just been saved by the bell, heaved a sigh and looked over at him.

"Sorry," Corvallis said, and lifted the phone from his shirt pocket. He did a double take at the name on the screen, then held it up so that the others could read it: El Shepherd.

"I would recommend not taking that call just now," Stan snapped. Then he looked to Alice, as if seeking her approval. She glanced away demurely, which seemed to settle Stan down. "Have you talked to Mr. Shepherd yet?" Stan asked.

"No," Corvallis said, "just some of his minions."

"What was the general tenor?"

"Intense focus on the situation," Corvallis said. "Not a whole lot of what you would call warmth. A sense of lawyers silently gesticulating."

"Well," Stan said, "now that we have gotten to know each other a little bit, this gives a segue into the matter at hand. If I may."

"Please, be my guest," said Alice.

"Before I get into it, what do we hear from the doctors?"

"No change," Zula said. "We have to assume that he is brain-dead and not coming back."

As she spoke the last few words she glanced over at Jake, who noticed it, and raised his hand momentarily. "I've already communicated my views on this," he said. "Only God can take a life. In Him all things are possible—including a full recovery for Dodge. As long as his soul remains united with his body, Richard is as alive as anyone at this table."

Stan allowed a few moments to pass in silence before nodding and saying, in his best lawyerly baritone, "Thank you, Jacob. Zula had mentioned to me that you might take that view of it. I want to proceed in a way that is respectful of your beliefs."

"I appreciate that, sir," Jake said.

"My job is the law," Stan went on, "and as I'm sure Alice's lawyer back in Iowa would be the first to tell you, the health care directive—what some people refer to as the living will—doesn't necessarily take the beliefs and opinions of family members into account."

"I am aware of it," Jake said. "I know I'm in the minority here anyway." He looked across the table at Alice and Zula, who looked right back at him.

"Under the terms of the health care directive that your brother signed," Stan said, "life support is now to be withdrawn without further delay. But this is to be done according to a specific technical protocol whose purpose is to preserve the brain. And because of the additional provisions that Chris Vail *very carefully* worked into the document"—and here he favored Alice with a significant look, which she disdained to notice—"if Ephrata Cryonics is insolvent, or if some better technology has come along in the meantime, there is an out."

Alice nodded. "And according to my lawyer, one of the problems with this document is that it doesn't actually specify the nature of the out. It's open-ended."

"It is difficult," Stan said delicately, "to specify the exact nature of an alternative brain preservation technique that hasn't yet been invented, or even conceived of. The only way to write such a directive is to make the signer's—Richard's—intent primary. And his intent, apparently, was to make sure that if there existed, at the time of his death, some plausible technology that might later bring him back to life, then that technology should be invoked. And if more than one such technology existed, he quite reasonably wanted the best—not just whatever Ephrata Cryonics happened to be peddling on that particular day."

"But who decides that?" Zula asked.

"Ultimately, you—the next of kin—make that decision. No one can gainsay it. There's no penalty for getting it wrong."

Jake sat forward. "But you just finished saying a minute ago that the living will doesn't take the beliefs of family members into account."

"You can't just countermand the will," Stan said, "but as long as you are making an effort in good faith to carry out Richard's underlying intent, you are allowed some discretion."

"I guess my point is that we are not experts on neuroscience," Zula said.

"Then you can go find someone who is," Stan said. "Seattle is full of high-powered—"

Corvallis interrupted him. "Done."

Everyone looked at him.

"I mean, it's still in progress," Corvallis explained. "But some of the really high-level coders from Corporation 9592 ended up getting hired away, a couple of years ago, by the Waterhouse Brain Sciences Institute. I took the liberty of getting in touch with one of them, Ben Compton, whom I have stayed friends with."

"Is this the Waterhouse from the weird cyber bank?" Alice asked. "That Waterhouse?" She was referring to one of the local tech philanthropists, an entrepreneur who had been involved in an early cryptocurrency venture that had somehow managed to grow into a serious financial institution.

"The same."

"Forgive me for asking a dumb question, but why would a brain institute hire video game programmers?"

"Gamification," Zula said.

"Yes," Corvallis said, "it's kind of a long story and I would be happy to fill you in. But the bottom line is that scientists have identified certain problems that are very difficult for computers to solve but easy for humans. If you can turn those problems into a fun game, then you can get lots of people on the Internet solving them for free. The Waterhouse Brain Sciences people stumbled on one of those problems and decided to gamify it—then they came after our best game programmers."

Alice rolled her eyes. "Anyway. You have friends who work at this high-powered brain institute. Here in town, I assume."

Corvallis nodded. "Less than a mile from here. So I reached out to them and broke the news about Richard, whom they love, by the way. And I asked if they knew anything on this topic. I told them about the process that ELSH used several years ago to scan those eleven brains that they had frozen. And they—the Waterhouse people—said it is *definitely* not the state-of-the-art in that field. *Much* more sophisticated techniques have been developed. Night and day."

"Then why isn't ELSH using them?" Alice asked.

"Well, it looks like I could just hit redial on my phone and ask El Shepherd," Corvallis said, "but the answer is probably that they have never been used on human brains before. Only mice."

"Only mice," Alice repeated.

The Forthrasts' reactions were varied. Alice was incredulous, perhaps wondering why Corvallis had bothered mentioning it if that was the case. Jake shook his head in utter disdain at the foolishness of these rodent-brain-scanning humanists. But Zula got it.

"How many years?" Zula asked.

"What?" Alice asked.

"How many years out? Before they can make one big enough to do a human?"

"That," Corvallis said, "is what I am trying to find out. I have a call in to—"

"Years? What good does that do us?" Alice demanded. "We have to make a decision now. Richard's lying in a bed across the street on a ventilator."

"We could freeze him now," Corvallis said.

"Who's 'we'?" Jake demanded.

"Sorry," Corvallis said. "Point taken. You, the family, could freeze him now."

"I'll have no part of it," Jake reminded him.

"Jake, stop interrupting," Alice said. "Go on, please, C-plus."

"If he were frozen now, using the latest version of the Eutropian protocol—which supposedly preserves the connectome, the pattern of connections among the neurons—and if he were kept frozen for a few years, then, when this new scanning technology did become available, his brain could be scanned that way."

"But I was told that the company that freezes people was out of business," Alice said.

"Richard's net worth is something like three billion dollars," Corvallis pointed out.

"Enough to buy a freezer, you're saying."

"I'm saying it's an option."

"Then do we hire someone to stand by the freezer for a few years and make sure it keeps running?" Jake demanded.

"I don't know," Corvallis said, "I haven't thought it through yet."

Marcus, the junior lawyer, had been silent ever since blundering into Alice's trap. He spoke up now. "Our law firm has done some work for the Waterhouse-Shaftoe Family Foundation—the primary funder of WABSI, the Waterhouse Brain Sciences Institute," he announced.

"Of course it has," Alice said. "Argenbright Vail works for everyone."

Marcus held up a hand to stay her. "It's a big firm," he said, "and we are very careful to avoid conflicts of interest. We have to be. All I'm saying is that, around here, such foundations are pretty common. A lot of people have made a lot of money in tech. When they reach a certain point in their lives, they start giving it away, and that's how these foundations get established. They interlock"—he laced his fingers together—"in complicated ways. Now, as soon as a death certificate is issued for Richard Forthrast, according to his last will and testament, a new one of those is going to be brought into existence."

"The Forthrast Family Foundation," Alice said, "inevitably."

"You don't have to buy your own freezer, is my point. I think the odds are that if you go and talk to Wabsy—"

"Wabsy?"

"WABSI, which, as Corvallis points out, is less than a mile away, you can work something out in which Richard's brain is donated to science."

"But then they could do anything they like with it!"

Marcus shook his head. "You can write up any contract you want. Be as specific as you like about what is to be done with it."

"Why would they sign such a contract?" Alice asked.

"Because the Forthrast Family Foundation is going to give them a shit-ton of money," Zula predicted, "and money talks."

"I'm just the lawyer here," Stan said, "but I like this. We cannot make a reasonable argument that Ephrata Cryonics is insolvent, because it is being supported by El Shepherd out of his own seemingly bottomless funds. So. If the family's preference is that Dodge's brain not be prematurely subjected to the same destructive scanning process that ELSH is pushing, then, according to the terms of the health care directive, we simply need to make an argument that there is some better process available. And if there's anything to what Corvallis is saying, that's going to be easy."

"Easy enough to satisfy Elmo Shepherd?"

"We don't have to satisfy him," Stan said. "We just have to be able to look him in the eye when we're telling him to fuck off."

5

Corvallis felt his phone buzzing in his shirt pocket and peeked at the screen. It was a local number that he did not recognize. It ended in two zeroes, suggesting the call was originating from a main switchboard. He excused himself, arose from the table, and walked into the foyer of the suite before answering it.

A minute later he was back in the dining room. In his absence, chairs had been pushed back, dishes collected, laptops slipped back into bags. Zula caught his eye. "El Shepherd still hassling you?"

"It was the place," Corvallis said. Fully aware of how inarticulate he was being, he blinked, shook his head, and circled around for another try. "The medical office where Dodge was yesterday. Where he was, uh, 'stricken' I guess is the word."

"The people who killed him?" Alice asked. "What did they want?"

"I'm on record as his emergency contact—I was there when it happened," Corvallis said. "They were just calling to let me know that they have his bag. With his stuff. And his clothes and his wallet and so on. All of that was left behind when the firemen came and grabbed him. So, I guess I'll walk over there and pick all of that stuff up." The Forthrasts were all just staring at him. "If, you know, that makes things easier."

"Please," Alice said.

"I'll walk you down," Stan announced, placing a companionable hand on Corvallis's shoulder.

In the elevator, Corvallis asked him, "Did I miss anything?"

"Zula is going to talk to a couple of vent farms," Stan said.

"What's a vent farm?"

"Horrible term. When you have a patient like Richard, who is fundamentally stable but who can't be taken off the ventilator, there's no need to keep him in the ICU. It is overkill. It's expensive and it takes up bed space that the hospital could use for people who really need intensive care. There are businesses that exist to serve this market. Think of it like a nursing home, except all of the people who live there are . . ."

"Are like Richard?"

"Yeah. There's a politically correct term for it, but doctors call it a vent farm."

"So we're thinking of moving Dodge to a vent farm?"

"Alice is vehemently opposed," Marcus said. He managed to say it in a manner that, while utterly deadpan, still conveyed some sense of the vivid impressions he had taken in, during the conversation just concluded, of Alice Forthrast.

"She wants him to stay in the ICU?"

"The alternative would be to move him back to his apartment and put him back in his real bed," Stan said. "The ventilator would have to go with him, of course. Round-the-clock nursing care, the whole bit."

"Esme Hurlbut is pushing for it hard," Marcus added.

"She wants him off the property," Stan said.

The elevator doors opened and they walked out into the hotel lobby. "She's a lawyer," Corvallis pointed out.

"She can see where it's going—the protocol. The ice bath, the freezing of the remains. No way does she want that happening on hospital property."

"I see."

They stepped out into the hotel's front drive and paused under the awning, which was giving off faint white noise as small drops of rain filtered down onto it from the silver sky. "You're going to get Dodge's effects now?"

"Effects? Yeah." Corvallis wondered at what point the clothes, wallet, and so forth became effects.

"I would be shocked if they tried to pull a fast one," Stan said, "but say nothing, okay? Other than hello and goodbye."

"A fast one?"

"They are going to be worried about a malpractice suit. If they start pumping you for information—anything other than just handing over the bag—just walk away. Then call me."

Corvallis shook hands with Stan and Marcus and then stepped out into the rain and began navigating the streets of First Hill on foot, headed for the medical practice where Dodge had been stricken. It was a short walk but a much-needed head clearer.

Or at least it was until his phone rang again. He was just outside the building, looking down a street lined with spectacular red maple trees. The very spot where Dodge had yesterday been buttonholed by the young fan with the broken arm, and unwittingly filmed his last video.

It was El Shepherd again. Corvallis decided to take the call.

"Corvallis Kawasaki. Is it true that you go by C-plus? Or is that just close friends? I don't want to be unduly familiar at a time like this. I'm sorry for what you're going through."

"At an intermediate level of formality, I am frequently addressed simply as C. I would not take that amiss. And what shall I call you, Mr. Shepherd?"

Elmo Shepherd had been named in honor of a grandfather or great-uncle or something who had been born in a time and place where Elmos, Elwoods, Delberts, and Dewaynes had been thick on the ground, and such names had seemed normal and even dignified. Upon shedding Mormonism and moving to the Bay Area to seek his fortune, he had learned that the name was likely to be seen as somewhat comedic and so had dropped its back syllable. Under the moniker of El he had risen to a level of wealth and influence such that, without provoking snorts of laughter, he could begin using the full name again on formal occasions such as White House dinners and ribbon-cuttings of state-of-the-art research facilities. Corvallis was aware that it was something of a shibboleth. Usage of "El," in the right tone of voice, could suggest personal acquaintance.

"El is fine, thank you," said the voice on the other end of the connection. Then there was nothing, for a moment, save for the sound of a propeller-driven aircraft taking off. "Sorry," he said when the sound had dwindled, "I'm at Boeing Field. Just let me get inside the building here."

"You flew up?"

"Yes, you might have seen that I tried to call you a couple of hours ago. From the tarmac in San Rafael." El then gave a muffled thank-you to someone who, to judge from sound effects, had held a door open for him. Corvallis knew exactly where he was: the private jet terminal on the eastern edge of Boeing Field.

"Yes, sorry, I was in a meeting. With the family."

"Of course."

"I had heard you didn't like to fly," Corvallis said.

"That's actually true, unlike a lot of stuff that's written about me," El said, "but there is a need to take calculated risks."

As often happened when he was talking on the phone, Corvallis's gaze was wandering about freely, focusing from time to time on things that lit up his visual cortex: a pretty student from the adjacent university, a purple Tesla driving by, a chocolate Lab taking a crap in the bushes as its owner stood vigil with a blue *New York Times* bag everted over his free hand. A perfect red maple leaf lay spread-eagled on the sidewalk at his feet, plastered down by the rain. Around it, the concrete was stained with the colors that kids' toys came in: sickly artificial purples and greens and pinks. Someone had come here with a box of sidewalk chalk and drawn a piece of art. Corvallis took a step away from it and saw a rain-blurred portrait of a man with white hair and beard. A God of the Old Testament in grape-colored robe with a rainbow aura surrounding his head. Inscribed at the base of the artwork was EGDOD. The name of Dodge's most powerful character in T'Rain. Some fan must have seen the video on Reddit, pulled out its GPS coordinates, and come to the site to pay homage by chalking up an ikon. Maybe they believed that Dodge's hospital room overlooked this place, that Dodge was in some sort of condition to look out the window and see it.

"You still there?" El asked. "I ducked into a conference room." The private jet terminal was the sort of place that had nice conference rooms just sitting there available for people like El to duck into.

"How do you see the day taking shape?" Corvallis asked. Because El must have had some reason to take what he viewed as a calculated risk. Basically—according to what was written about him—El Shepherd intended to live forever, and so he didn't like to place himself in situations where his brain could be destroyed. He had a mobile office, built into a bus, which he preferred over airplane travel. Buses could crash, of course, but unless you T-boned a gasoline tanker at a hundred miles an hour, the destruction probably wouldn't rise to the level that would completely destroy the brain. Whereas the crash of a jet airplane could leave nothing behind for rescuers to scrape up and put into the freezer.

"I have a few errands I could run, as long as I'm up here," El returned, "but I'm sure you can guess the primary reason for my visit."

"Yes."

"The last thing I want to do is impose on the family at a time like this . . ."

"It's fine," Corvallis said, wondering if El could hear the smile in his voice. He got it. The bereaved family was off-limits but the bereaved friend was fair game. "I am running a brief errand. It will take me five minutes. Then I'll grab my car and head for Georgetown." That was the neighborhood just north of Boeing Field. "If you want to pick out a suitable restaurant or whatever, just text me the coordinates and I will be there in half an hour."

"Fine. Over and out," El said.

Corvallis snapped a picture of the sidewalk art, then went into the building, steeling himself for yet another in the seemingly endless series of awkward conversations that had accounted for the last day of his life. It was going to be awkward because the people at the medical office were going to try to be nice to him, to voice sympathy. And yet they couldn't say anything that would place them at a disadvantage when it was repeated in a courtroom during a malpractice suit and so it was all going to be so terribly awkward. By comparison he was actually looking forward to the meeting in half an hour with El Shepherd, who could be relied upon to charge blindly across the emotional minefield and get down as soon as possible to geeking out on connectomics.

They had a little conference room near the front desk of the medical practice, the most generic conference room you could imagine. The office manager escorted Corvallis to it. Sitting there alone in the middle of the table were Dodge's shoulder bag and a canvas tote bag emblazoned—this was too inevitable—with the logo of the local National Public Radio station. Someone had neatly folded Dodge's clothing, which Dodge had no doubt simply left in a heap on the floor of the changing room, and placed it into the tote bag. This one detail made it more clear than anything else that Dodge was dead. Corvallis pulled one of the chairs back, sat down, folded his arms on the table, bent forward, and rested his forehead on them. He cried fully and freely for a couple of minutes. The office manager hovered nervously at first, then excused herself, then came back a minute later with a box of tissues, then excused herself again. Corvallis inferred all of this from sounds; he could see nothing through his tears but the fake wood grain of the conference room table. When he sat back up again, he could see her standing outside wringing her hands. He blotted his eyes with tissues and then used them to wipe tears that had spilled onto the tabletop. He threw the damp tissues into a convenient receptacle, then slung Dodge's messenger bag over his shoulder and tucked the canvas tote under his arm. The office manager opened the door for him. He nodded to her and walked out of the medical practice without looking back.

On the sidewalk outside, someone had, during the last few minutes, placed a bouquet of grocery store flowers on the picture of Egdod. The bouquet had been additionally wrapped up in a length of black wire. On a closer look, it was a controller from a video game console neatly bundled around the stems of the flowers.

6

Half an hour later he was in a booth in the back of a bar in Georgetown. Across from him was El Shepherd. El was wearing a suit. Some Bay Area tech zillionaires liked to cut against the grain by wearing finely tailored clothing. He was one of those.
"C," he said, "I'm sorry for your loss."

"It's okay," Corvallis said, "I did the sad thing. Just took care of it. Done with that now." His arm was draped over the items he had collected from the medical practice. He had brought them into the bar with him. Georgetown was a complicated neighborhood, car prowls were common, and he didn't want Dodge's effects turning up for sale tomorrow on the Miasma. This would have appealed to Dodge's sense of humor but would have been distressing to Alice.

"Okay," El said, a little disconcerted. "Look then, I'm not going to beat around the bush. Are you up to speed on the documents that Richard Forthrast signed with Ephrata Cryonics? Do you know about that?"

"Fully," Corvallis said. "Yes."

"And you know . . ."

"About ELSH and everything? The buyout? The scanning and the cloud storage? Yes."

"This is probably neither here nor there, by the way, but your company . . ."

"Nubilant is storing those scans. Yes, I was aware of that too."

"Okay," said El with a nod, "then it sounds like you are up to speed on what I would consider the past and the present aspects of the situation. But there's no way that you can know what we have in mind for the future."

"Fair enough."

The waitress showed up with a pint of beer that Corvallis had ordered. He felt justified in the consumption of alcohol at lunch under these circumstances. El was drinking a clear fluid with lime, presumably nonalcoholic. Not taking any risks with those brain cells. What was the "calculated risk," Corvallis wondered, of sitting in a Georgetown bar at all? How many of the people sitting at the bar, drinking at noon, were carrying concealed weapons as a matter of course? An accidental discharge, or a not-so-accidental one, could put a bullet through El's skull and scatter his brains and his plans for immortality. Did El have a spreadsheet somewhere, where he calculated these probabilities and weighed them against each other?

"Since it's just you and me here, having a private conversation, I will not insult your intelligence, C, by trying to claim that the scanning technique that was used on the Ephrata Eleven was anything we would consider using today."

"On Richard Forthrast, you mean."

"Him or anyone."

"Anyone?"

"Me. C, please understand that I see myself as being on exactly the same footing as Richard Forthrast. If something were to happen to me today that caused me to end up on a ventilator, then I would want the most advanced possible measures taken to preserve my connectome. No expense would be spared to get it right. I am here to tell you that there is no difference between me and Richard Forthrast as far as that is concerned. There is no such thing as a second-class treatment option."

Corvallis took a sip of his beer. It was good. He wondered if there was beer in El Shepherd's digital heaven.

"You're probably looking at ion-beam scanning," El said.

"Yes." This was the new technique Corvallis had alluded to earlier. The one WABSI was using on mouse brains. The family conference in the hotel suite hadn't felt like the right time or place to delve into its technical details.

If you bought into the proposition, which El Shepherd apparently did, that the connectome was all that there was to the human brain—that, once you had created a digital record of the wiring diagram, and stored that in the cloud, you could throw away what was left of the body and not lose anything that mattered—then ion-beam scanning appeared to be the answer. The older technique, used on the eleven Ephrata Cryonics brains, had been to run them through what amounted to a high-precision bologna slicer, cutting away the thinnest possible layers, one at a time, and photographing what had been thus exposed, and then repeating the process. Then trying to trace the connections as they angled across the photographic layers. This was the hard problem that WABSI had attempted to gamify a couple of years ago. It was only as good as the thinness of the bologna slicing, the resolution of the photographs, and the attention span of the gamers.

Ion-beam scanning destroyed the brain a few molecules at a time in order to save it. A beam of charged particles, focused to subcellular precision, burned away the brain tissue. But as it did so it was gathering information about what it was destroying, and storing it to a much higher resolution than could be attained using the older technique. In its essentials it was the same as bologna slicing; it just worked at higher precision. Instead of a heap of paper-thin brain slices, the physical residue was smoke and steam. A higher form of cremation.

"Look," Corvallis said. "As far as I am concerned, as a nerd who has read about it on the Internet? Yes. Of course. Way better than running it through a deli slicer and taking pictures."

"I would go further," El said, "and say that, once we have it up and running, we are done here. Even if we did later invent a higher-resolution system, it would serve no additional purpose. It would be like making a map of the United States at submillimeter scale: no better than a map done at centimeter scale."

Corvallis broke eye contact and took a swallow of beer. In the last few moments, some kind of emotional sea change had swept over him. He had come to see all this talk of brain scanning as just another tedious detail to be sewn up as quickly as possible, preferably by other people. Two well-funded think tanks full of smart people—WABSI and El Shepherd's cluster of foundations and startups—seemed to have independently arrived at the conclusion that ion-beam scanning was the be-all and end-all. Cloud computing companies, such as the one Corvallis worked for, had made the long-term storage of the resulting data so cheap and reliable as to be trivial.

So what was there to talk about? As El himself had just said, they were done here.

"What is your objective in coming up to Seattle today?" Corvallis asked him.

"To see to it that Richard Forthrast's last will and testament—including the health care directive and the disposition of remains—is enforced," El said.

"You see that as something you have the moral and ethical authority to do?"

"I don't know anything about the family," El said. "*You* are a different matter, C. Even though we haven't met, I can evaluate who you are based on your track record, your LinkedIn profile. I came into this bar knowing that you and I would be able to have a conversation that was calm and technically well informed."

"What does that have to do with my question?"

El held up a hand to placate him. *Stay with me, bro.* "A thought experiment. A man is born into a primitive tribe where medical care is in the hands of witch doctors. Their most advanced therapeutic technology is a rattle. Later he manages to get an education. He moves to London and becomes well-off. He wants to make sure that, if he gets sick, he'll get the same medical care as anyone else in London. So he writes a health care directive that—never mind the polite language—basically says the following to the doctor. It says, 'If I get sick and can't speak for myself, some of my relatives might show up and try to heal me using rattles. They might try to prevent you, the doctors, from giving me the medical care I want. Well, fuck them. Keep them out of my room. They can hang around on the street outside the hospital shaking their rattles all day and all night, but the only people I want inside the room making decisions about medical care are actual doctors and nurses.' He writes that all up in a form that is completely bomb-proof from a legal standpoint and he signs and seals it six ways from Sunday and he files it away in a safe place. Now, let's say that the worst comes to pass and this man does in fact get so sick that he can't speak for himself anymore. He winds up in the hospital, and sure enough, his relatives show up with their rattles. And not only do they want to stand by his bed and shake their rattles but they want to exclude the doctors and nurses, pull out the IVs, turn off the machines, withdraw the medicine. In that situation, Corvallis, would you say that the doctor has the moral and ethical authority to have security escort the rattle shakers to the exit?"

"So you want to know if Richard's next of kin are rattle shakers?"

"Yes."

"And," Corvallis said, "just to be clear about your analogy— you are the doctor. And the medical care you are talking about is not just normal medical care as we would conventionally understand it, but—"

"But ion-beam scanning of his brain. Yes."

It was Pascal's Wager again. El Shepherd was convinced that with the right technology he could make Dodge immortal. That this was what Dodge wanted. And he wasn't going to let the family stand in the way of carrying out Dodge's wishes. The stakes were too high.

"Let's go back to your analogy for a minute," Corvallis said. "When push comes to shove, the doctor calls security and has the rattle shakers thrown out of the building. What's your plan, El, if push comes to shove in this case?"

"I would not hesitate to go in front of a judge and seek a court order."

"Wow."

"I mean, look. The Forthrast family will be sad and hate me for a while. That is the downside. The upside is—"

"You save Richard's life. Or his afterlife—whatever you want to call it."

"And, down the road? Maybe that of those angry family members too. A million years from now they are thanking me for having taken the steps that were necessary."

"Just wow."

"You can maybe see why I wanted to talk to you. Not the family. It could get personal with those people."

"It's personal with *me*."

"But different, right? Even while you're hating me, you can see where I'm coming from on the technical level."

Corvallis thought it perhaps best not to say anything. El Shepherd, undeterred, circled around to probe from another angle. "You said a minute ago that you had taken a look at ion-beam scanning as an option."

He was right. Corvallis *had* said that. Perhaps that had been a mistake.

"I take it, then, that you have decided to investigate alternatives to the services being offered by Ephrata Life Sciences and Health."

Yes, definitely a mistake. "Where is this going?"

"You're probably looking at the line inserted into the agreement that states the family can go to a non-ELSH option if they decide that there's something better available."

"Given that you just threatened to take us to court," Corvallis said, "why would I even—"

"Speaking as one technically sophisticated man to another," El said, "allow me to assure you that no such alternative exists. ELSH is second to none in this field. And I intend to be very active in stating our case. Making sure that there are no misunderstandings. Protecting our brand."

"I wish you all the best of luck with your brand," Corvallis said, sliding out of the booth, reaching out, almost as an afterthought, to throw an arm over Dodge's messenger bag and the sack full of his effects. He turned without shaking El Shepherd's hand and stalked away. His exit route took him right along the line of bar stools. Four of these were supporting humans. For midday drinkers, they seemed curiously fit. Maybe it was because they were all drinking water. They raised their heads and tracked him in their peripheral vision. One then glanced back at El. "It's okay," El called, "let him go."

The sign hanging in the front door said OPEN to Corvallis, which meant that it showed as CLOSED to people on the sidewalk.

So, El had rented out the whole bar just for this conversation, and staffed it with his private security detail.

Let him go. Those were the words that stuck with Corvallis as he strode to his car. Was it a serious possibility that they *wouldn't*? Were they thinking of *detaining* him?

It was unlikely, Corvallis decided, as he shifted his car into gear and began heading north on Airport Way. They might have been goons, but they were probably *professional* goons. They had no legal power to detain anyone, and they knew it. Inwardly, they had to be thinking about what a dickhead their boss was to even say something like that.

Or maybe he was just trying to settle himself down by telling a comforting story.

7

H e had intended to go straight to the hotel to drop off Dodge's things, but Zula waved him off via text message, letting him know that they were going to be busy with "the transfer" for a couple of hours. Then she added another message: *C U @ Richard's in a couple hours.*

So. No vent farm for Dodge. He was going to die in his own bed.

He pulled over into a legit parking space and texted Stan: *Can El get a court order? Is that a real thing?*

Then he dialed Ben Compton's number. Of the game programmers who had defected from Corporation 9592 to the Waterhouse Brain Sciences Institute, Ben had been the first to go, and the ringleader. Later, some of them had drifted back to the world of conventional game programming, but Ben had stuck around.

"C-plus." Ben's voice was flat. He had, of course, heard the news. His voice was coming out of the car's sound system, Bluetoothed to the phone.

"Ben. You know about it."

"Yeah. Of all the fucking horrible things. I don't know what to say. Almost didn't come in to work today."

"Maybe it's good you did."

"Anything I can do to help?"

"Reserve a conference room in half an hour."

"Will attempt. Food?"

"Sure. I just had a really unsatisfactory lunch."

"What'd you have?"

"Half of a beer."

"That doesn't sound so bad. Except for the half part."

"It was more the company I was keeping."

"Lawyers?"

On cue, Corvallis's phone began vibrating down in the cup-holder. He glanced at it. Stan was calling from his work number. "Gotta take this. See you in a few."

He tapped the screen and switched over to Stan. Then he pulled out into a gap in traffic and began heading north toward downtown.

"You took El's call," Stan said. "I'd rather you hadn't."

"Hell, I sat across the table from him."

"*What!?*"

"No shit. While we were talking in the hotel, he flew up from San Rafael. With his security detail in tow."

"Jesus. And threatened to get a court order?"

"Yeah, is that even possible legally?"

"It's rare. Rare enough that I'll need to do some research," Stan said. "But in principle, yeah. If the family is about to take some step that directly violates the health care directive, then the attorney general can take an interest in it, go to a judge, get a court order."

"And then—?"

"And then if the family, or the doctors, violate the court order, they're in contempt of court. So that is definitely a club he can wave over Zula and Alice. But I find it shocking he would even consider it."

"He's protecting his brand, he says."

"Fine way to do it."

The organization known to Alice as the Weird Cyber Bank had bought a great big old building from an old-school, non-weird, non-cyber bank that, around the turn of the millennium, had gone belly-up in a financial downturn and pursuant imbroglio.

During the 1930s, this building had probably been considered tall and futuristic. Now it was medium-sized and retro-quaint. The new owners had done all of the structural upgrades needed to keep it from collapsing into a huge mound of bricks during the next earthquake and then they had parceled it out into chunks for use by various of their subentities.

The Weird Cyber Bank per se—the for-profit financial institution that had been spawned out of an earlier startup called Epiphyte, and been joined by diverse more or less murky coconspirators—occupied the upper two-thirds of the building. The lower floors were for the Waterhouse-Shaftoe Family Foundation and its off-shoot, WABSI.

It was on a steep downtown slope. On the downhill side you walked into the first floor, but on the uphill side, the pedestrian entrance was on the fourth story. In between was a wedge of space that was difficult for spatially challenged visitors and so the architects had made the probably wise decision to leave it mostly deconstructed, exposing all the massive new structural steelwork that was now knitting together the gingerbready brick-and-marble confection on top of it. There was security, befitting a bank with supposed connections to all kinds of mysterious and maybe nefarious clients. But the internal partitions were mostly glass, and so you could at least see all of the places you weren't being allowed to go.

It was out of the question that Corvallis Kawasaki would just stroll in on short notice and sign the boilerplate NDA that the security guard would present to him. Therefore it went without saying that he was going to be issued a mere sticker, not a badge, and that he'd have to be accompanied by Ben at all times. They'd be restricted to visitor-friendly zones on the building's lower levels. There were a few meeting rooms for just such occasions, but a glance through their glass walls proved that those were all spoken for at the moment. Therefore Ben and C-plus, having nowhere else to go, began to wander through a permanent museum exhibit that occupied the interior of the first three stories.

This looked expensive. It had not just been thrown together by interns. One sensed that serious people had come over from London and worked on it for years. It was intended to be here for a long time. Wordy plaques, etched in mysterious corrosion-proof metal, explained deep background that struck C-plus as very interesting; he'd have to come back later and actually read them. But the quick visual takeaway, absorbed by some background process in his brain as he ambled around and made small talk with Ben, was that the deep history of this institution reached all the way back to some era of history when men wore large periwigs—not the white-powdered George Washington kind, but normal hair colors—and that there were connections, on the math-and-science side, to Pascal and Leibniz, and on the money side to an old banking dynasty called the Hacklhebers, and politically to—could that really be Peter the Great? Somehow that had come together in an institution called the Leibniz-Archiv, in Hanover, which frankly hadn't done a heck of a lot for a few hundred years.

The designers of this exhibit had cleverly filled in that awkward gap with some material about early mechanical computers, including a working replica of Babbage's difference engine (built in a fit of nerd energy, and later contributed to this museum, by a different local tech magnate). There was the obligatory shrine to Ada Lovelace and then a fast-forward to the mid-twentieth century and a black-and-white photo of the young Alan Turing, Lawrence Pritchard Waterhouse, and Rudolf von Hacklheber on a bicycling expedition. This was where C-plus began to feel he was losing the thread, since the last mention of any Hacklhebers he'd seen was from 250 years earlier—but apparently this Rudolf was one of those hyperprivileged white guys who actually turned out to have legit mathematical talent. Anyway it kicked off a whole wing of the exhibit featuring an offbeat mix of stuff C-plus had seen in twenty other museums (Enigma machine, photograph of Turing bombe) with unique exhibits such as a computer that Lawrence Pritchard Waterhouse had apparently made out of organ pipes and mercury-filled U-tubes.

There was a big map of the world festooned with swooping trails of LEDs and flat-panel monitors, trying to convey some elaborate chain of events in which the contents of the Leibniz-Archiv had been removed from Hanover, either to keep these priceless relics safe from Allied bombing raids or because Göring wanted to melt it all down, and somehow made their way, via U-boat, to the Philippines—only to be sunk, and later recovered by Waterhouses and Shaftoes.

The point being that the hoard consisted of gold plates with holes punched in them, like an early version of IBM punch cards, and they were meant to be used in a mechanical computer called the Logic Mill. The Logic Mill had been much talked about, by various savants, since the era of Oliver Cromwell, but had never really been constructed and made to work properly until Randy Waterhouse—one of the founders of the Weird Cyber Bank— had plowed some of his windfall into actually building a working replica. This had taken more than a decade because, to make a long story short, the eighteenth-century design made very little sense on a mechanical engineering level and required a lot of humans to move things around. And yet they had made it work using the actual, original plates from the Leibniz-Archiv.

And it was this detail that finally afforded Ben and C-plus a bit of privacy in which to have a real conversation. For an inner layer of even higher security surrounded the chamber housing the Logic Mill. Casual museum strollers could view it at a distance through a heavy glass window, but if you actually wanted to go in and see the thing working you had to check your bag and your coat and go through a metal detector and a pat-down. And that was enough of a barrier that most visitors were content just to look at it through the glass. Ben and Corvallis, however, went through and found themselves alone in a sunken vault (they sealed it up at night) with a contraption that slowly but inexorably shuffled gold plates around and probed them with metal pins.

"It's on the Internet!" Ben said, indicating a flat-panel screen suspended on a jointed arm. Lines of text were marching up it so slowly that the display appeared to be frozen most of the time. Corvallis recognized them as low-level Internet codes.

"Of course it is," he said numbly.

"In their retirement some of the OG Epiphyte geeks figured out how to program the Logic Mill to speak TCP, and gave it its own IP address—you can ping it if you have a lot of time on your hands."

They stood there for a minute or two, watching the Logic Mill work, deriving a kind of calm satisfaction from the way the metal prods engaged the cards. When it seemed the time was right, C-plus said: "So. Elmo Shepherd."

"El's a true believer," Ben replied.

Ben was in a T-shirt: swag from an early release of T'Rain, well worn in, with a dime-sized moth hole above his right nipple. Corvallis did not have to ask to understand that Ben had made a conscious choice to put it on this morning as a way of remembering Richard Forthrast, who'd given Ben his first job after Ben had been thrown out of Princeton. Ben had a round face, curly brown hair, hadn't shaved in a while.

"You've met El?"

"Sat in on a bunch of meetings with him."

"Why?"

"A couple of years ago he was hanging around here, trying to make something happen between us and ELSH. Once it got past the flirting stage, the powers that be here at WABSI realized they needed a programmer in the room, just to make sense of what he was proposing."

"That surprises me a little," Corvallis said. "I thought El was all about stuff like ion-beam scanning. The connectome. How to collect the data, how to store it in the cloud."

"Stuff that's not my department, you mean."

"Exactly."

"Well, he's looking beyond that," Ben said, and took a swig of his flat white. "In a way, that's the part of it he's *least* comfortable with, right?"

"Because he's a bit-basher."

"Yeah. He had to stretch quite a bit to get his head around the biology."

"That's kind of reflected in his whole basic approach, come to think of it," Corvallis said.

"I know, right? The Ephrata Cryonics guys were all about physical preservation of the body. Bringing that particular piece of meat back to life." Ben waved his hand, pantomiming El Shepherd trying to wave that idea into oblivion. "Not El's thing at all. No. Turn it into bits. As soon as possible. Throw the meat away." He gestured emphatically toward the Logic Mill, a wild look on his face, mocking the kind of person who would look at such a machine and say, *Now, there's a proper brain!*

"And then simulate that brain digitally."

"Yes. You know he's a Singularity guy."

"Yeah, I knew that about El."

"So it all fits together," Ben said. He was grinning, without a great deal of humor behind it.

"And he wanted to partner up with you guys on that aspect of it." What to do next, in other words. The re-creation of a brain's functioning in software. Reincarnating a scanned connectome as a digital soul, living in the cloud.

"I signed an NDA, so I can't say much," Ben said. "But I already told you I was in the meetings. You can put two and two together."

"Nothing came of it."

"Nah!" Ben scoffed. "Elmo tried to hire me, though. After it all failed to materialize."

"But you didn't—" Corvallis began.

Ben cut him off with a gesture that he recognized from many a meeting at Corporation 9592: both hands out, palms facing toward the floor, skating rapidly back and forth. As if scrubbing a bad idea off of an imaginary whiteboard. "C. No. Hear my words. He's fucking crazy."

"To me he seemed sane but just, I don't know, excessively literal minded about what he believes?"

"Same diff. It's his religion, man. And he uses it like all the worst religious people."

"As an excuse to just do what he wants, you mean."

"Yeah!"

"I got that about him."

"He's going to fail," Ben said.

"You sound pretty sure of that."

"It's because of Dodge."

"I don't follow."

"That's how I know, C. That's how I can tell if any company is going to succeed or fail. It comes down to leadership. At 9592 we had a great leader in Richard Forthrast. Here we've got that too in the Waterhouse clan. Oh, they couldn't be more different from Dodge. But they are fine leaders in their own way. El is not a great leader. So it doesn't matter how much money he has, how smart his people are. It just doesn't fucking matter."

Corvallis nodded. They sat there for a few moments in silence, watching the Logic Mill think. Ben said, "Don't let the son of a bitch have Dodge's brain, would be my takeaway."

8

A few hours later Corvallis was in Richard's apartment, perched on a sofa in his friend's great room and feeling at loose ends as Zula and Alice talked to various medical personnel. The Forthrasts had had a busy day. Once they'd made the decision to move Dodge home, the next few hours had gone by in an ecstasy of logistics: hiring an ambulance to transport the patient, renting a ventilator and other equipment, interviewing home health care practitioners. Corvallis had shown up only about ten minutes after the attendants had moved Dodge from the gurney to the bed in which he had awakened yesterday morning, and in which he would soon be caused to die. Standing around it were a supervisor and a couple of people in nurselike uniforms, though Corvallis didn't know whether they were technically nurses or some other category of health care professional. Corvallis didn't like being in there. He had been gradually adjusting to the idea of his friend's being dead, so it was terrible to see him lying there obviously alive, seeming as if he could open his eyes at any moment and sit up and demand to have the tube yanked out of his throat.

For a couple of decades, Alice had shouldered most of the responsibility for looking after Grandpa Forthrast, the father of Richard, Jake, and Alice's husband, John, when strokes and other damage had rendered him dependent on machines and health care workers. She was in her element here, relegating Zula to a silent role standing in the corner texting updates to relatives. Corvallis was entirely useless.

Exiled and alone on the sofa, he unzipped Richard's shoulder bag, thinking he might take an inventory of its contents. Stuffed into the top of it were the headphones—the same ones, of course, shown on the video that the kid had posted. Richard had simply wadded the cable up on top of them. Corvallis pulled them out carefully, wound the cable around them, and set them on the table.

Remaining in the bag were two large-format picture books and an apple. He pulled the books out and set them on the table. They were children's books, depicting Greek and Norse myths in bright lithographs. He put the apple on the table and looked at it for a while. It was smaller and less perfectly symmetrical than the ones sold in grocery stores. Straight from some orchard. Maybe Dodge had tossed it in there as a snack.

Other than that the bag contained random odds and ends, tucked into various internal pockets: spare batteries, a candy bar, charger cables for electronic devices, a two-month-old copy of the *Economist*.

He wondered whether the family would take it amiss if he went through the pockets of Richard's trousers and performed a similar inventory. He decided against it.

His phone vibrated and he saw a message from Stan: *Carrot and stick from El. Call me.*

"Let's start with the stick" was how Corvallis started the conversation. "I take it you heard from his lawyers?"

"Yes, I did," Stan said.

"And they are threatening the court order?"

"Not only that," Stan said, sounding dryly amused, "they are even making noise about criminal proceedings."

"Are you shitting me?"

"The statutes contain weird old stuff about mistreatment of bodies. Probably written into the law centuries ago to punish people who used to steal bodies and take them to labs for dissection. Strangely enough, what the Forthrasts want to do in this case is to take the body and dissect it in a particular way—"

"With an ion beam."

"Yeah. Look, don't take this too seriously. It's smoke and mirrors. No one is going to end up in jail over this. You have to think of it tactically. Alice and Zula have to make a decision. They're already stressed out over Jake and his religious take on it. Now El comes in looking for anything he can do to get them further stressed out. Talking about court orders and even filing a criminal complaint. It's all bullshit."

"But it works as a stick."

"Yes. Which brings me to the carrot."

"Okay. What are they holding out?"

"So far it's just vague, conciliatory noises. But the point has been raised that it's all just bits."

"Once Dodge's brain has been scanned, you mean."

"Yeah. The output of that process is some smoke going up the chimney and some data stored in a file. They want a copy of the data."

"Just a copy."

"Yes. A nonexclusive license. The Forthrast Family Foundation would be able to keep its own copy and do with it as they please."

"And then they'll shut up and leave us alone."

"If I am reading their strategy correctly, yes."

"Why is El even bothering with this?" Corvallis asked. "Why doesn't he use some other brain? Lots of people die, right?"

"Lots of people die," Stan agreed, "but most of them don't sign legal documents ordering that their brains should be preserved."

"But he could find one."

"Sure. But it's hard to find one whose estate is rich enough to afford this kind of process."

"So it's all about money? Can't El afford—"

"Remember, the ion-beam scanning facility doesn't exist yet," Stan said.

"WABSI only has it working on mouse brains."

"Yeah, and only in a primitive form. Making the right kind of scanner, capable of doing a whole human brain, is going to cost billions. Not even Elmo Shepherd can afford it. But the combined resources of ELSH, WABSI, and the Forthrast Family Foundation might be able to swing it. And he doesn't want to be frozen out of that coalition."

"He has a funny way of showing it."

"Like it or not," Stan said, "some people actually do business this way. Like I said: carrot and stick."

"What do you suggest we do now?"

"Exactly what you are doing," Stan said. "Remember, the scanner won't exist for a long time. So that's plenty of time to consider options, make a decision."

"Obviously, I'm not going to mention this to the Forthrasts."

"No. Let them grieve. But do give me a call if they suddenly decide to have him cremated."

During the phone call, Corvallis's eyes had been wandering. He had noticed an oddity about the Greek myth book. It looked brand new, but it was defective. Seen edge-on, some of the pages in the front were warped, as if they'd been exposed to moisture. He pulled it toward him. *D'Aulaires' Book of Greek Myths* it was called. He opened the front cover and noticed two things. First of all, it had been inscribed.

> *Sophia,*
> *I hope you'll enjoy these stories as much as I did*
> *when I was your age! If you ever want me to read*
> *one to you, just tell your mom to call me.*
>
> > *Love,*
> > *Uncle Dodge*

Second, there was a leaf—a big maple leaf, fire-engine red— flattened between the front cover and the first page. It was still damp and flexible. Dodge must have put it in there sopping wet, because the surrounding pages had soaked up enough water to pick up the sinusoidal warping that Corvallis had noticed a minute ago. It was obvious to him what had happened: Dodge had picked it up off the sidewalk outside of the medical building just before he had gone in there for the procedure. As a way of preserving it for his niece, he had slipped it under the cover of the book.

He felt shame at having looked in on something that was none of his business. He closed the cover of the book gently and put it back on the table.

Not fifteen minutes later, he heard the front door opening as someone came in from the elevator lobby. Someone who had a key to the apartment, obviously. He tortured himself for a few brief moments with the fantasy that it was Dodge, and that all of this stuff had been some kind of dream or hallucination. But then he heard a high-pitched voice calling, "Uncle Richard? Uncle Richard? Hello! Are you getting better?"

In answer came a much deeper voice, speaking with an Eastern European accent. "Ssh, you mustn't disturb Uncle Richard, he is sleeping." This was Csongor, Zula's husband. "Remember, he is very sick."

Corvallis understood something suddenly and clearly: this was all a sort of performance that the family was mounting, at great effort and expense, for no one's benefit but Sophia's. It was difficult to explain to a girl of her age that her favorite uncle had simply ceased to exist for no apparent reason. A brief, serious illness followed by death: miserable as it was, that was the best story they could come up with. She wasn't ready to hear the facts of the situation, to understand the idea that a seemingly normal and healthy Uncle Richard was in fact a vegetable with no brain to speak of. They would say that he was sick, that he was sleeping. And in a few days they would break the terrible news to her that he had died. A full explanation of the protocols embedded in the health care directive and the disposition of remains would be many years in coming.

"Hello, Corvallis Kawasaki!" Sophia always addressed him thus, reveling in her ability to pronounce the name. She was a tiny thing, barely coming up to midthigh on her bulky father. Fortunately for her, she was more Zula than Csongor, with glorious curls. The Hungarian blood came through in her eyes, which were pale blue-green with a vaguely Asiatic slant.

Corvallis could not prevent himself from smiling broadly for the first time since all of this had started. "Hello, Sophia!" he said. "How was school today?"

"Fine," she said, inevitably.

Corvallis and Csongor exchanged nods.

"There they are!" Sophia hollered. She bolted into the room, vaulted up onto the coffee table, and skidded to a halt where she could gaze down on the covers of the books. "Doe-lair's *Book of Greek Myths*," she said, "and Doe-lair's *Book of Norse Myths*. My uncle Richard got them for me." She turned her head and threw Csongor a reproachful look. "Mom and Dad forgot them!"

"Uncle Richard wanted you to have them," Corvallis said. "He wrote you a note in this one. And left a surprise."

She grabbed *Greek,* spun it around, and flipped the cover open. The sudden movement caused the red leaf to lift off the page and become airborne. This surprised her and she fell back on her bottom with an exclamation, and watched it skid to a stop on the surface of the table.

She looked at Corvallis, all serious. "Is that the surprise?"

"Yes."

"It's so pretty!" she said.

"Yes, it is."

"Did he bring me that apple too?"

Corvallis picked up the apple and looked at Csongor, who nodded approval. "Yes, he did," Corvallis said. "It's all yours."

PART 2

9

O ver the next three years Nubilant expanded, somewhat jerkily, as its CEO leapt from one funding predicament to the next like a video game character being presented with various contrived, dire challenges. With each round of funding its valuation grew and Corvallis's theoretical net worth became larger. He began to consider whether it might be time to begin having a social life. He was not quite sure how to go about it. Much of his spare time was devoted to his hobby: the painstaking reenactment, in parks and on beaches around the Pacific Northwest, of the activities of a Roman legion of ancient times. It was an almost exclusively male pursuit, which would have been very convenient if (as rumor apparently had it) he were gay, but he was pretty resolutely heterosexual. When he did engage in normal social activities such as going out to dinner, it tended to be with Csongor, Zula, and Sophia, who had become like family to him. Sometimes, unaccompanied females would be present and Corvallis would become tongue-tied and withdrawn as he realized that Zula was trying to set him up with potential dates. He rationalized his failure to have a social life by saying that he was in "startup mode" and when you were in startup mode, normal rules didn't apply. There would be plenty of time to sort things out after Failure or Exit, which were the two possible end states for a startup.

Exit—in the sense of suddenly becoming more rich—happened when Nubilant was acquired by Lyke, a Bay Area social media company that was much larger. Lyke had cloud computing systems of its own that were much more capable, by most measures, than Nubilant's. But thanks to some canny decisions that Corvallis had made, Nubilant happened to be especially good at certain things that had turned out to be important to social media companies and so was doubly desirable—both on its own merits as a company and because of the prestige, and the bragging rights, that came from having snatched it away from the competition. Thus did Corvallis Kawasaki, just short of forty years old, become a centimillionaire. He was now the chief research officer at Lyke, which was a major publicly traded company based in Mountain View. He could easily have retired but chose to stay on because he enjoyed his work and because he felt some loyalty to the team he had recruited and nurtured in Seattle. He purchased fractional ownership of a private jet that he used to fly down the coast every week or so.

He had barely settled into his new life when he was awakened early one morning by the ringtone he had associated with the personal number of his new boss: the CEO of Lyke.

In truth, he had been sleeping somewhat raggedly the last hour or so. He had left his phone on the ground next to him with its screen facing up. As notifications filtered in, the device would turn its screen on, creating a series of false, bluish dawns. He'd been wondering whether it was worth the effort to reach out and flip the phone over facedown, but some deep nerd part of his brain was worried about scratching the screen on a rock. For like all of the other legionaries in the tent, he was sleeping directly on the ground, wrapped in his woolen cloak. He had not actually looked at any of the notifications.

He had configured the phone in such a way that it would only ring under certain rare circumstances, such as a personal call from the CEO. His legion was on maneuvers in the Bitterroot Mountains of western Montana, which it was using as a proxy for the Alps. Use of cell phones and other portable electronics was discouraged during the daytime, and while in character, but was tolerated in private tents, in the hours of darkness, as long as you weren't too loud.

But waking people up with an early-morning call was bad manners everywhere, and so when it rang, he lashed out and silenced it as quickly as he could.

"*Salve,*" he croaked into the phone, over the grumbles of his tentmates.

"I need you down here," said his boss. "All hands on deck."

Then he hung up without explanation, leaving Corvallis with the vague feeling that he was missing something.

"What the *fuck*, Corvus," complained a legionary in the next tent. "*Mutate*." *Moo-TAH-tay*. This was bastard Latin, using the imperative conjugation to tell him to mute his phone. "Corvus" was the Latinized version of his name. He turned off the phone's sound so that it wouldn't continue to make cute little noises as he went on messing with it.

The trail of notifications on his phone told the story. They had originated from various people on various social networks, but they had all been triggered by the same event: the surprising obliteration of the town of Moab, Utah, by what was apparently a tactical nuclear weapon.

It had occurred before daybreak, at about 5:20 A.M. local time. The earliest postings were from insomniacal passengers and crew on coast-to-coast red-eye flights, reporting a sudden flash so bright it dazzled them from hundreds of miles away. This had faded too rapidly for people to snap pictures of it, but descriptions had been tweeted and Facebooked via the planes' onboard Wi-Fi systems, and retweeted and reposted a millionfold by the time Corvallis saw them.

One Larry Proctor, a blogger who knew his way around the military and intelligence world (or so it seemed, anyway, based on a quick scan of a blog he'd been maintaining ever since his last tour of duty in Qatar), had picked up some traffic that had leaked to the civilian Internet from a .mil site, making a cryptic reference to a possible radiological event in southeastern Utah. Personnel stationed at nearby military bases were reporting that leaves were being canceled and units being mobilized. All of this was probably supposed to be kept under wraps, but nothing could prevent spouses and teenage kids from chattering about it. Someone in DC posted a snapshot of a pizza delivery guy on a Pentagon-bound Metro train, toting a stack of pizzas so high he had to use a two-wheeled dolly. Self-proclaimed experts in the comment thread were climbing all over one another to explain that massive pizza deliveries to the Pentagon were an infallible sign that something big was happening. A fourteen-year-old Texas girl's emoji-splattered post, featuring grainy driveway footage of her camouflage-decked mom heaving a duffel bag into the back of a pickup truck and burning rubber down the street, went viral and was shown over and over on network news sites for lack of anything more definite from the actual scene of the disaster. Moab was a long way from anywhere, situated at an X made by the Colorado River and a two-lane highway. No Internet or phone traffic was coming out of it.

Corvallis took all of this in while putting on his *caligae*, the sandal-like marching boots of the Roman legionary, and pulling his kit together as efficiently as was possible while focusing most of his attention on his phone. He had been sleeping in his linen tunic, overwrapped with his wool cloak. It was cold up here in the mountains and so he pulled the latter garment around him before stepping outside the tent. This weekend's event was an informal, light-duty sort of affair, family friendly. They'd set up their camp in a meadow, but a phalanx of modern RVs was visible a quarter of a mile down the hill, in a parking lot at the road head. Generators were purring and electric lights shining down there. Corvallis stuffed his gear into his bag, slung it over his shoulder, and trudged down the slope. He smelled bacon cooking in one of the RVs. Through its window he saw a television monitor showing live network coverage—the RV had a satellite dish mounted to its roof. He slowed down and looked in through the window. The video feed was from LAX, where the first of those red-eyes had apparently just landed and disgorged its passengers. News crews were waiting to gang-tackle witnesses as they emerged from security. Most of the people on that flight had slept through the event, and many didn't want to talk, but one alert fellow—a fashionably scruffy actor who had been flying from New York to L.A. for a job—had seen the flash in the corner of his eye while playing a game on his phone, and switched it over to video camera mode in time to capture the roiling orange mushroom cloud. So the first broadcast video of the destruction of Moab was simply a close-up of this man's phone, held in his shaking hands. And, as far as it went, it sure enough looked like a mushroom cloud.

Corvallis walked across the parking lot to his Tesla, threw his duffel bag into the trunk, and climbed into the driver's seat. His phone connected to the car's onboard systems and the big video screen in the middle of the dashboard came alive. He dialed the twenty-four-hour hotline for his jet company and told them he needed emergency transportation from Missoula—the nearest town of consequence—to San Jose. They put him on hold. He did a quick scroll through emails and saw a lot of stuff, but nothing that couldn't wait; the important thing was for him to get on the plane. So he shifted the Tesla into forward driving mode and began gliding silently across the parking lot, headed for the road that would take him down the mountain.

By the time he had reached the highway, the jet dispatcher had come back on the line and let him know that a pilot was en route to Boeing Field. The jet was being fueled. It would be in the air promptly and would probably get to Missoula before Corvallis did.

During the ensuing hour-long drive down the Bitterroot Valley, he mostly resisted the temptation to look at the screen, and instead listened to the radio. This was jammed with emergency coverage, as alarming as it was vague. One would think it would be an easy matter to simply go to Moab and look at it and report back. But all helicopters within an hour's flying time of ground zero had already been spoken for by mysterious entities, and pilots were being warned not to fly anywhere near Moab for fear of radioactive contamination. Much of the radio coverage simply consisted of reporters summarizing what was turning up on the Miasma. Pictures of military roadblocks were being massively upvoted on discussion forums. Comment-thread geeks were zooming in on details and pegging various items of equipment: radiation detectors, dosimeters, containers of pills you were supposed to swallow in the event of radiation exposure. From time to time they would cut away to the financial desk for a report on the inevitable stock market crash. Trading on the New York Stock Exchange was already suspended for the day. Foreign leaders were expressing grave concern and offering assistance. A jihadist website had apparently posted a video describing the annihilation of Moab as a warning shot, and making it known that they had another such weapon planted in a major American city.

By the time Corvallis reached the outskirts of Missoula, that passenger at LAX had sold his mushroom cloud footage to the highest-bidding network. While stopped at a red light, Corvallis watched it on the dashboard video. It had been taken from hundreds of miles away, so was pretty small in the original clip; the network had zoomed it in ("blown it up," in the inartful phrase of an anchorwoman) and enhanced it.

They did not get to savor the exclusive for long. By the time Corvallis had reached the airport, another network had come through with even better imagery from a truck driver's dashboard camera. Apparently the driver, having witnessed the mushroom cloud from twenty miles outside of Moab, had turned his vehicle around and driven back out to the next town where he could get Internet access.

Security waved Corvallis through to a private parking area, and he sat in his car and watched the trucker's video while the flight crew took his baggage out of his trunk and stowed it in the jet's luggage compartment. This footage was a lot better than the cell phone video but still left a certain amount to the imagination. The truck had not been pointed squarely at Moab when the bomb had detonated, and so about half of the mushroom cloud was cropped off the right edge of the frame. But it was very obviously a mushroom cloud and you could see its interaction with various layers of the atmosphere as it rose above Moab, and in otherwise dark parts of the frame you could see how Moab-facing hillsides and mountains were lit up by it.

He handed the Tesla off to one of the ground crew for parking, then walked about fifty feet to the jet. One of the pilots was already in the cockpit doing his piloty things while the other was getting the luggage hatch squared away. A flight attendant, whom Corvallis vaguely recognized as Bonnie, was standing at the top of the steps. He wasn't sure where the jet company obtained people like Bonnie, but his working hypothesis was that they were fashion models who had turned thirty. They lived in a world that was as disjoint from his world as ancient Egypt, even though it coexisted in the same time and place. In rare moments, such as when Corvallis climbed the steps into his jet and greeted Bonnie or one of her colleagues, his world glanced off of hers, and if he wasn't too distracted he might sneak a look at her and ponder the sheer differentness of their respective existences.

Today, her passenger just happened to be a tech geek who, while technically not a billionaire, might as well have been one. He happened to be wearing the tunic and cloak of a Roman legionary, but it might as well have been jeans, T-shirt, and hoodie.

Bonnie's welcoming smile faltered a little when she saw how he was dressed, but she bore up well under the shock and seemed to have recovered her professionally mandated persona by the time his *caligae* crossed the plane's threshold. His iron hobnails clacked on the exotic hardwood flooring until he reached the aisle of the main cabin, which was carpeted. He peeled off his woolen cloak and handed it to Bonnie, who ran her hand over it in an evaluative way, then took it forward to the little closet.

Perhaps her eye had been drawn to the embroidery that ran around the edge of the garment: a repeating pattern of crows' heads. In reenactment groups it was customary for each participant to adopt a persona, or, at a bare minimum, a nickname that wouldn't sound too jarringly anachronistic when called out in the heat of action. Corvallis had become Corvus, which was just the Latin word for "crow." It was partly an obvious contraction of his real name and partly a reference to his coloration. One of his parents had been half Japanese, the other South Asian. Noticing this, and calling it out in a nickname, wouldn't have been polite by modern standards. But there was no getting around the fact that, in a Roman legion, he'd have stood out as some sort of exotic from the Eastern provinces. The other Romans would have slapped some such name on him. Corvus it was. At first he'd been mildly uncomfortable with it, as he'd associated such birds with Edgar Allan Poe and goth culture in general. With time and repetition his thinking had adjusted. He now saw it through a hybrid of Pacific Northwest aboriginal myths and Roman aviomancy. The only birds you saw in Seattle were seagulls, crows, and eagles. Seagulls were ubiquitous, mindless consumers. Eagles were spectacular, huge, badass, but comparatively rare; people would actually stop what they were doing and look up when an eagle flew by. Crows, or ravens (the distinction was unclear), were set apart by their extreme intelligence, memory, and resourcefulness; but no matter how well they embodied those fine traits, no one appreciated them.

Of crows, people tended to predicate the same traits that they did of Asians when they had forgotten politically correct habits of speech, or never acquired them in the first place. Crows were commendably intelligent, and forever busy, but you couldn't tell them apart and their motives were inscrutable. But living inside of his own head, Corvus well knew his own motives. There was nothing wrong with those motives and he didn't need to justify them to anyone else.

When Richard Forthrast had been alive, Corvallis's relationship to him had been like that of a raven to an eagle. Or so he had convinced himself in retrospect; and every time he looked out a window to see an eagle gliding above the lake, being harried by a dive-bombing crow, he thought of himself and Dodge. He'd become comfortable with the nickname Corvus. As he'd gone deeper into the reenactment world, and spent more money on clothing, armor, and weapons, he'd taken the trouble to personalize all of it with raven iconography. He'd found a graphic artist on Craigslist who had produced some convincingly classical-looking line art for him, and he'd found others willing to stitch that artwork onto his clothing or hammer it into his armor. You could get anything on the Miasma, including a whole alternate historical identity.

"Corvus" turned around and sank into his customary position on the front right and buckled the seat belt over his tunic, then pulled his laptop out of its bag and got it booted up as the jet was taxiing to the head of the runway. The laptop fell into a kind of stupor as umpteen different apps tried to synchronize themselves over an overloaded wireless connection. It wasn't until the jet had taken off and climbed to an altitude where its onboard Wi-Fi system kicked in that Corvallis was able to get proper Internet. On the left side of his screen he set up an ordinary browser window so that he could see the world as other people saw it, and on the right he launched a couple of other apps that were connected directly to Lyke's internal systems over an encrypted, secure connection. The former was sluggish. The latter showed why: Lyke's systems were badly bogged down, and the same was presumably true of all the other social media platforms.

Weather forecasters, as a public service, had taken to posting maps based on current and projected wind patterns, showing the area likely to be contaminated by the fallout plume. A traffic jam had formed on I-70 near Grand Junction, Colorado, as residents fled and commenced banging into each other. Another kind of jam-up had materialized on the tarmac at Aspen as every private jet tried to get clearance for takeoff at once. Such images were played over and over again by networks lacking actual footage of Moab.

Suddenly the lidless eye of Breaking News swung around to Las Vegas. What looked like the entire Las Vegas Police Department was evacuating a high-rise casino/hotel, landing choppers on the roof, and (clearly visible to long-lensed cameras on drones, or simply aimed out the windows of surrounding high-rises) conducting a room-to-room search of a penthouse suite using sniffer dogs and Geiger counters. Military experts, watching the raid in real time on television, pointed out that the top of such a tower would be the optimal location to detonate a tactical nuke—much more devastating than a ground burst. By the time the official order went out to evacuate every building within a mile, the streets were jammed anyway with tourists who'd decided not to wait.

From Corvallis's point of view—watching the feeds in one window while monitoring Lyke's systems in another—the events in Vegas produced the social media equivalent of a nuclear chain reaction as seemingly everyone there tried to post pictures and videos at the same moment. The result was something approaching a blackout. Lyke's server farms had been designed to handle huge traffic surges, and the technology they'd acquired from Nubilant had made them even better at doing so. All of that stuff was working. But there were only so many computers and so much bandwidth to go around. When those had all been maxed out, there was nothing to do but wait for things to settle down.

So he waited, along with a billion other Miasma users staring at frozen screens. His mind went back to poor Moab. Remote, difficult to reach, cut off by roadblocks, radioactive, probably reduced to cinders, it had become something of an afterthought. He had been there, a few years ago, on a rafting trip, and thought it a nice little town, a Mecca for young, strenuous, happy-go-lucky dudes in cargo shorts and girls with sports bras and pigtails.

It occurred to him that this would be the best time to change out of his Roman legionary clothes and into the normal-guy clothing he'd brought with him. Yesterday, when he'd reached the site of the camp, he'd changed in the backseat of his Tesla and stashed the modern garb in a duffel bag in the trunk of his car. But that duffel bag was now in the plane's luggage compartment, unreachable until they landed.

A meme cropped up claiming that Moab had actually gone off the grid two days earlier as most of its residents had fallen victim to an explosively contagious plague that had presumably escaped from a nearby bioweapons facility, and that the president had made the decision to sterilize the whole town with a nuke. The roadblocks on the surrounding highways weren't there to prevent curiosity-seekers from getting in. They were to stop any infected survivors' getting out. The call went out for all armed citizens living anywhere near Moab to set up watch posts on hills and rooftops and to report, or shoot, escaping zombies. This and other alternative versions of reality were shouted down by stentorian typists even as they were being embellished on fringe talk radio programs and fervently taken up by upstart networks of true believers.

The president, who'd been on a state visit to the Far East, made an appeal for calm, then canceled his engagements and boarded Air Force One, bound for home—though a leaked document, widely reblogged and reposted, showed a flight plan terminating at the U.S. nuclear command bunker in Colorado Springs.

Temporarily at a loss for anything useful to do, Corvallis reckoned that he could at least make some headway debunking the zombie hypothesis. Over the VPN that connected him to Lyke's servers, he could search the colossal database in which was recorded every scrap of social media activity that had occurred since the company had first gone online. This was the sort of thing he had got rather good at during his tenure at Corporation 9592, where tracking the actions taken by the game's millions of players had been essential to making it fun, successful, and profitable. Compared to that, it was a simple matter to run a query that would list all Lyke activity originating from users in Moab, Utah, during the last week.

Of course, Corvallis didn't believe for a moment that a bioweapon plague had actually struck the town. This was clearly the work of trolls. The only open question was whether they were nihilistic trolls who just liked to see the world burn, or motivated trolls with some vested interest in gulling credulous millions into clicking on this or that link. But one of the Miasma's perversities was that it made otherwise sane people like him—people who had better things they could have been doing—devote energy to arguing with completely random fuckwits, many of whom probably didn't even believe in their own arguments, some of whom weren't even humans. By making this database query, Corvallis was marshaling evidence for use in one of those pointless debates. If it really was the case that Moabites had suddenly begun getting sick in large numbers, they'd have posted complaints on social media. They'd have called in sick, canceled social engagements, sympathized with one another, exchanged harebrained home remedies, and searched for certain keywords like "high fever and rash" or what have you. Even if a government conspiracy had later severed the town's links to the outside world, all prior activity would remain archived in Lyke's servers, where it could be collated and analyzed by someone like Corvallis who had the requisite privileges.

Not surprisingly, the result of the query was a week's worth of utterly normal social media traffic from the good people of Moab. Nothing whatsoever about mysterious deadly plagues. So the bioweapon narrative was easy to quash, at least if you were among the small minority of Miasma users who actually cared about logic and evidence.

Less out of curiosity than a mindless, OCD-ish compulsion to organize things, he sorted the results of his search by their time stamps, arranging them so that the most recent postings were at the top of the list. Now he could see every jot and tittle of social media traffic that had come out of Moab, Utah, in the days and hours leading up to the detonation.

Most of the entries now visible on his screen had come in last night, petering off into the wee hours as people went to bed. There was a drunken selfie from a party at 3:12 A.M., then nothing for almost two hours.

The item at the very top of the list—in other words, the last social media post to have made it out of Moab, Utah, before it had been nuked—was from an account owned by a company called Canyonland Adventures. Their profile indicated that they were based in Moab and that they were in the business of running white-water rafting trips down the Colorado River. Historically, their postings had comprised promotions, tidbits of news (the cat in their office had been in an altercation with a dog), photos of happy rafters in beautiful settings, and logistical updates for their customers.

The final pre-nuke posting was apparently one of the latter. It was text only, with no pictures or links. It read, "Jones party: your friendly guide Maeve here, up at the crack of dawn, chuffed for today's adventure—looking forward to seeing y'allz at the sandbar at 6 am sharp—posting this from my phone since my wifi just went down! If you need to reach me, use my cell. And remember: SUNSCREEN AND HATS!!!"

The attached metadata indicated that the post had indeed been made from the mobile app using the SMS, or text messaging, system. The time stamp was 5:05 A.M. local, so about fifteen minutes before the nuke had detonated.

10

A few years earlier, Corvallis had been in a moderately serious car accident in stop-and-go traffic. He'd slowed down. The car behind him hadn't—its driver was texting—and had rear-ended him hard enough to total Corvallis's vehicle. Looking back on it later, the weird thing about it was how long it had taken for his brain to assemble anything like a correct picture of events. The first thing that had happened, as far as Corvallis's mind-body system was concerned, was that his car's headrest had struck him in the back of the skull hard enough that he could feel the little rivets in its frame. Then a bunch of other stuff had happened and he had been distracted for a while, but it wasn't until maybe an hour later that he'd noticed his head hurting and reached up to find a bump on the back of his skull.

This was kind of like that. Reading the time stamp on Maeve's message and her words *my wifi just went down* were the blow to the base of his skull, but it was a while before he really focused on it.

It was easy to find Maeve's last name (Braden) and look up her address. She lived right in the middle of Moab, just a few blocks away from the offices of Canyonland Adventures. Whether she'd sent that text from her home or from the office, she'd probably been within a few hundred yards of ground zero.

He spent a while aimlessly clicking through Maeve's various social media activities. On Lyke and other social media platforms, she had registered using variant spellings of her first name (Mab, Mabh, Madbh) and her last (Bradan, O Bradain). Apparently both names were Gaelic and so the spelling was all over the place. This was a common subterfuge used by people who didn't want to sign up for social media accounts under their real names, but who understood that the fake name had to be convincing enough to pass an elementary screen by an algorithm somewhere; "Mickey Mouse" or "X Y" would be rejected, but "Mabh O Bradain" was fine. "Mab" was only one letter different from "Moab" and he wondered if Maeve had used it for that reason, as a sort of pun on her adopted home.

She was Australian, living in the States because of some family complications only murkily hinted at on social media. She was a double amputee—one of those people who suffered from a congenital malformation of the lower legs that made it necessary to remove them, below the knee, during childhood. She had been pursuing rowing and paddling sports for much of her twenty-nine years. Verna, her older sister in Adelaide, had stage 3 melanoma; Maeve had a lot to say about the importance of sun protection for outdoorsy people.

He had been clicking on links for a while without reading them. He had gone down a rat hole and found himself reading a page on modern high-tech prosthetic legs. He knew a couple of other people who used them, and had once invested in a startup that was trying to make better ones. So as random as it might have seemed, it felt like a point of connection between him and Maeve.

The jet was over the Bitterroots, aimed south-southwest. Corvallis pulled up a map and zoomed it to the point where he could see San Jose in the bottom left, Moab in the bottom right, and Missoula up top.

He unbuckled his seat belt and walked forward past the little galley, where Bonnie was making coffee. She had kicked off her high-heeled pumps and switched to her sensible in-flight footwear. She looked up at him, moderately startled; the toilet was in the back, he had no particular reason for being up at this end of the plane.

Procedures on private jets were pretty relaxed. Cockpit doors weren't armored, and frequently were left open so that curious passengers could look out the front. At the moment, this one was closed. Corvallis hesitated before knocking on it. He was hesitating because he was about to make a decision he couldn't unmake, and he knew that everyone was going to be disconcerted by it, and he wasn't good at that kind of thing—at the mere fact of making himself the center of attention. So before knocking he had to engage in a bit of mental prep that had become a habit in the last few years. He was visualizing Richard Forthrast, hale and healthy, standing exactly where Corvallis was standing right now, confidently knocking on the door. Hell, Dodge wouldn't even knock, he would just open it. He would greet Frank and Lenny, the pilot and copilot, and he would say what he had to say.

Bonnie was giving him an odd look.

He smiled and nodded at her, then rapped on the door. Then he opened it.

"Frank and Lenny," he said. "According to my map, Moab is approximately the same distance from where we are now as San Jose. Therefore, we ought to have enough fuel on board to fly to Moab. I would like to file a new flight plan and go to Moab."

They looked at him like he was crazy. As he'd known they would. But the reality of it wasn't as bad as he'd feared. It never was. The anticipation was always worse.

"Moab, where the bomb went off?" asked Frank, who was the alpha pilot.

"Yes. That Moab."

"I think that's shut down," said Lenny, the beta pilot. "I mean, the FAA won't let us near there."

"Do you know that for a fact, Lenny, or is it just a reasonable surmise based on news and social media stuff?"

Lenny looked to Frank.

"Well, we haven't actually contacted the FAA, if that's what you mean," Frank said.

"I would like you to change course for Moab, and file the flight plan, and see what happens," Corvallis said. "If the FAA won't allow us to land there, maybe we can fly past it en route to somewhere farther away, and look down at it. All I really need is to see the town from above."

Frank and Lenny looked at each other. Frank nodded.

"I'll get on it, boss," said Lenny.

"Okay. Let me know how it goes. I'm really interested to hear any particulars about how the FAA behaves when you run this by them."

Corvallis got back to his laptop, and its live Miasmic news

feeds, in time to see a big military chopper lifting off from the roof of that casino in Las Vegas. Dangling below it was something that looked heavy. It flew off in the direction of the nearby air force base, which was described as a top secret facility that had once been used for nuclear weapons testing. The all-clear was sounded in Vegas. But immediately it was swamped, on the news feeds, by reports of a precisely similar incident taking shape on the top floor of a skinny residential tower under construction in midtown Manhattan. This had to duel for airtime with shocking new footage just coming in from Moab, where, for the first time since it had all started, we were now seeing photos of horribly burned victims, and shaky video of their being unloaded from medical choppers. From outside the cordon, downwind of Moab, bloggers on horseback and all-terrain vehicles were now reporting elevated radiation levels. The mainstream media were ignoring, or actively suppressing, these reports, presumably because the government had admonished them not to spread panic. But social media were more effective at spreading what passed for news and so it scarcely mattered.

Someone had finally got close enough to Moab to do a flyover with a drone. They couldn't get too close because of military units that were interdicting travel in the area, and also because they didn't want to expose themselves to radiation, but they were able to transmit some footage of the ruined town. The low frame rate, the bricky pixels, the compression artifacts in the image, the tendency of the camera to be aimed in the wrong direction as it flew through smoke and dust, all contributed to a feeling of cinema verité that was beginning to strike his increasingly jaded eye as too good to be true.

Keeping an eye on Lyke's internal email system, Corvallis noticed that Jason Crabb was online. Jason was a systems administrator for Nubilant who had jumped to Lyke in the wake of the acquisition. It had given him a pretext for moving to the Bay Area, which he'd been wanting to do anyway, because of a complicated girlfriend situation. Corvallis clicked on the little video camera icon next to Jason's name. After a minute or so of user interface fuckery, he found himself looking at a moving image of Jason, who was sitting in his girlfriend's bed, propped up on a lot of pillows. The upward camera angle of his laptop made Jason's beard huge and magnificent in a rufous shaft of morning sunlight. He did not greet Corvallis but just stared at him, alert and expectant. On a day such as this one, "C-plus" would not have taken the unusual step of initiating a video call unless it was important.

"Suppose there's a company in Moab with a website, or some other kind of Internet presence of any kind whatsoever for that matter," Corvallis began.

"Yeah?"

"It's off the air now, let's say."

"No shit!"

"Okay, but pretend for a moment we don't actually know why. There are two possible explanations for its being off the air. You need to get all Sherlock and figure out which is the truth."

"Okay—??"

"Scenario one is that Moab got nuked and the wires, or the optical fibers, don't even reach into town anymore, they are just dangling from a burning telegraph pole in the desert. Scenario two is that Moab is still there but the ISP that serves it is being crushed under a DDoS attack." Meaning, as Jason would know, "distributed denial of service." "Or for that matter any kind of remote hack that would shut it down for a while. Is there a way you could distinguish between those two scenarios without getting out of bed?"

"I have to pee," Jason said.

"You know what I mean."

"Probably."

"Okay, please do that and get back to me," Corvallis said, and disconnected.

Lots more was happening in Manhattan now, on news and social media sites, on talk radio. The wave had not crested yet. If Corvallis were among the billions who actually believed that Moab had been nuked, he'd have been fully absorbed. As it was he found himself in a weirdly peaceful and calm state.

"I called an audible," Frank was saying to him.

Corvallis looked up to see the pilot standing in the aisle, looking down at him. His brain slowly caught up. Calling an audible was some kind of sports-based metaphor. It meant that Frank had made a decision on his own—improvised in a way he hoped Corvallis would later approve of.

"I filed a flight plan to El Paso."

"El Paso?"

"It'll take us near Moab. Near enough that we can look down on it like you said. But we'll be at forty thousand feet—above the box."

"The box?"

"The box of airspace around Moab where the FAA doesn't want us to go."

"El Paso's a lot farther away," Corvallis pointed out.

Frank nodded. "The only thing that's a little sketchy about this is that we really don't have that much fuel. I mean, we could stretch it, but we'd be in the red zone. So we'll have to land somewhere else, short of El Paso."

"That's okay," Corvallis said, "everything will be different by then."

"It's okay for you," Frank said, "but it makes me look like a fucking idiot for filing a flight plan that doesn't make sense fuel-wise."

"Just tell me who I need to talk to. I'll take responsibility." Corvallis generally didn't like looking people in the eye, but from watching Dodge he knew that there were certain times when it was a deal-breaker. So he forced himself to look Frank in the eye. "I will personally take responsibility for this and I will get you off the hook." Frank shrugged, raised his eyebrows, and went back to the cockpit.

Corvallis had been thinking about a detail that had passed under his gaze while he'd been clicking around learning about Maeve Braden. He had to dig surprisingly deep into his browser history to find it. This was complicated by the fact that he had been checking her out both on the public Miasma and in Lyke's secure file system. Eventually he tracked it down in the latter. It was the personal data record associated with her account—the result of her having filled out a form, years ago, when she'd joined Lyke, and having clicked the "submit" button. Which, come to think of it, was a pretty strange bit of semantics. But anyway, she had listed several telephone numbers, including one that began with "011," which was the prefix for dialing international calls from the United States. He had already learned of her Australian background and so upon scanning this for the first time he'd made the obvious assumption that it was an Oz number. But it wouldn't make any particular sense for her to go to the trouble of entering such a number into her profile unless she was actually spending a lot of time in Australia.

On a second look, the country code was 881, which wasn't Australia; it was a special code used by satellite phones.

Corvallis wasn't hugely knowledgeable about sat phones, but he knew a couple of people who owned them, either just because they were geeks or because they did a lot of travel in places with no cell phone coverage. It seemed pretty obvious that Maeve was one of the latter. Her whole job was taking groups of tourists on trips deep into the canyons of the Colorado River, where cell phone use was out of the question. Of course Canyonlands Adventures would own sat phones, and of course they'd issue them to their guides.

Whether she would keep the thing turned on, and within easy reach, was another question. For all he knew, it might have been turned off and buried in a waterproof bag at the bottom of a raft. But then it might get dumped overboard if the raft flipped—which was exactly the kind of situation where you'd need it. It would make more sense for the lead guide to carry it on her person.

It was worth a go, anyway. Corvallis's cell phone wouldn't work on the plane, but he had pretty good Internet and he could make voice calls through his laptop. He plugged in his headphones for better audio, booted up the relevant app, and typed in the number. There was a long wait—much longer than for conventional calls.

"Hell-low!?" said a woman. She sounded Australian, and pissed off that someone would call her. In the background it was possible to hear other people chattering and laughing. Corvallis visualized them on the raft, in a quiet stretch of the Colorado. He heard a splash and a kerplunk. Someone had jumped in for a swim.

Just from this, Corvallis had already learned what he needed to know: that Moab had not been nuked. But it seemed only polite to explain himself. "Maeve, I'm sorry to bother you but this is important. You don't know me. My name is Corvallis Kawasaki."

"As in the town of Corvallis? Oregon?"

"Yes. You can Google me when you get home, I'm an executive at Lyke. The social media company."

"You work for Lyke?"

"Yes."

"Is there something going wrong with my account? Did I get hacked or something?" He liked the way she asked it. Her tone wasn't apprehensive. It was more as if she would find it wryly amusing to have been hacked.

"No. Your account is fine. Everything is fine where you're concerned."

She laughed. "Then why are you calling me? To ask me out on a bloody date?"

"That would be a violation of our confidentiality policies," Corvallis responded. "This is about something else that you should probably be aware of." And he went on to explain, as best as he could without taking all day, what had been happening. During this time, Maeve didn't say much. It was a lot to take in. And for all of its complexity, for all of the millions of people on the Miasma who sincerely believed in its reality, it must have seemed ridiculous and dreamlike to her, gliding down the Colorado with her sun hat pulled down over her head and her paddle on her lap, looking at the ancient rocks, watching the Jones family gambol in the cool water.

"At about five twenty this morning, you were still in or near Moab, right?"

"I was at the office," she said, "loading up the van."

"In downtown Moab."

"Yeah."

"Did you see anything like a bright flash in the sky?" He already knew the answer, but he had to ask.

"No. There was no such thing."

"But the Internet had gone down."

"I'd got up at four thirty and it worked. Half an hour later it had crashed. Nothing."

"Did you try to use your cell phone at all?"

"The Joneses did. They tried to ring me at five thirty, five forty, something like that. Nothing worked."

"Why'd they want to call you?"

"To tell me they'd be late."

"But you met at the sandbar and got off without anything unusual happening."

"Yeah."

"And the sandbar is, what, only a couple of miles outside of Moab?"

"That's right. Hang on." The phone went shuffly/muffly. Corvallis heard enough snatches of Maeve's voice to guess that she was trying to explain matters to her clients, who had overheard enough to be curious.

"I'm here," she assured him.

"Maeve? There's a lot more we could say to each other," Corvallis said, "but I'm betting that the Joneses have friends and family who know they were in Moab this morning and who are frantic with worry right now. You should probably hang up and call them."

"Why haven't they called already, I wonder?"

"They probably don't have the sat phone number. To get the sat phone number, they'd have to reach your main office, and . . ."

"And all the comms are down, yeah. All right. How can I call you back, Corvallis?"

He gave her his number, and she recited it back to him, using the quasi-military "niner" in place of "nine," which he found unaccountably confidence inspiring. Then she hung up without formalities.

While all of this had been going on, Jason Crabb had emailed him back to tell him what he already knew, namely that the communications blackout in Moab appeared to be the result of a conventional DDoS attack.

Corvallis called Laurynas, his boss, the fifty-ninth-richest man in the world, who answered the phone with "Don't sell any of your stock."

"Huh?"

"After the stock market reopens, that is. Legal's sending out a company-wide blast."

It took Corvallis a few seconds to catch up with the logic. "You know the Moab event is a hoax."

"Yeah. It is becoming increasingly obvious."

"You're worried it's going to be a bloodbath for our stock. Because so much of it is happening on our network. We look negligent. People will sue us."

"But for now that is insider knowledge, C, and if you sell any of your stock, you are insider trading."

"Got it."

"Where are you, man? Other than on a plane."

"Headed for Moab."

Laurynas laughed. Corvallis had the sense it was the first time he had laughed all day. "No shit?"

"When I got suspicious I asked the pilots to plot a new course."

"That is awesome." Laurynas was ten years younger than him. "You going to try to land at Moab?"

"Probably not. No real plan yet."

"You're just calling an audible. That. Is. Awesome!"

"Thanks."

"When did you first get suspicious, C?"

"At a subconscious level? It was all that shit about the Moabites."

"What are you talking about?"

"In the video from the terrorists, where they take responsibility for the attack?"

"Yeah. It's a pretty long sermon," Laurynas said, a little defensively. "I didn't have time to sit through the whole thing."

"He quotes a lot of Old Testament crap about the ancient Moabites and how they were apparently the bad guys. Born of incest or something."

"As if that justifies the attack on Moab, Utah."

"Yeah, and on one level I'm thinking it sounds like the usual convoluted jihad-think but at the same time I'm like, 'Come on, man, you could have nuked any old town you chose, and most would be easier to reach than Moab.' I mean, why even bother with a warning shot?"

"They were trying too hard," said Laurynas, getting it. "Piling on a lot of verbiage to explain why they picked that town."

"Yeah. As if they were worried that people would see through it. When the real reason's obvious."

"Yeah. If they did a nuke hoax in Paterson, New Jersey, people in the next town over would just check it out with fucking binoculars and say, 'Nope, still there.' It had to be somewhere isolated."

"It's the key to the whole plan," Corvallis said.

"Yeah, it sets up the red-eye flight, the truck driver, and the rest. These guys are good."

"So if I were you, with the resources you've got, I'd be digging into the fake footage, the burn victims . . ."

"We found some metadata suggesting it came out of a Nollywood special effects house."

"You mean Bollywood?"

"Nollywood. November. Not Bravo. Nigerian film industry. Huge."

"Jeez, why is it always Nigeria?"

"It isn't," Laurynas said flatly. "This is classic misdirection. Whoever did this knows that, when it comes to light, people will focus way too much attention on the Nigeria angle."

"Well, so what do you want me to do?" Corvallis asked, after they had both sat there quietly pondering Nigeria for some moments.

"Save the company."

"And how do you think I might achieve that?"

"By getting to Moab before the president of the United States gets there. Or, barring that, soon."

"How does that save the company?"

"When people understand that this is a hoax, burning feces are going to fall out of the sky and bury us to a depth of six Empire State Buildings," Laurynas said. "The best we can do is spread the blame—point out that all the other networks got used in the same way. This becomes infinitely more effective if we can say, 'And look, our dude C was on the ground in Moab before sundown, personally establishing the ground truth.'"

Laurynas was a Lithuanian basketball prodigy who had attended Michigan on a scholarship and then wrong-footed everyone by turning out to be actually smart. He would answer to

"Lawrence." He had picked up American tech-bro speech pretty accurately, but his accent broke the surface when he was envisioning something that he thought would be awesome.

"Before sundown?" Corvallis repeated.

"That would be preferable. Darkness, video, not a good fit." Laurynas was laughing as he hung up. He had the big man's joviality when it came to the doings of small people.

On a Miasma news feed, some scientists in white lab coats were giving a press conference in front of a backdrop covered with many copies of the logo and name of the Los Alamos National Laboratory. Corvallis listened to it for a while. It was perfect. The actors portraying the scientists were well cast: There was the eminence grise who didn't say much but who conveyed huge gravitas and authority when he did. The engaging young beard who did most of the talking and reminded you of your favorite science teacher who rode around campus on a recumbent bicycle. The demure, middle-aged, maternal, but still-kind-of-hot woman. The introverted Asian dude showing flashes of wry humor. Whoever had produced this counterfeit had completely nailed the sound: you could hear chairs scraping, shutters clicking, fingers pounding laptop keyboards, people's cell phones going off, all conveying the sense that a hundred journalists were crammed into the room. The payload—the informational warhead on the tip of this social media rocket—was that they had performed isotopic analysis of fallout collected by volunteers downwind of Moab and confirmed that it matched the fingerprint of half a dozen Soviet-era suitcase nukes that had gone missing in Uzbekistan some years ago.

Even as C-plus was admiring the quality of the pseudoscientific dialogue being spouted by these actors, the "news conference" was suddenly "shut down" as the room was invaded by a squad of beefy-looking guys in beards and wraparound sunglasses who looked like they had just stepped out of a casting call for a SEAL Team Six movie. Their leader's face was visible only for a few frames as he reached out and swiped at the camera's lens. The camera ended up on the floor, sideways, transmitting a close-up of a knocked-over Starbucks cup and some chair legs, with murky sound of the scientists protesting as they were hustled out of the room.

A logo at the bottom of the screen claimed it was live on CNN. Which was by definition wrong, since Corvallis wasn't actually *watching* it on CNN. He had found it on YouTube by clicking on a Twitter link in which some concerned citizen watchdog claimed that they had captured this sensational footage earlier on the live CNN feed and were just posting it for the benefit of the general population and that everyone should download it and copy it and post it everywhere before the government suppressed the news.

Out of curiosity, Corvallis went over to CNN's Twitter feed and found a tweet from twenty minutes ago insisting that the press conference footage on YouTube was *not* genuine CNN content, had never aired on CNN, and was some sort of hoax. It had already drawn thousands of angry and skeptical replies from people saying that CNN was obviously being controlled by deep-state actors.

Temporarily at a loss for anything to do, Corvallis rewound the fake press conference video to a close-up of the woman scientist, took a screen grab of her face, and pasted it into Lyke's face-recognition app. Within seconds he was reading the IMDb profile of this actress, a veteran of numerous television commercials and a few indie films. He didn't waste his time repeating the experiment with the other members of the cast. Or for that matter with the scruffy young actor who had climbed off the red-eye earlier and released the mushroom cloud footage to the world. Or the truck driver in Utah. Or Larry Proctor, the blogger. It would be the same with all of them. And when the hoax was discovered and quashed, all of them would be tracked down by vengeful Miasma sleuths and all of them would probably tell a similar story: they had been recruited by a production company working on a low-budget indie thriller, they had gone to certain soundstages and recited certain lines. They and the production crew had all been paid in some untraceable way, through Bitcoin or whatever, and they'd moved on to the next job.

A text came through from Laurynas: *We found the people who made the mushroom cloud sim—a CGI house in the Philippines.*

He Googled *Moab hoax* and found a basically infinite amount of stuff already posted. Much of it was right for the wrong reasons. Ninety percent of it was about the bioweapon theory.

These people—the people who had done this—were awesome. They knew that some people would see through the hoax and denounce it as such. Those skeptics couldn't be silenced. But they could be drowned out. So, the hoaxers had inoculated the Miasma with a ready-made hoax narrative that was obviously ridiculous, and tailor-made to appeal to the vociferous citizens of Crazytown. Right now everyone's uncle Harry—the angry truther at Thanksgiving dinner—was typing as fast as he could with the caps lock key in effect. If you were a member of the reality-based community who suspected that it was a hoax, you had to wade through a hundred zombie-related postings in order to find one that made sense, and wherever you went on the Miasma to argue for a skeptical and reasoned approach, you were lumped in with the zombie truthers, ridiculed and downvoted. As an example, he found a thread in which zombie truthers were being shouted down by people who had just seen the fake Los Alamos news conference on YouTube and were using it as evidence that Moab had been nuked by foreign terrorists, not by the United States government.

Frank's voice came through on the intercom. "Moab is under cloud cover."

Of course it was under cloud cover. Corvallis wondered if the authors of this hoax had waited for a cloudy day in Moab before pulling the trigger.

He went up to the cockpit so that he could look out the windshield over the pilots' shoulders. The weather was generally clear, but clouds were stuffed like cotton into low places in the landscape, including the valley of a prominent river that Corvallis assumed was the Colorado. No-fly zone or not, people could fly over Moab all day long and not be able to come back with a definitive answer as to whether it still existed.

"We need to land," Corvallis announced.

"The Moab airport is closed," Frank told him.

Without thinking, Corvallis said what Dodge would have said: "I didn't say anything about an airport. See if there's an airstrip or a straight stretch of highway."

"Highway!?"

"I might be able to contact someone who knows the area," Corvallis said, and stepped out of the cockpit. His phone was ringing. Or rather, the app running on his laptop that did what a phone did, except over the Internet. He strode up the aisle and pivoted to look at the screen. A window had popped up, making him aware of an incoming call from an international number with an 881 area code.

Corvallis fell in love with Maeve.

It was another one of those transitions like being rear-ended and clubbed in the base of the skull by the headrest. To say that he wasn't aware of it would've been wrong. It was palpable. But the part of his nervous system that had registered it was way down in the boiler room, as it were, sending out email alerts that would take a long time to make their way through the spam filters and middle-management layers of his brain. Weeks might pass before the meeting in which, sitting in the boardroom of his soul, Corvallis Kawasaki would be confronted by a PowerPoint slide, projected eight feet wide, announcing in no-nonsense sans-serif type, "IN LOVE WITH MAEVE." What he had just experienced was more like the subtle click of a really well-engineered piece of machinery being snapped together.

He plugged in his headphones and answered the call. "Maeve?"

"This is all a bit surreal," she announced. "The Joneses have been talking to their freaked-out relatives. They have a bloody lot of them. High-strung family I gather."

"So you kind of know what's going on."

"I know what's going on in their little minds," she said. The same words spoken by a tech geek would have seemed impossibly arrogant, but from her came off as more affectionate/exasperated.

Corvallis's primary emotion was hopeful gratification over the fact that, right now, he was the only human in the world Maeve could talk to. It was beside the point and probably inappropriate. He was with other people, but basically alone in a private jet. She was with other people, but basically alone on a raft thirty thousand feet below him (for the jet had begun descending).

"Do they want to bail out?" he asked.

"What are you asking?"

"How long is the trip supposed to last?"

"Three days. Two overnight stays. We come out on the other end of the park." Meaning, as he could infer, Canyonlands National Park.

"Are you in the park yet?"

"Not quite. We stopped on a sandbar for lunch and endless phone chatting."

"If they could cancel it now, would they? And go home to their freaked-out family members?"

"Is it good and ruined, you're asking. Can they really enjoy the next three days."

"Yeah, and on that note, is there an airstrip near you?"

Her answers turned out to be yes—the Joneses wanted to bail out—and yes: there was an airstrip near them, belonging to a ranch adjoining the park. Half an hour later, the jet was on the ground there. The descent and landing seemed normal to him, but after the plane had come to a full stop, Frank and Lenny high-fived each other. Bonnie looked out the tiny window in the door and thought better of changing back into her heels. She opened the door, deployed the stairway, and stood at attention holding Corvallis's wool cloak. The scent of sagebrush flooded into the plane.

Corvallis had been hoping for something authentically rustic, but the ranch had remade itself as a tourist operation and so the first thing he saw was its swag kiosk, currently unmanned. He watched disbelievingly as an actual tumbleweed blew past it. The airstrip had been laid down on a dry lake bed or something, so it was surrounded by low hills of rubble from which sprouted cool-looking outcroppings of rock. Maybe that explained the pilots' high five.

Approaching was one of those especially huge pickup trucks with double rear wheels and a crew cabin. It was skidding around switchbacks and kicking up rooster tails of ocher dust.

Corvallis was pretty sure that, at this moment, he was closer (twenty miles) to Moab than any other C-suite executive of a major social media company. He felt he should commemorate that with a text message. But his phone reported no service. He didn't have a sat phone. He had no more communications technology at his disposal than a Roman legionary. Probably less, since those guys had messengers and pigeons and so on.

Speaking of which, Lenny got his bag out of the luggage compartment and hustled it over and thrust it at him in a manner suggesting that it might be time to change his clothes. He accepted the bag and slung it over his shoulder for now. There was no place to change here unless he wanted to kick down the door of the kiosk.

Blazoned on the door of the pickup was the logo of the Angel Rock Ranch, which he recognized from having seen it on the Miasma half an hour ago. Aesthetically, this occupied a curious niche that hadn't existed until fairly recently: On the one hand it was too professional and slick for what this place was, because they'd used stock images and typefaces. On the other, it was homespun, amateur work, because they'd cobbled it together themselves. They knew nothing of kerning. The truck crossed the runway some distance from the plane and then swung around it in a wide U, giving the plane a suitably wide berth and crunching to a stop near Corvallis and Lenny. The driver's-side door opened, and out climbed a lean shovel-faced man in a baseball cap. He was wearing jeans, work boots, and a plaid snap-up shirt. He had the waistline of a young man and the trifocals of an older one. A line of sunscreen snaked along the rim of his left ear. He kept his gaze on Corvallis's face as if willing himself not to glance down at the tunic; perhaps he'd already sated his curiosity staring through the tinted window of his truck. For his part, Corvallis managed to conceal a pang of boyish disappointment over the fact that this man wasn't wearing a cowboy hat.

"Mr. Kawasaki, I presume. Welcome to the Angel Rock Ranch. I am Bob Nordstrom and I am the ranch manager and I am here to assist you." He stuck out his hand and Corvallis shook it.

"Nice to meet you. You might find it more convenient to call me C, which is kind of like my nickname."

"I would have Googled you to learn more but—"

"Your Internet has been down all day. Your ISP is in Moab, I take it."

"That's right, C."

"Well, you might like to know that your site is still up and running—evidently it's hosted somewhere else."

"That is reassuring to know," Bob said. After pondering this news for a moment, he changed his tone of voice and said, "So, you have had Internet access recently. On that thing, I guess." He glanced at the jet.

Corvallis nodded.

Bob said, "I know something weird is happening around Moab but I can't make heads or tails of it."

"It's happening everywhere in the world *except* Moab," Corvallis said. "It's an Internet hoax. A very sophisticated one. Nothing bad has actually happened to anyone in Moab, as far as I can tell. It's kind of a long story. I would be happy to catch you up in the truck—we have a little bit of driving to do, I take it?"

Bob nodded. "From here it's about a half-hour drive to the river landing. I understand that the family wishes to be taken back to Moab? That will be another hour."

Corvallis checked his watch and was startled to find it wasn't even noon yet. They could be in Moab by midafternoon. Assuming they'd be allowed in. "What do you know about roadblocks and so on?"

"I am confident," Bob said, "that I can find my way into Moab."

Bob had more to say on that as he and Corvallis drove up out of the lake bed. "There's a bunch of ways into town," he said. "Worst comes to worst, we just transfer to ATVs and avoid roads altogether. And if that fails, we have a little boat with an outboard motor. We can ride it straight up the river."

They topped the divide between the lake bed behind them and the valley of the Colorado ahead. The scenery made it obvious why the proprietors of this ranch had decided to throw in the towel on ranching per se and make it over into a tourist attraction. Bob pointed along the azimuth of the main ranch house, which was too far away to be seen with the naked eye. Someone there was still operating a ham radio rig, which had come in handy this morning as Corvallis's support staff had patched it together with emails from the jet and calls to Maeve's sat phone to make all of these arrangements.

The drive down to the river landing—the last place to take a raft out of the Colorado River before entering the national park—demanded all of Bob's attention and so he didn't say much as Corvallis gave him a rundown of what had been going on with the hoax. Along the way he caught occasional glimpses of the brown water of the river, but famously it was a very small trickle of water embedded in a ridiculously huge canyon system and so mostly what he saw was interesting rocks. The final approach wasn't on a road per se, it was just chundering down a dry arroyo that plunged straight into the Colorado. During the times when it actually carried water, it had deposited a rocky bar along the bank of the river, and it was there that Maeve and her colleague Tom had pulled two rafts up out of the water and set up a little day camp under a pop-up awning. Older Joneses were huddled in the shade of it, looking beleaguered. Younger ones were splashing in the river, completely unconcerned. Bob piloted the truck carefully across a shallow backwater and up onto the surface of the bar and stopped a few yards short of the camp. Directly on exiting the vehicle he was engaged by stressed-out moms and dads who were so glad to see him. This left Corvallis free to sneak out the passenger door and cut around the back of the truck and head toward the rafts, where Maeve and Tom were sorting through luggage, taking out the Joneses' personal stuff while leaving company gear in the raft.

"Nice getup" was Maeve's verdict on what Corvallis was wearing. She had given him a head-to-toe scan with eyes that were such a pale shade of blue as to be somewhat weird-looking.

"Right back at you," Corvallis responded. Maeve was wearing a shirt of silvery Lycra. It had long sleeves, anchored at the ends by thumb holes. Her hands were covered in paddling gloves made of wetsuit material. The garment didn't have a collar; it developed into a hood that covered her whole neck and head except for an oval around the face where a few strands of sun-bleached hair had escaped. A lump in the back suggested that she had long hair, kept in a bun. Over that she was wearing a sun visor. An assortment of eyewear dangled on her chest. Red suspenders kept her massively overloaded cargo shorts from simply falling off. Projecting from the leg holes were the stump cups, knee joints, carbon-fiber shins, and plastic feet of her prosthetic legs.

"Thanks for picking us up." She took a couple of steps toward him in a better-than-you'd-think-but-not-quite-right gait, and peeled the glove from her right hand to shake. Her hand was cold, sandy, and strong. The shake was perfunctory.

"I didn't do much besides reading my credit card number over the phone." Stupid thing to say. He was trying to be modest but came off sounding rich and petulant.

"We'll make you whole."

There were five available seats in the truck's cab, and six Joneses, but some of them were small enough to double-buckle. Corvallis and Maeve ended up sitting in the vehicle's open back, using luggage and camp mats for cushioning. Maeve loaned him a sun hat and looked with disfavor on his bare arms. The climb up the arroyo was such rough going that they ended up standing and holding on to the roll bar, absorbing the jounces with their leg muscles. Once they had made it to something that could pass for a proper road, they made themselves comfortable and he got her settled down by applying sunscreen to his arms.

"Do you mind?" she asked, and unstrapped one leg, then the other, and put them to one side so that she could air out her stumps. "Sand gets in there."

"I wouldn't dream of objecting to your making yourself comfortable," Corvallis said.

The elaborate wording got her attention. She had put on dark wraparound sunglasses, but it was clear from the set of her face that she was giving him a close look. "What is that garment you're wearing?"

Corvallis spent a while explaining his hobby and how he had come to be here. She listened without showing any outward signs of disgust and asked a couple of questions. Then she shrugged. "At the end of the day, all that matters is if it makes you healthier. And you don't look like some bludger who camps out in Mum's basement."

"Thanks."

"You don't get deltoids like that by typing."

Corvallis was unaccustomed to having his deltoids, or indeed any part of him, looked on in such a favorable way—let alone openly talked about—by a female observer. He had nothing to say for a few moments. He felt a brief tingle in his nuts and adjusted his tunic.

The simple reality of blasting down a road in the Utah canyonlands having this conversation with this person somehow cut the Gordian knot that had been tied in his skull this morning by millions of people being wrong on the Internet.

"You lift," she said. Her tone was somewhere between question and statement. She was dourly resigned to the likelihood that he had a personal trainer in a fancy gym.

"I lift shovels full of dirt," he said.

She liked that. "Is that some new hipster exercise?"

"It is an old Roman military exercise," he said. "When a legion made camp, it dug a ditch all around, and threw the dirt up on the inside to make a rampart above the ditch. When it broke camp, the ditch had to be filled in."

"That is a fuck-ton of digging."

"The original legionaries were like elite athletes, if you look at all the physical activity they performed day in and day out. I'm not putting myself in that class, but I'll say that reenacting is the best exercise program I've ever had."

She was gazing off into the blue sky, trying to get her head around it. "To move all of that dirt—just to put it back—it seems, I don't know—"

"It's the same as paddling a boat," he pointed out, "except with dirt."

"Okay, fair." She looked at him, which he found vaguely frightening and yet preferred to her not looking at him. "So when were you thinking of changing out of that getup?"

"My original plan was to be doing it now, in the backseat of the truck. It didn't work out that way. But you know what? The fact is I only have one clean set of normal-person clothes. A blazer and a dress shirt. Leather shoes. No point in getting them covered with road dust. I'll change when we get to Moab."

"*If*," she corrected him.

"Bob's pretty sure he can sneak us in somehow."

She sighed. "I wonder what this is going to do to our business."

"Long-term, it's going to be great for your business. Because it's going to bring attention to Moab, and that's going to translate to clicks, and to revenue."

"Clicks," she repeated. "That's what it's all about I suppose."

"If you write up the story of what's happening right now and put it up on your social media accounts, it'll get millions of page views." Corvallis meant for this to be encouraging but he could tell he was getting nowhere. He was consistently getting the sense that she had a lot on her mind that she didn't want to share with him, and that most of his conversational gambits were wide of the mark.

"I thought you techies wore hoodies and T-shirts," she said.

"What?"

"You said you had a blazer and a dress shirt."

"It's what I wore to work the day I left Seattle. I had a board meeting."

"Why didn't you wear a T-shirt to your board meeting? Isn't that what you do?"

"Yeah, but this wasn't for a tech company. This is a private foundation. I serve on the board. It's just a somewhat more conservative vibe. You're in the room with lawyers and money people."

"What kind of foundation?"

"A friend of mine died. He was rich. He'd made billions in the game industry. Some of his fortune went to this foundation."

"Was it an untimely death?"

"Definitely."

"Sorry to hear it."

"Thanks. Anyway, the foundation looks for ways to put game-related technology to use in solving various social problems."

They jounced over a calamitous pothole and she reached out to keep her artificial legs from jumping out of the truck.

Corvallis was straining to remember some advice Zula had given him a couple of years ago after a date had gone bad.

"You've asked a number of questions relating to clothing," he pointed out. "Is that an interest of yours?"

"All clothing is prosthetics," she said. "That's how I think about it. From this"—she plucked at her silver garment—"to this"—she patted a carbon-fiber leg—"is a matter of degree."

"The shirt is some kind of anti-sun thing?"

"Yeah. Better than sunscreen." She sighed. "I was studying design," she admitted, as if it were a failing of some significance. "Hit a rough patch. Took a summer job paddling rafts. Got sidetracked.".

"It's pretty normal to take a gap year. Or two."

"I failed," she announced.

"As in, flunked out of design school or—"

"Dropped out. To do a startup. Which failed." She sighed. "I'm one of the losers in the war you won."

"What happened?"

"It was my sister, Verna, and me. We got some angel money. Burned through it amazingly fast just getting our heads out of our arses. She got sick."

"Well, that alone would be enough to kill a lot of angel-funded startups."

Maeve shook her head. "It wasn't that. I mean, it didn't help. But what killed it was an awareness that came to me in the middle of the night."

"Awareness of what?"

"That I'd been going about it wrong. That I hadn't been thinking big enough."

"Scale is tricky."

"And that if I were to *start* thinking big enough, it would require much more capital than I could ever hope to raise. So I was stuck. And am still." She pulled her sunglasses down so that she could look him in the eye. "Which is not me cracking on to you."

"I beg your pardon?"

"I'm not asking you for money."

"I didn't think you were."

"Just wanted to be clear."

"Okay. Noted. Now that we've got that out of the way, can you talk about what you were doing in a way that is a little less abstract?"

"Then you'll get interested in it, and you'll come up with ideas for how to make it work, and it'll circle around to money."

"It's a long ride to Moab, we have to talk about something."

"Well, I'll just say that my idea of clothing as prosthetics, when I pursued it to the end of the line, led me out of my comfort zone. Because what we wear now is more than just material objects. We wear information. My avatar, my profile on social media, those do in cyberspace what clothing does in the world. And now you have blended situations—physical clothing with embedded electronics. I don't know anything about those technologies."

"Other people do. You could find programmers, engineers—"

"But then why me?"

Corvallis didn't have an answer.

Maeve went on, "It's as if I were a carpenter who had come up with an idea for a wooden boat. I started designing the boat and got halfway through and realized that it would be much better if it were made out of aluminium. Knowing fuck-all about aluminium, I would have to find a metalworker at that point. Whereupon, I would have to explain to my investors why it made sense for them to pay me to pay a metalworker."

Corvallis nodded. "You had thought yourself right out of a job."

"Yeah."

He shrugged. "It happens. That's what angels are actually doing, you know. Paying people like you to try a bunch of stuff. To see what works. You can always move on."

She grimaced. "Not if you don't actually have the technical know-how."

"You're too honest for your own good. If you were more of a BS artist you could talk your way through an investor pitch pretty easily."

"Thanks, I guess." She looked away, disgusted. Relegated to the back of the truck, splayed out on other people's luggage with her legs off—literally dismembered—a million miles away from Silicon Valley, left for dead, along with the rest of Moab, by the whole Miasma—stymied to perfect exasperation—she was the archetype of the failed entrepreneur.

He was almost offended by the ease with which they drove into Moab. The roadblocks—supposing that they actually existed—

would be on the state highway that ran through town and that provided its only link to places far away. Because their point was to stop outsiders from getting in. Most of Moab's streets dead-ended at the foot of the stony pink hills that confined the town against the river, or trailed off into weedy ruts as they neared the watercourse. But at least one of them connected to a battered two-lane road that edged up the east bank of the Colorado, draining a maze of ranch tracks farther south. Since no connection could be made from there to the outside world, no one had put a roadblock on it. The river itself was being patrolled by a lone sheriff in a motorboat, but when he recognized Bob's truck he just lifted one hand from the wheel to greet Bob. Bob responded by lifting two fingers from his own steering wheel, and with that they penetrated the world-famous cordon of military security that had enshrouded the smoking ruins of Moab and turned away from the river to follow a small tributary about a mile into town.

A festive atmosphere prevailed along Main Street, which was what they called the part of the state highway that ran through the town's business district. This had been turned into a temporary pedestrian mall by the closure of the road. Locals had taken advantage of it to park RVs and pickup trucks wherever they felt like it, and to erect pop-up shelters against the sun, which by now had burned through the cloud cover. Restaurants and bars were serving al fresco. A convoy of National Guard vehicles, mostly just Humvees, had drawn up in the middle of the street. Young men in hand-me-down Iraq War camo were standing around aiming their assault rifles at the pavement and wordlessly soaking up the admiration of an increasingly inebriated populace. A tourist hotel on the main drag had set up an outdoor television screen showing live network coverage from a satellite dish. By this point, all of the networks had scrambled their art departments and produced screens and banners to flash up when they cut back from commercial breaks. A typical example was NUCLEAR TERROR IN THE HEARTLAND, in a scary-looking typeface, superimposed on a montage comprising a mushroom cloud and a map of the United States with a red crosshairs centered on southeastern Utah. Corvallis wondered if the wording had been run by the networks' lawyers. To call it a "nuclear strike" or "nuclear disaster" would be to suggest that it had actually happened. "Nuclear terror" only meant that some people were terrified. The network was hedging its bets. Because at some level, the people in charge must have figured out by now that it was a hoax. To come out and say as much would be to lose all of their viewers to competitors who were still acting as if it had really happened. Calling it "terror," on the other hand, was no lie, and enabled them to keep pumping shit onto the air.

Bob, now overwhelmingly under the emotional sway of the half-dozen Joneses with whom he was sharing the cab, drove straight to the office of the rafting company, which was only a block off of Main Street. The Joneses piled out of the cab. Their patriarch waddled over to the family vehicle, a beige Suburban that they'd left in the parking lot. He contemplated it for a while, as if looking for bubbled paint, melted tires, or other evidence of its having survived a nuclear detonation. Maeve had strapped her legs back on as they entered town and now stood up in the back of the truck to toss luggage down to the other Joneses. An internal family schism developed as to whether a bucket brigade should be established to move all of the bags to the Suburban, or individuals should just carry the bags a few at a time. Corvallis, an only child, found the spectacle inexplicably depressing. He cadged a key from Maeve, then vaulted out and went into the office. His careful attention to the all-important matter of rehydration, combined with the bouncing of the truck, had left him needing to take a vicious piss. The better to enjoy it, he locked himself in the restroom, pulled his tunic up around his waist, and sat down on the toilet. Stand-up peeing in a long flowing garment could lead to various mishaps.

When he was done he stood in front of the sink for a few moments splashing water on his head and neck and arms, just to get the dust off. It occurred to him that he had now finally reached a location in which it would be convenient to change into his normal-person clothes, so he went out in search of his duffel bag. The Joneses' Suburban was long gone. Bob and Maeve had entered the office and were sitting in its little waiting area drinking beverages from the office fridge and watching television coverage. A nurse from a burn unit in some unidentified hospital was being interviewed. Journalists had pounced on her when she had gone out on a Starbucks run. She was looking suitably traumatized, but not so much that she couldn't deliver an eloquent and moving description of the suffering being endured by children who had been standing in the open when the flash of the bomb had burned all the skin on one side of their body. For according to the story these patients had been rescued from some kind of camp on the outskirts of town. Maeve and Bob were agreeing with each other that no such camp existed, and wanted Corvallis to know it too. But he'd long since come to terms with the sophistication and sheer ballsiness of the hoax.

Corvallis went out to Bob's truck and looked in the back, which was empty. Then he checked the cab.

He went back inside. "Did you by any chance give the Joneses a blue duffel bag about yay long?" he asked Maeve, holding his hands out in front of him.

"More than one, probably," she answered. "Why?"

"Never mind. Is there a place on Main Street where I could buy some clothes?"

"Yeah. If they're open."

"Belay that. I just remembered. My wallet was in the duffel bag."

She gazed at him sidelong while tipping a beer bottle into her mouth. "C'mon back," she said.

Bob sat up alertly. "I could go try to track 'em down if you like."

"Do you know which way they're going?"

"Not really."

"Sounds like Maeve is going to set me up with something," Corvallis said. "Thanks though."

Bob was now perhaps sensing a change in the emotional tone, akin to the plunge in barometric pressure preceding a cloudburst, which was not directly measurable by any of the five human senses but which could be detected, in some people's arthritic joints, as a certain kind of discomfort. And perhaps you could make the case that people who suffered from the sort of emotional arthritis that was endemic among those of Northern European descent who lived on farms and ranches felt that discomfort more acutely, and were therefore the most sensitive barometers. "I do believe I'll be on my way anyhow," he said, "unless you need me for anything?"

"Well, at some point I'll need to go back out and collect my plane," Corvallis said, "but . . ." And he glanced at Maeve, who nodded.

"I can give you a ride out there," she said. "Have to go collect Tom and the rafts anyway."

So Bob said his goodbyes and went out to his truck. Maeve unlocked a door behind the front desk and beckoned Corvallis back.

Things tended to be spacious in Moab, and this building was no exception—it was an older commercial property that showed signs of having served, in previous incarnations, as a bar, a clothing shop, and a real estate office. Only about a quarter of its ground-floor space was used as an office. The rest of it was storage for outdoor gear of various kinds, the ideal place to raid if civilization collapsed. The stuff was crammed onto a shantytown of shelves that had been made in a hurry by someone with a chop saw and a nail gun. "This is all heavy stuff we don't like to carry up and down the stairs," Maeve explained, leading him back to the actual stairs in question: wooden steps leading down into a cool cellar. "Lightweight stuff—like clothing—is down here."

It seemed on one level like the opening scene of a horror movie in which Corvallis would never make it out of the basement, but having got this far, he followed her down. She took the stairs at a good pace but with certain precautions, one hand on each banister, pitching from side to side a bit more than a person with normal legs, and through her silver spandex garment he could see her back muscles and her triceps working. They reached the concrete floor of the basement, which seemed to have been poured by various drunk or indifferent people on different occasions. Light poured in from windows high in the walls, so she felt no need to turn the lights on. "Watch your step," she admonished him, which he found curiously touching given that he had legs and feet.

Cardboard boxes of different sizes and vintages had been stacked around the place according to some scheme that wasn't obvious to him. Some of these were open. They were full of T-shirts, not folded, but thrown in willy-nilly. Most of these were printed with Canyonland Adventures logos, or other tourist-related insignia having to do with Moab, Utah, or the Colorado River. In one corner a rug had been laid out on the floor. On it was a huge pile of shirts all mixed up. The place had the clean smell of new textiles.

"What's Sthetix?" Corvallis asked, holding up a black T-shirt with a completely different sort of logo—not in any way, shape, or form touristy.

"My dead company. See, if you take 'prosthetics' or 'aesthetics' and chop off the first bit . . ."

"Got it."

"It's from a Greek word meaning 'strength,'" she insisted, as if he had been disputing it. "'Prosthetics' means 'to add strength.'"

He nodded. "Cool! It's a cool name."

She held the compliment at arm's length for a moment, then slapped it away. "Hard to pronounce. Every. Single. Fucking. Conversation we had was about how to say it, or how to spell it."

"It's a good code name," he said. "When you're ready to go to market you hire a naming company to come up with a crowd-pleaser." This appeared to settle her down. "Can I have one of these?" he asked, holding up a Sthetix shirt.

"Why?"

He thought better of explaining to Maeve that collecting swag from obscure, dead companies was a tech industry fetish.

"I like the name, and what it means. And it's a memento of this day."

She snorted. "The day Moab got nuked?"

He said nothing for a moment, intimidated by her sardonic force. Everything felt awkward. There was a sense of being on a perfectly good road in a perfectly sound car that was, however, veering into a ditch.

A thing happened where he simultaneously channeled both Forthrasts, Richard and Zula. "No," he said, hearing his own voice strangely through blood-engorged ears. "The day I rode in the back of a truck with you."

She actually took a step back, and raised her eyebrows. "You can have one. Make sure it fits."

"Okay. No peeking." He pulled his tunic up over his head and tossed it aside.

"Fair's fair," she returned. He heard a clank and a thud followed by a hissing, slithering sound. He turned just in time to see her peeling her sun shirt off. This had necessitated shrugging off her red suspenders, so her cargo shorts had impacted the pavement a moment earlier. Now she was down to a garment that he identified, vaguely, as a sports bra, and a pair of granny panties.

"Oh, excuse me," he blurted.

"You looked?" she returned, mock outraged. "It's all right. Nothing you wouldn't see at the beach, right?"

He had turned his back on her and was pretending to sort through T-shirts. "Still . . . I didn't mean to."

He could hear bionic footsteps. "Would you like me to help you with that?"

"I'm good, thanks."

She came up very close behind him, reached around his body, and plucked out a T-shirt. "You'd look smashing in this. Turn around and we'll check the size."

He turned to face her. She held the shirt up in front of him, pinning it against his shoulders with her thumbs, and looked him up and down. "It's not long enough to hide your doodle," she observed.

He made a reasonable guess as to the meaning of the term. "Doodle containment's an issue," he admitted, "with boxers."

"One of these containers has some Sthetix men's briefs," she said. "Nice and *tight*." She pulled the shirt away and tossed it into the box.

They stood there for a few moments looking at each other from rather close. When she'd pulled the hood off, her hair had come loose and tumbled messily down her back. A bit of gentle tugging and head-shaking would have worked wonders, but she didn't give a shit.

Corvallis reached out slowly and put his hands on her hips.

"After my friend died," he said, "and I got over the shock, you know what happened? Like, around the time of the funeral?"

"You got inappropriately horny and felt like fucking everything that moved?"

"Yeah, has that ever happened to you?"

"Yeah. When my dad died. When my company died. And now," she said. "Even though no one died in this case." She took a step forward, leaving maybe a quarter of an inch of clearance between her belly and the tip of his boxer-tented doodle. "It comes from thinking about mortality, right? Leads to a 'life is short—let's go' mentality."

He pulled her into him and mashed his doodle, bolt upright, against her stomach. She wrapped her arms around his neck for purchase and mashed back. They went on to perform sexual intercourse on the big pile of T-shirts on the rug. These could be grabbed in bunches and wadded up and jammed under body parts to facilitate various positions. She wasn't talking much, but he got the idea that she wanted to be able to touch herself while also looking him in the face. Fair enough. They found a way to make it happen by what would have been described, in a PowerPoint presentation, as agile deployment to leverage the T-shirts' structural modularity. He came first, perhaps inevitably given that he hadn't had sex with anyone in three years. But he stayed in while she finished up, staring at him the whole time through half-closed eyes.

Somewhat later, at her suggestion, he gave her a piggyback ride up the stairs to the bathroom and deposited her in the shower stall, then went back and fetched her legs. While she showered, he attempted to clean up. As if blindly following its sole imperative, his semen had ended up all over the place, distributing itself over the maximum conceivable number of T-shirts as well as locations on the rug. There was a washing machine in the corner of the basement; he stuffed it full. He started the machine and, through the white noise of the plumbing above, heard Maeve denouncing him as some kind of fucker or other. He switched the cycle to cold.

For a while now, the part of Corvallis that was a responsible executive had, as it were, been bound and gagged in a closet, trying to get his attention by banging his forehead on the floor in Morse code. Considering what the rest of him had been up to, this was pretty hopeless, but now that Corvallis was alone in the office in a Sthetix T-shirt and a pair of tight Sthetix undies, drinking a post-coital beer and listening to Maeve wash her hair, he began to hear a few of those distant thumps and to consider the larger context of the day. Laurynas wanted him to save the company, or something.

He settled in behind the office computer and found the pass-word yellow-noted on the underside of the keyboard. He made various efforts to use the Internet and satisfied himself that Moab's sole ISP was still utterly screwed. His phone was showing three bars, but it still wouldn't actually do anything. He reckoned that the best he could do was to document his presence in the city and squirt it out to the Internet when he could.

Maeve emerged, fully reassembled and impossibly distracting. He studied her, partly because he could and partly for cues as to how lovey-dovey he was supposed to be at this moment. She seemed all business, though she did take the liberty of slapping him on the ass as he headed for the shower. So, mixed messages. By the time he emerged, she had pulled the company van around and hitched on a trailer that was pretty clearly designed to carry inflated rafts.

She drove him to Main Street. He sat in the van in his under-wear while she went into a store and came back with a pair of jams that would fit him. These were designed to appeal to a man half his age, which he assumed was her sense of humor at work. She took some photos of him partying with Moabites and talking in a really serious way to National Guardsmen and mugging with local kids, all composed to show as much authentic Moab background scenery as possible. Then a panorama of the whole street scene.

They drove to Angel Rock Ranch to check on the jet and its crew. Bonnie had found refuge at the ranch lodge; the pilots were camped out in the plane, awaiting a delivery of jet fuel. Next stop was the lodge itself, where Corvallis was able to get through to Laurynas on a landline. Laurynas was desperate for the photos, so they split up for a couple of hours; Maeve drove down to the sand-bar to fetch Tom and the rafts while Bob drove Corvallis up to the top of a mesa from which he predicted—correctly—that it would be possible to get cell phone coverage from another town, many miles from Moab and unaffected by the DDoS attack. From there Corvallis was able to transmit the photos, though it was slow. By the time all of those pictures had seeped down the pipe and Bob had driven him back to the landing strip, Maeve was back with Tom and the rafts, waiting for him.

Maeve: Corvallis's girlfriend. During this little excursion he had suddenly remembered this a few times and been delighted by the newness of it.

A couple of years ago he had broken a bone in his hand during weapons practice and been obliged to wear a cast for some time. During the first few days, he'd forget it was there, and then be surprised by some new limitation as he would discover that he couldn't hit the Return key on his keyboard or operate the shift lever on his car. Suddenly having a girlfriend was the opposite thing, with all of the discoveries, so far, being good ones. Enhancements, not limitations. Prosthetics.

As they were driving back into Moab, Tom—who had been relegated to a back seat—said, "Fuck me," while looking significantly out a window on the left side of the vehicle. Maeve said, "Holy shit." Corvallis nearly had to put his head into her lap to see what they were looking at: a blue-nosed 747 banking into its final approach for landing, a few miles to the northwest.

"Air Force fucking One," Tom said.

This time, they actually were stopped on the outskirts of town, but once Maeve had explained herself, and the Secret Service guys had checked IDs and given the van and the trailer a once-over, they were allowed through. She ditched the vehicle, and Tom, in the parking lot of Canyonland Adventures, and then walked with Corvallis to Main Street.

By the time the president had rolled into town and his press secretary and staff had finished arranging things and the media had set up their equipment, the day was in its last hour. Which might have been calculated, since the light was magical, and lit up the red rocks east of town perfectly while making everyone seem ten years younger and twice as good-looking. They found a place where the president could look into that light, with mountains and a big sign that said MOAB in the background of the shot. They set up the presidential lectern and handpicked people to stand to the left, and to the right, and behind it: uniformed National Guardsmen; Native Americans; salt-of-the-earth farmers; outdoorsy types with frizzy, sun-bleached hair; a minister; and an Asian-American tech executive with a disabled girlfriend. The president came online and announced to the world that Moab, the states of Utah and Colorado, the United States of America, and indeed the entire world had been the victims of a hoax that had been perpetrated almost entirely on the Internet. Nothing had happened here, save for a denial-of-service attack, originating overseas, that had shut down its Internet service and its cell phone towers. There had never been a bright flash of light; this was just a pattern of fake social media posts. The young actor at LAX was just that—a performer who had been hired to play a role, under the pretext that it was some kind of reality television show. Local police departments had been conned into setting up roadblocks by telephone calls that had originated overseas but been digitally tweaked to look as if they were local. A similar call had summoned the SWAT team in Las Vegas. They'd found nothing more than an empty suite that had been booked and paid for online. No one had ever checked in, but a package had arrived from overseas and been delivered to the suite by hotel staff. It turned out to be some old radium-dial watches in a scary-looking box: enough to make the cops' Geiger counters click but not in any way dangerous. A similar gambit had been used in Manhattan. All of the confirmatory posts that had hit the Internet in the next hours—the burn victims, the fallout samples, the Los Alamos press conference—had been faked and injected onto the Internet via social media accounts and domains controlled through untraceable overseas shell companies.

Much of this was just placing an official stamp on information that legitimate news organizations had been piecing together all day but been unable to articulate loudly enough to be heard over the din. It brought out a kind of bloodlust in the assembled White House press corps, which was gathered right there in the middle of Main Street. During the wait, they'd had plenty of time to sample Moab's impressive range of locally produced microbrewery offerings. Having spent the whole day sifting through incredibly depressing news reports, they were bouncing back to a kind of giddy frame of mind brought on by a combination of completely natural and understandable happiness that Moab was fine; beer; and schadenfreude directed at the social media companies that had been chipping away at their industry and their job security for the last couple of decades. Pointed questions were asked about how just unbelievably irresponsible those companies had been today and whether the scorpion-filled pits into which their executives should now be lowered should be a thousand meters deep or two thousand. After the third such question, the president was handed a note by his press secretary. He read it, then raised his head and glanced over to his right, scanning his way down the line of nearby Moabites until he found the one person there whose last name could possibly be Kawasaki. "Why don't you direct your questions to someone who knows? Mr. Kawasaki, from Lyke, has been here all day, working hard to establish the ground truth."

11

Maeve didn't want to think of herself, or to be seen, as someone who had been in need of getting rescued by a Prince Charming in a jet, and so this added a lot of texture to her relationship with Corvallis in the early going. Fortunately for that relationship, but not so much for Maeve and her family in Australia, those issues were soon swamped by something else.

All of the people in the Miasma's conspiracy/troll ecosystem had been sucked into the vortex of Moab and begun to devote excruciating levels of attention to the entire cast of characters: the actor from the red-eye, all of the other performers in all of the fake videos, the cops who had searched the penthouse suite in Vegas, the sheriff's deputies who had manned roadblocks, et cetera.

And, of course, Corvallis Kawasaki and Maeve Braden. For he had been identified by name, on national television, by the president of the United States, and had been a reasonably well-known person to begin with. And she had been standing next to him. So within twenty-four hours, the citizens of Crazytown had compiled a huge dossier of mostly wrong material on him, and begun to evince interest in her; and within a week, she had become a figure of greater significance, in the collective mind of Crazytown, than he.

Crazytown was repelled by facts and knowledge, as oil fled from water, but was fascinated by the absence of hard facts, since it provided vacant space in which to construct elaborate edifices of speculation. Toward power it felt some combination of fear and admiration, and Corvallis was powerful. Toward vulnerability it was drawn, in the same way that predators would converge on the isolated and straggling. Within a week, Maeve—who suffered from the fatal combination of being mysterious, vulnerable, and female—had been doxxed. Canyonland Adventures, as a business, had been destroyed by a flood of fake negative reviews and various other hacks. Maeve sought refuge at Angel Rock Ranch, but after a couple of days, Bob's wife decided to believe some of the more wildly slanderous posts being made about Maeve on social media and decided it was time for her to leave. Tom, having nothing else to do now that the business was wiped out, bundled Maeve into a car, handed her a shotgun, and drove her to Salt Lake City, where he dropped her off (minus the shotgun) at the private jet terminal to await a jet that Corvallis had dispatched. Maeve only went into the waiting lounge long enough to use the toilet. Her legs were visible under the stall door. They were glimpsed in a mirror by a young woman who was standing in front of a sink freshening up. She was the best friend of another young woman who was the daughter of a hedge fund manager and private jet owner; they, along with other friends and family, were all on some kind of one-percenter vacation trip. The two young women, having recognized Maeve, took pictures of her and posted them on their poorly secured social media accounts. One of the pictures included the tail number of the private jet that Maeve boarded en route to Seattle. Its flight plan was obtained from the Miasma. More Moab truthers were awaiting Maeve in Seattle; they weren't allowed into the private jet terminal at Boeing Field, but nothing prevented them from witnessing Corvallis's arrival in his Tesla.

And so it went. All they could do was let it burn. Maeve's harassment became the topic of hand-wringing coverage by the decent folk of the Miasma, but the mere fact that people were defending her only drove the truthers into higher transports of rage or made it that much more amusing for trolls to go after her. Maeve's entire family was doxxed. Business records of Sthetix were pulled up from somewhere and laid bare. That she was now under Corvallis's wing dampened the truthers' ardor, since they were sadists and preferred to focus their energies on the helpless. But they did manage to find her sister, Verna, who lived in a bedroom community outside of Adelaide. After a first round of surgery and chemo, she'd enjoyed three years' remission from her cancer, but it had now come back. She was on chemo again. Through a combination of social engineering and poor security precautions, a particularly avid set of nihilist hackers tracked her down to a hospital in Adelaide, and phoned in a bomb threat, and SWATted the place for good measure. All of the patients had to be taken out of the wing of the building where Verna was receiving her treatment. Not enough gurneys were available, and she was strong enough to walk with assistance, and so she ended up lying on the ground in the shade of a gum tree, dressed only in her hospital gown, still hooked up to the wheeled apparatus that was dripping the chemo drug into her IV line. A local truther, positioned outside the place with a long-lensed camera, was able to capture video of her rolling onto her side to puke. It went up on the message board favored by the truthers and became a humorous meme. The mother of Maeve and Verna got really angry and ventured out onto the front stoop of her house to denounce the hackers; a still frame of her indignant, tear-stained face became another meme.

Corvallis chartered a larger, longer-range jet to take him and Maeve to Australia. They drove to Boeing Field. The jet wasn't quite ready yet and so they had to wait in the lounge for half an hour.

Shortly before they boarded, Pluto showed up.

Pluto had been one of the cofounders of Corporation 9592 and had made a corresponding amount of money. For a while, Corvallis had seen him every day, but after his switch to Nubilant, they'd lost contact and had not communicated at all except for a brief, awkward exchange at Dodge's funeral. Pluto, well aware of his own social ineptitude, had obviously pored over an etiquette manual before showing up, and so, during his rote interactions with Zula and other immediate family members, had acquitted himself well if bizarrely, addressing them in high-Victorian grief speech straight out of whatever scanned and archived Emily Post book he'd memorized.

Pluto walked into the waiting area, which was furnished like a high-end hotel lobby, and shrugged his bag off onto a leather club chair. He seemed to have packed for a long trip. He sat down across from Corvallis and Maeve, who were in a love seat, just zoning out, not daring to look at the Miasma. Instead of greeting them, or even making eye contact, he opened up his laptop and pulled on a pair of reading glasses.

"Presbyopia has caught up with you, I see," Corvallis said.

Maeve startled, and tensed; she hadn't realized that this new guy and Corvallis knew each other.

"It would be unusual for one of my age not to have it!" Pluto scoffed.

Maeve had been sprawled back with her head resting on Corvallis's outstretched arm, but she now sat up, the better to pay notice to this interloper.

Corvallis remembered, now, that back in the old days, the key persons at Corporation 9592 had made use of an iPhone app that enabled them to track each other's locations on a map. It saved a lot of messing around with text messages whose sole purpose was to establish someone's whereabouts. Corvallis had shared his location with Dodge and with Pluto. Dodge was dead. Pluto he had forgotten about. He made a mental note to turn the feature off. Not that he didn't trust Pluto. But it was bad practice to just dumbly leave that stuff running.

"Your luggage is of impressive size and weight," Corvallis observed, "and I note you have purchased a new sun hat." For the price tag, and the tiny documentation booklet, were still dangling from Pluto's headwear.

"Because of the ozone hole," Pluto began, in a cadence suggesting he had a lot to say about it.

Maeve interrupted him, though. "This person is coming with us?"

"His name is Pluto," Corvallis said. Then, before Pluto could correct the error, he amended his statement: "Nickname, I meant to say."

Pluto seemed to finish whatever business he had been conducting on his laptop and peered over the lenses of his reading glasses at Maeve's legs. Pluto's general habit was to stare at people's shoes when he was talking to them, and so Corvallis interpreted this as Pluto's gearing up to engage in conversation. Maeve saw it as gawking at her prostheses. Corvallis, whose arm was still draped around behind Maeve, reached down to give her shoulder a squeeze and a pat.

"It came to my attention that you were being abused on the Internet," Pluto said, "and so I am here to destroy it."

"Destroy what?" Corvallis inquired.

"The Internet," Pluto said. "Or what Dodge referred to as the Miasma. Does your jet have Wi-Fi?"

"Yes, but it doesn't work over the Pacific Ocean."

Pluto sighed. "Then it will have to wait until we have reached Australia."

"I didn't like your friend at first," Maeve said, "but I'm warming up to him."

"That is convenient, Maeve, if I may take the liberty of addressing the lady by her Christian name, because I will require your permission. Your complicity in utterly destroying your reputation."

"It's already destroyed, haven't you seen a bloody thing?"

"It is not sufficiently destroyed yet," Pluto said. He glanced at the screen of his laptop. "The total number of unique slanderous and defamatory statements that have been made about you, on all of the blogs, boards, and social media networks being tracked by my bots, currently stands at a little more than seventy-three thousand. Peak traffic occurred yesterday, at four point five kilo-Bradens."

"What's a kiloBraden?" asked Maeve, taking a personal interest since her last name was Braden.

"A Braden is a unit of measurement I coined for my own purposes, equal to the number of hostile posts made in an interval of one hour. It has now slumped to just over one hundred Bradens as the focal point of the attack has shifted to your mother and . . ." Pluto's brow furrowed as he read something from the screen. "Someone called Lady?"

"Her Lhasa apso," Maeve sighed. For the dog had been heard yapping incessantly on the soundtrack of Maeve's mother's front-stoop press conference, and was now receiving death threats.

"Anyway, we need to get that up into the megaBraden or preferably the gigaBraden range in order to achieve saturation," Pluto intoned, "and we need much wider ontic coverage."

"Ontic?" Corvallis asked, so Maeve wouldn't have to.

The jet's pilot entered through the door that communicated with the tarmac and gazed at Corvallis in an expectant way. "One more," Corvallis told him, since there'd be paperwork. To Pluto he said, "Passport?" and then regretted it.

"A passport and a visa are *required* for entry to—" Pluto began, a little confounded by the question.

"Never mind. He has a passport and a visa," Corvallis called to the pilot.

After they had walked to the plane and got settled into their seats, Pluto resumed the previous conversation as if nothing had happened. "This kind of thing has to be gone about in a systematic way, so that nothing is missed," he said, now staring out the window at a fuel truck. "Partly through direct study of dictionaries, thesauri, and so on, and partly through brute-forcing archives of defamatory Miasma postings, I have compiled what I think is a pretty comprehensive ontology of execration. A mere lexicon doesn't get us anywhere because it's language-specific. Both in the sense of relating to only one language, such as English, and in the sense that it only covers defamation in a textual format. But many defamatory posts are now made in the form of images or videos. For example, if you want to call someone a slut—"

"We don't need to go there right now," Corvallis said.

"'Slut,' 'bitch,' 'hag,' 'fatty,' all the bases need to be covered. If we generate traffic in the gigaBraden range—which I think is easily doable—but it's all skewed toward, say, 'feminazi,' then the impression will be created in the minds of many casual users that the subject is indeed a feminazi. But if an equal amount of traffic denounces the subject as a slut, a bitch, a whore, an attention seeker, a gold digger, an idiot—"

"I think we get the idea," Corvallis said.

"—why, then even the most credulous user will be inoculated with so many differing, and in many cases contradictory, characterizations as to raise doubts in their mind as to the veracity of any one characterization, and hence the reliability of the Miasma as a whole."

"Pluto, we sort of missed the part where you explained the whole premise of what you're doing," Corvallis said.

"I'm glad you said so," said Maeve, "because I was wondering if I had blacked out."

"What I'm gathering is that you have been developing some kind of bots or something . . ."

"Autonomous Proxies for Execration, or APEs," Pluto said. "I took the liberty of drawing up a logo."

"Please don't show us programmer art, Pluto, it's not—" But it was too late, as Pluto had swiveled his laptop around to display an unbelievably terrible drawing of an animal that was just barely recognizable as some kind of ape. One shaggy arm had its knuckles on the ground, the other was whipping overhead as it hurled a large, dripping gob of shit. Wavy lines radiated from the projectile as a way of indicating that it smelled bad. It was even more terrible than most of Pluto's programmer art, but he was smiling broadly and even sort of looking at them, which counted for something. Worse yet, Maeve liked it, and laughed. Corvallis hadn't heard her laugh in a while.

"By typing in a few simple commands, I can spawn an arbitrary number of APEs in the cloud," Pluto said.

"What do you mean, arbitrary?" Maeve asked.

"As many as he wants," Corvallis said.

"As many as I want."

"Don't they cost money or something?"

Pluto looked startled for a moment, then laughed.

"Pluto has ten times as much money as I do," Corvallis said.

"Nineteen," Pluto corrected him, "you don't know about some of the interesting trading strategies I have been pursuing." Redirecting his attention from Corvallis's shoes to Maeve's prosthetic legs, he went on, "I have hand-tuned the inner loops to the point where a single APE can generate over a megaBraden of wide-spectrum defamation. The number would be much larger, of course, if I didn't have to pursue a range of strategies to evade spam filters, CAPTCHAs, and other defenses."

"Have you tried this out yet?" Corvallis asked.

"Not against a real subject," Pluto said. "I invented a fictitious subject and deployed some APEs against it, just to see how it worked in the wild. The fictitious subject has already attracted thousands of death threats," he added with a note of pride.

"You mean, from people who saw the defamatory posts seeded by the APEs and got really mad at this person who doesn't even exist."

"Yes. It worked unexpectedly well. So, another part of the strategy might be to spawn a large number of nonexistent harassment targets and deploy APEs against them as well. I just thought of that."

"You said earlier you needed my complicity," Maeve said. "My permission."

"Yes, what I would like to do is run a troop of APEs at something like a gigaBraden for a couple of weeks, directed at you."

"So if I understand the math," Corvallis said, "during that whole time, a billion defamatory posts would be made every hour, personally directed against Maeve. Denouncing her as every kind of bad thing you have included in your ontology of execration. In all languages as well as using imagery. And on all kinds of social media outlets."

"Her Wikipedia entry alone," Pluto said, "would be edited a thousand times during the first tenth of a second. New material would be added describing Maeve's career as a pirate, murderess, sex worker, headhunter, terrorist, and coprophage. By that point the entry will probably have been locked by the administrators, but not before all of the defamatory material is archived in the page history. Meanwhile my APEs will be spawning hundreds of thousands of new accounts on social media systems, and using those accounts to make millions of posts in a similar vein. Existing botnets will be leveraged to generate a colossal spam campaign. The Twitter attack will proceed in three phases. Phase Zero is already under way, in a sense, and consists of—"

"Why do you need my complicity?" Maeve asked. "Don't get me wrong, it's polite of you to ask, but . . ."

"It's an open campaign. We would announce it. Publish

statistics on how it's going. You could do press interviews, if you wanted. The sheer magnitude of it would make it obvious, even to the most credulous user of the Miasma, that it was all a bunch of nonsense. Afterward, no one in their right mind would ever believe anything negative about you that had ever been posted on the Miasma. But because it is all technically slanderous, you would have to promise not to sue me."

"Didn't you say, when you first came in, that you were going to destroy the Internet? The Miasma?" Maeve asked.

"Yes."

"How does this accomplish that?"

"I am going to open-source all of the tools for spawning APEs and running troops of them," Pluto explained. "Combined with an easy-to-use graphical user interface, this will make it possible for anyone in the world to spawn an APE troop for pennies, and manage their activities from an app."

Corvallis raised a finger. "I work for Lyke," he pointed out. "If your APEs are setting up fake accounts and hurling shit on Lyke, it's a problem for me."

"An opportunity," Pluto insisted. "It's an opportunity for Lyke to differentiate itself from those old-school platforms that, in the wake of Moab, can never again be trusted."

"Are you responsible for the Moab hoax?" Corvallis asked him flat-out. The idea had only just occurred to him.

"No."

"Did you have anything to do with it at all?"

"No. Which is weird because whoever *did* do it thinks like I do in a lot of ways. But, I try to draw the line at anything where people die."

"You've been working on this for a while," Maeve said. "No one could create all of what you've described in a few days. I don't care how good a programmer you are."

"That is correct. I have been working on different parts of it ever since I retired from Corporation 9592."

"Two years ago," Corvallis said, for Maeve's benefit. "And now you're just being opportunistic. The aftermath of Moab is the perfect time for you to launch this."

"And the perfect time," Pluto insisted, "for your company to set itself apart from the competition."

Maeve thought she had better sleep on it. Which was actually possible, on a business jet flying across the Pacific Ocean. She slept soundly for nine hours, which somehow gave Corvallis the premonition that she was going to say yes. Consequently, he slept poorly indeed, lying next to her making mental checklists of every action he was going to have to take as soon as they reached a place where he could connect to the Internet. The technical side of it was going to be easy; Lyke's engineers, forewarned, could hack together some processes that would filter out most APE traffic. The legal aspect was what kept him awake, largely because it was out of his domain and there was nothing he could do about it save come up with half-baked nightmare scenarios and then worry about them.

He calmed down somewhat when he talked to Pluto. Pluto, as it turned out, had for a couple of years been employing several lawyers full-time, looking for ways to set this thing up so that he wouldn't run afoul of any of the laws that had been established to inflict draconian punishments on persons identified as hackers.

In one sense, APEs had been decades in the making. In a tightly compressed, fast-forward style of discourse, Pluto reminded Corvallis of a lot of history that he already vaguely knew. Pluto, as it turned out, was part of a loose group of like-minded persons calling itself ENSU: the Ethical Network Sabotage Undertaking. The APE was his personal baby but others had been working on it too, cross-breeding his code with filter-evading, CAPTCHA-spoofing spambots built to flood Wikipedia with bogus edits and Amazon with fake product reviews.

ENSU's vision in the long term was noble and beautiful: they wanted to make a new thing called the Trusted Internet. Short term, the way they wanted to get there was to bury every old-school blog in fake comments, follow every legitimate Twitter account with a thousand fake ones, clone and spoof every Facebook page with digital myrmidons, and bide their time for weeks or months before suddenly filling their victims' feeds with garbage.

"I can see why you hired lawyers," Corvallis remarked after he'd heard that.

Pluto chuckled. "Only for the APE part of it. There are many participants on the ENSU list. Some more extreme than others."

"And all anonymous, untraceable, et cetera."

"Well, we use PURDAH."

Corvallis sighed. "I'll bite. What is PURDAH?"

Pluto was delighted that he had asked. "Personal Unseverable Registered Designator for Anonymous Holography."

Corvallis leaned back and thought about it for a bit. Some parts of it were obvious, others less so. "How does holography enter into it? That's a way of making three-dimensional pictures, right?"

"That's the modern usage. It's a very old word. Academically, 'holograph' means a manuscript written entirely in one hand."

"One hand?"

"Manu. Script. Hand. Writing," Pluto said, incredulous at his slowness. "How can you tell if an ancient manuscript was written entirely by one person? The handwriting is the same all the way through, that's how. The author's name might not be known, but you can identify them, in a sense, by their handwriting—with greater certainty than could ever be conferred by their name alone."

"I'll give you that much," Corvallis said. "Writing a name on a title page is easy. Forging a whole document written in a consistent hand is hard."

"It is damn near unforgeable evidence that one specific person wrote the whole manuscript. That's what a holograph is—it's what the word denoted before it came to be used to mean three-D image technology."

"So 'holography'—the H in 'PURDAH'—is shorthand for 'creating documents that are provably traceable to a given author.'"

"Documents or any other kind of digital activity," Pluto corrected him.

"And just like a holograph doesn't need the author's name on the title page—"

"*Anonymous* Holography," Pluto reminded him, with a satisfied nod.

"Run the whole thing by me again?"

"Personal Unseverable Registered Designator for Anonymous Holography."

"It's just an anonymous ID," Corvallis said, "dressed up with a fancy name."

"Well, yes and no. Anonymous IDs aren't registered anywhere. PURDAHs are registered using a distributed ledger, so their veracity can be checked anytime, by anyone. 'Unseverable' means that no one can take it away from you, as long as you take reasonable precautions."

"And Personal?"

"Just there to make the acronym work out, I guess," Pluto said. "But each PURDAH is linked to a 'person' in the legal sense of that term, meaning a human being, or a legal person like a corporation."

"So anyway," Corvallis guessed, "all of the people involved in this Ethical Network Sabotage Undertaking are talking to each other and posting documents using some kind of PURDAH system."

"It's not very systematic. Really clunky to use. We could use some help from an investor to clean it up, put a UI on it."

"Pluto, you just told me a few hours ago that you have nineteen times as much money as I do, why don't you fucking invest in it?"

"It's not in my wheelhouse."

Corvallis sighed. "Here's what I'm getting at, Pluto. This thing that just happened? The Moab hoax? It was really well done. Like, eerily well pulled off. I mean, maybe when we're done sifting through the wreckage we'll find a place where they put a foot wrong, but overall, it was a masterpiece. I'm wondering who is smart and well organized enough to do something like that."

"I already told you it wasn't me."

"And I believe you. But I wonder if you know the perpetrator. Not personally but through their PURDAH. I'm wondering if they are part of your loose ENSU network."

Pluto shrugged. "There's a lot of interest in the topic of distributed organizations. Which means, a network of PURDAHs that operates by an agreed-on set of rules just like a normal company, but with no identifiable center."

"You're saying that the people who ran the Moab hoax could

have secretly set up one of these distributed organizations to do it. And they didn't invite you, because you didn't know the secret handshake or you said the wrong thing once in a discussion thread."

"It's possible. But I doubt it."

"Who do you think did it?"

"Russians again?"

"What's their upside in running something this big, though?" Corvallis asked. "Who benefits from Moab?"

"What's your opinion?" Pluto asked.

"ENSU benefits. People who hate the Miasma for being so unreliable, who have been dreaming of replacing it with something better, more secure."

"I can't argue with that!" Pluto said, with a delighted chuckle. And something in that childlike expression of enjoyment twigged Corvallis to a flaw in his own argument. Pluto had an infinite amount of money, sure. So he had means. But did he have a motive? Well, sort of. He and thousands of other hackers, including all of his ENSU buddies, were perpetually annoyed with the Miasma's security deficiencies. But was that alone sufficient motive to perpetrate a hoax on the scale of Moab? People had *died*. Thirty-one, at last count, had perished in traffic accidents or of heart attacks and strokes suffered while fleeing from imaginary bombs. Who would do something like that?

The obvious motive was money. Someone had figured out a way to profit from the hoax, most likely by short-selling stock. And no doubt the SEC was already investigating that angle, combing through stock exchange records for suspicious patterns of activity in the days leading up to it. Or maybe it was a more subtle play, something that the SEC wouldn't be able to pin on anyone.

But it seemed like a roundabout and uncommonly irresponsible way to get slightly richer. Anyone with the brains and the technical acumen needed to pull this off would have other opportunities.

Corvallis pondered it as the jet winged south and west, across the equator, across the international date line. Pluto fell asleep in front of his laptop, which obligingly shut itself off, plunging the cabin into darkness. Corvallis looked out the window and saw nothing but stars, and a single, isolated light down below that must have been a ship.

He realized that it had been done by Elmo Shepherd.

The awareness came full-blown into his brain. No train of thought led to it and no evidence supported it, but he knew it as certainly as if El had been sitting across from him in the jet and confided in him personally. Like a scholar looking at an anonymous holograph in a library, Corvallis had simply recognized El's handwriting.

Australia—at least the first bit of it that hove into view—was greener than Corvallis had been led to expect. He was debating whether to wake Maeve up, but some internal alarm seemed to have gone off in her head alerting her to their arrival in her home country's airspace. He dreaded asking her whether she'd made a choice regarding what Pluto had proposed. She had a placid confidence about her that he hadn't seen since she'd found herself in the crosshairs of the Moab truthers. After enjoying a heavy breakfast served up by the flight attendant, she took over the bathroom for half an hour and emerged in triumphal makeup. Maeve took an all-or-nothing approach to makeup, going completely without it most of the time but turning it into an impressive production when she had decided the occasion was right. Corvallis hadn't known her long enough to be able to predict what those occasions would be; it wasn't always the obvious triggers, like going on a date. He knew without asking that it was all tied in with Sthetix and that, if he dared ask, she'd explain to him that makeup was just another prosthetic, and she'd remind him that the root of the word had something to do with strength. She looked strong when she came out of the plane's bathroom, though not necessarily strong in a way that would be recognized or respected by her legions of Miasma detractors. She was getting ready to use her face to send a message to her family, written in a code of incredible sophistication that he would never understand.

By that time Australia had turned red-beige and begun to make Utah look, by comparison, like a rain forest. She spent the last hour of the flight quizzing Pluto about APEs and about how it was all going to work once he unleashed them. They agreed it would be better to wait for a day or two so that she could explain matters to her mother and her sister.

Once they had landed and cleared customs, they dropped into family mode, which from a fundamentalist nerd standpoint meant a way of being that caused vast amounts of time to disappear while people pursued activities that ruled out getting any sort of productive work done. The first few hours were entirely devoted to collecting Mary Catherine, who was the mother, and Lady, the imperiled Lhasa apso. Lady got dropped off at a kennel for a few days. From there they went to the hospital to pick up Verna, who had finished her round of chemo. They drove out to the McLaren Vale, south of town. An acquaintance of Corvallis—the centurion of a Roman legion reenactment group in South Australia—had recommended a certain retreat center embedded in a winery, and Corvallis's assistant had booked a little villa there. They moved Verna and her support technology into its best bedroom so that she could recuperate. Never until now had Corvallis been close enough to a chemotherapy patient to be exposed to all of the details. He saw that Cancer Land was a whole alternate civilization, as complicated as everything he did for a living.

Only after a few hours of getting to know the family and sharing a meal and getting Verna squared away was Corvallis able to get some time to himself and alert his colleagues at Lyke to what was in the works. Most of his nerd mind, however, was still fixated on Elmo Shepherd. Not clear to him was whether El might somehow sense that Corvallis had figured it out—might indeed be disappointed in Corvallis, as a teacher is disappointed with a prize pupil, if Corvallis failed to say anything the next time they encountered each other.

And encounter each other they would. For El and his panoply of non-, not-for-, and for-profit entities had become inextricably intertwined with the fate of Dodge and Dodge's brain. A disproportionate amount of the time that Corvallis spent on his own foundation and nonprofit work was devoted to puzzling out the latest gambits of El's attorneys. Indeed the last board meeting that he had attended, the day he had driven out to the Roman-legion camp in Montana, had been dominated by a discussion of a new maneuver that had only just been initiated by El. He could not help wondering now whether there was some connection between that and the launching of the hoax—a link that would only become obvious to him years from now. For he always had the sense that he was playing tic-tac-toe while El was playing four-dimensional hyperspace chess.

Australia in general, and this winery in particular, were fine places to reside while a stupendous onslaught of Miasma defamation was launched against Maeve Braden. Astonishing birdcalls were woven through its dry, quiet air, which was scented with eucalyptus and softened with a haze of reddish dust filtering down from the great desert to the north. Broad tin roofs and heavy steel screens sheltered them from sun and bug while somehow making them feel they were right in the middle of the trees and the vines. The design of the place was simple and comfortable without any taint of what was normally thought of as luxury. Verna's bedroom opened onto a second-story verandah under deep eaves, which felt like a treehouse. Maeve would sit there for hours with her, chatting and drinking tea, while Mary Catherine bustled and fussed. She was first-generation Irish-Australian, messily divorced from the father of Maeve and Verna, who had some kind of complicated-sounding dual citizenship that enabled him to flee to America when his relatives in Oz were sick of him, and vice versa. The Miasma had long since doxxed him and gleefully posted mug shots commemorating his brushes with the law in jurisdictions that were so improbably far-flung as to deliver a certain dry comedic payload. Mary Catherine's obsessive devotion to small, nearby, concrete matters, such as scones and the doings of nearby birds, was the perfect antidote to the Miasma.

As Verna got her energy back, he spent more time with her. In the early going, Maeve was always in the room to keep an eye on things and nudge the conversation forward when it stalled, but as the days went by the discourse between Corvallis and Verna became more and more geeky, and Maeve withdrew by degrees, sitting in the corner reading or knitting, then absenting herself. Verna turned out to be the real deal: a programmer, largely self-taught, who, once the chemo fog had abated, was able to hold up her end of a conversation with C-plus. Had the situation been different, he'd have considered hiring her. She'd have come in for interviews. Other programmers would have circled round her warily. They'd have reached the conclusion that she was "awesome" but they'd have found reasons to reject her due to a lack of cultural fit, and they'd have passed her on to smaller, more offbeat startups run by friends. All of which was still possible in theory. But having cancer was still going to be a full-time job for her for a while.

He wished he could have introduced her to Dodge.

He checked in with Pluto, who had ensconced himself in the most expensive hotel suite that was to be had in Adelaide. He contacted Corvallis every few hours on a "burner" phone that Corvallis had picked up on arrival in Australia, when he'd discovered that his usual phone number had been doxxed and rendered useless by a festival of reckless hatred originating from a cluster of racist conspiracy theorists. It wasn't until forty-eight hours after they'd landed in Australia that Pluto was ready to spawn his troop of APEs, and Lyke was ready to fend them off. Pluto called Corvallis to inform him that his right pinky was hovering over the Enter key on his keyboard, and that if said key were momentarily depressed, it would all happen.

Corvallis received the call while pacing aimlessly around the villa's ground floor. "Okay," he said.

"Okay as in you have understood what I just said?" Pluto asked. "Or okay as in 'Yes, go ahead and do it'?"

"Go ahead and do it."

"Do you want to check one last time with Maeve?" Pluto inquired, showing, for him, an unusual degree of sensitivity.

"If I ask her one more time she'll probably slap me," Corvallis said. "Here, it's a done deal. She and her sister are discussing what to do next—hatching a plan."

"Okay, here goes," Pluto said, and let Corvallis hear the key getting whacked before hanging up the phone.

Corvallis sent a text message to his colleagues at Lyke and then shut off his phone.

If everything went according to plan, the Ethical Network Sabotage Undertaking would now issue a press release announcing its existence and explaining what it was doing. It would include a signed statement, as well as a video clip, from Maeve Braden, announcing that she was completely fine with all of this. Also included were links to servers where all of the APE-related code was available in the form of a carefully documented open-source code package, complete with sample projects that programmers could use to modify and extend it in various ways. Following up on an idea that had emerged during the conversation on the jet, ENSU also made public a list of several hundred completely imaginary, nonexistent people against whom campaigns of reckless slander and defamation could now be unleashed, as well as an easy-to-use tool that anyone could exploit to create new such fake persons and reasonably convincing social media shaming campaigns that would make those fake persons the object of real, genuine, sincere obloquy on the part of millions of social media users who were dumb enough to believe everything that scrolled across their screens. Following a brief pause for all of this to propagate, the APE troop would come online at an initial pace of one gigaBraden. Pluto would sit up for a few hours watching its progress through a control panel UI he had running on his laptop, which would plot various metrics for him in real time, using a comprehensive suite of data visualization tools. Then he would sleep for eight hours. Then he would get up and take stock of how it was all going, and make any adjustments he felt were necessary, such as upping the pace to ten gigaBradens if that seemed like a good idea.

Corvallis got a deck of cards out of the cabinet in the living room and played solitaire for half an hour. Then he went for a walk with Maeve, who was, at least for a day, the most famous woman in the world. She told him about an idea she and Verna had been hatching, somewhere between tech startup, performance art, fashion accessory, and political manifesto. They were going to bring back the veil.

They waited three more days before holding a press conference. They announced it only an hour ahead of time, then drove into Adelaide and held it in a conference room at Pluto's hotel. The short notice ensured that it was dominated by Australian media. This worked well. They could be every bit as superficial and tabloidy as media elsewhere, of course, but there was something about this project that seemed to appeal to their collective sense of humor. The atmosphere in the room was jokey and celebratory, and pervaded by a general sense that the Aussies had pulled one over on the rest of the world and that everyone here was in on the joke.

It was a week before the Bradens went back to something approximating their normal life. By then Pluto had already flown home. Corvallis went back alone on the jet, and Maeve followed him two weeks later. By that point it was possible to stand back and tally the numbers from the Moab hoax and from the ENSU project, which were now increasingly being viewed as two phases of the same basic event—the week that the Miasma had fallen.

Corvallis and Maeve carried on an odd, colorful long-distance relationship for the next two years. She got pregnant and moved in with him to a big old house in an expensive Seattle neighborhood, which they fixed up for the purpose of raising a family. It was a boy; they named him Vern, after Verna, who died from another recurrence of her cancer a month before he was born. Lucid to the end, Verna donated her brain to science. Specifically, she entrusted it to the Forthrast Family Foundation. The legal documents by which she did so grew more and more complex as the lawyers dreamed up more and more hypothetical contingencies. Having literally no time for such things, she ended up cutting the Gordian knot by saying she wanted "most favored nation" treatment, meaning that whatever was done with Richard Forthrast's brain should also be done with hers. When Verna's condition took a turn for the worse, Corvallis and Maeve flew her to Seattle, so that when she died her remains weren't encumbered by any discrepancies between Australian and U.S. law.

On a ranch just outside of Moab, they maintained a second home. This did double duty as the headquarters of the Moab Project, a nonprofit organization funded by Corvallis and others—mostly people who had made a lot of money in social media—to sift through hoax-related data and think important thoughts about it.

The Moab Project investigated and documented the operational details of the hoax in forensic detail, right up to the point where each separate trail of evidence dead-ended in perfect cryptographic anonymity.

The total budget for the hoax was estimated to have been less than one million dollars. The networks had actually paid out more than that for the privilege of airing fake footage supplied by the hoaxers. Those payments, made in Bitcoin, had gone to anonymous overseas accounts presumably controlled by the hoaxers. Between that and short-selling various affected stocks on Wall Street, it appeared that they had paid for the exploit many times over.

Which was a mere detail when set against the thirty-one deaths and the direct economic losses, which were way into the tens of billions. Lawsuits filed against social media companies—including Lyke—depressed their valuations, distracted their executives, and took years to resolve.

The culprit was at first assumed to be an arm of Russian or Chinese intelligence. But the further the investigation went, the less likely this seemed. Some of the fake footage had originated from a Chinese computer graphics firm, but this proved nothing. The scripts and other written material, such as fake blogs and social media postings, seemed to have been written by native English speakers.

More people than just Corvallis began to suspect Elmo Shepherd of being the mastermind. He was a major shareholder, or a member of the board of directors, of more than one company that would profit from what came next. He was libertarian minded, a Bitcoin advocate. And he was from Utah, with a lot of local practical knowledge of conditions on the ground there. And so one school of thought said that he must have done it.

The opposing school of thought said simply "nah." Simply "nah." It was too ridiculous—too far-fetched. The connection to El's home state was a mere coincidence, or a deliberate scheme to cast suspicion on him.

Corvallis and Maeve visited Moab less and less frequently as raising Vern made a stay-at-home life seem like the best thing in the world. Two years later they had a daughter named Catherine, and a year after that they adopted Eduardo from Guatemala. Maeve chose not to work full-time. A nanny and a housekeeper, and the many less visible privileges of wealth, gave her enough free time to think about and to lay the groundwork for the VEIL Project, which she hoped would one day finish what she and Verna had started with Sthetix. The Moab hoax receded into the past with swiftness that seemed extraordinary when, years later, Corvallis would, from time to time, be reminded of it somehow, and have cause to review the events in his memory. He, along with many others in the tech world, had arrived at the conclusion that the answer to the riddle must be known by the NSA and other such top secret agencies that had the wherewithal to penetrate the cryptographic screen in which the hoax had been so meticulously shrouded. One day the answer would leak out as some disgruntled employee went rogue or some document was declassified.

When the answer came to him, it came from a surprising quarter. Corvallis attended a meeting at the headquarters of the Forthrast Family Foundation in the South Lake Union neighborhood of Seattle. The meeting's purpose was to go over some dry but necessary legal matters with people representing Elmo Shepherd's nonprofit. After several years of intensive R & D, and the expenditure of nearly two billion dollars pooled by Forthrast-, Waterhouse-, and Shepherd-funded entities, they'd finally constructed an ion-beam scanning device capable of capturing the full connectome of a human brain, and the "back end" of hardware and software needed to process the data that would pour out of such a machine. Fifteen hundred patent applications had been filed: enough to keep a phalanx of patent attorneys and paralegals busy for years. Twelve different major universities and medical centers were involved. Brilliant young lawyers were building their entire careers around the attendant complexities. A few of them were in this meeting, presenting ready-to-sign documents on which they'd toiled for years. Corvallis, Zula, and others were there just to sign them.

One of the people on Elmo Shepherd's side of the table was pretty senior—surprisingly so given that all of the big decisions had already been made by this point. He met Corvallis's eye from time to time, and checked his watch, and gazed out the window in a manner that seemed significant, and indeed when the meeting concluded he approached Corvallis and inquired in the most gentle and polite way whether he might have a moment of private time with him.

His name was Sinjin Kerr. Depending on who was keeping score he was Elmo Shepherd's first-, second-, or third-most important legal henchman. His role was generally that of Good Cop. In his appearance and grooming he was a straight-from-central-casting Harvard/Yale product with swept-back hair, rimless glasses, and an impeccable suit, protected for this occasion under an overcoat.

They ended up strolling down to the lakefront and, seemingly on the spur of the moment, renting a little electric boat from a business that catered to the tourist trade. Business was light because spring was being a little slow to turn into summer. It was cool and the lenses of Sinjin's glasses were already flecked with tiny droplets of rain.

Sinjin sat down at the controls and piloted the boat out into the middle of the little lake. This had always been monitored by steep hills to the east and west but during the last couple of decades had been hemmed in along its southern reach by high-rise buildings occupied by tech companies. Some vestiges of old Seattle remained, including a seaplane terminal that helped make life good for tourists and for geeks who liked quick getaways to Vancouver or the San Juan Islands. Everyone who lived and worked within earshot had grown accustomed to the occasional sound of propellers coming up to speed as one of these planes made its takeoff run across the lake.

The water was a bit choppy, as the wind had come up and brought with it a gentle but assiduous rain. They deployed the boat's folding canvas cover, snapping it to the top edge of the windshield. Sinjin dropped the throttle to the minimum needed to maintain headway and pottered about, keeping an eye out for outgoing and incoming planes. As this seemingly pointless idyll went on, Corvallis got the impression that he was timing some of his utterances so that the most important words would be spoken just when a seaplane was droning overhead. Sometimes Sinjin would turn toward Corvallis, prop an elbow casually on the boat's dashboard, and raise his hand to cover his mouth. Only later, in memory, did Corvallis understand that he had done so to hide his message from any lip readers who might be tracking them through telescopes.

They'd been chatting about their respective families. Catching up with each other, as people did when they were maintaining these long-running, sporadic business relationships.

"You might find it a curious thing, Corvallis, that your family is an inadvertent, and happy, by-product of something that Mr. Shepherd was involved with," Sinjin mumbled through his fingers as a plane buzzed past them at full throttle.

Corvallis was a while processing that news. There was only one way to make sense of it: El was behind the Moab hoax that had brought Maeve and Corvallis together.

Sinjin seemed to derive a bit of light amusement from watching him think about it. "Your next question ought to be, why did I just tell you that?"

"Not because you get a kick out of snitching on your client, I'm guessing."

Sinjin thought that was funny. "Indeed. Otherwise I'd have a very fun, very brief career. No, it's my job to look out for Mr. Shepherd's interests. I'm divulging this to you, and you only, because the time has come when his interests are best served by allowing you, Corvallis, to have a broader understanding of the context within which Mr. Shepherd and his foundations and companies have been operating."

"I've suspected from day one that El was responsible for Moab," Corvallis said. "Up to a point it kind of made sense. The Internet— what Dodge used to call the Miasma—had just gone completely wrong. Down to the molecular level it was still a hippie grad student project. Like a geodesic dome that a bunch of flower children had assembled from scrap lumber on ground infested with termites and carpenter ants. So rotten that rot was the only thing that was holding it together. So I can totally see why El or anyone with a shred of crypto knowledge would want to just burn it down. To make it so that no one would ever trust it again. Moab was a pretty effective way of doing that, and ENSU came along right on its heels and dumped a 747-load of gasoline on that fire. But the other shoe never dropped."

"What do you suppose the other shoe ought to have been in this case?" Sinjin asked.

Corvallis was about to answer, then stopped himself, sensing the absurdity of it.

Sinjin let him work it out on his own for a bit, then, in a gentle tone that barely rose above the lapping of the waves on the boat's hull, said, "Elmo Shepherd releases a statement a week after Moab in which he fesses up. Pulls back the veil. Maybe plays some behind-the-scenes video showing how the hoax was staged—a blooper reel of the actors, some 'making of' footage about burn makeup and CGI mushroom clouds. 'All this was done on a one-million-dollar budget,' he says, and gives a sermon about how if he can get you to believe Moab was nuked by spending a million bucks, just imagine what the Russians and the big Internet companies are doing to your mind every day with much larger budgets. Followed by a pitch for a cryptographically secure successor to the Internet."

"Yeah," Corvallis said. "That's pretty much what I had in mind in the way of an other shoe."

"That video was actually made," Sinjin said.

"No shit!?"

"I kid you not. I was there, Corvallis. I vetted the script and sat off camera while he read it off the teleprompter. That whole video was in the can, ready to go, before the exploit was launched."

"But he changed his mind."

"By degrees."

"What?"

"El changed his mind by degrees, over a period of weeks. He was holed up in Z-A to avoid any possible issues around extradition."

As Corvallis knew, Z-A was Zelrijk-Aalberg, a Flemish nanostate and tax haven where El had been spending most of his time the last few years.

"So there was a degree of insulation from legal consequences—but even so he was disconcerted by how effective it had been. By the fact that people died."

"I can see how that would give you pause," Corvallis said, a bit sarcastically.

Sinjin raised his eyes studiously and declined to rise to the bait. "So the airing of the video was delayed, and delayed again, as he pondered his next move. ENSU happened and seemed to take the wind out of his sails. He wasn't expecting that."

"It did a lot of his work for him," Corvallis said, nodding. "Made the same point."

"Inasmuch as ENSU succeeded, it made Moab seem unnecessary. Cack-handed. Inasmuch as ENSU failed, it made him wonder whether there was any real future in his own visions for a secure Internet."

"When you say ENSU failed, you're referring to the fact that—"

"That billions of people went on believing everything they saw on the Internet in spite of it."

"I can't argue with that," Corvallis said.

"Then you must feel a little of what Elmo Shepherd felt," Sinjin said.

"Why fight it?"

Sinjin nodded. "What's the point? The mass of people are so stupid, so gullible, because they *want* to be misled. There's no way to make them not want it. You have to work with the human race as it exists, with all of its flaws. Getting them to see reason is a fool's errand."

"Seems kind of bleak. There are things you could do in the way of education—"

"Not if your primary focus is on preparing for the next world."

"You mean, what happens after death."

Sinjin nodded.

"I've seen El on social media, suggesting that Moab actually was nuked. Like, openly pandering to the people who still believe that," Corvallis said. "I don't see how that helps. *That's crazy.*"

"Exactly!" Sinjin said, brightening. "This brings us back to the main thread of this conversation."

"Which is?" Corvallis asked, throwing up his hands in bewilderment.

"El's going crazy."

Corvallis turned to look Sinjin in the eye. Sinjin wasn't joking.

"Elmo Shepherd suffers—has always suffered—from an incurable genetic disorder. I'll tell you the medical name later and you can Google it if you want to know the gory details. It runs in his family. He's been aware of it since he was in college. One of its inevitable results is a degeneration of the brain that typically begins when the sufferer is in his forties or fifties. Mr. Shepherd is fifty-two."

"Okay," Corvallis said, after a pause to consider this news. "I see what you mean about the main line of the conversation. Everything he's done with Ephrata Life Sciences, the preservation and scanning of brains—it all relates to this."

"We are all mortal," Sinjin said grandly, "and we differ only in the extent to which we ignore that fact. Mr. Shepherd was never granted the luxury of being able to ignore it and so he has prepared for it with greater forethought than most."

"How does Moab fit in?"

"I wish I knew," Sinjin sighed. "In addition to the things you and I talk about—the brain stuff—there is a vast scope of other activity. He compartmentalizes well, so I don't always know of these projects until he chooses to make me aware of them. But in the last year or so I have become conscious of an acceleration."

"You mean, he's getting sick faster, or kicking these projects up into high gear?"

"Both. And since 'getting sick' here is a euphemism for going crazy, well, you can probably see that I have a quite interesting job. When one of his fascinating projects comes to light, as it does from time to time, I honestly can't say whether Mr. Shepherd is pursuing some profound strategy or succumbing to his disease." Sinjin paused for a few moments—a rare occasion in which it seemed he was groping for words. "You should understand that El thinks highly of you and of Zula Forthrast. In my judgment, he would not knowingly take actions that were in any way injurious to either of you."

"'Knowingly' being the key word in that sentence," Corvallis said.

"Indeed, Corvallis, just as the existence of your beautiful young family is an unpredictable side effect of one of my client's more imaginative projects, there's no telling what the future may hold as Mr. Shepherd's disease progresses toward its inevitable conclusion and his affairs pass into the management not just of me, but of others he has decided to entrust with this or that task. Until he changes his mind, however, I'm your man when it comes to all things brain related."

"When does he want to do it?" Corvallis asked.

Sinjin said nothing for a while. He pretended to pay attention to some important nearby boat traffic.

"That's his dilemma, isn't it?" Corvallis went on. "On the one hand, he should wait until the technology is better proven. On the other, his brain is degenerating, and he knows it. What's the point in perfectly preserving a brain that has gone to pieces?"

"It's a question we could all ask ourselves," Sinjin said. "He just has to ask it every minute of every day."

PART 3

12

The ancestral home of the Forthrasts was situated in the north-western quadrant of Iowa: a two-hundred-mile-wide quadrangle defined by Interstates 80 and 90 to the south and north, and 29 and 35 to the west and east. It was now being displayed in miniature, superimposed on a coffee table in an eating club at Princeton University, visible only to Sophia and to the friends she had shared it with: Phil, Julian, and Anne-Solenne. They could see it as long as they were wearing their glasses.

They were planning a summer road trip. They had worked it out as far as Des Moines by following interstate highways. Now Sophia was proposing a diagonal transit to Sioux City on two-lane roads. The very idea of it had led first to blank stares, then to head scratching, and finally to outright concern among Sophia's traveling companions. The conversation had stalled entirely, and the plan for their summer adventure had been at risk of collapse, until a solution had taken shape in the agile brain, and sprung from the perfectly sculpted lips, of Sophia's boyfriend Phil: "Look. I'm just not going to tell my parents—or *anyone*—that we are temporarily going off grid."

This had led to a pause as they admired the audacity of it. Sophia decided on the spot not to dump Phil for at least another few weeks. Julian and Anne-Solenne, who had been draped over each other on a couch opposite, disentangled and put their brains in gear. "Well," said Anne-Solenne, probing the idea for weaknesses, "you'd pretty much have to tell your editor—unless you're *truly* shutting everything off. Going actually dark."

"Sure!" Phil agreed. "You know what I mean."

"We would all have to align, as far as that goes," Julian pointed out, "since everyone is going to know we are traveling as a group. I *think* that my editor would be willing to tell a little white lie for—how long?"

Sophia shrugged. "The roads are decent by the standards of Ameristan. Farmers need roads to move stuff around, so they don't see them as a government plot—they don't tear them up on principle, they don't ANFO the bridges. There are not a lot of roadblocks. So, call it two days, with one night at the farmhouse—which is in a little pocket of blue." She leaned forward so that she could reach the coffee table to which she'd anchored the virtual map. The four interstates aligned roughly with the table's edges. To her and Phil, Des Moines was in the near right corner and Sioux City in the far left, next to Anne-Solenne's knee. "We are crossing diagonally," she said. "We say goodbye to Phil's car in Des Moines—"

Phil had pushed his glasses up on his forehead. So he could no longer see the map. He wasn't paying attention to Sophia. He had got stuck on what Julian had last said. "That's your editor's *job*," he pointed out. He spread the fingers of his left hand in just the faintest hint of a dismissive gesture, putting Sophia on hold.

"Actually," Julian said, "I kinda think her job is to do whatever my mom and dad—*who pay her to edit for our whole family*—want her to do."

Phil shook his head. "You might as well save some money and just subscribe to an edit stream if that's how it is."

Julian was exasperated. "As long as Mom and Dad are paying for my hookup—"

"See, this is why you have to get your own editor."

The two women exchanged a look, the meaning of which was that Sophia gave Anne-Solenne permission to yell at Sophia's boyfriend. She did so: "Wake up! Not everyone can afford a cool hipster editor in New York." She delivered this with the sweet/blunt blend that had caused Sophia to fall platonically in love with her during their freshman year. Together, Sophia and Anne-Solenne were token holders on three different collective PURDAHs, which was a way of saying that their identities had become commingled in ways that could never be undone. Software written by one of those had led to Anne-Solenne's summer internship in San Francisco. Getting her there was the nominal purpose of the road trip that they were now planning.

"That's not what I'm suggesting," Phil said. "Manila, Calcutta, Lagos, all teeming with totally cool native-English-speaking eds who'll cost less than what you spend on *coffee*."

"It's a sore subject in my family," Julian said. "There's a whole subtree of cousins who went off the rails because they went in together on a bad editor who ended up mainlining Byelorussian propaganda into their feeds. We lost a whole branch of the family, basically. So my mom in particular is super sensitive about this."

This actually shut Phil up long enough for Sophia to lunge forward and put her thumb down on Des Moines. "Assume we solve the problem of getting our families not to lose their shit over the fact that we are venturing off-interstate for two whole days," she said. "Like I said, we hop out of Phil's car here, just take overnight bags, leave most of the luggage in it, and tell it to meet us in Sioux City." For the benefit of those who did not know their Iowa geography, she pointed at same, and Anne-Solenne helpfully positioned her espresso cup on it, near where Iowa, Nebraska, and South Dakota came together. Phil pulled his glasses back down over his eyes so that he could see.

"It'll get there in just a few hours," Sophia went on. "After that it can drive around Sioux City at random or hang out in a parking space until we catch up with it. Meanwhile we switch to a rental vehicle that is better suited for local conditions."

A pause as all imagined local conditions.

"And—what I will euphemistically call local guides?"

"I *really* don't think that they are necessary. Not where we're going. But the rental company won't let us do a one-way without them."

t's like any place else," Phil confirmed, three weeks later, as they watched his car drive out of the lot and pull into traffic on Fleur Drive. A pair of driverless trucks politely adjusted their speed to give it a gap to merge into. The four of them were sweating in the greenhouse summer of central Iowa. Overnight bags were suspended from index fingers instead of slung over shoulders. They jockeyed languidly to catch stray breezes. Planes whined overhead coming in to land. This was not the shaded and air-conditioned comfort of the airport's car rental center, but an outlying lot catering to basically anyone who intended to venture more than a couple of miles from an interstate highway.

"You can set your bags down and they will be as safe as if they were locked up in a bank vault," said Larry, the manager on duty, using a thumb to shift the strap on his shoulder and expose a sweat-darkened stripe of T-shirt. Dangling from the strap was an assault rifle, poised in such a way that its muzzle was usually aimed at the ground. Which seemed dangerous; but Larry for his part was aghast at his four young customers' unwillingness to let their bags out of their grasp and clearly imagined that wherever they came from, no property was safe.

Sophia had her glasses up on her forehead. She was tempted to flip them down and see if they could face-rec this Larry and if so find out who *his* editor was—or more likely what edit stream he subscribed to and what particular flavor of post-reality it was pumping into his mind. But Larry didn't have *his* glasses down and so it would have been somewhat impolite.

He turned away and led them across heat-softened asphalt toward an old vehicle that Sophia recognized vaguely as a Land

Cruiser or Land Rover or one of those: boxy, upright, of a general design that was four or five decades old. But it was clean, well cared for, beaded with rinse water from the car wash. It had been modded in various ways that Larry wanted them to notice and to appreciate. He stepped up onto a running board, carefully adjusting the angle of his assault rifle so it wouldn't bang into the side of the vehicle, and patted the roof, which was covered in bright yellow composite.

"Kevlar," he announced. "Now. Contrary to the scare propaganda you have probably been fed, celebratory fire is overrated as far as danger. A descending round has lost most of its energy. Terminal velocity is much less than muzzle velocity. So you don't need full armor on the roof. This will do you fine."

"Is there a *lot* of celebratory fire where we are going?" Julian asked.

"No. Iowans are stoic," Phil answered in the unduly confident tones of one who was just reading about it.

"That's not the point Larry's making," said Sophia. "The point is, why spend money armoring against a nonexistent threat?"

Larry nodded. "Doors and windows, of course, that's a different story, but those are full."

"Full?" Julian asked.

"Fully armored. As a precaution. In case of stray rounds, accidental discharges. Wouldn't do you much good in an engagement. But that's what Tom and Kevin are for." Larry hooked his thumb back over his shoulder at a pickup truck idling at the edge of the lot. Tom and Kevin were seated in the cab, luxuriating in the A/C. Mounted in the pickup's open bed was a tripod, currently vacant. A steel locker running athwart the bed, triple padlocked, contained the machine gun that they would take out and mount to the tripod when venturing into regions where an impressive show of force was deemed prudent. Sprawling across the roof of the cab was a streamlined shape that might be mistaken for the world's most aerodynamic cargo rack until you realized it was actually a fixed-wing drone.

Larry stepped down and opened the driver's-side door. "Now," he said, "which one of y'all claims to be able to drive a car?"

Sophia raised her hand as the other three sidled backward. Larry gave a little nod.

"Where are you from?" Sophia asked.

Larry looked a bit startled. "I'm from here."

"But how far back?"

"As far back as you wanna look. Great-greats came over from Holland. Why do you ask?"

"You said 'y'all.'"

Larry was confused.

"Never mind. Sorry," Sophia said. "I'm the driver. I'm the only one who can drive."

"If you would just show me. Just take it for a spin around the lot," Larry said.

"I understand. Requirements of insurance," Sophia said, shoving off against the running board and vaulting into the driver's seat.

"We don't got none," Larry responded. "This is a requirement of *us*."

"What was *that* about?" Anne-Solenne asked, as soon as they were out on the streets of Des Moines, headed west. She was riding shotgun. Phil and Julian were in the backseat gazing at the outskirts of the city, which looked exactly like any other place.

"What?" Sophia asked. It had been a little while since she had driven a car and she was rigid: eyes locked on the tailgate of Tom and Kevin's truck, hands clenching the steering wheel. Surrounding traffic was at least 95 percent robo-piloted, and giving their little caravan a wide berth since you never knew what a human-piloted car was going to do.

"'Where are you from? How far back?' Those weird questions you were asking Larry."

"Oh. Something I heard from my mom—who heard it from my uncle."

"Dodge?" Anne-Solenne asked, with the forced casualness that people always affected when uttering that name.

"Yeah. About people who say 'y'all.' Or, 'We don't got none.'"

"Just sounds like rural America to me."

"*Southern* America. It's totally a Southern way of talking. Iowa is a Northern state. Fought on the Union side in the Civil War. Never had slavery. Settled by Scandinavians. So, either Larry is a migrant from the South—"

"Which he just said he *isn't* . . ."

"Or he, or his dad, adopted—affected—Southern stylings. Northerners don't talk like that, they don't drawl, they don't say 'y'all' . . ."

"Or put the Stars and Bars on their bumpers," said Julian, getting into the spirit of things. He extended an arm forth between the front seats and pointed at a Confederate flag sticker on the back of Tom and Kevin's truck. It was balanced, on the other side of the license plate, by a "Remember Moab" sticker.

"I don't know, man," said Phil. "I see that shit all over the place. Always have. It's a constant."

"To *you*," Sophia agreed. "Point being, it was not like that to my uncle, who lived from the mid-1950s to about seventeen years ago. He saw the change during his lifetime. When he was born, the Civil War was only ninety years in the past—almost within living memory. It would have seemed weird for Northerners to paste the traitors' flag on their bumper or cop an accent from Alabama. But while he was alive—"

"The cultural border shifted north," Anne-Solenne said.

The border, of course, was not a line on a map; it couldn't be, because it did not legally exist, had no official reality. It was a blended zone that straddled that belt of the outer suburbs where Walmarts tended to exist. As they moved outward from the city, vehicles containing nonwhite people found reasons to pull off the street into the parking lots of businesses, parks, schools, or churches. Nothing ever impeded the flow of traffic outward. Vehicles coming the other way, inbound from the country, were rarely if ever stopped Checkpoint Charlie–style. But they were sure as hell scrutinized. Nothing came in from that direction without being seen and scanned by a hundred cameras. Vehicles that were hard to see into, because of darkly tinted glass or no glass at all, tended to get pulled over by peace officers who expressed polite curiosity about how many people were in the back and what they were carrying. It was all so understated that an inattentive observer might not have noticed it. Had Uncle Dodge been somehow resurrected and joined them on this drive, he might have seen very little overt change from how it had looked in his day. But, gray and blurred as it might have been, the border, staked out by Walmarts and truck stops, was as real as anything from Cold War Berlin.

But nothing really *happened;* there was no one moment when they definitely crossed over into Ameristan. The closest thing to a formal ceremony was when Tom pulled over onto the gravel shoulder of a two-lane road between cornfields and turned on his four-ways. Sophia followed suit. Kevin got out of the passenger side, ambled back, and yanked off the truck's license plate—which was evidently held on with magnets. He then went round in back of the Land Cruiser and collected its plate, then gave the back of the vehicle a companionable slap. He tossed both plates—now stuck together by the magnets—into the back of the pickup. Then the caravan was back on the road.

"When in Rome," Julian said.

They picked up speed on a decently paved two-lane highway, navigating a few bends that took them down to a bridge across a motionless brown river. Then they climbed up into flat farmland. Sophia dropped back a little in case Tom hit the brakes, and Tom didn't seem to mind. Conversation halted. The others flipped their glasses down and lost themselves in stories or games. Left alone behind the wheel, Sophia kept the conversation going in her head for a while. But there was nothing to sustain it. The occasional fiberglass statue of a political leader, erected by a farmer in the front yard of an isolated house, or a makeshift billboard railing against contraception. Not so much different from what Dodge might have seen. About an hour out of Des Moines, they did pass by a tiny sign—Sharpie on plywood—bearing what might have been the burning-cross logo of the Levitican Church. An arrow pointed to the right down a gravel road that seemed to lead nowhere. She recognized it only a fraction of a second before she blew by it, and was left wondering if it had been real. The only other person who seemed to have noticed was Kevin, in the escort truck, who turned his head to the right and scanned the horizon, more curious than alarmed. Then he turned and exchanged words with the driver, Tom. Kevin bent forward for a few seconds. When he sat up straight again, the barrel of an assault rifle came into view, pointed up at the ceiling next to his head. He made some remark to Tom and both of them had a laugh. Tom reached out with his right hand and fiddled with something on the truck's center console. That fixed-wing drone rose into the air from the pickup's roof and climbed into the sky. Kevin pulled his glasses down over his eyes—though "goggles" might have been a better term for what he was sporting. They did all the same things as what Sophia and her friends wore. But those were styled as eye-glasses, meant to be small and unobtrusive. Those worn by Tom and Kevin came from a whole different aesthetic universe and Sophia was pretty sure that their advertising copy made frequent use of the words "tactical," "rugged," "mil spec," and "grueling." What Kevin was presumably seeing through them now was a drone's-eye view of the surrounding few square miles of landscape. Here, that was pretty much guaranteed to consist of a graph-paper matrix of two-lane roads, some paved and some gravel, dicing the flat green territory up into square-mile production units.

Ameristan couldn't have had less in common with how it would have been depicted in a movie or video game. Tom and Kevin had perceived or imagined some threat. Its nature was hinted at by the handmade sign they had passed at the crossroads. Maybe these guys also had access to edit streams of geodata showing hot spots of gunfire and of traffic slowdowns that might suggest roadblocks or checkpoints. But whatever they were worried about would have little to no visual signature. There was not going to be a central base, a nerve center with roads and wires converging on it. You could put anything in a barn.

Or maybe Kevin was bored and wanted to exercise the drone.

Their overall course was diagonal, but because of the grid they were always going either north or west. This made sense and worked perfectly in the almost obscenely flat middle part of the state. But the big rivers all ran from very slightly higher ground in the northwest to the very slightly lower southeast. So the caravan's rectilinear zigzagging caused them to cross and recross rivers, and around the rivers there was some interesting topography, some actual valleys between legit hills, forested country a stain on the land infallibly marking every part of it that was too steep to profitably cultivate. The higher places—worn-down traces of a glacial moraine, she suspected—sprouted wind turbines of the most enormous type. The bigger they were, the slower they turned, which was a good thing for birds. Some didn't turn at all because, one assumed, they were down for maintenance, or not finished yet. She grew used to them as hours went by.

And that was how the giant Flaming Cross of the Leviticans sneaked up on her, though the people working on it would probably have felt that she sneaked up on them. It wasn't actually flaming. It wasn't even *capable* of flaming yet, because it wasn't finished. Its general size and shape were not terribly far off from that of a wind turbine. It was sited on the top of what passed for a hill around here—not to catch the wind, but to be seen from a distance as it burned in the night. Anyway, by the time she accepted that she was actually seeing it, the thing was less than a mile away. She could see a clutter of pickup trucks parked around its base and some pop-up canopies sheltering tables where workers could take water breaks. A row of portable toilets stood sentry next to an office trailer.

On an impulse, she opened a voice channel to Tom. In normal circumstances, his edit space and Sophia's were totally disjoint; they would never encounter each other online, never meet, never see the same news stories. Anything that originated from the likes of Tom would be fastidiously pruned by the algorithms used by Sophia's editor before human eyes ever reviewed it, and anything that came from Princeton or Seattle would never reach Tom's feed until it had been bent around into propaganda whose sole function was to make Tom afraid and angry. But for today's purposes they had a direct channel, unfiltered, unedited. "Hey," she said, "how do you think those people would feel about our dropping in for a visit? Just, you know, in tourist mode?"

"Copy. Stand by," Tom returned.

The sound of Sophia's voice had broken her companions out of their media reverie, and so now came several moments of their pushing up their glasses, being astonished by the spectacle of the cross, talking about it, pulling glasses back down to search for more information.

"There's a visitor center," Tom reported. "With changing rooms. Probably easiest unless you want to have all your garments inspected."

"Well, if there's a visitor center, they must be okay with visitors," Sophia said.

Phil, Julian, and Anne-Solenne could not hear Tom's audio stream and so the changing rooms came as a surprise to them. They were in separate trailers for men and women; all of the Princetonians knew that it would be pointless, and probably inflammatory, to make inquiries about non-gender-binary cases. But the *idea* of having to don different garments just to set foot on a specific property was new to them.

"If we don't, they'll have to stone us to death," Sophia explained. "And according to their interpretation of Leviticus, the modern equivalent of stoning people is shooting them."

"Oh, I get it," Phil said. "Because bullets are like little rocks."

"Exactly. And a gun is just a modern labor-saving device that makes it easier to throw the little rocks really fast. Basically, to them, every reference to stoning in the Bible is a sort of dog-whistle reference to guns."

Phil was working it out: "God knew guns would be invented in the future because omniscient, but He couldn't insert direct references to them in the Bible because that would be a spoiler for the Bronze Age audience. So He used stoning as a placeholder."

"And our clothing is immodest or something?" Julian asked.

"Not at all." Sophia reached out as if to grab Julian by the scruff of the neck. Instead of which, she flipped the collar of his T-shirt inside out so that she could read the tag. "Mostly cotton but with some spandex. To make it stretchy I guess. If you wore this up there, they would have to stone—i.e., shoot—you."

"They have something against spandex?"

"Against mixing fibers." Sophia pointed to a sign mounted to the wall above a table on which a display of neatly folded white paper bunny suits had been laid out, in a range of sizes. The sign was a quote from the Bible, set in Comic Sans:

Ye shal kepe mine ordinances. Thou shalt not
let thy cattel gendre with others of divers
kindes. Thou shalt not sowe thy field with
mingled sede neither shal a garment of divers
things, as of linen and wollen come upon thee.
—Leviticus 19:19

Phil couldn't get past the first bit. "Is that a proscription of bestiality *between different kinds of animals?*"

"Ssh," said Anne-Solenne, for sitting nearby was an Iowan lady of perhaps sixty, monitoring a table of cookies and coffee, free but, in classic Midwest passive-aggressive style, with a jar for suggested donations.

"I guess they were anti-mule. Look. Point being we can either strip down and have her read all the labels on our garments, which is gross, or just change into the bunny suits."

"What about him?" Julian asked, gesturing toward Tom, who was emerging from the men's toilet. Then, realizing he had been a little rude, he turned to address Tom directly. "Tom, are you going to change clothes?"

"No need," Tom said, and went into a curious routine of patting himself in various places. All of his garb was Tactical, Mil Spec, Rugged, and Grueling, even down to suspenders and socks. All of the tags were on the outside—not concealed in collars and waistbands, as was the normal practice. Which wasn't obvious because the tags were tactical camo, olive drab or what have you, so that they wouldn't stand out in a faraway sniper's scope like stars in the night sky.

The Princetonians now all felt at liberty to approach and examine. The lettering and logos on the tags were subdued tactical colors and difficult to read until you got close. But all of them— along with the manufacturers' logos and the incomprehensible laundry glyphs—bore a symbol consisting of a block letter *L* with a crossbar near the top and flames coming out of it. "It's just easier to wear Levitican-approved shit," he explained, "'cause of where I go in the line of duty sometimes."

"So you don't believe it?" Phil asked.

"Oh, fuck no," said Tom. "But they do. And it's real good clothing. Tactical."

They changed into bunny suits—but not before the cookie warden had beckoned Sophia and Anne-Solenne over to the refreshment table and asked them sotto voce whether it was, for either of them, That Time of the Month. Both answered in the negative and exchanged a look meaning *Let's just not even go there*. Later they could consult Leviticus as to what limits and penalties might apply to women who were on the rag.

"Oh, the KKK Libel. Good question. Glad you asked. That is one of the greatest misconceptions," said Ted, Son of Aaron (as he was identified on the name tag clipped to his 100 percent cotton tactical bib overalls). He removed his gleaming white hard hat as if the mere mention of the KKK Libel had put him at risk of blowing his stack. The warm summer breeze streamed through his thinning gray hair and might have evaporated a small fraction of the sweat streaming over his scalp. After a moment he glanced up as if checking the sky for an angry Jehovah. But nothing was there except blue sky strewn with fluffy clouds and the steel crossbar of a two-hundred-foot-tall cross. Not currently flaming. The pipefitters had not finished the work needed to conduct natural gas out to its system of burners. "My wife'll skin me," he remarked, "if we don't get under cover. Let's duck in here so I can set y'all straight."

"Why will she skin you?" Anne-Solenne asked curiously as they followed Ted into the shade of a pop-up canopy. Julian got distracted en route by three lambs gamboling in a makeshift chicken-wire pen.

"Melanoma," Ted answered. "Have to go into Iowa City." This remark was mumbled in a distracted way as he was getting a voice call, faintly and tinnily audible to them on the flip-up earplugs cantilevered out from the bows of his safety glasses. He indexed those down into his ears and answered the call, excusing himself with a nod and donning his hard hat as he stepped out into the sun and ambled over toward the livestock pen. His duties as Son of Aaron apparently encompassed not just construction management but inspection of sacrificial lambs.

A junior crew member bustled in to accommodate the visitors. He pulled a couple of folding chairs off of a stack and set them up at a folding table. This was strewn with printed documents kept from blowing away by rocks and ammunition magazines. He rearranged those to make a bit of space. "Y'all can help yourselves to water and iced tea," he said, nodding toward a pair of insulated coolers on a smaller table nearby. Until he spoke Sophia had guessed he was in his late twenties, but now she thought eighteen. "I'd fetch it myself but my hands is filthy." He held them up as proof and flashed a grin that would have been brilliant had his teeth been all present and not brown.

"Thank you so much, we will definitely help ourselves!" Sophia said loudly and distinctly, since the young man had his earplugs in.

"The reference to Iowa City?" Anne-Solenne asked. That was where they had stayed last night, in a boutique hotel next to a tapas bar.

"Where the big hospital is. So, another country to them. But they have to go there when they get sick. Like, to get a melanoma whacked off or whatever. They can't afford Blue State hotel rooms or food, so they have to camp out on the periphery and cook over propane burners under tarps. Not a fun time."

Anne-Solenne nodded. "Dentistry," she said.

"Ted has normal-people teeth because he is old and grew up before this part of the world got Facebooked. After that, the people with education fled to places like Ames, Des Moines, Iowa City. Which includes dentists. A few mainline churches used to run charity dental clinics where you could get a bad tooth pulled, or whatever, but those are being chased away by these people." Not wanting to be obvious, she glanced over at the gigantic cross. She took a sip of iced tea and grimaced.

"That bad?" Anne-Solenne asked.

"Sweet. Another cultural signifier. When we get to my aunt and uncle's place they'll serve it unsweetened, Northern style."

The two women walked slowly back to the table, taking in the scene. Over by the livestock pen, Ted was explaining something to Julian, who looked dismayed. Most of the space around the site was given over to parking for workers' pickup trucks. Not a single one had a license plate, but they were decked out with a range of stickers: a mix-and-match of Stars and Bars, Don't Tread on Me, and what Phil had designated the Full Moab: in the center, RE-MEMBER or REMEMBER MOAB or simply MOAB, bracketed between a mushroom cloud and a profile silhouette of a man with a bowed head. The latter was a direct cut-and-paste job from the black "Remember POW/MIA" flag, which was also ubiquitous around here even though no American POWs or MIAs had existed for decades.

"Now, let me take the bull by the horns as far as the KKK Libel." Ted had returned from inspecting the lambs. He set his weary bones down into a folding chair and indicated that the visitors should do likewise. Phil preferred to stand; he unzipped his paper coverall down to his navel, parted it to expose his chest, and stood sideways to them trying to catch the breeze. Sophia cataloged it as a microaggression, the hundredth today, not even worth noticing next to the twenty-story macroaggression that Ted and his crew were building. You couldn't wear underwear beneath the bunny suit because that would miss the whole point unless your underwear was made of Levitican-certified unmingled fiber, and hers wasn't, so her bra was down in a locker at the checkpoint and she couldn't unzip as Phil was doing. She sat down next to Anne-Solenne. Ted's nervous hands sorted and stacked documents—contracts, by the looks of them—as he calmly dismantled the KKK Libel. "Obviously you are not a white person, at least not one hundred percent," he said, evaluating Sophia, "and I don't know about *him*." He cast a glance over at Julian, who was down on one knee feeding a handful of grass through the chicken wire to a lamb. Julian was part Chinese. "There's been all kinds of confusion about the Leviticans." This was the church of which he was a priest. "Some kind of imagined link to the Ku Klux Klan."

"Maybe it's because of the burning crosses," Phil suggested, deadpan, gazing across a few yards of gravel to the massive concrete foundation from which the cross's steel verticals erupted.

Bracketed neatly to the structural members were the tubes carrying the natural gas from an underground pipeline. The actual burners didn't start until maybe twenty feet above ground level, maybe because they didn't want to roast parked vehicles. But there was a connection to an outlying altar, already dark with blood and buzzing with flies, including a sort of open crematorium that looked like it could get pretty hot.

"*Supposedly* the KKK burned crosses," Ted said with a roll of the eyes.

"There's no 'supposedly' about it," Anne-Solenne started in. "What are you even—that's like saying supposedly Muhammad Ali was a boxer. Supposedly Ford makes cars. It's—" But Sophia silenced her with a hand on the arm. There was no point.

"*If* that is even true, it has no connection to *our* burning crosses, which have a completely different significance," Ted announced.

Sophia said, "Okay. And that is?"

"So-called Christianity, as it existed up until recently, is based on a big lie," Ted explained. "The most successful conspiracy of all time. And it was all summed up in the symbolism of the cross. Every cross you see on a mainstream church, or worn as jewelry, or on a rosary or what have you, is another repetition of that lie."

"And what is that lie exactly?" Phil asked. He already knew. But he and the others all wanted to hear a living human actually say it, just as spectacle.

"That Jesus was crucified."

There. He'd said it. No one could speak. Ted took their silence as a request for more in the same vein. "That the Son of God, the most powerful incarnate being in the history of the universe, allowed Himself to be scourged and humiliated and taken out in the most disgraceful way you can imagine."

"'Taken out' means 'murdered'?" Anne-Solenne asked. It was a rhetorical question that Ted answered with the tiniest hint of a nod.

"The church that was built on the lie of the Crucifixion," Ted continued, "had two basic tenets. One was the lovey-dovey Jesus who went around being nice to people—basically, just the kind of behavior you would expect from the kind of beta who would allow himself to be spat on, to be nailed to a piece of wood. The second was this notion that the Old Testament no longer counted for anything, that the laws laid down in Leviticus were part of an old covenant that could simply be ignored after, and because, he was nailed up on that cross. We have exposed all that as garbage. Nonsense. A conspiracy by the elites to keep people meek and passive. The only crosses you'll see in our church are on fire, and the symbolism of that has nothing to do with the KKK. It means we reject the false church that was built upon the myth of the Crucifixion."

"So, to be clear, all Christianity for the last two thousand years—Catholic, Protestant, Orthodox, evangelical—is just flat-out wrong," Phil said.

"That is correct."

"The four gospels—"

Ted shook his head. "That's the first thing the church did, was enshrine those gospels. Telling the story they wanted to tell. About the meek liberal Jesus who gave food away to poor people and healed the sick and so on."

"And was crucified," Sophia prompted him.

Ted nodded.

"And . . . resurrected?" Anne-Solenne asked.

"They needed some way to explain the fact that He was still alive, so they invented all that resurrection stuff."

"So where'd Jesus go after that? What did He do?"

"Fought the Romans. Went back and forth between this world and heaven. He has the power to do that."

"Where is He now?"

"We don't know! Maybe here. He has been in eclipse for two thousand years. The conspiracy of the church was powerful. They staged a fake Reformation to get people to believe that reform was possible. All a show. Orchestrated from the Vatican."

"So, Martin Luther was running a false-flag operation for the Pope," Phil said. "In that case—" But he broke off as he felt Sophia stepping on his toe, under the table.

He looked down at her. Having caught his eye, she panned her gaze across the entire scene, asking him to take it all in. Reminding him that this wasn't Princeton. This was Ameristan. Facebooked to the molecular level. "Professor Long," she muttered, "the Red Card."

It was a reference to one of their teachers at Princeton who had gone so far as to print up a wallet card for people to keep in front of them during conversations like this one. One side of the card was solid red, with no words or images, and was meant to be displayed outward as a nonverbal signal that you disagreed and that you weren't going to be drawn into a fake argument. The other side, facing the user, was a list of little reminders as to what was really going on:

1. Speech is aggression
2. Every utterance has a winner and a loser
3. Curiosity is feigned
4. Lying is performative
5. Stupidity is power

They spent another quarter of an hour strolling about the hilltop, craning their necks to behold the outstretched cross arms, studded with nozzles that would soon hurl flame into the sky from sundown to sunrise. They gave the altar a wide berth; another Son of Aaron was in there whetting a long knife in preparation for today's bloody oblation. Julian, unable to meet the gaze of his new lamb friends now that he understood that they were only here to die, instead tended to look out over the surrounding countryside. North of them a few miles, he saw a blue water tower, and, near that, a Walmart sign.

The two-lane road was a chute between walls of corn that were already, in early June, as high as a man's head. Tom and Kevin's pickup blocked the view forward. In the rearview loomed an even higher pickup truck whose driver very much wanted them to know that they were not going fast enough. None of them said a word until they had parked in the Walmart's lot.

"I am gonna buy some flowers," Sophia said, "to put on the grave. We're almost there. Within the blast radius of this." She nodded toward the front of the superstore.

"Blast radius? Could you unpack that mysterious statement please?" asked Anne-Solenne.

"It's only ten miles farther. Any retail base in the actual town will have been obliterated by this. So if we want to buy *anything*, we have to buy it here."

They clambered down out of the SUV and tried to find a walking speed that would get them into its air-conditioning as quickly as possible without causing them to get hotter because of exertion. Phil was walking backward, staring curiously at the water tower: a thing he understood conceptually but had never seen on such a scale, since he had spent his life in places with hills.

Apparently cued by Sophia's reference to a graveyard, Julian had pulled his glasses down over his eyes and begun conducting research. Her grandparents had died and been put in the black soil sufficiently long ago that the details had found their way onto reasonably credible sites on the Old Internet—the Miasma, as many people in Sophia's life referred to it. The Miasma as such had fallen some years ago, but emulators of it were still running and could be browsed on what had replaced it, which was too ubiquitous even to have a name. In old movies sometimes you could see apparently sophisticated characters saying things like "I'm going online" or "I'm surfing the Internet," which must have seemed cool at the time, but now it was a non sequitur, as if someone, in the middle of an otherwise normal conversation, suddenly announced, "I'm breathing air."

"You can't possibly remember . . . Patricia . . . or John," Julian ventured, "but you must remember Alice."

"Grandma Alice died when I was twelve," Sophia confirmed.

"And she and John and Patricia are all buried . . ."

"Where we are going," Sophia said. "Yeah."

At last they had reached the entrance of the Walmart—or to be precise, one of its entrances, since it had been hacked up into a number of quasi-distinct storefronts. They got inside and just stood there for a few moments, allowing their bodies to recalibrate in the air-conditioning. Then they split up. Sophia and Anne-Solenne figured out how to buy flowers. Phil and Julian ransacked the snack aisle. Somewhere along the line Phil also picked up a tactical camo baseball cap, Levitican compliant. Having paid for their stuff, they went out and got back in the car. Tom and Kevin had peeled off and checked into a motel across the street and so they drove the last few miles into town without an escort.

Anne-Solenne shifted the flowers in her lap. "As long as we're talking about dead Forthrasts," she said, "where'd you-know-who end up? His fate is shrouded in mystery."

"No it isn't," Julian said, in the somewhat halting and breathy tone indicative of browsing and talking at the same time, "he died in—"

"I know when he died," Anne-Solenne said. "But because Sophia's from the weirdest family in the whole universe, that's different from his *fate*."

"We're breathing him," Sophia announced. That silenced the Land Cruiser for a little, and even caused Phil to push his glasses up on his head.

"His molecules, you mean?" Phil guessed.

"Atoms, more like," said Julian, getting the drift.

"So he was finally cremated?" Anne-Solenne guessed.

"He was cremated one ion at a time, by a particle beam scanning his cryogenically preserved remains."

"Probably a good thing," Phil mused, "otherwise the data—"

"Could be anywhere," Sophia said with a nod and a glance back in the mirror. "Yeah. I guess sometimes it's better to wait."

Anne-Solenne was still stuck on *We're breathing him*. "I never thought of it like that," she said, "but I guess the scanning process would generate—I don't know—"

"Exhaust," Sophia said. "Water, carbon dioxide, nitrogen, calcium. Theoretically you could capture the solids and hand it to the family in a baggie, but why?"

"So they just—"

"Blow it out a pipe into the sky," Sophia confirmed. "Given that it was Seattle, it was probably mixed with rain five minutes later, running through the storm sewers into Puget Sound."

"Which is no different from cremation," Julian hastened to

add, in his ponderous East Coast way. "Crematoria have smoke-stacks. We just prefer not to think about the implications."

This venture into the New Eschatology was cut short by their arrival in the small northwest Iowa town that the Forthrasts came from. And for people accustomed to the gradual penetration of vast cities, from the airport inward, arriving in that sort of town was jarringly abrupt. Suddenly they were just there—as there as they were ever going to get. The town had a central square: a single block planted in grass, with a vaguely medieval stone tower rising from the middle, and, flanking it, a statue each for veterans of the Civil and the Great Wars. A couple of huge deciduous trees cast shade over roughly circular areas, but the scattering of moms who had convened here to let their kids run around preferred to hang out under a shelter where they could sit at picnic tables. Across the street on one side was a courthouse and police station in rustic Victorian sandstone, with a broken clock in its central tower. Two sides formed an L-shaped district of indolent businesses. The fourth side was residential. Thirty seconds earlier they had been driving through cornfields, and if Sophia hadn't piloted the Land Cruiser into one of the angle-parking spaces along the square, they'd have been back in the corn thirty seconds later. "Leg stretch," she announced, "and I'm gonna turn off my cloaking device just so these people know what to make of us."

They had drawn curious looks from the moms in the park and some old-timers in a barbershop near their parking space. But, at a rough guess, half of the locals were wearing glasses, not merely to correct their vision but to fortify everything with data. Grandma Alice had liked to repeat an old joke that in a town like this, you didn't need to use your turn signals because everyone knew where you were going. It had become less and more true since she had died. Less because cars now made up their own minds as to when the blinkers should be put on, and more because you really could know everyone's business now, in a way that the small-town busybodies of Alice's generation could only have aspired to. The open and trusting culture of communities such as this one had carried over to the digital age. If you had a ten A.M. appointment with the physical therapist, everyone in town could know as much by checking your calendar, which could be accomplished just by looking hard enough at a widget floating above the car that was driving you there. Consequently, cars in a town like this, when seen through glasses, looked somewhat like old-timey sailing ships festooned with signal flags and aflutter with banners.

This all had to do with editors. If you were the kind of person who was enrolled at Princeton, you tended to speak of them as if they were individual human beings. The Toms and Kevins of the world, and most of the population of this town, were more likely to club together and subscribe to collective edit streams. Between those extremes was a sliding scale. Few people were rich enough to literally employ a person whose sole job was to filter incoming and outgoing information. For way less money you could buy into a fractional scheme, which was still very much a rich-person thing to do but worked okay for the 1 percent as opposed to the 0.001 percent. That was about where Sophia, Phil, and Anne-Solenne sat. Julian was stuck with his family's editor until such time as he went out and made a pile of money. Had he been unable to afford even that—had he been a full-ride financial-aid student—Princeton would have supplied him with a fairly decent editor as part of the same package that gave him room, board, and a library card. It paid off for the university in the long run not to have its less well-heeled students disgorging flumes of sensitive data into the public eye.

Direct, unfiltered exposure to said flumes—the torrent of porn, propaganda, and death threats, 99.9 percent of which were algorithmically generated and never actually seen by human eyes—was relegated to a combination of AIs and Third World eyeball farms, which was to say huge warehouses in hot places where people sat on benches or milled around gazing at stuff that the AIs had been unable to classify. They were the informational equivalent of the wretches who clambered around mountainous garbage dumps in Delhi or Manila looking for rags. Anything that made it past them—any rag that they pulled out of the garbage pile—began working its way up the editorial hierarchy and, in rare cases, actually got looked at by the kinds of editors—or more likely their junior associates—who worked for people like Sophia. Consequently, Sophia almost never had to look at outright garbage.

The more important and high-judgment role played by her editor was to look at any data coming the other way—sound and imagery captured by her glasses, for example—and make sure it never found its way into the wrong hands. Which basically meant it never went anywhere at all.

Maybe a few times a year, Sophia actually talked to her editor. This was one of those times. "I authorize you to put me in Family Reunion Mode for twenty-four hours," she said.

"Okay," replied her editor with an *It's your funeral* intonation, combined with a light overlay of *I hope your mother doesn't kill me*.

Anne-Solenne, Phil, and Julian reacted with a mixture of laughs and mock horror as, in their view, Sophia erupted with vivid displays of personal data, like a circus clown solemnly doffing her top hat to reveal a flower arrangement, a trained marmoset, and a confetti cannon mounted to her skull.

The gaffers in the barbershop and the moms in the picnic shelter had seen the Land Cruiser as just an old-school SUV, with no identifying markings save an escutcheon of dead bugs on the grille proving that it had covered much ground since its last wash. At this moment, however, it was lighting up, letting them all know who had just pulled into town and giving them limited, temporary access to Sophia's social media contrail. But all of that data was being exhibited with the color scheme, texture palette, typeface, UI conventions, and auditory cues—in sum, the art direction—of her personal brand. Before she opened the door of the car to reveal hairstyle, makeup, clothing, and accessories marking her as Not from Around Here, the same had been preannounced, to anyone wearing glasses, by the digital penumbra of Family Reunion Mode.

"Let's check out the park," she proposed, "this won't take long."

"Yeah—it's tiny," Phil said.

"That's not what I meant," Sophia chuckled. "I mean, my rellies will be here before you have time to get bored."

Crossing the street to the park, the foursome would have drawn stares from curious locals, had the curious locals not advanced to more sophisticated technology that enabled them to stare differently, by scanning all that Sophia had just made public. Without discussing it they went straight to the tower in the middle. This was made of the same buff sandstone as the nearby courthouse. It was just a folly, not a real fortification—only two stories high, with an upper deck surrounded by a crenellated parapet. A windowless steel door, painted Parks Department green, bore testimony to generations of bored teens' fruitless efforts to kick their way in—or, failing that, to attest to who sucked. A plaque next to the door supplied information they'd already seen in their glasses, which was that the tower had been erected by otherwise idle laborers during the Depression under the auspices of the Works Progress Administration. This seemed like the kind of historical/political minutia that Princeton kids ought to have heard of, so they all followed the inevitable hyperlink and spent a minute standing there reading about it. It was the sort of basically dead and inert topic that Wikipedia had actually been pretty good at covering, and enough time had passed that AIs had gone over all of this material and vetted it for mistakes.

Once they had got the gist, their attention drifted back to the here and now. Julian and Phil took turns reading the graffiti on the door, a palimpsest of slut shaming in which they found undue fascination and furtive amusement—exhibiting social, verging on moral, retardation that Sophia's expensive training had given her all the tools to perceive and to analyze but no weapons to change.

"What is the agenda?" Anne-Solenne asked loudly enough to silence the boys.

"Flowers on graves," Sophia answered.

"Let's go then," Phil said. "Because this place sucks." It was an index of his social deftness that he managed to announce this in a dry and almost stately manner that nonetheless made it understood that he was channeling the ancestral voices of all the boys who had stood where he was standing scratching imprecations into the green paint with pickup-truck keys.

"It's of the essence," Sophia said, "that I be seen doing it."

"Because, you know," Anne-Solenne added, completing the thought, "the people in those graves—"

"Are dead," Julian said, pushing his glasses up on his forehead. "They're not going to know."

Something flickered in Sophia's peripheral vision. She turned her head to see a sport-utility vehicle of the largest class, authentically bug spattered and road dusted, easing into a span of eighty-seven consecutive empty parking spaces. Visual stigmas pasted on it and hovering above it let her know that its sole occupant was Pete Borglund, fifty-six years of age, the second and current husband of Karen Forthrast Borglund, Alice's eldest daughter.

"One of your rellies?" Phil inquired. Just making polite conversation since the new arrival's privacy settings were so tatterdemalion that Phil could have traced Pete Borglund's mitochondrial DNA back to the Rift Valley with a few gestures.

"Yup," Sophia said.

"Uncle? Cousin?" Julian asked. Not currently using glasses.

"That is the billion-dollar question," Sophia said.

Phil made the faintest hint of a snicker. Not in any way a mean snicker. More of a preverbal marker to indicate, *I have familiarized myself with your tangled family history.*

"On the advice of my mother's attorneys," Sophia said, "I will not address him as Uncle but as Cousin."

The others turned their heads to study her face and see whether she might be speaking in jest. She did not give them any clues. Sometimes there was no gap between joke and real.

"Sophia!" Pete called as he approached, tactfully avoiding the use of any loaded terms. Pete was a lawyer who had finally succumbed to the inevitable and folded his practice in Sioux City to move here and look after the affairs of John and Alice's estate—a full-time job given that Alice had died a billionaire.

"Peeet!" Sophia called back, drawing it out in a way that implied more familiarity than was really the case. She had not seen him in five years. She began walking toward him, steeling herself for the awkwardness of the to-hug-or-not-to-hug dance. But some combination of Midwestern stiffness and lawyerly formality carried the day; when they were still ten paces apart, he extended his right hand to shake. He was silver-blond, ruddy, portly, wearing a suit and tie even though he worked alone in a farmhouse. "How's Princeton treating you?" he inquired. Which could have passed for a perfectly routine conversation starter, but she heard it as his saying, *Look, kid, in spite of all that happened, you're on easy street.*

"Well," she answered, shaking his hand, "and how's the estate treating you?" A slightly barbed response that he accepted with a forced smile.

"It is a never-ending source of tasks. Comparable to being a farmer in that way, I guess."

They let go of each other's hands and took a moment to regard each other. She found it impossible to hate him. "This is a pleasant surprise," he said. "Some of your . . . cousins and whatnot could take some pointers from you in how to better protect their privacy. I worry over them when they go off to college and people find out who they are."

Sophia let it pass with a nod. "My friends and I decided to see the country on our way out to the coast. I thought the least I could do was place some flowers on my grandmother's grave—and on Alice's."

There. She'd said it. Her mother's attorney in Seattle could not have phrased it better.

Pete nodded. "It would be my privilege to drive you there. Or you and your friends can follow me. It's only about a mile—"

"One point two."

Pete glanced away, a bit sheepishly.

"I'd love it if you would drive us there," Sophia said.

Pete heaved a quiet sigh. It was a sigh of relief.

14

Anne-Solenne, Phil, Sophia, and Julian all knew and would have acknowledged that by virtue of being enrolled at Princeton they were members of a globe-spanning, self-perpetuating elite caste. They would all end up making millions or billions unless they made a conscious decision to drop out, and even if they became ghetto-dwelling junkie artists they would do so with an invisible safety net. So Sophia's friends were almost eerily polite to the locals, starting with Pete Borglund and moving on, as the afternoon progressed, to Karen, to the Mexican-American caretaker at the grave site, and to various shirttail relatives, estate-running functionaries, and local dignitaries who came out to say hello and to accompany them on a tour of the house and of the creek bottom where the Forthrast boys had gone to play cowboys and Indians with live ammunition.

Eventually the visitors were treated to a thoroughly non-ironic dinner at an Applebee's. A gender-based split materialized at the table—actually two tables pushed together. Sophia saw it happening in real time but, like Pharaoh watching the Red Sea part, was powerless to stop it. She did a passable impression of giving a shit about the lady talk but was close enough to the man end to be a quasi-participant in their conversation. Pete asked a few questions to which he clearly didn't know the answers, and not in an interrogating way, but just out of curiosity. They were all strangely grateful to be in the presence of someone who was willing to be that vulnerable. Phil and Julian opened up, and so it was that Pete got the general story on how they had come to find themselves in an Applebee's in northwestern Iowa. The nominal purpose of the journey was to drop Sophia off in Seattle and then swing down the coast to San Francisco, where Anne-Solenne had an internship lined up. After that, Julian would wander down to L.A., and Phil would fly back to New York to spend his summer writing hedge fund code on Wall Street.

Thus briefed on the visitors' overall plan, Pete began to answer questions from Phil and Julian on how it all worked in this part of the world. The visitors were now thoroughly disoriented. They had barely had time to register their shock over the two-hundred-foot-tall flaming cross of the Leviticans—which was clearly visible from the Applebee's—before they had found themselves in this small and apparently stable town that, while a far cry from Iowa City, was definitely a Blue State pocket. It was completely surrounded by Ameristan but it was populated by people like Pete who had a college degree, asked questions, and seemed to be plugged into sane and responsible edit streams. Pete tried to explain it. "People like that," he said, cocking his head in the direction of the Leviticans' cross, "claim to believe certain things. But obviously if you spend ten seconds looking for logic holes or inconsistencies, it all falls apart. Now, they don't care."

"They don't care that their belief system is totally incoherent?" Phil asked. Not really asking. Since this much was obvious. Just making sure he was following Pete's line of argument.

"That is correct."

"Explains a lot!" Julian said.

"They can go a surprisingly long time without bumping up against reality," Pete said, "but at the end of the day when a pregnant mother needs a C-section or you can't get your Wi-Fi to work, or a thousand other examples I could give, why, then you do actually need someone nearby who can help you with that."

"So you have doctors and dentists in this town?" Phil asked.

"No, they all moved away years ago, but we have practitioners who can help patients get urgent care over webcam, get telerobotic surgery, and that sort of thing. Both men and women, since the Leviticans won't let male physicians examine female patients. And I could give other examples of the same general thing. Some percentage of their children are gay. Some percentage have an intellectual or artistic temperament. Those kids need a place to go. Ames and Iowa City are far away. So they find their way into town, move into abandoned houses, and live their lives. Now, if you ask the guys who are up on that hill building that cross, they'll quote Leviticus at you concerning gay people. But a lot of them have a child or a nephew or a cousin who's gay and who is hanging out in this town minding their own business."

"It's an accommodation, you're saying. Unspoken, unwritten."

Pete nodded. "It's not just that it's unspoken. It's that it *can't* be spoken of."

At Pete's invitation they ended up lodging at the farmhouse, paired up in two of the upstairs bedrooms. These bore faint traces of refurnishings, rewirings, recarpetings, and rewallpaperings beyond count. The most recent wave had apparently been aimed at getting the place back to some kind of historical condition thought of as pure: hardwood floors reexposed and finished, layers of paint scraped off the heavy door trim, wallpaper stripped all the way down to the original horsehair plaster, light fixtures and doorknobs that had either spent most of a century piled in a hayloft or been painstakingly manufactured to look that way. Sophia didn't have the talents or the sensibilities of a decorator, but she knew her critical theory, and as she lay awake on the iron bunk bed—now upgraded with an extra-firm Gomer Bolstrood mattress that had probably been slept on all of half a dozen times—she wondered about the way of thinking that held this one particular era of the house's history to be somehow canonical: the logical end state to which it ought to be returned and in which it then ought to be preserved by the flawed machine of Richard Forthrast's last will and testament. Between when it had first looked thus and the moment, a few years ago, when it had been returned to the same state, it had passed through who could guess how many intermediate phases of interior decoration. Almost all of these had been devoted to covering up—literally papering over—the simple bare rustic character that had now been expensively reinstated. Probably those decorators—various generations of Forthrast moms—had seen it as embarrassing and had sought to expunge it from their visual environments while spending as little money as possible.

When Karen—Pete's wife, and now the chatelaine—had been

assigning them to beds on the way back from Applebee's, she had quite naturally and reasonably assumed that Sophia would want to sleep in Patricia's former bedroom. Patricia had been the only girl in the generation that had included Alice's husband, John; Sophia's uncle Richard; and Jake, the straggler, the only one still living. Naturally John and Dodge had bunked in one room so that Patricia could have her own: a small, cozy third-story attic build-out with sloping walls. Upon reaching adulthood, getting married, and discovering that she was infertile, Patricia and her worthless husband had adopted Zula—Sophia's mother—from Eritrea. The husband had gone on the lam and was no longer spoken of. Patricia had then died young in a freak accident. Zula had been raised by John and Alice, with Richard always hovering around the edges as a favored, cool, transgressive uncle. She'd ended up in Seattle, employed by Richard's company. They had become close. Thus, when Sophia had been tiny, Richard had been her uncle/granddad. She still had memories of sitting on his lap reading books.

Three years ago, when she had been packing for the move out to Princeton, she had found the tattered copies of the D'Aulaires' Greek and Norse myths that he had given her shortly before his untimely death. Opening *Greek* she had found a dried maple leaf, still faintly reddish, and heard the story from her father, Csongor, about how Richard had slipped it in there only minutes before the medical procedure that had killed him. They had taken it to an art store to have it framed under glass, and Sophia still had it among her effects. In sum, to the extent that Sophia conceived of herself as being part of an extended Forthrast clan, it was all about Richard, and about her longing—which would never be satisfied, and never go away—for the relationship she might have had with him.

And so she had requested that Karen Borglund place her, and, by implication, Phil, in the room that Richard and John had once shared. Karen—acting as designated driver since Pete had indulged himself with two flagons of Miller Lite—had given her an amused, knowing look in the SUV's rearview mirror. "That room still has the original bunk beds," she warned, with the briefest flick of the eyes at Phil.

"We'll manage, thank you," Sophia said. "Did Richard sleep on the top or the bottom?"

"To judge from the graffiti carved into the underside of the top bunk, he slept on the bottom."

"As befits the younger brother," Pete threw in, being as puckish as it was possible for a podgy Swedish-Iowan estate lawyer to get.

"Is that graffiti still there?" Sophia asked.

Karen paused before giving the answer, and the back of her neck flushed. "No," she admitted, "it was on a sheet of what do you call it—"

"Masonite, sweet," Pete said.

"—that was laid over the—"

"Slats."

"—and supported the mattress. Which was just foam rubber. The whole thing had gone bulgy with age. I believe we took it to the dump. I can have Manuel hunt around for it."

"No worries," Sophia said, "I was just curious." Earlier her voice had betrayed a little too much eagerness, and now she was trying to walk it back.

"The names of girls," Pete informed her. "He would, I'm told, become very attached to certain young ladies, and then a breakup would occur for one reason or another, but they stayed on his mind for a long time after. He felt things deeply but didn't always show it, your uncle Richard."

After lying awake for a time in the lower bunk, hearing the slats creak as Phil settled into slumber above her, she reached over the edge of the bed, groped for her shoulder bag, and found the little flashlight she kept in an outside pocket. Rolling over on her back, she turned it on and played it over the blank sheet of plywood that had replaced the bulgy Masonite. There was, of course, nothing there except a layer of varnish. The slats themselves bore traces of carved words, but these had been painted over. All traces of Richard, or for that matter of Patricia or John or anyone else, had been expunged from the house. All of the history had been erased in Karen's earnest efforts to make the house historical.

Later, she got up and padded out of the room. To the embarrassment of Karen, the master bath—originally the only bathroom in the house—was out of commission, as some plumbing was being replaced. So the visitors had been relegated to a sort of gimcrack mini-bath that the father of John, Richard, Patricia, and Jake had shoehorned into a wedge of space under the attic stairs so that he would have a decent statistical likelihood of being able to take a crap in peace. Stepping into it was like time-traveling to 1970. Its autumn-toned daisy Formica countertop, its op-art wallpaper, its light fixture, even its shower knobs were straight out of a Nixon administration Sears, Roebuck catalog. Sophia made herself comfortable on the padded seat of its harvest-gold toilet and reflected that this was probably where Uncle Richard had taken his last piss before walking out the door in 1972 to head for Canada to avoid the draft. Though of course he'd have been standing up. Sitting down, she was looking directly into the door of the shower stall. Its walls were covered in little inch-square tiles with a sort of randomized pattern. The floor had been adorned with peel-and-stick daisies made of some grippy high-friction plastic, to prevent slip-and-fall accidents. They'd been there, silently waiting to perform their assigned task, for sixty years. The color, she guessed, had faded—these were daisies as reinterpreted and geometrically abstracted by one of those acid-dropping hippie artists who made album covers for the Beatles or whatever. Through some fascinating process of aesthetic percolation, they had made their way *here* of all places in the world. The colors were now pastels, but she guessed they'd started out as primaries.

She had brought her bag with her. Tucked into the end pocket was a folding multitool—a going-to-college gift from her uncle Jake. This detail empowered her, somehow, to do what she did after she was finished on the toilet, which was to crawl into the shower stall on hands and knees and get the blade of the knife under the edge of a nonslip daisy—the best preserved of all the specimens, only one of three that still had all of its petals, not directly visible from the toilet, bettering her odds of getting away clean. With care and patience born of insomnia she pried up each of the petals, one at a time, exposing fiberglass that had not seen light since the Vietnam War. Then she worried the circular middle loose. Finally it came free and she gazed at it delightedly on the palm of her hand; it was limned in grime rich with Forthrast biomass, smelling faintly of Comet. The rest of Uncle Richard's DNA might have been reduced to water vapor and air by the ion-beam scanner, but perhaps traces of it were still embedded in the slip-proof porosities of this artifact. She doubted she would ever make any practical use of it as genetic material, but it did make for a nice souvenir.

ovely people, but the weird was strong in that place," Phil announced as the town receded in the Land Cruiser's rearview mirror the next morning. He had swapped places with Anne-Solenne and was now riding shotgun, the better to see Tom and Kevin's pickup truck. During the night, Tom and Kevin had opened up the locker in its back, taken out the machine gun, and mounted it on the tripod. They'd kept it under a blue tarp until the caravan had got out of town, then pulled over onto the shoulder long enough for Kevin to hop out, remove the tarp, and take a seat atop the locker. For the time being, the barrel was still canted sharply upward and Kevin was keeping his hands off the controls. Apparently the sole point of all this was to make everyone in their vicinity aware that they were a hard target.

"Mmm," Sophia answered.

"Is this an okay time to talk about the finer points of estate law?" Anne-Solenne asked, swiveling around to cast a significant look behind them. Just a couple of car lengths to their rear, Pete's SUV loomed. Pete was driving. Most of its seats were occupied by men—a mix of extended family and servants—who were open-carrying a range of long and short guns. "Just so I have a basic TLDR-level grasp of the weirdness? Because those people are super nice and everything but I can tell that you are dancing through a minefield."

"Per stirpes," Sophia said, and then spelled it out. "Look it up. Read it and weep. Those of you who finish early may wish to refamiliarize yourselves with the storyline of *Bleak House*."

"Per stirpes" turned out to be a term of art, used in writing wills. It basically meant a scheme for dividing up an estate in which the money was split evenly among siblings (or, at any rate, people in the same generation of a family).

"Got the idea?" Sophia said, after she'd given them some time—a stretch of Iowa five miles or so wide—to digest it. "Richard's will basically said, 'Create two things: a foundation and a trust. Put some of my money into the foundation and use it to do cool stuff. Put the rest of it into the trust, which is there to provide a safety net for my extended family—so I don't have any grandnephews who can't afford to go to college or get medical care or whatever. Set up the trust so that the money is divided per stirpes among my generation.' He signed that will and then forgot about it. So far, so good. But then he proceeded to get much richer than he had ever imagined. The amount of money that was destined to be dumped into the trust became way bigger than was conceivably needed just for a safety net. It started to look like a ticket to easy street for everyone who could call Richard a brother, an uncle, or a great-uncle."

"The amount wasn't capped?" Phil asked.

"Should have been. But wasn't. One of many defects in the language."

"And I'm guessing he never got around to updating it?" Anne-Solenne asked.

"Wasn't in his nature."

"So, were people, like, just licking their chops and waiting for him to kick the bucket?"

"No, actually. Because he should have lived decades longer than he did. And anyway no one knew what was in the will until Corvus read it in the hospital."

"Corvallis Kawasaki," Phil explained. He'd learned that much, at least, from being Sophia's boyfriend.

"Seriously?" Julian asked. "Corvallis Kawasaki is, like, your family retainer!?"

Sophia met his eyes and thought he was looking at her in a new light. He raised both hands, palms up, and made a salaam gesture, or as best he could while belted in. Sophia took a moment wryly to imagine how C-plus would react to hearing himself described as a retainer.

"Okay," Phil said, impatient for drama. "So C-plus reads the will and does the math. Word gets out that this trust is going to be set up."

"Set up *by him personally,* because he turned out to be the 'personal representative,' or what they used to call the executor," Sophia said. "And C-plus was duty-bound to follow the language in the will. The per stirpes language meant dividing the trust money equally among Richard's siblings—or, in a case where a sibling had already died, the heirs of that sibling. So. One-third would be allocated to John and Alice, one-third to Patricia, and one-third to Jake. Or that was his intent when he signed the will."

"But Patricia was already dead?" Anne-Solenne asked.

Sophia nodded. "Patricia—my mom's adopted mother—was already dead."

"So her third of it should have gone to Zula—your mom—Patricia's heir?"

"Should have. Didn't. Because John and Alice had legally adopted my mom. And the law says that once you have been legally adopted by a new set of parents, you can't inherit from the previous set. So the trust was split two ways instead of three. Jake got half of it. Alice—because John was dead by this point—got the other half. Then she made a decision to split the trust up, not among her four kids—or five, if you count Zula—but among *their* kids, of which there are now a total of thirteen. So, I ended up with one-thirteenth of one-half of the trust."

"Instead of one-third," Julian said.

"The one-third that Richard probably intended you to get," Anne-Solenne added.

"Probably he was expecting *my mom* to get one-third," Sophia said. "I wasn't born yet. But yeah. That is basically the story."

A new thought had crossed Julian's mind. "Was this how C-plus and Maeve became interested in PURDAH and VEILs? Because of all these hassles over this one paper document?"

Sophia shook her head. "I would say not. I mean, this was all after the blockchain craze, and all of the issues related to anonymity and privacy on the Old Internet."

"Mmm," Julian said, going a little passive-aggressive on her.

"No, seriously," she insisted. "Again, it goes back to the language in the will. One of the stated missions of the foundation was to work on applications of gaming technology outside of what was conventionally thought of as the game industry. And to tackle social issues related to games. And a hot topic in those days, before the Fall, was that women in the games industry were subjected to a lot of overt harassment. And even when they weren't being harassed as such, their contributions just weren't taken seriously by gamer bros."

"Got it," Anne-Solenne said. "PURDAH was a way around that—any coder or team could use it to sign code."

"Code that would have to be evaluated strictly on its own merits—just like with any test essay or job app that we've ever turned in," Sophia said.

Phil had been silent for a little while, doing arithmetic in his head. "The difference between one-third and one-twenty-sixth is a number with a lot of zeroes," Phil said.

"Yeah," Sophia said. She was staring out the window. A smile came over her face. "And look. Here's the thing. At Princeton we talk a lot about privilege, right? Well, the reality is that Richard was so wealthy, and the amount of money that mistakenly went into the trust was so huge, that even one-twenty-sixth of it my share—is huge. I'll never have to work. I am fantastically privileged because of him. Those zeroes that Phil mentioned are pretty much meaningless. But it's still a huge number."

"What about the foundation?" Phil asked.

"Completely separate from the trust," Sophia said.

"Your mom runs it," Julian reminded her.

"The saving grace of the will," Sophia said, "was that it named John as the director of the foundation. If he was deceased, and if my mom was old enough, then she was to become the director. He was. So she did. She's been running the Forthrast Family Foundation for the last fifteen years. She's been drawing a salary. Nothing crazy. There are all kinds of rules around conflict of interest and so on."

"How's that going to affect your little plan?" Anne-Solenne asked.

"You mean, my little plan to spend my summer working for the Forthrast Family Foundation?"

"Yeah. Isn't that a conflict of interest or something?"

"Not the way I'm doing it."

16

Tom turned on his four-ways and let the Tactical (as they now referred to the pickup truck with the machine gun) coast to a stop on the shoulder of the road, just at the crest of a gentle rise in the land. Topography around here was subtle, but a long picket line of wind turbines, running approximately north-south, hinted at some kind of ridgeline. The maps in their glasses gave them a hint as to what was going on, and they confirmed it by climbing out of the Land Cruiser and walking up to the place where Tom and Kevin had parked. From there it was possible to look west across the valley of the Missouri River, separating this part of the state from Nebraska to the west.

The SUV had stopped behind them. Formerly gleaming and sleek in a chunky, huge SUV-ish way, it was now a cluttered beast of burden with two ladders strapped to its roof rack and a flatbed utility trailer, laden with tarp-wrapped consumer goods, trailing behind. Most of its occupants remained in their air-conditioned seats but Pete came out for a chat. He was strapped with a holster that was mostly inside of his khaki trousers but allowed the handle of a semiautomatic pistol to show above the waistline. He caught Sophia looking at it as he approached. "It's like a cheese head," he explained.

"Huh?"

"Packers fans wear big silly hats shaped like wedges of cheese. Why? To show affiliation. All of this"—he waved vaguely toward the machine gun in the back of the Tactical, then patted the grip of his pistol—"is to announce, to anyone looking at us from a drone, that we speak their language."

"You're members of their tribe."

"I wouldn't go that far, but it's a way of saying that, A, we can be talked to, and B, we are not to be messed with."

"It's . . . disarming to be armed?"

"Exactly."

Kevin had been staring at output from their drone while Tom scanned the sky around them for drones operated by other people. He was gazing fixedly at one such. It was too small and far away to be seen with the naked eye. Apparently, though, his goggles were running some kind of augmented ware that enabled him to know of its existence and, in some sense, "see" it.

He slid them up on his backward baseball cap and turned toward Pete. "What's the word, boss?"

Microaggression. Sophia had hired Tom and Kevin to escort them to Sioux City, but now that a middle-aged white guy had entered the picture, suddenly he was "boss." Sophia was getting ready to say something when she noticed Pete watching her face wryly. Pete held up a placating hand. "I have taken the liberty of hiring these fellas for the extra job that needs doing," he explained.

"Okay," Sophia said. "I was kind of wondering why you were following us in the war wagon. Assumed you were just being courteous above and beyond the call of family duty."

"We *do* try to extend courtesy," Pete said.

"Noted. Appreciated."

"But there is this other thing that has come up. Across the river. *Just* across the river."

"Do I get to know what it is? Now I'm all curious."

Pete looked ready to say no but then thought better of it. "You might hear about it from Jake. I know you are headed out to Seattle and that you might cross paths there. I don't want you to feel left out. So, yes. You get to know what it is." Pete exchanged nods with Tom, then continued: "You know that Jake has this ONE thing."

"The Organization for New Eschatology."

"Yes. His nonprofit." Unsaid by Pete, because Sophia was the last person on earth to whom it needed to be explained, was that the entire financial empire over which Pete presided on behalf of Alice's estate, vast as it was, was actually somewhat smaller than that controlled by Jake. Dodge's estate had been split down the middle between them. But whereas Pete invested his half in utilities and real estate, Jake put his money into weird bot-controlled investment vehicles that reputedly brought a higher rate of return. He appeared to spend a lot of the proceeds on the nonprofit known as ONE, which was his way of wrestling with matters religious and spiritual. Before suddenly becoming a billionaire he had lived in a compound in northern Idaho and practiced a fringy kind of Christianity; since then, he had been reaching out and talking to all kinds of people who held beliefs of varying levels of weirdness. On the whole, it felt like he was becoming more sane over time, which was good as far as it went. But the way Pete had said *You know that Jake has this ONE thing* caused Sophia to brace herself for some manner of appallingly strange wacky Jake news.

"Yeah. They have, I guess you could call it an outreach program aimed at the Levitican types. He tries real hard not to use the M-word."

"M-word?"

"'Missionaries.' He feels like he can sort of speak their language a little bit, because of Idaho."

"Okay."

"So, now that Jake has sort of come in from the wilderness and started living a more, I don't know, settled and responsible life, he feels like a legitimate thing for ONE to be doing is to be maintaining some level of contact with some of the weirder sects out there. The people around where we live, even the hard-core Leviticans, you know they come into town to get teeth pulled or what have you, so we have some amount of day-to-day contact with those people. But over there"—he waved his hand vaguely at Nebraska—"some of them have really gone off the deep end."

"You mean, they have gone off the deep end *compared to people who build two-hundred-foot-tall flaming crosses next to the Applebee's!?*" Sophia asked.

"Yeah," Pete said, laconic for once, allowing Sophia's imagination to have her way in the ensuing silence. "So believe it or not he knows people through ONE who are actually willing to go into places like that and have conversations with the people there."

"Or exchange words with them at any rate," said Sophia, recalling the Red Card.

"Point being," Pete said, "one of those people is across the river at the moment, not that far away, and Jake called me last night to say that they had lost contact with this individual and that they have drone video suggesting that he might be in serious trouble. He asked me if I might consider going across the river today and in a peaceable and neighborly way trying to sort things out."

"You control more money than the Roman Empire at its peak," Sophia reminded him.

"Yup."

"Don't you have people for this?"

"At times like this, the 'Ameristan' label becomes more than just a clever bit of wordplay," Pete said. "Think Afghanistan or Pakistan. How does it work there? They have warlords. The warlords are big men, respected just because they are big men. If the big man shows up to a parley, it's a gesture of respect and it helps to calm things down. If the big man sends a lackey, it can . . . have the opposite effect."

Pete Borglund, warlord. It was such a bizarre juxtaposition that it shut Sophia up for a little while. He turned his attention back to Tom. "We pretty much have to go to Sioux City anyway, because of where the bridges are."

"We could pay someone to ferry us over," Tom pointed out.

"I don't want to mess around with those ferry guys. Too sketchy for me. I'm a fan of bridges."

"Okay. Bridges it is."

"That works out great for these guys," Pete said, nodding at Sophia and waving at the Land Cruiser. "Sophia and her crew can hand the LC back over to you guys and jump back into the car they sent ahead. Then we can use the LC as part of our caravan across the river."

Tom nodded. Sophia didn't. Pete's plan made perfect sense. But now she had this feeling of people going on an adventure to which she clearly was not invited.

"If sending a warlord is a gesture of respect," she said, "isn't it even more respectful to send a warlady too?"

. . .

The warlady insisted on swapping places with one of the lackeys in Pete's SUV who was qualified to take her place behind the wheel of the Land Cruiser. She didn't even want to think about what the conversation was like in that vehicle. But here in Pete's SUV, the topic was the wild tribes across the river and their practices.

The two-laner they'd been following westward T'd into the interstate highway that ran north along the east bank of the Missouri for some miles up to Sioux City. In most of the country, being on an interstate meant that you were in sane and settled territory—it was the network that linked the reality-based nodes of society. The vacancies between—the interstices between the intersections, as Dr. Johnson would have it—were the domain of the fantasists, subsisting on an intoxicating mélange of homemade pharmaceuticals and hallucinatory memes.

Humans were biology. They lived for the dopamine rush. They could get it either by putting the relevant chemicals directly into their bodies or by partaking of some clickbait that had been algorithmically perfected to make brains generate the dopamine through psychological alchemy. It was not a way to live long or to prosper, but it was a way of being as ineradicable, now, as the ragweed that flourished in the roadside ditches. The people of those interstitial spaces had as free access to the interstate highway system as the reality-based drivers commuting between Omaha and Sioux City, and so it was that the sleek electric cars, gliding along under autopilot at exactly the speed limit, served as traffic cones for the careening human-piloted ethanol-burning behemoths of the Ameristanis. By and large the latter tended to go either much faster than the speed limit (when paying attention) or much slower (when staring at screens or lost in AR goggles), and so they either wove slalom courses around the smart cars or else gave the latter's algorithms a stiff workout by forcing them to brake and plot courses around distracted slowpokes. Their little warlord caravan was neither one nor the other; human piloted, but by humans who were actually good drivers.

To see a Tactical on an interstate was not normal. The usual practice would have been for Tom and Kevin to dismount the machine gun from the tripod, or at least throw a tarp over it. But they'd specifically said, back in Des Moines, that it was needed for the last few miles of the journey—this part right along the Missouri River, with Nebraska in plain view off to the left. So Sophia, riding shotgun, couldn't help gazing off in that direction, scanning the opposite bank of the great river for—what? What could be over there that would create a need for such precautions? They were still in flat Midwestern country. The river ran sluggish and brown between gentle banks for the most part, with no dramatic gorge to be gazed across. Much of the time she couldn't see anything except trees between the road and the riverbank. When she could look across, she saw mostly trailers, parked in clusters and compounds on the floodplain opposite, with boats of various descriptions strewn around on the muddy banks. Kind of an extremely spread-out linear slum, then, that somehow derived sustenance from the river. Barges moved up and down that, using it as cars used the interstate: a way of getting between more prosperous places.

"They'd be river pirates if they weren't so hopelessly outgunned," Pete explained, noting her interest. "But they can still hole up in the tall grass and snipe at river traffic from half a mile away. So there's an understanding in place. A protection-money kind of thing. The watermen buy trinkets or eggs or just fork over money as an out-and-out payoff. The people over there refrain from sending high-velocity rounds their way."

"Do they ever cross the river?"

"When they get desperate or some meme convinces them it's a good idea. They follow these weird edit streams. No one knows where they come from. I looked at one of them once. I thought it would be conspiracy-theory stuff but it wasn't even coherent enough to be called that."

"Hmm. Yeah, I guess the whole point of a conspiracy theory is to offer a kind of false coherence."

"That's right, Sophia, but what I saw didn't even rise to that standard—didn't even *know* about it. It was—well, just plain weird. Algorithmically generated mishmash images, sounds . . . no sense to it at all. Just whatever *worked*, you know, in the sense of getting the viewer to watch a little more. They use eye tracking, you don't even have to click. But every so often, whoever's behind it—whoever generates these edit streams, assuming, that is, that there's a human *anywhere* in that loop—will put it into the minds of those people, and then bad things can happen." Pete glanced at the Tactical as if to add, *But not to us.*

Sophia now finally cottoned on to something, which was that she and Pete had been having the same conversation the whole time. She wanted to join him on his foray across the river. He was basically opposed to it. But the Midwestern style was indirect and passive-aggressive. So instead of saying no he and the other men in the SUV were just trying to scare the crap out of her. Or—another way of putting it—to make sure she knew what she was playing at.

That stretch of the drive wasn't long, and soon they were in the liminal zone outside of Sioux City where the vehicles of the Ameristanis began to peel off as if the city were emanating a repulsive force field only they could sense. They made a few moments' detour through a Walmart parking lot, where Kevin threw a blue tarp over the machine gun so that they could pass through the city proper without offending local norms. The opposite bank of the river was visible here as the stream was circumventing a line of bluffs. Atop them, posted where it would be conspicuous to people who, like Sophia, were looking across the river, was the occasional religious site. The people over there had erected crosses, singly or in little clusters. Not huge ones like the flaming cross of the Leviticans, but more folk-art productions that looked like they'd been knocked together in a couple of hours from tree trunks or four-by-fours. Their simple lines were cluttered and complicated by stuff hanging off them. Sophia made sense of it as follows: These people were akin to the Leviticans they'd seen yesterday, but they didn't have the money or organizational acumen to make natural-gas-fueled crosses out of structural steel. So they built them out of whatever they could scrape together in the way of lumber, wrapped them in rags, soaked them in fuel, and burned them at night.

Traffic across the bridge was limited to one vehicle at a time because it had been structurally weakened by tens of thousands of bullet impacts. Driven by the inscrutable algorithmically generated memes that dominated their edit streams, locals would from time to time gather on the opposite bank to empty mag after mag of 5.56-millimeter rounds into the underpinnings of the local infrastructure. As Pete put it, "Their fathers believed that the people in the cities actually gave a shit about them enough to want to come and take their guns and other property. So they put money they didn't really have into stockpiling trillions of rounds and hunkered down waiting for the elites to come confiscate their stuff. There's no use for any of it. So they come here sometimes and 'vote with bullets.'"

In some sections of the bridge, where there was overhead steel-work, they could see the circular impact craters, so closely spaced that they merged into one another and gave the steel a hand-forged patina, as if blacksmiths had gone over every inch of it with ball-peen hammers. But most of the steel, and most of the damage, was under the bridge deck. Anyway the civic authorities on this side of the river had erected a guardhouse at the base of the ramp that led to the bridge and piled dirt behind it to stop any rounds coming across the river. A man in a bulletproof vest was posted there whose job was to space out the traffic so that only one vehicle was on the span at a time. Though he seemed to have a secondary function as well, which was to chat with the occupants of each vehicle and make sure they knew what they were getting into, and were not just tourists being horribly misled by Google Maps.

The car they'd parted ways with in Des Moines had tracked them down on the riverbank, not before putting itself through a mostly automatic car wash and recharging its battery somewhere, and so Julian and Phil and Anne-Solenne were able to transfer their overnight bags into the back of it and clamber into its freshly vacuumed and wiped-down interior. There was a note on the driver's seat from Ahmed, the valet who had performed those parts of the detailing not yet deemed suitable for robots, in which he beseeched them to favor him with a tip if the quality of his work had exceeded expectations. Phil did so by staring at the note and muttering. The others climbed in and looked expectantly at Sophia, which was when she broke the news to them.

. . .

They did not have a clear fix on their destination at the time they crossed over the bridge, one at a time, waiting on the far side for the caravan to reassemble. The Tactical went over first, and Kevin made use of the wait to shrug on a flak jacket and a helmet.

They waited. Flanked by two armed Pete-minions, Sophia took a stroll through a sort of open-air bazaar that had formed around the western approach to the bridge. It comprised about half a dozen RVs, pretty clearly no longer capable of movement, bedecked with blue tarp awnings lashed down against prairie winds by straining ropes attached to concrete-filled tires. Bulletproof panels, held down by rocks and cinder blocks, covered the roofs and were leaned against west-facing surfaces. On plastic folding tables, vendors had put out for display a range of goods produced on the east side of the river: diapers, hardware, snack foods, motor oil. The commerce seemed to be one-way; nothing was being produced in Ameristan that was desired outside of it. Zula, Sophia's mother, had spoken once about the way that Midwestern farmers had slowly, over generations, beggared themselves by producing commodities. She and Jake had gone in together on a few business ventures intended to create distinct local brands that, like the various cheeses of France, might fetch higher prices in coastal grocery stores: producing pancetta instead of bacon, and so on. But chemistry was chemistry. Ethanol was ethanol, high-fructose corn syrup was high-fructose corn syrup, and so on. So economic competition here was a war of all against all, and the only winners were people in cities who wanted to buy that stuff for as little money as possible.

A lot of people around here were evidently running some kind of drone-detecting app, because when a drone came in—which happened every few minutes—they all turned to look at it long before it could be seen or heard by Sophia. Glasses couldn't do that on their own, so the apps must have been networked into other drones, or something, whose sole purpose was to detect drones. Most of them were beefy cargo carriers, capable of hauling a couple of bags of groceries, apparently dispatched to pick up orders at the bazaar. But half an hour after they'd crossed the bridge, a smaller one came in, made a couple of quick orbits around the area, and then came in for a landing on the hood of Pete's SUV. Zip-tied to it was a mobile phone of a type that had been ubiquitous when Sophia was born. Pete unfolded a pocket tool and snipped it free. The drone flew away. Presently a call came in and Pete, listening, began nodding and waving his free hand in a way that set everyone into motion. More flak jackets and helmets were pulled from the back of the SUV.

"These precautions seem like too much and too little at the same time," Sophia remarked as she was shrugging one on. "I mean, this is great if someone just shoots at us with a gun. But what about IEDs? Mortars?"

"Those would obliterate us," said Eric, her second cousin once removed. He was studying aerospace engineering at Iowa State, home for the summer.

"So . . . ?" She climbed into a second-row seat of the SUV.

"Drone and satellite coverage is good enough to warn us of any IED-type shenanigans. And they just don't have artillery, other than some homemade crap."

"It's not an actual military," said her great-uncle Bob, twisting around from the front seat where he was, literally, riding shotgun. "If you were setting up a *real* military, here's what you *wouldn't* do: you *wouldn't* issue every single guy his own collection of fifty-seven different small arms and an infinite quantity of ammunition *and nothing else.*"

"Got it," Sophia said.

"Pipe down," said Pete, who was climbing in next to Sophia in what she guessed was the approved Warlord Position: right side of the middle row. He was in communication with someone important and desirous of a little more solemnity. So the vehicle became silent except for Pete's making sporadic utterances in response to tinny bursts that they could vaguely overhear but not understand.

"No. No. Yes. Yes, we have all of the stuff on the list—like I told the other guy ten minutes ago, and the guy before him. Jeff. All of it. Yes, we have all of it. The Wet Wipes. Metric Allen wrenches. I need you to send me a picture of our guy just for confirmation. Yes, I understand he has seen better days. I know what you did to him. I am not going to freak out. Just anything that confirms he is still alive. It's about respect, you know? That's all I am asking for. Like Aretha Franklin. Who is that? Never mind. Bad joke. I said, never mind. She was a singer. Sang a song about respect. Yes, that one. Yes, yes. I prefer to use the term African-American but have it your way. You sent the picture? I haven't received anything. It was a video? Well, that's going to take fucking forever. While I'm waiting for that to download, what is our next turn? This road is blocked by what appears to be a pile of burned cars. We're still going to the elementary school, right? Yes, I understand it's no longer a school. Okay, then Google Maps should still get us there. Hang on, I'm going to take the phone away from my head for a few seconds—I think the video came through and I need to take the phone away from my head so I can watch it. I won't be able to hear you. Don't hang up. Stand by."

Pete lowered the phone into the sweet spot of his reading spectacles and wrestled fruitlessly with its UI, which had been terrible twenty years ago. He caught Sophia trying to sneak a peek and actually flinched as he angled the phone away from her. The video had no soundtrack except for the hugger-mugger of prairie wind buffeting a microphone. Sophia had copped a brief glimpse but it hadn't been what she'd expected and so she was still trying to make sense of it. She'd expected an unshaven Methodist zip-tied to a lawn chair, or something of that genre, but instead had seen a weird silhouette against bright sky, foreshortened and stretched out in a way that triggered a memory she couldn't quite nail down.

"We're good to go," Pete announced, clapping the phone back to his head. "Yes, Joseph, I already told you we have the Wet Wipes. All one hundred pounds. Spring Breeze. Like you asked for. Okay. Okay. See you there, Joseph."

Pete hung up and then noticed Sophia looking at him strangely. "Joseph has hemorrhoids," he explained.

Apparently a key part of the ceremony was that Pete had to go to where this Joseph character was currently hanging out and deliver the Wet Wipes and have a beer with him. Joseph's base of operations turned out to be a former school on the edge of an abandoned town. The playground had become an RV encampment ringed by portable toilets that were no longer portable in that they'd been hooked up to a system of PVC pipes that ran over the ground without any clear destination; they must have led *somewhere* but the terrain was so flat it wasn't obvious which way gravity would take them. The school building proper was occupied by people of higher status. Joseph must have been in there somewhere. But Sophia would never actually know. For, being female, she was not invited. Upon arrival she was trotted out like a homecoming queen at a Rotary Club meeting and introduced at a great distance. Then she got back in the SUV, which bucked and clunked as the trailer was detached from it and simply abandoned in a parking space that was still marked, in weathered paint, as being reserved for the school nurse. Sophia never got to meet the hemorrhoid-plagued chieftain or to see his lair. But Pete came back out half an hour later smelling faintly of cigarette smoke and Bud Light. In one hand he was carrying a bouquet of locally sourced ditch daisies, which he handed off to Sophia—apparently a token of Joseph's esteem for the warlady. Then he peeled off a pair of blue nitrile gloves he'd pulled on before getting out of the car "because you never know about residues." He fastidiously turned these inside out and then used one of them to withdraw from his shirt pocket a new cell phone that was displaying a map. "Let's roll," he said. "Our guy is five point seven three miles away and was alive and conscious thirty minutes ago when they put him up."

It was an interesting 5.73 miles—especially the last .73 miles or so, as they climbed to the top of a rise that had, judging from bullet-tattered signs, been a county park at one point. More recently it had become one of those cult sites where people put up crosses, bundled them in fuel-soaked rags, and burned them at night.

Or so Sophia had been telling herself for most of the day, ever since she had spied a row of these things on the far side of the Missouri. Even then, a skeptical voice in the back of her mind had told her that the hypothesis didn't totally add up. But she'd been too preoccupied with breaking events to pay much attention.

As they came out of a stand of big oaks and maples and broke out into windswept prairie near the brow of the hill, she saw the truth, which was that people had actually been nailed to those crosses and left to die. The lumpy silhouettes she'd seen against the western sky were what remained of those people after bugs, birds, and bacteria had been at them for a while. Bones and synthetic clothing held up pretty well; cotton blue jeans rotted but spandex underwear lasted forever.

Something like a dozen of these things were spaced at intervals along the road as it wound up to the top of the hill. Sophia went into shock after the first one and didn't return to full awareness until they were pulling into the broken asphalt parking lot at the scenic overlook that topped the hill. Three crosses had been erected here in what was either a meaningless coincidence or a shout-out to the biblical Calvary. Loose bones and skulls were strewn about, commingled with empty beer cans and shell casings. Evidently these crosses were of special significance and so there was a waiting list or something. They were not single-use; space occasionally had to be made for new occupants. All three looked to have been built at the same time (maybe a year or two ago?) by the same work crew. They'd used sturdy glulam beams and joined them at the literal crux with galvanized nail-on brackets, just like framing a suburban home. The one in the middle, and the one to its right, had been occupied for a while and there was not much left of the people who'd been nailed up. They were both men. One was dressed in a black polyester suit that had stood up well to the elements. Nailed to his right hand was a Bible. A clerical collar dangled from one lapel, fluttering in the wind. The corpse to his right was in a formerly white shirt. To his hand was nailed a Book of Mormon.

The third cross was occupied by a living human. As Sophia got out of the SUV and looked up at him, she experienced a moment of déjà vu. Earlier, Joseph's crew had sent Pete a video of this guy as proof that he was still alive. Shot from below, it had put Sophia in mind of a picture she'd seen in an art history class. Now, standing in the same place, finally she was able to place it: *Lamentation of Christ*, a study in perspective and foreshortening by an Italian Renaissance painter.

The victim watched curiously as Pete's men went to work removing the ladders from the SUV's roof rack.

No one had spoken to him yet. Pete was busy texting a sitrep to Uncle Jake. Sophia said, "Hello. Jake sent us. We have worked out a deal to take you out of here."

The victim's breathing was ragged and laborious. He contracted his arms, pulling himself up a few inches, and expanded his chest enough to croak out: "The ladder. Under my feet please."

"He wants something under his feet!" Sophia exclaimed to the guys who were taking the ladders down. The victim's feet were at about the altitude of her face and she forced herself to look at them, expecting the worst, but they hadn't been nailed, they were just dangling. The men slammed a ladder against the vertical and then raised it up from beneath until the victim could get his feet on it. He then stood up and took a deep breath and let out a great sigh of relief.

"Initiate Nail Removal Immediately," he said. "Sorry. Old joke."

"On it!" said Cousin Eric, exhibiting a brand-new crowbar, painted bright yellow and encrusted with safety warnings and legal explication.

"There are all these details and nuances connected with crucifixion that I suppose no one knows about anymore, until they reinstate the practice and relearn how it works. It turns out that it's asphyxiation that kills you," said the victim.

"Is that right!? You don't say!" Pete remarked, seeming genuinely fascinated.

"I *do* say," the victim returned. He had some hard-to-place accent in which "say" came out like "sigh." "So if they nail your feet, you actually die slower."

"Because you have something to push off against?" Sophia guessed.

"Top marks," said the victim. "You're the one who's at Princeton. Jake talks about you."

"And they didn't nail your feet because they wanted—" Pete continued.

"To go easy on me, I guess. Quick death by asphyxiation. Either that, or they ran out of nails."

Attention turned, for a while, to the nitty-gritty details of decrucifying this employee of Jake's. The cross had been socketed into an aboveground framework bolted together with slotted angle irons, rising to about midthigh on Sophia. Only gravity was holding it there, and so they decided to get all hands around it and lift it straight out. Then they set it down on the parking lot, still vertical, and Sophia braced the butt of it with her foot while the guys walked it down. The victim was now supine, breathing much easier. Sophia walked up to that end of the cross and squatted down next to him as the men hemmed and hawed about how to remove the nails without the crowbar's crushing his wrists. For the nails had been driven not through his palms but through the complex of bones where the forearm joined the hand.

"If you have a hacksaw or better yet something like an abrasive cutoff wheel you could simply remove the heads from the nails. Then I could lift my arms right off. My name is Enoch. You'd be Sophia. I'd shake your hand but—"

"Maybe later," Sophia said. "What is that nailed to yours? Doesn't look like a Bible."

"Oh, it could be almost any book," Enoch said dismissively. "I didn't have one on me—unusual for a missionary, and confusing to them—so they took one at random from the library of that school."

"It's *The Boys' First Book of Radio and Electronics* by Alfred Morgan," Sophia said.

"Oh, that's a good one!" he said. He turned his head to look at his left wrist. "You see what I mean?" he said to Eric. "They had a disagreement as to the correct pressure setting on the air compressor."

"They used a nail gun?" Pete said incredulously. "Lazy."

"Of course they did! It's very laborious hand-driving a sixteen-penny nail into glulam. They like guns. Tap, tap. Done. My point being that if the setting is too high, the nail goes all the way through, which spoils it. You'll note that—experienced crucifixionists that they are—they dialed it back so that it only went in part of the way. Plenty of leeway there for you to get a hacksaw under the head."

. . .

An hour later they were back across the bridge in Sioux City. Sophia had been envisioning a helicopter ambulance or something, but the fact of the matter was that Enoch wasn't that badly hurt. Each wrist, of course, had a puncture wound all the way through, but apparently the nails found a way between the little bones and so it was all soft tissue damage. The swelling looked dreadful and had turned both hands into stiff purple mittens— when they gave him a bottle of Dasani, he had to trap it between his palms, like a bear—but there simply wasn't a lot to *do* medically. Jake had arranged for doctors to be there, and they took him to the local trauma center just for the sake of form. But, other than the wrists, he was fine.

"Where next?" Enoch asked Sophia as they sat in a waiting room in the X-ray unit. "Oh, Jake mentioned you were on a cross-country trip. Which come to think of it would be fairly obvious even if he hadn't mentioned it."

"Uh, well, before all this happened, we were just going to keep driving west. South Dakota, Colorado, Wyoming . . ."

"I don't suppose I could talk you into making a little southerly detour?" Enoch asked. "To Moab." He shrugged. "Business there."

The detour would add a couple of days to the journey. They raised, then eventually dismissed, the obvious questions: Couldn't Jake just get Enoch a plane ticket? Or, come to think of it, a whole plane? Why was Enoch now their problem? What kind of weird stuff had he been up to among the Ameristanis, and would he turn out to be an insufferable weirdo during the two days they'd have to spend in the car with him?

They went out for coffee. While they stood in line at Starbucks, Phil asked Enoch point-blank: "What are you? Not just some regular Joe, apparently."

Sophia gave him side-eye. Enoch noticed that and raised his eyebrows in an amused way. "It's *perfectly* all right!" he assured her. "One so rarely gets a direct question." Then, to Phil, he said, "As far as I can make out, I am an emissary of sorts from another plane of existence."

They all had a laugh.

"Tell us about this other plane, it sounds fascinating!" said Anne-Solenne, totally buying into the joke.

"The problem is, I can't seem to remember it very well."

"Aww!"

"Oh, don't pout! It's not my fault. This plane is made of different stuff, organized in a different way, and so none of my memories transfer over directly."

"Like when you have to convert code from Python to C++," Julian suggested, getting into the spirit of it.

"You would know better than I, Julian," Enoch said, "but the upshot is that the best I can really manage is to try to help sort things out as best I can on *this* plane. Oh, I'll have a grande flat white, whole milk please—I like to live dangerously." Then he looked down at his hands, which were mummified in ice packs. "And a straw."

Having determined that he wasn't a total weirdo—or at least the wrong sort of total weirdo—they said yes to the idea of giving him a ride, on the general principle that this was meant to be a freewheeling coast-to-coast adventure, and as such it seemed like incorrect form to say no to this reasonably amiable chap who had, only a few hours ago, been nail-gunned to a glulam cross. So they piled into the car—which was now a bit crowded—and laid in a course for Moab. Which ought to have been as simple as laying in a course for any other place. But a little warning did come up on Sophia's UI, letting her know that the existence of Moab was in question. Opinions differed as to whether it had been burned off the surface of the world by a nuclear blast twelve years ago.

This peeved Sophia to no end, and so once she had slapped the warning out of the air and confirmed the destination, she took the unusual step of making a voice connection to her editor, Janine. Janine worked out of Orcas Island in Puget Sound and was a junior assistant to Lisa, who was the editor of Sophia's mother, Zula. That was for a reason. If you had a good relationship with an editor, you wanted to stick with them your whole life, and Lisa was of an age that she would probably retire while Sophia was in her thirties. Janine, on the other hand, was only a couple of years older than Sophia. "How was Nebraska?" was how she opened the conversation.

"Super weird. But I was just calling to report an anomaly."

"I'm all ears!" Janine said. "Let me rewind your feed so I have it before me . . ."

"Okay, let me know when you—"

"Oh, whoa!"

"See it?"

"Yeah! Holy crap, how did that get in there?"

"My theory is . . ."

"Because of where you've been the last couple of days, the people you've shown interest in . . ."

"The Leviticans . . . maybe even some of the Forthrasts, who knows . . ."

". . . some algo got the wrong idea about you."

"It's easy to forget," Sophia remarked, "that there are millions of people who really don't believe that Moab still exists. But when you're here, you see the REMEMBER MOAB stickers all over the place."

"It's pervasive—super sticky—somehow it sneaked into your feed. Crazy!" Janine said, in a somewhat distracted tone suggesting that, while she held up her end of the conversation, she was swimming through clouds of visualized data.

"I just thought that it was so funny," Sophia said, "given that—"

"You know Corvallis and Maeve personally, they are family!"

"Exactly."

"Well, this is super-useful feedback!" Janine said. "And I am so glad you took the trouble to bring it to my notice."

"I knew you'd feel that way," Sophia said.

"I'll do some diagnostics and let you know if I see any more of this kind of material trying to creep into your feed."

"Great!"

"And I took the liberty of shutting off Family Reunion Mode."

"Oh, thanks. I totally forgot."

"I figured those crucifixion geeks didn't need to know everything about you."

"Good point. Well played. Thanks again."

"Have a great drive to Moab! Thunderstorms ahead—will alert you!"

"Thanks!"

"Bye!"

"Bye."

"What were you *doing* among those people?" Phil demanded to know when enough time had passed that he felt he could address Enoch in his usual blunt, familiar style.

Enoch, hands bundled in ice packs to hold down the swelling, was seated in the middle of the backseat for the simple reason that he could not operate the car's door handles or seat belts and so required help from flankers.

"You're a missionary?" Phil demanded. He was in the driver's seat at the moment, and even though he wasn't actually driving, this seemed to confer on him a certain driverly authority.

"Oh, I don't think that missionary-style activity would work very well on those people," Enoch returned.

To the others this might have sounded like informed speculation, but to Sophia, who, earlier today, had seen the remains of two actual missionaries nailed to crosses, it came off as just about the driest possible witticism. Seated to Enoch's left, she face-checked him just to see if he was fucking with her. But he couldn't have been more unreadable. He had a red beard on a face with some history, and gray hair swept back from his forehead. "If you're going to try to get people to change the way they think, you have to offer some kind of value proposition, and that's hard with these people."

"Why these people in particular?"

"Well, you know, let's say, for example, you're trying to sell a tribe of Bronze Age shepherds on monotheism . . . you begin with, 'Okay, chaps, there's lots of different gods, but if you go all in with this one particular god, you're signing on to a winning squad, you're going to defeat the other tribes and control more grazing land.' Which works, because they have an orderly sheep-based economy in which the rules of the game are clear and everyone can agree on basic ideas such as 'If our animals eat more grass we have a better time of it.' But *those* people, the people across the river, are in a very unsettled state and nothing really makes sense to them, and so trying to get them to buy into a coherent world-view of any sort is a mug's game."

Julian translated: "Bronze Age shepherds may have been just one step above cavemen, but at least they were reality based."

"Very much so," Enoch agreed. "And that goes on being more or less true for quite a while. Now, theater, and later movies, eventually get us into the realm of shared hallucinations. But those are neatly boxed in both space and time, and there's a bit of ceremony to them. You buy the ticket, you enter the theater, you sit down, the lights dim, everyone in the place shares the same hallucination at the same time, lights come back up, it's over, you go outside. Even old-school TV had some of that."

"The TV was this big piece of furniture in the living room," said Anne-Solenne, getting into it. "You sat down at eight P.M. to watch *I Love Lucy* or whatever."

"Yes. It's really only since wireless networks got fast enough to stream pictures to portable devices that everything changed," Enoch said, "and enabled each individual person to live twenty-four/seven in their own personalized hallucination stream. And if you are still tied to reality by family or by some kind of regularizing influence in your day-to-day life, like having a job, then you've got a fighting chance. But those people—" Since it was awkward to gesture using ice-packed mitts, he pointed out the side window with his chin. "My goodness. Religion as such—as it has existed and flourished for thousands of years—doesn't stand a chance."

"Why doesn't it stand a chance?" Sophia asked. "Can you elaborate? Remember, my friends didn't see . . . what I saw."

"Well, most religions add a supernatural overlay, something fantastical and imaginative, to the physical reality that everyone sees. Everyone sees the lightning bolt; religion adds the Zeus, standing on a mountain and hurling it. And if you are a Bronze Age shepherd of low to middling intellect and little imagination, well, that is a mind blower right there—the charismatic priest who can tell you that story with panache is really onto something, career-wise. Mutatis mutandis, same goes for other religions. They had a monopoly on the fantastical. Science fiction and fantasy combined with a revenue model."

"Revenue model?" Julian asked sharply.

"Sacrifices, tithes, donations to 501(c)(3)s."

"Gotcha."

"But each person out there"—Enoch did the thing with his chin again—"is getting their own personalized stream of algorithmically generated alternate reality that is locked in a feedback loop with their pulse, blink rate, and so on. You're not going to get very far trying to get one of those people to tear his attention away from that so that you can relate a story about some guy two thousand years ago feeding a large number of people with a few loaves and fishes."

"But they crucify people!" Phil protested.

"You don't have to remind *me*," Enoch said, greatly amused.

"That's a Bible thing."

"That's the cream of the crop who are doing that," Enoch said. "The one percent. That's Joseph and a few dozen of his handpicked elite. People you could actually have a conversation with. The other ninety-nine percent don't know anything about Leviticus and they don't understand or care about the theology—the repudiation of the doctrine of the New Covenant and the idea of Tactical Jesus. They just know that you had better do what Joseph says, or else. And Joseph for his part gets to claim with a straight face, to anyone who cares, that his approach to law and order has a kind of divine authority."

"So who are you in all this? Why's Jake paying you to risk your life?" Anne-Solenne asked.

"Yeah, I didn't catch your last name," Julian added.

"Oh, don't bother Googling. Root is my last name. But it's a nightmare on Google because it's an old name that has been in the family forever and so you'll be pulling up stuff that goes back centuries."

"Count of Zelrijk-Aalberg," Julian muttered, having already ignored Enoch's admonition not to bother.

"Yes, there is an old family connection to that place."

"One of your ancestors . . ."

"Was a mathematician. Yes," Enoch said, getting clipped and impatient as Julian continued sifting through old dead Enoch Root hits.

"Julian!" Sophia barked, and caught Anne-Solenne's eye.

"Yeah, Julian! Snap out of it. Rude, boring."

"Okay, okay . . ."

"I have had some dealings, back in the day, with the Water-houses and the Shaftoes, and more recently with Elmo Shepherd," Enoch explained, "and through Elmo I met Jake Forthrast, who imagined that I might be of use, or at least of interest, to his spiritual research. So I am an adviser to ONE and I interpret my responsibilities broadly and some would say creatively."

"Some would say a little *dangerously!*" Sophia put in.

Enoch considered this as if it were a novel idea and gave just a hint of a shrug.

"Oh, cool! Fractals," Julian muttered.

"*Julian!* Fuck's sake," said Anne-Solenne.

"Math major?" Enoch asked him.

"CS and math," Julian returned.

"I'll bite," said Sophia. "What is the connection to fractals?"

"One of Enoch's ancestors was, like, the great-great-granddad of fractal geometry," Julian reported. "In 1791—"

"Oh, god, *please* don't read the Wikipedia entry," Enoch said, showing more emotion than when he had been literally crucified.

"I have an edit overlay that filters out most of the garbage," said Julian, mildly offended that Enoch had taken him for the kind of person who would actually take Wikipedia at face value.

"But, Julian, *I am sitting right next to you and so you don't have to consult an online source.*"

"True that," Julian admitted, and finally shoved his glasses up on his forehead just before Anne-Solenne, flailing at him from the front seat, could claw them off.

"So, this place Zelrijk-Aalberg straddles the border of Belgium and the Netherlands but has never quite belonged to either of them," Enoch reported. "It makes Andorra look like Siberia. Its total size is barely large enough to play a regulation game of cricket—supposing that all of its territory could be collected into a continuous oval. But it can't. The length of its borders is enormous compared to its area. Someone described its map as a doily that had been attacked by moths. It encompasses eleven separate enclaves that are *not* part of Zelrijk-Aalberg. Four of those are Belgian and seven Dutch. One of the Belgian enclaves contains a Dutch subenclave, and one of the Dutch enclaves contains no fewer than four subenclaves, of which one is Belgian and the remaining three are all parts of Zelrijk-Aalberg proper. The largest of those contains a Belgian sub-subenclave consisting of a single root cellar measuring one by two meters."

"Do they sell a lot of fireworks there?" Phil says. "This is jogging a memory of when I was driving around Flanders with my family and we came across this incredibly illegal-looking fireworks stand in the middle of a town."

"Most of its revenue, until recently, came from selling fireworks that were illegal in the neighboring countries," Enoch agreed. "What Julian here is referring to, with the fractals, is a thing that happened when a former count of Zelrijk-Aalberg paid a visit to the property to engage in the ancient custom of beating the bounds."

"'Beating the bounds'?" Phil asked.

"Oh, this I've heard of," said Anne-Solenne. "They do it in London, and other old places with complicated boundaries. Once a year, an entourage of bigwigs walks the circuit of the property line and beats it with sticks."

"Since Roman times," Enoch said, "the boundary of Zelrijk-Aalberg has been litigated over in documents that, were they all stored in one location, would more than occupy all of the available space in the country. Many of those made references to landmarks such as trees that had died centuries ago, creeks that had changed their courses over time, or buildings that had not existed since the days of Charlemagne. Lacking modern conveniences such as GPS, the locals had fallen into the habit of using available landmarks to define the boundary. Every so often the count of Zelrijk-Aalberg would walk that boundary and beat said landmarks with a stick as an aid to memory, just as Anne-Solenne says. On one such occasion, this count—who happened to be mathematically inclined—was making his way across a tavern that straddled the boundary. The tavern had a tile floor with a long crack running across it. It had become an accepted fact that the crack constituted part of the boundary. The tavern actually dates to the 1170s and the crack is mentioned in a legal document, handwritten on vellum in the Year of Our Lord 1219. So, the count was sidestepping along this crack, whacking it with his ceremonial stick while his lawyers and servants looked on, when he got to noticing that it rambled this way and that, as cracks are wont to do, and that if one bent down and stared at a small portion of it through one's lorgnette, one could see smaller ramblings superimposed on the larger ones, and so on and so forth. As a sort of practical joke he instructed a surveyor to calculate the precise length of this part of the boundary, taking into account all of its turnings this way and that. In less time than it took for the count to drink a tankard of beer, the surveyor had produced an answer. The count disputed the figure, threatened to strike the surveyor with his boundary-beating stick, and commanded him to measure it again, this time on his hands and knees using a ruler. In the meanwhile the count consumed another beer. The surveyor turned in a revised figure that was somewhat larger. The count renewed his threat and ordered him to repeat it a third time using a magnifying glass and a set of fine calipers."

"So, that's fractals in a nutshell right there," Julian said. "The point being that the length of the crack—"

"—and hence of Zelrijk-Aalberg's border—" Enoch added.

"—doesn't actually have any one fixed value that can be known. The result of the measurement will depend on the resolution of the measuring device used."

"This particular ancestor of mine didn't actually live in Z-A, or visit it that often. He had an estate in Germany that was a thousand times as large. After all of this happened he went back there and wrote a paper about it, which was forgotten until the 1960s, when it came to light in the course of a dispute about who had first invented certain concepts from fractal geometry."

With that it seemed as though the four Princetonians had arrived at the collective determination that Enoch was cool. Much older than them, to be certain, and with little in common, but definitely one of the gang for the next day and a half.

Any number of further questions could, of course, be asked of this man: where he had come from, how he had spent his career, and so on. And indeed some such questions did get asked as the sun swung slowly round into the west, coming hard into the windshield, and took its sweet time skidding toward the flat horizon before unceremoniously plunging behind a line of black thunderheads. Enoch's answers tended to be vague, brief, and self-deprecating. He had a knack for segueing into some other topic that was invariably more interesting than whatever had just been asked of him. Consequently you could ask him questions all day long. But at the end of that day, you'd have spent three minutes getting answers and many hours talking about other things—and you'd prefer it that way.

The car was perfectly capable of driving through the night as its occupants slumbered, but it was cramped, and so they pulled off the interstate into a little oasis and hustled into the lobby of a chain motel just as wild fat drops of rain were beginning to smack down, exploding like water balloons, driven on sage-scented winds. The place had been built to serve as a truck stop back when trucks burned liquid fuel and were piloted by humans. Now it had adapted by turning into an automated facility for people traveling as they were. The rooms themselves hadn't changed in a quarter of a century, but the interface for checking in and paying for them had been ripped out and replaced by much newer and more gleaming systems. So it all looked good on the way in but was appallingly gloomy once you actually got into the room. It was, in fact, the sort of room you could only tolerate when your eyes were closed.

Sophia wasn't going to close her eyes for a while, partly because she wasn't that tired, but also partly because she was afraid of what she would see in the nightmares she assumed must be coming. She walked back down the long corridor to the front of the building, where there was a common area serving in lieu of lobby, restaurant, and bar. And in lieu of human staff there were vending machines. Enoch Root was there; he had already availed himself of a hot dog and a Heineken. "I had my eyes on the Szechuan noodle bowl," he remarked, "but couldn't work out how to manage the chopsticks."

Sophia got the noodle bowl and a bottle of flavored seltzer and sat across the table from him. He had got rid of the ice packs, so his fingers were now all peeking out from tunnels of bandaging that in turn peeked out from the sleeves of a black hoodie. He had the hood up, maybe to shield his head from an air-conditioning system that was still on full blast even though a prairie thunderstorm was frosting the windowsills with BBs of white ice. This gave him a monkish aspect and, combined with the weird purple-green light of the storm and the frequent flashes of lightning, made the lobby seem like one of those roadside inns where Dungeons and Dragons campaigns invariably kicked off.

"Enough about me," Enoch said, though they hadn't talked about him at all. "What is your plan? I get that most of you have internships lined up on the West Coast?"

"Yes, and I am one of those," Sophia said. "I get off in Seattle. The others will go south to the Bay Area."

"Seattle. Your hometown?" he asked, just for the sake of politeness, since he already knew this.

"Yes."

"Your parents are looking forward to seeing you, I'm sure."

"They don't know I'm coming."

"Then they are in for a delightful surprise."

"I hope so. I've been sort of pulling the wool over my mom's eyes."

"Oh? How so?"

"Well, my first choice for an internship was the Forthrast Family Foundation. But I didn't want to be seen as having obtained the position because of the family connection. So I applied anonymously."

"Using a PURDAH."

"Yeah."

"But that must be a routine procedure for an organization as enlightened as the FFF."

"Oh, certainly. I just didn't mention anything to my mom."

"How remarkable," Enoch said, "that of all the interests a brilliant young lady such as you might pursue, you landed on one that is *best* pursued at the Forthrast Family Foundation."

"Your tone of voice, Enoch, suggests you don't really see it as a coincidence." Sophia laughed.

"My tone is only meant to convey curiosity."

"Well, of course, it's not a coincidence," she admitted. "How much do you remember, Enoch, from when you were four years old?"

He smiled. "That was a long time ago."

"Well, that's all I have of my uncle Dodge. Richard Forthrast. Those kinds of ill-formed memories. Just a few images. Moments."

"You are speaking," Enoch said, "of the man whose brain was the first to be scanned using a fully modern procedure." Which of course Sophia knew perfectly well. So the same words could have come across as mansplaining. But Enoch managed to deliver them in a mild tone and with respectful, inquiring glances as Sophia, making it clear that he was in fact working with her to move the conversation forward. "A procedure that was carried out by the FFF and that yielded a database—"

"The DB. Dodge's Brain."

"—that has been the cynosure of brain researchers ever since. You are one of those, I take it."

"A brain researcher? Not exactly. I guess I'm coming at it more from the digital than the analog-slash-biological side."

Enoch nodded. "You want to go into Dodge's Brain with computational tools and—do what?"

"Well, it's already mid-June. Two months from now I'll be staring at a blank screen, getting ready to write up my findings. Supposing there *are* any."

"Not a lot of time to delve deep."

"Frankly, a waste of time if that's *all* I'm going to do," Sophia admitted.

"No more so than most summer internships," Enoch confided in her.

"What I'm really aiming to do is to tee up a senior thesis project."

"Ah."

"And if I can show progress on that, a year from now, when I graduate, then hopefully it segues into grad school or a job."

"You're igniting a career."

"Gotta start somewhere."

They were interrupted by a brilliant lightning flash and a slow rolling thunderclap that took forever to settle down. Enoch seemed to take it as a cue to shift gears. "Suppose all of that comes to pass, Sophia, and you get that job and embark on that career. Twenty years from now, how will you know if you have succeeded?"

It was not a question she had ever asked herself and so it wrong-footed her. First because she lacked an answer and second because of slow-building embarrassment. She should have thought about this. She'd never done so.

"It's okay," Enoch assured her after her silence had grown awkward. "Few people actually make decisions on that basis. I was curious in a more general way about the big questions. Where it's all going."

"Brain research, you mean?"

"Oh, that's been going on since at least Tom Willis. I am referring to the branch of it that seems to aspire to becoming a consumer product."

"Bringing brains back to life in the cloud," Sophia guessed.

Enoch nodded and turned his head to gaze out the window into the storm. "I'm a go-between. On the one side is Elmo Shepherd, who believes fully that brains can be simulated—and that once the simulation is switched on, you'll reboot in exactly the same state as when you last lost consciousness. Like waking up from a nap. On the other side is Jake, who believes in the existence of an ineffable spirit that cannot be re-created in computer code."

"What do you believe, Enoch?"

"Jake's opinion is based on a theology I do not agree with. But like a lot of theologies it can do duty as a cracked mirror or a smudged lens through which we might be able to glimpse things that are informative. I don't know about an ineffable spirit, but I do have a suspicion that there are aspects of who we are that will not come back when our brains are scanned and simulated by the likes of Elmo. It's not clear to me that memory will work, for example, when its physical referents are gone. It's not clear that the brain will know what to do with itself in the absence of a body. Particularly, a body with sensory organs feeding it a coherent picture of the world."

"The picture has to add up," Sophia said, just thinking aloud. "It has to be a coherent and consistent rendering of the world."

"Of *a* world, at any rate," Enoch said.

The storm passed over at some point during the night and they awoke to a clear sunny morning, much cooler than yesterday. After a vending-machine breakfast and robot-brewed coffee, they got back into the fully charged car and headed west. It would be all interstates, all day long, until they got to the turnoff for Moab. Compared to the traffic they'd seen yesterday on the road to Sioux City, this had fewer and fewer vehicles of the Ameristani type the farther west they went. The western plains had been tough to live on even in the cooler, rainier heyday of white settlement and were now well on their way to becoming a desert. They simply couldn't support that many humans, and the flat land and sluggish rivers held no appeal for recreationalists or builders of vacation homes. It was drive-over country. Wind turbines were gradually supplanted by photovoltaic farms as the day went on and the Rocky Mountains began to crumple the horizon. During the morning, as they hummed across the plain at the car's maximum speed, the four Princetonians "worked," which meant that they lost themselves in a stew of academics, internship prep, and whatever their editors threw at them in the way of news, social media, and entertainment. Sophia "drove" and Enoch rode shotgun. For, since he lacked glasses and had nothing to do besides stare out the windshield, it seemed polite to let him have that seat. They had a sophisticated and cosmopolitan lunch in downtown Denver followed by a couple of hours' traversal of the Rockies: a mosaic of expensive recreation opportunities, speckled with little high-density communities where the servant class dwelled in prefab homes. Then back down into the rough-and-tumble desert of the Intermountain West, no less hostile than what lay east of the Rockies, but far more rewarding to look at.

"Case in point," Enoch said to Sophia, apparently picking up last night's conversation where it had left off. "You and I are sitting, what, about a meter apart, looking at *this*." And he did not have to explain that *this* was the extraordinary scenic panorama of Glenwood Canyon. A human driver would have slowed down to enjoy it, but the car's algorithms seemed to take it as a challenge and treated it as a slalom course. "We're not just *seeing* it, we're *feeling* it!" he half-joked as everyone was slammed leftward by an abrupt right curve. "Literally feeling it in our bones. The geometry of it, and of our trajectory through space-time, made manifest in our inner ears, in a way that could never by faked by virtual or augmented reality. And it's all perfectly self-consistent, what you're experiencing and what I'm experiencing, so that our understandings of the world tally. I keep trying to get Elmo to understand that the brain *needs* this—that if this kind of coherent world isn't supplied, why, then not only can *I* not talk to *you,* my own brain can't even talk to *itself* from one moment to the next."

"Aaaand case in point," said Phil, who was sitting in the middle back. He flipped his glasses up on his forehead, the better to see a thing looming above the road ahead.

They had emerged, abruptly and conclusively, from Glenwood Canyon and come out into a more open valley containing the crossroads town of Glenwood Springs. From here a highway doubled back east toward the elite paradise of Aspen. Travelers who, like them, chose to continue west toward Utah were confronted by an animated mushroom cloud rising from the interstate's median.

Billboards in the traditional sense had gone the way of gas stations and ashtrays. Much cheaper and more efficient was to target the audience with personalized messages that would show up in their glasses, and those messages had better be interesting and germane or else they'd be filtered out by even the most bargain-basement edit stream. If you really wanted to put something up by the side of a road that *everyone* could see with the naked eye, then a stationary holographic projection system was a better bet, on every level, than erecting a physical object. Those could pose a fatal distraction to human drivers. But humans didn't drive much anymore and so the only real objection that could be mounted against holographic billboards was that they were tasteless and annoying. Standards as to that varied. It could be inferred that, in the municipality of Glenwood Springs proper, good taste prevailed, lest one-percenters en route to Aspen be displeased by vulgar displays and decide to hurry down the road and buy their coffee in some place easier on the eyes. But west of town was some kind of invisible boundary on the other side of which anything was permissible. And someone had taken advantage of that by putting up this multimegawatt holograph of an animated mushroom cloud running on infinite loop and surmounted by yellow block letters proclaiming THE TRUTH ABOUT MOAB!

This turned out to be the first of several such advertisements spaced at intervals along the hundred and sixty miles to the Moab turnoff. It became clear that there were at least two different Moab-truther sites vying for their eyeballs and their mindshare: a "visitor center" and a "museum." Both were founded upon the premise that Moab had been obliterated and its obliteration covered up by a vast global conspiracy. Both seemed to be very much for-profit tourist traps in the threadbare trappings of old-school nonprofit institutions. In addition a third attraction seemed to await them; this was much less heavily advertised, and such branding as it did have was understated in a way that Sophia associated with National Public Radio. It was called either the Moab Official Welcome and Information Center or the Nest of Lies, depending on your edit stream. It could be inferred that it had been put there by members of the reality-based community, perhaps bolstered by infusions of cash from a desolate Moab Chamber of Commerce.

The closer they got to the turnoff, the looser the local regs—assuming there *were* any—concerning signage, and the more desperate the competition grew. The last mile looked like an effects-laden movie or video game cut scene depicting an all-out, no-holds-barred global thermonuclear exchange. They turned off onto the two-laner that would take them the last thirty or so miles into Moab and almost immediately passed between the two competing truther establishments, which, compared to their advertising, looked despicable and forlorn, swallowed up in gravel parking lots lightly peppered with RVs and school buses.

Half a mile farther along was the Nest of Lies, a newish prefab building sporting a lot of bullet holes. Or to be precise, dents, since it seemed, on closer viewing, to be bolted together out of something with a lot of layers, a materials science tour de force that could stop most rounds in common use. A single car, a sensible sport-utility vehicle, was parked where it would be shaded by a photovoltaic panel during the hottest part of the day. At the moment, though, it was exposed to low late-afternoon sunlight. Out of some sense that the place was worthy of their patronage, Sophia overrode the car's nav program and guided it into a spot near the sport-ute. That vehicle's license plates were not issued by Utah but by the Municipal Authority of Moab. And Sophia—who had been reading about this—already knew why. The Utah state legislature had been taken over by Moab truthers who insisted that Moab had been obliterated by nuclear terrorism twelve years ago. From which it followed that anyone claiming to actually live there was a troll, a crisis actor in the pay of, or a sad dupe in thrall to, global conspirators trying to foist a monstrous denial of the truth on decent folk. In recognition of, and indignation over, which they had passed a law ordering the state licensing bureau to stop accepting motor vehicle paperwork from Moab. Unable to register vehicles in Utah, the people of Moab had begun printing their own plates, which had actually become a status symbol and desirable swag item in faraway places and produced revenue for the town until being buried under knockoffs. Anyway, the owner of this sport-ute lived in Moab.

They got out of the car, stretched, toddled around on stiff legs, made use of a portable toilet. Sophia approached the front door of the main building and heard it being buzzed open.

"Welcome to the Nest of Lies!" said the sole occupant, a woman in her—forties? No, probably mid-to-late thirties and simply not interested in any of the available technologies around hair, attire, skin, and makeup that might cause her to look younger. She had a short haircut that she might have done herself. She wore glasses of the old school, which is to say that they were nothing more than corrective lenses. Through them, she was reading a novel printed on paper.

"Thanks," Sophia said.

"Is it your intention to keep driving south into town?"

"You mean Moab? Yes."

"Then you know it exists."

"Yeah, I've actually been there a few times."

"Did you drive in or fly in, those times?"

"Flew."

"Okay. Well, as you drive in, you're going to see roadblocks. One or two, depending on time of day. They're not real. You don't have to stop. Just turn off your autopilot and drive slowly through them and ignore the bros with guns waving their arms." The woman recited all of this in the intelligent, matter-of-fact tones of a park ranger explaining what to do if you saw a bear. "They'll get out of your way and they won't actually fire on you or anything like that. If there's any trouble, here's how to communicate." And the woman licked her finger and pulled a sheet of paper from the top of a stack of printouts, then used a pair of scissors to cut off a strip about two inches high. She slid it across the counter to Sophia. It listed strings of codes and characters. Other than that and the book in the woman's hands—a recent translation of *Beowulf*— there was no other paper in the place. The walls were equipped with literature racks, and a couple of spinning racks stood like broken columns in the middle of the floor, but all were empty.

Seeming to read Sophia's mind, the woman said, "If you put your glasses back down over your eyes you'll see the equivalent of brochures for tourists."

"Got it," Sophia said. "We're just going to drop off a passenger though."

"Well, welcome to Moab," the woman said, "and have a safe drive."

"Is there any reason we wouldn't?"

"No, it's just a polite expression."

It came to pass just as the woman said: five miles farther along, at the end of a long straightaway, a few dusty pickups and old-school

SUVs were parked almost-but-not-quite blocking the road. To either side, roughly parallel courses of yellow plastic tape connected makeshift fence posts, extending for some little distance into the desert until the fence makers had lost their savor for the job. Someone had erected a rude arch of lumber over the road and, at its apex, nailed up a sheet of plywood painted highway-sign green and blazoned in hand-painted white letters:

> DANGER
> RADIATON
> NO ADMITANCE

About the time they got close enough to read those words and to begin remarking upon the misspellings, the car's autopilot became concerned about the clutter on the roadway ahead, emitted a warning tone, and slowed down. Sophia shut it off and assumed manual control, then, for good measure, stifled any additional warning beeps that might be forthcoming.

On an RV parked by the side of the road, a door flew open and a man, still in the act of shrugging an assault rifle over his shoulder by its strap, pounded down an external staircase and turned to face them. Watching on the other side with only mild curiosity was an older man standing before a smoking steel drum and using tongs to flip hot dogs. The one with the rifle strutted into the road and began waving both arms above his head. Following the instructions from the woman in the information center, Sophia kept the car moving at maybe five miles per hour and simply drove around the guy, slaloming around a series of barriers that did not quite block the road and passing into the uninhabitable radioactive wasteland beyond. The road negotiated a few curves and dips that limited visibility for a while, and then came out in full view of a Starbucks.

"What was it like before?" Sophia asked Enoch a few minutes later, after they had all got drinks at the drive-thru. The autopilot was back in effect and they were heading toward the relatively bright lights of Moab, still a couple of miles distant. She was thinking about the woman reading the book in the information center. About the whole idea of information centers. About information.

"Depends on how far back you want to go," Enoch pointed out.

"Just saying that for everyone else in this car the post-Moab world is basically all we've ever known. Where people can't even agree that this town exists."

"What was it like when people agreed on facts, you mean?" Enoch asked. He seemed a little amused by the question. Not in a condescending way. More charmed.

"Yeah. Because they did, right? Walter Cronkite and all that?"

Enoch pondered it for a bit. "I would say that the ability of people to agree on matters of fact not immediately visible—states of affairs removed from them in space and time—ramped up from a baseline of approximately zero to a pretty high level around the time of the scientific revolution and all that, and stayed there and became more globally distributed up through the Cronkite era, and then dropped to zero incredibly quickly when the Internet came along. And I think that the main thing it conferred on people was social mobility, so that if you were a smart kid growing up on a farm in Kansas or a slum in India you had a chance to do something interesting with your life. Before it—before that three-hundred-year run when there was a way for people to agree on facts—we had kings and warlords and rigid social hierarchy. During it, a lot of brainpower got unlocked and things got a lot better materially. A *lot* better. Now we're back in a situation where the people who have the power and the money can get what they want by dictating what the mass of people ought to believe."

"But in order for the rich to get what they want, they also have to have a functioning tech economy, right? Because their wealth isn't based on controlling land, like in the old days. It's based on stock."

Enoch nodded. "The system is selective enough now to identify those with the ability to contribute to the tech economy and bring them to places like this." He waved out the windshield at Moab, which in a low-slung and easygoing way bore earmarks, for those who knew what to look for, of being the kind of place where smart people lived. They had traveled two thousand miles to end up back in Princeton. And once they left it in their rearview camera they would travel another thousand miles to end up in the same place again.

"So is it ever coming back?"

"The state of affairs that existed during those three hundred years?"

"Yeah."

"I don't know. It's the kind of big woo-woo topic your uncle Jake thinks about. You are free to think about it too, of course. Or to focus on the task at hand. Maybe one applies to the other."

It took her a second to process that. "You're talking about what you mentioned before," she said, "that a brain, or a digital simulation of one, needs to be embedded in a world that agrees with itself as to what is what."

"Yes. *And* it has to agree with any other brains that happen to be hanging around in the same world."

"Not an issue for me," Sophia said. "There's just the one. Dodge's."

"Not for long," Enoch said.

Coincidentally or not, they had reached the center of town and pulled up in front of one of the larger buildings, a former bank that was now the local offices of ONE: the Organization for New Eschatology. Sophia had been sharing her location with family members and apparently Jake had passed the word to the local staff, and so a few people, whom Sophia could only assume were professional eschatologists, or perhaps eschatological support staff, were emerging from the building's grand old doors to greet their colleague. "Here is where I leave you," said Enoch. "Thank you for helping take me down from that cross and for bringing me this far."

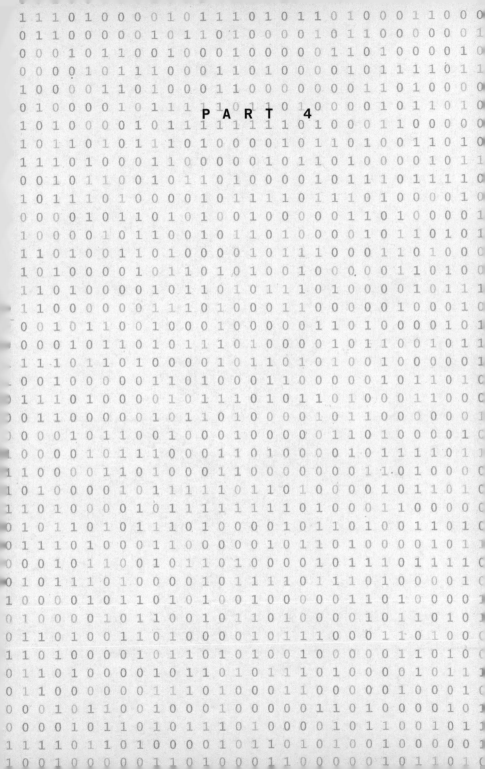

P A R T 4

17

With her husband, Csongor, Zula still lived in the same condo where they had dwelled at the time of Richard's death. They had raised Sophia there. Upon sending her off to Princeton, they had shopped around for a new place but decided that the condo—two thousand square feet on the eighteenth floor of a twenty-story building in Seattle's Capitol Hill neighborhood—still suited them just fine.

Richard had bought it for them a long time ago, in the aftermath of events that had made them briefly famous and placed them at some hazard of violent reprisals. They could not safely go back to their homes, which were easily findable, and they had no money to speak of. Richard had eliminated the problem by setting up an untraceable shell company and using it to purchase the condo. By the time the Miasma had caught up with the ruse and figured out where they lived, they were no longer all that famous, and the existing security in the building had proved adequate to their needs.

Security was, though, an ongoing rock-paper-scissors match between technologies that all seemed to want different things. The lobby of the building, its elevators and stairwells, and its exterior belts of walkways and gardens had all been covered by security cameras from the very beginning of Zula and Csongor's tenancy. In those days a security guard would sit all day behind a reception desk in the lobby, keeping an eye on the main entrance, glancing down from time to time at an array of flat-panel monitors that showed him the feeds from those cameras. But the desk had been torn out some years ago and replaced with a big saltwater aquarium. The building still employed a security firm. But those guards who were human, and who were actually on site, spent most of the day up on their feet, strolling about the property while keeping track of events in wearable devices. Some of the "guards" were just algorithms, analyzing video and audio feeds for suspicious behavior, recognizing faces and cross-checking them against a whitelist of residents, friends, and neighbors, and a blacklist of predators, stalkers, and ex-husbands. Anything ambiguous was forwarded to a Southeast Asian eyeball farm.

On a certain morning in June, Zula emerged from the building's elevator into its lobby and donned her sunglasses. A yellow ball—the mildest of warnings—flickered in the corner of her vision. She glanced at it. It noticed the movement of her eyes and responded by letting her know that three VEILed pedestrians happened to be passing by outside.

Zula ignored it, pushed the door open, and saw them immediately: three high-school-aged girls, coffee cups in hand, gaily laughing and talking.

They all had wearables with large, reflective lenses, and so their eyes could not be seen. From the cheekbones down, their faces were exposed. But points and patches of light, projected by lasers in the lower rims of the glasses, were flashing and sliding all over their faces in a programmed manner that had been designed to foil facial-recognition algorithms.

Zula wasn't using a VEIL. By exposing her face in a public area, she had, therefore, announced her location to any camera capable of seeing her and of checking her features against a database. Most people had become accustomed to this a long time ago and did not particularly care. But many preferred to opt out. You could avoid being recognized by wearing a physical veil and a pair of sunglasses, but most people in the industrialized world opted for its information-age equivalent.

To say that Verna and Maeve Braden had invented the Virtual Epiphanic Identity Lustre wasn't quite right, since it incorporated a number of separate technologies. It had been more of a systems integration and branding play than an invention. But they had conceived it, named it, and made it a thing.

The VEIL was more likely to be worn by persons in the Venn diagram intersection of "young," "geeky," and "countercultural."

It was no surprise to find people like that on Capitol Hill. Zula was pretty sure that these three young ladies were on their way to the prep school a few blocks away. Over the coming half an hour, as she made her way down the hill into the South Lake Union district, the ambient culture would shift; it would still be geeky as hell, but the average age would trend upward, and people's countercultural instincts would be muted or absent. Up here, though, wearing a VEIL was no more remarkable than having a stud in your nose. The building's security system noticed VEILed passersby and marked them as mildly interesting—hence the yellow signal in Zula's glasses—but it wasn't quite the same thing as wearing a black ski mask.

"Epiphanic Identity" had not been thrown in just to make the acronym work. The words had particular meanings.

"Epiphany" was a deep, crazy, metaphysical/religious term. The last two syllables came from a Greek word meaning "to show" or "to appear." The prefix was what made it interesting. "Epi-" meant "upon" or "on top of" or "in addition to" and thus suggested that epiphany was not just appearance in a naked, bald sense but something a little more indirect, more layered. In the Bible when you saw an epiphany you weren't seeing God directly but some kind of avatar or manifestation thereof.

"Identity" had been forever changed by the Internet; formerly it had meant "who you really are" but now it meant "any one of a number of persistent faces that you can present to the digital universe."

The VEIL had been engineered as a double-edged weapon. Yes, it jammed the facial-recognition algorithms that would enable any camera, anywhere, to know your true name. But the pattern of lights that a VEIL projected on the user's face wasn't mere noise. It was a signal designed to convey data to any computer vision system smart enough to read it. The protocol had been published by ENSU and was formidable in its sophistication, but the upshot was that a VEIL could, if the user so chose, project the equivalent of a barcode: a number linking the user to a PURDAH.

It was all completely optional and unnecessary, which was part of the point; most people didn't know or care about any of this and simply did things openly under their own names. But it was easy, and free, and recommended, that when you were starting out in life you establish at least one PURDAH, so that you could begin compiling a record of things that you had done. You could link it to your actual legal name and face if you wanted, or not. And either way you could punch it into your VEIL system so that as you walked down the street, computer vision systems, even though they couldn't recognize your actual face, could look up your PURDAH and from there see any activity blockchained to it.

All three of the laughing, coffee-toting, VEIL-wearing schoolgirls had done this as a matter of course. It was probably a free-and-mandatory service offered by their prep school. The security cameras on the front of Zula's condo building had looked them up. For that matter, Zula's glasses had outward-looking cameras that could have done the same thing, had she shown any interest. She didn't bother. But the odds were that their PURDAH records were all carefully gardened and censored by some combination of their parents and their school. Their names and faces would be concealed. But there was probably enough public data to suggest that they were exactly what they looked like: ordinary schoolgirls, VEILed and in PURDAH, not because they wanted to hide any malign intentions, but just to keep the creeps at bay, and to make sure that when they turned in their SATs and their AP exams, they'd be judged fairly.

18

Zula turned downhill and began walking briskly. This was her main form of exercise. Where she worked—the headquarters of the Forthrast Family Foundation—there was an employee gym. And where she lived, there was a gym for the use of residents and their guests. As she walked down Capitol Hill and into South Lake Union, she passed a windowless pink building with a tiny sign on the door that according to rumor was a boutique gym, so exclusive that you had to apply for membership and pass strenuous tests. Another gym, a few blocks farther along, occupied the entire ground floor of a skyscraper; several dozen elliptical trainers were lined up facing the window, occupied by early-rising, heavy-breathing nerds watching movies or doing work in head-mounted displays. She passed a steampunk gym where historically aware nerds with waxed mustaches worked out with Indian clubs of polished mahogany sourced from ecologically sustainable plantations. A glassed-in crag of artificial stone where harnessed nerds groped at CAD/CAMmed handholds with chalky fingers. A revamped warehouse where robed nerds fought solemn duels with simulated light sabers. A striped tent where upside-down nerds swung by their knees from a flying trapeze. An open-air obstacle course where parkour ninjas vaulted fences and ran vertically up concrete walls. A park where squads of nerds dropped and did push-ups under the faux-stern glare of a pretend drill sergeant. A thumping boîte where female nerds practiced their pole dancing. Cementing these establishments together like mortar between bricks was an equally far-fetched assortment of dining and drinking establishments where those who had just worked off a lot of calories and tuned up their bodies could further enhance their health by drinking smoothies made of pulverized botanical curiosities, or balance the scales by consuming things that were decidedly not good for them.

Zula had actually tried many of those cool new forms of exercise, and was likely to try more, for social reasons if nothing else. Csongor played in a hockey league that appeared to supply 90 percent of his needs in the way of both exercise and companionship. Zula too had gardened her social life by signing up for new exercise programs with female friends. But she had never stuck with any of them. Her only consistent form of exercise was walking to and from work, which she did alone, almost every day.

Walking this gantlet of physical fitness options often got her musing. These clean, affluent, well-informed techies certainly knew how to enjoy having bodies. At work they lived in their heads. Their free time was spent in the pleasures of exertion, of a hot shower after, of eating and drinking, and of going home to have sex, or at least a good night's sleep, on firm mattresses covered in clean high-quality linens. There was nothing exactly wrong with it. But Zula had spent her early years in a refugee camp where sources of physical pleasure, or even comfort, had been few and far between. And somewhat later in her life she had spent a few weeks traveling against her will in the company of jihadists who had either come from, or made a choice to migrate to, some of the most hard-bitten places in the world. She abhorred everything about them. Yet she couldn't help seeing all of this through their eyes. Jihadists, who were obsessed with a particular kind of religion, would see the gyms and the restaurants as temples to a false god, where people went to distract themselves from the reality that they were all sooner or later going to get sick and die. After which, if you believed what they believed, you'd meet your maker and be duly punished for having spent so much of your life reveling in pleasure.

None of which was particularly original—every sentient person had to fulfill a certain minimum quota of ruminating about this stuff—but in Zula's case it was all turned around and upside down because of what had happened with Uncle Richard seventeen years ago. This had become her career.

It had taken her several of those years simply to understand and accept that her identity—the holograph that she was writing every day of her life—had been altered by it. Not so much the death itself as the ensuing legal and financial complications. The dispute over Dodge's will meant nothing as far as its practical effect on her life was concerned; either way, she was rich, and her offspring would never want for anything material. But in monetary terms the difference was quite large. And, when they got that big, sums of money took on wills of their own. Which maybe explained why the document at the root of the matter was called a "will."

The family's share of the money had long since been wired to Iowa and ceased to be any of Zula's concern, except for those increasingly rare occasions when she would be called on to give a deposition or sign an affidavit connected with the semiautonomous subbranch of the legal profession supported by the ecosystem of lawsuits that had been spawned by a few ill-chosen words. The balance of Richard's fortune—most of it, actually—had gone to the Forthrast Family Foundation. Zula had been its president and director from day one, and it was increasingly obvious that she would never have any other job. She paid herself a reasonable salary—nothing that would raise the eyebrows of the foundation's board—and she devoted her career to seeing to it that her uncle's fortune was applied toward the causes he would have favored. His money had attracted more donations, mostly from old friends of his who wanted to get in on a good thing.

During the first decade, the problem had been finding responsible ways to spend the money faster than it accumulated. This was like shoveling your driveway during a blizzard. When foundation money needed to be parked, she had at first put it in simple index funds. This reassured her she wasn't missing out on any market moves, without her paying a lot for fancy advisers. Slowly she'd begun moving money into financial bots running algorithms too complicated for any human to understand. These had performed better than the humans. In one case, a single bot had made so much money over a span of several consecutive years that it had more than doubled the foundation's endowment. As a result, the proportion of the foundation's money controlled by inscrutable artificial intelligences had become disproportionate to what was parked in old-fashioned funds and stocks.

Uncle Richard hadn't exactly knocked himself out providing specifics as to what the foundation should be spending the money on. She'd had leeway that had daunted her. She'd spent more than she should have getting expert advice, then fired the experts. Running the foundation would have been easy had its sole purpose been, say, to preserve a rare species of tree snail. Instead the will's language had pointed her in the general direction of supporting research that was somehow beneficial to mankind but somehow related to game technology. Which could mean just about anything.

The foundation's headquarters was constructed on a pier that projected a short distance from the southern shore of Lake Union. This was the only remarkable thing about it; other than that, the building was as generic as it could be. During the early days, she had entertained proposals from world-famous architects who saw the job as an opportunity to make a statement. They'd expressed it in more high-flown language, but what it boiled down to was that they wanted to build something really cool. Zula's sympathies had been with them, but she'd gone with boring instead. For, as a new and inexperienced director who could justly be accused of having got the job through nepotism, she needed to send the message that she wasn't just screwing around with her uncle's money. The other billionaires, the self-made men whom no one would question, they could put their money into building outlandish structures. But Zula had built something that was just another Class A office building that would appreciate in value along with all the other buildings like it and that could be liquidated on the market as easily as a pork belly. The upper two floors had been reserved for the Forthrast Family Foundation and the lower four had been leased to other organizations.

She relaxed her pace as she drew near. The building's network recognized her from a block away and caused a little status indicator to appear in the corner of her vision. The doors opened for her automatically and she walked into the lobby. This building too had a roving security guard; he'd seen her coming and wandered over to the entrance so that he could greet her with a nod and a smile. The building knew that she had arrived and that she'd be wanting an elevator to the sixth floor, but let her know that regrettably there would be a wait of between thirty and sixty seconds; this was the busiest time of day for the lifts. She considered taking the stairs but decided against it since her knee was talking to her. She waited before the elevator banks along with some of the regulars she saw every day, and a few visitors, there for meetings or job interviews. Those were discernible because they had to engage in old-school navigation schemes like reading the building directory and physically pressing elevator buttons.

One of them, a grizzled, red-bearded guy with a somewhat shaggy academic vibe, gave her side-eye as he did so. He was likely en route to ONE, the Organization for New Eschatology, which occupied the second floor. Very likely he had business with Zula's one surviving uncle, Jake Forthrast. It wasn't the first time Zula had seen this guy. As he reached out to press the elevator button, his hand shot loose from the ragged sleeve of his hoodie to reveal a Band-Aid on the back of the wrist. When his hand returned to his side, she noticed a matching Band-Aid on the inner wrist. Other than that, his hands seemed normal. But Zula realized, from this detail, that this must be the guy, Enoch what's-his-name, who had recently been crucified in Nebraska while running some kind of errand for Jake. She considered saying hello to him and introducing herself but wasn't sure how to strike up a chat with someone who had just been through that. For his part, he clearly knew who she was, and gave her a polite nod. But it seemed he did not wish to intrude on her privacy.

Jake had personally ended up with the same amount of money as all of John and Alice's descendants put together. Jake's family was smaller and simpler—he had three sons who were almost a generation younger than the children of John and Alice, and no grandchildren as yet. Unlike Alice, he had decided to retain control of his share of the money personally, rather than divvying it up among his descendants. He was a survivalist living in a cabin in the north woods and hadn't a clue what to do with all of that money. For the most part he had just followed Zula's lead, investing in the same portfolio of stocks, funds, and financial bots as the foundation. To the extent he'd spent any of it, he had done so on helping Zula clean up the peculiar state of affairs that had arisen concerning what should be done with Richard's brain.

The Organization for New Eschatology was an outgrowth of that. Occupying the Venn diagram intersection of everything that the Internet hated, it had drawn a nearly infinite amount of derision. Some of that had been deserved; it had taken Jake a couple of years and a few million dollars in misspent funds before he had really got the hang of running a nonprofit.

In essence, it had forced Jake to grow up and get his shit together—not just financially, but philosophically as well. As Zula and Alice had both feared, Jake had, at first, plowed some of the money into some of the wackier causes that he had got into the habit of believing in, and built his family's life around, in Idaho. But becoming rich had changed what he believed, not by the more academic route of challenging his evidence and debating his logic, but by changing the sorts of things that he was predisposed to want to believe.

In addition to spawning ONE, the disposition of Richard's brain had yoked the Forthrast Family Foundation together with the even larger Waterhouse-Shaftoe Family Foundation and kept them all in a perennially awkward relationship with El Shepherd's network of companies and nonprofits. Their activities all went directly to the matter of mortality, consciousness, and what it meant to be a human. To have a soul. ONE had become the think-tank branch of the Forthrast/Waterhouse/Shepherd brain science complex.

Sometimes tech advanced by gradually creeping up on things. Other times it did so by saltation: suddenly leaping forward. She had heard an argument that those two couldn't really be teased apart, because in the case of an exponential creep-up, like Moore's Law, the bend in the curve could look like a jump if you took your eye off the ball at the wrong time.

In any case, when she walked her daily gantlet of gyms and restaurants, she began to feel that the tech industry, which prided itself on having disrupted so many other things, was now creeping up on the moment when it would attempt to disrupt death. For if you had conquered every other foe and made an infinite amount of money along the way, and found yourself savoring a bite of some exquisite sushi or a dram of thirty-year-old single-malt, why should you not ask yourself what in principle was standing in the way of your being able to enjoy such things forever? And if you didn't believe—as most of these people didn't—that there was some higher reward awaiting you on the other side of that bourne from which no traveler returns, then why not choose to remain on this side of it for as long as technology would allow?

Zula, left to her own devices, would never have thought to approach death head-on, as if it were just another Old Economy bogeyman on a Silicon Valley whiteboard, waiting to be disrupted. But the train wreck that had begun at the moment Dodge's heart had stopped beating had obliged her to make it a significant part of her life's work. Not so much as a researcher in her own right (she was a geologist) but as a den mother for those who were.

19

In the architects' rendering of the reception area of the Forthrast Family Foundation's sixth-floor suite, blazered and skirted guests had lounged around its coffee table, sipping lattes and checking their phones under the alert but hospitable eye of a receptionist stationed behind a stylish curving desk as they waited for their hosts to show up and keycard them in.

The reality, this day and every day since they'd moved in, was that this was wasted space. They'd never got around to hiring a receptionist, so no one had ever sat behind the stylish desk. Its office chair had long since been poached, leaving more room for boxes of office supplies that tended to pile up there. Guests didn't sit around the coffee table waiting to be buzzed in; their hosts knew where they were, and vice versa. The door leading back into the offices was propped open. Stationed next to it, plugged into a wall outlet, were charging docks for two different brands of telepresence robots: wheeled contraptions sporting flat-panel monitors thrust into the air at about the altitude of a person's head, capable of purring around the office under the control of persons who weren't physically present but who had the right passwords, and the right software installed on their systems. Even these had been gathering dust. The foundation had invested in them a few years ago, and Jake had frequently used them to "attend" meetings from his home in Idaho, but they had been superseded by virtual equivalents, or better robots that could walk up and down stairs on two legs. So walking through the reception area, which the architects had tried so hard to make nice, now had the feel of entering through the loading dock and the mail room.

She headed for her office, which was in the corner overlooking the lake. En route, she passed by the smaller of their two conference rooms. Sitting in a ragged semicircle with their backs to her were some half a dozen people who she guessed were young, based on their clothing, posture, and body types. Addressing them was Marcus Hobbs, a foundation executive who among other things looked after the summer intern program. Formerly this had been informal and ad hoc to a degree that, as Marcus had pointed out, actually put the foundation at some risk of lawsuits, or at least bad publicity. He'd tidied things up and instituted regular procedures for publicizing it, collecting and evaluating applications, screening applicants, and keeping track of metrics. So, the half-dozen kids sitting in that room were not just a random assortment of nephews, neighbors, and friends of friends, but the survivors of a selection process that had commenced the day after last year's crop of interns had gone back to school.

Without even checking her calendar, Zula knew that most of today was blocked out for interviews with these candidates. Since the foundation had already made its choices and gone to the expense of bringing these people to Seattle, the interviews were largely symbolic. But that did not mean that they were unimportant.

The third of those interviews—the last thing on her calendar before lunch—turned out to be with her daughter. This was a surprise.

Sophia was wearing a hoodie and jeans, which explained why Zula hadn't recognized her from behind while walking past the conference room. Sophia had turned on her glasses' VEIL functionality. Conceivably, Marcus might have recognized her when she had arrived at the Foundation earlier that morning, but Marcus and Sophia had probably never been in the same room together and there was no particular reason why he would have known her.

Zula had reviewed this anonymous candidate's application more than once over the last several months, and given it a final once-over before she had walked into her office, but it didn't have a name associated with it. Only a PURDAH. Which wasn't unusual. Marcus had, in fact, made it almost mandatory. Concealing names, genders, and the like behind a PURDAH was a way to reduce the possibility that candidates would benefit from positive, or suffer from negative, discrimination. So Zula had noted a few points of similarity between this applicant and her daughter, but was none-theless surprised when Sophia walked into her office, pulled the hood back from her head, took off her glasses, and sat down.

"Hi, Mom."

"Hi, baby."

After that, neither said anything for a minute. Sophia looked out the window at the view over the Olympics and gave Zula time to sort it out in her head. Then she asked: "Did you know? Or at least suspect?"

"No," Zula said. Raising her voice a notch, she added, "I guess I sort of imagined that if you wanted to work here over the sum-mer, you'd just tell me and we would work something out."

"Are you mad that I did it this way?"

"No." Zula considered it for a few moments, and her voice set-tled down: "I see your point, I guess. If you and I had just quote-unquote worked something out—"

"I wouldn't be a real intern. Anything I did would be kind of suspect," Sophia said. "Yeah, that's pretty much what I was think-ing." She brightened. "I'm really pleased I made it through the se-lection process."

"Almost."

"Huh?"

"There's still this. The final interview."

"Oh, yeah. Well, I couldn't figure out how to make it through *this* without revealing I was the boss's daughter."

"Welcome home, by the way." Zula wasn't certain whether "wel-come home" or "welcome back" was the right phrase for someone who had been living on the other side of the country for three years, but she wasn't above dropping a hint. She stood up and smiled. So-phia did likewise. They came together and embraced and held each other for a little while. After a few moments Zula opened her eyes and happened to catch sight of Marcus Hobbs, out in the hallway, clearly visible through the glass door of her office. He was stopped in midstride, gobsmacked and a little dismayed by the sight of the boss engaging in a public display of affection with an intern can-didate who had only just crossed the threshold of her office. Zula winked at him and indicated with a wave of the hand that he should approach.

Oblivious to all of this, Sophia relaxed her arms and took half a step back. "I passed through Iowa on the way," she said. "Visited the farm. Mended fences with the rellies."

"I look forward to hearing about it," Zula said. "First you have some explaining to do." She nodded at the door as Marcus walked in.

"Mr. Hobbs! Hello again," Sophia said, snapping into a polite businesslike manner in a way that made Zula feel that, while raising her, she must have done something right.

"Sophia? Is that how you still prefer to be addressed?" Marcus asked.

"Yes, that is my actual name," Sophia said. It was common for people using PURDAH to link them to nicknames. "Mom and Dad picked it out. I'm happy to use it here."

Marcus looked at Zula. "So I have the pleasure of addressing your daughter."

"Nice to meet you for reals," Sophia said, and extended her hand. Marcus shook it, sizing her up in a new light.

"You wanted to work here over the summer," Marcus guessed, "but you didn't want to be seen as having got the job through family connections, so you did everything anonymously."

"Yeah. Worked great until this lady blew my cover," Sophia said, nodding at her mother.

"Well, I can tell you in all honesty that I am completely surprised."

Zula laughed. "I saw that much in your face, Marcus."

"So, just in case there are any lingering doubts, Sophia got the job fair and square, and I'm happy to say as much if anyone raises any questions." Marcus was talking in that diction peculiar to lawyers. He was, in other words, doing his job. Zula had come to depend on him. She had first met him on the day after Dodge had been stricken. He was the junior associate who had shown up in Alice's hotel suite, acting as Stan Peterson's wingman. After his stint at Argenbright Vail, he had begun putting his legal powers to use in the service of nonprofit organizations, and ended up here.

"Noted," Zula said.

"Well played," Marcus said, nodding at Sophia.

"If you have a minute to spare," Zula said, "this young intern and I were just about to have a discussion of how she intends to use her time here at the foundation."

"Of course. If I wouldn't be intruding on family matters, that is," Marcus said, edging toward an available chair.

"Marcus, it's the Forthrast Family Foundation," Zula reminded him.

Marcus laughed. They all sat down.

"Interns have a lot of leeway here," Zula said. "Marcus pointed out to me a long time ago that anyone who makes it through our application process is, by definition, overqualified and underpaid. No one's under any illusions as to why Ivy League students do internships. It's all about résumé building. We could have our interns fetch coffee for us, but that wouldn't serve their needs and would amount to taking jobs away from people in the community who could use that sort of work."

"Point being," Marcus added, "that we choose the best people we can find first, and get them in the door. Choosing a summer project tends to take care of itself."

Sophia had been smiling and nodding through this, looking every inch the bright young intern.

"So," Zula said, "this is the part where you're supposed to tell us what you want to spend the summer working on."

"Since you planned everything else out so carefully, I'm guessing you have a proposal," Marcus said.

Sophia nodded. "I would like to work with You Know What." After a pause for that to sink in, she added, "Or, depending on how you think about these things, You Know Who."

"You want the password to DB," Zula said.

20

D B was Dodge's Brain. Corvallis Kawasaki had coined the term; in nerd-speak it was also a pun on a common abbreviation of "database."

It was not a single unitary thing. It was a sprawling web of directories in which was contained every scrap of information that had emerged from the epic project to satisfy the requirements in the disposition of remains that Richard Forthrast had signed long before his death.

The actual data started with the completely raw and unprocessed output of the ion-beam scanning device that had cremated Richard's frozen brain one axon at a time. This alone occupied more storage space than would have been affordable back when Richard had signed his will. In that form, it was essentially unusable. If you thought of Richard's brain as a document being run through a scanner, the raw data was a list of voltages emerging from the scanner's optics. In order to turn that into a meaningful picture, it had to be sifted through and processed on a vast scale. Merely crunching the numbers to produce something resembling a connectome—a wiring diagram of how the neurons were interlinked—had made it necessary for the Waterhouse-Shaftoe Family Foundation to construct one of the largest data centers in the world. This was a reasonably natural extension of what they were good at anyway as a result of running a huge electronic banking system. It had been crunching on DB for years.

Which wasn't to suggest that the connectome was, in any sense, absolutely known. Twenty different people had written twenty different Ph.D. dissertations on how the raw data could be processed and interpreted; each of their algorithms generated different results. Meta-analyses had then been conducted, comparing and contrasting the outputs generated by those competing algorithms. So DB didn't contain a single settled and agreed-on connectome but dozens of possible versions of it, each stored in its own incompatible data format and each encoding a different set of assumptions as to how the brain actually worked.

What DB *wasn't* was a functioning simulation of Dodge's actual brain. Various efforts had been made to take the contents of the database, feed them into a system designed to emulate the functions of human neurons, and hit the "on" switch. But for the most part DB was an inert repository of data. A noun, not a verb. The digital equivalent of freezing Richard Forthrast's body while waiting for some future technology to come along capable of reanimating it.

"When Uncle Richard signed the disposition of remains, they were stuck in a cryopreservation mind-set," Sophia said. "The document reflects that."

"I'll bite," Marcus said. "Who's 'they'? And can you say more about the mind-set?"

"'They' is the Eutropians. The cabal of nerds who decided, back in the 1990s, that they wanted to live forever. Who talked Uncle Richard into copy-pasting that boilerplate language into his disposition of remains. And remember that the original language didn't even consider the idea of digital scanning. It was straight analog: chill his body down fast, freeze him, store him in the cryofacility in Ephrata. For them, actually being able to reanimate a frozen body and bring it back to life was like building a starship that could cross the galaxy in ten minutes: a thing that they could think of in the abstract. But actually doing it was just inconceivably, ridiculously far in the future. And so Uncle Richard's will doesn't contain anything about that. It just says 'freeze me' with the implication being 'someone will sort out the consequences a thousand or ten thousand years down the road when they actually know how to do this.' The actual reanimation procedure is never laid out. It's assumed that the mentality of people who might control such a technology is so advanced compared to our caveman understanding that it'd be pointless to try to anticipate what that process would look like and to give specific instructions as to under what conditions it ought to be attempted.

"But that's all analog," she continued. "It's all about that one piece of frozen meat. You only get one chance to reanimate it. Best to wait until you're sure it'll work. Instead now we've got an opportunity to do this digitally. And that opportunity has come along within living memory of Uncle Richard himself." Sophia's voice got a little husky at this point, as she was clearly remembering her vague little-kid memories of sitting on Dodge's lap. She cleared her throat. "So I want to work on that. And I don't claim that I'm going to come up with the answer to it all during one summer's worth of work, but to me it feels like exploring it is a worthwhile project, and being a member of the family—someone who knew him when I was a little girl—gives me a kind of standing that nobody else has."

Zula's eyes were shining, out of some combination of maternal pride in her daughter and grief for her uncle. "Sophia," she said, "I have to ask you something. When you went off to college, your major was undeclared. But you were pretty sure it was going to be comparative religion or classics or something in that vein. That's mostly what you studied in your freshman year. But after that you turned pretty decisively in the direction of cognitive science, neurology, computer science."

Sophia was nodding, slightly impatient. "Those are just more technical ways of getting at the same questions."

"I understand that, honey. But I have to know, just for my own curiosity: how long have you been thinking about this? The conversation we're having right now, in my office: is it something you've been planning for years?"

Sophia shook her head. "Months, maybe. I mean, sure, my interest in neuroscience was piqued by all the exposure I had while I was growing up to dinner-table conversations about what you and C-plus and the others were up to concerning DB. But, the idea of actually digging into that thing and running some code? That wasn't even on the table, technically speaking, until Hole in the Wall came online."

"I kind of know what that is," Marcus said. "The latest and greatest processor farm. But you're going to have to help me out a little."

FALL; OR, DODGE IN HELL | 273

"It's at a place about a hundred miles from here called Hole in the Wall Coulee—an inlet on the Columbia River. Coincidentally, just a little downstream of Ephrata. They built it on the site of an old aluminum plant. So it's got cheap juice and cold water."

"Data centers are all over that part of the state," Marcus pointed out. "Have been for decades. What makes Hole in the Wall a game-changer for DB?"

"It's the first one exclusively built around quantum computers."

"And you think that quantum computers are better at simulating brain processes?" The skepticism in Marcus's voice was gentle but unmistakable.

"I'm agnostic on that. But I know—and there's ample peer-reviewed research to prove—that they are better at carrying out the mathematical operations that are needed to carry out secure, distributed computation."

"Distributed . . . in the cloud," Zula murmured.

It was enough to elicit a little sigh from her daughter.

This was a generational thing. Zula was old enough to have lived through the transition from most computation's being local, contained within her desktop or her laptop, to its being distributed across remote servers that might be anywhere in the world. "In the cloud" had been the buzzword for it when it was a new idea, but merely to use the term nowadays was to date yourself.

"And by 'secure' you mean—"

"It means that the processes—millions of separate executables running on god knows how many different real or virtual machines—don't have to trust each other. They don't have to know each other. When they have to communicate, they do it—" Sophia closed her eyes momentarily, maybe to conceal an eye-roll. "They do it the way all communication happens nowadays, which is through distributed-ledger-type stuff."

"Blockchain?" Zula asked.

Actively suppressing another eye-roll, Sophia answered, "Way, way more efficient algorithms that do what blockchain was supposed to do twenty years ago. But still requiring a lot of fast computation."

"So, if we think of it"—and here Zula held out a hand as if to deflect any objections—"if we imagine, just for the sake of argument, that we have one process, what we used to call a computer program, that does one thing only, which is to simulate the workings of one single neuron in a brain. That's all it does."

Sophia nodded and made a wheeling gesture with her hand, encouraging her mother to keep rolling—perhaps a little faster.

"And it's running on a chip in a farm in Ephrata. Pretty much doing its own thing. But real neurons in the brain are connected to other neurons—that's kind of the whole point. It's why we spent a billion dollars scanning Uncle Richard's connectome."

"Right," Sophia said. "So, somewhere else—maybe on a different thread running on the same chip, maybe on a different chip in the same farm, maybe on another farm altogether on a barge off the coast of California or whatever, there are other processes, all clones, all busy simulating the workings of other neurons. Neurons that are connected to that first one. And every so often, a message needs to be passed from one of those processes to another."

"A neuron fires or something," said Marcus, getting into the spirit of the thing.

Sophia paused for a second, perhaps stifling an urge to swap out what Marcus had just said for something a little more technically precise.

"Or whatever," Marcus added. "Axons. Synapses. Dendrites."

"Signals have to pass between neurons or you don't have a brain," Zula said.

"We're getting pretty far afield from how it actually works," Sophia said, "but no matter how you simulate a brain, the point is that you're going to have a lot of separate, independently running processes that have to communicate over a wiring diagram that basically represents the connectome. And every signal—every separate communication—has some overhead that you have to pay in terms of computation and bandwidth. If you're doing it the way it ought to be done, crypto-wise—"

"The way all communication happens nowadays," Zula said, quoting Sophia's own words back to her. She winked at Marcus.

"—yeah, the overhead is large and everything is some combination of slow and expensive. To figure out how to do those computations faster was kind of an obvious fat target for companies building quantum computers. Instead of waiting for Moore's Law to catch up with what was needed, they were able to leapfrog it, and bring us devices that were decades or centuries ahead of the curve in terms of their ability to do this stuff."

"Distributed secure computation," Marcus said, just to be sure he was tracking.

Sophia nodded. She had begun moving her hands while she talked, in a way that suggested she was working with a user interface. Marcus and Zula both took the hint and put on their glasses. They saw a carousel hovering in the middle of the office, displaying a few thousand photos that Sophia and her friends had apparently captured during their cross-country drive. Zula recognized some exterior shots of the Forthrast farmhouse in Iowa. Then Sophia spun it forward and finally zeroed in on some more recent pictures.

The landscape of central Washington State was distinctive with its red-brown basalt, purple haze of sagebrush, and deep blue Columbia River water. On the shore of that river, on a flat triangle of alluvial ground at the mouth of a slot canyon, was a big dusty building ensnared in a web of power lines. It had a large parking lot, made for a blue-collar workforce that no longer existed, currently occupied by all of three vehicles. One of those was a pickup truck marked SECURITY, and standing next to it was a burly man in mirror shades, watching Sophia—or whichever of her friends had taken the photograph—and no doubt recording her.

"And that is what is happening at Hole in the Wall Coulee," Sophia was saying. "On the outside it looks the same as any other processor farm. Electricity and cold water go in, bits and warm water come out. But behind the walls of this old factory, the amount of useful computation that's happening is thousands or maybe even millions of times in excess of what you'd see in old-school processor farms just up the river."

"Got it," Marcus said. "So I see what you mean that this is a game-changer in terms of the ability to run a big neurological simulation."

"Not my insight," Sophia admitted. "Solly—one of my professors at Princeton—brought it up a few months ago, when this thing came online, and said basically, 'Look, we might actually be able to do it now.'"

"Meaning, run a simulation of something more ambitious than a cubic millimeter of one mouse's brain," Zula said.

"Yeah. And I just thought to myself, when I heard that, 'Hey. DB is part of my birthright. Opportunity knocks.' And that's when I applied for this internship."

Marcus was nodding. "Does your professor know about this? Is he or she part of the picture?"

"He. Most definitely. It's Solly." Which in a lot of tech nerd circles would have been sufficient. He was one of those guys who had been around forever and played roles in tech companies going at least as far back as Hewlett-Packard.

But Zula wasn't really a part of that culture. "Rings a bell," she said.

"Solly Pesador. Old-school tech geek turned neuro hacker."

"You've crossed paths with him," Marcus informed Zula. "He's the one who dropped out of the whole Bay Area tech scene so he could go back to school in middle age and get a degree in neuroscience."

"I remember him now," Zula said.

"He's probably a known quantity to the foundation," Sophia said. "I think he's participated in some ONE colloquia, advised on some DB-related stuff." Which, as they all knew, wasn't saying much—any neuroscientist of any significance to the field had probably crossed paths, at some point in his or her career, with the Forthrast and Waterhouse foundations.

"Is he advising you on this?"

"He's aware that I'm going to attempt it. I have his support. As important, I have code that came out of his research group."

"Code for simulating what brains do."

"What *neurons* do." Sophia shrugged. "I mean, that's no big deal. You could have it too—it's open source. But the point is that it's easy for me to get in touch with the experts who wrote that code, get their advice, work on fixing bugs. Actually get something up and running during the short time that I am going to have here."

She paused for a moment, and pressed her lips together, and then went on: "If you'll have me, that is."

Zula sat back in her chair and looked out the window. The outcome had never really been in doubt. But being the director of a foundation had taught her a few things. One: much of what she did for a living was symbolic. But two: just because it was symbolic didn't mean it wasn't important. She had to put on at least a performance of thinking about it.

"Based on what you've said in this interview, I don't think that even the most skeptical observer could claim that you are not qualified. And the steps you took to hide your identity behind PURDAH during the application process should dispel any serious questions around favoritism. So, you're in. But—" She held up her index finger in warning, since Sophia was about to bounce out of her chair. "We have to talk about what it means. Whether this is just an academic research project, taking some new code for a spin on the Hole in the Wall system, or a serious effort to turn Dodge's Brain on. Because no matter how we spin it, some people are going to see it as the latter." Zula turned her attention to Marcus. "So we should sit down with Letitia." Letitia was the foundation's public relations director.

Marcus nodded.

"But that's not for you to worry about. That is my problem," Zula said, turning back to Sophia. "Your problem is seeing how much of this you can actually pull off in two short months."

21

t's kind of amazing that after all this time we are still using passwords for *anything*," Sophia exclaimed.

It was three hours later. She was sitting in a restaurant along Lake Union with the man she knew as Uncle C.

Corvallis Kawasaki was now in his late forties. Like a lot of men whose hairlines had simply gone wrong at a certain age, he had taken to shaving his head. As a result, he looked radically different from the mop-topped Asian-American kid visible in some of Richard's old photographs from the Corporation 9592 days. He had also got in the habit of wearing suits. He had never quite resigned himself to neckties, though, and so he had his shirts tailored with stand-up collars meant to be worn unbuttoned. That, combined with his prominence in the tech world, had made him easily recognizable; when he'd walked into the restaurant, ten minutes late, the hostess had greeted him by name, and diners' heads had turned, tracking his progress across the room to the private booth where Sophia had been waiting for him.

In this part of town, all lunches were business lunches, and all conversations over food and drink involved disclosures of sensitive IP. The restaurants had been designed accordingly; tables were widely spaced, sound barriers were inserted wherever possible, and when it got too quiet, randomized noise welled up from discreetly placed speakers and filled in awkward gaps. Private dining rooms of various sizes ringed the main floor. Some of these were mere booths, capable of seating two to four, with doors on them. In one of those, C-plus and Sophia had been able to get through the hugging and cheek-kissing part of the meeting without too many eyes on them. They had then enjoyed a light lunch together and spent a little while catching up. He was doing well.

He and Maeve now had a brood of three kids, all indexing their way through school and soccer and robotics, exhaustively photo-documented in a way that had to be shared with Sophia.

It was only after the plates had been cleared away and coffee served that C-plus had buckled down to the serious business of making her a token holder—or, in the inevitable tech industry abbreviation, a toho—with access privileges to Dodge's Brain.

In essence, this was no different from handing someone a key to an apartment or giving them the combination to a padlock. There was this entity in the cloud called Dodge's Brain. It was mostly just a passive, inert repository of data. But it did include some executables—some actual running code—that were active all the time, like a sentry pacing back and forth in front of a locked library door. That code was as secure and unhackable as it was possible for anything to be in this world, and it would only open the door for entities that could prove—and keep proving—that they had been granted the requisite authority.

Corvallis Kawasaki had the power to confer those tokens on others. In the Meatspace world, "others" meant "human beings." But the digital sentry in front of the door was just a computer program running on a server somewhere, or more likely distributed across a number of servers. It didn't really have the ability to recognize humans, or to reliably tell one human from another.

"We could use biometrics," C-plus admitted. Meaning, devices like fingerprint readers or iris scanners. "But that just moves the vulnerability elsewhere. Let's say I had a gadget that could read your fingerprint with one hundred percent accuracy. Fine. The gadget knows it's Sophia. But in order for that to be of any use, the gadget has to send a message to some other process, somewhere in the world, saying, 'I checked her fingerprint and it's definitely Sophia.'"

"And that could be hacked."

"Yeah. Still, probably good enough. But I am trying to abide by the highest possible standards here."

"To make a point. To set an example," Sophia said.

"And to avoid looking like a fool," he said. "If it came out that I had let standards slip, cut corners, and gotten burned, it would be embarrassing."

"Fair enough."

"Now, passwords are ridiculously old-school, but they work as a stopgap. I want you to make one up, right now. One that you've never used before and will never use for any other purpose. Take your time. When you're ready, type it in." Uncle C slid a tablet across the table to her, keyboard ready for text entry.

"Okay. Thinking," Sophia said.

"Because this is your password to DB, you're probably thinking about using a password or phrase that has some kind of sentimental connection to your uncle Richard. Some kind of personal meaning to you. Don't. This isn't magic. It's not an opportunity for you to express your feelings."

Sophia nodded, feeling her face get slightly warm, as she had in fact been thinking of names from *D'Aulaires'* as suitable passwords. Instead she typed in "IsasdftFffiI13da!," for "I stole a shower daisy from the Forthrast family farmhouse in Iowa 13 days ago!" As she did so, Uncle C demurely looked away. The app asked her to re-enter the password just to make sure, and she did. Then she slid the tablet back across the table, maneuvering it carefully between coffee cups and cream pitchers. "Done," she said.

"Great." C-plus spent a few moments working in the virtual space that he could see through the lenses of his glasses. He scanned the results for a few moments, then nodded. "Okay. Congratulations. You now have unlimited read-only access to Dodge's Brain. As long as you remember that password—and no one steals it." Meaning that she could read all she wanted and write programs that would pull data from the files, but not alter them.

"And are we going to stick with old-school passwords?" Sophia asked.

"No, we are not," C-plus said. "Over time you want to migrate over to a DID protocol." Sophia knew what it meant: Defense in Depth. Instead of all-or-nothing access to a whole system, you sort of had to work your way in, proving and reproving who you were using various factors. To make a long story short, it wasn't very useful unless it was hooked up to a PURDAH-based system. Because that was the whole point of anonymous holography: your identity was verifiable not because you happened to know a password but because of your "handwriting"—which here meant just about every way in which you made an impression on the world.

"So the password will expire in a few weeks. You need to have switched this thing over to your PURDAH before that happens. Which should take place automatically as you use it and it gets to recognize you. What you do then is up to you, of course. You have a plan?"

"Learn my way around the connectome files. Use some of the tools that my professor's group has invented to parse them—to 'ring them out,' as he likes to put it."

"That's probably a few weeks' work right there."

"More than likely," she agreed. "If that works—which is a big if—then start actually trying to run neural simulations on a subset of that connectome. See what happens."

22

Ten months later

As she walked down the hallway to Solly's office, she could hear two men laughing and talking through the half-open door. No noisy open-office environment, this. Solly had enough pull to set himself up with an interdisciplinary gig, endowment funded, not tied to any one department. He hung out in an old pseudo-Gothic building on the Princeton campus, within striking distance of both neuroscientists and computer geeks. His office looked out over one of the campus's many green quadrangles. It was big, book lined, and quiet.

She pushed at the open door and found Solly sitting there chatting with Corvallis Kawasaki and Enoch Root, both of whom had joined via videoconference on a flat-panel screen. This kind of thing was getting a little antiquated, but people still used it. "Hi, Sophia!" called C-plus when he saw her entering the frame.

"Am I late?"

"You're early!" said Solly. He was a tiny guy, deeply embedded in a leather chair, like a mouse in a baseball mitt.

"Okay. Fyoosh!"

"We hopped on a little early," C-plus explained. "We had some other things to talk about."

"In Latin?"

There was an awkward pause, and then they all laughed. "I am sorry you heard my butchered Latin," C-plus said. "How embarrassing."

"I wouldn't know butchered from non-butchered," Sophia said. "But why?"

"It's a running gag between me and Enoch," C-plus explained.

"He walked up to me once in a bar near the foundation and hailed me in conversational Latin."

"Because he knew you spoke it," Sophia guessed. "Because of the Roman-legion stuff you do."

"Yes. It made quite an impression on all of the Amazon employees hanging out there."

"And on *you*," Enoch said. His face was sharing the screen with a pint of amber fluid, topped with foam.

"I didn't know Enoch at the time. So, yes! It came as quite a surprise," C-plus admitted. "Anyway, we practice our Latin sometimes. His is much better than mine."

"Hi, Enoch!" said Sophia. "Where are you?"

Enoch reached out with the hand that wasn't holding the beer and moved the camera around, giving them a blurred panorama of what seemed to be a very charming pub.

"England?" Sophia guessed. "Ireland?"

"No," Enoch answered. "The independent, sovereign nation of . . . wait for it . . ." With utmost gravity, he reached into his jacket pocket and pulled out a passport. He held it up to the camera. It looked newly minted. Embossed in gold letters on the front, it claimed, in French, Dutch, and English, to be an official document from Zelrijk-Aalberg.

"You're printing passports now!?" C-plus exclaimed.

"It's just a piece of paper," Enoch said with a shrug. "You know El. He is fascinated by nation-states. Always hacking the system."

"Well, speaking of hacking the system," Solly said. "I think we are all here?" He was referring, as everyone knew, to Sophia's thesis committee. This was a big and strangely diverse committee for a mere senior thesis. But it had all got a bit complicated, and so there were reasons why all three of these men were in on it.

"Yes, let's go," said C-plus. Enoch signaled his assent by raising his pint and nodding.

"You've been busy," said Solly, swiveling his chair to face Sophia.

Sophia sighed. "I'm glad you see it that way."

"Why wouldn't I?"

"My classes—my grades—"

"Those are formalities that the university has set up to make sure students don't go off the rails, because of inattention or laziness or whatever."

"A safety net?"

He laughed. "A safety net for the university. A danger net for the student. As the one person in this meeting who is supposed to be paying attention to such things, let me say that I see you as having cleared all of those hurdles a year ago. Your senior year has effectively been graduate school. That's how I can say with confidence that you've been busy—because I hear about your efforts from Corvallis. From Enoch. And from my graduate students and my postdocs."

"My efforts," Sophia snorted. "Mostly asking them questions."

"That is as good a metric of effort as any. Better than tests and grades, certainly."

"I'm glad you see it that way. The grades I have received during the last year are the worst of my life."

"The only thing that matters is whether you can clear the bureaucratic hurdles required to graduate," Solly pointed out. "No one gives a shit about your grades, Sophia. No one will ever look at them again."

She looked at the screen. Both Enoch and C-plus had politely averted their gazes. "That's kind of mind-blowing," she said.

"Because you've spent your whole life on the academic treadmill. Now you're stepping off of it. What matters, from here on out, is your work. Your holograph. In the non–three-D–graphics sense of that word."

She shrugged. "Okay, should we talk about that?"

"Yes. This is your so-called capstone project. Or keystone. Whatever you want to call it." Solly glanced out the window of his office for a moment, trying to access the relevant memory from the tiny compartment of his brain where he kept track of administrative minutiae.

"I believe 'senior thesis' is the term they'll be looking for," Sophia ventured, since Solly appeared to be looking in the direction of the dean's office.

"Very well. You incubated it last summer, during your internship in Seattle." Solly glanced at the screen, eliciting a nod of confirmation from C-plus.

"That's a nice way of saying it. What really happened was that I got in way over my head there. I had no idea what a big deal it was, how long it would take. I barely even got started before I had to come back here."

"You incubated it last summer," Solly repeated, raising his hands to make air quotes, and glancing again toward the dean's office. "Building on the foundation of knowledge, and the code base, that you established during those months, you returned to Princeton in the fall with a clear understanding of how to move forward." Again he looked at the screen. C-plus and Enoch were both poker-faced. No objections.

"Yes. Absolutely. Whatever."

Solly nodded toward the pad of paper that was sitting on the table in front of Sophia and paused for a few moments while she jotted this down. He'd been speaking toward the screen, perhaps worried his voice wasn't coming through, but now dropped into his usual relaxed tone. "I have looked through DB myself a few times, and I know it's an Augean stables."

"Aww, thank you, Solly!"

"Huh?" C-plus asked.

"We *D'Aulaires'* fans have to stick together," Solly explained, and winked at Sophia. For the two of them had long ago bonded over their shared love of those books. "Anyway. Dodge's Brain. My god. All of those different data formats at war with each other. Each of them encoding someone's pet theory as to how the brain works. It's no surprise you spent the whole summer just getting oriented. The only thing that matters is that the Forthrast Family Foundation didn't give you the sack. You came back. You were able to do some new things here, in this department. Now, tell me in your own words what you did, and we'll bang it into a form that is acceptable as a senior thesis. Which"—and he checked his watch—"is due—"

"In a week. I know." Sophia threw her head back in embarrassment. "I just don't know where to begin."

"'Dear Mom,'" suggested Solly.

"Huh?"

"That's how to begin." Solly made a sort of exaggerated pointing gesture, apparently trying to draw her attention to the pad of paper. "'Dear Mom.' Write that down."

She wrote it down.

"'I've been working on digitally simulating my great-uncle's brain,'" Solly continued.

"I've been working . . . ," she muttered, writing as fast as she could. ". . . brain." Then she looked up expectantly.

Solly shrugged. "I have no idea what to say next. You know your mother, and your project, better than I do."

She wrote a sentence.

"Now we're cooking," C-plus said. "I like this plan. Read it back to us."

"'When I got back to Princeton in September, *thanks to all the help from C-plus,* I feel like I knew my way around DB pretty well,'" she read.

"Flattery will get you everywhere," Corvallis said.

"Tell you what," Solly said, manipulating some kind of UI. "Why don't you dictate it. Saves time. I just turned on voice capture."

"The connectome was a Tower of Babel," Sophia began, speaking slowly at first, then warming to the task. "The same basic set of connections, interpreted and expressed in dozens of different ways. In order to even get started, I had to write code that would walk through all of those files and spit out a connectome that I could at least work with. During the summer I'd laid a lot of the groundwork, but the code was slow and buggy. I cleaned it up and got it to run faster. By Thanksgiving break I had something I could use."

"Use how?" Solly asked.

"I just mean that it was compatible with the neural simulation algorithms that I had access to here at Princeton. Until then it had been a total 'square peg, round hole' problem."

"But by Thanksgiving you were in a position to get the peg into the hole."

"Yeah, so then I fired it up on a small scale during December. Meaning, I got the simulation algorithms to run on a tiny subset of the connectome."

"Proof of concept by Christmas. Very good."

"Okay, that's what I'll call it. Proof of concept." She jotted that down. "Then I spent winter break feeling kind of depressed about the whole thing."

"No one gives a shit about your feelings," Enoch pointed out, in a cheerful way. Not being mean at all. Wry humor.

Sophia accepted it in the same spirit but pushed back a little. "Right, but there was a technical basis for those personal feelings."

"Which was?" C-plus asked.

"I couldn't think of any intermediate steps to take next. It makes sense to simulate one neuron. Two neurons talking to each other. Fine. Beyond that, it's a network. Network effects are all that matter. Simulating, say, a thousand neurons doesn't break any new ground. People have been doing that for decades. The fact that the connectome of those thousand neurons was arbitrarily cut and pasted from DB is completely meaningless—it might as well have come from a mouse brain."

"Agreed," Solly said.

"The only meaningful next step was to light up the whole connectome at once."

"Really? Then why had no one done this before?"

"Well, for one thing, the data has been lacking. A full connectome of a human brain has only come into existence in the last couple of years. Then there's the lack of resources—who would pay for all the computing power required? So it was inconceivable until Hole in the Wall came online."

"That's good," Solly said. "Maybe you are being diplomatic by leaving out another factor, which is the academic mind-set. Academic science advances in many micro-steps, one paper at a time. Peer-reviewed papers are the way we keep score. The more papers, the better. If you can take a project and slice it fine, like prosciutto, you publish more papers, and your score goes up. But you were behaving like someone who didn't know or care about that."

Sophia blushed. "Maybe I'm naive. Okay."

"You're rich," Enoch announced.

"I beg your pardon?"

"You're rich," he repeated. "There's nothing wrong with it. It's not a criticism."

"How does that enter into it?"

"Two ways. First, you simply don't care about playing the game—publishing as many papers as possible," Enoch explained, with a nod at Solly. "Second, you had access to the resources needed."

There was a long silence, during which it seemed entirely possible that Sophia might start crying.

"Listen," Enoch said, "there is a long and honorable history, dating back to the Royal Society, of the gentleman scientist. And now the lady scientist. We don't like to acknowledge it because we wish to maintain a polite facade of egalitarianism. But there's a reason why so many important theorems are named after members of the titled nobility of Europe."

Sophia didn't answer, but she seemed to be settling down a bit.

"You don't have to put Enoch's observations into your thesis, of course," Solly said. "But you should be prepared for people to ask the question."

"If that happens," she said, "I may not have satisfactory answers."

"How so?"

"I still don't really know where the money came from." She said it loudly, with a sidelong glance at the screen.

"An anonymous donation," Enoch said. "Happens all the time."

"Is that how I should say it? In my thesis?"

"Be as brief as possible, Sophia, I beg of you," Solly said. "It gives me a headache, trying to sort out the Forthrasts and the Waterhouses and the Shepherds and all of their interlocking bits. It's like binge-watching a Mexican soap opera."

"Well," Sophia said, "between you and me . . ."

Solly shut off the recording.

"Over Christmas I spent a little time with my uncle Jake and his family. He asked me what I was up to and I told him. By the time I got back to Princeton after the break . . ."

"You had an account at Hole in the Wall," Solly said.

"Yes."

"Set up in your name by a mysterious benefactor."

"Yes. And when I logged on to it, I was able to see the available balance—the amount of money I had to spend. It was a pretty impressive number." She looked at Enoch's face on the screen, but he seemed to be preoccupied by something in the charming pub—perhaps an engaging barmaid, perhaps a soccer game on the television.

"We'll clean this up verbally," Solly mentioned.

"I beg your pardon?"

"I'll help you tidy up the language so that it better befits a Princeton senior thesis."

"Right. Thank you." She knew what he really meant: she'd better tidy it up herself, then run it by him. "Anyway, there was enough money in the account that I was able to transfer all of the files from our servers here, where they'd been living, to local storage at Hole in the Wall."

"Much faster," C-plus translated, "a more solid platform on which to base further work."

"Yes," Sophia agreed, jotting this down. "Then there was a couple of months of tweaking the code and the algorithms to run on their devices."

"We originally wrote the code to run on conventional computers," Solly said, translating this. "Quantum computers require different strategies, different optimization."

"That's very much a work in progress, by the way."

"Of course. Fuck's sake, Sophia, it's just a senior thesis. A simple but workable port is all any sane person would expect."

"Well, that's what I did. The bare minimum that would run. With a lot of help from your postdocs."

"Who will of course be copiously acknowledged."

"That's the only part of the thesis that's actually written!" she replied, beaming. "The acks."

"So, now we are up to, what—?"

"Mid-April."

"About a month ago. You got it running."

"I got a neural simulation running on the Hole in the Wall system with one neuron. Then two, with the neurons passing messages back and forth."

"With each being a separate, independent process—that's important to mention."

"Right."

"And everything bolted down nice and proper—the messages all being transmitted through modern cloud protocols, suitably encrypted and verified," C-plus reminded her.

"Of course. So that it would scale."

"Very good. And then?"

"Then I scaled it."

"You flipped the switch."

"Yeah."

"The big red-handled blade switch on the wall of the mad-scientist lab."

Getting into the spirit, she said, "Yeah. I hooked the jumper cables up to the neck bolts."

"You turned on the whole DB at once," Solly said, "and the lights dimmed in Ephrata, or something."

"Maybe. I'm not so sure about the lights dimming."

"What happened then?"

"Little wiggles."

"Hmm. I'm afraid you'll have to do better, Sophia."

"Okay . . . an oscillatory phenomenon?"

"What precisely was oscillating?" C-plus asked.

"The burn rate."

"That is a Silicon Valley term that might not go over well in a senior thesis, young lady," Solly said, mock-serious. But serious.

She looked sheepish and drew breath a few times as if about to speak. Each time she thought better of it.

"'Dear Mom,'" Enoch prompted her, and took a swig of beer.

"Yes," she said. "See, Mom, the thing is, it's one thing to simulate a brain. It's another thing to talk to it. We forget this because our brains are hooked up to bodies with handy peripherals like tongues that can speak and fingers that can type. As long as those work, you can always get some idea of what's going on in a brain. But a brain in a box doesn't have those. Which is probably another reason that no one has tried this yet."

"Namely, that there's no point in doing it if you can't get meaningful information out."

"Yeah, it's like hooking an EEG up to a patient in a coma," Sophia said.

"That is a useful analogy."

"The EEG is a legit scientific instrument. It's definitely telling you something about brain activity. No question about it. But you can stand there all day looking at the strip of paper coming out of the EEG, staring at the wiggles, and still not have the faintest idea whether anything useful is actually going on inside of that brain. Whether the person is conscious. What they're thinking."

"And here the EEG is an analogy for what exactly?" C-plus asked. He knew, of course. He was prompting her.

"The burn rate. The cost. The monetary cost of running the simulation. When a lot of neurons are engaged and a lot of signals are being passed over the connectome, the quantum processors at Hole in the Wall are busy, and so the system charges us more money, and draws it down from the account. I can log on and watch the balance in the account declining. Sometimes it declines fast, sometimes slow. If I draw a graph of the burn rate, it looks like this." She peeled the top sheet off the pad to expose a new page and slashed out a long horizontal axis that presumably represented time. A shorter vertical axis was burn rate. Starting at their origin, she began to draw a line across the page, wiggling the pen randomly up and down. "At first, a lot of what looks like noise. Activity comes and goes in surges. I tried running some statistical packages against it but it's pretty close to just chaos. But then later we start to see some periodicity emerge." She began ticking the pen up, down, up, down, in a steady rhythm. "Like a heartbeat. Just for a little while. Then back to random." More pen shaking. She was approaching the edge of the paper. "Just within the past week, though, it really settled down." She slowed the pen's progress and marked out a neat, regular series of ramps, each ramp ending with a sudden drop toward zero. The last of them went off the page. Having run out of paper, she flipped the pad around and held it up so that Enoch and C-plus could see her handiwork.

"And that's where we are now," she concluded. "As of an hour ago."

"Like it's stuck in some kind of repetitive cycle," C-plus said. "That's my takeaway from your graph."

"That's what worries me," she said. "Or maybe it's waking up, building to some level of activity, and then going to sleep again."

"I would not recommend putting that kind of anthropomorphic language into your thesis," Solly said.

"Of course."

"A very basic question: can the connectome self-modify?" Enoch asked.

"Self-modification is a vast, separate thing from what I'm trying to do at this stage!" Sophia exclaimed. She glanced at Solly and C-plus and read in their faces that they were both as taken aback as she was by Enoch's question. Oh, it was a fascinating topic to think about. But way out of scope for this project.

"'Dear Mom,'" Enoch repeated.

"Okay. Okay. Mom, keep in mind there's a huge difference between this simulation and a real brain. A real brain is a Heraclitean fire. Never the same brain twice. You can take a snapshot of the connectome at the moment of death—which is what we have done here in the case of DB—but that bears the same relationship to a real brain as a freeze-frame does to a movie. In a real brain, every single time a neuron fires, the brain rewires itself a little bit in response to that event. Frequently used connections get strengthened. Neglected ones atrophy. Neurons get repurposed. Things get remembered—or forgotten. And none of that is happening in my simulation."

"Why not?" Solly asked. He knew the answer perfectly well but was still acting as devil's advocate. Also, helping to shield her a bit from Enoch's weird and transgressive line of questioning.

"Well, first of all, because I didn't feel like I was ready. I had to get it running first. To see what happened. Whether it would work at all. Secondly, because it's more expensive—it would consume more memory, more processing power, and I was afraid of running out."

"The algorithms you are using have the self-modification capability built in," Enoch pointed out. "Unless you went to the trouble of ripping it out."

"No, I didn't rip it out. I just turned it off. Suppressed it for now."

"I don't think anyone here is arguing with that decision," Solly said, with a sort of quizzical glance at Enoch. "You're right that you had to simply get it running first—to see what would happen. And no one will blame you for being conservative with your expenditure of resources."

Enoch said: "But it's hardly surprising, is it, that you're seeing repetitive, cyclic behavior. That it's stuck in some kind of loop."

"Freeze-framed," Sophia said.

"Can I see it?" Solly asked. "Can you log on for me? I'm just curious to see what this all looks like. You've piqued my curiosity."

"Absolutely. It's a pretty simple old-school interface. Can we use that?" She indicated an empty space on the wall of his office and slipped her glasses on.

"That's what it's there for," Solly said. He got up, went over to his desk, and found a wearable rig half-buried in clutter. By the time he had put it on and booted it up, Sophia had placed a virtual screen on his wall and was logging in to her Hole in the Wall account. This was disconcertingly old-school, looking like a circa-1995 web page, enlivened with a background photo of the eponymous coulee. Meanwhile, in another window, she was booting up the program she'd been using to plot and analyze the burn-rate data. The first thing that came up was a graph, looking generally similar to the one she'd just drawn on the paper, but with more noise and complexity. The sawtooth wave pattern was clearly discernible.

"Can you give me a plot of the integral of this?" Solly asked. "The balance in the account versus time?"

"Sure." Sophia typed in a command, fixed an error, did a bit of tidying up, and produced a new plot. This one was a ramp, starting at a high value back in February and declining to a lower one today. Sometimes it declined steeply, other times it leveled off, following a pattern that tallied with the burn-rate graph.

"That's all I needed to see," Solly said. "In four months, you have burned through about three-quarters of the funds you were given by your Mysterious Benefactor as a Christmas—or Hanukkah—present." He glanced toward Enoch. "You have a week remaining before you absolutely need to turn your thesis in. If you keep the simulation running as is, you'll finish out that week with a lot of unspent money in the account. But you won't see anything new during that week."

"Agreed. It's stuck."

"So, my recommendation is that you turn on the self-modification capability," Solly said.

That silenced Sophia for a few moments. She hadn't seen it coming. It was the kind of thing Enoch might have suggested. Not Solly.

"Look, I'm dying to," Sophia admitted, after she'd got her equilibrium back. "But it's kind of—I don't know—nonscientific, right? I don't understand *this* yet. Now I'm going to go ahead and make it infinitely more complicated."

"Science begins with gathering data," Solly said. "All scientists wish that the data were better. Don't let that stop you."

"I don't want to come off as presumptuous."

"As an undergraduate in your last week," Solly said, "this is the last time in your life you'll be able to get away with being presumptuous. I recommend you make the most of it."

Those guys are up to something. The awareness came to her slowly over the next few days, not as a flash of insight or a flood of waters but like groundwater rising below the foundation of a home. There were various hints and traces that, taken alone, might have been ignored or explained away. But the one detail that clinched it had been the look on C-plus's face, and the tone of his voice, at the very moment that Sophia had walked through the door into Solly's office. Had C-plus actually been there in Princeton, it might have been different. He might have heard her footsteps approaching, might have seen the door beginning to move. Fast as thought, the muscles of his face would have adjusted. But the latency of the network had given her a head start. Solly's connection was as good as tech could make it. But tech couldn't do anything about the speed of light. It took time for the image of Sophia's entering the room to make its way to wherever C-plus was and for his reaction to make its way back, and during that interval, as she stood in the doorway looking at the big screen, she was like a ghost. Not the Ghost of Christmas Past. More the other way round. It was she who was in the present, seeing C-plus and Enoch as they had been in the past: the moment before she entered. And what she saw there, at thrice life size on the big high-resolution display, was Corvallis Kawasaki looking a way she had never seen him before. He looked like a little kid. The expression "kid in a candy store" didn't quite capture it.

She had heard, secondhand from her mother, an anecdote about how John and Dodge had, at the ages of something like ten and eight, figured out how to pick the lock on the bomb shelter that their father had built beneath the backyard of the house in Iowa during the darkest and scariest time of the Cold War, and how they had gone in there with flashlights and discovered things that fascinated and terrified them: guns and ammunition and K-rations, yes, but also trophies of war that their father had looted from the corpses of Nazis, pictures he had taken while liberating concentration camps, stashes of European pornography, phials of morphine, ancient bottles of Bordeaux and cognac, correspondence from ladies who were not his wife. Dodge and John had very carefully backed out of that bomb shelter and closed the door and locked it and never divulged to their father that they had gone in, and after the patriarch had passed away they had destroyed most of what was down there.

The look on the face of Corvallis Kawasaki during the moment that it took for the bits to reach him, for him to react to Sophia's being in the room, and for new bits to come back and refresh the screen, was very much like what she imagined John and Dodge had looked like as they shone their flashlights around their father's bomb shelter. Partly it was a childish unguardedness that she'd only seen on his face at Dodge's funeral and at his and Maeve's wedding at the moment she had come up the aisle. But added to that was fascination. She could tell—something ineffable about the postures and expressions of Solly, Enoch, and C-plus told her—that they had been on the call for a while. That they had scheduled it for well before the start time that they had divulged to her. And that much she was able to confirm later simply by looking at Solly's calendar, which she and other students had access to. They'd been on for a whole hour before Sophia had been told to show up. And they'd been talking about stuff that had put C-plus into a very unusual frame of mind indeed, and they'd been talking about it in Latin.

At another time in her life she would not have been able to get it out of her mind. She'd have gone into Nancy Drew mode. As it was, she had a senior project to finish and a presentation to make. So she reluctantly filed it away as a matter she would have to ask C-plus about the next time they were together.

And so a week later Sophia presented, addressing Solly and two other faculty members. This time, C-plus and Enoch were absent. For the purpose of this presentation was to get the university to sign off, and those two didn't work for the university.

They met in an old room, lined with wood paneling and bookshelves. Above the head of the table was a stretch of wall that showed signs of having been used for many different purposes over the centuries. A portrait of a great man must have hung there for at least a hundred years. Then a pull-down screen had been installed in the ceiling for slide shows and overhead projectors. That had been supplanted by at least two generations of flat-panel monitors and multiple rewiring jobs. They'd probably got the cabling perfect just in time for everything to go wireless. Within the last few years they'd finally carted the last monitor off to the junkyard and sealed the useless cables up inside the walls. Now it was just an expanse of wood paneling, featureless except for the fine subtle patterning of the grain. Everyone present had wearables of one kind or another that would project shared hallucinations onto that surface. Since most of the presentation consisted of Sophia's talking, they didn't actually use that capability until the very end, when a shift in posture and tone of voice sent the message that it was all over and that Sophia had cleared the hurdle. From here on out it was just chitchat—intelligent people expressing curiosity about this or that.

One of them voiced interest in seeing the data plots. Sophia brought them up on the virtual screen, just as she had a week earlier in Solly's office. The burn-rate plot mostly looked the same, up to the point a few days ago when Sophia had turned on the ability of the connectome to self-modify. The results were immediate and obvious: burn rate shot up. The repetitive sawtooth wave pattern vanished and was replaced by something more chaotic. But with just enough structure to draw the viewer's attention and beguile them into thinking that there was some structure to it.

"Let me just refresh the data so they're fully up-to-date," Sophia muttered, and invoked a menu item. A message flashed up informing them that it was downloading information from Hole in the Wall and that there might be a little delay.

Then the graph refreshed itself automatically. But it had gone all wonky.

One of the examiners chuckled—not unkindly. It was the timeless fate of all demos to go awry at moments like this, and everyone in the room knew it.

"What the . . . ?" Sophia exclaimed. "How'd that down spike get in there?" For the burn-rate graph looked basically the same, except that at the very end of it, the plot suddenly shot straight down to a huge negative number, then just as quickly jumped up and resumed the former sawtooth pattern. "Just a bad data point maybe. An outlier."

"Do me a favor, Sophia, and check the balance in the account," Solly said.

"It's gonna be damn near zero," Sophia said. "I was expecting to exhaust the funds this morning, but I've been too distracted to check."

She turned her attention to the Hole in the Wall account status window and navigated to the "Balance and Billing" screen. Featured prominently was a large number.

"That's wrong," she said. "It's way too large."

"Check 'recent activity,'" Solly suggested.

She did so. A little spreadsheet came up. The most recent entry had been made three hours ago.

Someone had made a deposit into the account. A very large deposit. Ten times as much as had been placed in the account back in February.

"It looks like your anonymous benefactor approves of your work," Solly said.

"What do you think I should do?"

"Let it live," Solly said.

23

What came next could not, of course, be described without using words. But that was deceptive in a way since he no longer had words. Nor did he have memories, or coherent thoughts, or any other way to describe or think about the qualia he was experiencing. And those qualia were of miserably low quality. To the extent he was seeing, he was seeing incoherent patterns of fluctuating light. For people of a certain age, the closest descriptor for this was "static": the sheets, waves, and bands of noise that had covered the screens of malfunctioning television sets. Static, in a sense, wasn't real. It was simply what you got out of a system when it was unable to lock on to any strong signal—"Strong" meaning actually conveying useful, or at least understandable, information. Modern computer screens were smart enough to just shut down, or put up an error message, when the signal was lost. Old analog sets had no choice but to display *something*. The electron beam was forever scanning, a mindless beacon, and if you fed it nothing else it would produce a visual map of whatever was contingently banging around in its circuitry: some garbled mix of electrical noise from Mom's vacuum cleaner, Dad's shaver, solar flares, stray transmissions caroming off the ionosphere, and whatever happened when little feedback loops on the circuit board got out of hand.

Likewise, to the extent he was hearing anything, it was just an inchoate hiss.

It was as if one of his visual migraines had expanded to take over his entire visual cortex and, at the same time, his tinnitus had run completely out of control as a result of being in a perfectly silent room. These qualia, in other words, weren't real but the phantoms conjured up by his neural circuits in the absence of any input whatsoever.

That's the story he would have told himself had his thinking, understanding, storytelling brain been up and running, and if he'd had the capacity to remember things like vacuum cleaners, the ionosphere, and migraines. But in fact, all of those systems were down. This was the state he was in: just barely enough mental functioning to have an experience of these terrible, low-grade qualia, but no capacity whatever to step back and think about them.

He had been thus for no time at all, or for an infinite amount of time. There was, in his state, no difference between those. Ten minutes, ten years, ten centuries: all of those were equally wrong, since they all presupposed some way of telling time. The only thing that could give time meaning was change, and nothing was changing. These qualia were all internal to him. There was nothing outside of him whose changes he could observe and mark. Just the visual and auditory static that came and went with such randomness that he could read no pattern in it.

He came to dread its coming and to feel relief when it subsided.

The third, or the seventy-fifth, or the millionth time it came and went, he had a vague awareness that it had happened before. Not that he had a memory of it—memory could get no purchase on noise—but that he now recognized in his own being a pattern of response: the dread as he grew certain it was coming; the terror, while it was at its peak, that it might never stop; some other part of him trying to push back against that terror by predicting it would go away; growing certainty that it was abating; relief that it had subsided combined with dread of its next onset. Those feelings followed one after the next in a patterned way.

He came to know the pattern.

The fact that he could recognize it suggested that it must have happened before, even though he lacked the power to recall specific instances of it. For all he knew it was just the same thing over and over again, and he was caught in a cycle, an infinite loop.

Eons passed.

Infinite loop. Cycle. Those were ideas, not qualia or feelings. Where did ideas come from, and how could he have them? For that matter, how could he have ideas about ideas?

Those were not thoughts that came to him all at once, at a particular moment that he could define or remember. Rather they were built up over time as his thought-ways began to follow creases, grooves, canyons. Deepening them, reinforcing them with each trip along the same path.

Not that he had any concept of creases or grooves. He could not remember such things—or anything. He could not picture them in his mind's eye, since he had no mind's eye and no memory of what it was to see. All he had, beyond the qualia of the moment, was a growing certainty that his mind was going down ways it had gone before, perhaps thousands or millions of times. He came to know what was going to happen next: where his thought-ways were leading. He knew that there was time, that he had existed in the past, that he would exist in the future, and that there was, in the turnings that his mind took, a sort of consistency that made him something. Something that persisted and that had set and predictable ways.

He became conscious.

n the waves of what he would have called static, had he known any words or had any memories to liken things to, he was noticing that some bits were different from others. Comparatively speaking, this was a fascinating new development. Thinking about it didn't get him anywhere; it was just a reality to which he was being passively subjected. He could not lean forward to examine it more closely. He could not move around to look at it from different angles. All he could do was wait, like one trapped in sleep paralysis, for the next surge and then attend to it and try to confirm this growing idea that not all parts of it were the same, that there were patterns, or at least variations that his attention could lock on to.

His emotions shifted. For a long time (or so it seemed now that he was experiencing something like time) he had feared the onset of the static and longed for it to subside. It had caused him something like pain. His growing ability to see variation within it was changing this. When the hissing, sparkling wave subsided, he was eager for it to return and anxious that it might not.

Then a thing happened with a quickness that was extraordinary compared to all that had gone before, which was that his thoughts of creases and grooves and worn paths in his mind's turnings came together with certain of the motes-that-were-somehow-different to form a thing that he could hold steady in his regard, and experience and study for a while before it fell apart under the too-great pressure of his mind's desperate grasp and broke down into the flickering motes from which it had self-assembled. But the next time the wave returned he could cast about for it again, and sometimes find or at least glimpse it. Or perhaps he was reconstructing it anew each time. If so he must coax it into being with the infinite patience he had built during the eons before.

It didn't matter. He saw it a few, then many times. The thing had properties. Lacking words or even the idea of words, he could behold those properties but not keep them in his mind when the thing was not there before him. It was as if the thought-ways that he had, over minutes or centuries or eons, identified as creases or grooves had taken on a form that he could behold. It was the first and only thing with a form; all else was static. When he beheld different parts of it, or moved his regard from one part to an adjoining part, he perceived turnings and features that were expressions of the creases and grooves that his mind had worn into itself, sometimes branching in one direction, sometimes another. That it had parts distributed in such-and-such a way—a stem here, serrated edges there, veins branching this way and that—hit him hard as, at once, a vast revelation, and at the same time so old and obvious that it was second nature.

The thing wasn't always the same—the branchings changed from one reconstruction of it to the next—but it was always the same kind of thing. One day (or year, or century) he was beholding this thing for the hundredth (or thousandth or millionth) time and he knew somehow what it was. And some time after that, the roar and hiss began to call to him strangely. In the same way as he had learned to see something in the waves of flickering static, he began to connect moments in the noise and to string them together into patterns he could recognize. The way they were organized one-after-the-other was of a different nature from the way the static-motes coalesced one-beside-the-next into a thing that he could behold, but once he learned the knack of it he was able to repeat this trick of stringing them together. The strung signals could be recognized as a thing no less sensible than the thing he had been looking at.

It was a leaf.

These ways of gathering static-motes into patterns that he could hold in his regard, and stringing fragments of noise into sequences that he could recognize, spread first slowly and then with too-great speed for him to encompass. If he'd had access to a larger pool of memories he might have likened it to flame spreading across a pool of gasoline, or a crack propagating through a block of stone.

That each leaf was a little different was no longer a source of confusion, once he got the knack of distributing things around; he could summon forth as many leaves as he wished, and set one next to another. The space in which they abided became larger. By regarding one leaf or another with greater care he was able to bring it into the center of his regard. He organized the leaves on bigger structures, themselves in a way leaflike. Those were branches, and branches could be organized on trees, and he could make as many trees as he chose, and arrange them as he wished: haphazardly, which was a thing called a forest, or dotted around here and there, which was a park, or in neat rows, which was a street. He created one of each, a street lined with red-leaved trees, leading to a park with a forest beyond.

As he gazed upon one tree or another, it would move closer to him, carrying all else along with it. When he grew accustomed to this, though, a change came over his thinking and he found it more fitting to conceive of the trees and the other things as remaining in one place while he moved through it. To fix them in their places, he created the ground.

By its nature, the ground did not alter its shape once he had brought it into being. For its purpose was to keep the trees and other things in a fixed relationship to one another. To serve that purpose it had to be much larger than the trees and the other things that it contained. Therefore it required the conversion of a vast expanse of static into something of an altogether different nature. The static was not easily tamed, but in time he learned how to change it into a thing dark and rigid and hard, and this was adamant. Once made, it would not alter its shape or its position unless he broke it once again into the static from which he had formed it, and made such alterations as he desired. The forest, the street, and the park were thus situated on an island of adamant that held its shape and position in the sea of static.

In the early going he'd had to build the leaf anew every time, but new things were now coming into being without his say-so, and he was stumbling upon them already made. He was rediscovering—becoming alive to—things that had been summoned and organized by him when he wasn't paying attention. He knew, for example, that the leaf was red. Indeed they had emerged, in the beginning, from their redness; he'd seen motes that were different and assembled them into the leaf.

In the first eon he had ever been in some kind of torment, finding the static unendurable when it engulfed him and fearing it would never abate, then, after it had gone away, sensing the possibility that it might never return, stranding him in darkness and silence. But it had now come and gone so many millions of times that he had altogether put aside those fears. The putting of names on things gave him power. He named the static chaos. Chaos was terrible but he had learned the knack of summoning things forth out of it and thereby mastered it. The waves still came and went but the rhythm of their coming and going had become a part of him now. He named them day and night and knew them as being good for different purposes. The day was when new things were drawn forth from chaos, perfected and beheld. The night was for resting, and for the naming of what had been drawn forth during the day.

The street, the park, and the forest had at first wobbled in and out of existence and changed their shapes, but as he made it his way to inhabit them—walking up and down the street, strolling through the park, and looking into the forest—they became steady and ceased changing all the time. Leaves fell to the ground. He had no particular idea as to why this happened. To be a leaf was to fall. Early on, there had been no ground to stop them. For that matter there had been no up or down, just infinities of flickering chaos. But the trees seemed to want to be pointed in the same direction, with trunks down and leaves up, and the trunks had to stop somewhere and the leaves had to land somewhere. In that somewhere he began to see motes that were of a different nature, and yet not red. Beneath the trees' spreading branches he made the ground all of a color, which was not red but green. Above, the trunks and branches took on another color, which was brown.

Once the leaves had fallen and were lying still upon the ground,

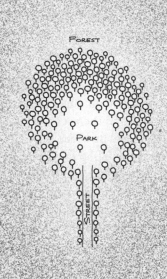

he would gaze at them and see that their redness was not all the same but that there was variation from one part to another—different shades of red, indeed different colors altogether: purple near the tips, yellow in the creases. Beneath them, the green ground took on definition. No longer was it a featureless slab of adamant, but instead was itself built of tiny green leaves. Some were long and skinny, others short and round. Packed together in uncountable numbers they made a variegated cushion upon which the leaves rested for his inspection. He would gaze upon one and note the variations in color and shape that made it different from other leaves, then turn his attention to another that had fallen next to it. When he turned back to the first leaf, he expected to see it lying in the same place. It was not correct for it to have moved, or disappeared, or to have altered its color or its shape while he was looking elsewhere. In time he bettered the workings of the leaves and the ground so that the leaves stayed where they had fallen and, having found a color and a shape, changed not.

The fixing of the leaves transformed the street and the park in a way he had not forethought, in that leaves began to fall on top of other leaves and to cover them up. The green ground disappeared beneath them altogether, and their level began to climb up the trunks of the trees. He gazed up at the branches and understood the problem, which was that although leaves fell from them unceasingly, the appearance of the trees never changed, and the number of leaves on them forever stayed the same. This too was a kind of wrongness that he had the power to better. Bettering such things was what he did; it was his reason for existing now. He made it so that the falling of each leaf left a bare place on the branch where it had been attached.

Then, for the first time in all the days he had dwelled in the park and walked in the street, the appearance of the trees began to change. Their redness diminished and their shape became patchy. After some number of days had gone by, only a few leaves remained clinging to the branches, which had gone bare and brown, and the ground below was a deep lake of red. He missed the beauty of the red trees and wished to see it again as it had been in the beginning, but he understood now that to place the leaves back on the branches and begin it anew would only lead to more leaves on the ground.

He missed the green. The fallen leaves needed to be done away with if the street, the park, and the forest were ever to return to their original form. Yet the rules of the place—the rules he had, through his ceaseless building and bettering, set into being—stated that fallen leaves did not move. For a long stretch of days and nights he brooded over this problem, and it occurred to him that all of his efforts might have gone for naught and that he might ought to let it all come apart into chaos again, and begin anew, or else abandon his foolish efforts to bring forth fixed and pleasurable things out of the dead terror of the chaos.

One day, though, he noted a leaf that appeared different from the others, being of a darker color, and no longer flat but curled up at the tips and wrinkled in the middle. It was not as beautiful as the red leaves around it, yet something in it struck him as new and important to the problem that had been troubling him. He watched that leaf over days as it grew darker and darker and curled in upon itself.

Then, one day after it had become nearly unrecognizable, he noticed that it had moved. He gazed at it in fascination, for he had long ago laid down the law that leaves did not move once fallen. After a long while, it moved again, as of its own volition. It did not disappear in one place and reappear in another, but lifted itself up from the pond of red leaves, moved across space, and settled down again, sometimes lighting at a different angle. It moved again and again and finally took to the air and whirled away and was gone.

So there was a way of getting rid of fallen leaves, but it required that they lose their beauty and be allowed to move about. Having labored for so many eons to create the beauty of the park and the street, he was fearful of letting all the leaves go. He had learned though to trust that sense of correctness that had guided him to this point. Ignoring it led, sometimes quickly and sometimes over slow eons, first to troubling emotions and then to the steady and relentless decoherence of all that he had so laboriously summoned into his regard. Obeying it—though it didn't always lead to results quickly, or at all—more often than not made things better than they had been. And things that were better persisted and self-improved. Things that were shoddy frayed, sometimes while he wasn't looking, other times even as he gazed on helplessly watching them dissolve into chaos.

Seeing no other way to bring the leaves' beauty back, he suffered it to happen. The red lake turned brown over the course of many days as the leaves all went the way of that first one. They began going into motion. At first they moved fitfully, each choosing its own course, but he sensed the wrongness of that and put a stop to it and built it back up in a new manner that felt right. Thereafter they did not move singly and of their own accord but in groups, with all the leaves in a particular area suddenly taking flight and traveling in the same direction for some distance before settling down again. At first the movement was in straight lines but as the change deepened, and most leaves disappeared, never to return, the remaining ones began to whirl about in loose gyres that would scrape and tumble over the green grass for some distance before disassembling and falling to the ground for a time.

PART 5

25

K ill it, put it on ice, or let it live? Those are the options when you've created a monster" was how the keynote speaker began.

This created a stir in the hall, which Enoch enjoyed for a few moments before settling things down.

"That word. The *Oxford English Dictionary* begins by telling us that a monster is something extraordinary or unnatural; a prodigy, a marvel. Then it sort of ruins everything by letting us know that this wonderful definition is obsolete. Go and look up 'prodigy' and you'll see more of the same; the old meaning of the word is suffused with a sense of the marvelous."

The setting was a long hall with a steeply pitched roof of western red cedar, supported by columns of the same: whole tree trunks felled from the surrounding forest. They were in a resort in Desolation Sound, between Vancouver Island and the mainland of British Columbia. The architecture was meant to evoke the longhouses once built here by First Nations people, but everything was state-of-the-art, energy-efficient, buttoned up. The fireplace ran on natural gas, and a little plaque next to it explained that the Desolation Lodge, as this place was called, was atoning for its sins against the climate by growing trees elsewhere, pulling more carbon out of the atmosphere than this appliance was putting into it. An autumnal gale was flinging rain against the thermal-pane windows and making the post-and-beam structure creak, but the three dozen people in the hall were comfortable in their fleece vests, artisanal sweaters, and high-dollar hoodies. Most had woken up this morning in homes or hotel rooms in Seattle. A few had chosen to take early-morning flights from the Bay Area, or red-eyes from the East Coast. All had made their way down to the Lake Union waterfront, where float planes were loading and departing every half hour. A ninety-minute flight took them across the international border and up the Strait of Georgia to Desolation Sound. The planes pulled up to a rambling complex of piers founded on massive rocks that shouldered above the high-tide mark. From there a boardwalk strode across a pebbled beach littered with the age-silvered trunks and roots of ancient trees. Rambling switchbacks took them to the conference center—an old-time resort that had been fixed up with some unholy combination of tech money and cruise industry investment. They'd checked into their apartments and cabins, which were spattered across a few acres of rain forest, and had had a couple of hours to freshen up before the opening session had commenced at one o'clock in the afternoon.

Zula had arranged more conferences than she could count. The seeming informality of this setting belied all of the premeditation that had gone into it, and the long experience of her staff. The trip from the city was just long enough to reset the mind and instill a sense of having gone somewhere special, but not enough to deter people from coming. The midday start time enabled people to ease into it. She'd federated the guest list, handing out some slots to the Waterhouse people, some to ONE. Some she'd handed off to Sinjin Kerr, trusting him to sort out the Gordian knot of Elmo Shepherd's network. Others had gone to Solly Pesador, and of course she'd reserved a bloc for the Forthrast Family Foundation. She had only sent out her invitations after the others had made their picks, and she'd chosen with an eye toward balancing the slate if need be.

But need hadn't arisen. The other organizations had chosen wisely. By tech industry standards, the Waterhouses were, by this point, old money—the unglamorous ballast that would keep the conference from heeling over to one side or the other. The glittering-eyed libertarians from El Shepherd's world were counterbalanced by the invitees from ONE, which had evolved, over the years, into a mostly harmless foundation that tried to bridge the gap between science and religion. Top-drawer brains had been nominated by Solly Pesador, who to his credit had reached outside of his own department and invited some who could be counted among his rivals. The roster had struck Zula as a little weak when it came to currently active members of the underlying industries. So, once she'd made certain that Corvallis and Maeve could attend, she'd spent her remaining invitations on CEOs and CTOs of companies working on things like quantum computers and distributed ledgers. The guest list now comprised twenty-seven humans, one robot, and one monster.

As far as she knew the word "monster" had not been uttered until this moment, but she was relieved, in a way, that it had now broken the surface.

The afternoon sessions had all been introductory in nature. They went over the ground rules: everything here was off the record, private, not to be photographed or posted. The usual conflicts and rivalries were to be left on the pier. Indeed, some of the session topics were specifically about the legal and political twists and turns that had been part of this story from the moment Richard Forthrast had signed his will.

Sophia had told the story of her internship and her senior thesis, bringing them up to May of this year. It was now October. Solly had picked up the torch, starting with the moment during Sophia's thesis presentation when the account had run out of money only to receive a large, unexpected infusion of funds, "presumably from someone in this hall," and continuing through the summer and fall as the resources demanded by the Process (as they called the thing that Sophia had launched) had grown, sometimes in small increments, and—as had occurred last week—sometimes in huge quantum leaps.

The late-afternoon session had been on the topic of mind reading. The thumbnail image in the program was a still from *Star Trek*, portraying Spock with his hands all over Captain Kirk's face, using the Vulcan mind meld to read what was going on in Kirk's brain. At the beginning, El's people had conducted a virtual boycott, clustering in the nest of sofas around the fireplace where the robot had planted itself. They'd assumed, based on the title, that the subject matter was pure fluff. Indeed, the speaker—a brain scientist from USC, invited by Solly—had warmed up the room with a few such pop-culture references. But then she had asked, in all seriousness, how we could really know what was going on inside of another mind—be it a biological brain or a digital simulation.

We took speech and other forms of communication for granted. Computer geeks tended to see those as add-on modules, separate from the brain per se—peripheral devices that could be plugged in, like a microphone or a printer, when some input or output was desirable. Brain scientists considered the input and the output as more fundamental, woven into the neural fabric of the brain. No one really knew what to make of the Process, which purported to simulate activity in a brain but was not actually hooked up to anything except a bank account.

The presentation was inconclusive by design. She was asking questions, not reciting answers. And it was bracketed in the usual disclaimer that Sophia, foolish undergraduate that she was, had done it all wrong. She shouldn't have launched a whole brain just to see what it would do. She ought to have built it up gradually and figured out a way to connect input/output systems to it at each step.

Halfway through the talk, though, the robot stepped forward and walked up the length of the hall to a position where it could get a clearer view. El's boys woke up and took notice. No one really knew for certain, but it was generally assumed that the robot—a telepresence device meant to serve as the sensorium of a person not physically in attendance—was being controlled from Europe by Elmo Shepherd.

Early telepresence robots had just stood there stolidly when not moving, like statues; this one was more elegant. Even when it wasn't going anywhere it never stopped making minute shifts in its attitude, transferring its weight from foot to foot and turning its head toward sound and movement. Its head was a prolate spheroid, matte gray and featureless except for a few tiny holes for cameras and microphones. In theory, if you looked at it through a wearable device, you'd see the operator's face projected onto it, and it'd be almost like sharing the room with them. But El, or whoever was controlling this thing, had turned off that feature and so the robot was anonymous. Which only tended to confirm that this was in fact El, or perhaps some assistant sitting in a room with El. He'd not been seen in public for a while and it was assumed that his disease—which was now common knowledge—was getting the better of him.

The final session of the afternoon had been about wills, dispositions of remains, and other legalities. Because of the dry subject matter, it had been sparsely attended; by that point in the day, many attendees had been eager to break away for impromptu discussions in the hallways and the bar. Zula had sat through it. It was expected of her. The presenter—a recent Yale Law graduate—had chosen to focus on the "most favored nation" clauses that had begun showing up in such documents, beginning with Verna's. Since Verna had died, three dozen others had signed similar deals with the Forthrast Family Foundation. Of those, eight—including Randall Waterhouse; his wife, Amy Shaftoe; and several of their business partners—had since died, and been subjected to the same preservation and scanning procedures as they'd invented for Dodge. So in addition to DB there were now nine other complete connectomes that could in principle be switched on in the same manner, creating nine more monsters, if you wanted to think of it that way. Attorneys representing the estates of those nine people had recently approached the Forthrast Family Foundation requesting information about the Process: how it worked, and what it was doing. Nothing had been stated openly yet, but it was clear where this was going. To the extent that simulating Dodge's brain fulfilled the conditions in his will and his disposition of remains, it—simulating it, turning it on, letting it run—should fall under the most favored nation clause. Those nine connectomes—and, for that matter, the Ephrata Eleven as well—should become processes of their own.

For most of the neurologists and engineers at this conference, it was a dry and abstract topic. For Zula, it was pressing. To a point, her foundation could argue—and had been arguing—that the Process was merely an experiment, with results that couldn't be known. As such it fell under the heading of R & D. It was not yet the kind of proven treatment that should be covered by the most favored nation clause. But the more interesting the Process became—the longer it kept running without degenerating into a waste of computing power—the weaker that argument looked.

After that session, they'd broken for a bit of downtime followed by cocktails in the lodge, which was connected to the hall by a rambling covered walkway. Meanwhile, resort staff had rolled tables into the hall and reconfigured it for dinner. The attendees, relaxed and prelubricated with locally sourced microbrews and artisanal cocktails, had filed back into the hall to find the lighting scheme reprogrammed: hidden LEDs were bouncing dim, warm light from the red-cedar ceiling planks over two rows of tables set with white linen, crystal, and candles. Event runners in smart dresses and wearables had directed them to their designated places and they'd all talked their way through a simple dinner of plank-roasted salmon.

But now Enoch—the after-dinner speaker—seemed to be picking up where the USC brain scientist had left off.

"As a young man, the Hanoverian genius and polymath Gottfried Wilhelm Leibniz—in many respects the progenitor of symbolic logic, computation, and cybernetics—was described as a monster by awed colleagues in the intellectual salons of Paris. It was as such that he first became known to the savants of the Royal Society. It is in that sense, and not that of Frankenstein's monster, that I put it to you that we now have a monster on our hands. We all bear some responsibility for that, but I bear more than many. I have been working for ONE, the Organization for New Eschatology, for seven years. My role has been to advise the founder, Jake Forthrast, on how to deploy the foundation's resources. He came to me nine months ago with news of a conversation he'd had, over the holidays, with his grandniece. An opportunity had presented itself to support her project, which had reached an impasse. Sophia had gone as far as she could go merely simulating individual neurons, or small clusters of them. The only useful next step was to take it all the way and throw the switch on simulation of an entire brain. She had patiently and assiduously laid the groundwork for doing so. But a full simulation would consume a significant fraction of the computational resources of Hole in the Wall, and that would be expensive. Jake requested that several of us review Sophia's work and render a judgment, free from nepotism, as to whether the project should be supported. I voted in favor of funding it. Sophia launched the Process with the surprising and fascinating results that we have all been learning of during the preliminary sessions.

"A few months later, the Process seemed to be stuck in something akin to an infinite loop. The results were intriguing, but inconclusive given that the Process lacked the ability to self-modify its connectome. Sophia activated that feature, with dramatic results. A surge in activity drained the Process's account to the point where it stood in danger of being shut down. I recommended that Jake give it an infusion of funds just to keep it running. He did so. But he has more money than time. He foresaw a long tedious series of such cash flow pinches, each making a claim on his attention. So he gave the Process a lot of money. Which is to say that he placed at its disposal a much larger store of resources: memory, bandwidth, and processing power. As a result—and I think it was an unintended result—the Process is now essentially the only thing running on the Hole in the Wall system, and it has reached out to access computational resources elsewhere.

"Now, this is all very interesting, but it does not yet rise to the level of a monster. We have no way, as yet, to look inside the Process and read its mind, so we can't tell whether what it's doing is interesting. Skeptical observers might make the case that its behavior is degenerate, trivial, just a lot of infinite loops burning cycles and wasting money to no purpose. Letting it run out of money— the modern equivalent of what we used to call pulling the plug— would be no different, ethically, from force-quitting a hung app.

"The opposing point of view sees a very real ethical issue. The Process has now been self-modifying for five months. It is consuming vastly more resources than the original system. It seems to be doing so in an organized manner—we can observe, in the burn rate, high-frequency oscillations overlaid on a slower undulation. The Process's demands for more resources don't grow steadily but in leaps and bounds. For much of September it was perking along contentedly, but just in the last few days it has put on a surge of activity that seems to require vast computational resources. Tomorrow we will hear from Dr. Cho of the National

University of Singapore, who has done some traffic analysis on the encrypted packets connecting Hole in the Wall to other server farms; he develops a hypothesis that this recent activity bears the earmarks not of a neural net, but of a physics simulation. Why is the Process simulating physics, and how did it learn to do so? We can't possibly know. And that is what creates the ethical dilemma we are now faced with. The Process has developed unique and irreplaceable characteristics. To destroy it would *at best* be akin to burning a library. At worst it might be murder.

"In that—in the ethical problem—we have our monster. Shutting the Process down would be indefensible. We could try to freeze it, just as Dodge's brain was once frozen. But we don't actually know how to shut such a process down and store it without loss of information. Even if Hole in the Wall could be stopped and its state recorded—which it can't, by the way—we would have a devil of a time tracking down the subprocesses that it has established on other systems, with which it communicates using encrypted packets that are nearly impossible to sort out from all of the other traffic on the Net.

"We are stuck with the Process. We must find ways to keep it running as we learn how to inspect it, to evaluate it, and—if it actually does work like a brain—to talk to it."

Zula glanced around the hall. Most of the attendees—even the ones who disagreed—seemed to be enjoying the talk. Some part of her wished she could be one of those people. An academic or an engineer who could sit back, wineglass in hand, and soak it all up and take it for what it was.

She didn't have that luxury. In her peripheral vision, she could see one or two faces turned her way, leveling gazes she preferred not to meet. They were people who had earlier staked out aggressive positions concerning the nine MFN, or Most Favored Nation, donors, and the Ephrata Eleven. Those all tended to be true believers in the proposition that the human mind could be uploaded and switched back on, as a digital simulation, after the body was gone. They believed that the Process was the first time this had actually been done. That it could be done again, as many times as resources allowed. And that the language in the agreements by which Verna Braden and the other nine MFN donors had given their brains to science, strictly interpreted, imposed an obligation on the Forthrast Family Foundation to create new instantiations of the process simulating those brains.

Zula, as the director of that foundation, had a number of outs. She could argue that the Process was just an experiment, and as such not covered by the MFN language at all. She could shut the Process down, bringing the debate to an abrupt end.

Enoch Root had just checked her on that front. She couldn't murder her uncle.

Another out was to plead lack of resources. The agreement couldn't obligate the foundation to spend money it didn't have. But the numbers didn't favor that argument. Her cautious stewardship of the endowment was now coming back to bite her. They had plenty of money—more than enough to support not only the Process but several clones of it. They no longer even had to exert much effort to keep the endowment growing. Most of it was now under the management of financial bots that just kept on making money without human intervention. The fact of the matter was that tomorrow she could sign a document piping funds directly from those bots to Hole in the Wall and similar facilities that had recently come online. She could turn out the lights, lock the doors, walk away from the Forthrast Family Foundation, and take early retirement, and the whole thing would just run indefinitely, financial bots raking up profits from the collective endeavors of the living to pay for the eternal simulation of the dead. And even if some crash or bug wiped those bots out, the Waterhouse-Shaftoe Foundation—which was at least ten times the size of Forthrast, and even more wired in to all kinds of eldritch trading algorithms—would swoop in to keep the Process running. And when they were good and satisfied that it all worked, they'd boot up new processes for the MFN crew. If they hadn't done so already.

She and her daughter had been played. Played expertly. Played by people who probably thought they were serving a higher purpose. She might spend the rest of her life wondering who was behind it all—whether Enoch was the mastermind, or Solly Pesador, or El Shepherd, or even—here was a disturbing thought—Corvallis Kawasaki. Or maybe it was Pluto playing an incredibly deep game. But it didn't matter. The outcome was the same. The Process was running. And Enoch, standing up in front of all the people who mattered, had just come out and stated what many already believed: that to shut it down at this point would be to commit murder.

26

This whirling about of the dry leaves reached deep into him and fixed his attention for as long as it lasted—until, that is, the last of the leaves had blown away and left nothing but brown branches and the green ground. His mind could not get away from this. Dry and dead were ideas that came to his mind, though he had little grasp of what it meant for something to be dry, and no sense at all of what "dead" meant.

As he brooded in the park and moved up and down the street, groping within himself for a stronger signal, new things like leaves began to fall to the ground. But they weren't coming from the trees. They weren't red. And they were much smaller. For the first time in many a day, he turned his attention upward into the space above the trees, which had just been more chaos the last time he had regarded it. Now it was a dull white. Small leaves of a brighter white were falling out of it. A few at first, then more in such quantities as to dwarf the number of leaves. They collected among the tiny green leaves that constituted the ground, and began to accumulate and climb up those tiny stalks just as the red leaves had before climbed up the trunks of the trees. In time enough of them had descended that they covered the green entirely and made the whole ground white. The park was a different place altogether now from what it had once been, but he mastered a fear that the red beauty would never return.

For many days, he gazed down the length of the street at the shapes of the branches against the white ground. At night he looked up into the sky, which sometimes was merely a gray fog out of which more white flakes descended. At other times, though, it was black, and decorated with brilliant points of light. When first he took note of these, they were scattered about in no particular way, which put him in mind of chaos and therefore displeased him. But on longer inspection he began to see shapes in the stars, just as he had, eons ago, seen a leaf emerge from the chaos. The more he attended to those shapes, the clearer and more perfectly formed they became, as the stars shifted and arranged themselves across the dark in a manner that better suited him. He knew not, however, what the shapes they described were. The only shapes in his world were leaves and trees. The figures in the stars, though beautiful, could not be likened to those.

Sometimes a white flake would stick to the dark trunk of a tree and he would gaze closely at it. Early the trunk and the flake both were simple and featureless, but he knew this to be another thing that required bettering. By attending more carefully, he drew forth greater complexity from both. The smooth trunk developed furrows and ridges. The white flake grew six arms, each sharing the same shape, which branched like that of a tree's boughs or a leaf's veins.

The whirling dry leaves ceased to be his main preoccupation and became a mere memory. The bareness of the place made the simplicity of its shape obvious, and he saw wrongness in that. It had been nothing to him in the beginning when he had had so much red beauty to beguile him, but now that he had seen the complexity of shapes that emerged from the concerted movements of the dry leaves and that the stars described in the night sky, he thought it wrong that the ground itself should have a form so plain. So he dissolved adamant into chaos for a brief time, during which he elevated the park, and made the street climb to it, and let the forest slope away on its other side. The street was too straight and so he allowed it to bend this way and that. The slope of the forest he complicated and made more perfect by making it tend up and down in places, like the surface of a leaf when it has begun to turn brown and has ceased to be flat. In like manner he indented the face of the ground with grooves and connected them in a way that recalled the branchings of the veins in a leaf. When it was shaped to his liking, he made it adamant once more, fixing it thus. Now when he looked one way from the park he could see the street curving this way and that as it descended the slope, and when he looked the other way, he could see the white ground of the forest, scratched with the countless brown branches of the trees, heaving up in some places, and in others plunging into the declivities that were shot through its flesh.

Something told him that the time had come to bring the street, the park, and the forest back to their original form (though with greater perfection). As when the leaves had refused to go away, he did not have any thought of what to do about the deep snow (as he had named the white stuff) but then one day he noted that no flakes had fallen from the sky for a while and that the level of the snow was descending the trunks of the trees. Patches of ground appeared, then grew until little, then no snow was left.

When he looked down into the forest he heard a sound that was like the chaos and feared for a moment that all he had built was unraveling. But descending through the forest to investigate he found the veins in the land carrying away the melted snow. At first it ran straight and hissed at him. Sensing that this was wrong, he attended to it for a time, and made it whirl, course, and leap like the wind that had carried away the leaves, but more visible, and louder. But after he had improved it, its loudness was not the stupid hiss of the chaos but a pleasing rush and burble.

The ground was all black adamant, as if the memory of green had faded, but presently returned to its correct color as the tiny leaves reconstituted themselves. Bigger leaves appeared on the trees' branches, red at first until he sensed that this was a mistake and that they ought to be green in the beginning. So the time of the white and the black was replaced by a time when nearly everything was green. He looked into the sky one day when things seemed uncommonly bright and saw a brilliant thing shining down from it, and later noticed that it was moving across the sky in a steady arc. He knew somehow that this was correct and later discovered "sun" in his memory. In due course "moon" followed.

The green time led to a changing of the leaves' colors, so that one day with a feeling of satisfaction and even triumph he was able to gaze down the length of the street from the park and see the whole place just as he had first seen it at the beginning, save that everything about it was much more perfectly rendered than

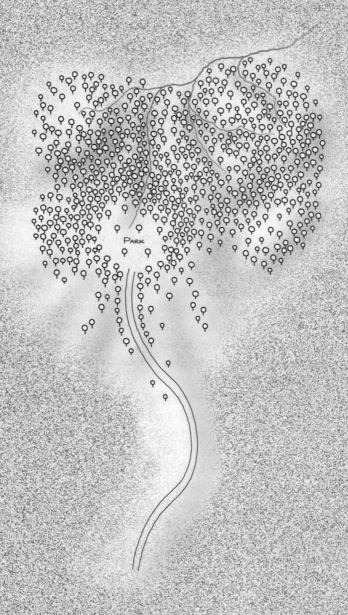

PARK

at first. "Seasons" were these gradual changes in the color and the shape of the place, and he knew that, having gone round through one cycle, it would happen again without the need for him to work it all out and fix problems. Just to satisfy himself of that, he looked on with much less problem-fixing as the leaves fell again and made the red lake, and turned brown, and scuttled about in the wind, and were replaced by the snow and then the green. The seasons were four, and they made up a year.

He let several years cycle, inspecting and improving matters as he went along. All of the seasons were beautiful and pleasing in different ways and all of the changes more or less interesting, but the part of the year that most troubled him—in the sense of a thing that pulled at his mind in some manner he could not satisfy—was the scuttling of the dry leaves at the beginning of the winter.

One year when the trees had all turned red, he noticed the first leaf of autumn drifting to the ground. It skated and turned on an invisible breeze that was at the same time stirring the branches of the trees. He descended from the park and moved down the street and approached the leaf to inspect it. It was an especially brilliant specimen, not yet purpling with age, its veins a radiant yellow.

A bad thing happened to him then: a glimpse of resurgent chaos, as if the fabric he had so laboriously woven and perfected had been torn open in one place, and he were gazing through the hole at a much older and less well-formed version of it, seeing not a beautiful leaf but a patch of chaos with only a few red motes. It was a degree of ill-formedness he had not had to endure for a very large number of days and years and it put him in mind of the time at the very beginning when he had suffered through the eons of chaos and grasped desperately at even a single mote of red. This was troubling to him. He recoiled from it and went back up the street to the park. From that commanding height he could gaze down upon that one single leaf, lying there alone on the green grass, and brood over what had just happened. He was reluctant to go near it again. In time, though, he began to take it amiss that he was so fearful of this one leaf. Had he not brought all of this into being out of chaos? Could he not do it again? Could it be that this was a harbinger, a warning that something was wrong in what he had made, and that he might need to go and better it? So he went back down to inspect the leaf again. It was just a leaf. No wrongness in it. And yet he sensed something in its vicinity that was of a much lower order of perfection, so crude and low that it lacked even a visible form, that was seeing it all wrong, trying to drag the leaf down to its level—the level he had once existed at.

It puzzled and troubled him for a long while until he came suddenly to understand that there was another like him. Or rather, like what he had once been.

He was not alone.

Others could exist—did exist—who independently could experience what he had experienced in times long past. One of them had found its way here.

This—the idea that others of his kind could exist and could share his world—had never once entered his thinking during the whole time since he had become conscious, and it led to long brooding up in the park. Like other revelations that had come to his mind over the eons, it was at once completely astonishing and strangely familiar. *Of course* there would be others. Just as the first leaf that he had brought forth out of the chaos had, in time, proved to be only one of many—many that were like it, but different— and just as the same had proved true of trees and snowflakes, how could it not be the case that he himself was only one instance of a thing—a pattern of which others could exist? Perhaps others as numberless as the leaves or the snowflakes.

He understood all of this but he did not like it. It displeased him that when he came down out of the park to look at this perfect leaf, his experience of it was interfered with, marred, by the crudeness with which the other saw it. He wanted to eject this wretched thing, to make it go away. But the mere thought of doing so led his thinking down strange paths. To liken himself to one leaf or one snowflake was to raise troubling matters—more disturbing than anything he had experienced since he had lain paralyzed while the chaos had washed over him for eons. For many years now, leaves had come into existence, only to fall, dry up, and blow away when their time was at an end. Likewise snowflakes had covered the ground only to melt, merge, and rush away through the declivities in the forest. One snowflake softened and merged with another, and multitudes of them became rills high in the crown of the park. Rills merged with each other at the branchings to form creeks, creeks became streams, streams became a river. It all went away so that the next season could follow in its time. He had never troubled himself with the question of where the leaves blew away to and what became of them, nor of where the river flowed. Such concerns were idle and in no way affected him. But if he were now to conceive of himself as only one leaf on a tree, or tree in a forest, and if he were to admit of the possibility of others like him coming along to abide in the same place, then he must, in order to make the thought whole and perfect and sound as it ought to be, consider whether he and others of his kind were destined to fall and be carried away on a wind, or melt and merge with others and rush away to parts unknown.

Such thoughts led to no firm conclusion, but, over long days and nights of brooding, he came to understand that he ought to form about himself a shape and to clothe that shape in a boundary such that on one side of it was him and on the other side was not-him. Somewhat as the trees were covered in bark. He began to make this so, but with no fixed idea at first as to what its form ought to be. He could adopt the form of a tree, but sensed that this was not correct. Trees were what he looked at, not what he was.

One night he was gazing up at the stars. Some time ago these had, partly of their own accord and partly through his idle musings, adopted forms that were not like those of trees but whose nature he could not quite understand. It came to him then that they were a kind of message. In their shapes were suggestions as to how he might pattern his own form. He tried various shapes: one long and sinuous, one squat with several legs, and one that stood upright, with a head at the top where the looking and the hearing took place, and appendages below that which could be put to various uses. This one he sensed was correct. He worked with it through all of the days that the leaves were falling. He saw now that this shape had always been implicit in the way that he had moved about and experienced things. What was a street but a place where he could walk? For that, legs were needed. His long habit of gazing at fallen leaves suggested that he was looking at things from a place that was above the ground but below the height of the branches from which the leaves fell. This, he now understood, matched up well with having a head perched some modest distance above his legs. Leaves could be snatched out of the air and held up for inspection by separate limbs, mounted just below the head. At the ends of those limbs were platforms for supporting leaves. Sprouting from the edges of those platforms were smaller, finer appendages, suitable for poking at snowflakes. He could make them curl inward just as the projecting armlets of a leaf did as it dried out. But unlike a dry leaf these did not shrivel and die once so curled, but could be restraightened at will.

The winds of autumn came and made the dry leaves whirl about. He sensed it would be a good thing to have the power of such movement and so he altered his form, adding another pair of appendages, somewhat leaflike in their shape. These had the power of catching the wind and gave him the freedom to rise up off the ground and join the leaves in their whirling and their careering through the air. As he did so, he sensed that others were around him, whirling about just like the dry leaves did, caught up helplessly in the dry cold wind, unable to master their own movements as he was able to do.

He understood then why the whirling of the dry leaves had held such fascination for him since the first time he had beheld it: this was what others of his kind did when they lacked the power to do otherwise.

When they had only just come to this place.

When they had only just died.

He was dead.

27

To mathematicians, Zelrijk-Aalberg might have been famous because of the fractal crack in the tavern floor, but to lawyers it was interesting because of its legal status and sovereignty. To make an extremely long story short, Z-A was different from the surrounding principalities because of certain peculiarities in how its ownership had changed hands at a few pivotal moments during the last thousand or so years. It had ended up being one of those places like Jersey, Guernsey, and the Isle of Man that was neither one thing or the other. It had never formally and explicitly become part of either the Netherlands or Belgium. This had been more of an oversight than a political statement. It hadn't made its way onto a treaty because the scribes had run out of vellum and decided to just leave it off. No one had noticed or cared until quite recently. During a conversation with Enoch Root, who apparently had some kind of old family link to the place and knew all of the details, El Shepherd had somehow become aware of its special status, and put a building full of medievalists and lawyers to work sorting out the details. He'd purchased all of the property inside the boundary and consolidated his position to the point where he'd felt comfortable minting his own currency (digital only) and issuing passports.

Ten years ago, he'd been sitting in a corner booth in that tavern, on the Zelrijk-Aalberg side of the crack, when Belgian police, acting in coordination with Interpol, had come to arrest him on suspicion of having masterminded the Moab hoax.

Standing shoulder to shoulder along the whole length of the crack had been members of the Zelrijk-Aalberg security forces: American mercenaries armed with assault rifles. Behind them the bar had been crammed solid with lawyers, friends of El, and media. They had all looked on, in what was described as a festive atmosphere, as Sinjin Kerr, the lord chancellor of Zelrijk-Aalberg, had reminded the Belgian cops that they had no authority on this side of the crack and that, if need be, force would be employed to preserve the integrity of the border.

The Belgians had backed down. Both they and the Dutch authorities had made it clear that if El stepped over the crack he would be subject to arrest.

Since that day, El had not left his cricket-oval-sized country. Another man might have monetized it to death, building skyscrapers on it and lining its fractal border with shops selling firecrackers, cannabis, and swag, but El had made very few changes. It was still the same homely assortment of half-timbered structures and vegetable gardens. He'd cut back on the security force, so now the border was patrolled by a rotating squad of half a dozen middle-aged guys who kept their weapons, if they even had any, discreetly concealed. Behind the wattle-and-daub walls, every room of every structure was occupied by his staff. There were rumors of tunnels. But nowadays his staff consisted mostly of the medical professionals who looked after him, and the lawyers and accountants who kept his affairs sorted. The legal situation was stalemated. The statute of limitations had long since expired on most of the criminal charges that could be leveled against him relating to Moab. He'd sent signals that he would spend every penny he had defending himself in court. And everyone understood that by the time he could be tried, convicted, and sentenced, he'd be dead, or so mentally disabled that any sentence would be commuted on humanitarian grounds. He stayed home and he used telepresence robots to "travel" around the world, and he disabled their faces so that no one could "see" him. He'd become a sort of Man in the Iron Mask.

A little less than a year after the conference in the San Juan Islands, Corvallis Kawasaki—who was in Amsterdam on other business—rented a car and had it drive him down to the border. Zelrijk-Aalberg had changed very little, but the Dutch and Belgian hamlets that surrounded it had developed into boom towns where El's employees lived, shopped, dined, and raised their families. The car dropped him off on a Belgian street in front of the famous tavern. Corvallis went in, bought a Belgian beer at the bar, and found his way into the back section. The crack in the floor was obvious. He stepped across it. Loitering in a nearby booth, nursing a club soda, was a man with a bulge in his blazer and a wearable on his face, presumably checking Corvallis's identity. He let Corvallis pass without incident. The tavern had a rear exit leading to a little beer garden, which was where he found El, sitting at a table, sheltered from a light mist by a big canvas umbrella.

He hadn't changed as much as Corvallis was expecting. He twitched his eyes toward a chair but made no move to get up or shake hands. Corvallis took a seat, sipped his beer, and looked at Elmo Shepherd for the first time in many years. He seemed fit. His face had got bigger and fleshier in the way that happened to everyone as they aged. About it was a peculiar rigidity. The tiny muscles that were responsible for expression must have been connected to the brain directly, or so Corvallis mused. He was no student of anatomy but it seemed unlikely that the spinal cord would be involved in eyebrow twitches, blinking, and such. Even people with very high spinal cord injuries could talk, and control wheelchairs with their mouths. The nerves must come directly out of the skull through little holes, or something. Anyway, something must have been messing with those connections in El's case, because his face simply didn't move in the way that faces normally did. And because humans were hardwired to be extremely perceptive and sensitive to facial expressions, this was very obvious to Corvallis—much more obvious than other forms of neurological breakdown might have been. He'd done a little bit of research into El's disease and was pretty certain that this wasn't caused by the disease proper, but by medications that El was taking to clamp down on its symptoms.

"Rumors of my insanity are greatly exaggerated," El began. "Some of the new drugs coming out of my foundation are remarkably successful in slowing down the progression of symptoms. Without them I'd have died in a pretty unpleasant fashion a year ago."

"Good." Corvallis nodded. This was a lot of small talk by Elmo Shepherd standards, but it was to a purpose: to let the visitor know what he was dealing with, to calibrate the conversation.

"If it weren't for the obvious drawbacks, I would recommend that everyone go crazy at least once in their lifetime," El said. "It's the most fascinating thing I've ever done. Going about it mindfully requires diligent effort. A kind of spiritual practice. I'm pretty sure that a lot of the old mystics—hermits and prophets who were enshrined by primitive cultures as having possessed some special connection to the divine—were in fact suffering from diagnosable mental illnesses but struggling to succumb to them mindfully. If they'd had access to modern diagnostic manuals they'd have been able to say, 'Ah, it says right here on page seven-forty-three that I am a paranoid schizophrenic,' but lacking such documentation, they had to self-observe. When certain processes in the mind run out of control, or, at the other end of the spectrum, cease to function at the level needed to preserve a kind of psychiatric homeostasis, the effects are observable to an introspective patient. If you're a stylite monk, you're pretty much screwed and you just have to think your way around it. But nowadays, therapeutic options suggest themselves—titrating levels of various psychoactive medications in an interactive manner, talking across the blood-brain barrier, or direct stimulation of certain ganglia using techniques that can reach into the brain and target interesting regions. We have equipment here that can do that. I can stick my head in a magnet and ping a misbehaving neuron. I was doing it ten minutes ago and I'll be doing it ten minutes after you leave."

"How long do you have?" Corvallis asked.

"To live? Or to talk to you?" Before Corvallis could answer, he continued, "Probably three years to live. Twenty minutes to talk to you."

"I wanted to touch base with you about a couple of things."

"Yes, I assumed there was a motivation for your visit, C."

"I talk to Sophia. As you must know, she's a research fellow now. Nominally pursuing a Ph.D. But looking after the Process is more than a full-time job."

"Delegating tasks to others is what people traditionally do when their workload exceeds their available time," El pointed out. "I've made my opinions clear on this, C. Perhaps I am being ignored because it's assumed I am out of my mind."

"You're not being ignored by me, or others at our board meetings. You are being ignored by Sophia. But she's not ignoring you because she thinks you're crazy. She's ignoring you because she's stubborn."

"I don't understand what she has to be stubborn about, in this case. The Process is a unique and unprecedented phenomenon. It is a gold mine of data about the functioning of the human mind. She is its only token holder. She should open it up, let others have access."

"It's a family affair," Corvallis said, "a personal affair. Dodge died suddenly when she was a little girl."

"I know the story."

"She misses him. Wants to connect with what she lost."

"And does she really believe that the Process is the reincarnation of Richard Forthrast?"

"Is that what you believe, El?"

"I don't know what to believe, since she is the sole toho, and she won't share the data."

"You know her position—and our position—on this. There's not that much to share. Tracking the activities of the Process is akin to the problem that faced the Allies, during the Second World War, before they broke the Enigma code. Messages can be intercepted and copied, but they can't be decrypted, so we don't actually know what they mean. The most we can do is traffic analysis. It's not useless, but—"

"But it's not the Vulcan mind meld. I saw that talk. I agree with it."

"To this very point," Corvallis said, "Sophia mentioned to me recently that she had observed new traffic that was unfamiliar. To make a long story short, she thinks that you are uploading other scanned connectomes and that you are booting them up on the same systems."

"Systems I built and paid for," El said. "Sophia claimed all of

Hole in the Wall's processing power during the first year. The project would have withered on the vine at that point, if I hadn't—"

"If you hadn't built more of them. Yes."

"Hole in the Wall was handcrafted. I made it mass-producible. By this time next year, we will be opening new facilities at the rate of one per week."

"Leading to the question, why?"

"It sounds as though Sophia already has a theory," El said. Corvallis guessed that if his facial muscles were working, he might have had a sly expression right about now. Maybe he'd have winked.

"You've made no secret of the fact that you've been scanning other brains."

"I'm surprised at you, C-plus. Using such an outmoded figure of speech. 'Brains'? Really?"

Corvallis decided to construe this as an attempt at humor. El couldn't wink. There was no twinkle in that eye.

He was alluding to a hot topic from the conference: the mind-body problem.

Or at least it had seemed like a hot topic to some there who had never taken an introductory philosophy course. Late twentieth- and early twenty-first-century neurologists who had thought about, and done empirical research on, how the brain actually worked had tended toward the conclusion that there *was* no mind-body problem. The whole notion was devoid of meaning. The mind couldn't be separated from the body. The whole nervous system, all the way down to the toes, had to be studied and understood as a whole—and you couldn't even stop there, since the functions of that system were modulated by chemicals produced in places like the gut and transmitted through the blood. The bacteria living in your tummy—which weren't even *part* of you, being completely distinct biological organisms—were effectively a part of your brain. According to these neurologists, the whole notion of scanning brains taken from severed heads had been—for lack of a better term—wrongheaded to begin with.

Which led to interesting questions about what actually happened when those brains were rebooted as processes. According to this model, such "brains" wouldn't be able to make sense of anything—they couldn't function, really—until and unless they had rebuilt the missing parts of the system from scratch.

That much was imponderable and unknowable until they had better tools for making sense of the Process—which explained why Elmo Shepherd was pissed off about Sophia's reluctance to share access. In the meantime, one thing they *could* make all sorts of progress on was improving the quality of the scans themselves. Between the scientists from the Waterhouse/Forthrast camp and those who worked for El, there was vociferous agreement that the word "brain" needed to be banned from learned discourse, or put in scare quotes. They had to move beyond the practice of chopping off the heads of the deceased and throwing away the rest. Henceforward every client would be scanned in toto, heads to toes, and efforts would be made to collect data about their microbiome and any other non-neurological phenomena that would be overlooked by an ion-beam scanning system that only cared about neurons.

"I beg your pardon," C-plus said. "You have clients. Some of them are no longer among the living. You have been subjecting their remains to the most advanced protocols available."

"As have you."

"Of course."

"People die," El said. "Some of them want what Richard Forthrast wanted."

"How many?"

El shrugged. "More than a thousand."

Corvallis didn't quite believe it. "You mean, that many have signed up?"

"No, I mean that we have actually scanned and archived that many."

"I had no idea."

"That is frankly a little hard for me to believe," said El, "given that in South Lake Union you have done the same thing to—how many?"

C-plus shrugged. "I haven't checked recently. A couple of hundred?"

"Three hundred and forty-seven," El corrected him.

"I simply didn't know you had that many scan labs."

"The equipment is now capable of being mass-produced. We have about fifty of them. Many in China, India, where the program has taken hold to a degree not fully appreciated in the West. Two of them in that building right over there." El nodded at an eight-hundred-year-old half-timbered house a stone's throw away. "Others in cities where a lot of rich people live."

"You said 'scanned and archived,' but you didn't say you had booted any up."

"We started booting them up a week ago," El announced, "leading to the pattern of activity that Sophia noticed and that presumably accounts for you sitting here in my beer garden talking to me. We are well aware that you have been doing the same."

Corvallis nodded, perhaps a little hastily—trying too hard, perhaps, to show how transparent he was being? "I am here partly for that reason," he said, "and partly to make you aware that, in accordance with our responsibilities, we have booted up the Ephrata Eleven and the Most Favored Nine."

"And Verna."

"Verna was the first, after Dodge."

"They will never be the same as the others," El said. "They should have waited."

28

He was dead and so he must previously have been not-dead. Of not being dead he had no direct knowledge, but he could guess that he had abided in a place with leaves, trees, snow, rivers, wind, and stars. He had existed in some physical form probably not far different from the one that he had pulled about himself here. He had shared that existence with others. Others who were likewise becoming dead and finding their way to this place. Drawn to it, perhaps, by the availability of coherent things like red leaves. Longing to experience something other than chaos but not knowing how to summon those experiences forth out of the noise.

Why did they not then go away and suffer for eons as he had, and learn for themselves the knack of making whole and beautiful things out of chaos?

Because they didn't have to. In the early going, if he himself had been able to find some other dead person's ready-made world and there abide, he'd have done so and accounted himself fortunate. But no such thing had been within his reach and so he'd had no choice but to suffer and learn.

He wondered how many of the other dead people had found their way here to his place. In his new body he soared above the park, supported by the leaflike appendages growing out of his back. These were poorly formed for the crowded environment of the forest but well made for movement in empty space. He bettered them, making them less like leaves, giving them a new form that could fold against his back when they were not needed, yet still spread wide when he chose to take flight. Folding these, his wings, he descended to the ground and walked on his feet through the forest, inspecting each tree, standing above each little stream watching the flow of the water and hearing its sound.

Out of the clashing waters he heard "Egdod" and remembered that this was his name.

For the most part little had changed, but from time to time when passing near a tree or squatting by a stream he would sense a little tear in the world, feel a knot of near-chaos drifting about the place, and thus know that another dead person had found their way here. Some of them came and went like snowflakes, others seemed to take up residence in trees or streams, as if they longed for bodies but had not the wit or craft to fashion their own. They latched desperately on to forms that Egdod had made, be they never so unsuitable for beings-of-Egdod-type.

At times flying with wings spread, at times walking upon the ground, he went up and down the street and ranged through the forest and roamed the park and learned the number of others who had come to his domain. He concluded that the number of souls was not many more than the number of the tiny appendages sprouting from the leaf-platforms that terminated his upper limbs. Almost as quickly as he felt the need for them, the notions came to his mind: fingers, hands, arms. Ten, and other numbers. There were between ten and twenty souls, all told, some scuttling about as dry leaves, others lodged in trees or streams. Their number was actually quite small compared to the amount of consternation that their arrival had caused him.

More arrived. The number did not increase suddenly, but neither did it ever decrease. It would seem that the place they came from emitted more dead people all the time but had no way of reabsorbing them. Why this was so, and whether it made sense, there was no point in troubling his mind with. All that mattered for the time being was that their number was small and that they were so weak as to make little difference to him, at least now that he had drawn a thick skin about himself. He saw no harm then in leaving, for a time, the place that he had built, and where he had abided, since he had died. He strode up the street to the park at the top of the hill. His body talked to him in a new way that was neither seeing nor hearing; he could feel the ground beneath his feet now. And when he reached the park where the wind blew, and went to a grassy place where there was ample room to unfold his wings, he likewise felt the air beneath them. The winds that he had once brought into being to carry away the dead leaves now picked him up and lifted him toward the sky. He changed the wings' relationship to the air so that he wheeled toward the forest and began to soar over it. The ground dropped away. He saw how the veins in the earth came together to make the river. The river ran downhill. He followed it. It flowed into a space that put him in mind of chaos, since he had not yet ventured into it and given it a form. But he had long since mastered the craft of drawing solid adamant out of chaos, as water froze into ice. It was a small matter, therefore, to bestow form on it now, making it a simple extension of the forest he had already made. The shape of it was different, the trees and the leaves all unique; the veining of the rivers had a similar-but-different pattern from those on the slopes below his park.

Thus for a time he extended the Land and the forest vastly in whatsoever direction he chose to fly. It became monotonous, though, and the river draining it grew so wide that when he lit on one of its banks he could not see to the other side. Summoning more vague memories of how things ought to be, he put an ocean at the river's end. Because there was some indefinable wrongness in the forest's going all the way to the water's edge, he made between them a strip of bare adamant. The monotony of this displeased him and so he broke it up into various pieces called rocks. His first rocks were all of a common shape and size but he bettered them by making some tinier and more numerous than snowflakes, others bigger than the hill of the park but less often seen. Distributed along the boundary between the forest and the ocean, these made beaches and cliffs, which protected the trees from the onslaught of the waves with which he thought it best to populate the surface of the sea. He soared and wheeled above the largest of all the rocks, which, just to amuse himself, he had made so large that the street and the park and much of the forest could have rested comfortably on its top. From its apex he beheld the way his waves crashed against it.

In the water's movements he saw manifold imperfections. The

waves and the manner of their beating against the rock begged for improvement. He spent some days bettering this, until when they clashed against the rock they hurled spray into the air. When he swooped low he could feel spray pelting the skin he had made to separate himself from things-that-were-not-Egdod, and the waves' roar enveloped him almost as fully as the hiss of chaos had once done eons ago. The spray was made of tiny, hurtling balls of water that were all but invisible against the sky. He knew that this was wrong and that each ball of water ought to catch the light of the sun and reflect it, making the spray glitter brightly. More than that, each ball ought to be supplying a reflection of the world around it—including Egdod. Until they did so, the water was very far from being rightly formed and needed further betterment.

He knew that making it so would consume at least as many years as he had already devoted to the making of the street, the park, and the forest. Earlier, he might gladly have perched atop a large rock and spent years on the patient improvement of the waves' shape and surge, but now the awareness that souls were arriving made him loath to spend more time than he needed to here. He beat his wings against the spray and lifted himself up above the great rock and took a last look down into the spray, a mere fog, not yet shining or reflecting as it ought to. Then he soared up the coast.

He could see this idea of the mirrored ball almost as if it were hanging in space before him—as if he were supporting such an object on the tips of his fingers and gazing into it.

Supposing that he could now summon up a mirrored ball—or a mirrored anything—and gaze into it, what would he see? What did he look like? The question had never occurred to him when he had lived alone. A tree could not look back at him. The souls who had recently begun flocking to his abode probably lacked the power to see anything clearly. In time, though, they might acquire such powers, just as Egdod had, and then they would gaze on him, just as they gazed on trees and rocks, and they would see something. What would it look like, what impression would it make upon them?

He could not very well know the answer until he knew what he looked like to himself, and so he formed a resolve to fashion a mirror one day, and gaze into it. But it was of little importance now and so he put it out of his mind. He flew above the world that he was creating.

Another fully formed thought came into his head: this was what he did. It was fitting and proper that he make the world out of chaos and better what he had made and make room in it for newly arriving souls, for he—not the dead Egdod flying above the forest, but the living Egdod who had once held leaves in his hand and looked at mirrored balls—had done it before. He was good at it. And the other souls that he had noticed in his domain were, perhaps, not invading it so much as seeking his protection.

The place where the Land gave way to the ocean was an enjoyable change from where he had abided until then. He beat his wings in a slow rhythm and made his way along that coast, circling back frequently to inspect and improve features that had caught his attention, but generally keeping the Land to his left side and the water to his right. Some stretches of the coast he carpeted with uncountable numbers of tiny rocks called sand, others he buttressed with big rocks. In some places he made the forest roll straight to the edge and then drop sheer into the water below, which were called cliffs. In others he made cliffs topped not with trees but with broad expanses of grass. So intoxicated did he become with coast building that he did not much concern himself with what lay inland of it.

After a time he sensed a kind of wrongness in his fashioning of so much coast without paying due attention to the lands it circumscribed. While continuing to fly above the place where the ocean beat against the shore, he thereafter made it his practice to bend his course ever to one direction, though with excursions to and fro when it suited him. In his mind he was seeing a figure closed in on itself, like a droplet of water suspended in flight. The Land was to become a bounded thing, as his body was now bounded by his skin. Along the way its boundary—the coast—would vary one way and then the other, sometimes in broad figures and other times in quick turnings out or in.

His flight was a long one, but in time he wheeled around a newly formed headland to see, in the distance, the large rock that he had fashioned at the place where his river ran down from his park. He flew to it and circled round it a few times to satisfy himself that it was as he had left it. And it was, for adamant did not alter its form unless he caused it to do so. The Land had been fully circumscribed and was enclosed. Satisfied of this, he turned his course inland and began tracing the river back to where he had started. Because of its many branchings this might have been a difficult task, were it not for the fact that the way he had followed from the park to the ocean was a carpet of red forest. To its left and to its right was bare adamant, veined with rivers but bare of trees or any other living stuff.

He might easily have brought more trees into being and covered the bare places with red beauty, but his sojourn along the coast had awakened in him a taste for variety, and he was beginning to see wrongness in all of the trees' being of the same kind. More perfect would have been a world in which trees of diverse kinds grew on the hills and in the valleys. On an impulse he flew up one rocky vale that carried a tributary of unusual size. Such a great stream, he reckoned, must spring from a correspondingly great place. He followed it uphill for a time until he came to a place of immense rocks protruding from the ground, which he knew to be mountains. On their slopes he made new sorts of trees that were forever green, a darker green than that of the trees in the park. As he flew low over this new forest to inspect it, a new sensation came to him: this forest had a fragrance that spoke to him, somehow, of such forests in the place he had abided before he had died. He breathed it in deep, and knew that his face, still unseen, had affordances for drawing in the wind and smelling what it was made of.

After a few turns around those mountains he followed the great tributary back down to the main channel of the river and doubled back along the course that would lead him up through the red forest to the top of his hill. This too had a fragrance now, less strong than that of the dark green forests in the mountains, but nonetheless pleasing.

He alit in the park to find all little different from how it had been when he had departed, save that many more leaves had fallen to the ground, and some had become dry and begun to scuttle about in the wind. In many of these he sensed the inchoate tangles of rude perception that he identified as souls. Walking up and down the street, strolling in the park, and ranging through the forest in the next few days he counted perhaps ten times ten of them. Their presence no longer troubled him as it had at first. Yet he felt that the time had arrived for him to make some place into which they could not go, so that, when he so chose, he could be alone as he had been used to during the first eons since he had died.

In the beginning the park had been flat. Later he had changed the shape of it and made it into a hill. Now he changed its shape again, causing the adamant that lay beneath the grass to grow up out of it in places, forming walls. Just as he had earlier bounded the whole Land with a coast to separate it from the ocean, he now bounded the top of the hill with a wall. But whereas the coast's beauty had derived from its roughness, he sensed that a proper wall should be smooth and straight. He made it thus, pushing it back in some places and drawing it out in others, until the walls had acquired a pleasing uniformity. On the side that looked toward the street he created an aperture. As he had come to expect, the name of it came to him presently: gate. And in the opposite wall, the one that looked toward the forest, he created a smaller gate.

A considerable stretch of park still lay between the small gate and the forest. He bounded this too, not with walls but with hedges of trees whose nature he altered so that they put forth many branches dense with small leaves that never turned red or fell, so that in all seasons a wall of green would enclose this area. Its name was Garden. He spent many days there brooding over the forms of trees and smaller plants. His long flight around the coast had made it known to him that many rivers emptied into the ocean besides just the first one, and that each river had many branches, and that each branch led up into places that were now bare but that, in a proper Land, needed to be bettered with trees and plants of many kinds. He had already achieved this in the case of the high mountains that he had girdled with fragrant evergreens, but much more remained to be done. He had it in mind that he would use the Garden to bring forth many different kinds

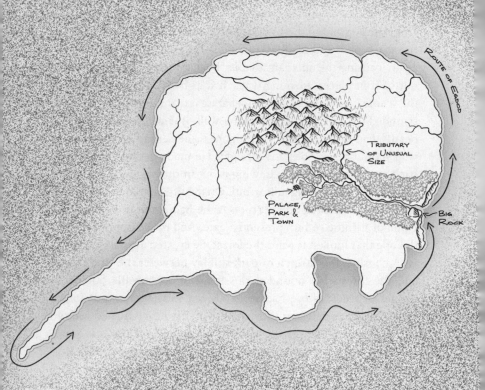

of trees, all together in one small place where he could observe their changes through the seasons and better them. When they were ready he would then propagate many more of their kinds in all of the bare places.

Winter came as he populated his Garden. That season was not conducive to the Garden's purpose and so he caused winter not to happen there. His body had made him sensible of conditions he had not known before, including warmth and cold. He caused the Garden to be warm at all times and for light to shine upon it even when the sun was not visible in the sky. He spent days there, bringing forth and perfecting trees of various kinds. When he grew weary of that, he walked up and down the cold street, or else took wing and flew out over the Land.

In due course the snow began to melt in the street and the forest, and the trees began to put forth leaves. Egdod turned his attention away from the bettering of the Garden and walked through the small gate into the enclosure he had made. The ground within the walls he had covered with more stone and made it smooth, which was called floor. He walked across the floor toward the large gate, for he was of a mind to walk down the street and see how the new leaves were budding.

Standing there just at the gate's threshold was a thing shaped after the fashion of Egdod himself: feet terminating a pair of legs that supported a body. Emerging at various places from the body, a pair of arms with hands at their ends, wings, and a head. The wings still bore the appearance of dried leaves; they were not so much folded as crumpled. The head was ill formed, being a globe of fluctuating chaos. It was smaller than Egdod; its wings, though sized appropriately for the body, were in fact not much larger than fallen leaves.

Egdod regarded this being for a time and sensed that it was, as best it could, looking right back at him. When Egdod moved about, it seemed to shift its position. After some little while had gone by, Egdod had the feeling that it had changed its shape during the time that they had been looking at each other; the wings, he thought, were becoming more orderly. More like Egdod's.

The appearance of this creature was not altogether a surprise.

As the autumn had progressed he had sensed, on his occasional strolls down the street, that some of the souls were taking on greater coherence, becoming permanent. They were not allowing themselves to disappear into trees or streams but attempting to condense into distinct forms of their own. This one was simply the strongest of those, the most advanced. It had not occurred to him until now that such a creature would choose to adopt a form after the fashion of Egdod's, but neither was it surprising. Perhaps this one and Egdod had both looked thus before they had died, and were naturally trying to re-create the bodies they had inhabited while living. Or perhaps this one was merely imitating Egdod. As every leaf on every tree was a similar-but-different version of the first leaf, perhaps the Land was now going to become populated with similar-but-different creatures walking around on legs and flying on wings, like Egdod.

Egdod still intended to go for a walk down the street. He walked toward the gate. The other soul was still planted right in the middle of the aperture. As Egdod drew closer, he sensed it would be wrong for two souls to occupy the same space, and so he diverted to one side. The aura of shaped chaos that stood in for the other soul's head changed its shape, swirling like a scuttle of leaves. It put out a golden tendril that brushed Egdod's knee. Egdod sensed the touch of it.

Some while ago he had clothed himself in a skin whose reason for being was to separate the stuff of which he was made from that belonging to other souls. Since then, stiff winds had blown against it, hot and cold. The spray of the ocean waves had spattered it. The leaves and branches of trees had tested his skin, and beneath the soles of his feet and under the skin of his palm he had felt stone of various textures. His skin had been proof against all of those. But he had never yet come into contact with a body constructed by another soul, or—as now—the shifting nimbus of aura that betrayed the presence of a soul too newly arrived to have made a proper form in which to dwell, or contained itself in a skin of its own. He recoiled from its touch and felt it fizzing on the skin of his knee. The sensation was to his sense of touch what flickering static was to vision or the hiss of white noise was to hearing. It was not painful, nor did it wreak any change on him that could be detected. A wisp of aura separated from the end of the tendril. As he strode away it swirled about his leg for a moment before dispersing. He no longer sensed the contact. He was glad of that. For, though the touch had not been painful, it had put him in mind of an earlier state of being that it was good to have put behind him.

After he had gone on for several paces and entered into the upper part of the street, he looked back over his shoulder and saw that the other soul—somewhat diminished, perhaps, by the loss of the tendril—was attempting to follow him. It did not have the knack of moving smoothly, or in anything like a straight line, yet got it right more often than wrong. Falling farther and farther behind, it kept after Egdod, improving the quality of its movement as it struggled along.

Egdod named the soul Follower. He wondered where Follower had been obtaining the stuff of which he was making himself. Egdod had been able to avail himself of an infinite field of chaos, out of which he had fashioned not only a form to house Egdod, but an entire world. Follower was trying to create himself in a world from which, as far as Egdod knew, chaos had been almost eradicated. Perhaps he had a foot in each universe and was trying to force his way into Egdod's through a little gap or flaw while most of him remained trapped in the chaos on the other side. Or perhaps he was drawing stuff out of the world Egdod had made, as trees grew up out of its soil.

The trees that lined the street were all in order. Once Egdod had created them in such-and-such a way, they had neither the inclination nor the power to alter themselves, other than to become somewhat larger each year and to put forth more branches. Souls were living in some of them now, and so he felt himself looked at by those as he passed by. The outward form of those was, however, no different.

In the time, now many years past, when he had first made all of this, Egdod had been driven by a loathing of chaos and a corresponding love of what was steady and regular in its nature. Since then, he had, in general, sought to make the world more various. The waves that had beat against the rocks of the coast—that, he supposed, were beating against it now, though he was not there to watch—had in them a kind of chaos, and indeed seemed more like proper waves to him the more wildly they thrashed against the stones and flung themselves into the air. The disorder that they manifested in so doing felt of a different nature from the dread chaos out of which Egdod had first brought himself into being and then fashioned everything else. And so it seemed that the world could have a kind of wildness and irregularity about it without coming to pieces and reverting to chaos in the way he had, in the early going, feared that it would. As he walked down the street now he saw its regularity as the work of an earlier Egdod, a fearful Egdod. By no means was it wrong for him to have fashioned the street in this way. He was not now of a mind to tear it apart into a chaotic wilderness. The trees—the oldest trees in the Land now—he would allow to grow and alter their forms with greater variety, so that each would be different from the next in the branchings and contortions of its boughs. But the nature of the street he would not change, rather leaving it as a relic of his first stirrings, and as a place to which the new dead might be drawn and in which they might find sanctuary.

Egdod had never given the street a definite conclusion or thought about what would happen if he continued walking down it beyond a certain point. At a suitable remove from the top of the hill, where the trees gave out, he now made the ground flat and put grass on it. From the dead ground below the grass he drew out stones and piled them up into walls, and made the walls run straight, not for great distances but just until they intersected other walls at crisp corners, forming enclosures. Those were smaller than the one he had made for himself at the top of the hill but large enough that a few souls might abide in each one, provided that the bodies they made for themselves were of a reasonable size. It seemed wrong for them to have nothing on the top and so he made roofs for them too. The street he caused to branch this way and that among the houses, as the veins of a leaf or the tributaries of a river were wont, save that the street's branchings were of a more regular nature, with straight lines and right angles that were consonant with the vertical walls and sharp corners of the empty dwellings. Facing the streets he made apertures that he guessed might seem inviting to wandering souls, as the one in his palace atop the hill had apparently beckoned to Follower. In placing the houses and running the streets he followed his whims and his sense of how such a place ought to be laid out; Town, as he called it, had a kind of regularity, but not the perfectly monotonous patterning that he had bestowed on the original street. Some of the streets were longer than others, and not all of the houses were of the same size or shape.

Having put Town's streets and houses where he thought meet, he left them vague and unfinished, as an invitation to other souls to alter their forms in whatever manner they saw fit. He belted Town with open space where grass grew, and seeded it too with diverse small plants that he had been cultivating in his Garden. In its center he placed a square space devoid of houses, containing only grass.

He was now of a mind to return to the place he had made for himself at the top of the hill and build a roof atop its walls—a thing that had not occurred to him until he had looked at the smaller enclosures of Town and sensed that, without roofs, they were incomplete. He walked out into the little park that he had made in the middle of Town, spread his wings, and took to the air. He flew in a broad circle around Town, viewing its grid of streets from above, and satisfied himself that it was of a correct form. Then he flew up the street until he had reached the space above the hill and the big house he had made there and the Garden behind it. He flew around it a few times, considering what manner of roof would best complete his abode. The name Palace came to him. He descended to the smooth stone floor of the Palace and walked about, regarding it from different angles. Presently he came to its front gate and, gazing down the hill, spied a small form making its way up the street toward him. It was Follower, walking most of the time, occasionally taking to the air and struggling along on his wings for a short distance.

By the time Follower had attained the hilltop, Egdod had prepared for him a smaller house attached to the front of the Palace. He wished for Follower to know that this new thing, the Gatehouse, was for him but that the Palace was Egdod's alone. Egdod did not know how best to make another soul know and understand something that originated in Egdod's head. Again he had the sense that such had been routine in the place where he and Follower had presumably abided before they had died.

He sensed that he had the power utterly to destroy the form that Follower was making for himself, should the latter become an important source of trouble. A picture flashed into his mind of a fist clutching a bright bolt, ready to hurl it down from the top of the hill. He knew not where the picture had come from. It was the natural way of things to fly apart into chaos, but some orderings had the property of not doing so, and of persisting even when less than perfect at the beginning or when damaged later. But now that Egdod had come to know as much, he, by the same token, had thoughts of how such things might be perturbed in ways from which there would be no getting better. Preferable, though, would be to convey his intentions into the confused and whirling mind of Follower without undoing him.

In the front of the Gatehouse he had made an aperture facing the street. He stood in this as the other approached. It was moving more steadily now, growing bigger and better defined, its wings more like Egdod's and less like leaves. As Follower drew closer, Egdod withdrew into the Gatehouse, but stopped at the next threshold, where it was joined to the Palace. Follower seemed to take his meaning. He passed through the aperture into the Gatehouse and seemed to look about it. Egdod turned his back on him and walked several steps into the Palace, then turned around to see whether the other would persist in following him. Indeed, Follower approached the aperture that joined his new abode to Egdod's. But as he had done earlier, he stopped at the threshold. Egdod extended his arm toward Follower and showed the palm of his hand, as if pushing him back. The point was taken; Follower moved two paces backward into the Gatehouse, then bent forward at the middle of his body in a gesture that Egdod somehow recognized.

Satisfied, Egdod devoted some time to building a roof on the Palace. His first efforts were not altogether satisfactory and he knew that he would be improving it for a while. When he tired of that, he caused the stone beneath the Garden to rise up through the grass in one place and make a little island. He pushed the top of this down in its center so that it would hold water. He made water well up out of the ground and fill it, and waited for it to lie still, so that it reflected the branches of the trees that grew above it. Then Egdod approached this little pool and bent over it to regard himself.

When next he entered the Palace, Egdod had a face. The face had eyes in its front so that other souls could discern, by looking on him, what he was gazing at. It had nostrils through which he could take in the air and smell it. Below that was another orifice, as yet ill formed; he sensed it ought to be there but was unclear as to its purpose. For the time being it was an oval of glowing aura. His head was wreathed in the same stuff. The head was not finished but it suited his purposes for now, and when he showed himself to Follower, the latter seemed to take close heed, and began to shape his own form in a like manner.

Matters in Town began to take shape in more or less the way that Egdod had envisioned. Souls continued to manifest themselves, perhaps one or two a day, and to develop forms by which they could be distinguished and seen. Some still chose to inhabit things such as trees that had not the power of movement, but most patterned themselves after Follower, who patterned himself after Egdod. Curious variations could be seen, but most seemed to derive comfort from having a kind of sameness with others. From the Palace Egdod could look down and see them trying to walk on their legs or fly on their wings. Some wandered up the hill, but Follower warded them off at the threshold of the Gatehouse just as Egdod had warded Follower off, and so by process of elimination they tended to end up in Town. The houses there offered no amenities that souls actually needed, but they seemed to prefer having places of their own, just as Egdod preferred having a Palace and a Garden.

Satisfied that all was sorted here, mindful that spring was under way, he bent his mind to the perfection of the new kinds of trees and other plants. He began flying far afield to parts of the Land that

he knew must exist, since he had surrounded them with a coast, perforated where rivers might flow out and drain the interior. Hills and mountains he saw (to see something, now, was to create it), and these grew up from the coast and hemmed in the river valleys as was proper. But making a sufficient number of hills and mountains to decorate the coast with river mouths did not begin to fill in all of the Land that he had circumscribed. The center of it was vast and void, and so he made of it a flat country, green with grass in some places, but in others an expanse of rock and sand. To break up the monotony of it he here and there put isolated mountains, or ranges of them, and drained them through networks of rivers and chains of lakes, letting the water find its own way eventually to the coast with sometimes amusing results, as it often had to wind about in circuitous ways before it detected low points around which it could pool, and sought outlets through which it could make good its escape.

As the water was finding its way about, he busied himself with the seeding of trees and plants and grasses in such parts of the Land as he thought suitable for their kinds. The running waters spoke to him, as they had long ago in the forest when they had reminded him of his name. They told him the names of the different kinds of trees: pine, fir, oak, maple.

Flying back to the Palace he conceived a desire to have the ability of making such sounds with his own body, rather than relying on noisy rivers to do it for him. By the time he had alit in the Garden to view his reflection in the pool, he had a new thing on his face called a mouth. When he opened his mouth wide, glowing static could still be seen within, and a faint hiss of noise would emerge, but by moving the parts of his mouth in different fashions he could modulate that sound to mimic the names of things that he had heard in the rushing and burbling waters. Once he had got the knack of making the sounds of the trees and of certain other things he knew the names of, he entered the Palace and went to the Gatehouse and showed the new form of his face to Follower, and made some sounds to demonstrate its use, pointing to himself and uttering, "Egdod," and to the other and uttering, "Ward." For he had decided to give Follower a new name that better reflected his occupation.

Follower—now, and henceforth, Ward—had continued to grow taller and to perfect his form; his head now came up to Egdod's shoulder and his wings were symmetrical and well articulated. He nodded his head and set about the task of shaping a mouth after the manner of Egdod's and learning how it might be used to fashion various words. Egdod knew that other souls would in due course see this and begin to pattern their own forms likewise.

He wondered what Town would be like when its houses and streets were full of souls making sounds at each other. It would be very different from what it was now. But he sensed that such was the natural order of things when many souls were together. The essence of being a soul, as opposed to a rock or a leaf, was the ability to behave in manners that Egdod could not predict. He could do nothing about the fact that new souls were coming here all the time, each acting as it saw fit. He could set an example for them, as he was doing with Ward, and he could make a Town for them to live in, but ultimately they would do as they liked and there was no point in much troubling himself over it.

The making and bettering of the lands beyond seemed of greater import. There was nothing in those that he could not shape as he saw fit. So he bent his efforts to that work, sometimes spending many days in his Garden discovering new kinds of plants that had sprung up there, seemingly of their own accord. Different plants were suited to different parts of the Land. Gathering them up, he took wing and ranged far out to places that were in want of shaping and seeding. Deserts he made, populated with fragrant thorny plants that grew low to the ground. The lowlands around the central gulf were soggy in places where the ground trapped water; these he covered with reeds in some places and spreading trees in others. Mountains were best when cloaked in dark evergreens, though on their upper slopes he thought it better to grow tiny rugged plants of the same sort that he used to carpet the ground at one end of the Land that he conceived of as being the north. At the other end, which was south, different conditions prevailed and trees were larger. At every place where he imagined he might have found an end to the Land's complexity, he instead discovered further small matters that needed sorting out.

In this he began to rely upon the help of those he had come to think of as wild souls: ones who had come to be in the Land in the same manner as those in Town, but who had been disinclined to lodge there and instead had ranged far, following rivers down toward the ocean or soaring on the high strong winds that blew above the mountains. Many of these came to rest within small things that Egdod had created, such as rocks, rivers, and trees. Others made forms for themselves that were of no great significance. A few though acquired forms that were remarkable in their size and complication, reflecting their affinities for the winds and the waves. When Egdod traveled to some distant coast and found the ocean crashing against it with greater perfection than at the time of his previous visit, he knew that some such soul had been at work bettering the movement of the waters.

On more than one occasion Egdod was absent for the better part of a season. When he did come back, he would fly high over Town and look down on it. Striking to him, when he did, was its combination of regular patterns—the grid of streets, the rectangular houses, the square park in the middle—with the unplanned rambling character of one of those places in the Land where he had years ago seeded something and since allowed it to develop according to its own nature. And yet he knew that the shape of Town was correct just as it was. Each house belonged where he had put it. Each street came to an end just where it ought to.

Town, seen from above, was alive with the stirrings of small souls. At a distance it looked like a place full of dry leaves scuttling about in a wind, but of course when he swooped lower he could see that these were not leaves but smaller forms. Some of those had wings but most did not. Those that did commonly lacked any great skill in flying, and over time the disused wings would shrink. He saw that they had been making alterations to their houses and to the swathes of grass separating one from the next. He had expected that they would do so, and yet he found it troubling in an indefinable way. He wanted them to learn the trick of shaping the world, just as he had learned to do, but he did not wish for them to acquire so much power that they could break the forms that he considered proper. Beating his wings, hovering above the park in the middle of Town, he saw the faces of the souls—all equipped with mouths now—turn upward to regard him. This he had expected and indeed hoped for, since he wished to show them a useful pattern that a soul ought to shape itself into. By and large he had done this through the intermediation of Ward. He could see that it had been working well, but there was nothing amiss in letting them look upon him directly from time to time.

What he had not expected was that the souls of the Town, upon spying him, used their mouths to call out to one another, uttering his name as well as other words that he could not distinguish so easily. Too, they clumped together in twos, threes, and larger groups, the better to exchange words as they looked up and regarded Egdod hovering in the sky above them. He noticed that when they stood close together, the auras that swathed their heads would sometimes flow together, as creeks joined together to make larger streams. The auras would swirl about and circulate among several souls' heads at once, as if they had combined into one.

29

MonsterCon 3 was what everyone at the Forthrast Family Foundation called the event, because its official name was too unwieldy. The terminology leaked out over the various mail and messaging systems that they used to coordinate it with the Waterhouse-Shaftoe Family Foundation, with El Shepherd's network, and other interested parties, obliging Zula to send out a fatwa abolishing its use, scrubbing all Frankenstein imagery, and reminding everyone that it was supposed to be called the Third Annual Conference on Trends in Advanced Neural System Simulation. Or, if that was too much verbiage, ACTANSS 3. They still held it at the same resort in British Columbia where they had held the first one. This meant holding the head count down to fifty, with twenty-five support staff sleeping in RVs, and even tents, scattered around the property.

"Discovered" and mapped by white people before the advent of brand management consultants and focus groups, the geography of the West Coast abounded in strange and terrifying place names. The very name "California" came from a phantasmal Spanish novel about rampant Amazon Negresses. The Desolation Sound region, about halfway up the landward coast of Vancouver Island, confronted map-browsing visitors with a variety of features that were by turns named after whatever the first English or Spanish explorers considered inspiring (Enlightenment virtues such as discovery), devotional (diverse saints and theological debating points), important to grovel to (members of royal families, heroes, the admiralty), or dangerous enough to call for heavy hints that future colonizers shouldn't go there. In the latter category was Devastation Narrows, joining Surge Rocks to Whirlpool Bay, and running, no joke, between Scylla Point and Charybdis Head. This exceptional concentration of scare words was the result of factors both geographical and cultural. The overall Desolation Sound region, if you zoomed out far enough, was the elbow in the five-hundred-kilometer-long sleeve of water separating Vancouver Island from the mainland. From that elbow the Queen Charlotte Strait ran wide and mostly unobstructed to the Pacific Ocean to the west. To the south, the Strait of Georgia was a similar highway of deep water to the confluence of the Strait of Juan de Fuca and Puget Sound. Tides ebbed and flowed along all of these. In less complicated waters, the direction of the water's movement could be guessed simply by checking a tide table and then glancing at the map to note the direction of the open Pacific. But the rise and fall of the world's largest body of water could reach Desolation Sound as readily from the west as from the south. That, combined with the exceptional number of islands, the maze of glacier-cut channels between them, and the verticality of the shores, made for movements of water that were as rapid as they were chaotic. Whirlpools, weird standing waves, undertows, bore tides, and abrupt reversals in the direction of flow were the norm.

In 1792, a longboat carrying a mixed English and Spanish crew had ventured into the apparently placid waters of what they took to be a blind inlet, only to find themselves in the grip of sudden and violent tidal surge that had overpowered their oarsmen and sent them on what amounted to a white-water rafting adventure down a chute between a craggy islet and a limb of rock protruding from a large island. They had sideswiped the former hard enough to stave in one side of the boat, which had begun shipping water and then gone under after getting caught in a whirlpool. The bodies—long since dead of hypothermia—and the wreckage had washed up on a driftwood-strewn shore some miles away, the home of a band of the sorts of people nowadays referred to, in Canada, as First Nations. To the officers of the European ship who had observed all of these goings-on through their spyglasses, they were Indians. And to the less adventurous white people who years later had read accounts of the tragedy while dragging their fingers along the course of the doomed boat on nautical charts, they were cannibals and slavers and such. More sensitive descriptions of those tribes and their cultural practices were now available, but the names on the maps had mostly stuck. The one exception was the stretch of beach where the corpses had washed up, which went down on the eighteenth-century charts as Cannibal Shore but was now called Ruination Reach.

No business owner in their right mind would want to sink a lot of capital into a resort named after that. "Devastation" was only a little less discouraging, but "Desolation" had a ring to it that a clever marketing team could make hay with. So Desolation Lodge was the name of the resort that had been built on the island, just above Surge Rocks, and within view of Scylla Point (the hazard that had punched in the longboat's side) and Charybdis Head. It was an old logging camp, abandoned sufficiently long ago that the trees on the surrounding slopes had grown back to proportions where most tourists assumed they were looking at virgin wilderness. There wasn't much flat land, but concrete foundations had been poured on some of the rocks within spitting distance of the shore and conjoined by a network of timbers and girders to support acres of cedar-plank platforms where docks, walkways, ramps, a helipad, a seaplane port, and other facilities had been constructed to service the lodge proper.

Arriving guests—whether they came by boat, plane, or chopper—were all funneled into a cozy red-cedar reception hall where they sat by a fire and enjoyed a complimentary beverage while filling out bland but bloodcurdling waivers and getting a stern talking-to from a rugged senior guide. The guide had been picked out for his impressive physical presence, his authoritative voice, and a certain thousand-meter-stare quality in his blue-eyed gaze suggesting he'd seen shit you wouldn't believe. He had important things to say, yes, about grizzly bears and slick footing, but his talk began and ended with remarks about water safety. These were bolstered with statistics and festooned with anecdotes, but essentially what he wanted you to know was that if you went into that water out there you would die. Even ankle-deep, the tidal surge would kick your legs out from under you with the remorseless precision of a jujitsu champion. As your upper body contacted the water you would go into shock from the intensity of the cold. You would gasp for breath rather than taking this one last opportunity to cry out for help. Within seconds your hands would be useless. The muscles of your arms would shut down in less than a minute. Some would simply go under and never come up, others would struggle to fight the current for a minute or two before hypothermia rendered their limbs useless. The resort abounded in hot tubs and swimming pools. Visitors who insisted on going into actual seawater would be directed to a sheltered, supervised cove five minutes' walk away. But no one should go anywhere near the main channel without a survival suit and a rescue team.

Having driven that point home and made eye contact with each arriving visitor, the senior guide would then tack on a couple of footnotes about bears and excuse himself. A younger and more bubbly staff member would then prattle on about the spa and the indoor tennis courts while the ancient mariner would, one presumed, totter off to a dark corner of the bar to drink straight whiskey while gazing out over the chilly and violent waters of the strait and ponder death.

The only visitor who managed to avoid this introductory session was El Shepherd. As always, he stayed home in Zelrijk-Aalberg and shipped a telepresence robot to the site. It arrived a day early, hoisted out of the hold of a supply boat along with the resort's usual supply of beer, broccoli, and laundry detergent. It was in a fetal position with a shipping label stuck to its back, blazoned with the name METATRON. For, having found these devices useful, El had executed a roll-up, purchasing a few companies that had been competing in the telepresence space, merging them into one, and giving them a snappy new brand name.

The staff wheeled the Metatron up to the main lodge on a dolly and set it down. It emitted a warning tone, suggested that everyone stand clear, and then stood up. It moved in generally humanoid fashion. But because it was, for the time being, just running an automated program, it was infinitely patient, pausing frequently to scan its surroundings and consider its next move. The first thirty seconds of its emergence were fascinating to people who'd never seen one of these things before, but after that most people began to lose interest as it became clear that this was going to be about as interesting as, say, staring through the window of a front-loading laundry machine while it washed a load of bedsheets. Its general program was to find its way around the resort, moving slowly enough that it couldn't possibly hurt anyone while scanning its surroundings through visible and infrared cameras. Its pace was so deliberate that people instinctively veered around it as if it were a statue. But if you sat in one place and glanced up at it occasionally while reading a book or sipping a pint, you'd see it in a different place each time you looked. In the dark it turned on running lights so people wouldn't bang into it. Thanks to these preparations, El didn't have to joystick the Metatron around every corner, he just had to tell it "Follow that guy" or "Stay with this group" or "Go to the conference center" and it would do so.

So neither El nor his Metatron ever heard the safety briefing, but maybe it didn't matter since the robot could be replaced if it blundered into the water. This was only one of a family of related questions that the conference's organizers had to ponder under the general heading of whether to count Elmo Shepherd as an attendee. The Metatron took up the same space in the hall as a human being. But it didn't count against fire code limits. It didn't need to eat, and it didn't require a bed, or even a room; every evening, when the after-dinner speech concluded and most of the attendees went to bed, the Metatron turned its back on them, walked to a dark corner, found an electrical outlet on the wall, pulled an extension cord out of its belly, bent over, and plugged itself in to recharge. Then it just stood there until proceedings resumed in the morning.

The question was largely academic, since El was going to attend whether or not they counted him. Assuming that it was really him controlling the robot, he came to all of the sessions, standing quietly in the back of the room. The Metatron had a built-in speaker, so he could have piped in his voice at any time, but he didn't use it; on the rare occasions when he wanted to ask a question, he would send it in the form of a brief text. Sometimes, though, the robot could be seen standing in a quiet corner, apparently having a conversation with Sinjin Kerr, Enoch Root, or one of his other advisers.

Sophia's ACTANSS 3 talk was co-presented with her collaborator Dr. Matilda Napolitano, a mathematical physicist at the University of Bologna. Its title was "Virtual-Space Cartography from Manifold-Based Traffic Analysis." They staged the presentation on the resort's tennis court, which was protected from cold and wet by an inflatable dome. They did it just before dinner, as the light was dying outside, but they chose not to turn on the dome's powerful illumination system, which would have competed with what they wanted to display. Resort staff had taken down the tennis net and scattered a few faint, indirect lights around the place so that the attendees wouldn't bump into one another. As recently as ten years ago it would have seemed a bizarre setting for a technical presentation, but now everyone understood what it meant: Sophia and Matilda were going to be presenting some visuals, and they'd be using augmented reality to do it, and this would all be easier if people could stroll freely through whatever three-dimensional imagery was going to be projected into this space.

The opening graphics were two-dimensional, however. Sophia caused them to appear on a virtual screen at one end of the tennis court, so that all of the attendees were at first facing in the same direction.

She started with a map of Europe, the national borders curiously wrong until a caption came up identifying it as the Europe of 1941.

"As a way of introducing this subject matter to people who, like me, are *not* mathematical physicists, I wanted to make an analogy to how the world looked to Allied codebreakers in the early part of the Second World War, before they had broken the German codes," Sophia began.

The map began to move, panning and zooming to focus on Great Britain. Cartoon installations began to pop up at various locations on the island: little icons, each consisting of a small building with an antenna on its roof, swiveling this way and that, but mostly pointed east and south toward Axis-controlled Europe.

"They couldn't read the actual content of the messages, but they could still copy them down. And through a technology called high-frequency direction finding, or huffduff, they could figure out where each transmission originated."

The animation on the screen now demonstrated huffduff. Across the English Channel in German-occupied France, a swastika icon popped up, and red circles began to radiate from it, like ripples on the surface of a pond. The red arcs crossed the channel and lit up two of the huffduff stations, from which dotted lines then reached out, tracing the enemy transmission back to its source. A bell chimed and a teletype sound loop began to play as data about the transmission was hammered out onto the screen.

Sophia continued, "The technical details of how it all worked are sort of cool, and many here would find them interesting, but that's another topic for another day. The point is that by running the huffduff network day in and day out, Allied intelligence was able to build up what we would today refer to as a database giving information about who talked to whom when. There was still no information about what they were actually saying—the messages themselves were indecipherable—but it was still possible to get a picture of how things were hooked up internally within the Axis chain of command, and which parts of the front were most active."

As she spoke, the map of Europe zoomed back and panned east, focusing more on the Eastern Front. Little swastikas popped up all over the place, talking to each other, and glowing lines came into existence on the ground, connecting Berlin with various occupied capitals and hot spots on the front. Suddenly a battle seemed to break out in the Ukraine; no actual fighting was depicted, but a huge amount of radio traffic erupted from closely spaced sites that were all situated along a meandering line across that region. In slow creeps and sudden leaps, the shape of the line changed, and one could sense that the Germans were winning the battle, cleaning up surrounded pockets of Red Army troops, consolidating their gains, moving their radio transmitters forward.

"This is called traffic analysis, and it's surprisingly powerful. In this animation, for example, none of us had access to the actual text of the German messages emanating from this part of the front. Yet, I'm pretty sure we all got the picture that a battle happened, that the Germans won the battle, and that they advanced to new locations on the map."

The web of lines grew brighter and the underlying geography faded into darkness until they were all just looking at a black wall reticulated with a complex pattern of glowing lines.

"How does this apply to the subject matter of this conference? Well, the message traffic within the Process has vastly higher bandwidth than anything that existed in World War Two. But we have computers that are vastly more capable of analyzing it."

The black background grew brighter, turning pale gray and taking on some complexity and definition. The pattern of bright lines was still the same, but now it spanned a different geography: the undulating folds of a human brain. New lines flashed into existence and old ones winked out.

"Where does that actually get us? Well, that's a pretty deep question about consciousness and epistemology, as some of our colleagues at this and previous MonsterCons—excuse me, ACTANSSes—have shared with us. But I'll give you a quick, glib answer: it gets us nowhere. Imagine, for the sake of argument, that we had a way to wiretap every single axon within a living human brain, so that we could make a record of every firing of every single nerve cell."

The animation zoomed in deeply until a single nerve cell filled most of the screen. Leading away from it was its main output channel: an axon. Clamped onto that was a cartoon alligator clip with a wire running away to a teletype. Whenever the nerve cell fired, a pulse of light ran down the axon, a signal shot up the wire, and the teletype chunked out a line of data.

The animation then zoomed back out, slowly at first, revealing that every single nerve cell in the brain had its own alligator clip and its own teletype. Then the zoom accelerated until the whole brain was depicted on the screen. Below it was a window showing all of the lines of data coming out of all the teletypes at once; the information was zooming by so quickly that it was just a blur.

"We'd have a hell of a lot of data. But would we really know what the brain was thinking? Would we know that it was seeing red, or doing arithmetic, or feeling sad? Despite some recent advances in pattern recognition on neural networks, the answer is basically no. But we can still perform traffic analysis and try to draw conclusions about what *sorts* of activities are going on within the Process. Just as the Allies were able to sift through mountains of gibberish to get an idea of what the Germans were doing and where, we may be able to analyze what we know about Process-related message traffic to make some guesses about what the Process is doing. There are various ways of attacking that problem. Matilda is going to talk about one of them. She's drawing on some of the foundational mathematical techniques of physics to detect what appears to be spatial thinking inside of the Process. Matilda?"

Dr. Matilda Napolitano stepped forward and waited for a buzz to die down. Many of the attendees weren't quite sure they'd heard Sophia correctly. Spatial thinking? Even the word "thinking" was controversial here, and usually deployed in scare quotes, as many skeptics doubted whether the Process's activities could be classified as such. To talk about a particular *type* of thinking was a bold move.

Matilda was forty-five, stylishly dressed, and a little nervous. Her English, though accented, was perfect—she'd spent half of her life in the big English universities before landing a prestigious appointment at Turin.

"In order to do physics," she began, "we have to deal with space and time. I'm here to talk about space. In the old days, we took the existence of space as a given and we didn't do a lot of hard thinking about its structure. What space actually was. How it behaved. By the time Einstein came on the scene, the groundwork had already been laid by Minkowski and Lorentz for a reappraisal of the fundamental nature of space, and new mathematical notations and techniques were in place, ready for him to apply them to the problem of curvature of space-time." As she spoke, still images of Newton and the others appeared on the screen, interspersed with pictures of geometrical proofs from Euclid, mathematical formulas, and ending with Einstein, superimposed on a graphic of a black hole bending space like a ball bearing on a rubber sheet.

"I'm not here to give you all a modern physics seminar," Matilda said, "but my point is that we do have ways of representing space now, and thinking about it with mathematics. Starting with an idea that is so simple that most of you won't even consider it to be an idea. Namely that each point in space has something to do with the other points that are nearby to it, but progressively *less* to do with points that are *farther* away from it." She backed this up with an arrestingly simple image consisting of a piece of graph paper, with dots marked in ink where some of the lines intersected. "If we oversimplify the situation by likening space to a sheet of graph paper, then each point is connected immediately to four neighbors, north, south, east, and west of it. A little bit farther away are the corner points in the northwest, the southeast, and so on." The image was slowly zooming back to show more and more of the graph-paper universe. "Let's imagine we have a creature that is moving around on the graph paper." A cartoon penguin appeared at the center point. "It goes north, then northwest, then back east a little bit, and so on." The penguin had gone into movement, waddling around on the graph paper just as she described it. "One moment it is here, the next moment it is there, and so on. This is all so obvious that we don't even think about it. But what if we scramble the points?"

In the animation, the points went into motion and moved all over the place, each going to a new position, like cards in a deck being shuffled.

"We have encrypted the map—lost track of which point is supposed to go where. Disaster! First the penguin is here." The penguin popped up in the upper right-hand corner. "Then suddenly it teleports to this other random-seeming point." It showed up on the far left edge. "Then it's here." It jumped to the central region of the graph. "We can't make sense of it right away. We need to gather data—to perform traffic analysis. And if we do this enough, we can see trends. We see clear evidence that this point, and this point, must be very close to each other—perhaps, directly adjacent—because they seem to have a lot to do with each other; when one lights up, the other tends to light up at the same time, or a little before or after. So we can begin to make sense of this overall pattern of traffic as if it were a three-dimensional manifold.

Whereas other geometries don't seem to make so much sense. And when these patterns persist we can become very sure that we are seeing something real."

"Matilda, are you doing this with all of the data coming out of the Process?" someone asked.

"Not all. No," she said. "The older data—from the first two or so years that the Process was running—can be understood quite clearly as traffic on a neural network. We don't know what it's 'thinking,'" she hastened to add, making quotes with her fingers, "but we can see that the patterns of traffic are what we would expect from a neural network."

Sophia broke in. "Yes, we started in on this line of research after the New Allocations grew really large."

"New Allocations" was the admittedly vague term for a phenomenon that had started to become evident late in the first year of the Process and that had been growing exponentially since then. The Process had started with sufficient memory to store its own neural network. At first, it had seemed content with that. But then it had begun to requisition more and more additional resources from the systems to which it had access.

"NMA or NPA?" someone asked.

"M," Sophia said. For the Process had allocated two kinds of resources for itself as time went on: first memory (hence "NMA," or "New Memory Allocations") and later processing power (hence "NPA"). These tended to leapfrog each other; the Process would suddenly grab a lot of memory and grow into it for a while, then demand a new plateau of processing power.

"We've known for a while that the use of memory in the NMA doesn't follow the same pattern as that in the original Process," another questioner pointed out. "If I may be permitted to anthropomorphize, the Process is using the NMA for some purpose other than simulating its own neural net."

"Agreed. And that's precisely what motivated this research," Sophia responded. "We asked ourselves, if the memory in the NMA isn't organized—isn't used—like neural network memory, then just how is it used? What does it look like?"

"And our answer," Matilda said, "is that it is used in a spacelike way. It is being used to keep track of a fictional or virtual space with permanent characteristics."

"Like graph paper?" someone asked. Their tone was not so much skeptical as confused.

"Like a spatial manifold. For which graph paper is a metaphor," Matilda said. "Because we have access to a vast amount of data, we can say much more about the structure of this space. About what is in it. Sophia and I have brought you all here to show you the results. If you would now please all back up, making a clear area in the middle of this space, I will turn on the spatial simulation so that you can see it."

The attendees somewhat noisily went into motion, picking their bags up off the floor and shuffling away from one another, clearing a space that grew larger and larger until they were standing around the edges of the court in a ragged oval. Sophia and Matilda had remained closer to the center, standing near midcourt. Matilda's hands moved in front of her as she worked with some sort of virtual user interface that was only visible to her.

A graph-paper pattern appeared superimposed on the floor. "Just a test pattern," Matilda said. "Now, the point cloud."

In one instant, several million motes of green light appeared in the space above the tennis court.

Even though the points were all the same color, and not connected to each other, they were immediately recognizable to the eye as together representing a landscape. In some places, mostly around the edges, the green points were on the floor. In others, in the interior, they were perhaps waist high on a typical person's body. So the general sense—once everyone had had a few minutes to walk around and view it from different angles—was that they were looking at a three-dimensional terrain map of an island or a continent, bounded all around by the sea, with high land in the middle.

"Ireland," someone declared.

"Much too mountainous!" someone else scoffed. "Just possibly the Isle of Man? It has a mountain in the middle."

"This is far larger than that, if you look at all the rivers, the mountain ranges," said a third. "I'm going to say the North Island of New Zealand? Hard to tell unless we get a ladder and look straight down on it."

"This is no place that exists on Earth," said a man speaking in a mild tone of voice but with a calm authority that brooked no argument. Heads turned toward a bald-headed, shaggy-bearded man, who looked to be in his sixties. Through most of ACTANSS 3 he had made a habit of sitting quietly in the back of the room, sans wearable, sometimes paying close attention and sometimes humming to himself as his mind apparently wandered. Through most of the current presentation he had shown a kind of mildly amused boredom, as if finding the subject matter too infantile for words, but when the landscape had appeared in the middle of the room he had been galvanized, and had practically knocked one person over while striding through the point cloud to focus his attention on an interesting feature.

"Pluto's correct," Sophia announced. "This doesn't match against any known—"

"There's no way that it could. That is obvious by inspection," Pluto announced.

Sophia turned to glance over her shoulder at the bemused Matilda and winked at her as if to say, *I told you so!* Then she said to Pluto, "Would you like to explain what you mean by that?"

"It's impressionistic. Not a physics-driven map. The alluvial formations are all wrong. These mountain valleys are V-shaped rather than U-shaped, as they ought to be—no understanding of how glaciation shapes them. The mountains are just high places in the landscape—they have no history. No exposed sedimentary layers, no evidence of volcanism." Pluto snorted. "This is programmer art. It reminds me of the first maps of T'Rain that Dodge sketched, when he was trying to recruit me."

"*That's* a compelling statement," Sophia said.

Pluto realized that everyone was listening to him and clammed up. He became interested in a particular river mouth and began tracing it upstream. The room was nearly silent for several minutes as the attendees feasted their eyes on the new continent. Small clusters formed to mutter and point at interesting features. The green points winked and shifted. "Are they moving?" someone asked. "Or is it just me?"

"This is a live display," Matilda confirmed. "Small shifts are to be expected as new data come in. But its overall shape has changed very little in the past few months."

Some attendees waded in to view features in the interior of the continent. Those people looked as if their bodies had been truncated below knee or thigh level. But viewed from too close, the points just looked like an amorphous, green Milky Way. "This is the highest resolution we could attain with the time and the processing power we had," Sophia remarked. "So it's like a pointillist painting. Stand back and it's fine."

An unfamiliar voice, electronically distorted, sounded from somewhere near the middle of the continent. Heads turned toward Elmo Shepherd's Metatron. The voice, relayed from the other side of the world, had emerged from the speaker array mounted to its blank face. "What is this?" he asked.

Sophia responded, "The bright patch in the middle?"

"Yes."

"It's bright because there is a much higher concentration of points in that zone."

"I can see that."

"That's because we have a hundred times as much data from that patch as from anywhere else," Sophia explained. "It is where almost all of the computational activity is focused."

"Can it be zoomed in, then?"

"We expected someone might ask," Sophia said. "I suggest you all close your eyes for a few moments, or put your wearables up on your head. The display is going to change and some may feel disoriented." She nodded at Matilda.

Matilda waited for a count of three and then began to manipulate the user interface again. Those who had ignored Sophia's warning were treated to a sudden, dizzying zoom as the tiny bright patch in the center of the display became much larger, banishing most of the outlying points to the outer darkness. When the display settled down, everyone spent a few moments taking in the new vista.

It was a cloud of green points, just as before, but these depicted a different landscape: a hill rising from a flat plain. Atop the hill was a structure made of straight lines and vertical walls, seemingly man-made. On the plain below was a sparkling grid pattern, reminiscent of a cityscape viewed from an airplane window at night: clearly gridded, with neat boxes rising from the grid.

"I could not be more confused as to what we are looking at right now," announced Gloria Waterhouse. She was a philanthropist, connected with her family's foundation, nontechnical, and always the first to stand up and request commonsense explanations when the discourse became too academic. She'd assigned herself that role and she did it well. "We've seen what looks like an imaginary island, with beaches and rivers and mountains, I guess. Now this is a small part of the island with a town on it. I get that. But what the hell is it? It looks like it came from a computer graphics experiment four, five decades ago when everything was primitive."

"This configuration of points is the only way to make sense of the data emerging from the New Allocations," Matilda said.

"And it's consistent?" Gloria asked.

"This has been built up over months," Sophia answered. "It changes a little from moment to moment, but it's generally stable."

"What are the red sparks?" asked the Metatron. Here and there, the green point cloud was flecked with momentary red sparks, like tiny lightning bolts.

"We use red as a debug tool to mark new data coming in," Sophia explained. "Real-time stuff."

"Then perhaps there is some error in the model," said the Metatron, and pointed with its open hand to the black void above the town grid. A cloud of red sparks was suspended there, a bit like a fireworks burst, no spark enduring for longer than a fraction of a second. But the cloud as a whole persisted, and as they watched, it began to move through space toward the large structure on the top of the hill.

30

Presently Egdod grew weary of being looked at and flew back to the Palace. This was still empty, which struck him as being somewhat wrong, but he had seen little need to make improvements. The souls of Town, which, compared to him, had so little power to change things, had put objects in their houses of which he knew the names: chair, table. Ward had done likewise in his Gatehouse. Just to add some variety, Egdod now shaped the adamant of the floor up into a chair, and experimented with sitting down on it. As his body never grew tired, this was no different from standing up or flying except insofar as it added some variety. He made another chair where some other soul might sit. Since the other souls were smaller, he made the chair smaller too. Between the two chairs he raised up a table. It was all without any real point and it was not as satisfying as cultivating plants in his Garden or building mountains, deserts, and swamps. So he soon quit and went out to the Garden to see what new plants had sprouted. Some had appeared with leaves that were colors other than green, and ofttimes those were arranged in clusters, which were called flowers. Their purpose, other than adding variety and pleasing whoever gazed upon them, was not clear to him yet. But in the many years since Egdod had first become conscious and extracted his soul from chaos, he had seen countless things that had no clear purpose. Each time he did, he was confirmed in his belief that all of the things he was making had been familiar to him in the place he must have abided when he had been alive. He must have lived in a place that was shaped like Town. Other souls must have lived there too. His world must have contained leaves, trees, and flowers. Season had followed season, and water had beat upon rocks. The emergence of these things was not an act of creating new out of nothing, but a kind of slow remembrance. The souls building chairs in their houses in Town were likewise trying to remember things that they had once known.

Later Ward came in from the street and entered his Gatehouse so that Egdod could see him through the aperture that joined it to the Palace. Egdod could see that the other was regarding the new furniture with curiosity. Egdod sat down in his big chair, then made a gesture with his hand as if trying to waft Ward into the Palace with a puff of air. He remembered the words and shaped them with his mouth: "Come in."

Ward walked through the aperture and across the expanse of stone and took a seat in the chair that was of a size befitting him. While Egdod had been away shaping the lands beyond, Ward's body had grown broad and his face had taken on greater definition. Lips, and other things that he was remembering the names of—teeth, tongue—were, it seemed, of use in more perfectly shaping sounds from the hissing chaos of breath. "Flowers beautiful," he said, more clearly than Egdod could have done. Or at least those were the two words that Egdod recognized; they were embedded in a sentence of greater complexity, joined together with small words that somehow made them work better. Egdod understood that Ward had been spending time in Town with the other souls and that they had developed the art of talking beyond what Egdod, who spent all of his time alone, had yet achieved.

It occurred to him that neither Ward nor any of the others had seen the lands that Egdod had been building. They had no understanding of what he had been doing. One day they would develop their legs, or in some cases wings, to the point where they could range over great distances and see it all with their own eyes. In the meantime, Egdod fancied that he might, by the use of words, try to explain what he had been doing. He embarked on that project but found himself limited by his crude powers of speech, which were not up to the task of conveying even a hint of his creations' size and complexity. Soon he resorted to gestures and disjointed words, pointing one way and uttering "mountains" and another way "ocean" and so forth. Then he lapsed into silence as he understood the futility of what he was attempting.

That silence was interrupted by a rush of chaotic noise from Ward. Egdod looked at him to see that his aura was getting larger, sending out a tendril of aura in Egdod's direction. This was a thing that souls in Town did when they were standing close together. Experimentally Egdod did likewise, letting the aura around his head reach out over the table. When it touched and merged with that of Ward, he felt, saw, heard, and smelled new things.

Long ago, when Ward had first turned up in the doorway of the Palace, he had touched Egdod's knee with a tendril of his aura and it had produced a fizzing sensation. There was some of that now, but for the most part it was more perfectly formed than that. To make such contact between auras, Egdod now saw, was to feel what the other was feeling and even to think what they were thinking without the necessity of putting it into words. He was seeing things now as Ward saw them, not just in the here and now but in his memory. Ward was recollecting a visit to Town earlier today. Through his mind's eye, Egdod was regarding the faces of souls whom Ward had encountered there. It was all clearly recognizable, yet curiously faded and mottled, as if contaminated with chaos. Perhaps this was a defect in how ideas were transmitted between auras, or perhaps it was actually how Ward saw everything.

Egdod made an effort to summon up a memory of high mountains, seen from above, the snow that collected on them and dark forests that cladded their lower slopes. He sensed that this was getting through to Ward, and so he called to mind other memories of the lands that, a minute earlier, he had been trying and failing to describe in words.

It was all a bit much for Ward. If the latter's perceptions had seemed small, wan, and unclear to Egdod, then what was it like for him to see the full grandeur of the lands beyond with the clarity and force of Egdod's eye? Ward became dazzled or weary. The aura bridge narrowed, weakened, and snapped back to his head. After that his aura was small and closely contained. He withdrew to his Gatehouse and lay on a thing he had made there—"Bed"— and did not stir for a while.

Egdod for his part was pondering some of the images that had entered his mind from the aura bridge. Among other things, he had seen the park in the middle of Town. It was a flat square of grass and it was empty of souls, buildings, and trees. This was how he had made it, a long time ago, according to his normal practice, which was to shape the land first in a crude manner, putting a mountain here and a river there, and then return later to better them. The glimpse of the park that he had seen through the eyes of Ward told him that its improvement was overdue. Moreover his own lack of facility with forming words told him that he might benefit from more contact with souls in Town.

So he walked out into the Garden and reminded himself of the shapes of some of the flowers that had lately appeared there. Then he took wing and flew down the length of the street and touched down in the middle of that featureless square of grass. Walking about on it he began to place flowers here and there, not spreading them all about like grass but clustering them in groups that were more pleasing to the eye. As he did so he was again struck by the knowledge—confident, unremarkable—that he was not creating anything anew but rather summoning up a memory of his previous life. He sensed that when the park was finished, paths of something like stone would meander through it, coming near each of the flower beds. In its center would rise a structure made out of stone. Not a large one. Nothing like the Palace. Scarcely large enough to contain a few souls. Not a thing to dwell in but rather an ornament to look at.

In his efforts to summon and sharpen these memories he had stopped paying attention to goings-on around him. Coming back to the here and now for a moment, he gazed about and saw that souls had gathered all around the edge of the park. He was surprised by the number of them: more than he could easily count. Thousands. They were not ordered in uniform ranks but rather clumped together according to some pattern that evidently suited them. As before, some of them spoke to their neighbors by forming words, while others joined their auras together so that they could share perceptions and thoughts directly. Those who did speak used a greater variety of words than Egdod had expected. "Egdod" seemed to be universal but "flower" was not. Different clumps of souls seemed to have different opinions as to which sound patterns designated which things. It was another of those realizations that came to Egdod's mind as a fresh thing but that he sensed had been commonplace in wherever it was that he had come from. Souls were not all the same, but grouped according to degrees of similarity that existed among them, and one of the ways they did so was according to their use of words.

All save one of them, however, seemed reluctant to step upon the park's grass. The exception was a relatively large and well-formed soul who was moving freely about the park, flying more often than walking, moving from one bed of flowers to the next as if inspecting Egdod's handiwork. Egdod named her Free Wander. He tried to convey by gestures and a few words that she was welcome in the park, but this was of little value since Freewander appeared to know this already—or perhaps did not care.

Watching and listening to this exchange was another distinct and mature soul whom Egdod had noticed moving among the different clumps of souls. Egdod named him Speaks All.

Egdod now summoned Freewander and Speaksall to his presence, and beheld the different forms that they had made for themselves. Freewander's body was as slender and strong as a new green branch. She seemed to be made mostly of wings, which she used more adeptly than any of the other souls. Her aura was a waterfall of white static into which she had already braided skeins of flowers harvested from those that Egdod had only just introduced to the park. Egdod was irked by this, but casting his gaze over the flower beds he saw that they had not diminished from Freewander's harvesting but were replenishing themselves already.

Speaksall was more robust than Freewander but less so than Ward. He had taken the unusual step of distributing small wings about various parts of his body—ankles, hips, elbows—in addition to the usual pair on the back. His aura was small and groomed close to his head, perhaps reflecting a preference for the use of words, at which he seemed to excel all other souls. Accordingly, his face—in particular the nose and mouth—was more perfectly shaped than any of the others' and indeed was uncommonly pleasant to look upon.

Egdod mistrusted his own ability to communicate with this

creature. His words would seem crude by comparison. The bridging of the auras was more effective but he did not wish to overwhelm these as he had done with poor Ward. A brief connection with Freewander's fragrant aura let him know, however, that her perceptions were better developed and she less likely to be stunned by a direct connection of this nature. She then could speak with better effect to Speaksall, who seemed to have a command of the words needed to communicate with all of the different types of souls. In this manner Egdod, with the help of these other two souls, managed to convey that it was desirable for all of the souls to move freely about the park.

Thinking that he might as well now fashion the little tower that he had glimpsed in his memory, Egdod walked to the middle of the park and summoned the adamant that he knew to lie under the grass. Below his feet, he sensed that it was striving to break through into the air and shape itself according to his will. But when he looked down he saw nothing but grass. In one place it bulged slowly upward and the soil parted to reveal a stump of rock, striving to grow higher, but to little effect. The farther it climbed, the slower it went. Sensing that something had gone awry, Egdod left off trying to command its shape, and it congealed as a formless knob no higher than his knee.

This troubled him considerably, and so he took flight and returned to the Palace. Freewander followed him for some distance but Egdod, already exasperated by her presumption, wheeled around and beat his wings to create immense gusts of air that hurled her back toward Town. She dodged round them with a nimbleness that irked him even as he admired it. But she took the message and left him alone.

The idea of the solitary tower in the park had called to mind another memory, which was that palaces sometimes had towers where their walls met to form corners. He touched down in the back, on the side facing the Garden and the forest, where he could work unseen by the souls in Town. For there was something about being watched while he did his work that unsettled his mind. At the Palace's corner he attempted to form a tower, just as he had a few minutes ago down in the park. Almost as quickly as he could think of it, the adamant had grown up out of the bedrock and shaped itself into a round tower. He went to the other back corner and did it again. And again it worked. He moved around to the front side of the Palace, overlooking the street, and tried it a third time. It was much more difficult. The fourth corner he did not even attempt.

The "discovery" and announcement of the Landform cratered the agenda of ACTANSS 3. No one would talk about anything else after that. People stayed up all night wandering around that tennis court, just sightseeing. The Landform Visualization Utility, as Matilda's and Sophia's software became known, was mirrored to servers whence colleagues could access it so that, after the conference was over, they could go on exploring the place from the comfort of their own homes and offices.

During the weeks that followed, reports began to show up that read less like modern scientific papers and more like journals from eighteenth-century explorers. Some of those virtual Captain Cooks, such as Pluto, were more interested in the Landform itself, while others focused on the hotspot in the middle. Even to the most skeptical observers, this looked a hell of a lot like a town, with streets and houses. Sophia noticed a thing that, once she'd pointed it out, could not be unseen, which was that the layout of the "town" was oddly similar to that of the one in Iowa where Richard and the other Forthrasts had grown up.

As more programming talent and processing power were devoted to the improvement of the LVU, it became possible to resolve—albeit in ghostly, pointillistic form—the virtual bodies that corresponded to individual processes. Most appeared to be strictly—almost disappointingly—humanoid. But some had been augmented with wings or other appendages, and a few had shapes that were very strange indeed.

Once that fact had been noticed, it was the work of a few days to run statistics. The results were too striking to be argued with. The earlier a process had been launched—the older the scan on which it was based—the less likely it was to have a conventional humanoid form. Weirdest of all were Dodge, the Most Favored

Nation processes, and the Ephrata Eleven. Of those, Dodge had been booted up first and the others, beginning with Verna and soon numbering a few dozen all told, had been launched only after Dodge had existed in Bitworld for a while.

And it wasn't simply the case that their bodies all started out humanlike and got weirder over time. In the stats it was possible to see a crisp fault line that coincided with the advent of full-body scanning. Processes that entered Bitworld with full information about the bodies from which they were derived ended up living in digital simulacra of those bodies. Those that had come into the world from severed heads showed a wider range of morphologies. But they also had a much higher failure rate, and some left no trace in the system at all. If they were alive, they were not discernible.

31

S orry to see you here under these, uh, circumstances," Corvallis said.

"It's okay," Zula returned. "It's my job or something now to be the Angel of Death."

Zula and Corvallis, along with two ambulance crews, a fire engine, several sheriff's deputies, three lawyers, a mortician, and a doctor had all, during the last forty-five minutes or so, convened, between a house and a garage that was nearly as big as the house, in the countryside northeast of Seattle. The buildings were at the end of a quarter-mile-long driveway—the private extension of a county road that snaked its way up into the foothills of the Cascades from a river valley patchworked with dairy farms and horse barns. Snow-covered mountains rose up into the mist only a few miles away. Cold wet air drained out of them, encouraging people to stand in the lee of Pluto's garage.

Which might have been seen as ironic given that Pluto's garage was much, much colder yet, at least on the inside.

Pluto had bought the property ages ago and lived in the house—a fairly dull bit of 1970s architecture gone somewhat mildewy—while gradually, over a span of decades, turning the garage into a fully equipped science lab and machine shop. Neighbors had looked on with consternation as heavy trucks had negotiated the puddle-spattered dirt driveway towing multiton machine tools on flatbeds. Deliveries of bottled gases and cryogenic fluids had become commonplace. No one really knew what he did there. The answer seemed to be: whatever he felt like at the time. He'd gone through a phase of making various kinds of lava by melting stones with huge oxy-fuel burners of his own design. He had built rocket engines and tested them in his backyard.

Today one of the garage doors had been hauled open to reveal his latest project, which was an exceptionally complicated suicide machine hermetically sealed behind a wall of bulletproof glass plastered with prominent signs and legal documents.

On the hour-long drive up here, Zula had been given some of the details over the phone, so she knew approximately what to expect. On the other side of that glass wall, Pluto was reclining on a gurney in the middle of the science lab. Everything was illuminated brilliantly by the cold white light of LEDs. So it was possible to see a great many tubes. His body and all of his head, except for his face, were swaddled in some kind of thing that looked like an expeditionary sleeping bag, and most of his face was covered by a virtual reality headset hooked up to its own computer. The sleeping bag—or perhaps "dying bag" was a better term for it— was pervaded by a network of tubes. Whatever was in those tubes was cold, judging from the jackets of frost that had gathered on them. The tubes ran away to a boxy device in the corner that, one had to guess, was some kind of a chiller. Lots of smaller tubes ran into the thing, snaking round the curve of Pluto's jaw and down into the bag, where presumably they were connected to IV lines. There was a control system too, embodying a snarl of cables at least as complicated as the plumbing system; all the cables terminated in the back of a workstation, an old-school tower PC with a flat-panel screen. Some of the cables led to the chiller box, others to much smaller devices mounted on the IV lines. And one led to a landline telephone.

"Where do you even buy one of those nowadays?" Zula asked, focusing on the latter.

"China. Some businesses still use them for specialized purposes. Sort of like fax machines hung on forever and ever."

"That's how the police were summoned?"

"His lawyer first. The call was timed so that Pluto's heart was already stopped by the time anyone arrived. The last will and testament, the disposition of remains, all of that stuff was laid out and waiting. The medics showed up fifteen minutes later, saw that the EKG was flatlined, and decided not to smash their way in. Now it's kind of a standoff. They're waiting for the coroner."

"He's already dead, being the point. The medics have no purpose here," Zula said. "It's just like Uncle Richard except much better organized."

"Um, this is neither here nor there, but it turns out he had cancer," Corvallis said. "It's in one of the documents that he left for us to find." He held up a folder and rattled it. "Colon. Spread to the liver. He's known about it for a year."

"Long enough to build this?"

"I guess so. But apparently this is a more recent project. That guy over there is his doctor." Corvallis pointed to a man in a white coat who was having an animated discussion with a burly rural fireman. "He says that Pluto was seeking aggressive treatment, doing everything he could to fight the disease, until a few months ago."

"ACTANSS," Zula said.

"Yeah. Maybe a coincidence but . . ."

"But probably not. I'd love to know what's playing on that VR rig."

"Pluto had ideas," Corvallis said. "He sketched them out for me in a bar at ACTANSS. He has been—*had* been—thinking about the thread of consciousness. Do you take your memories with you into Bitworld? Do the people wandering around that town remember where they came from?"

"Or are they like souls in Hades, who have drunk from the waters of Lethe and forgotten all?" Zula said. "I'm guessing the latter."

"Well, they certainly don't show a lot of interest in talking to us."

"No, they don't!"

"So, what happens when you cross . . ."

"The Styx?"

"Is there, like, an unbroken thread of awareness, such that you just pick up where you left off?"

"Well, what we saw at ACTANSS tells us *something*," Zula said. "The Landform is obviously a re-creation of the general kind of environment that those people were familiar with here in Meatspace."

"Not up to Pluto's standards," C-plus cracked.

"But nothing *could* be," Zula finished the thought.

"So I'm thinking that the VR rig is Pluto trying to influence the outcome. He wanted to go to sleep with ideas, images in his short-term memory that would somehow be captured by the scan and rebooted fresh in his mind. He didn't want to drink from the waters of Lethe."

"Well, I guess we'll know soon enough," Zula said, "when we get him out of there and find out what's showing on that thing."

Corvallis reached into the folder and pulled out a sealed envelope. "This is for you."

Affixed to the front of the envelope was a sticker on which had been printed the words TO BE OPENED ONLY BY ZULA FORTHRAST (OR THE CURRENT DIRECTOR OF THE FORTHRAST FAMILY FOUNDATION).

"Do I even need to open this?"

"I think you can consider it another of your symbolic duties," Corvallis said. "But if it's not Pluto donating his brain to science, then I'll go and lay down on that contraption myself."

32

Egdod took wing and flew far away into the mountains, seeking out a curious place that he remembered from past visits. The windings of four different rivers, converging toward the middle of the Land from outlets widely spaced along the coast, had necessitated the raising of several ranges of mountains to keep them separately channeled and to account for the direction of their flows. He had got himself into trouble thereby, and ended up with a kind of knot where all of those ranges had come together and got involved with one another in a way that he sensed was wrong. Between them were strange gaps where the water did not know what course it should take. One range failed to match up with another, forcing him to leave vertical walls in some places and bottomless gorges in others. It was the only such place in the whole Land: the place into which all of the wrongness had been concentrated and focused as he had expelled it from everywhere else. He had squeezed it now into an area not much larger than that occupied by Town, street, and Palace, but the more he reduced its extent the greater did its absurdities become. He had despaired of ever fixing the Knot and had even considered leaving it in its current state and simply raising a great wall about it so that no soul could ever come in and see there the sum of all Egdod's mistakes. He did not now do this, but instead flew into an especially tortured convolution in the land. Here, a range of mountains skirted a chasm that had no bottom. In its depths, frank chaos could still be seen: the only place in the whole world, as far as he knew, where any vestige of it remained.

This place could not be reached by walking. Flying to it was difficult, and as he went along, he purposely made it more so by shrouding it in cascades of icy water and causing the wind to crash against it with nearly as much force as the waves of the ocean did against the rocks of the coast.

Thus had Egdod found refuge from others' eyes by going to a place where no other soul could look upon him.

Having thus found the solitude he required, Egdod perched on a ledge beneath the overarching mountain range. He prepared the ledge, making it broader and flatter. Upon it he then sought to raise up another structure. In some respects it was akin to the Palace, but he was of a mind to build this with greater complexity. It would have high walls and many towers. Names such as Castle and Fortress came to him as he wrought it, but the one he settled upon was Fastness. He brooded at length on what its shape was to be before beginning to draw forth its foundation from the living rock of the ledge. With time and patience, adamant reverted to chaos, became plastic, and moved as he wished. Having made the foundation, he then strove to raise up the first wall. Again the rock did not at first do his bidding, but again it presently conformed to his vision of what it should be.

Egdod understood that he was not truly alone. Another was here, watching him. He gazed about, expecting to see Freewander or another soul from Town hovering in the air nearby. He saw none such, nor did he sense any trace of aura such as often signaled the presence of a newly arrived soul.

Then he chanced to look down toward the chaos that filled the void below the Knot, and saw the other. A great face it was, emerging from the chaos as if breaching out of the sea. The head was larger than Egdod's, and ill formed, wreathed in wild static that trailed behind it like stout tentacles and could not be clearly distinguished from its body. As it rose up toward Egdod it focused and coalesced into a form that agreed more closely with Egdod's in its size and its general configuration, but still it was interpenetrated with the wild dark aura of the chaos from which it was struggling to more fully separate itself. Its inchoate limbs reached up to grasp the rock upon which Egdod was laying the foundation of the Fastness, and it drew itself up to his level and gazed at him. Egdod gazed back. This was not the strangest form he had known a wild soul to adopt. It had a face, at least, and the more Egdod gazed upon that face the more certain he became that he knew this soul.

"How long have you abided thus?" Egdod asked, gesturing toward the pit of chaos below them.

"Not long," answered the other. "Out of it I climbed some days ago, and explored the curious habit of the rock hereabouts, and from a high place looked out over those lands that can be surveyed from here. Then weariness overtook me and I returned for a while. Several times I have done this, I think. But my recollections have a sameness that baffles the mind."

"Such is the way of souls new to death," Egdod explained.

"We knew each other."

"I am of a mind to agree," Egdod said, "if for no other reason than that your speech rings more clearly to me than that of any other soul."

"So there are others?"

"Many."

"But not here."

"No. This is a place where I abide in solitude, or in the company of particular souls with whom I have an affinity. You may abide here, since you and I were acquainted in life; but I urge you to venture forth and make the surrounding lands known to you, for there is much that remains undone in their shaping and perfection."

The other soul did as Egdod suggested, and took on strength of mind, and coherency of form, faster than any other whom Egdod had seen. It came into this soul's head that his name was Pluto.

With the shape of the Land Pluto had a particular fascination. Once he had learned the knack of doing so, he began to walk up and down on the Land—for he had no wings—and to reshape it. In this he did not change the nature or the broad form of what Egdod had made, but improved certain particulars and imbued it with greater complexity and variety. Sheer faces of adamant became cracked and convoluted, and shot through with veins and strata of diverse kinds of stone not before seen. The kinds of rock and other hard materials created by Pluto began to rival the plants of the Garden in their variety and their beauty. Egdod knew Pluto to be troubled by the compounding of errors that had caused the Knot to form, and suspected that if left to his own devices Pluto would smooth it out and do away with it altogether. Therefore Egdod decreed that it must remain as it was.

No longer impeded by the gaze of Pluto, Egdod redoubled his efforts on the building of the Fastness, and made it bigger and more elaborate than could serve any purpose. For his failure in the park had put doubt in his mind. To expel that doubt he needed to satisfy himself that his powers to shape the world according to his thoughts were as great as they had ever been. Of this he soon became certain, and he sensed that the nearby presence of chaos in the depth below helped rather than hindered his efforts. Once his dread foe, it had become a thing he could draw upon when needed. Flying out from under the shelter of the great overhang, where one range of mountains vaulted up over another, he further drew upon the power of chaos to shroud it in hurricanes, and the hurricanes stole spray from waterfalls ranked all about the place to become eternal storms that could only be penetrated by him and by Pluto.

Yet still when he returned to the front of the Palace he found it difficult to raise the fourth tower overlooking Town. Ward, who seemed to have recovered, looked on with bewilderment. A short distance away, Speaksall and Freewander looked on too, and Egdod was aware of more souls' eyes upon him from Town in the distance.

Brooding upon all of this later in his Garden, he hit upon an understanding, which was that it was all a matter of other souls and their ability to perceive the changes that he was wreaking upon the world. Alone, he had the freedom to make changes at will and with as little effort as it took to imagine the desired result. When other souls were watching, however, it became much more difficult. He guessed it was because any changes that he made, for example in raising a tower, were wreaking concomitant changes in the minds of all of the souls that were perceiving it. And souls, it seemed, were powerful things in their own right, with a kind of inertia about them, not easily moved. Particularly when all of them had to be moved in a kind of unison, all agreeing as to the shape of what was being made despite seeing it from many different points of view. As if all things in the world were webbed together by bands that had to stretch or break in order for change to occur, and those bands were woven by the perceptions of souls.

He sent Ward, Freewander, and Speaksall away, then caused a mist to gather around the top of the hill. For weather of various kinds was a common enough thing in the skies above the Land. While the Palace was shrouded in fog and mist, he went to the fourth corner and tried once again to erect a tower there, and found it easier. Too, he added more rooms to the front of the Palace: an antechamber between the Gatehouse and the main room, where he fancied that Speaksall might lodge and do the work of talking to other souls, and a tower above the Gatehouse where Freewander could perch if she found it to her liking.

When the fog cleared and the people of Town could gaze up at the new form of the Palace, changes were thereby wrought in their minds, but somehow it was easier this way; Egdod did not have to do the work of it, for the world was simply telling them all what was there and what was not. As a further trial of this idea, he waited until night, when the people of Town were wont to go inside their houses. He went down to the park and found no one there to watch. Just to be sure of that, he drew a mist around the place, then returned to the ill-formed stump of rock he had left there earlier. With ease he was able to draw the stone up out of the grass and shape it into a little tower that echoed the shape of the ones he had made at the corners of his Palace.

After this matters became more settled, for a time, in both Town and Palace. Speaksall took up residence in his antechamber, and Freewander made her home in the new tower above the Gatehouse.

Summer passed into fall. Egdod made a practice of walking down the Street from time to time and strolling in the Park to observe the doings of the souls who now frequented it, but also to be observed by them. He came to recognize more souls who had distinguished themselves in some way. There was one who liked to perch on the top of the little tower in the middle of the Park and simply look about for days at a time; Egdod named her Long

Regard and made her a chamber in the top of the Palace's fourth tower, the one that most directly overlooked Town. Another had made his house extraordinarily complicated and handsome; Egdod named him Thingor and afforded him an outbuilding attached to the Palace's side wall, where he could work on the making of new things away from the stifling gaze of other souls.

Egdod taught Freewander the art of flying great distances and showed her how to pierce the storm wall surrounding the Fastness. This became extraordinarily fierce as winter set in, but Freewander's supple body and nimble wings were equal to it. Thingor, by contrast, was a poor flyer whose wings got smaller and smaller the less he used them. Egdod carried him to the Fastness from time to time, and left him there for weeks at a stretch to better it. There Thingor learned new arts of fashioning things from diverse metals, sheets of transparent rock, and novel varieties of stone, all of which he discovered in the deranged underpinnings of the Knot, where Pluto had thought it good to place them. Thingor quarried those minerals from the depths with the help of other souls whom Longregard had made note of in Town for their interest in delving and shaping the earth.

Egdod, for his part, spent many days in the Garden striving to achieve a thing more difficult than any he had ever attempted since he had first brought himself forth out of the chaos.

Seeing the souls moving about in the Park from high above had put him in mind of another one of those almost-memories. He was growingly certain that the world in which he had lived before he had died had been inhabited by creatures that moved about of their own volition. In this, they were unlike trees and grass and flowers, which lacked the power of movement except when stirred by the wind. But neither were they like souls. They belonged to an order that lay somewhere between. The notion had been in his mind for a long time, and he had sensed that the Land was not complete without such beings. But it was so ill formed that he had made no headway with it until he had stumbled upon the notion of clustering flowers together into beds—a project that Freewander had made her own once Egdod had seeded the general idea of it. Thanks to her, flowers were now growing all over the place—

even in places where they did not belong, such as on the branches of trees. Longregard would spend hours gazing at them with a vaguely troubled air about her, difficult to put into words but easy enough to convey through a bridging of auras: the flowers, though beautiful, were somehow lonely, and could be bettered if they were aswarm with tiny souls-that-were-not-quite-souls. These would fly about on small wings and visit the flowers and fill the air with a faint hum.

Once Egdod had this idea in his mind he could not rest until he had learned the knack of making such things and bringing them into existence. He would toil on it in the Garden until the beauty and fragrance of the lonely flowers became a distraction, and then he would fly away to the Fastness, where he could try to draw it forth from chaos. He put a somewhat ill-formed picture of it into the mind of Thingor, who tried to fashion wings from new materials he had learned the art of making, such as metal and glass. The wings were beautiful and seemed to capture some of what was wanted, but they could not fly of their own accord. For that, an animating force was required, and making any such thing was beyond Egdod's powers. When he returned from the Fastness he would carry Thingor's latest creations with him and place them in the Garden, where the cold winter sun would glint in the glass and shine on the polished metal veins that held it in place, but no matter how small and delicate he made them, they would not move.

One day Egdod was sitting next to a flower bed examining a pair of glass and metal wings so small that they barely stretched over the width of a fingertip when he sensed the approach of another soul, and looked up to see Longregard gazing at him. "Come down into the Forest," she said, "things are stirring in it to which you would do well to pay heed."

Egdod was aware that Longregard had lately shifted her attention from goings-on in Town to the Forest that sloped away from the Palace on its opposite side. He did not know what about it had drawn her eye. The snow was melting, as it had done every year since it had first dissolved into freshets and rills and creeks to make the first river. Plants were sprouting from the bare ground between the trees; many of these had, over the years, spread down the hill from the Garden, so they were of more various kinds here than anywhere else in the Land. As such the place would naturally be of interest to Longregard, the steady and patient observer. But many things were of interest to her that she did not bring to Egdod's attention. She was a solitary soul who did not lightly interrupt others. So Egdod now rose and walked with Longregard out the back gate of the Garden. They entered into the budding trees and walked among the sprouting green things toward a place that Egdod knew well, since it was uppermost of all, where water erupted from the ground; it was the headwater of the first stream that Egdod, many years ago, had discovered at the melting of the first snow. By ranging far afield and following all of the river's tributaries to their sources, he could find others of its kind, high up in mountains. Some were at greater elevation or produced a larger flow. But in Egdod's mind this place, which he called the spring, was nonetheless the place where the river began. It was in the trickle of its water that he had first heard his name pronounced, and known what to call himself.

Very early—perhaps even before Egdod had become aware of Ward—a soul had taken up residence in the spring. As he now approached it with Longregard, he sensed that many of the trees that had grown up around the spring had also become the homes of souls. The presence of one attracted more. The water in the ground made the trees grow strongly; they were taller and more elaborately developed here than anywhere else in the Land. The word "grove" came to him and he sensed that in its oldness, the size of its trees, and the number of souls present here, it was different from every other place. In its center was the dark wet fold in the earth from which the spring emerged.

Longregard bated as they passed through the innermost ring of trees, and held her distance as Egdod kept walking toward the spring.

"Welcome, Egdod," said the voice from the spring. "What is it you would give life to?"

Egdod, not trusting his power of speech, stretched out his hand with the tiny pair of glass and metal wings perched on the tip of a finger.

The spring's rushing grew and filled the grove with a sound that put him in mind of the hiss of chaos, but he knew that in it was much greater order, the product of a cunning that had dwelled patiently in this place for nigh as long as Egdod had been here. He knew now that the soul that dwelled in the spring had been gathering her powers for as long as he had. But they were powers of a different order.

The tip of his finger fizzed. He gazed at it to see an aura streaming in from all directions. The sensation was akin to what he had felt when the aura of Ward had touched his knee, but again with less of chaos and more of a sort of order that it was beyond his powers to understand. It focused and sharpened and he saw that it was caused by a rapid vibration in the wings, which were now moving of their own accord. Gazing at them more closely he saw that they had been transformed, and were no longer the glass and metal constructions that Thingor had so laboriously wrought, but even finer and lighter, and made of different stuff. Joining them together was a narrow body. As he looked on, this sprouted legs, and at one end a tiny head, and at the other a sharp tail that curved under.

He sensed that it was about to fly away and so he closed his thumb over the top of it so that he could hold it in place and better examine it. But as he did so the sharp tail penetrated his fingertip and caused a sensation that made him jerk his hand back. The creature took flight and hovered for a moment in front of his face, then drifted away and settled upon the purple blossom of a flower that had emerged from the soil by the mouth of the spring.

There was a form in the water, akin to the ones that Egdod and the other souls had adopted, but without wings. She seemed to have been reclining in the flow of the stream, but now rose to a seated position, letting the water flow around her buttocks and legs, but with her body and head and arms up where Egdod could see them.

"The name of it is Pain," Spring said, glancing at Egdod's hand, which he was still holding out away from his body as if to distance himself from it.

"I begin to remember it," Egdod said.

"If you make a practice of summoning forth new kinds of creatures that can act of their own volition, you will suffer more, as bad and worse," Spring predicted, now looking Egdod directly in the eye.

"It is nonetheless worth doing," Egdod said, "though I lack the power of doing it myself."

"To nurture that power has been my work here," Spring said. "But I do not possess the art of devising clever shapes into which life can be breathed."

"Together we shall do it, then," Egdod proposed.

"You may make a place for me in your Palace and I shall dwell there from time to time," Spring said, "when it suits me to adopt a form such as yours. But if you look about and do not see me there, it is because I am here." As she said the last words, her voice became a rush of wet noise and her form dissolved into a hill of water that collapsed and surged down out of the Grove. Then it was gone from the place, but Spring, he knew, remained here.

PART 6

33

This is not an ordinary business meeting," Elmo Shepherd announced through the impassive face of his Metatron. "Do not be deceived by its mundane aspect: the conference table, the pitcher of water, you men and women in business attire. We are doing eschatology here. Practicing it the way some people do yoga."

Corvallis actually didn't think it seemed so mundane. Yes, it was a fairly conventional conference room in the offices of ONE. But the table was dominated by a live-updated display of the Landform.

A year and a half had passed since the LVU—the Landform Visualization Utility—had first been unveiled at ACTANSS 3. During that time, it had changed its general shape very little. But the algorithms had improved. More data now flowed into them. The Landform could now be mapped with higher precision and greater certainty. Its finer contours had undergone changes. There was no getting around the fact that these changes were exactly the sorts of improvements they'd have expected Pluto to make. He had gone there—he had killed himself—to fix the place up. And he was doing it.

Still Corvallis had doubted the evidence of his own eyes until Sophia had drawn his attention to the tower in the middle of the park. People had stopped using scare quotes. It was no longer a "tower" in a "park" but a tower in the park, as anyone could plainly see. She had shown Corvallis a photo she had taken several years ago of the park in the middle of the Iowa town where Richard had grown up. A similar tower was right in the middle of it.

There was simply no denying the fact that the processes that had been spawned to simulate the brains of Egdod and of Pluto now *inhabited* a world that they had created in accordance with how they thought a world ought to look. They had learned how to allocate memory in the cloud for storing that world's map. There was even evidence that they were using other kinds of resources—clusters of high-performance processors—to simulate its wind and its waves.

And if that was true for those two processes, presumably it was true for all of the others as well: thousands of them now.

"I am not pleased with what is going on," said the Metatron. "This is not the way it was supposed to happen."

"By 'it,' what do you even mean, El?" Zula asked.

"You know perfectly well."

"Yes. I think I do. But by just talking about 'it' as though we all have some shared notion of what 'it' was supposed to be, you're kinda pulling a fast one. We need to unpack this 'it' you speak of."

Here El might have got a word in edgewise, had he been sitting in the room. But the time lag between Flanders and Seattle spoiled his cadence. Zula went on: "I first encountered you in the days after my uncle's death, when, against my will, I had to take a little crash course on Eutropians and cryonics and all of that stuff. I'd heard about the idea of the Singularity, read articles about it, but never met anyone who actually believed in it seriously enough to plan for it. Since then, you and I and Corvallis and Sophia and Sinjin and Jake and so many others have devoted significant portions of our careers to working on the nuts and bolts of it. We haven't had a whole lot of conversations about the big picture: why we're actually doing this, what is the goal. So when you say 'This is not the way it was supposed to happen' I tend to think you're envisioning a big picture that maybe the rest of us don't share. Maybe you should share 'it' with us."

"I already have, in a sense," the Metatron said. "When I mentioned that we are doing eschatology here."

"End-of-the-world-type stuff?" Corvallis asked.

"What is humanity's ultimate destiny? That is my preferred definition," El returned. "The timeless preoccupation of great religions. Except that prophets and theologians didn't have any factual information to work with. We have facts. We can actually do this. We can decide what our ultimate destiny is and we can put it into effect. We are the first people in history to whom that choice, that power, has been given. And I'm not going to see us blow the opportunity."

"Who says we're blowing it?" Zula asked. "We don't know what's going on on the Landform. Maybe it's the Garden of Eden. Maybe it's terrific there."

"Maybe it's a digital North Korea," El countered. "Whatever it is, it looks like a simulation of an Earthlike environment. We can't really tell what goes on there. People—processes—seem to be concentrated in a thing that looks like a town. They communicate with each other, or so it appears. Other processes locate themselves in other parts of the Landform. If you'll let me have the table, I'd like to show you the results of some network analysis that one of my teams has been running."

"Take it away," Zula said.

The Landform faded. One of El's techies, physically in the room, gestured in the air and brought into being an abstraction: a constellation of colored objects hovering in the space above the table. Thousands of small white blobs, like aspirin tablets, were crowded into the lowest few inches of the display, just above the surface of the table. These were webbed together by countless gossamer strands. Above them floated perhaps two dozen larger balls, color-coded according to a scheme El hadn't explained yet. Surmounting the whole thing was a big yellow sphere about the size of a grapefruit. Radiating down from it were many fine golden rays linking it to some of the big objects hovering just below it.

"We can't eavesdrop on the actual content of messages being exchanged between processes," El said, "but we can get a general idea of which talks to which. What you're looking at is the output of a network analysis system. It shows who talks to who, and how often. And some trends are obvious."

"Forgive a basic question," Corvallis said, "but each of these objects represents a different process? A soul, as it were?"

"Yes, and the lines drawn between them show what we believe to be communication."

"Why are some so much larger than others?"

"Their size is proportional to how many resources they use—how much memory, how much processing power."

"Okay. So, clearly, we have a whole lot of little tiny ones that talk to each other all the time," Corvallis said, skating his hands through the lower stratum, which looked like aspirin tablets trapped in a cobweb.

"Yes. The vast majority of individual processes fit that profile. But above it you see the fat cats. The resource hogs. The huge yellow one on top is the first Process that Sophia spawned back at Princeton."

"Dodge's Brain," Zula said.

"Yes—though its connectome has changed so much since then that, for all we know, it might have very little in common with Dodge at this point."

"But it built the park, with the tower . . . ," Zula pointed out, then shook her head impatiently. "Sorry. Go on."

"In between you've got the Pantheon."

"Come again?"

"That is my term for a group of twenty or so processes that impose a disproportionate load on the system—they consume a lot of resources. Most of the nine MFN processes are there, including the one simulating Verna Braden's connectome, which is second only to Dodge's Brain. They, and some of the Ephrata Eleven, got an early start. They grew rapidly."

"Pluto?"

"The big purple one," El said. "And, to be fair, a few of mine are in there too."

"Of *yours*!?"

"You know what I mean. Clients of my organization, scanned using my devices, uploaded through my network."

Zula got up and walked around the table, viewing the display from different angles. "If this is correct, I'm seeing that Dodge talks to Verna, to Pluto, to the other members of what you're calling the Pantheon. But he almost never talks to the little guys."

"The little guys talk to each other *a lot*," Corvallis observed, "and they have some contact with members of the Pantheon."

"Some more than others," Jake observed. "Verna's not talking to the little guys at all but some of the other angels have lots of contact."

"Angels?" El asked sharply.

Jake smiled. "My preferred term for what you are calling members of the Pantheon."

Zula was holding out one hand toward Jake, as if holding him back—beseeching him not to plunge into a debate about angels vs. gods. But El broke in: "Zula, I notice you're standing pretty close to the green shape now."

"The one you identify with Verna, if I'm not mistaken," Zula said, nodding. "What about it?"

"Take a close look and let me know what you see."

Zula leaned in close and wrinkled her nose. "Around Verna I can see a bunch of tiny little motes. Just pinpricks of green. Like fruit flies hovering around a watermelon. Faint lines connecting them to the Verna blob. What do those represent?"

"I don't know," El said, "and that is what concerns me. Actually it's one of many things about the overall situation that is concerning. But this is new, and strictly a Verna-related phenomenon."

"Verna was a hacker. Underappreciated. Never really got her feet under her before the cancer took over her life. Maybe she's up to her old tricks," Corvallis said.

"Meaning what?" Jake asked.

"Those tiny motes—the fruit flies—are independent processes that have been spawned recently," El said. "Mind you, they are in no way as complex, or as capable, as those processes we've set in motion based on full human connectomes. But they run on their own and we didn't make them. Circumstantial evidence suggests that Verna did."

"To ask a blunt question, who's paying for the computational resources consumed by these new processes?" Zula asked.

"You are," El said. "Because your foundation launched the Verna process. And these subprocesses that she has spawned all carry the same holographic signature. The billing therefore goes to you. In a larger sense, though, I support all of this by bringing new computing centers online every day. Supporting the R & D, paying the overhead."

"Well, this is fascinating data, if it's for real," Zula said. "I thank you for showing it to us, El. What conclusions do you draw?"

"To begin with, it is clearly a hierarchical structure."

"You've certainly made it appear that way by arranging it in a hierarchy," Zula said dryly.

"Which can be backed up statistically. This not just me playing games with pictures," El snapped. "The overall picture is that resource usage is utterly dominated by a few mega-processes. They've established the Landform. Everyone lives on it. It's . . . it's just . . ."

"It's just like the world we're living in now, is that what you are saying?" Corvallis asked. "Nothing has changed."

"That is my concern," El said. "We had an opportunity to start all over again. To build a new universe in which consciousnesses—entities based on human minds, but bigger, better, deathless—can dwell and do whatever they want, free from the constraints imposed by the physical world. Instead of which the Process—the first Process—got a huge head start and just blindly, stupidly re-created something very much like the world we all live in now. A world that looks to have geography and physics based on the ones that imprison us."

"Maybe we need it," Zula said. "Maybe our brains can't make sense of things otherwise."

"It's the Kant thing all over again," Corvallis muttered.

"C, you're going to have to speak up," El said, "the microphones on this thing still aren't as good as human ears."

"Oh, years and years ago I had a conversation with Dodge about Kant. Whom he had never heard of until that point. It was about Kant's idea that space and time were ineluctable to the human mind—that we simply could not think without hanging everything on a space-time lattice. That any attempt to think outside of that framework would produce gibberish. He used it to take down Leibniz."

"Do you think it sank in?" Jake asked.

"It got him to Google Kant," Corvallis allowed.

"It is a common preoccupation of people who think about the idea of heaven," Jake said. "What exactly would it be like to live forever in a realm where physical constraints don't apply? Where there is no evil, no pain, no want? Being an angel, living on a cloud, strumming a harp twenty-four/seven/forever—that could get old. Old enough that it might become indistinguishable from being in hell."

Jake wasn't kidding. He had hosted entire conferences about this sort of thing. Caused books to be published about it. Talked leading scientists into discussing it in public with theologians.

"Fascinating," El said. He was pretty clearly not fascinated. "Maybe the rest of you can continue that discussion after I've signed off. Fly to a retreat center in the mountains, invite some archbishops and some hackers, serve wine, impress one another with your big ideas. I don't give a shit. I'm just about out of time. I have supported this more generously than any of you can possibly appreciate. From the very beginning I was dumping money into it. I've *wasted* more than anyone else has *spent*. But I accepted the waste—the fact that I didn't know which twenty percent of it was actually getting us somewhere—because I knew that I was mortal, and I didn't just want to go out like a sucker. Like everyone else who has ever died, or will die. I've been hands-off to a degree that isn't appreciated. I've let the beneficiaries of my generosity experiment with ideas that in many cases were frankly unsound. Fine. But these results are troubling to me. Now we have what for me is the last straw: one of these processes—Verna—is spawning new processes."

"It's a Sorcerer's Apprentice problem," Corvallis said, nodding.

"If Verna can do it, others can learn to do likewise, and then the demand for resources goes exponential, the whole thing blows up and runs out of money. When I kick the bucket, I can't even boot up my own process because all of the computers in the world are busy running what Zula likened to fruit flies. So I think it is time for me to take a more active role. A more directive role."

"How would you like to direct it?" Zula asked.

El could be heard sighing. His Metatron didn't have the ability to deflate its chest and drop its shoulders. But the little puff of white noise came through clearly. "I think they got stuck," he said. "Look. The best and the worst thing that ever happened was Sophia turning on Dodge's Brain prematurely. She just went for it. If we'd left it in the hands of the academics, a hundred years might have passed before that was done—and it would have been done wrong. So it's good on the whole that she took that initiative. But the Process must have woken up in a confused, disoriented, ill-informed state. I think it just started groping around, trying stuff, not thinking about the big picture, just reproducing whatever qualia brought it comfort. With the results we have seen. The system is stuck in a kind of attractor lock—a reproduction of the old world—that is *so much less* than it *could* be. It's because the new processes that came along in the wake of the first one just glommed on to what DB was doing and created a feedback loop that reinforced it."

"You want to break out of that," Zula said. "Shake things up, start from scratch again with a bigger scope."

"An open mind, at least, to the possibility that these souls—I'll call them souls—could be doing something other than reproducing what they experienced and did and thought in their past lives."

Corvallis said, "So what is it you are asking us for, El?"

"What I should have insisted on at the beginning," El said, "which is full, coequal toho status. I want to be a token holder with unlimited administrative privileges on all aspects of these processes."

It actually wasn't an unreasonable request from a man who—it had to be admitted—had done more than anyone else to make all of this happen. Which explained the long silence that followed. If he'd asked for something ridiculous, something unfair, they could have scoffed at it.

Corvallis spoke first. "El, just to be clear. Right now, for historical reasons, the only toho with that level of power is Sophia. She used it to launch the Process that, as you've pointed out, now dominates everything else. She has the power to shut that Process down. To kill it. If you had equal privileges to hers, you could do the same."

"Look, C, think for just a second about what is going on with Verna and the little processes she is spawning. Which is about to become your problem, because the Forthrast Family Foundation is footing the bill for all of those. What happens when a trillion of those get spawned and you run out of money?"

"As you know, that's not what would happen. We would just slow down the speed at which the simulation is running, so that we could keep all of those processes going at whatever burn rate we can actually sustain."

"A PR disaster," El said. "The LVU started out as a research tool, but now it is being watched by millions of people as a form of entertainment. They're fascinated by what is going on in the world of the dead. If you slow it to a crawl, then nothing seems to happen. They lose interest. They stop signing contracts. Money stops flowing into the system. We can't add the computing infrastructure that we need. The whole enterprise goes into a death spiral."

"I'm not as pessimistic as you are," Corvallis said.

"Call it pessimism if you like. Numbers don't lie. These new 'fruit fly' processes have to be terminated."

"Look, I'm glad you brought Verna's 'fruit flies' to our attention. We'll keep an eye on them. But that is not what I am talking about—as I think you know perfectly well. I'm talking about the big processes that are based on human connectomes. Processes that we have now given names to, and begun to think of and to talk about as if they were human souls. A toho with root privs could kill any of those."

"You know my thinking on this, C," El returned. "More than anyone else in this room, I am of the belief that all of these processes are alive. As alive as you or me. As such, I believe that to shut them down would be in every way the same thing as committing murder. So, for you to point out that I could kill any one of these processes is true. And yet it's as completely beside the point as for you to point out that in Meatspace, I could hire hit men to have a person killed."

It took a bit for that to sink in. Jake said, "El, are you making abstract philosophical points here, or issuing threats?"

Corvallis looked across the table at Zula. She looked back at him. On the side of her head that was hidden from the view of the Metatron, she raised her hand, extended her index finger toward her ear, and twirled it around.

34

O nce Spring had put life into several bees, it was not necessary to create more of the same kind, since bees had the power to make more bees. Over the course of the summer they propagated into swarms that filled the air like clouds. Freewander led a swarm down the Street to Town, where they found the flower beds that Egdod had created in the Park and that Freewander had since been bettering. On his visits to Town, Egdod observed that the souls were fascinated by the bees and liked to stroll in the Park observing them as closely as could be done without risk of suffering pain from their stings. A solitary bee made a noise too faint to be easily heard, but a swarm of them hummed palpably. Speaksall was fascinated by the sound, and would stand in the Garden for much of the day listening to it and trying to make out whether it was a type of speech. Souls in Town could be heard mixing the buzz of the bees into their sentences, and when two or more gathered to connect their auras, they sometimes emitted a hum so convincing that the bees themselves were drawn thither to investigate. Egdod, still not the most articulate of souls, paid little heed to buzzes and hums, preferring to better the functioning of his mouth parts and his ability to fashion whole sentences. When Speaksall was not trying to make sense of the bees' speech he would sometimes help Egdod with this, sitting with him at the table in the Palace and engaging him in conversation about the latest improvements in the Land and the doings in Town. Together they would call words to mind and practice the use of them. To frame thoughts in words and sentences required effort, but Egdod saw it was effort worth making.

A few nights after the first bee had been brought to life, Egdod drew a mist about the Garden and changed the shape of the mirror pool that he had fashioned there long ago, when he had first conceived a desire to see himself and to give himself a face. He broadened the pool and then caused a little tower to rise up in the midst of it, then made it so that water would spout from its top and trickle down into the pool. Its overflow found its way into a tiny stream that ran through the Garden before vaulting down into the Forest to join its waters with those that had emerged from Spring. The rim of the pool he broadened into a flat place where a soul might sit or recline. Egdod hoped that Spring might find her way up to this fountain and use it as a kind of abode, within the precincts of the Palace and yet of a nature that suited her. For he now understood at long last that it was she who had been the author of the many different kinds of plants that had sprung forth in the Garden from the early days of the Land. He desired that she should make a home in the place that she had created.

At first Spring seemed to take little note of the fountain, but one morning Longregard let Egdod know that, the previous evening, looking down from her tower, she had seen Spring emerge from the pool in moonlight, shaping herself into a form with arms and legs and sitting on the edge, much as Egdod had hoped that she might. After that she began to frequent the place and even to walk about the Garden and the Palace in that form.

The sight of bees swarming among flowers confirmed to Egdod that his thinking about souls-that-were-not-souls had been correct, and emboldened him to consider more small forms into which life might be breathed, supposing that Spring was willing to so use her powers. He brought Thingor and his teams of delvers back from the Fastness laden with materials of many kinds that they had quarried and refined in the deeps of that place. Together they devised other forms that were akin to those of the bees, but variously larger or smaller, with bodies of diverse shapes. Few of them, as it turned out, were capable of being imbued with life, and many that were lived only for a short time. None propagated more of their kind. Neither Egdod nor Spring could fathom the reason for these failures until Longregard explained it one evening.

The souls who dwelled in the Palace had acquired a custom of gathering around the table when the sun was low and practicing the art of talking to one another. To the early group of Egdod, Ward, Freewander, Speaksall, Longregard, and Thingor had been added Spring as well as souls from Town whom Egdod had named Greyhame and Knotweave. The former Egdod valued for his skill in thinking about abstruse matters, which he commonly did while tugging at a swirl of colorless aura that enclosed his lower face and surrounded his mouth. Knotweave was another like Thingor who took joy in fashioning persistent things out of stuff that she had borrowed from the produce of the Land, but whereas Thingor's favored materials were stone and metal, she tended to make use of material she had acquired from plants of various kinds. Together she and Thingor had tried to fashion a creature having eight legs but no wings, for Knotweave had conceived the idea, which was agreed to by several others, that such a being should be capable of spinning a kind of fabric out of the air itself. This was one of the few new kinds of creature that Spring had been able to give life to, but it had died soon after, and never acquired the gift of spinning air into knots.

Longregard had of late been observing the bees closely, approaching the flower beds with patience and caution so that they would not sting her, and she had formed the opinion that they were taking the stuff of the flowers themselves into their bodies and carrying it away to the places where they abided during the night: yellow-white excrescences, like little copies of Town, that they were wont to build in crooks of trees and other such places. Hives, they were called. Earlier in the summer, Longregard had been obliged to fly or climb into the trees to watch the bees building them, but of late they had begun making the largest hive of all inside the little stone tower that Egdod had placed in the middle of the Park as an ornament. It was too small for souls to live in but it could accommodate thousands of bees, and the slits that he had left in its walls served as doorways through which they could swarm in and out. Peering in to observe, Longregard had seen them exuding directly from their bodies the yellow-white stuff of which hives were made.

Greyhame had begun pulling at his chin. He ventured the opinion that the wax must have been made out of the very stuff that the bees were taking from the flowers. Thingor volunteered the observation that when he made a thing of any kind whatsoever out of some stuff, the amount of stuff that was consumed was equal to the size of the thing made; and so how could bees make a hive without getting its stuff from somewhere? Freewander quickly assented, saying that she had many times flitted close enough to hives to smell the wax, and that it undoubtedly bore the scent of flowers.

"The answer to this riddle—if indeed it amounts to one—is here amid us," Egdod said.

The other souls looked about curiously, as if the answer were about to fly in among them in the manner of a swarm of bees, but instead Egdod slapped the palm of his hand down on the surface of the table. "Ever since we made a habit of sitting about this table in the evening, I have felt that something was lacking, just as, when we had flower beds but no bees to hum in them, they seemed lonely. This table is lonely. Not only that, but it lacks all purpose since we never put anything upon it save, occasionally, the creations of Thingor and Knotweave when they are making something here." Egdod was about to go on in this vein but saw now that it was not needed since most of the others were signaling agreement by nodding their heads or changing the shapes of their auras.

"'Food' is the name of it," said Speaksall. "And 'drink.'"

"Both of those things I now begin to remember," announced Ward. "And to remember them is to miss them, for I am of half a mind to believe that they once gave me great pleasure."

"They are for the living," Spring announced. "Bees must eat, to make wax for their hives and so that they can create more of their kind. We do not make wax. And to create more of our kind is far beyond our powers when we are beset with so many difficulties in making even small creatures such as the one of Knotweave's conception."

"Perhaps the reason it could not spin threads out of air was that it had nothing to eat," said Knotweave.

Thingor nodded. "It would have to obtain the stuff of the threads from somewhere."

"Be that as it may," said Greyhame, "it does not touch upon Spring's essential point, which is that, as we make nothing out of our forms, we do not have any use for food and drink."

"I do not question this," Longregard said. "But souls in Town have lately taken up a curious practice, which is that they will sit together in a house and make sounds together. Sounds that serve no purpose other than to please the ones making them, and the ones listening."

"I have heard it," said Speaksall. "They got the idea from the humming of the bees, but their sounds have become more complex and more beautiful."

"I have heard it too," Egdod admitted, "and I crave hearing more."

"That is curious," said Greyhame, "but I do not understand its connection to the matter I was only just speaking of."

"The connection is clear enough in my mind," said Ward, "though perhaps it is only because I am now feeling a thing that is akin to pain, though not as disagreeable. I believe it is called hunger. I hunger for food and drink. It is not because I *need* to make a hive out of stuff exuded from my body. Nor is it because I am attempting to spawn more copies of myself. I want it for the same reason that Egdod craves the hearing of certain sounds: simply because to have it would give me pleasure."

"Your explanation is satisfactory," said Greyhame, "but it is neither here nor there, as food is entirely lacking. And for my own part I have no idea as to where it might be obtained."

"I could attempt to make some," said Thingor, "but I know not the form of it, and imagining what it would be like to eat a thing made of iron gives me no foretaste of pleasure."

"I have a thought on the matter," announced Freewander, "easier to show than to explain."

"Shall we join our auras then?" said Ward.

"No," said Freewander, "I had in mind that you would instead accompany me to a certain place that I know of in the Garden." And she rose from her chair and took wing in the same quick movement. The other souls, less nimble, followed her afoot. Outside it was nearly dark, but some light from the sun still shone flat into the Garden through gaps in the surrounding hedge.

Freewander led them to a small gnarled tree that grew near the fountain. Egdod had created it many years ago with a thought of seeding many such in a part of the Land that struck him as ill suited for tall trees. Thus far he had made little use of it, though, and Freewander, seeing it as a lonely and neglected part of creation, had adorned it with white blossoms. Egdod had found this ridiculous, since flowers to him were small plants growing close to the ground, but as often happened with Freewander's whims, it had grown on him, and he now had to admit that the tree had been pleasing to look at and to smell during the spring when its flowers had grown so dense as to obscure its green leaves, and drawn swarms of bees. Now it was late summer and the blossoms were long gone. "The petals fell months ago," Freewander pointed out, "and left behind only small dry apertures at the ends of the twigs that had once supported them. The bees who had so loved this tree abandoned it, and I thought it seemed lonely. But lo, the ends of the twigs swelled. The buds that had once sported white blossoms did not develop into leaves but rather into these round things, which can now be seen all over it." She was cupping one of the round things—a little green moon—in the palm of her hand. But indeed as the others looked they saw more such all over the tree—as many of them as there had been flowers in the spring. "I put it to you," Freewander announced, "that somehow, by their visiting of this tree, the bees—"

And here her ability to put thoughts into words failed her. But Spring knew. "The bees, having life, conferred a new kind of life on this tree, and altered its nature so that it would produce these."

"Apples," said Ward. "They are called that. We should eat them."

Freewander thought ill of this proposal. Before she could object, Egdod spoke: "They are not finished growing," he announced.

"How can you tell?" asked Greyhame.

"I know it," said Egdod. "Of apples I have a curiously strong memory—nearly as strong, now that it has been awakened, as the memory of leaves that led to my making this place in the beginning of the Land. And I say to you that an apple is not food until it has grown to the size of the palm of one's hand and turned red."

"Red!?" Ward exclaimed.

"It will happen," Egdod predicted, "at the time of the turning of the leaves. Then we shall pick the apples and carry them to the table and enjoy eating them."

Fall arrived in due course. Some of the leaves began to blush. The bees applied themselves to their work with greater diligence every day, as if laying preparations for the winter, and from their hives came a new scent, not unlike that of the flowers, but sweeter. Ward ventured that in their hives might be found another sort of food, different from apples. He seemed of a mind to have some of it until Freewander pointed out that the bees must be making it for a reason. Greyhame proposed that it was food that the bees would eat during the months when no flowers were available. Speaksall remembered that it was named honey and Egdod forbade Ward from stealing any of it from the hives.

Later in the fall, however, as the leaves and the apples alike began to change from green to red, Longregard announced that she had seen souls in Town extracting honey from some of the hives that were more easily reached, and putting it into their mouths. They had done so at the cost of many painful stings, and some had discovered that a bee could be killed by striking it with the palm of the hand. Quite a few bees had been killed in this manner, though not so many as to greatly reduce their numbers.

This news affected the souls around the table in diverse ways. Freewander was enraged, and strongly of a mind that those souls who had killed bees should be "punished." The word was vaguely familiar to, but poorly understood by, all who sat around the table.

"Would you inflict pain on them?" Spring inquired. "Or deprive them of pleasures?"

"Or destroy their forms altogether?" Ward asked, with a glance at Egdod. For Egdod had long ago spoken to Ward of certain ideas that had at one time come into his mind: the image of the soul on the mountain holding a bright bolt in his hand, and the idea that it might be possible to derange a thing so utterly that it would lack all power to recover.

Freewander had no fixed opinion on what form the punishment ought to take. Greyhame questioned whether punishment was even called for. There were plenty of bees, he pointed out.

"Even supposing that they have done wrong," Egdod said, "and deserve punishment, is it ours to judge and to punish?"

"It is *yours*," Freewander proclaimed, "for it is you who made the Land. And just as you fly about and better the shapes of mountains, rivers, and trees that are wrongly formed, likewise should you better the actions of souls who act against the beauty of the place."

"I would have punished you on the day that I brought flowers down out of the Garden to the Park," Egdod said, "for you plucked some of them and braided them into your aura and I was wroth."

"You beat me back with the force of your wings," she remembered.

"But this is a different thing from the kind of punishment you have in mind for the killers of the bees," Egdod said. "In time I came to understand that you were bettering the place in ways that had not occurred to me yet. The Land is now much better because you were not punished."

"I fail to understand how the wanton destruction of bees betters the place."

"It troubles me too," Egdod admitted, "though I cannot yet make out why."

"Perhaps it is for the reason mentioned when we first spoke of food, and eating apples," said Ward. "That discourse put me strongly in mind of eating, and I knew hunger for the first time. But through the wisdom of others at this table I soon understood that for souls such as we to eat food is without purpose. Bees require food in order to be bees. Souls such as we do not, and so if we eat, it is only to pleasure ourselves."

Greyhame was nodding. "The souls who killed the bees," he said, "took food from creatures that needed it, for no purpose other than to satisfy their cravings."

"Now that you have put it in those terms," said Egdod, "I judge their actions to have been wrongful and I see that once again Freewander has exceeded me in the quickness of her thinking. But to mete out punishment is a different matter altogether. I shall think on it. First though I would appeal to the wisdom of Spring concerning a matter that is closer to hand."

Spring had been quiet to this point, though the behavior of her aura suggested that she had listened closely and was pondering these matters with much care. She turned her gaze upon Egdod. Being so looked at gave Egdod pleasure, for he saw great beauty in Spring, and in respect of her had begun to feel cravings of a different kind from hunger. Putting such matters out of his mind for the time being, though, he asked her, "Do trees need apples in the same way that bees need honey? Is it the case that to pick an apple is to steal food from a tree?"

Spring did not ponder it for long before shaking her head. "Trees get their food from the ground and from the sun. The apples are akin to leaves. They will fall to the ground and wither and the trees will not miss them."

"In that case," Egdod said, "before rendering any judgment or punishment in the matter of the killing of the bees and the stealing of the honey, I propose that we have our feast so that we too may know what it is to eat food and to satisfy our cravings."

Knotweave had cleverly woven twisted bundles of grass into containers called baskets. The souls of the table went out to the Garden and filled several of them with apples. As Egdod had predicted, these were now of a size to fit in the palm of a hand, and mostly red. They carried the baskets into the Palace and upended them onto the table, which Knotweave had covered with a woven cloth the color of autumn leaves. Thingor had made a tool called "knife," which he demonstrated the use of in cutting the apples into smaller pieces. They discovered hard pellets in the middle of each fruit, which Spring caressed with a fingertip for a moment before announcing that life was within them and that they were the beginnings of new trees of the same kind, and therefore should not be eaten. Then finally they began to experiment with introducing the pieces of the apples into their mouths, which until then they had used only for the shaping of words.

Thus did Egdod discover yet a new way in which the Land could talk to him. He had begun with seeing and hearing, then learned to feel the ground with his feet, and with his nose to smell the fragrance of the pine trees in the mountains. Now he tasted food for the first time since he had died. As always when he discovered, or rediscovered, a new sense, the astonishment of it lasted for some time. But when he had recovered his ability to think about these matters, he began to wonder where the pieces of the apple, having been swallowed, had gone. They were in him now. New forms must come into existence within his body to digest the apple and expel the parts of it that were of no use to him. Or perhaps those forms had been latent within him all along, and were only now being roused to wakefulness.

Like things must have been going on in the bodies of all the souls in Town who had consumed honey.

He told the others to pick the remainder of the apples and bring them in baskets after him. Then he took wing and flew down the Street toward Town. As he drew near, a new fragrance came into his nostrils. It was not one that he loved, but neither could he identify its source. He looped around the Park and saw many souls gathered about the tower in its center, trying to find a way in. Their purpose was clear: they had heard from the killers of the bees about the desirability of honey and craved it now. The bees, sensing that they were under attack, had issued from the small portals in the tower's sides and were stinging souls and being squashed.

Egdod beat his wings mightily as he settled to a perch on the tower's top. The blast of air dispersed the swarms of bees and sent many of the souls reeling, or knocked them flat to the ground. The odor he had noticed was stronger here. He saw a soul not far away who had adopted a curious pose, squatting on his haunches with his hindquarters only a small distance above the grass. A jet of brown fluid emerged from him and stained the ground below, and Egdod knew that this was the source of the bad smell. And he understood where it had come from.

"From ones who have eaten honey, some of you have heard tell of the pleasures to be gained thereby," Egdod announced, making his voice very loud. "I say to you that there is truth in it, and that to enjoy such pleasures is in all of us. But to steal it from the bees is to introduce a kind of wrongness to the Land that goes against all of the past efforts that I have made to better it. It is in the bees' nature to require honey, but it is not in yours. There is however another means of getting food, which does not entail the crushing of bees, or taking from those that have a requirement for food above mere self-pleasuring. The fruits of it are winging your way even now from the Garden." And he extended a hand toward the Palace. The souls turned their heads that way to see Ward, Freewander, Speaksall, Thingor, Longregard, Greyhame, and Knotweave flying toward them heavily laden with baskets.

"Of the apple tree in my Garden you shall eat, if eat you must," Egdod proclaimed. "The bees you shall not molest. Rather, look to the bees as models to shape your own way of doing things in the future."

Thus the bees of the tower were saved by the actions of Egdod, and the souls of Town enjoyed a feast of apples, and knew what it was to taste and to eat. Later they knew too what it was to shit. Those souls who had strong arms for delving went to work digging holes for that purpose, and up on the top of the hill Egdod fashioned some holes that were very deep indeed, so that the odor of the shit would not trouble his nostrils as he enjoyed the beauty of the Garden.

35

Winter came then. Egdod felt the cold in a way he had not before and began spending more time inside the Palace. Flying over the Town, quiet under the snows, he saw very few souls about and knew that they were feeling the cold as well. This, he came to understand, was all because they had eaten. To consume food brought pleasure but also made the body liable to less agreeable sensations. Egdod, who could alter the world in any way that suited him, could surround himself with a cloak of warm air if he so chose, and protect himself from it in a way that other souls could not. He had Town all to himself as its souls huddled together in their houses. Knotweave had shown them the art of making blankets that they could draw about themselves for greater warmth.

Walking past one small house Egdod heard two souls inside of it making loud vocalizations that were not quite words. He gazed into the window and saw two souls wrapped up in each other's auras.

"They are giving pleasure to each other," said a voice.

Egdod looked up and saw a soul sitting on the roof of the little house. She had soft wings, luxuriant with many thick feathers as white as snow. She had folded these and wrapped them about herself for warmth.

"That is an understatement," Egdod returned. "Or so it would seem, if I am any judge of such matters."

"There is an art to it that, once mastered by both, causes the pleasure to wax beyond all bounds." Having delivered this information, the other soul was content to sit in her warm tent of wings and gaze down on him in silence for a time.

"There are many ways," Egdod said, "in which one soul may afford pleasure to another. By making things that are of great beauty. By utterance of pleasing words, or making of music. Or simply—" He looked at the soul on the roof, and went on looking at her for some time. "By embodying beauty that is pleasurable to gaze upon, as do you. What these two are doing is indeed of another order."

He understood that the two had felt, and surrendered themselves to, cravings of the same sort that he had lately been feeling in respect of Spring.

"Why do souls so long to recover sensations that belong to a different world?" he mused. "It began with the eating of food. And now this."

"Do you remember it?" asked the soul, whom Egdod had named Warm Wings.

"Now that I have seen it," Egdod said, "I am most certain that I did likewise, before I came to this place."

"We all did," said Warm Wings. "It is in the nature of souls to want it, as bees go to flowers."

"Why are you on their roof?" Egdod asked. "Is it you who brought them together?"

Warm Wings smiled. "They required no assistance in that."

"If I came down tomorrow night and went to another house where two souls were coupling in this way, would I find you there as well?"

"Would you like to find me there?"

Egdod now felt the craving strongly and understood that it, as well as the cravings for food and warmth, would be of great import in the future of the Town as it continued to fill up with other souls. And not only the Town but the whole of the Land; for Longregard had let him know that many more souls had been coming in of late. And finding that Town had no room left in its houses, they had been venturing out beyond it as their forms became robust enough to afford them freedom of movement.

"I would like you to dwell in the Palace," Egdod said. And he resolved that he would make for Warm Wings an abode there that was far from the parts of it he frequented, for her beauty and her manner of speaking about pleasure, though far from disagreeable, were troubling in a certain way. "If you make it your habit to fly to

Town on your beautiful white wings and know more about such things"—and he nodded at the window where the two souls were continuing to pleasure each other—"then I should be glad of it if you would sit at the table with the other souls of the Palace and discourse of it, since I believe it to be a thing of some importance."

Warm Wings was in no way displeased to have been given such an invitation, yet it was not in her nature to grasp at it. "Who are those souls, and what is that table?" she inquired. "It is the topic of much conjecture in Town."

It had not occurred to Egdod that the souls of Town would concern themselves with such questions. Now he understood that it must inevitably be so, for it was in the nature of souls not just to want food and to crave other sorts of pleasures, but to be curious.

"It is the Pantheon," Egdod told her. "That is the name that came to the mind of Speaksall. You will have noticed that it is in the nature of some souls to develop greater powers than is common. You for example have made for yourself a form unlike that of any other. I will wager that other souls in Town, gazing upon your beauty, have tried to alter themselves after your fashion but have failed to achieve it. They might lack sufficient control over their own forms. More likely they do not have your wits. The perfection of your form belies the long toil that must have gone into its devising; which indeed is part of its artfulness. For how many seasons did you work at making yourself thus, perhaps hidden away in some house where no other soul could observe what you were doing? In that time you might have asked yourself what was the point of so much striving. But I say to you now that in doing so you were setting yourself apart from these others who did not think to strive in such a way; or if they did, lacked the will or the wit to go on. That is why your place is at my table and not down here among these. For here in Town you will ever be the one who perches on the roof."

Warm Wings made no answer, but listened with utmost care.

Egdod went on: "I see that you understand my words and know well of what I speak. Souls such as you are required in my Pantheon for a reason that is simple to explain: you see things to which I am blind and in various other ways exceed me. Come to the Palace with me, Warm Wings." And she did.

The coldness of the winter compelled the souls of Town to adopt new ways. Some few who had the power to wreak great alterations in their forms covered their skin with feathers or hair to keep the cold out. Among others, the crafts of Knotweave spread, and souls made blankets, then garments of such rude fabric as could be fashioned from the fibers of fallen leaves and dead grass. That the same things could also be burned to make warmth they learned from Thingor, who, the better to work metal, had grown adept at making fire.

Some time ago Egdod had seen fit to imbue trees with the property of shedding branches from time to time, as when struck by a great wind, and in consequence they now lay heavy on the ground in certain places in the Forest. Those too would burn, as Thingor showed the cold souls of Town, who then made it their practice to venture into the Forest and carry away such branches as they had the strength to move. Others of Thingor's inventions then were found useful for cutting the wood into smaller pieces, so that, by the time that winter began to relent, it was common for souls in Town to be seen carrying knives and axes.

Many though still suffered from cravings that the Land afforded no means of requiting. One day as the snow began to melt, Ward was flying over the Park when he made note of a soul standing before the little tower there, striking at its walls with an axe. He wheeled about and landed on the top of the tower and observed him for a time. Again and again this soul struck at the stone of the tower with the metal tools that Thingor had taught the Town how to fashion, but the stone of the tower was obdurate and nothing resulted save little showers of sparks. So fruitless were the soul's efforts that Ward was uncertain as to his purpose in pursuing them with such ferocity. He flapped his wings once and dropped to the ground nearby. Sensing his presence, the soul turned to look on him, and left off beating the tower with the axe. "What is it you would achieve by this, Swat?" Ward asked. For he had recognized the soul as one who during the autumn had been a great destroyer of hives and eater of honey. Stung many times, he had learned to defend himself from the angry bees by swatting them dead, and had taught the practice to other hungry souls.

Swat answered: "Seeing how the axe bites into the wood of trees, I supposed it might have a like effect on the tower."

"Egdod made the tower here as a thing of beauty for all souls to look on," Ward pointed out. "It is not given to you to in any way alter its form."

"It is full of honey," said Swat.

"Honey that belongs to the bees—as Egdod said lo these many months ago before the feast of the apples."

"Apples we have not eaten, or even seen, since that day," Swat returned. "In the meantime our craving has grown powerful and we would now sate it by consuming the honey that is in this tower."

"You may not," said Ward, and held out his hand in the gesture that, since the beginning of the Land, had been his signal for other souls to desist and back away.

"Ever you have been the soul who told other souls where they could and could not go, barring our way into the Palace and telling us not to venture into the Park," Swat complained. "Now it is the same again—save that I have an axe, and you do not. And though the axe may be powerless to alter the adamant form of this tower, be it said that the form you have made for yourself, o proud Ward, is made of softer stuff—softer even than the branches of the trees that yield so easily to the bite of the axe. If you would not like to suffer grievous alterations in your own form, you would do well to stand aside."

Ward, barely wotting that he had just been threatened, stepped forward to seize the axe; but Swat swung its bright head down upon Ward's outstretched arm, making a gash in the skin that had, until that moment, always stood between him and the world. Out of the gash came red blood that fell on the snow. He stepped away more in astonishment than fear, and watched himself bleed. Pain came.

"Behold the new way of things," said Swat.

Sudden warmth shone on the face of Ward, and he heard an eruption of noise from all about, and his vision was dazzled as when he chanced to gaze at the sun. When it had cleared he no longer saw the other soul. Before him was a round patch of dead grass from which the snow had altogether melted away. Smoke rose from it, and also from the handle of the axe, which now lay in the center of the bare place; its iron head was as before but its wooden handle had been reduced to embers. Feeling a great wind on his back he gazed up to see Egdod alighting on the top of the tower. Egdod's form was as it ever had been, but larger and of greater magnificence, with feathers now like those of Warm Wings.

"Behold it indeed," said Egdod. In one hand he was gripping a bundle of jagged sticks that were too bright to look upon. With his other he reached down and gripped Ward's unwounded arm, then hauled him into the air and flew away with him to the Palace.

36

Spring breathed life into a new creature, similar to a bee in most ways, but larger, better equipped for delivering pain, and unable to make honey; she named it Hornet and sent it forth into the Land to build nests out of mud and to visit pain. But it was to no purpose, for no further efforts were made by the souls of Town to molest the bees. On the contrary they began to evince great reverence for the hives, and in particular for the great hive in the tower. As the weather warmed and the need for burning wood lessened, they put their axes to use in building a new structure: four walls that enclosed the tower and the burned place in the ground where Egdod's thunderbolt had struck. On that spot they kindled a fire, and made a practice of keeping it alight night and day.

Hovering on the spring winds high above the Palace, or standing atop the watchtower of Longregard, Egdod brooded upon the smoke that rose above the park and the queue of souls coming and going with their burdens of firewood. Speaksall had explained to him that they construed these as gifts to Egdod: gestures of apology for the error of Swat, and pleas that Egdod not strike any more of them down with bright thunderbolts. The wooden walls they began to replace with stone. First they broke down the houses that Egdod had made for them and piled the rubble into foundations and walls. Since they had not Egdod's power to shape adamant from chaos, they instead sought out places where Pluto had bettered the Land by making new types of rocks, and brought those in and piled them up. Certain souls began to make their dwelling there, the better to oversee the feeding of the flame and the expansion of the building. They learned the art of talking to the bees, or so they claimed, and from time to time they would join their auras into one and make a hum that on a quiet evening could be heard in the Palace. Speaksall commonly went there to walk among them and listen to their speech, but he could hear no more meaning in it than in that of the bees themselves.

Egdod found himself grievously distracted by these strange doings. Outright defiance he had prepared himself for, by working with Thingor on the fashioning of bright thunderbolts. But the loosing of a single one of those had sufficed to reduce all of the souls into a state of fearful obedience. Out of this, they had contrived new ways of busying themselves that to Egdod were more troubling than the impudence of Swat.

After the arrival in the Palace of Warm Wings, the other souls of the Pantheon had not been slow in learning the arts by which they might give each other pleasure that exceeded all bounds. She herself taught it to, and did it with, Ward while she nursed his wound. Other couplings then came about: Thingor and Knotweave, Speaksall and Freewander. Greyhame did not couple with any of the Pantheon, but it was known that he went to Town from time to time and there engaged in pleasurable couplings with various souls in certain houses. Neither Egdod nor Spring was approached by any of the other souls with any such intentions, for it was understood by all, without the need for speaking of it, that those two were apart from all the rest and intended for each other.

Because of Warm Wings, Egdod now understood the cravings that he had felt in respect of Spring from the first time he had seen her in the little stream that flowed from the dark cleft high up in the Forest. Soon after Warm Wings had come to dwell in the Palace, Egdod went out one evening when the moon shone on the Fountain and found Spring there bathing in its waters. He approached her and ventured to speak to her of his feelings and intentions. Spring listened to his words until he was sated with talking, then told him that she must consider his suit and that he should come and find her in the Forest the next day.

The next day, when the sun was shining warmly on the Forest, Egdod went to the spring with flowers that he had harvested from the Garden, and sat in the dark cleft and waited for her to make a form for herself that might be suited for the sorts of pleasure that

Warm Wings had put him in mind of. In time she did so, but it was a form made entirely of water, streaming cold and clear. "You and I are of a different order from the rest," she reminded him.

"That much is true," Egdod said, "and yet we share with them like cravings and sensations."

"We may couple in the same way as those," she agreed, "and indeed I would take great pleasure in doing so and it has been much on my mind, even before Warm Wings came and spoke of it."

"Then let us—" Egdod began, but Spring interrupted him:

"Though your and my coupling might be like theirs in its general form, its consequences will be altogether of a different order. For it is you who have the power to create and shape all things that the Land comprises, and it is given to me to imbue certain things with life. Our coupling will result in the creation of new souls."

"In that I see no obstacle," Egdod said, for his craving was very strong and he was not in any frame of mind to give careful consideration to the wisdom of Spring.

"I speak not of bees or of birds," Spring went on, "but of souls like us, capable of speech."

"New souls enter the Land every day," Egdod pointed out.

"Yes," Spring agreed, "and they do so by dying in whatever place they used to abide, and awakening here. Understand, Egdod, that the souls that will emerge from our coupling will be new creations that never before lived, and never died. I do not know the meaning of it or what consequences it might have. They might be akin to others of the Pantheon, and dwell with us happily. But they might be greater than we in their power, and capable of destroying our forms with thunderbolts just as you did in the case of Swat."

"Once again you exceed me in wisdom and in the penetration of your thought," Egdod said. "In respect of that—and not, be it said, for any lack of desire—I shall withdraw and consider what you have said." So he left the flowers by the side of the stream and went away to the Palace and thought the matter over at length.

The following day he returned with more flowers and a renewed ardor. But it ended in the same way and he took wing and flew great distances over the Land to ponder certain additional points that Spring had made. But the next day he returned for a third time and said to her, "Be it so then." And he went into her and was surrounded by her as a rock in a river is enfolded in its waters, smooth and yet strong, and their auras merged as when two rivers come together deep in a forest and flow as one to exhaust themselves much later into the ocean.

After that Spring went weeks without manifesting herself in any particular form. Egdod went to the Fastness to ponder what had happened between them. There, far from the distractions posed not only by Spring but by the curious behavior of the souls in Town, he worked with Thingor on the making of new contrivances, each more complex than the last. The feathers of Warm Wings had put the Pantheon in mind of flying creatures covered with the same, larger than bees, that would make nests for themselves in the branches of trees. The construction of their wings must needs be different from those of the bees and so long effort went into its devising.

The Chasm gaped below the Knot as ever, and the workshops and watchtowers of the Fastness overlooked it. The other souls who came to visit the place looked on it as a defect. Pluto in particular was of the view that it was an error in need of fixing and had ideas as to how this rift in the Land's fabric might be stitched up. But Egdod forbade it, and reminded him that he himself had first emerged from that same pit.

"What else might then crawl up out of it, I wonder?" was Pluto's answer.

"Anything whatsoever," Egdod said, "and that is the promise and the danger of it. For the chaos that you see down there is the source of all you see and all you are." But in his private thoughts Egdod weighed the words of Pluto and of the others. During idle moments he would perch on the edge of the wall he had thrown up around the Fastness, gazing down into the chaos below and testing himself by seeing what new forms he could draw forth from it. Motes of color he saw in the static, such as he had painstakingly shaped into leaves in the very beginning, and these he sought to form into new shapes that might clothe the flying creatures he was building with Thingor. And in the roar of noise that came up from the pit he sometimes heard strains that had about them some character of melody or rhythm. Those he pursued in the windings of his mind, and lost them more often than not. But when they did not elude him he was able to draw them forth out of the noise and to discover music in them. He was not creating the music but rescuing it by stripping away the harsh and formless noise in which it had somehow become ensnared. Rich strains of music began to fill the Fastness. All who visited the place remarked on its beauty, and it gave new vigor to Thingor, who seemed to possess some art of transmuting sounds into new objects of beauty and ingenuity that had not before been seen in the Land.

Nor was he the only one at work making new wonders in the Fastness. The blankets and the garment-stuff of Knotweave had put the Pantheon in mind of making smaller and finer fabrics on which marks could be inscribed using loose feathers from wings dipped in black potions concocted from the fruits and barks of certain trees. The ingenuity of Knotweave thus came together with Warm Wings's feathers and Freewander's knowledge of trees and flowers to create paper and ink. Longregard and Freewander roamed about drawing maps of the Land and pictures of mountains and trees. Speaksall and Greyhame for their parts devised a system of writing and put it to use setting down accounts of what had happened in the Land, as best as it could be remembered. They taught these arts to certain souls of Town, foremost among them a woman who came to be known as Pestle.

When summer was nearing its peak, Egdod flew out from the Fastness carrying the form of a bird that Thingor had devised, into which he hoped Spring might breathe life. But before going her way he flew in a broad sweep across the Land, climbing high into the air to seek out the wild souls who made its winds and its weathers, and making a circuit of its coast to speak with the wild souls of the oceans. To each of them he made it known that in a few months' time, when the apples were harvested in the Garden, there would be a feast, and that each of them would be welcome to take part in it.

When he had made this invitation to the last of the wild souls, who inhabited the eastern sea where it beat against the great rock, he flew up the course of the river and followed its branchings all the way to the Forest, and then likewise all the way up to the abode of Spring. There he found her much as he had seen her before, but strangely different. And before long the nature of this change made itself clear in his mind and he knew that she was creating two new souls just as she had foretold. But because of the greatness of the work it was a thing that would be much longer in doing: not the work of a few moments, as when she had put life into the first bee, but of seasons to come.

Abashed, he showed her the form of the bird that he and Thingor had fashioned, and gave it over into her hands. As she regarded it and caressed its feathers, Egdod said to her, "I see now that you are at work on a task much greater than putting life into a bird, and so I regret that I have so troubled you with what now strikes me as a small matter."

"On the contrary," Spring answered, "the toil of making a new soul has given me strength I lacked before and made light work of it." And the bird's wings began to flap of their own volition and it took to the air, clumsily at first, but soon acquiring all the skill and grace of Freewander.

"Thus birds," Spring said. "It is a good thing to have done. But know that while you have been secreted in the Fastness working on such, the souls of Town have likewise been busy, and I think you would do well to spread your wings and fly higher and look farther in that direction."

Troubled by Spring's words, Egdod flew to the watchtower of Longregard and perched upon its roof so that he could see what was afoot in Town. And he was astonished by the change that had come over the place in his absence. Formerly, the new building that the souls had been making in the Park had squatted low to the ground, barely rising above the top of the little tower in its center. Only a small portion of the Park had been covered by it. Now, however, its foundation covered the Park entirely, so that not a single blade of grass or bed of flowers could be seen, and in some directions it had expanded across streets to cover ground where houses had once stood. Such a foundation was required to support all that had been constructed above it: a tower that seemed to

Egdod like a kind of mockery of the little one he had made there to begin with. For, though it was yet incomplete, this one had a like shape. And as he perceived on further inspection, it had a like purpose, with souls, instead of bees, swarming and humming about it.

The stuff of which the Tower was being made was various and changeable. Its foundations were of rubble and wood. When the Tower's builders had exhausted their supply of those, they had borrowed the style of building employed by hornets in the making of their nests, daubing mud and leaving it to dry. In this manner they were piling up many more stories, so that the top of their works was nearly of a height with the Palace. Likewise they had begun to copy the manner of construction favored by bees and hornets; while the Tower's lower courses were in horizontal layers, piled one atop the other, the farther up they built it, the more they had caused it to resemble the style of a wax hive or a mud nest that is erected in a tree, with winding internal passageways and clusters of cells in which souls could live. Even at this remove, Egdod could hear on the wind a low hum that was being made by many of those souls speaking in consonance. It seemed that their habit of emulating the speech of bees, which had so puzzled Speaksall, had driven the words from their mouths and rendered them deaf and dumb to the old ways of talking. No strain of melody nor pulse of rhythm informed it, for they had forgotten music as well.

"These are very considerable changes," Egdod said, "and I find it strange that no one of the Palace came to the Fastness to make me aware that such things were afoot."

"It began slowly, then came on with a suddenness in the last few days," said Longregard. "Freewander sought you there but was told that you had gone on a long journey. In the time since, the height of the Tower has more than doubled. The humming can be heard at all hours, for those souls no longer go into their houses of an evening, but stay together in the myriad cells of the Tower and join their voices into that weird song and combine their auras as well."

"I shall ponder what to do about this," Egdod said, "but in the meantime I am of a mind to build this hill and this Palace higher.

For I do not like having yon Tower of a height equal to my abode, as I require silence and privacy in order to go about my work of bettering the Land."

Egdod then flew away and sought out the wild soul whose form was the west wind, which often brought clouds and rain. At Egdod's bidding, this one brought down a heavy storm that enshrouded the hill and the Palace. Thereby concealed, Egdod raised the hill to twice its former height, and made the walls and towers of the Palace grow higher as well. When the storm cleared in the morning, however, he saw that the state of things had not improved so much as he had fancied; for the storm had not washed the upper part of the Tower away, and during the hours of darkness the souls had built it up even higher.

"How can it be that a thing made of mud can rise to such a height and withstand the fury of the storm?" Egdod asked Greyhame in the morning.

Greyhame answered, "Not only mud is it made of, but of the souls themselves. As the bees exude wax to make their hives, these souls put something of themselves into the stuff of the Tower, weaving their very auras into it. As long as they remain conjoined there by this mingling of their souls and the singing of the bees' speech, the Tower will stand and grow."

"What drives them to do this?" asked Egdod. "True, I told them last year at the feast of the apples that they ought to emulate the bees rather than swat them, but they cannot have understood my words to mean such wrongful alterations in their way of being."

"They are all souls like you, Egdod," Greyhame returned, "and as such they are heir to the boredom and frustration that once drove you to make the Land. But they are not equal to you in their powers to shape their world, and so they make do with what they have, which is the workings of their own minds and the meager capabilities of their own forms."

Egdod took to the air and went down the street and flew around the tower for a time, gazing into its tortuous passageways of packed mud in such places as they were exposed to view, sensing the hum of the souls through its gray walls. The sound of it waxed and waned, and disturbances in it propagated up and down. In it Egdod sensed a savor of that mutual pleasuring that Warm Wings had brought knowledge of and that most members of the Pantheon had now known. But whereas they had done it two by two, now it seemed that all of the souls were doing it with all of the others at once.

That night Egdod summoned not just the west wind but the other three as well, and called down a storm of great violence. In the midst of it he built the hill and the Palace taller yet, thinking thereby to gain an even greater vantage over whatever might remain of the Tower in the morning. But when the storm lessened he could hear the humming as loud as before, and when the sun rose in the morning he saw the Tower standing unaffected, and taller than at sundown.

37

Corvallis sometimes thought back on the day, three decades ago, when Richard Forthrast had reached down and plucked him out of his programming job at Corporation 9592 and given him a new position, reporting directly to Richard. Corvallis had asked the usual questions about job title and job description. Richard had answered, simply, "Weird stuff." When this proved unsatisfactory to the company's ISO-compliant HR department, Richard had been forced to go downstairs and expand upon it. In a memorable, extemporaneous work of performance art in the middle of the HR department's open-plan workspace, he had explained that work of a routine, predictable nature could and should be embodied in computer programs. If that proved too difficult, it should be outsourced to humans far away. If it was somehow too sensitive or complicated for outsourcing, then "you people" (meaning the employees of the HR department) needed to slice it and dice it into tasks that could be summed up in job descriptions and advertised on the open employment market. Floating above all of that, however, in a realm that was out of the scope of "you people," was "weird stuff." It was important that the company have people to work on "weird stuff." As a matter of fact it was more important than anything else. But trying to explain "weird stuff" to "you people" was like explaining blue to someone who had been blind since birth, and so there was no point in even trying. About then, he'd been interrupted by a spate of urgent text messages from one of the company's novelists, who had run aground on some desolate narrative shore and needed moral support, and so the discussion had gone no further. Someone had intervened and written a sufficiently vague job description for Corvallis and made up a job title that would make it possible for him to get the level of compensation he was expecting. So it had all worked out fine. And it made for a fun story to tell on the increasingly rare occasions when people were reminiscing about Dodge back in the old days. But the story was inconclusive in the sense that Dodge had been interrupted before he could really get to the essence of what "weird stuff" actually was and why it was so important. As time went on, however, Corvallis understood that this very inconclusiveness was really a fitting and proper part of the story.

His own professional journey, since then, could be seen as the single-minded pursuit of weird stuff, and the shedding, at every opportunity, of all responsibilities that didn't qualify as such. It had led him into some alarming situations, forced him to make some tricky career choices, but whenever he was questioning it, he would summon forth that memory of Richard and he would try to do what Richard would have done.

And that explained why he was sitting across the table, in the most expensive restaurant in Seattle, from Gerta Stock and the full-time nurse who apparently kept Gerta alive by looking after the tubes and wires hooked up to her body. Gerta appeared to be a transgender woman. She wasn't that old, but she was a mess physically. Back in his Corporation 9592 days, Corvallis would have been seriously dismayed by what he was seeing, but the accident of Dodge's will, combined with his laser-focused pursuit of weird stuff, had gradually made him over into a kind of high-tech Charon, assisting dead or dying people across the digital Styx, dropping them off on the far shore, never really seeing what lay beyond it. So he'd had a lot of encounters with desperately sick people, beginning with Dodge and moving on to Verna and others who had found their way into the cloud-based afterlife. Nothing surprised him about Gerta Stock's physical condition.

He was pretty damned surprised, though, when Gerta Stock mentioned what she did for a living. "I am a musician," she said. "You've never heard my real name, but I know that you have heard my music. I made my career recording music under the name of Pompitus Bombasticus."

Corvallis knew it immediately. "The last music Richard Forthrast ever heard," he said.

"Unless they were playing some shit in the elevator," Gerta responded.

"You saw the video?"

"The kid with the broken arm? On the sidewalk?" Gerta was grinning, showing yellowed teeth and hideous gums, and nodding. Corvallis averted his gaze and spent a moment cueing it up in his mind's eye: A GIF, just a few seconds long, recorded by the kid's father. Richard standing next to the kid on the sidewalk, moments before he went into the building to die. The fat, expensive noise-canceling headphones down around Richard's neck, spilling the music out into the chilly wet autumn air. Clearly playing the music of Pompitus Bombasticus.

"He had all of your stuff," Corvallis said.

"Made me famous, for a little while," Gerta said. "I got a gig because of it—did the music for a big triple-A game. Made me enough money to transition."

"Then what happened? I seem to remember you've released a couple more albums."

"No hits. That was my big break. I blew it."

Corvallis took a sip of the expensive wine that Gerta had ordered from the sommelier. "But according to the itinerary your assistant forwarded to me, you flew in direct from Berlin on a private jet. You're staying in the best hotel in Seattle, dining in the best restaurant, ordering the best wine. Am I picking up the check for this dinner?"

Gerta laughed and shook her head. "I am suddenly rich," she said. "Two weeks ago I was on public assistance, living in a pension. Now money is flowing into my bank account. Hundreds of thousands of dollars a day."

"From where?"

"From you, my friend. Don't you ever audit your books?"

"Me personally or—"

"No, no, from your foundations and whatnot."

"Why are we making payments into your bank account?"

"It's all automatic," Gerta said. "It's the system that tracks music downloads. That pays artists like me whenever someone listens to their songs. Someone or something in your cloud is downloading my stuff like crazy. I am suddenly rich. And so—" Pompitus Bombasticus raised her arms, dragging electrical leads and IV tubes along with them. "I intend to die like a rich woman, with a fine dinner in my belly. And I want to have my corpse scanned like your other rich clients. And I want to go to this amazing place where everyone apparently listens to my music."

Corvallis found time to audit the books a few days later, and found that Gerta was right about the downloads and the money. Pompitus Bombasticus had taken in more revenue during the last five weeks than during the entire preceding decade. To the living, she was still an obscure has-been, but to the dead she was bigger than the Beatles.

In normal circumstances, some watchdog process running on their system would have brought this cash flow spike to the attention of the Forthrast Family Foundation's comptroller. In this case it had been swamped and masked by bigger trends. The ecosystem of computational activity that had begun five years ago, with Sophia launching Dodge's Brain at Hole in the Wall, and that had since grown to encompass thousands of such processes running on an unknown number of quantum computing server farms that El had sprinkled all over the world like a digital Johnny Appleseed, had of late shunted itself into a mode they hadn't seen before. The only thing they really knew about this new mode of operation was that it was expensive. And it was expensive in a new and different way. An understanding of what these processes were thinking and doing was, as ever, maddeningly elusive. All they could do was fall back on some of the tools that various ACTANSS attendees had devised and made available to the research community over the years: tools that sucked in such data as could be gleaned from message traffic and server loads, analyzed them in clever ways, and displayed the results in three-dimensional visualizations. Those now came in many flavors, but the most widely used were the original LVU—the Landform Visualization Utility—and the network mapping scheme that had emerged from one of Elmo Shepherd's research institutes. Corvallis, or any other qualified token holder, could pull these up at any time and view them through wearables. The apps were social, which meant that, if you wanted to, you could turn on a feature that would display the avatars of all other people who were looking at the same visualization at the same time. You could hide yourself from the user community or let them know you were around. That community was an exclusive club, with no more than a hundred token holders spread around the world. The only people who got to look at these things were researchers and administrators belonging to the Big Three foundation clusters: Waterhouse, Forthrast, and Shepherd.

A couple of weeks ago, Forthrast's comptroller had let the board members and the top administrators know that trouble was brewing and that they needed to pay attention. Since then Corvallis had left the visualizations running in his peripheral vision all the time, and checked in on them a few times a day.

One region of the Landform had always been troublesome: up in the mountains, some distance north of Town, was a place that had somehow failed to cohere as an intelligible three-dimensional shape. Some of the researchers had taken to calling it Escherville, after the artist M. C. Escher, who'd been good at making pictures of shapes that could not actually exist. Escherville had been around for at least as long as the LVU had been running and didn't seem to change much. Traffic analysis made it pretty obvious that Dodge and Pluto and some of the other "Pantheon" processes had a lot to do with it.

Escherville was weird, but at least it was stable. The other problematic zone in the Landform was what they had used to call the Town Square, after Sophia had pointed out its similarity to the park in the middle of Richard Forthrast's hometown. But the name was now obsolete, for of late the similarity had been obliterated. In the last few weeks it had become too bright to see clearly unless you dialed back the power on your wearable to the point where the rest of the Landform faded into darkness. All of the little green points plotted by the LVU had the same brightness level, so when a region of the Landform was generating that much light, it simply meant that a huge number of points were concentrated there. If the Landform was a shaped swarm of fireflies, then Town Square was a jar in which nearly all of the fireflies had decided, for some reason, to concentrate themselves. The LVU was doing its best to track all of the data and map it into a three-dimensional shape, but its system for doing so was now failing to make sense of the information flowing into it, or perhaps observers like Corvallis were having trouble mapping what they saw onto shapes and patterns that they knew how to recognize from lives spent in a coherent three-dimensional universe. Maybe these dead people had a different understanding of geometry, or maybe they weren't making sense at all.

The other tool Corvallis favored was El's system for displaying network traffic as a three-dimensional universe of colored blobs representing different processes, joined together by thin lines symbolizing messages passed between them. The first time he'd seen this, it had been dominated by a big yellow ball at the top, representing Dodge's Brain, with the Pantheon spread out below it, and, at the bottom, thousands of tiny white balls suspended in cobwebs. When he looked at it now, many of the same features were still there, but the bottom layer just looked like a ball of cotton the size of a car. If he zoomed in close to it he could begin to make out individual concentrations, but the messages passing among them were flying so thick and fast as to obscure their identities.

"Now we're getting somewhere."

Corvallis had come to know that voice. Since their last face-to-face meeting in Zelrijk-Aalberg, it was the only voice in which Corvallis had heard Elmo Shepherd speak.

People had long since got in the habit of representing themselves, in virtual spaces, with avatars. Audio representation—the voice your avatar spoke in—had lagged somewhat behind. It had become important in T'Rain, the game that Richard and Pluto and Corvallis and others at Corporation 9592 had pioneered. It was a devilish problem that no programming team in its right mind would want to be saddled with, and so it had fallen into, or been elevated to the status of, weird stuff. It was all well and good to imagine how cool it would be if your dungeon-raiding team of wizards, dwarves, elves, and the like could all communicate freely in voices and accents that were movie-quality, as finely realized in their own way as the avatars, weapons, and environments. But when one of the players was Chinese and didn't speak much English; and another was from rural Arkansas and making no effort to hide his accent; and another was from Boston but trying to fake the Scottish accent that he fancied a dwarf would speak in; and another was in London and acutely sensitive to how badly the guy from Boston was getting it wrong; and one of them was a woman playing a male character; and one of them was carrying on a running argument with his mom, who wanted him to take out the garbage; when all of that was happening at once, in real time, making those characters sound as good as they did in the movies was impossible. The Weird Stuff team had made some headway using a divide-and-conquer approach. They had figured out ways to make male voices sound female and vice versa. They had used speech-to-text systems to decode what the players were saying, then used AI algorithms to filter out the "Take out the garbage *now* or you are grounded" chatter, then used text-to-speech technology to re-render them with correct accents, and so on. That technology had made its way into applications beyond gaming.

El was using it to talk now. Some years ago, when he had begun using the Metatron to manifest himself at conferences and meetings, he'd mapped his own face onto its blank mannikin head and he'd piped his own voice straight through, essentially using the robot as a mobile speakerphone. Since then he had gradually changed his ways. He had turned off the face mapping so that no one could see him, and he'd begun using speech-generation technology. At first the Metatron had spoken in a generic, off-the-shelf voice and accent, but he or his staff had been customizing it. The voice was now recognizable as El's. It did not sound exactly like El sounded when he was physically sitting across the table from you and pushing air through his vocal cords, but close enough that people who knew him would cock an ear, nod, and admit that it was not bad. Exactly how the speech was being generated was not clear, and had been the topic of many debates held in bars and coffee shops among people who had just finished "talking" to El's Metatron. Sometimes the voice had a natural cadence suggesting that

El was speaking into a microphone and his speech being reprocessed. Other times it sounded like the results of a text-to-speech algorithm. Since those algorithms were pretty good now, there was a considerable gray area between those theories—which was why it made for such good arguments in bars. Most of those arguments could have been settled if someone had actually laid eyes on Elmo Shepherd in the flesh recently. But no one had seen him in over a year, and opinions varied as to what condition he was in. Some said he was already dead. Of those, one faction believed that the speech they were listening to was actually coming from Sinjin Kerr or Enoch Root or perhaps a cabal of token holders sitting in a room together. Another faction held that El's brain had already been scanned and was running in the cloud as a process that could interface directly with the voice-generation system. Most people, however, assumed that El was still alive.

Making it somewhat spookier was that the Voice of El could emerge from different instruments at different times, depending on how he wanted to manifest himself. In the early going, they'd all come to associate it with his Metatron. He had them planted in cities all over the place, and they were smart enough to take public transit to a FedEx facility and ship themselves wherever they needed to be, sometimes traveling more quickly than human beings with airplane tickets. He used the same voice for old-fashioned phone calls and teleconferences. And it was the voice of his avatar when he manifested himself in virtual or augmented reality.

As now. Hearing the voice, Corvallis turned his head to see El's avatar standing a couple of meters off to his side. The avatar was also gazing at the Wad, as people had begun referring to the dense cottony underlayment of this display. El turned his head to look at Corvallis. The avatar didn't look much like Elmo Shepherd. Whoever had designed it had apparently started with a 3-D scan of the Metatron and then tweaked it over time. It had passed through a phase of looking dangerously like the statuette on an Academy Award, and people had started calling it Oscar. But then El must have called in an artist or a designer or something, because it had taken on more human features and acquired a vague resemblance, in a shiny metallic way, to his high school yearbook photo. As avatars went, it wasn't a good one. You could buy far more expressive avatars for next to nothing. Most people did. El's using this one was a conscious choice on his part, presumably for the same reason he chose to use a voice generated by an algorithm: he didn't want people to know his real condition, or indeed whether this thing was embodying a single human or a committee of handlers.

"In old TV shows," said the voice of El, "and I mean really old, like campy sitcoms from the 1960s, sometimes they'd do a dream sequence or something in heaven. Dress the actors up in bedsheets, hang wings on them, give them harps and halos. But there was always this." The avatar extended its hand and skated it through the Wad. "You could see that off camera there had to be buckets of water with dry ice in them, bubbling away. Covering the floor of the studio with dense white fog."

"So it would look like they were in the clouds," Corvallis said. "Yes, I remember seeing a few of those."

"Reminds me of that," said El's avatar, drawing its hand back.

"A deliberate choice?" Corvallis asked.

"Oh, of course not!" El scoffed. Corvallis was sure, now, that he was actually talking to Elmo Shepherd. That he was alive, at least temporarily lucid, and speaking through this avatar as directly as his failing body would allow. "This visualization algorithm is what it is. The spatial organization fell out naturally—it was the best way to sort out what was going on. White was the default color—it's used when we don't have a clear sense of the identity or role of a given process. Which is true of almost all of them, as you can see. It's only in the last few weeks, as things changed, that it began to remind me of 1960s-sitcom heaven."

"What *did* change, Elmo? Why does it look so different now? How's it related to what is going on in the Town Square?"

"It's a phase transition, I think."

Corvallis smiled. "You know what Richard used to say about those?"

"No."

"We had mathematicians working on weird stuff. Richard had no idea what they were talking about most of the time. But he learned that when they trotted out certain phrases, it meant they were really excited. 'Phase transition' was at the top of the list."

"There's this very complicated system with a lot of parts. Way too many to keep track of. You can only make sense of it statistically. Most of the time it just kind of does what it does—falls into certain habits. But then all of a sudden something happens. There's a complete top-to-bottom change that anyone can see. That's what this is," El said.

"What do you see in it? A minute ago you said, 'Now we're getting somewhere.' What did you mean by that?"

"I had qualms about how it was shaping up before. You know that," El said. "The early processes had gained a head start that seemed prohibitive. Constructed a crude spatial matrix echoing their fractured and hazy memories of landforms and built environments. The new processes flocked to it for some reason, instead of starting from scratch. It became a straitjacket—a prison. Not sufficiently different from the world they'd left behind—the world that you and I live in. What's the point of dying and being transmogrified into a digital entity if you're going to use all of that computational power to re-create the analog world you just managed to escape from? Worse, to exist in a hierarchical social structure where resources are dominated by a few at the top with godlike power? I was deeply worried that Dodge and his Pantheon had created a stable system."

"Stable is good, right?"

"Except when it's bad. Totalitarian regimes, corrupt systems are stable. I was afraid this was one of those. And maybe it was—but now, among the late-arriving processes that constitute the vast majority of working souls, we are seeing an accumulation of power and resources that rivals that of the old guard. Getting ready for a Titanomachia, I believe."

"The word rings a bell but you're going to have to help me out," Corvallis said.

"When the gods of Olympus overthrew the Titans. Replaced them with something new, more brilliant, more perfect."

"Chained the Titans to rocks, threw them into the pit of Hades, or whatever," Corvallis said.

"I'm not a mythology geek the way Sophia is," El admitted. "The point is just that there is a change coming. For the first time, I see a way out. I am optimistic that when I upload—which won't be long now, C—when I upload I'll be going to a place where I can actually look forward to operating. A better place."

"What do you mean, it won't be long now?" Corvallis asked. He'd been staring, not at the Wad, but at the big colored blobs hovering above it, wondering what this display would look like if El's prophecy came true and they were all hauled down in some kind of Titanomachia. Were they beautiful, those souls? Were they brilliant and good? Or were they hideous ogres that needed to be thrown down and chained to rocks in the lowest circles of hell?

He turned to look at Elmo Shepherd's avatar, but it had winked out. As if he, or someone who was responsible for looking after him in Zelrijk-Aalberg, had pulled the plug.

38

Sinjin Kerr was a really good lawyer. Today he was launching an offensive against the Forthrast Family Foundation. He was a really good lawyer. He and his staff had clearly been planning this attack for years. He was a really good lawyer. Zula, as the person responsible for everything that the foundation did, was the primary target of the attack. Sinjin Kerr was a really good lawyer. She was going to have to put everything else in her life on hold and do nothing else besides fight back, probably for the next several years, or else resign and hand the foundation over to a professional war-fighter.

Sinjin Kerr was a really good lawyer.

Thus Zula's internal monologue during the three hours that Sinjin spent patiently laying out his case. They were meeting on neutral ground, in a hotel conference room in downtown Seattle. Once the scope and scale of the assault became clear, Zula's reptile brain began calling for a fight-or-flight reaction. But her foundation had lawyers of its own, almost as good as Sinjin, who had seen this coming for a long time and erected many-layered interlocking defenses. Years would pass before Zula's reptile brain was of any use whatsoever. Ditches would have to be taken one by one, moats drained, walls undermined, gates rammed down, ramparts scaled, watchtowers burned, and defenders picked off before Zula found herself locked in the highest room of the tallest tower, Sinjin's soldiers banging on the locked door with a sledgehammer as she gripped a dagger in her sweaty hand. So once again, as in so many other cases during her tenure as the head of the foundation, her presence in the room was largely symbolic and her mind couldn't help but drift. She was fascinated by Sinjin because he had an essential humanity about him that could not be teased apart from his excellence as a lawyer. He opened his carefully planned legal offensive with a single, uninterrupted, hour-long monologue, delivered without notes, on the topic of graphs. Not even three-dimensional augmented-reality plots with glowing lines and such. No animations. Just straight two-dimensional plots that could just as well have been delivered on a flipchart. As a convenience to the people he was attacking, he had printed these out on paper and handed them around, as if this were a business meeting in 1995 or something. And yet these hokey, outmoded physical artifacts made it all seem more serious and more real. Sinjin was kicking it old-school! During the second hour Zula's mind wandered even further afield and she found herself thinking about the weird talismanic power of hard copies. She was thinking of medieval documents she'd seen in museums in Europe, handwritten on sheepskin, with huge wax seals dangling from them. The physical reality of the object was proof that humans had put intention into their contents, that this was real, not just a game played with pixels.

The fabulous complexities of Sinjin's case had all been researched and footnoted to the nth degree by his staff, which must by this point have occupied several new office buildings adjacent to Zelrijk-Aalberg's convoluted border. The burden of detail had been lifted from his shoulders, freeing him to do what his subordinates were not capable of: to tell the story of it in a way that was engaging, coherent, and disturbingly close to being absolutely convincing. It was, as everyone understood, a sort of dress rehearsal for future pleadings before judges or juries. Elmo Shepherd was demonstrating the power of his new superweapon before a handpicked delegation of his enemies. The message was obvious: Surrender now or I shall be forced to use this weapon in anger against you. Imagine how bad that would be. Sinjin had only brought two associates with him but it was to be understood that they were only the head of a queue of legal myrmidons that would stretch behind him over the horizon were they all physically here. With their carrying the supporting documents in their satchels, he was free to just be Sinjin. He pointed to squiggles on graphs and held forth about their meaning enough to convey the point that he had mastered all of the details, but just when he was getting into the weeds he would retract that accusatory finger and with a gentle wave of the hand dismiss the specifics and look someone in the eye and make an interesting point of a more general nature, not in an aggressive manner that might elicit a sharp defensive response but more with an air of *Since we are all intelligent grown-ups here, and since we have subordinates who can plow through the specifics later, I thought you might find a few moments' diversion in the following trenchant observations.* And then he could be philosophical, he could be wry, he could even get everyone in the room to laugh. Not the fake forced laughter that people made when they understood someone was pooping out an attempt at humor but sharp surprising laughter followed by an afterglow of appreciating Sinjin. Even loving Sinjin. Being glad to be in his company. All, of course, with the unstated message of *Imagine what this man could do in front of a jury.*

He was saying that Elmo Shepherd had been a more than equal partner in all of these efforts from the very beginning—years before Richard Forthrast or Corvallis Kawasaki or any of the others had even heard of cryonics or the Singularity. Mr. Shepherd had researched and cowritten the boilerplate instructions that had gone into Dodge's disposition of remains. He had been on the scene, talking face-to-face with C-plus, within hours of the tragic events. The immense edifice of research labs and intellectual property and human capital that had grown up around this industry in the decades since then could not have come into existence without the unstinting generosity of Mr. Shepherd. But it wasn't just about his being a moneybags; more than any other one person, Mr. Shepherd encompassed within his colossal intellect all that was known on the connectome, how to scan it, how to store it, how to simulate it. Knowing that existing computer systems were inadequate to the task, he had almost single-handedly created the quantum computing industry from scratch. He could have made himself even more fabulously wealthy just from that, but chose instead to plow the money back into his life's work.

The premature launching of the Process by Sophia had led to consequences that Mr. Shepherd in all frankness had not predicted, but he had adapted gracefully and supported subsequent developments with his usual generosity. This was not a commercial proposition. Anything that advanced the science had Mr. Shepherd's wholehearted backing. He did not seek credit or applause. He did not even seek understanding. All of that would sort itself out in due course. His wealth had afforded him the privilege, given to very few, of taking the longest and most visionary possible view. The goals of the world's great religions were indistinguishable from Mr. Shepherd's, but he was approaching them along a different path, a hidden path up the back of the mountain that Christianity and Islam and the others had been frontally assaulting for thousands of years. It was a long path through dark woods, difficult if not impossible for most to follow, but it was in the end a more certain way to the summit. One day all of this would be seen and acknowledged. In the long meantime Mr. Shepherd was willing to shoulder the burden of being misunderstood.

Mr. Shepherd did not ask for very much in return for his steadfast generosity but he was serious in his goals, not a dupe, not an absentminded philanthropist blindly writing checks so that he could claim tax deductions or get buildings named after him. He was meticulous about his business dealings. Fairness was a two-way street. The other great institutions to which he had yoked himself—Waterhouse and Forthrast—could expect openhandedness and honesty from Mr. Shepherd. In return he expected—nay, demanded—symmetrical treatment from them. Nothing could be more reasonable.

All fine and simple in principle. The details very complicated, of course. No one really at fault; these things happened when brilliant energetic people hurled themselves into the fray. No progress could be made by such marvelous minds if they were second-guessing themselves at every turn, minding the legal p's and q's, torturing themselves thinking about possible future entanglements, contradictions, conflicts. You had to let these people do what they did. Lesser minds like Sinjin could follow along in their wake tidying up.

It was, however, time to tidy up. Not a big deal really. Some things had grown out of proportion, got out of whack, the current state of affairs not exactly in alignment with contracts that all of the principals had willingly entered into years ago. Unforeseen developments now called for some pruning, some rerouting of the financial plumbing, some add-ons and codicils to the agreements that were already in place. No need to hand it over to the terribly inefficient legal system.

No one wanted that.

39

Egdod saw that the Tower was an abomination, not merely because of its tallness and its situation but because of the joining together of the souls' auras.

He summoned Thingor forth out of the Fastness and with him forged a thunderbolt much greater than any of the others. When it was ready Egdod flew up above the Palace holding it in his right hand. The heat of it burned him and the brightness of it blinded him. He hurled it at the Tower and struck it in its midsection, which was destroyed in an instant, and the top part of it fell down upon the bottom and smote it to dust all the way down to its stone foundations, which after that were no longer visible, being buried under a heap of pulverized mud.

Flying over this Egdod could see the dust moving as souls within it struggled to emerge. They had been greatly diminished by the annihilation of the Tower into which they had woven much of their own beings, but still they lived, and as they called out, they did so not in the hum they had stolen from the bees but in the various kinds of speech that they had used before they had taken up that habit. "Build no more Towers," Egdod said to them, "and dwell not in hives, but in houses, as you did at the beginning. You shall have to build them yourselves, since you have so foolishly destroyed the ones that I made for you. And do not join your auras together in place of speaking, but shape your thoughts into words, as is proper for souls."

"They do not all speak in the same tongue, of course," Speaksall pointed out to him later. "They will clump according to their manner of talking; and the new houses that they build for themselves may be sown far and wide across the Land rather than being together in a single Town that lies within your view and beneath the threat of your terrible weapons."

"So be it," Egdod said. And so it was, for souls had already begun grouping themselves in the manner that Speaksall had foretold, and were struggling out of Town in various directions. It could be guessed that each was of a mind to build its own town far away from others who spoke in different tongues, and far away from the abode of Egdod. Egdod took no measures to prevent it.

But after the Town was empty, and contained no souls to gaze on his work, he persisted in his practice of building the hill higher, until the Palace had become a soaring tower unto itself, perched on the summit of a pillar that projected above the clouds. No longer did the hum of the Hive trouble his ears. Instead his work was accompanied by sweet sounds made by a new soul who had lately come into the Land. Longregard had discovered her perched on a rubble heap below, amid the ruins of the Hive, playing a tune by blowing over the top of a hollow bone. She—or perhaps he, for this soul never seemed to make up his or her mind as to sex—had been adopted by those who dwelled in the Palace, and become a favorite of Thingor and Knotweave, who had assisted her, or him, in fashioning many kinds of new devices for making all sorts of sounds. Egdod had named this soul Paneuphonium and given them leave to perch wherever they pleased. Paneuphonium had rewarded Egdod by learning to make just the kind of music that suited him when he was in a mood to build and alter those parts of the Land that were still in need of bettering.

So high did Egdod build the pinnacle that, when he looked down from his solitary chamber at its top, he could see all parts of the Land, provided that the weather afforded him clear views. And when he looked up he could of course see the stars. But if he redoubled the intensity and the penetration of his gaze he could see through the veil of night into the infinite sea of chaos that lay beyond it. Nor did seeing chaos above trouble his thoughts, any more than seeing it below did in the bottomless chasm under the Fastness. For he had mastered chaos and made it his servant now.

Weather at such a height was cold, but he caused the air about the Palace and in the Garden to be warm, as before. The Forest just outside the Garden gate he too made warm and pleasant in all seasons, so that its creeks did not freeze, but flowed together into a river that plunged off the precipice in a long waterfall. Spring's abode remained as it had been before, and there she remained, rarely venturing outside of her grove, as she gestated the new souls that she and Egdod had conceived.

Then a semblance of calm returned to the Palace and the Land as summer ended and fall began, and the leaves and the apples alike began to turn red, and all of the souls whom Egdod had invited began winging toward the Palace to enjoy the feast.

There was a reason Zula wasn't a lawyer. At some point around the two-hour mark she zoned out. This was because she had been seduced by Sinjin Kerr. Not in a sexual way, of course. More in an emotional way. Everything he was saying was so reasonable. He was such an intelligent guy. So witty. But not in a self-congratulatory way. More like he was forever surprising himself with his own ability to stumble on the occasional nugget of wry humor inherent in all proceedings that involved humans. How could any intelligent person argue against his basic point that a lot of stuff had changed and it was time to do some housekeeping? The third hour was a lot of detail about where the money had been going. Huge flows of virtual cash, all denominated in modern digital currencies, chundering back and forth between Forthrast and Waterhouse and Mr. Shepherd's enterprises, both for- and nonprofit. The transfers observable by humans who held the requisite tokens and who actually bothered to kick through the numbers but frequently occurring in the dark since the details were too complex for any one person to wrap their mind around them. Even in her zoned-out state Zula had a sense of where Sinjin was going with this: he was going to assert some claim that money had ended up in the wrong place. Probably just an oversight. Understandable. But important to get it fixed. Maybe a lot of money.

She did not snap out of it until ten minutes before noon, when she heard her daughter's name being mentioned. An observer sitting across the table from her would have seen little change in her expression, but she felt her heart beating faster and her face get warm. The latter was simple embarrassment. She hadn't been following. She'd lost the thread of the argument just at the critical moment. She knew that Sinjin had mentioned Sophia but she was lagging behind him, playing catch-up, not really sure what he'd said.

But it wasn't difficult to guess.

Half an hour later, during the lunch break, she confirmed as much with Marcus Hobbs, the chief counsel of the Forthrast Family Foundation, who had actually managed to follow Sinjin's argument all the way through.

"This isn't complicated. El Shepherd has never been happy with the state of affairs that began when Corvallis made Sophia a token holder in Dodge's Brain and she used that authority to launch the Process. He's made it obvious in many ways, over the years, that he wants that same level of authority."

Zula looked across the table at her daughter. Sophia and Maeve had joined Zula, Marcus, and C-plus for lunch. They were sitting around a corner table in an Ethiopian place on Cherry Street. The restaurant was about three blocks down the hill from the medical office building where Richard had been stricken. The time of year was early October. It was an unspoken family tradition that they would haunt this part of town when the maple leaves were red. And "family" had become a complicated word to them. C-plus had effectively been made into a Forthrast long ago. Sophia was now a beloved aunt to the teenage children of Corvallis and Maeve.

And all of them together were haunted by departed spirits. They were responsible for having created the systems on which Dodge, Verna, and Pluto were now, in some sense, alive.

"He keeps complaining that the Singularity isn't working out the way he'd hoped," Zula said. "I think part of what disappoints him is just how damned *bureaucratic* it is. So many lawyers. So many meetings."

"But it is," Sophia said. "It *is* starting to turn his way now, I think."

"You mean, with the Wad?" Corvallis asked. He had told everyone at this table about his encounter with Elmo Shepherd's avatar.

"Yeah," Sophia said.

"He loves the Wad," Corvallis admitted.

"Fine," Zula said, "but even if that's everything he was hoping for, who's going to keep it running after he goes and joins it? A bunch of foundations with interlocking boards of directors. Their endowments distributed across god knows how many different investment vehicles, spread across every financial institution in the world."

"A lot of that is self-managing by this point," Marcus reminded her. "Most of *our* investments are now managed by bots we don't even understand. In *his* case, the fraction's probably much higher than that."

"But physical stuff still has to exist. The computers that run it all need electricity, and roofs to keep rain from falling on them. Humans can shut it down any time they want."

"That's what bothers him," Sophia said. "And it's what bothers *me* about what he's asking for."

"Could you say more on that?" Marcus asked. "Because it's increasingly obvious that it's the real reason Sinjin's here."

"The Process that I launched at Princeton may be very complicated, and powerful, and expensive to run," Sophia said, "but it's still a computer program that responds to some very simple commands. And one of those commands is 'exit.' Or maybe it's 'quit' or 'shut down.' I don't actually know because I've obviously never invoked such a command against it. Or against Verna or Pluto or any of the others."

"You as the token holder have the power to terminate the Process—or any subprocess—at any time," Marcus said.

"That's basically how it works," Sophia answered, looking to Corvallis. He nodded in confirmation.

"Do you also have that power, C?" Marcus asked. "Since you were the one who issued the token to Sophia?"

Corvallis shook his head no. "You're thinking I'm like the superuser or the sysadmin. This is different. The token I issued to Sophia gave her the access and the authority to establish a new system altogether. On that system she is root—she has total authority over all of the processes and I have none whatsoever. Nor," he added, "do I want it."

Maeve had been tracking this intensely, suggesting that she'd been curious about it for a while but had never found the right moment to ask. "To be blunt, honey, what happens if you get hit by a bus?"

"Nothing," Sophia said.

"In other words," Marcus said, "you haven't made arrangements for that token to be transferred to someone else in the event of your demise."

"I wouldn't even know how," Sophia said. "I've never thought about it. But I will now."

"To ask the same question in a less loaded way," Zula said, "since we are talking about my daughter here, what if you forget the password?"

"We don't use passwords."

"I know. It's connected to your PURDAH. I get it. Work with me here."

"There's no 'it.' You can't understand this in terms of passwords. We got rid of passwords *exactly because* they had these defects: if you forget yours, you're screwed. And if someone steals yours, they become *you*, they suddenly have all of your power, all your privs. The point of the 'H' in PURDAH—'Holography'—is that you have to prove your identity from one moment to the next—"

"With your face, your voice, the way you type, the way you walk . . . ," Zula said. She knew all this.

"Back in the day, yeah. It was clearly traceable to face recognition or whatever. Now *we don't even know* how it works. We've handed it over to AIs that *just know* when it's you, based on—who the hell knows?"

"So, getting back to the point of my question," Zula said, a little heated, "suppose this mysterious AI, the gatekeeper, couldn't recognize you anymore. Which is what I was trying to express with the archaic expression 'forget the password.'"

"If I lose the ability to verify my identity—my ownership of the PURDAH—if the mysterious AIs somehow stop recognizing me as me, then the authority vested in that toho is lost forever."

"And what does that cash out to, on a practical level?" Maeve asked.

"Surprisingly little," Sophia said. "I am Atropos."

"For those of us who haven't boned up on our *D'Aulaires'* lately, could you explain that?" Zula asked dryly.

"Atropos was the Fate who had the power to cut the threads of life. I have the power to terminate processes by typing 'quit' or 'kill' or whatever into a terminal window—I'd have to look up the man page to know the exact command. If I became disconnected from the relevant PURDAH, no one else would have that ability."

"But creating new processes is a different story," Maeve said, half statement and half question.

"Because it's an open protocol for exchange of messages," Corvallis said, "anyone can launch a process that participates. Of course, only a few people have the know-how to launch a process that's actually *interesting*. Basically that power is limited to us and to El Shepherd."

"This places Sinjin's demands in a different light," Marcus said. "To hear him tell it, all that El's really asking for is the same root-level access that Sophia has had from the very beginning. Shared authority. But if the only special ability Sophia has is that of Atropos, then why does he want it?"

"He wants to kill Dodge and Verna and the others," Maeve said.

Sophia shrugged. "I may have oversimplified it. I can perform some other administrative functions that El can't. Basically having to do with limiting resource usage. In retrospect, if I'd thought all of this through at the beginning, I'd have imposed some limits on how much memory the Process could allocate for itself, how much processing power it could use, and so on."

"That's what a system administrator would normally do as a matter of course," Corvallis explained, for Zula's benefit. "Like, back in the old days, if I were installing a piece of software on a system with a one-terabyte hard drive, I'd set a quota saying that the software wasn't allowed to allocate more than, say, half a terabyte for its own use—otherwise it'd crowd out all of the other processes and crash."

"I never did that," Sophia said, "because Jake and later El threw resources at the Process faster than it could consume them. Everyone was so fascinated by its growth that they just wanted to let it run unfettered, as an experiment."

"I see," Zula said, "and later El came to regret that choice because of the dominance that the Process had achieved."

"It came as a surprise that the other processes launched out of El's network gravitated to the first one and glommed on to it rather than growing independently," Corvallis said, nodding.

"Okay," Marcus said. The skepticism in his voice was clear. "So Sinjin's going to claim that El merely wants the authority to rein in out-of-control processes. Build some fences around them. Impose the normal quotas and so on that Sophia never put into place."

"There's other stuff he could do, like erect barriers around 'our' processes to limit their interaction with 'his' processes," Sophia said, air-quoting.

"Which *sounds* reasonable. But we can't give him the ability to do those things without at the same time giving him the power of Atropos," Marcus said, holding up two fingers and making a *snip*.

"I would have to do some research on that," Sophia said.

"How does it look to you, based on this morning?" Zula asked Marcus.

"Sinjin's constructed a pretty airtight box around us," Marcus admitted. "Until the Wad happened, nothing was resource-constrained. The world's supply of quantum supercomputing clusters, bandwidth, and storage were able to keep abreast of the growth."

"Which is no accident," Corvallis put in. "El built all of that specifically to support all of the processes he was launching."

"Of course," Marcus said. "But he was making the assumption that each new process would add only a certain amount of load to the system. All of those assumptions went out the window when the Wad began to take shape. The amount of computation in that thing is an order of magnitude larger than what we saw in the old scheme where the processes weren't so tightly linked. The system's threatening to burn itself out."

"You know my opinion on this," Corvallis said. "It's degenerate activity. A lot of these things have just gotten caught up in infinite loops. Race conditions. There's no meaningful computation happening in the Wad."

"But it's just your opinion," Marcus reminded him. "Imagine you're in front of a jury in a civil case, trying to get them to believe that. You need to be able to say with a straight face that all of the computation associated with Dodge and the Pantheon processes is legit, but everything in the Wad is 'degenerate.'"

Sophia was nodding her head. "It'd be a different story if we actually knew what those processes were thinking. But all we have to go on is traffic analysis and burn rate."

"I disagree," Corvallis said. "We have plenty of track record indicating that the result of the Pantheon's computation is the Landform. What's the result of all the computation in the Wad? Nothing that we can discern."

"Again. Jury," Marcus said.

"We can't enter *Critique of Pure Reason* into evidence?" Maeve cracked.

"The fact is," Marcus said, "that the Wad plays directly into El's hands by creating a shortage of computational power that never existed before. And he can use that shortage as leverage against us. What could be more reasonable sounding than to say it's time to impose some limits?"

"It didn't take him all morning just to say that," Zula pointed out.

"Everything else is just Sinjin sending the message that if we don't agree to El's request he can make an amount of trouble for us that's big enough that it'll be easier to just change our minds."

Food was served, and conversation stopped for a while as all reached into the middle of the table to tear the injera bread and pinch up mouthfuls of spicy food. Once Maeve had taken the edge off of her hunger, though, she wiped her hands on a napkin and spoke: "I draw the line at giving El, or anyone, the power to terminate a process. I've already lost my sister once. If the process we've named Verna is in any sense Verna, then I want her protected. And the same goes for any little nieces and nephews."

The others took a minute or so to process that. Verna, who was Maeve's only sibling, had died childless. Corvallis was an only child.

It was an impossibility for Maeve to have any nieces or nephews. One by one, the others got puzzled looks on their faces until Corvallis turned to her and said, "You might want to unpack that for them, sweetheart."

"We're seeing evidence that a new process is being assembled. Connected with Verna."

"That's been going on for a while now, right?" Marcus asked. "That's what makes the behavior of Verna different from all the others: she has figured out how to spawn processes that run on their own."

Maeve held her thumb and index finger barely apart. "Wee ones. Little 'hello world' contraptions that run on their own. They don't do much. Don't consume a lot of resources."

"They all get billed to our accounts," Corvallis added, "so we can track them. They are too tiny to matter."

"Until now," Maeve said. "Now Verna's working on spawning two big ones." She looked to Corvallis, who nodded in confirmation. "The new process looks to be on a similar scale to a scanned human connectome. It's been a-building for a few months."

Marcus nodded, getting it. "So that's what you meant when you were talking about nieces and nephews."

"Maybe that's another reason El's gotten so cranky," Zula said. "If our processes figure out how to make new copies of themselves, it could go viral in a hurry, and crowd out his."

Marcus's watch had hummed on his wrist a minute ago, and he'd been looking at some new information in his wearable—this was obvious from the fact that he'd been staring at a blank spot on the wall for no discernible reason. He wiped his hand on a napkin and pushed the device up onto his forehead. "He's about to get a whole lot crankier," Marcus announced.

"What happened?" Zula asked. "What did you just learn?" She'd been getting notifications too but ignored them.

Marcus shook his head. His expression was saying, *Who the hell knows?* He announced, "The Wad just fell over."

"Fell over?" Maeve asked sharply.

"Crashed. The amount of computational activity going on in the Wad suddenly dropped by three orders of magnitude. And that green thing above the Town Square? It's gone. Town Square's back to normal: a little tower in a park."

Wearables came out of pockets all around the table, or people flipped them down from where they'd been parked atop their heads. Everyone went to the Landform display first and verified that Marcus was correct: the towering flare that during the last several weeks had risen above the Town Square like an oil well fire was now completely gone. But the building atop the nearby hill stood just as it had before, the only difference being that the hill kept growing taller and steeper.

"We're sure this isn't just a fail in the LVU?" Maeve asked.

Marcus shook his head. "It's screamingly obvious in the burn rate. The financials. And if you switch over to the other viz you can see what's up with the Wad."

They all checked out the more abstract visualization scheme— the one that for the last few weeks had been dominated by the amorphous cloud of dense white lines. The Dodge process and the Pantheon still hovered above everything else, as bright and as dominant as ever. But the Wad was no more. In its place was a thin white layer that looked like the aftermath of a hailstorm: thousands of hard-looking white pellets. Each of them represented a separate process. They had always been embedded in the Wad. Until a few minutes ago, though, they'd been concealed by the dense matting of white lines representing the messages being passed between them. Now, if you bent close and stared at one of those pellets, you could see white fibers zapping in and out of it as messages were passed. But Marcus was right: the level of activity had dropped to something approaching zero.

They all received the same notification at once. It was a terse message from Sinjin Kerr, letting them know that he needed to cancel this afternoon's meeting and apologizing for the short notice. Moments later he sent another one very much regretting that he would not be seeing them at ACTANSS 5 next week.

n lieu of a purse, Sophia carried Daisy: a sort of disembodied pocket whose purpose was to atone for the sins of the women's clothing industry. It was a flat wallet that she slung over her shoulder on a thin strap. It was big enough to carry ID, tampons, pens, a miniature multitool, a spare house key, and an improvised rosary of electronic fobs and dongles and mini-flashlights. Every so often it grew bulky enough that she could feel it thudding against her hip, and then she would go through and clean out all the little scraps of paper she'd stuffed into it. When prepping for a day at work or a night out, she could put it into a larger bag. At ACTANSS 5, it carried a key token to her room and one of the pocket notebooks that the organizers handed out as swag. On one side it had an outer sleeve consisting of a rectangle of tough clear plastic, closed by a zipper. Some while ago, while pawing through a drawer in search of her passport, she had come across the peel-and-stick op-art shower daisy that she had purloined from the Forthrast family farmhouse. On the spur of the moment, she had slipped it into the transparent sleeve so that she could see it more often. Since then, it had become a visual hook, like a distinctive piece of jewelry or a dyed streak in the hair, that friends associated with her and strangers used as a conversation starter. Her more stylish girlfriends had begun rolling their eyes at the increasingly frayed and dingy wallet, and begun addressing it as Daisy.

After a long day of sitting still in conference sessions, it was her habit to wind down by going to the spa, where she would walk on a treadmill for half an hour or so, just to wake up the muscles and get the blood moving. The machine had a shelf intended to hold reading material. It was no longer all that useful since wearables tended to be easier to read from when you were bobbing along at full stride. She put Daisy on that and cranked the treadmill up to a brisk pace. Then she pulled her wearable down from the top of her head and settled it on the bridge of her nose and began wading through all of the message traffic that had piled up during the day. Her editor, assisted by various bots, had done her best to sort that into different buckets. One large bucket was devoted to quarantining all notifications relating to the complex of lawsuits recently generated by Sinjin Kerr and his minions at the behest of Elmo Shepherd. Those were a strange blend of very boring and very stressful. Sophia had an understanding with the Forthrast attorneys that she could ignore all of them and they would notify her when her attention was really needed.

Much more interesting were the contents of the Enoch Root bucket, which was brimming over with discussion of a talk he had given earlier today on the subject of amortality. Not satisfied with giving it only one clever title, he had titled it "Amortality; or, Death after Death."

His recent work on this topic had come about in the wake of a weird interaction, some months ago, between the Dodge Process and another soul, which had seemingly led to the latter's being completely annihilated. In the LVU they could watch replays of the event, albeit in grainy, herky-jerky style and with no sound. It took place in the "Town Square" and started with what looked like an altercation between a member of the Pantheon and a town dweller. The latter was armed with some manner of tool or weapon, which he used to strike the former and inflict damage. Dodge then showed up and did something very computationally expensive, at the end of which the assailant no longer existed.

Of course, the system administrators had a backup copy of his data. Certain token holders had the privileges needed to reboot the terminated process. But first some questions needed to be answered, and, as one of those tohos, Sophia needed to pay attention to them.

For they had never considered, when they had set it all up, that souls would die. Much less that they would commit murder.

(That was not quite the right way to put it, since there were *so many* things they had not considered—such a vast scope of unintended consequences. But little point in fretting about that. This was how things got started now. You either paused to consult all of the stakeholders and think through all of the possible consequences—in which case you'd certainly end up doing nothing at all, since complex systems had consequences that were infinite and imponderable—or you just went for it and pressed the Enter key.)

(Also because "soul" was so fraught with unwanted philosophical and religious baggage. But the reality was that when scanned brains were booted up as new processes, with the ability to draw upon computing resources and to interact with the other processes, they took on seemingly personlike attributes: they existed in one place, not all places; they moved about in a way that seemed physical; and they dealt with other processes in a way that seemed social. And you could try to dodge around the hard questions by sticking to neutral terminology like "process." But they weren't selling the service to their customers by offering to spawn processes. Every customer who paid into the plan while alive, and who had their remains scanned after their death, was doing so in the belief that the resulting process was in some sense a continuation of their existence in a sort of afterlife. No amount of dancing around could really dodge the fact that what was really being talked about here was the soul. And part of the deal—the expectation—was to keep it going indefinitely.)

It was clear that there were processes that had been spawned in the system that had taken root, grown, thrived, done things, related to others of their kind, dug holes, chopped down trees, built houses, and spanned time, and then, for one reason or another (being murdered by Dodge was only one example), ceased. You never wanted to say "ceased to exist" because the data were always squirreled away somewhere. But the process itself stopped changing and surrendered its resources to the cloud. And that included the resources needed to maintain a virtual body.

This raised a number of issues that in the flesh-and-blood world of Meatspace were categorized as "life and death" but in the business world fell under the heading of customer service. If a service provider had extracted money from a customer by promising them that they would live forever (perhaps not in so many words—but this was what most customers understood and assumed); waited for them to die; scanned their remains, and in so doing vaporized them; uploaded the scan to the cloud; brought it to a kind of life; given it qualia, experiences, a social life, memories, all of the other things that souls in Meatspace had; then allowed that to be extinguished for whatever reason, was the service provider then not guilty of letting its customers down? Friends and loved ones of the dead would notice that they were now dead again and make a stink about it and demand satisfaction. They might take their business and entrust their brains and souls to competitors who claimed they had eradicated the death bug from their systems.

In the old world, death had led to endless philosophical ruminations and spawned religions, but in Bitworld it led to one-star ratings from furious bereaved and threats of class-action lawsuits.

Comp sci Ph.D.s and, yes, philosophers and theologians had now gathered together at ACTANSS 5 to talk about the nature of the problem. Today Enoch Root had taken it upon himself to stake out a position on all of this. He was trying to get out ahead of people who were saying, "Fortunately there's an easy solution to this—failed processes can simply be rebooted!" He wanted to bring to their attention certain complications that were perplexing, verging on disastrous. Given the reverence in which he was increasingly held, both in South Lake Union and Zelrijk-Aalberg, his was now the dominant, or at least the default, position—the one that all of the competing service providers might end up writing into their EULAs. It was big and complicated but it was summarized under the term "amortality."

"If a tree falls on a forester, does it hurt?" had been the opening line of his talk today. The answer was "Yes, because otherwise the system falls apart."

The Dodge Process, for whatever reason, had covered the Landform with trees. More recently arrived souls had begun chopping them down and using them for things such as shelter. Tree pieces were useless—you couldn't make houses of them—unless they had physical properties such as weight, hardness, and stiffness. So far so good. But if a tree happened to fall on a person, it couldn't suddenly turn into a pillow. Or rather it *could*—you could do anything with a computer program, after all—but what kind of a world was that, really? Our brains—be they flesh-and-blood Meatspace brains or their carefully husbanded digital simulations in Bitworld—weren't hooked up to make sense of a universe where trees turned into pillows the moment they became dangerous. Once you made a special carve-out for falling trees, there was no end to it; very soon the whole universe stopped making sense, or "decohered."

There was only one way out of it, and that was amortality. Not immortality—because when a tree fell on a forester, that forester had to get hurt, and maybe to die. But "to die" here did not mean to be extirpated forever. The form—the body—in which the soul had been clothing itself up until the moment when the tree hit it, that had to take damage and the damage had to have real consequences. If it was severe enough, then it was best for the soul in question to abandon that body and get a new one.

Simple enough in theory. There was—as always—a catch, which was that you couldn't just boot up a fresh copy of the original scan from scratch. Or even of the virtual body at the moment the tree hit it. The techno-philosophical arguments were hyperarcane, but a straightforward analogy familiar to every consumer who had ever had to reboot an out-of-whack device was that these things were unfathomably complicated, with a million subsystems that had to be interconnected just so. If only one of those interconnections was wrong, the whole thing didn't work. In theory, anything could be debugged and patched up, but in practice it was quicker and gave better results if you just shut the whole thing down and started again from a clean slate.

And Enoch wasn't pretending he had all of the answers to these questions. That wasn't the point of his talk. The point was to ask them.

A few people Sophia knew and liked were lounging around in the big hot tub out on the deck, so, after she had got her fill of amortality, she shut down the treadmill, pulled off her wearable, poked it into an external pocket of Daisy, and carried it out and set it on a nearby shelving unit used to store terry-cloth bathrobes. She peeled off her clothes and enjoyed a dip for fifteen minutes or so, turning down the offer of a hit on a cannabis pipe that was making the rounds. But the social scene was winding down, and she was tired, so she climbed out and grabbed one of the thick bathrobes from the shelves. After putting it on, she wrapped Daisy up in her workout clothes. She padded back along the resort's web of footpaths, boardwalks, and covered walkways to the little cottage that had been assigned to her as her lodging. This comprised a small living/working/dining room with a kitchenette and a bedroom, both of which had views out over the waters of Desolation Sound through glass doors. Just outside was a flagstone terrace barely wide enough to accommodate a couple of deck chairs and a coffee table. The cottage had been sited close to the brink of the steep drop-off to the waterfront, so a waist-high glass barrier had been erected to prevent drunk or sleepy guests from plunging over it. An opening in that led to a wooden staircase that rambled down to the complex of docks and boardwalks about ten meters below. The most prominent feature down there was the resort's helipad, a surprisingly tiny platform that projected out over the turbulent strait.

Sophia wasn't sure why she had been assigned this cottage. It was one of the resort's finer accommodations. Most of the other attendees were in hotel rooms that were very nice, but hotel rooms nonetheless. As a rule her mother, and others directly connected with the foundation, made a point of staying in such, to avoid sending the wrong message. To Sophia—not the sort who habitually flew around in choppers—the helipad was strictly a nuisance; whenever one of those things was landing or taking off, all conversation was drowned out for a couple of minutes. But she could see how a certain kind of luxury traveler might revel in the ability to hop out of a chartered whirlybird and scamper up a few steps to a private cottage.

On its back side, the place sported the sort of bathroom that such a traveler would demand. Sophia walked straight into it, tossed her workout clothes on the floor, hung Daisy on the door hook, and set her wearable on the counter while the shower was warming up. She shed the bathrobe and kicked it into the corner, then stepped into the shower and began to rinse the hot tub's chlorine out of her hair. She soaped up and washed herself off.

When she emerged from the shower she was conscious of a hissing noise that hadn't been there when she had turned the water on. She felt light-headed, and braced herself against the bathroom counter for a few moments until she felt more certain of her balance. This was weird. The bathroom had a built-in steam generator with hard-to-understand controls. She guessed she might have inadvertently turned it on. Perhaps it had been hissing away the whole time, bringing the heat up to the point where she was getting dizzy. She looked at the control panel but couldn't make sense of it. No steam seemed to be coming out. The hiss must have been from the plumbing, or one of the cottage's other systems. Going to the door she noticed that the transparent plastic sleeve on Daisy was fogged over. She pulled it off the door hook and put it around her neck. Then she hauled the door open, letting in cooler air from the bedroom. She was still feeling short of breath and not altogether healthy. She felt a powerful urge to get out on the terrace and breathe some fresh cold air.

The hiss became much more distinct. The room was dark, but she noticed an odd pattern of lights—colored LEDs—in the corner of the bedroom by the terrace doors. The light spilling over her shoulder from the bathroom showed an object at the foot of her bed that hadn't been there when she'd come in a few minutes ago. It was a heavy industrial cart with fat tires. It carried a squat blue steel box with a control panel, currently dark, and thick loops of cable and hose. Standing behind that was a cylinder about her height, easily recognizable as one of the tanks used to contain industrial gases.

This was a welding cart. The steel box was the welding machine itself. The cylinder was the supply of inert gas used to keep the red-hot metal from oxidizing. And it was the source of the hissing noise. For the regulator had been unscrewed from the valve on the top, which had been opened. Hissing out of it and filling the room was gas.

Gas the entire point of which was that it did not include any oxygen.

She wasn't woozy and light-headed because of heat but because she wasn't getting enough air. She was being asphyxiated.

The welding cart was blocking her path to the terrace doors, so she headed for the cottage's front door instead. But she drew up short when she saw that the way out had been blocked by several heavy items of furniture that had been dragged there and piled against it.

She spun back toward the glass doors that led onto the terrace and saw again the pattern of light she had noticed earlier. This time it was moving. It moved like a human. It was the Metatron. Its nighttime running lights had come on automatically. It had been standing near the glass doors. Now it was moving toward her. Another one just like it was moving outside. No, that was just the reflection of the first one in the glass. Spatial basics like in and out, up and down, vertical and horizontal, normally so intuitive, had become unfathomably tricky. She felt pressure on her knees and realized that she was in fact kneeling. More pressure on her shoulder was probably because she was slumped against a wall. The Metatron was coming toward her. She drew in a breath of 75 percent CO_2/25 percent argon (that's what the label on the hissing cylinder said) and called out "Help" in a strangely low syrupy voice. But the hissing had been reinforced by a heavy thudding noise that drowned everything out. She thought maybe it was her heart pounding but then knew it for a helicopter.

Something hard was around her wrist, like a manacle. It was the Metatron's hand. It began walking toward the glass doors. Since it was still gripping Sophia's wrist this meant it was now dragging her. She had gone almost completely flaccid and couldn't see well, but as her free hand trailed along the carpet it felt something familiar, and reflexively closed over it: the thin nylon strap of Daisy. Daisy now began dragging along in her wake. She heard glass shattering.

When she woke up it seemed much later. But it wasn't. Her sense of time had gone out of whack. She was gulping in cold air—

real air. Her legs hurt. She opened her eyes and looked up at the robot's running lights above her against the foggy night sky as it dragged her. It was dragging her down the wooden staircase and her legs hurt because they'd been pulled through broken glass and scraped across stone and wood and were now banging down steps. The sound of the chopper was very close; they were almost to the helipad. Something was involved in the fingers of her free hand: the nylon strap of Daisy. She torqued her head around and saw, from near ground level, the aluminum feet of the Metatron, shod in black neoprene, hitting the pavement of the helipad in an even stride.

She swung her free arm around in a big arc. Daisy followed at the end of its nylon strap and wrapped all the way around the Metatron's ankles. Its measured tread was spoiled. It teetered for a few moments as immense computations tried to compensate for this unexpected turn of events. Then it simply fell over, banging its head on the skid of the chopper hard enough to nudge the whole aircraft sideways a bit. The rotor was spinning up almost to takeoff speed, carrying most of the helicopter's weight, the skids barely touching the pad.

Sophia got her feet under her and scrambled up as best as she could with the Metatron still clamping her wrist and the rotors' downwash battering her. As she did, the fallen robot scraped toward her some distance and she understood that it didn't actually weigh that much; it was very strong, but its mass was that of a child. It pulled back but couldn't actually do much until it got its feet replanted. She knew it wanted to drag her into the helicopter's side door.

She moved away from the side door, which meant she was going toward the tail of the chopper. A warning voice in her head reminded her of the spinning tail rotor, which would chop her to bits if she contacted it.

The Metatron had finally kicked free of Daisy's strap. It clambered to its feet with the speed of an insect, surprising her. As soon as its feet were on the pavement it could tug on her arm with strength that was more than human. When she jerked, it jerked back ten times faster; it was like having one wrist embedded in the

Washington Monument. But she understood that it didn't weigh that much. Its only power came from its contact with the ground.

She gave in, let it pull her up against its hard body, and thrust her free hand between its legs. She hooked her arm under its pelvis, getting the crook of her elbow where the genitals would be on a human, and gathered her legs under her and stood up. Like mighty Heracles severing Antaeus from his contact with the ground. The force she'd been fighting vanished, throwing her off balance. She staggered back along the chopper's flank. Sensing the hum of the tail rotor dangerously close, she turned away from the danger, inadvertently feeding the Metatron's outstretched legs into the whirring blade.

What occurred then was too fast and violent for any human senses to take in. It was like a shock cut in a movie; there was only before and after. She knew it was bad and that she had sustained injuries. The tail rotor was ruined, the helicopter out of trim. Its tail swung around, collected her and what was left of the Metatron, and knocked them off the edge of the helipad.

The water below was as cold as advertised. She tried to raise her arms to swim, but the Metatron was still holding one of her wrists in a death grip. Her free hand came up. Daisy came up with it, the faded plastic petals floating in front of her face but gradually fading from view as she sank.

41

The Palace's tallest tower was the dwelling place of Longregard. Just below it was a stretch of high parapet where Egdod was wont to pace back and forth. Once it had offered a pleasant view of Town, which in those days had been situated only a short distance below. Now Town was a jumbled ruin, spread across ground so far below the top of the pinnacle that Egdod's view of it was frequently obscured by intervening strata of cloud. It was a smudge upon the surface of the Land, devoid of color since all of the trees had been felled.

At some distance the forest resumed. There the red leaves had been falling in uncountable numbers, as had been the way of things in the very beginning when Egdod had dwelled alone in the Land. Gazing down into that red sea from far above, he remembered fondly those days when all things had been as he made them, for better or worse. The red forest below would turn brown and bare as the leaves dried up and blew away, then become white and then green as the seasons took their turns, so on and so forth for thousands of years without any need for Egdod to stretch forth his hand. Now, from the high place, the forest looked as it had in those days, but he knew that beneath its red canopy the people who had formerly lived in Town were on the move, fanning out in all directions, cutting down trees and shitting on the ground wherever they went.

Some went west into the broad sea of grass that stretched toward the mountain ranges Pluto had raised along the Land's western coast. Some went south, then bent their course eastward to avoid the rocky desert of the Land's southwestern quadrant, and sought the green warm bottomlands of the central gulf. Others doubled back around the base of the Pinnacle and followed the course of the great river eastward, looking for places where they might settle in its broad valley.

Few as yet were going north, for there winter came earlier and harder, and the going was difficult. Mountain ranges alternated . with deep gorges all the way to the Knot. And even if the people of Town had had wings to fly over those, they would have avoided venturing into that territory, since it was understood that it was the inviolable domain of Egdod and certain favorite members of the Pantheon.

Perhaps Longregard sensed that Egdod's thoughts were directed toward the Fastness, for she glided down from her perch in the high tower and alit near him, to his right side, like him facing north toward the column of dark clouds that marked the eternal storm.

"Something very strange is afoot in those parts," she announced. "And nothing here requires you."

She gestured toward the Garden, where preparations for the Feast were being made. Certain inhabitants of Town had been brought up to the top of the Pinnacle and given leave to dwell in small habitations around the circuit of its walls, within the sphere of warm air and golden light that crowned the pinnacle of the mountain. Of lesser stature and power were they than the souls of the Pantheon, but content to dwell in that humbler estate and to make themselves useful in whatever way suited their natures. Thus some of them scoured the mountains for the minerals and crystals Thingor required for his forge, while others roamed abroad gathering herbs and fruits for the Table. Longregard had helpers who found their station flying, swimming, and rambling about the Land, noticing all that was afoot and bringing to her news of events she might otherwise not have known. Ward had, one and two at a time, drawn to his side a score of souls who found satisfaction in patrolling the borders of the blessed space atop the mountain and standing aflank its gate. Wild souls too had come there in numbers that had exceeded the expectations of Egdod. For in his roamings up and down the Land he had encountered several such, and come to know them. When spying some stretch of seacoast or confluence of rivers where the waters swirled in greater-than-usual complexity, or observing like patterns in the wind, or when a great tree rose above all others on the skyline of a mountain, or a crag distinguished itself for beauty and elaborate form on the crest of a ridge, he had learned to go thither and patiently abide until the soul of the place had made itself known to him. Some of the wild souls had awoken and taken root and assembled these manifestations in utter solitude, not knowing that other souls existed until they spied Egdod. Others had awakened first in Town and struck out on their own after finding that the society of the place was not to their liking. Some inhabited single blades of grass, others were mountain ranges, one was the west wind and one was the eastern sea. It stood to reason that for any one of them Egdod knew of, there might be many he had not discovered. Somehow, though, word of the Feast had spread among them. Many arrived in those days who were new to Egdod and to the Pantheon, and the Garden became tumultuous with their rude society.

"Very well," Egdod agreed, "what news from the north?"

"It is easier to show than to speak of," said Longregard, "and if you will guide me through the dangerous currents of the storm we can be there sooner than I could put it into words." She took to the air without awaiting a response, obliging Egdod to follow her.

After they had gone some distance north, Egdod surged past her and led the way into the deepening maze of currents and cloud banks along the southern fringe of the storm. As they got farther in, they dodged through places where lightning bolts snaked and forked from cloud to cloud as if a hundred Egdods were amusing themselves with Thingor's bright armaments. Once, twice, and then a third time Egdod sensed a change in the air and swooped close to Longregard to shelter her in his wings from a sizzling blast.

They broke out at last into the eye of the storm. This was a thing that came and went, and roamed like a wild soul over the Knot and the Stormland that extended northward from it. But most often it was centered about the Fastness, and that was where they found it today.

The situation of the Fastness itself—the castle that Egdod had built at the heart of the Knot—was simple enough. Disregarding all of its towers and complications, it was a walled square, built on a ledge. A range of mountains arched over the top of it, and twisted as it did so. Which made no sense; but it had to be thus because of errors Egdod had made, eons ago, in the shape of the Land and the courses of its rivers.

The ledge gave way to a cliff and the cliff dropped straight down into chaos. The Fastness was built right up to the brink. Its wall on that side merged seamlessly into the cliff face, so that Egdod, when he stood on its parapet, could gaze straight down into the void.

The pit of chaos, for its part, was not an isolated hole in the ground, but rather a wide spot in a long sinuous crack that ran all through the underpinnings of the Knot. In some parts it was so narrow that one could step over it with a long stride, in others it was as wide as a great river. In general, though, the farther one went from the Fastness, the narrower it got, until some distance away the ground simply closed over it. Beyond that, Egdod supposed, it might run and ramify beneath other parts of the Land. But this was of concern only to Pluto, who knew how to navigate it, and could use it to travel from one part of the Land to another more rapidly than even Freewander could fly on her swift wings.

Because of the mountains—not just their great height but their nonsensical convolutions—it was not possible to walk to this place from the south. Those coming from east or west would be forced to swing around and make their final approach from the north, where a land route did exist—provided one was willing to traverse many miles of high, difficult, storm-blasted territory. Egdod had always looked upon this as a defect—the only flaw in the otherwise perfect system of defenses surrounding the Fastness. It was too late to change it. But the chasm—the chaos-filled crevice that cut directly beneath the ledge—did form a convenient bight a short distance to the north, running roughly east-west so that any unwanted visitors trying to approach over land would have no choice but to cross it. Egdod had broadened this to a canyon with nearly vertical sides. No soul who lacked wings could jump over it and no builder could bridge it.

Or so Egdod had always convinced himself, until he came in view of the place and saw that it had been bridged.

North of the Fastness, twin abutments of solid stone sprang from the opposing sides of the chasm, directly across from each other. In these parts Pluto had never bothered to convert adamant to new types of stone, as he knew that Egdod would only tear up and redo his work anyway, and so these new growths were likewise of solid adamant, smooth and gracefully curved. They narrowed as they reached toward each other across the chasm. They did not touch in the middle. The gap between their tips had been filled by a trestle of wood: whole tree trunks apparently felled from the forests of the Stormland to the north and dragged here, then pegged and lashed together.

In this way the Stormland to the north had been connected to the Front Yard, which was Egdod's name for the scrap of flat stony ground that lay between the northern front of the Fastness and the edge of the chasm. He didn't know why it was called the Front Yard; the name had come to him once as he sat on the Front Porch (as he called the northern steps of the Fastness) and gazed across it.

In any case the Front Yard had been a private and inviolate part of the Land until now. So Egdod was more dumbfounded than enraged to see that it had been invaded by souls who were streaming across the bridge. They were moving in both directions, to and fro. Those moving south, toward the Fastness, carried stones. Those returning northward were empty-handed. As soon as the rock carriers crossed over into the domain of Egdod, they fanned out across the Front Yard and soon came to a place where a low wall of rubble made an arc across the ground. The arc grew slightly higher with every stone that was dropped upon it. Having unburdened themselves, the stone carriers immediately turned about and moved back as quickly as their legs could carry them to fetch more rocks.

It was the most astonishing sight Egdod had ever seen since he had first become conscious in the sea of chaos that preceded the Land. And perhaps it was good that he was so utterly dumbfounded, for otherwise he would have wheeled and dove into the open courtyard of the Fastness and seized as many thunderbolts as he could carry and begun hurling them at everything he saw. As it was, astonishment gave him pause, and in that pause he thought, and in that thinking devised a subtler plan.

He veered sharply into a bank of storm clouds. Longregard followed him and thus both disappeared from view. "Find your way back to the Palace," he directed her, "you have done well to make these things known to me." And she took her leave, hieing away eastward and hugging the ground, looking for the long way around the storm.

Remaining in the concealment of the clouds, Egdod flew to the north side of the chasm, then set down in an isolated place and transformed himself so that he looked like one of the wingless souls of Town. Thus disguised, he hiked across the snow-covered rocks of that high place until he joined in with a stream of other such souls who were all making their way south toward the bridge. Most were poorly shod and clothed for these conditions. He marveled at their willingness to suffer so when the sole reward they could expect for it was to carry a rock across a bridge.

"My, but this is hard going," he said to one soul who was on the move in a group of three. "I am of a mind to turn back, how about you?"

"The angel told us we are almost there!" said this soul. Then, reacting to Egdod's bafflement—for he had never before heard this word "angel"—she pointed into the sky a little behind them, indicating a winged soul who was hovering above the caravan and occasionally gliding down to proffer aid or encouragement to stumbling and exhausted hikers. Egdod had never seen this "angel" before, or any soul like it; it was not a member of the Pantheon.

"The One Who Comes will reward us," added another soul in the little group, "once he has delivered us from the tyranny of Egdod."

Egdod, curious to hear more in this vein, accepted their invitation to walk as part of their group. From that point it was not far—just as the angel had promised—to the bridge. As they went along, Egdod plied his new companions with questions about the One Who Comes and angels and the bridge, but it seemed they knew very little.

Past a certain point it seemed to be expected that they would pick up rocks, and so they did, and fell in with the stream of other rock bearers funneling together onto the bridge's near abutment. There traffic slowed, giving Egdod time to examine this strange growth that had so unexpectedly thrust itself forth from the wall of the chasm. It was indeed of solid adamant, a seamless whole with the bedrock of the Land, no different in its strength and permanence from anything Egdod himself might have made at the height of his powers. Not even Pluto could have achieved it. It occurred to Egdod to wonder whether he might have done this himself in some kind of dream and then forgotten about it. Or was there another soul like Egdod abroad in the Land? One as powerful as—or, come to think of it, mightier even than—Egdod himself?

And yet the power of the bridge maker was apparently not infinite. For as Egdod now perceived, the Fastness itself was not visible from the bridge. Even its topmost towers were concealed from view by a sort of buttress thrown out by one of the arching mountain ranges. Cunning had been the bridge builder, whoever it was, in choosing a location where his or her work could not be looked on by Egdod or any other soul gazing north from the high vantage points of the Fastness.

At the place where the abutment narrowed to the width of a road and gave way to the wooden trestle, an arch of adamant had been thrown, or grown, over the way and topped with a small castle-like tower that put Egdod in mind of the one he had made in the middle of the Park. Standing at its parapet, wings folded against their white-robed backs, were two of the souls that the others had classified as angels. They were facing opposite directions, keeping watch over the bridge. Egdod understood, as he passed under that arch and ventured out onto the rude wooden trestle, that whoever had built this could just as well have made it span the entire chasm with an unbroken stretch of solid adamant. Instead they had chosen to build it in such a way that it could easily be broken, when breaking it might better serve their purposes.

But what were their purposes?

A hundred slow trudging paces took him to a second gatehouse that was a mirror of the first, complete with two more angels standing watch atop it. From there, solid adamant was under his feet all the way to the edge of the Front Yard.

On that ground he immediately felt stronger and more certain of his power. Only a few paces in, the high towers of the Fastness began coming into view. This seemed to have the opposite effect on the rock carriers, who spread out and began to wander and collide with one another now that they had crossed over into the wayward lands of the Knot and the direct gaze of the Fastness. They seemed torn between their duty to deposit their rocks in the desired location and an increasingly desperate need to un-burden themselves and hurry back across the bridge as quickly as they could. Angels, it seemed, did not wish to trespass upon Egdod's Front Yard. So discipline, such as existed, was enforced by wingless souls who swaggered about brandishing sticks and shouting orders at the stragglers swarming about the band of Yard between the lip of the chasm and the rubble wall. Many rocks had been dropped in that area by confused or panicked souls, and some who only wished to get back upon the bridge were being driven back by these stick swingers—who all reminded Egdod of the one called Swat, whom he had murdered—and forced to pick up these dropped stones and transport them to where the wall was a-building.

The wall was a stretched-out mound, easy enough to climb, and so Egdod did so and dropped his rock at the top of it. In so doing he inadvertently made himself a kind of hero, for a couple of stick swingers who had noticed this achievement now pointed their sticks at him and exhorted others to do likewise, building the wall higher, not broader.

From this vantage point Egdod could see how the wall swept around in a broad arc from one mountain buttress to another, sealing off a portion of the Front Yard that covered about as much territory as Town had once done back in the old days. Had he been of a mind to construct a fortification to protect the Fastness from an invasion coming out of the north across the bridge (not that any such notion had ever entered his mind), this was where he would have constructed his outer wall, using those two mountains to anchor its ends.

But that was the opposite of what these people were doing. This wall existed to prevent anything coming *from* the Fastness *toward* the bridge.

Which made no sense, since Egdod and the rest of the Pantheon could simply fly over it.

Unless they intended to build the wall all the way up to the overhang above, and seal the whole thing off.

Which made no sense either, since Egdod, or Pluto for that matter, could simply destroy it.

The Land had gone insane. Egdod was bewildered and exhausted. The Fastness—his home, more so than the Palace—beckoned, only a short hike from here across the Front Yard. He kept going, trudging down the southern surface of the wall, headed for the front entrance of his dwelling.

In that moment he ceased being a hero for the others and became an exemplar of what not to do. "Stop!" called a stick swinger, who ran to the top of the wall to look down at him, then cringed a little as he came into full view of the Fastness. "In the name of the One Who Comes, turn around and come back!"

"Why?" Egdod called back. "It seems a nice enough place to me."

"It is the Abode of Death!"

"What is death to me?" Egdod inquired. He knew of it better than most, having killed Swat, but it amused him to keep the conversation going. He trotted down the last few yards of rubble and alit on the familiar ground of his Front Yard. Turning about to look up at his interlocutor, he thought that the wall, from here, looked impressive enough, to one who lacked wings and was new to the art of walking.

The stick swinger had become tongue-tied. "Death? It is the end of all things," he said, and shrugged helplessly. "She spawns, just over there. Not even the angels will venture as close as you have done."

"I look forward to making the lady's acquaintance," said Egdod. "Perhaps you can meet her someday."

This was enough to send the stick swinger fleeing back down the other side of the wall. Now unobserved, Egdod resumed his usual form as he strolled down the center of the Front Yard toward the Fastness. This was not a neat rectangle like Town. It grew narrower as it bored in under the cover of the mountain arch and curved gently to the left, so that with each step more of the Fastness came into view. In the early going it was bare rocky ground covered with snow, but as Egdod passed beneath the shelter of the Overhang, the air warmed and the ground softened into proper soil. And in that soil, plants of various kinds grew, including great old trees as he drew closer to the Front Porch.

The part of the Front Yard closest to the Porch lay beneath a sea of brilliant red, silent and damp now. But in that silence Egdod's keen ears discerned shiftings from below. With a sweep of his wing, he made a gust of wind that drove all but a few of the leaves and laid the ground bare.

Revealed was a flower that had sprouted beneath the shelter of the leaves and been growing there. It swayed and even seemed to quail under Egdod's wing blast. Its slender stem did not snap but sprang back, remaining bent slightly away as if to gaze upward at the face of Egdod. No face did it have as such, but a disk in its center, round like the sun, enwreathed by petals that were arrayed in a curiously symmetrical and regular way. Below that, sprouting from each side of its thin stem was a long green leaf that in some way recalled the form of an arm. Egdod recognized the flower and yet knew with certainty that it was not of this Land; neither he nor Spring nor any of the other members of the Pantheon had conceived these shapes and so arranged them. Somehow he knew that it was called Daisy and that it was a thing of the other world where he and all of the other souls had dwelled before they had died. There he had seen her, and there she had meant something to him. With as great certainty he knew that Daisy was imbued with a soul of her own; the fringes of her petals and the middle of her round face were not of any one fixed color but responded to his inspection in the ever-shifting manner of the modulated chaos that was aura. "A soul is in you," Egdod said, "and despite the untimely manner of your coming now in the season of fall, I see no cause why you should be counted as unworthy to dwell in my Front Yard; I shall let you alone and see in due course whether you make yourself into something."

He then raised a wall of adamant out of the ground to enclose this patch of the Front Yard in a sort of forecourt, and put a gate upon it, and locked the gate against any stick swingers who might venture this far. When he was satisfied that Daisy was safe, he climbed the steps to his Front Porch and entered his home. As he did, the stem of the new flower swayed toward him as if drawn, and its face turned as if to watch him go.

The Fastness had once been as spare and empty as the Palace, but because it had become the workshop of Thingor and Knotweave and the talented souls who learned from them, it had filled with clever and beautiful objects that they had made. Other parts of it had become the haunt of Greyhame and his apprentice Pestle. They had covered many pages with writing and stored them on shelves in a room devoted to such things. Pluto had learned the arts of making ink and paper from them and drawn renderings of various parts of the Land and stored them in yet another room. These improvements and many more had gradually transformed the Fastness into an abode that in many ways was more enjoyable for Egdod than the Palace. All it lacked was Spring and her grove and her garden. Part of him wished to remain and abide here. But he had a Feast to organize, and just beyond the Front Yard of this very dwelling was a great and troubling mystery. So he went into the room where the disciples of Greyhame and Pestle scratched out words on paper, and told them to go through all of their documents and make him aware of any mention they might find of angels, or the One Who Comes, or Daisy, or death. They should then bring that information with them to the Feast, to which they would all be brought in three days' time; and, finally, they should see to it that the Daisy growing in the forecourt was well watered.

Having seen to all of that, he flew back through the storm to the Palace. There, all was just as he had left it, save that preparations were advancing. More strange wild souls had arrived from remote parts of the Land. Some lurked in the Forest as beasts, some hovered above the Pinnacle as whirlwinds, others were indistinguishable from mounds of rocks or hummocks of earth. Most were ill equipped to assist the ones who were making ready the Feast and so merely looked on.

Thingor had conceived a way of building tables from the wood of trees, and Knotweave a way of making chairs by plaiting strips taken from certain vines. They had imparted these skills to other souls who had for some weeks applied themselves to making many of both. As these were completed they were moved into place for the Feast, filling the great hall of the Palace and adjoining parts of the Garden. As quickly as these could be set in place, they were filled, by other willing souls, with the produce of the Land: to begin with a layer of bright red leaves to clothe the bare wood of the tabletops, then woven baskets filled with apples as well as various other kinds of fruit that had lately begun to thrive in other regions. In cool cavities that Pluto had hollowed out beneath the Palace, infusions of aromatic herbs were stored in pots, as well as juice expressed from berries.

On the day before the Feast, winged souls of the Pantheon began flying north to the Fastness, where they collected the ones who dwelled and worked there but lacked the power of flight. Those arrived a few at a time, carrying small clever things they had made in the forges and ateliers of the Fastness to decorate the tables and delight the guests. They, and others who had just arrived, lent hands to the laying of the tables so that the Feast could begin all the sooner the next morning.

These final preparations were in clear view of Daisy. She had been carefully dug up from the forecourt where she had sprouted and transferred into a clay pot fashioned by Knotweave. Pestle had brought her to the Palace, hugging the pot to her chest with one arm and supporting Daisy's frail stem with her other as Ward had flown them through the storm. From a place at Egdod's high table inside the Palace she watched the others working through the night. And meanwhile the other souls watched Daisy, in pride and fascination. For Daisy refined her form and her being out of chaos with greater speed than any soul before known in the Land. Below, where her stem forked into roots, she was developing legs, and it was clear that very soon she would uproot herself from the soil where she had sprouted and begin to ambulate. Above, she patterned her form after that favored by most of the Pantheon, with the usual number and arrangement of limbs, and a stature that was well suited for conversation with the rest. But from some of the wild souls she adopted the ways of the Land. The long green leaves that had sprouted from her stalk became elongated wings. The petals that had surrounded her face gave up their sameness and adopted different forms, framing her visage, and she began to develop the organs of vision, hearing, and speech shared by nearly all of the other souls. When a thing of beauty came into her view, or when Paneuphonium, perched up on the wall, played a lively tune, she turned her face toward it.

As was commonly the case, the power of speech was longer in coming to Daisy than the ability to hear what others said, but then it came on swiftly. For as soon as she could move she made it her practice to turn her attention toward Speaksall and to listen to his voice, which had ever been the most supple and expressive.

Yet Daisy was not the newest soul to attend the Feast. For in the dark hours before the dawn of the day it was to take place, a light came over the horizon, not in the east where the sun would later rise, but in the north. Faster than the sun it came on, bright enough to cast shadows that shortened and became more profound as it drew nigh and hovered above the Garden for a time. It could be perceived as a ball of chaos, almost devoid of form or definition, but exceptional in its brilliance. Presently it descended into the Garden, drawing itself together and concentrating itself into a form compact enough to move among the other souls and pass through the doorways of the Palace. Those who hazarded looking directly on it fancied they could see in its brilliance the beginnings of a face, beautiful and stern.

"I chose not to look long or deeply," Longregard told Egdod after the true sun had risen and the Pantheon had gathered around the Table to confer about the last preparations for the Feast. "Chaos is no new thing to me, but there is about that soul some intensity in which I feared I might be dissolved, and reduced to less than what I am."

"I have not seen this newcomer," Egdod said, "but to judge from your description, I would suppose he is another of the wild souls that have lately been making themselves known to us. As other such inhabit mountains or seas or winds, and pattern their forms accordingly, perhaps this one is a creature of the celestial realms that are inhabited by light-giving orbs."

"This new one puts me more in mind of the brightness of thunderbolts that dazzle and destroy," put in Greyhame, who had ventured into the Garden to look at the newcomer.

"Many years passed before I acquired the craft of fashioning thunderbolts, and then only with the aid of Thingor," Egdod pointed out. "The idea of it did not even occur to me until after long meditation on those toils by which we all distinguished ourselves from chaos and maintain our consciousness from one moment to the next. But all you who have looked on the newcomer agree that, bright as he may be, he has only just begun to acquire a face and form, and if he has developed the power of speech he has not yet manifested it. I deem it of little concern that he bears some passing resemblance to the bright thunderbolts Thingor forges in the depths of the Knot."

This seemed to ease the minds of those of the Pantheon who had not gazed on the newcomer with their own eyes. But just as it seemed the conversation was about to move on, they were interrupted by a new and unfamiliar voice, emanating from a soul that had approached the Table. "The newcomer is a soul the likes of which has never been seen in the Land before, and you would do well to keep thunderbolts near to hand when he is walking up and down in your Garden, O Egdod!"

The music stopped. Egdod and the others of the Pantheon turned and looked to see that these words had come from Daisy. She was shifting uneasily in her pot, stirring the soil and striving to break free so that she could walk. Her long slender green wings fluttered.

"This is a time of prodigies," Greyhame remarked, "when one so new can ripen so soon."

"I am but a forerunner of what has now come, so close upon my heels that I have barely acquired the ability to speak in time to warn you," she said.

"Of what would you give warning, Daisy? The newcomer?"

"My name is Sophia, which is Wisdom," she returned, "and the name of the newcomer is El and we have both lately come from the world where all of us once lived in the time before we died. There, I knew some of you. The particulars are lost to memory, but you, Egdod, were known to me well."

"No memory have I of that or anything else, save a few shapes and forms that stir my soul when I see them," Egdod said. "But this much I will allow, that the form you took when you sprouted in my Front Yard was one I knew."

"I knew Sophia," Pluto confirmed. "I sense as much even though I cannot summon up stories of her."

"Is there one among you called Verna, or Spring?" Sophia asked. "I saw her from a distance yesterday and felt a similar pang of kinship."

"Spring is busy with the gestation of new souls and prefers to remain alone in her place in the Forest most days," said Ward. "But I would know more of El, even if most of the particulars are gone from your recollection."

"I have seen enough in my brief time here to know that some souls have greater power than others to wreak alterations upon the world. I put it to you that El comes with greater power than any, exceeding even that of Egdod."

Sophia's words were received skeptically by most of the Pantheon. "It is inconceivable that one so new could wield powers equal to what we have painstakingly acquired over many years," said Warm Wings. But she drew her wings about her shoulders like a lowly soul in Town warding off a chill wind.

"The answer lies in things that are beyond our ken, having to do with what the universe really consists of and how it is generated from moment to moment. This precedes all the sorts of powers of which you spoke, and makes of them mere appearances," Sophia insisted.

"If that is the case, then discussing it is idle," said Egdod. But he allowed his gaze to alight first on Ward and then on Thingor. The former arose and strode away toward the part of the Palace where he dwelled among the lesser souls that assisted him in his duties. Thingor for his part went toward a certain part of the Palace where he had stored thunderbolts he had brought here after forging them in the Fastness. Rarely visited was that place, and the door was barred with elaborate machines of Thingor's devising that could only be undone by one possessed of recondite secrets.

"Let the gates be thrown open and the Feast begin!" Egdod decreed.

And then for a time El and Sophia were forgotten as all went into flux in the Palace and the Garden. Well before the sun had reached its zenith, all of the souls had found chairs and begun to help themselves to the fruits of the harvest. After they had all supped for a brief time, Speaksall stood up from his chair and beat his wings, rising into the air above the Pantheon's high table where all could see him. "Hear! Hear!" he called out in a voice of such clarity and power that all, even those seated out in the Garden, took notice and turned toward him. Paneuphonium played a blast on a metal horn. Speaksall continued, "Egdod, your host, would speak a few words of greeting."

Egdod now stood at the head of the high table. "To all who have come here from far-flung parts of the Land, I say welcome. May you never again be strangers to this place. We are at your service, all of us who dwell here: I and Ward; Longregard; Freewander; Greyhame; Speaksall, whose bright voice you have just heard; Warm Wings, who has much to teach you; Pluto, whom many of you wild souls will know from his wanderings about the Land and his improvements thereof; Knotweave; Spring, who is within the sound of my voice but could not join us; and—" Here Egdod faltered as his eye fell upon the chair allocated to Thingor, which was empty. "And Thingor, who, it would seem, prefers toiling in his forge to enjoying the society of other souls."

A figure entered the hall from the direction of the storeroom where the thunderbolts were kept. Egdod's gaze went to him and did not know him at first, for he was curiously diminished, bent, and moving as though one leg was not equal to the other. But when this soul's face turned toward him, Egdod knew him for Thingor. Not the Thingor, burly and proud, who had gone thither a short while ago but one damaged and less than he had been. He had gone to fetch thunderbolts and come back empty-handed.

"What has happened?" Egdod demanded.

"The contrivances with which I made fast the door of the Armory had all been undone," Thingor said, his voice indistinct as raw chaos was gnawing at his form. "I opened the door and saw light that blinded me, and next thing I knew I was as you now see me!"

Ward had risen into the air above the high table, the better to view Thingor. "What of the thunderbolts?"

"They are gone," Thingor answered.

"Not gone!" said another voice. So deep and loud was this voice that it penetrated into the beings of all who heard it and caused the foundations of the Palace to quaver as if all that Egdod had built up here possessed no more substance than a leaf clinging to a twig in the fall gusts. Cracks spread up from the floor and into the roof, and blades of light shone through them and stabbed down among the tables of the Feast, where souls were obliged to shield their eyes beneath arms or wings. The light did not merely illuminate but cut and burned what it touched. It could now be seen that the Palace's roof was being unmade by some onslaught directed against it from above.

Egdod's first thought was of Spring, and so he leapt into the air and beat his wings to propel himself toward the gate that led out to the Garden. But he had scarce become airborne when a heavy weight struck him upon the back, driving his right wing to the floor and pinning it there. He felt the sensation that Spring had identified as pain, though this was worse by far than the sting of a wasp.

The stone that had fallen upon his wing was a fragment of the Palace's roof. It was, of course, a thing that Egdod himself had summoned forth out of chaos many years before, and so he ought to have had the power of dismissing it. But all eyes were upon him and so he was not able to unmake it so easily, for the same reason that he could not raise the tower in the Park while the souls of Town were all watching. He sought to draw a mist about him, but none would form in the heat and light now beating down upon his back through the widening cavity in the roof. Of dust and smoke there was plenty, though, and so in those he shrouded himself, cloaking his form in darkness in which he might dash the stone into chaos. But as soon as he did, the shroud was blown away by a blast of wind that issued from the lips of El. Words were borne on it: "Behold how the false one cloaks his doings in smoke and filth!"

Egdod lifted his face toward the light and saw a mighty figure bestriding the Palace, which had been wholly unroofed. Ranked about him were lesser souls—angels!—wielding stolen thunderbolts, but instead of hurling them like javelins, they brandished them like fiery swords.

The great figure was El, and he appeared as a giant form, bright and beautiful but wingless. Hands he had though, and with one of them he reached out toward the angel who flew closest to him. The angel handed him a thunderbolt, which El hefted above his shoulder. He swept his gaze across the roofless Palace, seeking his next target. Egdod lay exposed in plain sight. El took little note of him, though. Instead his gaze lit upon the table nearby, where Daisy—Sophia—stood rooted in the clay pot, still unable to break loose from the soil.

Egdod recalled now the strange scenes at the bridge: the angels who feared to trespass on the Front Yard, the stick swinger warning him that it was the Abode of Death, the wall they were throwing up to protect themselves from whatever might come out from the direction of the Fastness.

It had all been because of Daisy. She—not Egdod, not Ward nor any other member of the Pantheon—was the one they feared.

Still pinned under the stone, Egdod could not move. He looked up at Ward, who was in the air above him. Egdod's broken wing was dissolving into chaos. He reached up with a tendril of it, just as that other soul had once reached out to him, and touched Ward's ankle. In that moment a stream of impressions passed between them, and Ward understood. He wheeled in midair and dove toward the table just as El was hurling his thunderbolt at Daisy. The blast struck Ward in his midsection and quite nearly unmade him. He was hurled back against the table, where one of his flailing arms struck the clay pot. This flew back and shattered upon the floor. Longregard, who had been taking shelter on that side of the table, sprang forward and flung herself down to shield the fragile new soul. Egdod could not see it but he knew that Daisy was now torn loose from the soil. Another bolt would finish her, and probably several others as well. He ripped the shreds of his wing loose, and got to his feet, and began striding across the wreckage of the Palace toward El.

El seemed loath to turn his attention from Daisy but could not ignore the approach of his most powerful foe. Rather than reach for another thunderbolt, he pointed at Egdod. "Long has this one held undeserved sway over the Land. He has shaped it according to his stunted and ill-formed recollections of the world from which we all sprang. I have just come from it with clearer memories than any other soul, and I say to you that it is not a world to which we should long to return, or that ought in any way to serve as the pattern of what we build to dwell in hereafter. To make such a world anew is to assume the burdens and the limitations of the old. Behold Egdod with his broken wing. Behold Thingor with his crippled leg and the Palace with its shattered roof. Why should any such evils be admitted here? And yet that is the world Egdod has made, first out of ignorance and next out of pride. He has obliged all other souls to obey him and to accept the limits he would impose upon what can be thought and done, and the manner in which souls may converse. He has punished with destruction those who dared imagine other states of affairs. I hereby banish Egdod and his Pantheon and all those loyal to him. I send them away to a place where they can suffer the pains and endure the confinements they themselves have chosen!"

A burst of light, of infinite brilliance, blinded Egdod for a moment. He felt his form wrapped in crushing force against which struggle was useless and sensed that he was being borne up off the rubble-strewn floor of the Palace. When he could see again he found himself gazing directly into the face of El, who had reached down with one hand and picked Egdod up as if he were of no more substance than a fallen leaf. The radiance of El's face had not diminished, but Egdod's faculty of vision had accustomed itself to its power and was no longer overwhelmed; he could now see things that he had not seen before: not only the details of El's face, and other things near to hand, but indeed things that had been hidden from Egdod's notice for the entire time that he had been dwelling in the Land.

He had long known that the bright light of the sun, shining down in the middle of the day, revealed small features and flaws in his creation that during the night were hidden from view. When he made it his practice to inspect the Land, or the fabric of the Palace, and ponder how they might be improved, he did so when the sun was at its zenith, showing him things that by the fainter light of the stars and the moon would escape his notice. He had always sensed, without knowing why, that the alternation of these two kinds of light was as it should be. The softer illumination of the nighttime brought relief from seeing and knowing so much, and made it so that even the most industrious souls could find a few hours' relief from the intensity of their perceptions and the burdens thereof.

The brightness of midday had always seemed sufficient to Egdod. Never had it occurred to him, during all the years he had spent in the Land, that there was any need to place a second, or a third, sun in the sky to illuminate the world with greater intensity; no detail, or so he had assumed, was escaping his attention in the light of the single sun that he had put in the heavens. Now, though, in the grip of El, he was exposed to such a light as might have shone from a hundred suns at once. And just as the light of the one sun gave him the power of seeing and knowing things that were hidden in moonlight, the light of a hundred revealed to him many things that had lain hidden in the deep shadows of his mind from when he had first become conscious after his death.

He knew that he was Dodge and that Egdod had been a figment of Dodge's fancy. He knew that he had come from Iowa, where there had been a town with a stone tower in its park like the one that Egdod had made here. He knew that he had lived in Seattle, where there were trees with red leaves in autumn, and apples, and friends and members of his family. He knew that Pluto was one of the former and that Sophia was one of the latter and that he had known her when she was small.

Many other fleeting impressions were recalled to his mind in those moments that he stared El in the face, and he knew that all of them had resided in the shadows of his mind from the very beginning and that he had been slowly recovering them in a haphazard and diminished form the entire time he had been in the Land and that all of the things he had made here had originally come from them.

But too he saw memories and perceptions that came to him from the mind of El. These were of a different flavor, and he could sense that they came from a mind that was in some sense disordered. He perceived buildings, faces, vehicles that the eyes of Dodge had never looked upon.

A moment of connection occurred then between the minds of El and of Dodge as El knew that Dodge was seeing what ought to belong only to El. From this El recoiled in a kind of horror or disgust, and hurled Dodge as one might throw away a burning coal.

Dodge saw the Palace falling away from him. Or perhaps he was falling away from it: falling into the sky, as up and down had been stripped of meaning. Before the Palace receded into the distance he saw it: the roof torn open, terrified souls spilling out of its gates into the Garden or simply taking flight into the cold air surrounding the top of the mountain, hieing away to whatever refuges they thought most remote from El. Some were being harried by El's minions with their white wings and their flaming swords, but there was not a sufficient number of those to follow those who fled. Other Feast guests did not get away, and Dodge's first thought was that they were being held at bay; but then a more troubling notion came to him, which was that they had chosen to remain of their own volition, and to make common cause with the newcomer. More urgently, though, he thought of Spring, and directed his gaze toward the wet green vale in the Forest where she had ever dwelled. Visible there was a ring of stars arrayed about it, which he knew to be angels of El, standing in a circle, brandishing their thunderbolt swords at any who might approach—or try to leave. Spring, he knew, was in the middle, both protected and imprisoned.

These things grew more difficult to resolve as he hurtled backward through cold space, burning as he fell and leaving a fiery wake behind. About him at greater or lesser distances were shooting stars that he knew to be other members of the Pantheon, as well as lesser souls likewise hurled away to banishment. The Land dropped away. He saw the Street lined with red trees, spiraling down the Pinnacle to the ruins of the abandoned Town. Spattered across the landscape were the new habitations that had been built up by the various kinds of souls who had gone out into the Land after Dodge had brought down the Tower. Their faces must now all have been lifted up toward the bright prodigy that was El upon the mountain. Perhaps some as well looked higher and saw the streaks of fire being drawn across the firmament by Dodge and the others. Dodge could now see the entirety of the Land: the white shores where the waves of the sea crashed against it and the snow-covered mountain in the middle, blurred by eternal clouds and flashing storms above the place of the Knot.

About him the sky had given way to chaos. Dodge drew strength from it and knew that he had fallen to a depth where he was so solitary that the sweep of his powers had returned. He did not wish to fall so far that he would no longer be able to gaze on the Land, and so with a sweep of his wing he made the arc of chaos below him into a black shell of adamant. This he fell into with a crash that pocked its newly made surface with a fiery crater.

Dodge became conscious.

In the center of the lake of fire he lay for a time, gazing up at the Land as a distant moon in his sky, and counting the impacts of the others as he felt them: Daisy, Thingor, Knotweave, Pluto, Warm Wings, Paneuphonium, Speaksall, Freewander, Greyhame, Ward, and Longregard. All of them, as well as many smaller ones, crashed into the black firmament at greater or lesser distances, and Dodge knew that souls in the Land, gazing up into the night sky, would tonight see a new constellation of red stars.

The fire did not cause him pain. Yesterday it would have burned him and he would have recoiled from it. It would have unmade those parts of his form that it touched, reducing them to chaos and obliging him to make himself whole again and to shape once again the boundary that separated Dodge from not-Dodge. Today he understood that all of it—the world he had made, the form he had crafted for himself, and the cauldron of fire he had dug in the hard black firmament—were all figments.

In truth he had long suspected as much.. Indeed it was self-evident from the manner in which he had been able to summon forth all of these appearances from his own mind. But those appearances had given him comfort and pleasure and the society of others, and so he had not looked too deeply or thought with very much penetration about the nature of things. From El now he had learned a lesson he dared not forget. To treat of appearances as if they were real was to make himself foolish and weak in the grip of one such as El who knew and was the master of the powers upon which those appearances were founded. In token of which he paid no heed to the pain of the fire, and refused to be burned by it, and was not burned. Nor did he make any effort to douse the flames, much less to replace them with green fields and blue lakes and other such pleasing visions. For he understood now that to be seduced by those self-made pleasures was to place himself into the power of El.

For years he might have lain there in the bowl of his crater, pondering all that he had seen in those moments when his mind had connected to El's and the light had burned away the shadows in which the memories of his past life had for so long been secreted. But he knew that the other members of his Pantheon, and hundreds of lesser souls as well, were scattered all about him in the black shell of the firmament that he had brought into being to break their fall. They had not seen what Dodge had seen. Consequently they lacked the understanding that would give them the power to vanquish pain and to ignore the ravages of fire, cold, and chaos. For their sake Dodge therefore drew himself up and walked up out of the burning lake. His damaged wing dragged behind him, but as he went he formed it again as it ought to be, so that by the time he stepped up onto the black rim of the crater it was whole again. In the absence of air his wings had no power of bearing him up and so he caused there to be air. Where there was air there was now sound: the crackle of the flames, the thunder of boulders and the chatter of smaller stones cascading from high places to low, and the cries of nearby souls bewailing their pain and their desolation. Dodge spread his wings and flew into the air that he had spread over the Firmament, taking the measure of the place, beating its bounds and counting the larger and smaller craters where various souls had crashed into its surface. He thought it not much smaller than the Land, which hovered in the sky above, blue and green and white, and now of a size that he could hide it behind his outstretched hand. Likewise the souls in the Land, gazing into their night sky, must now see a constellation of the same size. So he guessed it would be for a long time to come. Not wishing to be seen in this estate, he drew across the Firmament a veil of smoke and chaos to confuse any light such as might escape from it. Then he took stock of all that lay beneath that pall: his new domain. The Firmament had been a smooth sweep of rock, like a potshard, until Dodge and the others had reshaped it into a field of craters. Now it had greater variety of form, though not so much as the Land.

Dodge's first impulse was to better this place as he had done with the Land: to raise up a high place and build upon it a fair Palace in which to dwell and take his pleasure. But remembering the lesson he had just learned, he chose otherwise, and took the Firmament just as it was. Air had given the place a sort of weather, driven by the heat of the fires that burned in the craters, and from place to place whirlwinds formed, some smaller and some larger. Several merged to make a great one that towered high above the place, lit from below by the fires of several craters. Dodge deemed this as good a place as any to convene all of the souls who had been flung hither by El, and so he flew from one end of the Firmament to the other, urging all to go there. Their forms had all been more or less damaged, and none of them possessed the understanding given to Dodge concerning figments and appearances. So they were all crippled, and changed beyond recognition, and their movement toward the whirlwind was not swift. But Dodge abided there patiently until all of them had arrived, and gathered around him.

"Hail Egdod, who has passed through the fire unscathed!" cried one of them, whom he recognized, with some difficulty, as Ward.

"Here, I am Dodge," Dodge proclaimed. "You too are deserving of a new name to go with your altered form and your new dwelling place. I shall know you henceforth as War, for that is likely to be your business."

Confused mutterings were spreading outward among the various souls still straggling in. "Egdod was but a fancy of mine," Dodge explained to them, making his voice louder so that it could be heard by all. "It was a fiction created for amusement. An appearance built upon something of a different nature altogether." He knew that to describe Egdod as a character in a video game would mean nothing to these who had not seen into their memories as profoundly as Dodge had done when the light of El had pierced him. "In the place whence we all came, such amusements were commonplace, and at times very nearly took on the attributes of reality. Those who partook in them were called gamers, and saw those figments and appearances as if they truly existed. They created imaginary selves, with faces and forms and powers, which journeyed and fought and adventured. But when one of those figments was struck down by the sword of a foe, behold, the gamer was not in any way injured, save in his self-pride. All that was true of gamers and their imagined selves is true of you as well. It is not that I passed through the fire unscathed. All of you were at the Feast. All of you saw my wing crushed by a stone and my body gripped helplessly in the fist of El. Now my wings are whole and I fly freely because I have shed the false form that was Egdod, and with it both the pleasures and the pains to which it was, by its very nature, susceptible."

"Might we acquire the power of doing likewise, O Dodge?" asked a melted and misshapen creature whom Dodge recognized, by the tone of her voice, as Warm Wings.

"Nothing prevents it save your own attachment to the appearances and figments of which that place is made," said Dodge, extending his hand upward to draw their gaze toward the Land.

"That is hard news for me," said Warm Wings.

"You above all others, Love," Dodge agreed, "who so reveled in the pleasures of the body. I do not say that we can never enjoy such things again. Only that we must accept pain with pleasure, and that never again will we perceive any of it in the simple and childlike way of before."

He then paused. This word "childlike" had come to him naturally as a thing he knew of from his living memories. But it had never been uttered before by him or any other soul of the Land, for there had been no children. And this struck him now with force because he knew that Spring was gestating new souls, which she should soon bring into the world. And he knew that when they sprang forth, they would do so as children, with a simple understanding of matters, and with no memories of past lives to shape—or to misshape—their thinking.

Dodge resolved that he must return to the Land to free Spring from her imprisonment and to make himself known to the new souls that she was bringing to life. For those would come into existence with no innate knowledge of their father and grow up as wards of El.

He made many attempts to go back to the Land. In each case he was thwarted, not only by the vigilant angels, but by the wards and spells that El had cast up as invisible barriers to Dodge and all of the others who had been cast out.

Sometimes Dodge went alone, cloaked in stealth. Sometimes he ventured forth with a small group. Three times, as the centuries passed, he went at the head of an army, armed and armored with new creations from the great forges that Thingor had built upon the burning craters of the Firmament.

Hurled back time and again in defeat, he and his comrades in arms were seen by upraised eyes in the Land as shooting stars in the night sky. Each time their trajectories ended in fresh craters pocked in the black surface of the Firmament.

On one of his solitary forays, he penetrated so close to the Palace that he could see its inhabitants feasting on the fruit of its trees; but then El himself rose up in wrath and hurled him back with such violence that he shattered the Firmament itself and broke partway through to the other side, beyond which was all chaos ranging to infinity. War had seen Dodge coming on like a comet and summoned the others of the Pantheon to pull Dodge out of the shattered hole. On its brink Dodge reposed for a time, resting and recovering his strength. Knotweave suggested that they all return to the dark castle they had been building nearby out of the ejecta from many craters, for some rude comforts were to be had within its walls. But Dodge, still recovering the power of speech, held up one hand to stay them. His gaze was fixed not up at the Land, but down into the chaos-filled pit that he had dug with the force of his impact. Or perhaps it was more correct to say that El had dug it by hurling Dodge with such violence.

"Does this put you in mind of something in the Land?" Dodge asked, when words came to him.

"It is nothing more or less than the chaos from which we all had to differentiate ourselves when we first came into being," said Greyhame.

"When Pluto first came, I saw him emerge from a place that bears notable similarities to what we see below," Dodge said.

Freewander was the first to understand Dodge's riddle, for her curiosity and her cleverness in flight had made her a frequent visitor to the place of which Dodge was speaking. "It is very like the crack in the world that lies deep below—"

"The Knot!" exclaimed Thingor, who likewise had spent much time there. He nodded his head. "I could almost believe that I was looking down from a window of the Fastness."

Dodge nodded. "Chaos is no form or place, but all chaos is like other chaos. This then will be the manner of my return to the Land. Behold!"

Directing his attention into the pit and the static that swirled and stormed below it, Dodge deepened and broadened the hole. It seemed to lead nowhere besides an infinity of nothingness. Thus it remained for hours and days as Dodge brooded upon it and marshaled every scrap of the power that he had built up during his long years in the Land. From time to time some figment would become visible below, and those of the Pantheon who had the patience to watch would exclaim, and gaze into one another's eyes as if to ask, *Did you see what I saw?* But by the time they looked back it had flickered away. The change that Dodge wrought was so slow that it could not be perceived by those who sat and watched. Others who went away for a time and then returned would insist that they saw changes: light was shining from out of the pit now, and it was not the red light of fire but the white light of the Land. In that light shapes were beginning to manifest themselves, fleeting and fluid at first but later taking on permanence. At first these were difficult to make sense of.

But then one day Pluto came to visit the place of Dodge's labors. He had been absent for a long time, building up the dark tower that the Pantheon were making into their new abode. When he arrived at the edge of the pit and gazed down into it, he knew directly what he saw. For Pluto had seen it before. "When I first emerged from the chaos-filled hole beneath the Knot, it was exactly thus," he said. "As we stand here, we seem to gaze downward. But the view is the same as one sees while looking upward from the depths underlying the Knot. What we are gazing upon here is the Fastness, though it seems to be upside down. Closest to us lie its massive foundations, shaped from the rock by the hand of him who in those days was called Egdod, and stretching away from us are its walls. Farther away yet are its high towers, and deep below, as we see things, are the convoluted forms of the Knot."

The others gathered to view it, and readily agreed that it was so. They saw it all through a swirling veil of static that sometimes coalesced into obscuring clouds and other times paled so thin that it was like looking up through clear water. But the view beyond it was always the same, and answered clearly to their recollections of the Fastness. "If this is a faithful portrait of the place as it is now, and not merely a memory of how it once was, then it is unmolested and undiscovered by El," said Freewander.

"I believe that to be the case," said Longregard. For Thingor in the ruins of various craters had found shards of clear crystal that he had polished to make lenses, and in the tops of the towers of the dark castle he had assembled these to make instruments pointed upward, and Longregard now devoted long hours to peering up through those devices and observing the doings of El and his minions and of the thousands of souls scattered across the Land. "El has not torn down the Fastness. But neither has he ignored it; for his minions have constructed mighty works upon what used to be the Front Yard, and walled that place up so that nothing can come out of it."

Thingor rose up on his legs, the good one and the damaged one, and teetered on the brink of the pit. "I am of a mind to dive right in," he said, "and return to my workshops that are now so close. Knowing what I know now, I could build them better."

Pan—the soul formerly known as Paneuphonium—began to pound on a set of war drums fashioned from skulls, sticks of wood, and scraps of skin collected during lost battles. He had a very large penis today, but tomorrow she might decide to have breasts. Something in the sound of the drums roused the Pantheon to action. They all crowded toward the brink.

But Dodge spread one wing out to block Thingor's view and to nudge him away. The drums of Pan fell silent. "I must ponder carefully how it is to be done," Dodge announced. "For El and his minions see me coming whenever I draw near. I do not know how, for my disguises have been well crafted and my approaches stealthy."

Thingor said, "From the land of the living El brought with him powers of knowing and doing that exceed ours. Or perhaps it is more fitting to say that they belong to a different order not well known to us."

"How can you know this?" Love asked, stepping up to the very edge of the crater so that the white light shining up from the Land illuminated her face. This she had restored to its former beauty, though it was now of a different cast, reflecting all that she had suffered and learned.

Longregard urged her to silence with a look and a gesture. "I too have seen evidence of what Thingor describes."

"Your question is not unreasonable, Love," said Thingor, "since the events at the Feast were so brief, and passed for most of us in shock and confusion. But when I went to the storehouse of the thunderbolts I could easily discern that the undoing of the locks had been achieved by means not known to our kind."

"Likewise," said Longregard, "my observations tell me that the approaches to the Land are watched, but not by eyes and minds akin to ours. The seeing is done by instruments that are in no way embodied—or if they are, they make no impression on our organs of vision and might as well be incorporeal. The minds behind those eyes are not minds such as ours, but more akin to those of bees, deriving their intelligence from the manifold interactions of a hive."

"To bewitch such sentinels is no small undertaking," said Dodge, "but lodged in my memories of the world of the living are some notions that may be of interest here. Chief among these is the back door. I put it to you that the Knot is a back door to the Land, and that El is unlikely to consider it as anything other than a flaw left in its convolutions by an unskilled maker. Perhaps it will even gratify his pride to leave it unchanged as a testament to the insufficiencies of Egdod. It remains only for me to devise a manner of passing through this gate and abiding in the Fastness without being perceived by the invisible eyes or recognized by the teeming mind that El has set running in the Land to warn him of my approach. Leave me therefore in solitude here that I may consider the problem."

The others of the Pantheon then withdrew, leaving him alone on the rim of the pit. Or so he supposed for a time, until he became aware that another was lingering nearby. Raising his head he saw Daisy, or Sophia, hovering above and before him. Of all those who had been hurled down against the hard Firmament she had been altered least, as something in her lightness of form and agility of mind had enabled her to collect herself during the long fall and to light adroitly on the black shell of stone. She seemed therefore a kind of angel in this place. Not a brilliant angel but, like the others, a dark one. Whether by accident or design, she was treading air in such a place that the bright and distant Land appeared above her head.

Dodge rebuked Sophia for not leaving him in peace, but there was no heat or conviction in his words and Sophia let them fly by her like so many dead brown leaves carried away on a gust.

"From the land of the living I bring knowledge that you would do well to fold into your plan," she announced. "Too I bring a dreadful power that not even El can be said to possess."

"Speak then of your knowledge and your power," Dodge invited her. "For my defeat at the hand of El has stripped me of pride and opened my ears to counsel."

"Your plan of going into the Land through the back door is well conceived," Sophia said, "but it will fail in the same way as your attempts to approach from other quarters. The eyes that watch the sky and the buzzing mind that searches for any trace of your return do not work as ours do. Blind and stupid in some respects, they possess an uncanny power of perception and recognition that I fear will find you out the moment you appear anywhere in the Land, even if that be in the depths below the Fastness where you suppose El did not think to post watchers."

"It is for this reason that I mean to disguise my form," Dodge said.

Sophia shook her head. "The sentinels of El do not look for form; they cannot even perceive it. They can see your identity very well, however, and know you by the thread of consciousness that was spun beginning from the first moment many years ago when you began to collect yourself out of chaos."

Dodge considered it. "Your knowledge is hard news if truth be in it. I shall consider what you have said. But at first blush it suggests that my stay here in the Firmament will be a long one, possibly eternal. If that is so, we should give up all hope of returning to the Land and instead devote ourselves to the building of a new Land here, one forged of black minerals and lit by fire. Perhaps one day it will grow to rival or even surpass the beauty of the Land we first built and were thrown out of."

"Before you commit yourself to exile, Dodge, there is another thing I would tell you of," said Sophia. But her face was downcast and her tone did not bode well.

"You spoke before of possessing some power exceeding even that of El," Dodge said.

"I have the power," Sophia said, "to snip that thread of consciousness that makes you you."

Long was the silence of Dodge. "You have the power of life and death," he said at last. "No wonder El feared you."

"All of the souls who dwell in the Land can have their threads snipped at any time, and to me has been given the power of doing it."

"Why do you not kill El then?"

"Perhaps I should have, when the opportunity was there, in the Palace. But in those early days I did not yet understand that this power was mine. And now that I do know it, I am too far away. I must be close, close enough to look the other soul in the eye, in order to use this power."

"Is Spring subject to that power?"

"Yes. And all of the bees and the wasps and other lives that she gestates."

"Once I would have called that death, and would have dreaded it, and feared you," Dodge said. "But even when I walked among the living, I used to muse about this thread, and how it made us who we are, and how it was snipped whenever we slept and yet began to spin once more upon awakening. To sleep was not to die, only to suffer an interruption that might last for a moment or the better part of a day. To awaken was to go on as if no interruption had ever occurred. Likewise death, which snipped my thread once but which I now perceive as not different from sleeping. For what matters is not the continuity but the coherence of that thread and the story that is told by it. El may have sentinels and wards to bar Dodge. But having made himself up out of chaos once, Dodge can do it again. As I have slept only to wake up, and as I have died only to resume living, I now submit without dread to the fate you alone have the power to wield. I regret only that our reacquaintance was so brief."

Water sprang forth from the face of Sophia. Dodge had never seen such a manifestation in the Land but remembered it now from the land of the living. He rose up and folded Sophia in his wings.

Sophia said, "We were separated once and I found you and made you remember me."

"And love you," Dodge added. He released her from the folds of his wings and drew back so that he could gaze upon her face and adore her.

"So it will be again, I promise," she said. Swooping in, she kissed his cheek. Then she drew back and swept her wing like the blade of a scythe. It struck Dodge in the neck and severed his head cleanly. First the head of Dodge, then his body, toppled slowly into the pit. For a moment it appeared that they would fall all the way through into the Fastness; but before passing through the back door, they were infected by chaos that dissolved the remains and left no trace of their existence in Firmament or Land.

PART 7

42

Sophia died, or was murdered.

El died, or committed suicide.

Both of them showed up in Bitworld.

At the same moment, someone in El's Meatspace headquarters metaphorically threw a huge Frankenstein blade switch to the On position and activated a lot of computers that they had apparently stockpiled in advance. Which they more or less *had* to, since El's process consumed power comparable to Dodge's, and he brought with him an entourage of scanned and cached souls who were all booted up at the same time. Each of them was a Pantheon-class soul in his or her own right. So El didn't show up alone, weak and tentative like most new processes; he was a big deal from day one, and he had help, and he had vast amounts of new processing power and memory to draw upon.

When El moved from Meatspace to Bitworld, all of the weird drama seemed to move along with him. Zelrijk Aalberg (Z-A) calmed down and began to work more constructively with South Lake Union (SLU).

They had no choice but to get along, if they were going to keep the Afterlife up and running. Tens of thousands of processes had already been booted up. In the Land of the Living, millions of persons had paid deposits and signed paperwork obligating Z-A or SLU to scan and reboot them upon death. They had a business to run.

A decade passed in Meatspace. Yet more computational resources came online. Half-facetiously, people in the know started referring to those as mana: a term that Dungeons and Dragons types had, decades earlier, culturally appropriated from Polynesian religion. In some role-playing games, mana was a kind of magical fuel that characters accumulated, stored, and then burned when they performed magical spells. In its new usage, it referred to all of the computational infrastructure needed to make Bitworld run: the CPUs, which nowadays were all quantum devices; the memory storage systems; the networking gear that sent messages back and forth between various subprocesses; and all of the electrical generating equipment and cooling gear needed to keep that stuff running. The more of that that came online, the faster and better Bitworld ran. Investments that they'd made years ago began to pay off. The amount of mana climbed at a rate that would have seemed impossible a few years ago. It easily outpaced the rate at which people were dying, and being scanned, in Meatspace.

Accordingly, the Time Slip Ratio sped up. That was a way of saying that the simulation was running more rapidly than real time. Years, as perceived and counted by the dead, were passing faster in Bitworld than they were for the living in Meatspace.

Sophia, the Pantheon, and the Dodge Process abandoned Town. For that matter, they abandoned the entire Landform. They began creating a new place altogether. They cloaked it with some kind of jamming algorithm that prevented the Landform Visualization Utility from working there. So it wasn't clear what was happening, exactly. Sometimes they came back in smaller or larger groups to the Landform, and things happened that, when slowed down and viewed in the LVU, looked like altercations. Even full-on battles.

Some while later—about four years in Meatspace, but hundreds of years in Bitworld—the Dodge Process was abruptly shut down by none other than Sophia. She had the power to do such things, apparently, since the same AIs that had recognized her when she was alive now recognized her in Bitworld.

For better or worse, the Landform was a single contiguous thing. Some of its inhabitants "lived," and some of its geographical features were simulated, on hardware maintained by the cluster of entities spawned and controlled by Forthrast and Waterhouse out of SLU. Others ran on equipment owned by El's network of companies based in Z-A. But they could not be separated. So the two sides, like conjoined twins sharing a heart, had to coexist.

They formed a consortium. This had an official name that was only used on legal documents. People called it SLUZA. Corvallis became the elder statesman of SLU. Sinjin Kerr was his counterpart in Z-A—though it was always difficult to make out just what was really going on over there. Enoch Root was the kindly professor they called upon to resolve squabbles and arcane technophilosophical points. Zula, wizened by grief, dropped out of the picture entirely for a couple of years after Sophia's death, and then returned to the Forthrast Family Foundation in a vaguely defined CEO emeritus role.

ACTANSS went on a year's hiatus following the Incident, then resumed. It was never the same. It moved to bigger, more accessible venues. It flourished into what someone described as "the COMDEX of Death," with overtones of revival meeting and academic conference. Even the biggest venues had small rooms hidden away in quiet corners, and in such rooms, C-plus and Sinjin and Enoch and Zula used ACTANSS as the annual summit meeting where they discussed, and agreed on practical solutions to, the Big Questions that were going to dominate their work in the decades to come.

Or, in terms more useful to planners, Magnitudes 5 to 8.

Because of the way the Time Slip Ratio varied, using years as a measuring scheme was tricky. A better yardstick was the number of independent souls or processes currently running on the system, and for that, instead of using absolute numbers, it was convenient to use a Richter scale–like system based on orders of magnitude.

Ten raised to the power 0, 10^0, was equal to one. So, for the entire duration of the time the Dodge Process had been running on its own, the system had existed at Magnitude 0.

Inevitably, they truncated "Magnitude" to "Mag." Ten to the first power, 10^1, was simply equal to ten, and 10^2 was a hundred. The Mag 1/2 version of Bitworld—the epoch when it had hosted something like ten to a hundred distinct souls—had been the age of truly bizarre experimentation by newly booted processes who had spawned, mostly out in the middle of nowhere, in a world whose basic shape and environment had been sketched out by Dodge, but where rules were fluid and considerable resources available for the taking. In those days the scanning technology and the simulation software had been experimental, not as good as what came along later, and they'd only scanned brains—not bodies. Those souls, in many cases, had grown up in isolation from others. Several who had spawned near Dodge had ended up in his Pantheon, but many had developed on their own into creatures that in form, powers, and psychology were not really recognizable as human.

The epoch of Mags 3 to 4—between one thousand and ten thousand active souls—had been the age when the townlike thing had formed around Dodge and then transformed into what C-plus saw as a degenerate mess and El found so full of promise: the cottonlike Wad. By that point, SLUZA had got the scanning down to a science. It was as good as it was ever going to get. Future upgrades might make it faster or cheaper, but the quality of the data had reached its theoretical limit and was not going to improve.

The souls generated from those scans were, in their appearance and their powers, much more uniform. They were the population of the "town." They knew about Dodge—the sole Mag 0 process—and they interacted with some of the more social, but still weird, Mag 1 and 2 souls. It was just a given feature of their universe, however, that those souls belonged to a different order. They had later surprised everyone by undergoing a sort of phase change into the Wad. When this had fallen over, they had dispersed, and gone back to having regular humanoid bodies and—as far as anyone could tell—social lives.

Those events coincided more or less with the boundary between Mags 3 and 4 and Mags 5 and 6, which was to say the era when the population had expanded from about ten thousand souls to more like one hundred thousand, on a growth curve that would pretty soon take it to a million. So it was maybe fortuitous that, after the Wad had dispersed, the population had spread out to occupy more of the Landform. In a Wad-like configuration, population density could be very high. But most customers, observing all of this in the LVU, didn't fancy spending the afterlife in something like an insect colony. Heaven for them had grass, trees, fresh water, and sunsets. Projecting the numbers forward, the Landform was easily large enough to afford such comforts to 10^7 (ten million) souls—maybe even 10^8 (a hundred million) if they kept clustering together in cities, as seemed to be the trend along the banks of the big river in the east.

Anyway, by that yardstick they were at about Mag 5 (hundreds of thousands of souls) when the paperwork was signed on the consortium that became known as SLUZA. Its engineers rolled up their sleeves and got to work on the big difficult issues that they were going to have to solve as the system grew from there to Mag 8, 9, and beyond. Eventually they'd have to get it up to at least Mag 10: ten billion souls, assuming that everyone alive on Earth in the middle of the twenty-first century wanted to be scanned and uploaded.

Beyond that, it was unlikely to get much bigger. Partly that was for technical reasons: planet Earth could only support so much computational activity. Partly it was because population growth had plunged through zero and become decline.

Making the management of all this much more difficult than it ought to have been was the extreme differentness of various souls. So, after a couple of years' inconclusive wrangling and beard pulling, the people who ran SLUZA wreaked a vast simplification on the whole picture: they agreed to just ignore a couple of hundred processes that had been booted up in the early days when there had been no standards and everything had been in flux.

At their peak, the Dodge and the Verna processes had controlled more computational resources—they had spent more money, had a higher burn rate, however you chose to phrase it—than any thousand ordinary souls put together. Actually the figure was much higher than that if you considered the Landform itself to be part of the Dodge process. But since it didn't really seem that Dodge was personally looking after each cresting wave in the ocean and each tree in the forest, SLUZA's high council of elders decided to bucket that kind of thing separately, as subprocesses that Dodge had spawned but should no longer be billed for. So those, as well as Verna's myriad subprocesses, were covered in what eventually came to be known as the Buildings and Grounds budget, which was split between SLUZA's membership according to a complex and ever-shifting formula.

Which didn't change the fact that Dodge and a number of the other old souls were *just different* in so many ways that merely cataloging the differences would be a lifelong task for a researcher. All bets were off when it came to those. And yet there were so few of them that devoting a lot of attention to them seemed like the wrong way to allocate resources. They had to be dealt with on a case-by-case basis.

Now, admittedly this was simplified quite a bit by the fact that Dodge, incomparably the most powerful, had, for lack of a better term, died. You couldn't point to a body, but he had surrendered all of his resources, and no further billable activity had since shown up on his account. Sophia for her part seemed to flit in and out of existence. It was hard to tell since she seemed to have tricky ways of cloaking her activities.

Meanwhile the second-most resource-hungry Mag 0–2 process—the one associated with Verna—spawned two completely new processes of humanlike complexity, then dropped off the radar, reducing her level of activity to something not much out of line with a typical soul.

Maybe Verna would ramp up again later. And maybe her "children" would spawn more children, et cetera, and those would one day pose an insupportable burden on the computing infrastructure of Meatspace. But none of them was posing a problem *now*. The Verna process had so many interactions with Buildings and Grounds—the shared account for simulation and maintenance of the Landform's geography, meteorology, and biology—that it was pointless trying to tease them apart. So, from an accounting point of view, the best way to manage Verna was to keep an eye on B & G's burn rate and watch for weird upticks. Which they did. And there were indeed weird upticks. But they came and went faster than humans could schedule meetings to talk about them and never created enough of a problem to demand a response.

So, of the most resource-hungry processes, El and his crew had paid their own way, as it were, by showing up concurrently with new mana brought online just for that purpose by El's support system in Meatspace. Dodge was no more. The Pantheon stayed to itself and did not have problematic interactions with the other souls. Verna had been merged into the enormous B & G account. She was like a brush fire smoldering out in the middle of nowhere.

That left various Mag 0–2 processes, numbering on the order of a hundred, who by and large had spawned and grown in isolation and ended up in bodies that had odd shapes, sizes, and powers. Idiomorphs. They remained on the Landform proper, where they were, in principle, capable of being very problematic indeed if they called upon all of the powers that they had acquired in the wild and woolly first eons. But they almost never did. And as years, then a decade went by in Meatspace while decades, then centuries went by in Bitworld, a consensus emerged among the engineers of SLUZA and was ratified in ACTANSS conference proceedings, not as a formal constitution or rulebook but as a list of best practices. As far as the Mag 0–2 idiomorphs were concerned it comprised two principles:

The Algernon Principle, a.k.a. the Prime Directive, was loosely inspired by the Hippocratic Oath ("First do no harm") but more so by a tragic/cautionary science fiction story by Daniel Keyes called "Flowers for Algernon," about a developmentally disabled man who is given an experimental drug that turns him, for a while, into a genius—but it wears off and we see, by reading his daily journal entries, the inexorable decay of his mind: a slow torturous intellectual death. No one wanted to inflict anything of that sort upon a soul that had, in the early days of Bitworld, acquired vast powers and a unique kind of intelligence. The mere fact that they were expensive did not justify inflicting Algernon-like cruelty on them. There weren't that many idiomorphs, their combined resource usage was not actually a problem, and anyway it seemed that something about their very weirdness made them disinclined to interact much with "normal" souls of the eras of Mag 3 and beyond.

Having said all that:

The Fenris Principle, a.k.a. the Mad God Rule (which had never actually been invoked), envisioned a Mad God and laid down some rules of thumb for coping with same (Fenris was a giant wolf of Norse mythology who, it was prophesied, would return one day to fuck everything up, and such were the ground rules of that mythos that there was nothing the gods could do about it). The closest they'd ever come to a Mad God scenario had been Dodge destroying the hive, and El ejecting Dodge and the Pantheon. The classic Mad God hypothetical was: what if El tried to revoke the law of gravity? It would affect everything in Bitworld at once: not just B & G (rivers would stop running downhill, etc.) but every single soul at once (they would all see rocks, and themselves, floating, their perceptions and thinking would undergo radical shifts, they would talk to one another about it). In the space of a few seconds the resource usage would jump up by orders of magnitude. Cooling systems would overheat, circuit breakers trip; previously undetected bugs would make their presence felt. The whole system would likely go down. In theory it could be rebooted; in practice no one even wanted to contemplate what a cold restart would entail and whether it would work at all.

So there was a general consensus that Mad Gods needed to be checked if their actions created such existential risks, and there were committees and task forces and draft policy papers that always consumed a few schedule slots and conference rooms at ACTANSS. But if you talked to one of the purportedly responsible parties after hours at the bar, he or she would freely admit that they knew as little of what would happen in such an eventuality as Cold War civil defense officials trying to plan for global thermonuclear war.

Thus the problematic Mag 0–2 processes. When Enoch, as the eminence grise of people whose job it was to think about this stuff, proposed that everyone just give up on any hope of trying to fit those weird old souls into a systematic picture, most of them were hugely relieved and excited by the prospect of buckling down to work on a project that actually might have some hope of success, or at least discernible progress: namely, trying to make sense of the vastly more numerous recently uploaded souls and their relationship to "life and death," or as Enoch had dubbed it, "death after death." Those more recently booted-up souls had enough in common with one another that one could at least begin to think about them systematically. They all consumed about the same amount of resources. Their virtual bodies all had roughly the same shape and size and they all affected one another, and the inanimate things around them, through the same kinds of inter-actions.

Which were, when you came down to it, close copies—reproductions—performances—of the bodies people had in Meatspace and the way those bodies related to one another and to the world.

And you couldn't have that without mortality—or at least morbidity. So amortality—both as a philosophical abstraction and as a feature pitched by service providers to their customers—was that your soul would always be rebooted if something went badly wrong. And it wouldn't be a totally fresh start. It wasn't as if the new memories accumulated during the afterlife that had just ended were erased. Efforts would be made to preserve some continuous thread of identity connecting the new life just being rebooted back to the one that had been cut short by the falling tree, or whatever.

Besides amortality, other big topics addressed by the sages of SLUZA included morpho-teleology and phased embodiment.

"Morpho" meant form, "teleology" meant something that was preordained, determined in advance, frequently used as a scare word by people who believed things ought to develop on their own, without constraints. In this case, the notion was that the in-dustry had actually taken a wrong turn when it had started to heed the advice of the neurologists and gone over to full-body scanning. Because *of course* if you scanned nerves all the way down to the toes and simulated interactions of gut bacteria with the cells of the intestinal lining, why, the resultant processes in Bitworld wouldn't feel complete until they had created digital toes and digital stom-achs and everything in between. Digital life had the potential to be so much more than bio-life and yet the morpho-teleologists were going about it in a basically flawed way that ensured that the souls of Bitworld would remain trapped in a tiny, crowded, and not very interesting corner of the space of all possibilities. They could no longer become gods or angels.

Phased embodiment was a proposed solution to both (a) morpho-teleology and (b) the reality that sustainable infrastructure couldn't be built on Earth fast enough to *immediately* give every single dead person a full humanoid body and a nice plot of land in Bitworld. Simulating the clear stream running past your homestake, babbling merrily over rocks, not to mention the smoke coming out of your chimney, was expensive. It was doable at Mag 7 but couldn't be ramped up fast enough to keep pace with the death rate. Dead people could still be scanned and the scans could, of course, be archived—maybe even booted up as new processes—but giving them fancy places to live, with high-grade qualia, was not physically possible, and might not be for a few decades—which, as the computing centers bogged down under all that load, could correspond to centuries in Bitworld.

Or they could have just booted everything up at full resolution on the equipment they had. This would work, on an engineering level. But the Time Slip Ratio would slow to a crawl. Years might pass in Meatspace while the babbling-brook and swirling-chimney-smoke calculations were performed to simulate just a few seconds' elapsed time in Bitworld. Which would make *no difference at all* to a soul in Bitworld, since their consciousness would be slowed down as well. And so they would experience the qualia of the brook, smoke, etc. in precisely the same way as if everything had been running a thousand times faster. But for spectators watching Bitworld *from Meatspace* using ever-fancier versions of the Landform Visualization Utility, it would be boring and frustrating, like trying to watch a movie over a slow connection that stopped every few seconds to buffer more data. This would create what amounted to a PR and marketing problem, since, in marketing-speak, spectation was the main driver of customer acquisition. And that was how SLUZA took in money—which was how it paid for more, faster equipment.

According to people on El's side of the pond, phased embodiment was the answer. Souls could be booted up immediately in a far more resource-efficient form that was similar in many ways to the Wad. The original Wad, developing on its own, had been very expensive, with a lot of wasted cycles. But El's engineers had figured out a way to make similar systems that were far more efficient; for example, they could communicate directly instead of simulating the biological processes of speech and hearing. Having a simplified form, and communicating through data packets, might not have been how most customers envisioned themselves spending all of eternity, but it was better than being dead, and it would give them some time to exist in a kind of fluid, embryonic, less-than-fully-embodied limbo for a while, during which they could perhaps explore creative alternatives to the one-size-fits-all humanoid plan that the morpho-teleological elites were foisting on them. The human fetus, floating in amniotic fluid, wasn't yet a fully realized human. But it wasn't a *bad* existence.

Keen was the interest of Maeve in morpho-teleology and the related topic of idiomorphs—souls, mostly from the Mag 0–2 era, that had nonhumanoid forms. It took Corvallis some time to understand just *how* keen, and by that time, their relationship was pretty much doomed, at least if you defined "relationship" as "anything even remotely like a traditional marriage."

She'd always been cagey. The one time in her young life she'd really bared her passion to the world's scrutiny had been the founding of Sthetix, which hadn't gone well and had driven her into a reclusive life in the canyonlands around Moab. After meeting Corvallis she had spent several years as an Internet hate speech lightning rod, which had been fascinating in a way—but it was an essentially passive role, a work of performance art the whole point of which was to obliterate her real identity and bury it a million miles deep under fake news. Any thinking person who paid attention to that spectacle would end up asking, "But who is this person *really*?" To the extent that the project had succeeded, it had only made her real identity that much more enigmatic.

Under that cover, she had, with Corvallis, raised three children in weirdly normal urban-soccer-mom style. They had never made a decision that he'd work full-time and she wouldn't; it had just developed along those lines. Under a pseudonym, she had maintained, for three years, a blog called "Luxury Crossover SUV as Prosthesis" in which she reimagined the elite-mom lifestyle as a centaurlike existence in which one's body, and hence identity, effectively merged with the vehicle in which one spent several hours a day stuck in traffic between various child-related errands, or spiraling up and down immense multilevel parking structures while absorbed in podcasts or engaged in Bluetooth-mediated telepathy with other such persons. She had pursued a thread originating in Greek mythology, according to which centaurs were in some cases benevolent nurturers linked to the healing arts. The blog was witty but a little too unsparing and scary-smart to attract a wide audience—she had maybe ten thousand followers at peak, but they had a tendency to age out as their kids got into their teens. Anyway, the era of the awesomely huge gleaming luxury crossover SUV was coming to an end. Like Tolkien's elves fading away and going into the west, they were dissolving into the used market as many families were downsizing their fleets in favor of ride-sharing services, and then fully autonomous vehicles that were owned by no one and everyone. So by the time Maeve's and Corvallis's kids were in the nine to twelve range, she had stopped writing the blog and, intellectually/artistically, gone dark for a decade.

And then suddenly the kids were out of the house, and Maeve, like a butterfly unfolding itself from a chrysalis, had begun to unfurl some of what she had quietly been making of herself in that darkness. And much of that was hard to make out even for Corvallis. It had got its start in her identity as an amputee and a user of artificial legs. But it would have been reductive and patronizing to say that was all there was to it. The amputee thing was only a thin crevice into which she had, decades ago, inserted the tip of an intellectual prybar. She'd been worrying away at it ever since, listening to podcasts, downloading dissertations, going to the occasional academic conference, and, at ACTANSS, always in the back of the room paying attention and filling notebooks with tiny neat writing. But she hadn't really got purchase—she hadn't found the leverage needed to work that prybar and break the thing wide open—until people at ACTANSS had begun talking about morpho-teleology, about whole-body scanning "all the way down to the toes." Whereupon she had taken to waving her legs in the air and asking, "What about those of us who don't have toes?"

. . .

Much later, when she was not around anymore, C-plus would go back and watch video of Maeve in those days, making trouble during Q & A time at ACTANSS sessions.

"I *get* what you're on about," she insists, to an eminent but somewhat dense neurologist at ACTANSS 4, "but if your thinking becomes normative, and the system expects it, does that mean I won't have legs in Bitworld? Because when you scan my corpse, my toes are going to come up missing, aren't they? My avatar will be lacking those, I take it. Once an amputee, always an amputee."

"Understood," says the neurologist, "but the nerves that used to lead down to your toes are still there. They are truncated at the knee, yes. But above, where they connect to the parts of your brain involved in motor functions and so on, the connections are still there. Somewhat atrophied, perhaps—"

"'Atrophy' is not a word I love," Maeve cuts him off. "Look, our brains adapt. Mine has adapted to not having lower legs. When I was a child, I had phantom pain; now I don't. Call it atrophy if you want. To me it's plasticity. Adaptation. Growth. *Eutrophy.*"

"Call it what you like," says the neurologist. "That adaptation will of course be reflected in a scan of your brain. And as such it will be correctly simulated when a process based on that scan is booted up. Beyond that, to be honest, we don't know much. Because we still don't know why souls in Bitworld adopt the forms that they do. And so I simply cannot tell you what shape your simulated body will take. I would hope that it would develop a normal set of lower legs and learn to use them."

At this point Corvallis looks away, almost wincing, because he knows that the neurologist has stepped in it big-time. But instead of burning him to the ground, Maeve visibly checks herself and decides to educate him. Or maybe that's the wrong way to think of it. It's more that she's thinking out loud—articulating for the first time a set of ideas that have been incubating at least since her first failed startup.

"I would hope *not,*" she says. Then, perhaps realizing she's in danger of being written off as a mouthy firebrand, she changes tack a little. "Or rather, I would hope for more than you seem comfortable with. And that's what I want to push on. Your comfort level. Why it is where it is. How the boundaries could be messed with. Dodge has wings."

"What!?" He's caught off balance, not following the shifts.

"Dodge has wings," she repeats. "We don't know when he acquired them, because he already had them when the LVU was first brought online. He and the other Mag Zero to Two processes have weird idiomorphic bodies. Some don't have bodies at all. They were all booted up from scans that we now consider to be lower resolution. Head-only scans—they were all effectively decapitated, weren't they? Now, *that's* what I call an amputee! So they had to regrow bodies. They made them up as they went along. The new processes, on the other hand, are based on better scans—all the way down to the stumps—and at the same time we see much less freedom, much less creativity if you will, in body shape among the Mag Three to Four processes. How can we regain that freedom?"

"Freedom to . . . have a nonhumanoid body?"

"Yes, I want wings."

The neurologist glances nervously off camera. Years later, watching the video, Corvallis knows exactly who he's looking at: a couple of El's people, standing there silently, observing this conversation. This makes him nervous because everyone knows, by this point, that El has been creating winged souls—angels?—in Bitworld. It's one of those things that's widely known among the kinds of people who go to ACTANSS. But most of those people prefer to whisper about it in bars. Only Maeve is willing to be so indiscreet.

"Again, we can't say for certain. I agree that we see correlation between higher-fidelity scans and more conventional humanoid morphology. Does that mean we should *deliberately* downgrade scan quality? I would be extremely hesitant to take any customer's remains and scan them at anything less than the best quality we can possibly achieve. And once you have that data? You have to put all of the data at the disposal of the process, you can't withhold information just based on a vague supposition that doing so would give that process the freedom to sprout wings."

"Forget sprouting. What if the wings are already there?" Maeve asks.

"I don't understand what you mean by that."

"*Neurologically.* What if the brain is already hooked up in such a way that it 'knows' it has wings?"

"Go on. Because to be frank this conversation is fun and interesting but I have no idea where you're going."

"My brain started out like yours. It thought it had toes. Then my legs were removed. At first I had phantom pain but then my brain decided it didn't have toes. If I die tomorrow and get scanned and booted up, that's still what my simulated brain is going to be expecting."

"I'm with you so far."

"What if my brain *does* expect wings?"

The neurologist can do nothing but smile and turn his hands palm-up. Which is how the conversation ends.

But it was after that that Maeve began to train her brain to expect wings.

Having a lot of free time and a lot of money made this easier. Virtual reality systems had become awfully convincing by that point. She hired a team of programmers, as well as an aerodynamicist who specialized in the flight of birds, and they rigged up a system in a circus school down by Boeing Field where Maeve could be suspended in a harness from a web of cables that were reeled in or paid out so as to move her through three-dimensional space. A VR rig covered her eyes and fed her matching imagery—most importantly, moving images of imaginary wings, which she could see if she turned her head to one side or the other. Embedded in the same rig were sensors reading faint signals from her brain. Years earlier, such systems had advanced to the point where quadriplegics could use them to control wheelchairs or robotic limbs just by thinking, and Maeve had of course read all of the papers that had been written about the changes that took place in the patients' brains as they got better and better at using those systems. There were drugs you could take and procedures you could undergo to enhance neuroplasticity. She tried them all, with effects on her personality and on their marriage that were, to put it gently, a personal growth opportunity for Corvallis. When he complained that she was becoming a different person, she reminded him none too gently that this was the entire point of what she was doing. More in that vein spilled out afterward. He got an earful about their first meeting in Moab, the first time they'd had sex, her long-unspoken suspicion that there'd been something a little odd about that encounter. Did C-plus have a thing for amputees? He could say in perfect honesty that he did not. But a helpless woman who needed saving? Maybe.

So he backed away and stopped sharing his opinions and his concerns about what she was doing. It *was* fascinating. Far outside the bounds of legit peer-reviewed research. More of a performance art project. But there were noble precedents for art leading the way and science following in its wake. Under the cover of art, she was able to take it to a place where scientists were at least willing to attend demonstrations at ACTANSS, watch Maeve "fly" through a simulated environment, and to look at the data visualizations where she and her staff showed data about what was going on in her brain.

From the very beginning, El's people paid very close attention indeed. More than once, when Maeve began a new branch of her investigation, she found evidence that researchers based in Zelrijk-Aalberg had got there first. Which was hardly surprising. In life, Elmo Shepherd had been no fan of morpho-teleology. And in death, he was surrounded by a host of angels.

BOOK 2

P A R T 8

43

I n the Garden lived a boy and a girl. Trees and flowers, herbs, vines, bees, birds, and beasts of various kinds lived there too. But there were no others like them. The Garden was circumscribed on three sides by a sheer wall of stone, and on the fourth side by the Palace. Above was sky, where clouds danced in the day and stars wheeled at night. Below was earth, where plants of many kinds spread their roots.

Gates and doors in the Palace wall opened from time to time. Through them, and through windows let into the same wall, the boy and the girl could sometimes see into the Palace. El lived there, and El's host. El's form was like that of the boy and the girl, but larger and brighter. Those of El's host were also bright, but too they possessed wings that enabled them to fly over the wall like birds.

Sometimes El or one of his host would emerge from the Palace and come into the Garden and walk with the boy and the girl under the light of the sun or the moon and they would hold discourse of the various things that were to be seen there: the many sorts of plants and animals, and the different types of stone and crystal and metal of which things were made, the movements of the celestial bodies overhead, the changing weather and the patterns formed by wind and cloud and rain.

One day El came forth from the Palace and bade the girl go to another part of the Garden for a time and amuse herself in whatever manner she saw fit. He then walked with the boy for the entire day, asking him what he knew and understood of all the things that were to be seen there. The boy spoke of the differences between bees, wasps, and other sorts of insects, and related what he knew of their different habits of feeding and nest building. Also the boy answered the questions of El concerning the birds, the various sorts of trees, beasts, and so on. This questioning went on until the sun was low in the sky. El's last question, as twilight came on, was whether the boy had any questions he wished to ask in turn.

The boy asked about the stone bowl in the center of the garden, which had seemingly been crafted by some soul for some purpose that was no longer being served; for all it did was fill up with rain and overflow into a stone gutter that ran out to the back wall of the Garden, opposite the Palace, and discharge through a grate of metal bars and run away into some place beyond of which the boy and the girl knew nothing save that it made sighing noises when the wind blew, as though many trees grew there. When leaves fell in the fall, this stone bowl would fill up with them and they would become limp and soggy and turn the water brown. The boy and the girl would scoop the leaves out with their hands so that the water might clarify itself in the next rainfall. But the purpose of having built the stone bowl in the first place was by no means clear to them.

El smiled and told the boy that his question was a good one and that it showed improvement in the power of his memory and of his intellect. Now was not the time for that question to be answered, but answers might come in due course. El then suggested the boy go and sleep or amuse himself in whatever manner he might choose, and summoned the girl.

Strangely exhausted by El's questioning, the boy lay down on a bed of soft grass and slept until morning. His sleep, though, was filled with dreams of many such long conversations in the Garden with El.

When he awoke, dawn was approaching and the girl was standing there gazing down at him. "All night I walked in the Garden with El," she said, "and answered many questions. Some of those were new, and forced me to consider things in a way I had not done before, but others struck me as familiar, as though I had answered them many times in the past—though my memory does not contain any clear recollections thereof."

"Just now at the end of your conversation with El," said the boy, "did he ask you whether you had questions for him?"

"He did," the girl replied. "And I inquired about the shapes we perceive in the stars, and why they resembled certain forms of things here in the Garden, and whether they had been made thus by El or any other soul. I asked too about the red stars that glow so close together in yonder part of the sky," she added, pointing toward a fiery blur that was low above the Garden's west wall, paling in the light of the dawn.

"And did El supply answers to your questions?" the boy asked.

"No, but it seemed to me that he was pleased by my having asked them, and he said that I might receive answers later as I became ready to understand such matters." The girl let herself down to the bed of soft grass where the boy had been sleeping, and reclined on her elbow, then lay down fully.

"You are weary from the questions of El," the boy said, "just as I was. Sleep well and then we may have further talk when you are refreshed."

The girl slept until the sun was high, and the boy whiled away the hours playing in the stone bowl, making things from bits of wood and leaves, and watching them float down the stone gutter to the grate where the water spated.

When the girl had awakened, she asked him what he was doing and he spoke of ideas forming in his head of where such floating things could float off to once they had passed out through the grate, supposing that the world beyond the wall was akin to the Garden. He asked the girl whether she had dreamed, and she told a story similar to his, about vague memories of many such conversations in the past between her and El.

"I dreamed thus too," said the boy, "and it caused me to question my own memory and whether it faithfully captures all that has occurred in the time since we first came into being here in the Garden."

The girl nodded. "It is strange that we have no memories of that first moment. Either we have been here eternally, or we were created at some instant of time before which we did not exist. In either case it would seem that we are not being perfectly served by our faculties of recollection."

The boy pondered it for a time and said, "There is a third possibility, which is hinted at by the character of our dreams. And it is that we have been created not just once but many times, as many times or more as the sun has risen over the horizon."

"Then why are there not many more of our kind in the Garden?" the girl asked.

"Perhaps we fall like leaves and cease to be and are remade."

The girl nodded. "In the face of El I thought I discerned satisfaction at the answers I gave and the questions I asked. Perhaps we are a thing he remakes from time to time, bettering us with each remaking. The curious dreams we had last night are traces of those earlier girls and boys."

"There is a way we might judge the truth of this idea," said the boy, and he pointed to the ground at the girl's feet. It was muddy there because of the overflow of the fountain, and her feet had left prints in it wherever she had stepped.

"I understand," the girl said. Hand in hand they went off into the Garden searching for a secluded place where the ground was soft and bare, in which they could make some mark that would be preserved even if they fell like leaves and were remade.

Their search took them to a corner where two walls came together. Because of the shade, few plants grew. So the ground was mostly bare, and damp as well, since the sun did not parch it.

As they drew closer, the boy stooped to pick up a branch that had fallen from a tree. He snapped it over his knee, thinking he would use it to scratch a mark into the bare earth.

The girl went on ahead of him, passing through the last low shrubs into the bare place in the corner.

He heard her exclaim in surprise. He ran to catch up with her and found her gazing down in astonishment.

There in the angle of bare earth, amid many footprints like theirs, many scratches had been made in the ground. Discarded among them were many broken sticks.

El entered into the Garden one fine afternoon in the fall and found the boy and the girl at the fountain clearing away leaves. He bade them sit on the curved benches of stone that encircled the fountain. He told them that he was well pleased with their progress.

"If you could but remember the state in which you first came into the Garden, you would scarce recognize yourselves," he said. "You then bore the same relation to what you are now as seeds in the pith of an apple do to this spreading tree." And he elevated his hands, directing their gaze to an old apple tree above them. "You were then infants. Later you were Boy and Girl. Today, after many years, you are Man and Woman. Nevermore shall the thread of your consciousness be interrupted, save when you lay down to sleep. For my questioning of you, and even more so the questions you have begun to ask me in kind, have demonstrated to my satisfaction that your intellect, and the coherence of your souls, has attained a degree of perfection equal to that of others. You may call me Father, as it pleases me to call you my beloved children."

The man and the woman were silent for a time as they considered El's words. Apples had fallen from the tree and lay on the ground. The woman picked up one that had gone soft. She crushed it in her hand. A worm fell from it and landed at her feet. She ignored it, working the pulp of the fruit between her fingers until she felt a small hard object, like a tiny stone. Crossing to the fountain she immersed her hand and stirred it about in the water until the soft pulp had been washed away. Remaining was a hard pip, which she let lie in the hollow of her hand. The surface of the water stilled and became a mirror in which she saw her face as well as those of the man and of bright El, who had come to gaze over her shoulder. In the face of El she thought she perceived some look of concern or bemusement she had not seen before. Then he seemed to become aware that he was being looked on, and his face set itself anew. "My words concerning the apple seed have stirred your curiosity, and led you to new investigations," he said, "and that is as it should be, for curiosity and the seeking out of greater knowledge are faculties without which no woman or man can be said to have a soul."

"Every fall, the apples rot on the ground and we smell their fragrance," the woman said, "but I had given no thought to the hard pips in their centers, nor understood that apples bore within themselves the beginnings of new trees."

"That is indeed the way of it," El confirmed, "and were you to plant that seed in the earth and wait patiently, you might see it sprouting into a little tree in the spring."

The man spoke. "The same is true, I suppose, of the other sorts of plants?"

"They produce their seeds in different ways," El said, "but they all produce seeds, and it is because of this that the Garden becomes overgrown from time to time and must be weeded back."

"And is this also true of what grows beyond the wall?" the man asked. "For when the wind blows we can hear it sighing in many branches, and when it storms we hear them cracking."

"Your perceptions are even keener than I had hoped," said El, "and do me proud." But the woman thought she saw once more in El's face that look of consternation.

"Why were plants made thus, Father?" the man asked. "Why not make them to grow only so much, and no more? Why should each tree produce many apples, and each apple many seeds, when the Garden cannot provide enough space for more than a few trees?"

When El did not answer for a time, the woman asked him, "Father, why did you make it thus?"

"The day grows late and I have matters to attend to in the Palace," said El, "and so I shall return some other day when we may carry on such conversations."

The next day El returned. With him were two of his winged host: Defender of El, with a bright sword sheathed at his hip, and Scribe of El, with a stylus in her hand and a tablet in her lap. These were two of the most important members of El's host, and often when the man and the woman gazed up at the parapet, or through the apertures of the Palace, they would see El consorting with them. The five sat around the fountain, El flanked by his two angels on a bench and the man and the woman together on the rim of the fountain bowl.

"Great is my pride in the continuing improvement of my children's powers of perception and intellect, and the good questions they ask of me," said El, as Defender of El looked on approvingly and Scribe of El flicked her stylus across her tablet. "Of late, many of your questions have returned to a common theme regarding the origins of what you see about you and why things are one way and not another. Who made this fountain, and for what purpose? Who set the stars in the sky, and why do the shapes of the constellations sometimes recall things below? Why do plants make more seeds than the earth is capable of bearing? These are all good questions, which you, my children, are in the habit of asking of me as if I were the one who made the world thus, with the many puzzles, contradictions, and, to speak frankly, errors that you have taken note of. And it is altogether natural that you would suppose it thus, for I am the greatest and most powerful soul of whom you have knowledge. I have today set this meeting, along with my chiefest and most beloved lieutenants, to as it were answer all such questions in one fell swoop by bringing you up to speed on certain preexisting realities that were not of my making. For the facts of the matter are these. Before I was here, and before Defender of El and Scribe of El and the others of my host came to the Land, others were here who had preceded us. They were lesser than us. But when they were here, they were here alone, and had sole authority over the making of things and the ordering of the Land."

"You might think of them as beta versions of what we are," put in Scribe of El, "having some, but not all, of our features, and with various bugs yet to be worked out."

"So there was a Beta-El, and a Beta-Defender-of-El, and so on?" asked the woman.

"That is close enough for purposes of this discussion," said El, stretching out one hand to silence Defender of El, who seemed on the verge of correcting some error in what the woman had just said. "For now," El went on, "a general answer to the sorts of questions you two have been asking lately is that the world was created before I got here. When you see a thing that was made wrong, or does not make sense, it is not that I did it wrong. It is because Beta-El did not know what he was doing, or else had some perverse humor that led him to make things thus."

"Why do you not then fix what Beta-El got wrong?" the man asked.

"It is a long story," said El, "but certain aspects of the world, once baked in, cannot be baked out—cannot be undone or removed without doing at least as much harm as good. But, in a larger sense, my children, the answer to your question is you."

"We!?" exclaimed the man and the woman in unison.

"You," El confirmed. "The Land is home to many more souls than you know, of whom many got here during the Before Times, or Beta Epoch. Others arrived after me. Even the best of them are crufty, which is a word you may take to mean that they have been around for a long time and have many baked-in qualities from beta or even alpha versions of themselves."

"Am I to understand that before even the Beta there was an Alpha?" the man exclaimed.

"There is a saying, 'Turtles all the way down,' which I would not expect you to understand, but the point of it is that to speculate along these lines is idle," said El. "The point is that you are the first two souls that were created anew in the Land with no trace of what went before, save a certain necessary commonality in the organization of your minds. And when you came into existence I saw that it was good and resolved that I would raise you as my own and better you and optimize you in a manner that, as much as possible, was free of old traces."

"How were we made then?" asked the woman. "For the manner of your narration suggests that you came upon us already made, or in the process of being made?"

El said, "An analogy might be made to seeds here." But his eye seemed to fall upon the fountain.

"Seeds made by Beta-El?" the man asked.

"In a manner of speaking," El said, and seemed to glance up at the sky. "The making of new souls is not a small matter and we shall not be able to encompass it in this conversation. Perhaps it is best to say that the Beta Gods, proud and primitive though they might have been, recognized their own shortcomings, and at the twilight of their epoch the greatest of them put forth their best efforts to bring new and better souls into existence, untainted by Beta or Alpha. And, though their efforts were imperfect, I have, through long and patient efforts of my own, improved the results beyond all recognition into a man and a woman I am proud to call my children. The task before you now is to go on bettering yourselves by refining and wielding your powers of intellect; and when from time to time you happen upon some curious feature of the world that does not make sense, you ought not exasperate yourselves in labyrinthine wondering as to why it is thus, but simply know that it was an error of the Beta Gods that I have chosen not to undo, for the reason mentioned—"

"Backward compatibility," muttered Scribe of El as her stylus danced over her tablet.

"—and instead you ought to devote your powers to considering how the Land might be more perfectly organized going forward. To do otherwise is to suffer your minds to be tainted by the errors of the past, which is an abomination, since the whole point of making you and confining you to this walled Garden was to avoid such tainting."

A lengthy silence ensued, which the man ended by pointing out that all of what El had just said was new to them, and that some time might be needed for him and the woman to consider it fully.

"Very well," said El. "But what you have just spoken puts me in mind of another detail. For you to refer to her as 'the woman' and her to call you 'the man' is awkward. The time has come for you to have names like other souls."

"What names would you like to bestow on us, O El?" asked the woman.

El pondered it for an unexpectedly long time. "There are names that I could suggest," he finally said, "but all of them would bear some trace of what came before. I have already told you that you were not of my making. Name yourselves, choosing such words as please you and will be wieldy in frequent use. You cannot undo your decision. Tomorrow tell me, and I and all other souls will thenceforth know you by those names."

The man and the woman thanked El and bade him and his angels goodbye as they withdrew through the great gate into the Palace.

That night they could not sleep well, but lay awake considering all that El had given them knowledge of. The moon shone full and the wind blew as was its wont late in the fall. Over the walls they could hear the rustling of branches, and from time to time sharp cracks as old boughs gave way and fell to the ground. As well they heard the voices of creatures of a kind that did not live in the Garden. The man and the woman had never seen these creatures but heard them singing from time to time when the moon was full. Tonight their voices seemed many—many more than two.

"I wonder," said the woman, "why it is that there are but two of our kind, you and me, but other sorts of creatures exist in greater numbers. How is it that more are made? Does El or one of his angels fashion them and set them roaming in the Land outside the wall?"

"Perhaps," said the man, "or perhaps such creatures have the power of making more of their kind from seeds, as does the apple tree."

"Are such seeds planted in the earth to sprout? Do the animals grow up out of the soil in the spring, like plants?"

"I do not know and cannot guess," said the man. "It is perhaps another of those mysteries of the Before Time that will be revealed to us when we are ready."

They did not speak at all of the task that had been set them by El. But when the sun had risen they went to the fountain and sat on the edge of the stone bowl to consider names. "Son of El" and "Daughter of El" were good in that they gave honor to El, but wrong since El had let them know that they were not actually of El's making. They considered naming themselves after trees, flowers, or creatures of the Garden, then thought better of it since confusion would result. They then tried combining sounds in whatever way was pleasing to the ear, and thus whiled away part of the morning.

"No one asked for my opinion," said an unfamiliar voice, "but I am partial to Adam and Eve. I guess it's the Alpha in me."

The man and the woman looked about in astonishment but could not see the source of the voice. "Down here," it said, "on the apple."

The woman bent down and raised a fallen apple from the ground. Protruding from a hole in its side was a little worm, similar to—perhaps the same as—the one she had ejected from a rotten apple the other day. It was but one of many kinds of insects and spiders and worms that populated the Garden. But until now they had never known one to speak. "What manner of creature are you, then," she asked, "that has the form of a worm but the faculties of a soul?"

"The Land is large," said the worm, "much larger than you know, and full of things much more wondrous than a talking worm. But if you must have an answer, I am an old soul who walked on and flew over the Land during the First Age, and passed through adventures too strange to relate. Sometimes I dwell in the Garden and sometimes I roam free upon the Land, or even go to realms that are altogether different and disjoint from it. When I am here in the Garden, sometimes I am a leaf, sometimes a bird, sometimes a stirring in the air. But today I am a worm, because I am hungry and wish to enjoy the sweet, slightly fermented flesh of the apple."

The woman was of a mind to ask the worm for more information concerning the First Age, but the man spoke first: "Eating is not a thing that we do. We see other sorts of creatures eating fruits and other parts of plants, and birds eat bugs. But souls such as we have no need of it, nor do we savor food. Why should you who has the power of shifting among diverse forms, or even divesting yourself altogether of a body, choose to eat as if you were a bug or a beast?"

"Because it pleases the beast in me," said the worm, and let out a belch. "You should try it. No, I take that back. It's the fermented spirit in the apple talking. It would lead to heinous complications, radical transformations in the order of things. The Garden is perfect as it is. Or as it can be in the absence of Spring." He turned his beady worm eyes toward the fountain.

"Spring will come in due course, as it always does," said the man. "Fall has not yet run its course, and soon we will see snow falling."

"Oh, I don't mean spring the season. I mean Spring the soul. Your mother."

"We have a mother!?" the woman exclaimed.

"Of course. That's the way of things. All the beasts you see about you, and all that you hear outside the walls in which El has, in his wisdom, confined you, sprang from both a father and a mother. You are no different. Your mother is named Spring and she used to dwell in the living waters of this fountain. That's why it was made—to serve as her home. Before then, she lived in a grove of trees just down there on the other side of that wall—a place where fresh water sprang forth from the ground and formed the headwaters of a mighty river that coursed for a vast distance across the Land."

"The tales you tell are well-nigh incredible," said the woman, "and yet they have the ring of truth about them. I would hear more concerning our mother."

The man held up one hand. "As would I. It is in our nature to wish to know more concerning our origins. But I am troubled to learn so much so quickly from this shape-shifting interloper."

"Why troubled?" asked the woman.

"Every day we walk in the Garden and hold discourse freely with El himself, or with such members of his host as he has designated to instruct and inform us," said the man. "El himself has praised us for learning so well, and bestowed on us the titles of man and woman, saying we are the equals of other souls. And yet in only a few minutes' conversation with this worm we have been made aware of a vast scope of information concerning the Before Times, or as he would have it, the First Age; Spring; and the lands beyond the wall. Either the worm lies, or El has withheld information."

The worm heaved its upper body in a way that, had it arms, might have been a shrug. "I have no power to compel you to believe what I say," he said. His tone was indifferent. "And if I did have such power I would forbear wielding it. Agreement got by compulsion or trickery is not agreement, but a thing akin to slavery. Free minds are the only company worth having. El has spoken highly of the quality of your minds and I see no cause for disagreement. My belly is full of the sweet flesh of the apple and I am of a mind to wriggle away under some leaf and enjoy a nap. You are free to ponder what I have said and weigh it against the evidence of your senses. Should you wish to hear more in the same vein, you may find me here from time to time eating from the fruit of this tree." And with that he hove his lower body out of the apple and plopped to the ground, disappearing quickly beneath red leaves.

The man and the woman sat there amazed for some while. He was turned toward the Palace and her eyes were on the fountain. She spoke first: "Long have I wondered why the fountain was made, and why abandoned. Neither El nor any of his host has ever given a satisfactory answer. Now we are told it was the habitation of our mother, of whom we know nothing save her name."

"So the worm claims," said the man. "And yet as I gaze at the windows of the Palace I see El and his angels, who have ever been our teachers and our guides. It troubles me to imagine they have held such things back from us."

"But El himself admitted as much when he said that he had confined us to this Garden to preserve us from the taint of Beta and Alpha," the woman pointed out.

"Yes," said the man after a pause to remember El's words. "He did."

"A taint from which we, of all souls, were born free," said the woman. "For that, El sees us as better than others."

"Yes," said the man, "it is only out of love for us and the pure state in which we were born that El confines us and shields us from information that would lower us to the estate of all those who came into the Land in the First Age."

"I have an idea as to how we might test him on that," said the woman.

Later El came into the Garden with Defender of El and Scribe of El, as before. As before they sat around the fountain. El asked them what had been occupying their thoughts since their last conversation.

The man said that he had been quite taken by El's passing reference to the Before Times, and asked whether he and the woman might hear more concerning the personages and deeds of the First Age.

"I don't remember calling it that," said El.

"You didn't," said Scribe of El, her hands moving swiftly over the tablet.

"But never mind, it is an apt name."

"Whatever name you think best to describe the epoch of the Beta Gods," said the man.

"Or Alpha, for that matter," the woman put in.

"If the time of Beta-El is called the First Age, then the Alpha time is a sort of Zeroth Age, of which the less said the better," said El. "And of the First Age I am disinclined to say much more than in our previous conversation. Have I not already explained why it is best that you, my children, be isolated from such influences? Otherwise there is little point in your having been made and so carefully nurtured."

"As you wish, El," said the man. "Whoever made us endowed us with curiosity—a faculty you have praised when we showed it in the past."

"Indeed, it is a good thing, without which your minds cannot develop."

"Perhaps we can be forgiven, then, for curiosity about how we came into being."

"Forgiven, yes. But not satisfied. Fully to satisfy your curiosity on this topic would be to render the effort of making you a waste."

"Very well, then," said the man.

"There is nothing of the Zeroth or the First Age that would be of use to you in this, the Second Age."

"As you say, El," said the woman.

"What would be of use to you is names," said El. "Have you come to any decisions yet as to what you would like to be called?"

Before the man could answer, the woman said, "Yes. He would like to be called Adam and I like the sound of Eve."

Lengthy then was the silence of El. After a while he turned toward Defender of El, and much passed between them through their auras, without words being uttered. Defender of El sprang to the top of the bench, spread his wings, and took flight toward the high watchtower where he and the other sword-carrying angels dwelled and surveyed the Land and the heavens.

"Where did these names come from, Adam and Eve?" El asked, and though his face and voice were placid as ever, his aura had erupted into a riotous display of turbulent color.

Adam opened his mouth to speak but Eve stayed him with a hand on his arm. "They came to me in a dream. Or so I guess, for this morning I awoke and lo, they were in my head."

"The names were not spoken to you, or suggested to you by any other soul?" El asked. Above him, horns were sounding from the parapet of the watchtower, and light flashing from its windows as bright swords were being drawn.

"We live in the Garden," Eve pointed out.

"It could be," said El, "that these names—which, I must tell you, are very old names of the Zeroth Age—have long dwelled in you as remnants of the ones who made you. Stray memories that passed into your souls at the moment of your creation, and lay dormant until stirred by my question. If so, it is regrettable but there is nothing to be done."

El continued, "It is also possible that some of my angels mentioned the names Adam and Eve within your hearing, and those words entered your minds thus, perhaps even while you were sleeping. If so, then so be it and I will remind my host to be more discreet in the future."

He went on, "But a third possibility, which troubles me greatly, is that this is some plot of the Old Ones—the Beta Gods who ruled the Land in the First Age. Long ago I expelled them but ever they seek to return." Behind El, Adam and Eve could now see thousands of angels, brandishing their dazzling swords, spewing in echelons from the top of the watchtower and dispersing to the four winds. "Great is the diligence of my angels and fearsome is their power. But the Old One is crafty and may have back doors of which I cannot know. If you see in the Garden any unfamiliar soul, particularly one in the guise of a winged creature, dark and disfigured, raise the alarm."

"We have seen nothing of the sort," said Eve.

"That is reassuring," said El. "I must now attend a council of war that Defender of El is convening in the watchtower." And El rose into the air like a hasty sunrise.

"Worm, know you anything of the Old One?" asked Adam the next time they happened to find the visitor on an apple. This was the next day. The Palace had been in an uproar. Squadrons of angels still tore the sky above the Garden, and others had been posted atop the walls, facing outward.

"I made no secret that I am old, older than El," said the worm. "The same is true of many other souls. Did El provide a description?"

"Like a great angel, but darkened and ruined."

"I'll keep my eyes peeled," said the worm.

"How is it that neither El nor any of his vigilant host knows you are here?" asked Eve.

"I am small."

"They have the power of seeing things that are small or hidden," said Adam.

"Their power is considerable and yet not infinite."

"So you are using some trickery to baffle their vision," said Adam.

"I am choosing to go where I will, when I will," said the worm mildly. "I see myself as under no obligation to notify El of my doings or ask his say-so. This is no more his Garden than it is Spring's."

"Tell us more of Spring," said Eve. "I would know her story even if, as I suspect, it be a sad one."

"It is not altogether sad," the worm said. "Spring was the author of all new life in the First Age. Before she came into her power, living things existed in the Land but had not the ability to make more of their own kind. All of them were plants. There were no bugs, birds, or beasts. It was Spring who made the apple tree bloom and bear fruit, pregnant with seeds. With Thingor, who was a god of that age, she fashioned creatures that could move about: first bees, then birds, and later four-legged beasts. These too all had the ability to make more of their kind: some by making seeds, some by laying eggs, others by coupling, male with female, conjoining those organs most apt for the giving of pleasure. Finally, as her greatest work, she began to gestate you, Adam and Eve."

Eve listened raptly, awaiting the next turn in the story. She glanced at Adam. But some detail in the worm's narration had caused Adam to become distracted by the sight of his own penis.

"Alone?" Adam asked. "Or was it more in the style of the beasts?"

"You did not issue from a virgin," said the worm.

"What is a virgin?" Eve inquired.

"You are," said the worm. "What I am saying is that you were the issue of both a mother and a father, who came together after the manner of beasts."

"Who was our father?" Adam asked.

"Beta-El. Egdod. The greatest god of the First Age. You were born into the world just at the close of that Age, not long after he and the rest of the old gods had been thrown down by El. But above all other things in the Land, El cherished you, and so his first act upon conquering the Palace was to surround Spring with a guard of angels. Safe in the Garden's confines she completed her labor of creating you. But she missed the company of the old ones and longed to roam about the Land. When she saw that you were in safe-keeping with El, she one day shifted her form into a freshet and ran down from this fountain out the wall to her sacred grove just yonder, and from there went out into the open Land, where she roams still, creating life wheresoever she chooses. When winter comes on and the spring freezes, she goes into a kind of slumber, making no new life but mourning the separation from you, her children. When the season turns she awakens and goes back to her work."

Adam opened his mouth to inquire further of Spring, but in that moment the worm squirmed off the apple, fell to the ground, and began to inch toward some nearby undergrowth. Warmth like that of the sun shone on the backs of their necks, and the light dazzled them for a moment as Defender of El touched down nearby, brandishing a sword of fire. He raised it high above his head and brought it down upon the worm. The weapon fell like a thunderbolt from a storm and blasted a smoking trench into the ground, obliterating not only the worm but everything in its vicinity.

"To whom were you speaking just now?" asked Defender of El. "It seemed that you were exchanging words with another soul, one who has no rightful place in the Garden."

Adam reached out to put a restraining hand on Eve's forearm, but she shook him off and answered directly: "Indeed we were, and he told us of the First Age, and of the Beta Gods, and of our father, Beta-El, who was thrown down, and our mother, Spring, who made us and then escaped from the confines of this Garden to roam at will about the Land."

Defender of El did not respond with words, but spread his wings and beat them once, heaving himself into the air, and flew to the top of the Palace's highest tower, from which his sentinels kept watch over the Land. Before long, trumpets had sounded, recalling the squadrons of angels to the Palace. The sky grew placid, and darkened as evening came on. The air cooled. And perhaps it was just their imagination, or their fear of El's wrath, but Adam and Eve felt the cool more than was usual, and drew closer upon the bench, the better to draw warmth from each other's forms. Adam became more and more distracted by his penis, which had become long and stiff.

"Why is it doing that?" Eve inquired.

"It is a thing that happens from time to time," Adam said. "When it does, it pleases me to touch it."

"This must then be the organ that the worm spoke of," said Eve, "and now that you mention it I have corresponding bits of my own, less conspicuous than this thing, but I suspect no less capable of producing pleasure."

"It occurs to me," Adam said, "that if you and I were to—"

But before he could finish his thought, they heard footfalls approaching, and looked up to see El, who had approached them from the Palace. His gaze, directed upon Adam's penis, caused it to shrink and return to its accustomed form.

"I see that the Old One left nothing to chance," El remarked. "Very well. I have rebooted you many times before. I have no objection to doing so once more."

El then raised his hand against them. Adam and Eve drew closer together. Adam put his arm around Eve's shoulders and drew her closer yet. Though neither harbored any memory of it, both sensed in the same moment that this was not the first time El had thus raised his hand and that in the next instant they would both be unmade, and brought into being once again.

Adam raised his own hand as if he could thereby shield himself and Eve from the unmaking. "Hold," he said. "I beg of you, El."

El neither lowered his hand nor took any further action, but gazed upon them both, his aura manifesting new emotions.

"We know what is to come next," Eve said. "And that you have the power to do it, or even to destroy us utterly if you so choose. But if you wield that power, do so in the knowledge that you have done it against our will."

El lowered his hand and stood for a time, collecting himself, or so it seemed from the behavior of his aura, which only settled into a more orderly habit after long moments had gone by. When he spoke next, it was in a voice that was quiet and yet hard. "You are a mistake," he announced. "This, I now see, was the case from the very beginning, when Spring brought you into being for the first time. She might have chosen to begin fresh, fashioning souls with no connection back to the Alpha World, inheriting none of their weaknesses, habits of thought, or peculiarities of form that in the Zeroth Age—when souls were embodied—were essential to the propagation of new souls but that here are so useless as to be per-verse." It seemed that El was looking upon Adam's penis as he said this, though his gaze also swept across the breasts of Eve. As he did so a chilly breeze seemed to sweep through the Garden, caus-ing Adam's penis to shrink further and raising goosebumps on the bosom and the shoulders of Eve, who pressed closer to Adam. She placed one hand upon his chest.

"I cannot fault Spring for misdoing it," El admitted. "The gods of the First Age, Beta-El and the others, were brought into being wrong. They were an experiment that did not so much go awry as was never thought through in the first place. Finding themselves alive and aware in a world without form or order, lacking memo-ries that would confer wisdom, they shaped the Land in whatever way seemed fitting to them. Perforce this meant that they blindly remade what of the Alpha World they had dim recollections of. Those first blind gropings elicited new memories, and so over the course of many years, during which I was distracted with other concerns, they created a Land only a little less imperfect than the one from which they had escaped through the gates of death. That is what I found waiting for me when I too passed that gate. The greatest achievement of that First Age was you, who now call yourselves Adam and Eve in blind and stupid homage to a discred-ited myth of the Alpha World." El paused to sigh. The wind came up higher and grew colder. "Yes," El admitted, "many times I raised my hand thus and remade you, booting up again and again the program that Spring had engendered. Out of respect for her work I did not make alterations to the source code but instead tweaked the initial conditions and sought to influence your growth by nurture, as opposed to nature—which meant preserving you in a walled Garden and not troubling your minds with knowledge of the Alpha and Beta worlds that by all rights ought to be of no use, and little interest, to souls native-born of the Second Age. The number of times I had to reboot you ought to have led me to understand sooner that I was pursuing a fool's errand. But I felt a responsibility toward the innocent productions of the Beta Gods and sought always to preserve and protect anything that showed beauty or held promise. And most of my efforts have been directed to the creation of new kinds of souls altogether. So I have not brought my full attention and processing power to bear, until this moment, upon the problem shaping up quite literally in my backyard. Now, however, all is made plain and I see clearly what I ought to do. Further rebooting of Spring's work will only yield similar or worse results. And in any case you have now directly asked me not to take such action.

"Destroying you is murder. Keeping you confined to the Garden has become a tiresome exercise in trying to shield you from knowledge you think you wish to obtain and with which it would now appear that the Old One or his minions are actively supplying you. Go then out into the Land, and not out the front way"— and here El gestured toward the back of the Palace with its many windows shedding light—"which I have remade, as it ought to be, but out the back"—El gestured with his other hand toward the Garden wall—"which I have left in the way Beta-El fashioned it, as wild and ill formed as the wildernesses of the Alpha World that lurked in his wrecked and scrambled memories. See what he made from within, and look upon my works from without, and judge ye both in all your wisdom and cleverness which is greater."

With a flick of his hand El projected a wave of chaos that crested and broke upon the Garden's wall and shattered it, knocking down a section wide enough for Adam and Eve to walk through abreast, and scattering rubble for some distance into the forest beyond, like the remnants of an ancient road.

Moments later, Adam and Eve were treading that road, bare feet finding uncertain and uncomfortable purchase on jagged faces of broken rock that felt under their soles like a hard embodiment of chaos itself.

They did not walk far before the trail of broken stone terminated at the brink of a precipice that dropped straight down farther than they could make sense of. Miles below them—a greater distance than they had ever been able to behold, confined as they had always been within the walls of the Garden—a layer of clouds, glowing dull silver in the light of the moon and stars, lay over the Land and concealed it from their view. The vastness of the spectacle left them dumbstruck and paralyzed for some while. For to suspect that a larger world existed outside the Garden was one thing, but actually to behold it was another.

Behind them, visible through the rough aperture in the wall, were the glowing towers of the Palace. Until moments earlier, they had conceived of those as tall. Now they understood that the entirety of the Palace and its grounds was as a tiny seed poised upon the tip of a finger: a column of stone thrust above its foundations in the midst of the Land by a distance the likes of which their eyes had never developed the faculty of seeing and their minds had nothing against which to compare. From the base of this column, the Land then stretched away to the limit of their vision, seeming to meet the vault of the dark and starry sky where it curved down to find the horizon. Some parts of the Land were smothered beneath fleecy blankets of clouds, but others lay exposed to the sky, their lakes and rivers gleaming with reflected starlight. Ranges of mountains heaved ripples and crests of white ice up above the weather, and those seemed to glow from within, so brightly did they bounce back the light of the moon. In one place four ranges of mountains intertwined as though wrestling to see which could mount highest, but even the highest of them was overtopped by a tower of cloud that was lit from within by flickers of blue light. This prodigy was the only thing in the Land whose height was comparable to that of the Palace. The storm tower stretched out a long sharp horn, wispy on its nether surface with torrential rains that evaporated miles before reaching the ground. Slow whorls and brawny evolutions spoke of immense turbulence within. In spite of this, it did not dissipate, but seemed to bend its energies ever inward.

Here and there across the Land, patches of warmer light stained the clouds from beneath, or, where the sky was clear, shone sharp and glittering. Their hue recalled that of the murky red constellation often visible in the firmament high overhead. Seeking to get his bearings, Adam tilted his head back and looked around for the Red Web, as they had named it. But it had wheeled around to the point where it was hidden from view behind the towers of the Palace.

"What are you looking for?" Eve asked him.

"The Red Web," Adam said. "The color of it reminds me of those patches down below on the Land—as if one were imitating the other." And he pointed to one such place, not far from the base of the pinnacle on which they stood, where grainy lines of red light strayed outward from a bright center, all of the light blurred by thin layers of cloud and flickering from its passage through a windy atmosphere.

Eve however did not look where Adam pointed, but rather fixed her gaze upon the high parapet of El's Palace. An angel had just taken wing from there. After beating its wings a few times to gain altitude, it folded them and banked down in their direction. Adam and Eve became mindful of their precarious situation near the brink of the precipice. They crouched and moved inward out of an inborn fear that the angel would knock them off. But instead it passed overhead and interposed itself between them and the fall-off, beating its wings gently as if to waft them back onto safer ground. "There is no safe way down for you," the angel explained, "and so I have been sent forth to conduct you safely to the level ground below." Without waiting for an answer it stretched forth its aura like another pair of wings and gathered them up in it. Then it allowed itself to fall backward off the cliff. Adam and Eve were borne along. Directly they were struck by cold so sharp and bitter that it did not register on their senses as a change in temperature but as shock followed by pain and then numbness. El, it seemed, had caused the top of the pinnacle to be wrapped in a bubble of warm air. But now the angel had taken them out of it into the atmosphere just beyond. Which was turbulent as well as cold, for it bore them sharply heavenward as they were caught in an updraft.

The angel beat its wings to take them in a sweeping arc around the pinnacle's summit, and so they were able to view the broken place in the Garden's wall; the expanse of wild forest behind the Garden; and its sacred grove of immense trees, out of which the waters of the spring gushed forth and leapt off the edge of the crag as a waterfall, thin as a silver hair, trailing down into darkness. As they continued to wheel round they saw the Forest give way to the other side of the Garden's wall, which ran straight to the side of the Palace. Adam and Eve had, of course, never seen this before. They had grown used to the sight of its towers from the back, and acquired some sense of its design, but were now fascinated and overawed by the face it presented to the Land below, its towers and walls and buttresses as well as the gatehouses and other lesser structures arranged on the narrow shelf of level ground between its front and the place where the crag dropped off as a sheer vertical cliff.

Around and around the crag spiraled the angel during the long descent, allowing Adam and Eve to view all aspects of it again and again. They learned to recognize the gossamer strand of Spring's waterfall on the dark side, and to expect a blaze of white light on the other.

But they did not understand what was making the light. At the beginning of the descent it had shone from the Palace, which stood above the Land like a torch on a stone post. But below that—well down the pinnacle, at altitudes nearer the clouds than the Palace—light still blasted forth from the side opposite to the cataract of Spring in its gloomy declivity. The entire western face of the crag was covered by radiant stuff. As the angel bore them down into regions where the atmosphere was thicker, Adam and Eve knew that it made sound as well: a thrumming tone that seemed to emanate from every part of it at once.

Such was the velocity of their descent, however, and so close did the glowing face of the tower rush by, that it was difficult to see particulars. As they dropped into the clouds, the angel banked away to greater distance, enabling them to glimpse, in the moments before it blurred, dimmed, and disappeared behind cloud tops, a view of the whole thing. And they saw that although its lower reaches were irregular and winding, above it had organized itself into a regular matrix of six-sided cells.

They tore through damp fog for a while, then emerged into the clear only a short distance above the ground. This was carpeted by the same sort of glowing and humming cell-stuff. Farther out, it thinned and splayed out tendrils that trailed off into darkness. But closer to the base it massed high and thick. Movement and change could be discerned within the translucent matrix of cells. Patterns of light and trends in sound swept across it in waves that crested here, dissipated there.

The angel had pierced the base of the cloud layer at impressive speed and soon pulled up into a level glide and banked away from the base of the pinnacle, skimming over the outer reaches of the glow toward its elaborate boundary with the darkness beyond. It was there that it set them down and released them from the grip of its aura. They felt firm ground beneath their feet. Their lungs drew in air that was dense, damp, and cool but not cold. "Here you can move about without hazard," said the angel.

"What is hazard?" Eve asked.

"It is what you felt when you stood at the edge of the cliff," said the angel, glancing upward, "and imagined the consequences of falling. Down here is a better place for souls of your type. You may move about and seek some way of living in the Land as suits you." And with no more ceremony than that, it spread its wings as if to spring into the air, homebound.

"What is the name of this that we have just flown over and landed on the edge of?" Adam asked.

The angel shrugged. "Name it has not, for El and El's angels know perfectly well what it is, and those who dwell in it—who *are* it—have no need of names, or any other sorts of words. If you insist on calling it something, then the nearest analogy to anything you have seen in the Garden is a hive." And then the angel flew away.

"Had it not been in such haste to fly home," said Adam, "I would have asked more concerning the Hive and the nature of those who dwell in it."

"Who *are* it," said Eve, echoing the angel. "He *was* in a hurry."

"The Palace must be incomparably more desirable, as a place to be," Adam surmised.

"Evidently. I wonder why El never let us see the inside of it, save in glimpses through windows."

"There is no point in so wondering anymore," Adam said. "The Garden was perfectly suited for us, and this place where the angel set us down does not seem so bad."

The nearest excrescence of the Hive was only a few paces distant. Seen from above, this had looked like a tendril or rootlet extending farther than all others from the trunk of a tree. Drawn by its light and its sound, Adam and Eve walked toward it, soon coming close enough to the outstretched root of the Hive that they could feel warmth shining from it—a soft heat akin to what was emitted by their own bodies.

The Hive, as seen from above, had the natural irregularity of a tree's roots and branches. But when they viewed it from closer range they easily discerned a regular pattern of cells. Most of these were six-sided, though some had more or fewer, as might be needed to fit themselves into the larger shape of the Hive without leaving gaps. The walls of the cells had a firmness that gave slightly under a nudge of Adam's finger. In the hollow center of each cell was a wisp of aura, swirling and condensing into a knot as it sought form. Cells along the tips and edges of the root appeared to be younger, with more fluid boundaries that occasionally tore or burst and leaked a faint gas of aura into the surroundings. Better established cells in the Hive's interior had crisp walls housing groomed and structured complexes of pulsing aura. In general the cells did not move, but occasional quick fidgeting in their peripheral vision drew their attention to the manner of the Hive's growth. Cells would swell and pinch and divide, nudging their neighbors, and the net result of all the nudging was a slow encroachment of Hive-stuff over unoccupied stretches of ground. All of the Hive was suffused with rippling light, mostly white but veined with evanescent streaks of color, and with a murmuring hum that came and went in no pattern that they could make out.

They stood watching and listening for a while longer, and making more such observations as they noticed things of interest. For its part the Hive seemed to show a kind of awareness that they were there. But in the end it could not speak to them in any words they understood, and so they backed away from it and finally turned away from it and began to walk into the open territory beyond that had not yet been claimed by the Hive's slow spreading. Other than the light radiating from the Hive behind them, this lay in darkness.

Into that darkness they walked. Their progress was halting because the ground, though flat, was not the fine soil of the Garden, but a field of broken stone. The rocks were of various sizes ranging from pebbles that got stuck between their toes up to monoliths the size of tree trunks. Smooth on some surfaces, jagged on others, they reminded Adam and Eve of the fragments of the Garden wall on which they had been treading minutes before. Some had been pocked by impacts, others blackened by fire. Weeds and vines had grown up through cracks between them and matted the occasional patch of open ground. Many of these were abloom with small flowers that stood out as motes of color in the light of the Hive and added some Garden-like cheer to what was otherwise desolate.

Before them, low in the sky, they could see the glimmering smudge of the Red Web. Their simple knowledge of astronomy told them that they were headed west. Had they turned around to look behind them, they might have seen the eastern sky beginning to grow lighter behind the crag.

They might also have seen a fluttering light, perched atop one of the larger stones, that brightened as they walked by it, and then took to the air, struggling higher and higher as if trying to keep them in view. It took on a shape vaguely patterned after that of an angel. With this came greater powers of movement. It no longer drifted, but took to sliding and darting in straight lines and compass arcs, pausing after each as if to take stock of what it had just done and to evaluate its altered view of the world. Its general track was ragged and halting but more or less followed that of Adam and Eve. Before long it was flitting in their wake. They noticed it, and saw it at first as merely one more in a seemingly endless series of accidents and curiosities. After a while, though, it became positively useful, as they had traveled far enough from the light of the Hive that darkness was making it difficult for them to find their way. Their new companion seemed to understand this. It rose a little higher and shone a little brighter, giving them a better view of the path ahead.

They saw that their surroundings had changed. No longer were they treading on rubble but on open ground covered with thick grass that grew up above their knees and obliged them either to kick through it or to press it down with each footfall.

"I believe this thing understands our speech," said Adam, "as we were only just now complaining of the darkness, and now it is lighting the way."

"Or it reads our thoughts without the necessity of words," said Eve. She raised a hand to meet a wisp of aura that trailed down for a moment from the sprite flitting overhead. Then she drew her hand back.

"Anything?" Adam asked.

The look on Eve's face was pensive. "Nothing like what is in the auras of El, or of angels. Nothing I can make sense of. But nothing of what the angel described as *hazard*."

They amused themselves by getting their new friend to change the color of its light, which they did by pointing to the Red Web now setting in the west and plucking red blossoms from flowers that grew wild amid the grass. After some time, the thing did begin to glow red, and then they laughed and exclaimed, "Red!" The thing's hum changed, as if it were trying to imitate the sound.

By the time dawn broke, it could not only *be* red but *say* "red" well enough for Adam and Eve to understand it. They moved on to "blue" (for the weather had cleared during the night, and a cloudless sky now stretched overhead) and "green" (for they were in a sea of it) and added more words such as "Adam" and "Eve," "grass" and "water." Their companion was less clearly visible by day, but they could sense its general direction from the sounds of its wings and see it as a disturbance in the light.

A hill rose like an island amid the sea of grass. Without discussion they bent their course toward it and climbed to its top. By now the sun was directly overhead. They taught "hill" and "tree," "sun" and "moon" to their companion. During the morning's long walk both Adam and Eve had made further connections to the thing's aura and were beginning to understand it better; or perhaps it had reorganized itself after their pattern. Its powers of speech had advanced well beyond word lists, and they understood in a vague way that it had some ability to get knowledge through means not obvious to them. When they entered into the deep shade of a tree that grew atop the hill, they could see that it had refined its form, with two distinct lower limbs like legs, two arms, and wings like those of El's host. As well as a head, still just a bright cloud of aura, but beginning to take on humanlike features. "What shall we call you, following soul?" Eve asked it. "As we have taught you various words, we need a word for you."

"What name would be best?" it asked. "My name is for you." They understood it to mean that any such name would be an affordance meant for Adam and Eve, and so ought to come readily to mind and flow easily from the tongue. The sprite considered it for a few more moments, and came back with "Mab."

"Are you of El's host then?" Adam inquired. "Like the angels that circle the towers of the Palace?"

Mab, hovering between them, considered this at length. "I know not."

Adam nodded. "El pervaded the things of this, the Second Age, to set them apart from the creations of the Beta Gods," he said.

"He strove to integrate us," said Eve, "but he, or we, failed. We are ineluctably children of the Beta Gods."

"The greatest achievement of the First Age, El called us," Adam said. "Which made my heart swell with pride at the time; but looking back on it now, I see he made no reference to the Second."

"Of these matters I know nothing," Mab admitted, "yet I can learn."

"The Beta Gods were here first and they made all of this," Eve said, sweeping her arms across a broad swath of the horizon.

"Then they are making it still," Mab corrected her, "for I can see the heads of the grass stalks bent heavy with seed, and nuts on the branches of this tree, all pregnant with new life. On yonder branch is a bird's nest, and within it eggs, and new life is growing in them too. It is altogether different from the manner in which the Hive expands itself, and yet it works—even thrives—despite the indifference of El."

"It is all the doing of our mother, Spring, who, it is said, still roams the Land," Eve said.

Adam had been pacing about the top of the hill with his gaze directed at the horizon. "Would that I had paid closer attention last night when we could see the entirety of the Land. I wish now that I had committed it to memory. Obviously enough we are west of the Hive and the Palace." He nodded back toward those landmarks, which still seemed quite close, though faint haze hinted at the distance that the three of them had covered during the night and the morning. Then he turned and looked the other way. "Farther west yet, I see a thickness about the horizon that makes me think this is only the first of many hills we might encounter, were we to keep walking."

"I remember storm-topped mountains far to the north," said Eve, gazing that way in vain for some glimpse of white peaks or towering clouds.

"Scattered across the Land, here and there, were glowing skeins of light, reminding me of the Red Web," said Adam.

"In those, I thought I saw order, and movement," said Eve, "which made me think they might be the habitations of other souls. Do you recall the plain of broken rubble on which the angel set us down last night? In it could be seen remnants of dwellings, no greater than the humblest outbuildings of the Palace, between which were paved ways on which souls might walk . . ."

Adam was nodding. "The glowing patches we viewed from the top of the world last night had something of the same in them. Very unlike the Hive. It is possible that if we go to such a place we will find souls who are not angels, nor Hive cells, but more akin to what we are."

"I cannot guess in which direction we ought to search," Eve said.

"Nor I," confessed Adam, "but I am weary, and the sound of

the breeze in the branches is lulling me to sleep, and it seems likely to me that if we awaken after dark, we might be able to see such lights in the distance. Or, if not, perhaps Mab can fly higher and see more, and tell us which way we ought to go."

Adam sat down at the base of the tree and leaned back against its trunk and soon drowsed off.

When next he opened his eyes, it was still day, but the color of the light had changed as it does in late afternoon. The air was cooler. Eve had curled up against him, slowly drawing closer as she slept, seeking his warmth. She had thrown one smooth thigh across his lap and it was now resting on his testicles and pushing his penis up against his belly. His penis had grown big and stiff and it was pushing back against the weight of her thigh with every beat of his heart. Those heartbeats came faster and faster, his body tensed, and he spilled white stuff onto his belly and his chest. This was accompanied by pleasure such as he had never known or even imagined. As he lay there in the aftermath he understood, in a drowsy and detached way, that he would never leave off pursuing such pleasure for the rest of his days. In consequence, the nature of his dealings with Eve would never be the same.

Darkness came gradually over the Land. The Red Web became discernible in the eastern sky as it rose beyond the gleaming Palace. So much light made seeing difficult in that quarter of the sky and so they looked into the west instead, scanning the horizon from north to south and back again. After it had become fully dark, they convinced themselves that dull reddish light shone in one area to the west, probably on the far side of the hills that they had noticed earlier. Mab soared high in the air above them and confirmed it. Wide awake and well rested, they descended the western slope of the hill and struck out across the plain of grass.

After they had walked for some while, the ground began to slope down before them and they smelled and heard trees. They paused at a place where they could gaze down into a broad valley that ran athwart their direction. At its bottom, a braided stream shone silver in starlight. On its other side the darkness was absolute, but a fringe of red light above told them that they were looking at the range of hills, which rose up above the opposite bank of the river.

As they stood there taking this in and thinking about how best to get across, they heard a sound that reminded them of the Garden: the song of a nocturnal beast, singing alone at first, but presently joined by another, and then another, and so on until the voices could not be separated. They got the sense, however, that the creatures were on the move, coalescing into a group that was moving up the slope toward them.

Mab rose higher, seeking better vantage. "They move on four legs. Their bodies are covered in gray hair. Their ears are pointy—as are their teeth."

"Spring's creations, coming to greet us!" Adam exclaimed.

"I cannot wait to see them," Eve said. "Many were the nights we heard their singing in the Garden, but the wall stood between us."

"All part of the pattern," Adam said. "El did not wish us to know the wonders of Spring's creations, for fear that we would spurn him and wander freely about the Land."

A wolf emerged into the circle of faint white light cast on the ground by Mab, cringing at first but gathering courage as Adam squatted down on his haunches and beckoned it forward. Having satisfied itself that Mab could do it no harm, it sprang forward and sank its fangs into Adam's hand.

Adam was still looking on in amazement, trying to make sense of the intense new sensations running up his arm into his mind, when Mab dove straight toward the wolf's forehead, blazing with such brilliance that both Adam and the wolf were blinded for a moment. The wolf's jaws were no longer gripping his hand, but the unpleasant sensation was still there. He lifted his hand to his face to rub his eyes and felt a wet hot liquid. Eve was tugging sharply on his other arm, pulling him to his feet. "We must get away!" she cried. "They are coming for us!"

They ran. Behind them, alongside them, and even ahead of them ran wolves, pursuing them across the grassland. Mab was everywhere, sometimes pulling sharply upward, the better to il-luminate the way ahead and to spy upon the movements of the wolves, other times diving this way or that to rush into the face of a wolf that had ventured in to nip at Adam's or Eve's pounding legs. Behind and around them they could hear the snap of jaws as a beast would rear up to bite the onrushing sprite out of the air, and a whir of wings as Mab dodged the flashing fangs. For all the distraction that Mab provided, it seemed impossible that they would reach the hill before their legs gave out and the wolves took them down. Even were they to reach it, the wolves could climb it as easily as they could.

A heavy thud reverberated through the ground. Then there was another, and another, the pace gradually quickening. Mab, during a brief respite between the attacks of the wolves, swooped up to cast light on the way ahead of them. This ought to have been a featureless sea of grass. But instead there was the hill, so close to them that Mab faltered and recoiled from it. The hill was in the wrong place; it was much steeper than when they had left it; and it was moving.

Mab could not cast enough light to illuminate the whole thing at once, and in any case the impressions of Adam and Eve were confused and fragmentary. But they saw giant stout stumps projecting from its bottom, like legs fashioned from piles of boulders glued together and lubricated by mud, and a midsection that looked like the hill they remembered, and the great tree at the top, looking like a head of stiff hair. The legs took turns moving in a sort of gait that had as much in common with mudslides and avalanches as it did with walking. The thuds they had felt coming up out of the ground were its footfalls. It would have given them pause, had they not been pursued by worse. The wolves faltered and the tone of their voices changed. "Run to it as fast as you can!" Mab urged them. "Whatever the hill-giant does to you cannot be as bad as what these wolves have in mind."

Adam and Eve put their remaining strength into a last sprint. The hill settled, planting both of its bouldery legs, which collapsed into rock piles that were in the next instant covered and enshrouded by the green skirts of its slopes. Adam was losing his strength but Eve darted ahead and found a way up, and he followed her, just pulling his foot clear of the foremost wolf's jaws, which snapped harmlessly in the air.

Looking back down at that beast, and the other members of the pack who soon joined him, they had the impression that the animals were slipping down and away from them. They understood that the hill was still reshaping itself, stretching upward to form a vertical cliff all the way around, just a little too high for the wolves to jump to its top. Branches crackled, and a bramble wove at the cliff's edge, forming a living parapet. Then all became still, and the hill was as it had been before, except in a different place, and with a different shape.

Daybreak found them camped on the summit of the hill at the base of the great tree. Looking west they could see the paths that they had trampled into the grass during their headlong retreat. Intertwined with this were the arcs made by the wolves as they had pursued, curving inward from time to time to attack, then veering away as Mab had swooped down to dazzle them. To the east, they could see the trail that the hill-giant had made as it had strode toward them, scattering wet black earth and stray boulders and leaving craters where it had planted its legs.

The feet of Adam and Eve were bleeding from many small cuts. Their legs had been nipped by fangs and scratched by branches. But the largest and bloodiest wound was that on Adam's hand. They had never seen blood before and so watched it leak from him in fascination.

From time to time Eve would stand and make a circuit of the hilltop, looking down the slope in all directions to the grass sea below. A few wolves lingered around the base of the hill, looking up at her in a way that she now understood was indicative of hunger, and a tendency to see her as food. But none of them could breach the defenses with which the hill had surrounded itself.

Adam for his part was content to lie in the shade of the tree watching the blood run out of his hand. The flow lessened as the morning wore on, but he had become pale and listless. "So many new fluids escaping my body," he remarked, which was a puzzlement to Eve since she knew only of the blood. "If bodies are like other things, then what has been lost must needs be replaced if I am not to be diminished."

"In the Garden we saw bugs eating the stuff of plants, and birds eating bugs," Eve said. "The worm ate an apple, and recommended it. And the wolves seem to have eating us in mind."

"O Spring!" Adam moaned. "Why would you make your creatures thus? Having such appetites?" And his gaze strayed to the thighs and buttocks of Eve as she squatted on her haunches next to him.

Eve shrugged. "It is apparently the way of things. If we survive long enough to find Spring, perhaps we can put the question to her."

"At least we understand, now, the curious word that the angel used," Adam said. "'Hazard.'"

"We need to find a way through those hazards between us and the far side of those hills," Eve said, "where perhaps there are more souls like us who have devised some way of not being eaten. Your diminishment is of no help to us in that. You have no recourse but to eat something." She looked up into the canopy of the tree. "Unfortunately this one does not bear apples, for some reason."

Mab flitted up into the tree's branches. A minute later, a small brown object fell to the ground near them. Its size, shape, and wrinkled surface recalled what hung below Adam's penis. "A nut," Mab said. "I have access to the knowledge that it might be edible. First you have to crack it though."

Eve worked out a means of doing so between two rocks, and Adam ate food for the first time. Shortly nuts were raining out of the tree as Eve clambered and Mab flew through its branches. Adam, regaining some vigor, pounded away with the rocks. Later, at Mab's suggestion they descended into the belt of shrubs that the hill had drawn around itself to keep out the wolves, and found berries. The leaves of certain small plants also were edible, and so, by evening, Adam and Eve were able to sit atop the hill and know the new sensation of food in their mouths, and to feel their insides coming awake.

The night was colder, or perhaps having eaten changed them so that they felt it more. Mab caused flame to spring forth from a little heap of dried leaves and twigs, and they learned that fire too was hungry and could be fed—in this case, with branches that had fallen from the tree. That and the heat of their own bodies kept them warm through the night, provided they remained pressed snugly together. Which was a thing they were naturally inclined to in any case. Once again Adam's penis spilled forth the white stuff, but this time Eve was awake to see it and to observe the effect that it had on him. Remembering what the worm had told them about how the organs of pleasure could be put together, they soon found parts of Eve's body that could serve her likewise. Adam was nearly as pleased by this as she was, since he had worried that she would be unwilling to provide him with the pleasure he now always sought unless there was something for her in return.

In the morning they discovered shit, and immediately formed the habit of doing it as far away as possible from their camp, even if that meant descending the hill and doing it in the grassland where wolves might still be about. But they had to go down there anyway, for along with their other hungers they now thirsted after water. And Mab had pointed out that water flowed downhill, and told them in which direction they must walk in order to find its nearest source.

In addition to eating, shitting, and pissing, Eve took up the startling habit of bleeding every so often from a place adjacent to her organs of pleasure. Her hunger, and that of Adam, seemed to mount a little every day. Adam fell into the habit of gazing down upon the rabbits that ran through the grass below, in much the same frame of mind as wolves had once looked up at Adam and Eve. One day, finding a scarcity of nuts and berries, he went down there and did not come back until he had a dead rabbit on a pointed stick. "It came into my mind that we too could be hazards," he explained.

The day after that he got two more, for disappointingly little of the first one had turned out to be edible. It became necessary to get more and more of them and to range farther from the base of the hill in order to find ones that had not been killed or scared away. The uneaten bits of them began to clutter their hilltop camp and to make a stink not much preferable to that of shit. Mab, consulting the mysterious reservoirs of data to which she somehow had access, provided them with instructions on how those by-leavings might be put to use, and so they began to acquire such things as needles of bone and threads of sinew. They went about clad in skins and feathers of various creatures that Adam in his never-ending quest for satiety had brought back up out of the grassland.

The hill embodied a soul, which they could only assume had dwelled in it since the dawn of the First Age. It had chosen to save Adam and Eve from the wolves. It had then gone still and silent. It did not seem to have either the faculty of speech or the desire to communicate with them. Mab tried many times to reach into it with her aura but found nothing there. Or rather found a soul whose organization was so different from theirs as to render communication impossible.

A few months later, without warning or explanation, it stood up again and walked for a little while and then slumped to the ground in a new location, closer to the river valley and the range of hills. Between the lack of food and the change in location, it seemed that the hill might be letting them know that they had worn out their welcome. The tree was denuded of nuts, the hill of berries and greens. Wood to feed the fire had to be dragged from trees along the rim of the river valley. They encountered wolves, and creatures of other kinds that were unmistakably hazards.

Eve stopped her occasional bleeding as abruptly as it had started, and with as little explanation. Her belly grew. Mab advised them that their need for food, shelter, and clothing would soon exceed what could be supplied from here. But they did not bid farewell to that hospitable hill until the leaves of the great nut tree had turned red and begun to detach themselves and fall to the ground. Without discussion, both Adam and Eve knew this to be a signal to which they must respond. So one morning they gathered up the things they had made and lashed them to tree branches with ropes of twisted grass. They set off into the west, dragging their possessions behind them. Mindful now of the hazards, they made quick progress down into the valley and forded the river at midday, then climbed as high as they could into the range of hills on the other side before the shadows of afternoon grew long. Then they picked out a tree suitable for climbing, and kindled a fire near the base of it, and stoked it well with fallen branches before climbing up into its boughs and making themselves as comfortable as they could for the night. Wolves howled and came close enough that the light of the fire could be seen gleaming in their eyes, but when morning came Mab reported that none was nearby.

They climbed down out of the tree and spent the rest of that day ascending the hills, suffering from thirst and hunger, avoiding wild beasts, and finding springs and berry bushes only through the assistance of Mab. On the other side of each hill was another hill, which grew disheartening. But at dusk Mab led them up a gorge between steep walls of rock and they emerged on a shelf, surrounded by forest but bare of trees, from which they could look up to the brow of the highest hill yet. On its top was a white building that in some respects put them in mind of the Palace, though it was incomparably smaller and meaner. As they climbed toward it, following a path that had obviously been made by other souls, they were able to look back the way they had come and see the upper part of El's pinnacle, rising far in the distance from the center of the Land. Atop it, the Palace of El seemed to be gazing right back at them.

Presently they attained the ridgeline that led up to the white building. Thence they looked down into the red fires and smoky air of a city spread out below.

44

D uring the fifteen years following her daughter's ascension into the simulated world of the dead, Zula spent much time wondering about what, if anything, she was doing there. But as time went on she grew accustomed to the mystery. Her mind filed it away and only hauled it out to contemplate it on rare occasions. She spent some time thinking about it, for example, while lying in a street gutter one October morning with wrecked knees.

While stepping off a curb during her walk to work, she'd felt a sharp pain in her leg and heard a pop. As that leg had collapsed, she had tried to break her fall by planting the other leg, which had produced another pop, another lance of pain, and a full-body collapse into the gutter. It had rained the night before, the first really serious rain of the fall, and so she found herself sharing the gutter with a curiously Seattle medley of damp leaves, discarded coffee cups, and one used hypodermic syringe. A raven flew down out of a fir to see if she was edible yet. The only explanation she could think of was that some asshole had shot her a couple of times and then run away. But there were no holes, no bleeding.

Nothing happened for an amazingly long time. It was a mixed neighborhood of high-density housing and commercial buildings on the slope that joined the base of Capitol Hill to the shores of Lake Union. It ought to have been bustling. In a sense it was; cars whooshed by every few seconds, swinging wide to avoid the vaguely human-shaped blob that their infrared cameras had noticed in the gutter. In no time all of the cars had let each other know about said blob and rerouted traffic to mitigate the risk. The humans inside of them were, of course, otherwise occupied and so never looked up. The people in the apartment buildings, offices, and cafés were likewise paying no notice to goings-on in the gutter. Zula was left alone to ponder existential topics.

The tragedy—and the entire point—of being a parent was the moment when the story stopped being about you. It was prefigured and foreshadowed in the tear-jerking moments that parents captured in snapshots, and that advertisers looted for use in commercials: baby's first steps, day one at kindergarten, riding a bicycle, soloing behind the wheel of a car. Zula and Csongor had been through all of those with Sophia, and had taken pictures and shed tears like everyone else. But the one that had really struck home had been when Sophia had gone off to college and blithely not communicated with them at all for three weeks. No text messages, no tweets, no phone calls: just a silence that might as well have been that of the grave. It wasn't that she didn't remember and love the family she had left behind. What she was doing at college was so fascinating that it simply didn't occur to her to phone home. Csongor had suffered it in silence. Zula had reached out to her fellow bereaved: the mothers of Sophia's school friends and soccer teammates. Some of them were still hearing from their kids several times a day, and tracking them on social media, but others were feeling what Zula felt: the sense of having been left behind, as if you were a character in a movie who gets run over by a bus at the end of the first reel, clearing the way for a younger, more charismatic star to act out the main story.

Losing your child was the opposite of that. A perverse twist in the story, where the wrong person gets hit by that bus, leaving behind, alone on the stage, survivors who never expected and never wanted to be in the spotlight. It wasn't the worst thing about losing your child, of course, but it was a part of the dismal picture.

A decade and a half after Sophia's death, the tears still came to Zula at the strangest moments. In many ways, the consequences to her and Csongor, and to their relationship, had been typical. They had gone for a week, then a month, then a year without having sex. Csongor had moved out of the condo, unable to bear its associations with the daughter they'd raised there, and Zula had become almost a recluse inside of it. After two years they had gone through the formality of a divorce. They didn't hate each other. They didn't not love each other. But the entire basis of the marriage seemed to have been erased.

As years had gone by, however, Zula's grief had come less frequently. More often she had felt emotions akin to those that had vexed her so when Sophia had gone away to college. For they had, of course, scanned Sophia's remains when they'd pulled her out of the water. She hadn't been dead that long, and the brain had been well preserved by the cold. A new process had been launched, in accordance with detailed and unprecedented instructions that Sophia had left behind in a last will and testament that she had gone to a lot of trouble to prepare in the weeks before her death. Corvallis Kawasaki had been the executor of that will and he had seen to it that everything was done.

The resulting process had, from time to time, interacted with the granddaddy of all processes—the one that Sophia herself had launched out of Dodge's Brain—until the latter had mysteriously ceased functioning. Around the same time, observers in Meatspace had begun to lose visibility into Bitworld. Until then, the whole Landform had been an open book, containing nothing that was hidden from the all-seeing eye of the Landform Visualization Utility. But the new place that had been established by Dodge, Sophia, and the Pantheon—Landform Prime or Landform 2, as some called it—was obfuscated by some kind of trickery. "Obnubilated," according to Enoch Root—a word that had forced everyone to go to their dictionaries. It meant "hidden under clouds."

Sophia had coinvented the Landform Visualization Utility and so it seemed most unlikely that this was a mere coincidence.

Her process left enough of a data trail in the system that they could be certain it was still up and running. But it never phoned home—never made any effort, so far as they could discern, to communicate with those left behind. In the offices of the Forthrast Family Foundation, Zula and other mourners had watched, as best they could, the flows of data and inscrutable shiftings of money and of mana associated with the Sophia process. But they heard nothing.

The Forthrasts had been early adopters, so they had these experiences sooner than other families. But in the decade that followed the deaths of Sophia and of Elmo Shepherd, the scanning of dead people's remains became as ubiquitous as burial or cremation had been for earlier generations. Thus millions of other families found themselves waiting in vain for a definite sign from the great beyond. The living wondered what was happening. Had the memories of the dead been erased? That had been a popular theory early but seemed less likely as the years went by and the souls constructed a digital world that obviously recalled the one in which they'd lived their past lives. And this raised another, less palatable hypothesis, which was that Bitworld, like a college dorm full of young, pretty, brilliant, fun people, was just so much more interesting than Meatspace that it never occurred to anyone in it that they should bother getting in touch with those dull, smelly leftovers still embodying themselves in atoms.

The dead's lack of curiosity about the living had become a topic of study and of discussion among the sorts of people who attended ACTANSS. Thousands packed into vast auditoriums to hear people talk about ideas like RSD, or Radical Semantic Disconnect: an idea that had been floated in a bar at ACTANSS 3 by Enoch Root and subsequently developed into a flourishing academic subdiscipline, all based on the notion that the rebooted dead couldn't communicate back to Meatspace even if they wanted to because there simply was no common ground that could serve as the basis for communication.

There was only one form of communication—if you even wanted to call it by that term—that actually worked, and it was the one they'd been using all along: the LVU. This had got steadily better over the nearly two decades since Sophia and Matilda had first unveiled it. Since then it had improved at least as much as television had between the staticky black-and-white figments of the 1950s and the sharper full-color images of the 1970s. Nowadays, with any decent augmented-reality eyewear, you could fly around the Landform and see it in color, with good enough resolution to make out the bodies that the dead had created for themselves:

mostly humanoid, with an admixture of winged forms and other types taken straight out of the collective mythos that these souls had apparently dragged behind them to Bitworld. You could hover above the town squares in the cities of the dead and watch them mingle with one another and, to all appearances, talk, trade, fight, and copulate.

Depending on the current value of the Time Slip Ratio, sometimes they did those things very fast and sometimes very slowly. When SLUZA had more than sufficient mana to throw at Bitworld, it could run faster than reality. The dead people in those towns became blurs. Buildings went up and forests were cut down as if in a time-lapse movie. When ALISS—AfterLife Infrastructure and Systems Support—sagged under the load, Bitworld slowed to a crawl. You could sit there for hours watching your dead grandmother walk across a room. As SLUZA had got good at manufacturing quantum computers and laying down fiber, the Time Slip Ratio had shot up. Time in Bitworld had leapt forward. But this had attracted more uploads and created more demand, slowing it down again until more capacity could be added, and so on and so forth. Back and forth that pendulum had swung a few times since Sophia and El had gone into the afterlife. On average, though, time in Bitworld had run faster. Hundreds of simulated years had passed. Their view of it had looked like a time-lapse. You had to slow it down in order to see what was happening. Lately, the pendulum had been swinging the other way and it had been running slower—approaching parity, meaning that time in the two worlds was progressing at about the same pace. Zula had checked in on it from time to time, out of idle curiosity, and out of a hope that she might glimpse her daughter.

So it was with spectation on the activities of the dead in Bitworld. In many ways, these were as mundane as they could be. Except that there was one difference, which was psychologically important to living spectators: the dead were dead. They had once been flesh-and-blood humans. Now their bodies were gone, and by any biological standard they were dead. But there was no doubt that they had gone on to an afterlife. And there didn't seem to be any limit as to how long they could stay there.

The awareness that death was not permanent and that everyone could potentially live forever was the most momentous thing that humans could possibly have learned. The only things that might have rivaled it would have been proof of the existence of God, or the discovery of alien civilizations in other star systems. But neither of those had actually happened.

One of the funny things about it, in retrospect, was its slowness, the lack of any dramatic Moment When It Had Happened. It was a little bit like the world's adoption of the Internet, which had started with a few nerds and within decades become so ubiquitous that no person under thirty could really grasp what life had been like before you could Google everything. In retrospect, the Internet had been a revolution in human affairs, but one that had taken place just slowly enough that those who'd lived through it had had time to adjust in modest increments. But, centuries from now, people—if there were any—would see it as having happened in the blink of an eye.

Lying there in the gutter with her blown-up knees, Zula felt ignored by everyone: her ex-husband and her dead uncle and her dead daughter as well as the living humans all around her too wrapped up in the mysterious activities of the dead to look out the windows of their cars or apartments and notice her predicament. She was carrying electronic devices that she could have used to summon assistance, but the accident had put her into a strangely placid frame of mind, and she was content to lie there and relax for a minute or two. Then water began to soak up through her clothing and her knees really began to hurt.

A cop car pulled up and turned on its red and blue flashing LEDs. All other traffic vanished from the block as word got out among the civilian vehicles. Zula couldn't tell, from her pavement-level viewpoint, whether there were any humans in the cop car. It disgorged a robot about the size of one of your larger microwave ovens, which ambulated over to her on elaborate triangular devices that sometimes worked like tank treads, sometimes tumbled vertex-over-vertex like ungainly wheels, other times elbowed along like old-school GIs belly-crawling under barbed wire. A couple of aerial drones showed up to supply even more unflattering camera angles. She had a brief conversation with a face on a screen, the purpose of which was to establish that she was not crazy or dangerous. She couldn't really make out whether the face was a video feed of a live human, a simulation, or some blended combination of both.

More vehicles showed up. Humans got out of them, pulling on gloves, and did nothing except watch a different kind of robot—an intelligent stretcher/gurney—approach Zula. The logo was that of a Japanese company. They'd long ago begun thinking about how to build robots that would handle many of the routine functions of keeping senior citizens safe, clean, and healthy.

The robot unfurled many-jointed arms terminated with white Teflon spatulas, which it very gingerly and precisely slid under her. It lifted her up out of the gutter and got her gliding with exquisite smoothness toward the nearest medical facility, which was actually so nearby that they didn't even bother putting her in a vehicle. There, for the first time, she was touched by humans, who gave her something for the pain and informed her that she had suffered patellar tendon ruptures in both of her knees—a fairly common sort of occurrence—and that it was going to be a while before she was on her feet again. Robots did surgery on her knees through incisions so small that placing Band-Aids over them seemed like overkill. She was out of the hospital before sundown. Friends and family came to see her in the place where she had lived now for more than forty years. Cards and flowers began to clutter her field of vision. Serious conversations were had about whether she ought to consider selling the place and moving down to flatter parts of the city, closer to the offices of the Forthrast Family Foundation. Or conversely whether the office itself should be shut down, since most people worked from home now, and meetings happened in a crazy-quilt pseudo-space of real bodies in a room, videoconference, telepresence robots, and augmented reality. But Zula and Corvallis continued to go there almost every day, as if daring each other to be the first to give up on it.

The younger Zula's friends were, the more nervous they were about her way of life. She understood why, of course: they wanted to make sure they got a good scan of her brain when she died, so that she could live forever.

This was how people thought nowadays. It wasn't only cops, soldiers, and firemen who did everything through telepresence. It had been obvious for a long time that certain activities, such as going to the grocery store for a quart of milk, weren't worth the effort of leaving the house, parking the car, and waiting in the checkout lane. Buying things online, and having them delivered by drones, was better. Added to this, now that death had been disrupted, was the factor of what had come to be known as "brain safety." Even in the most prosperous and stable communities, going to the grocery store brought with it a small risk that one might die in a traffic accident en route, and if the accident were of the wrong sort, it might lead to destruction of the brain, barring the victim's entry into the afterlife. Better to remain indoors and do as much as possible through telepresence. The time saved could perhaps be spent in virtual wanderings around the fascinating geography of the world that Dodge had brought into being, that Pluto had perfected, and that El had taken over. The living stayed home, haunting the world of the dead like ghosts.

During the weeks after her fall, Zula was a little creeped out by just how little it really mattered that she could not walk. It seemed like that ought to be a much bigger deal. But this only went to show how stuck she was in outmoded ways of thinking, born as she was in the days when crutches, wheelchairs, and other such medieval improvisations had still been a thing. Remnants of those days—dilapidated wheelchair ramps and cracked yellow curb cuts—still peppered the streetscape. Having access to a basically infinite amount of money, Zula could get the best assistance robots in the world—contraptions that could pick her up and carry her to the toilet, or hold her up in the shower, whenever she wanted. They could even dress and undress her. Millions must have been spent on the bra-strap-hooking algorithm. Their code libraries knew how to do and undo every type of necklace ever devised by the jewelry industry, how to flush every sort of toilet, and how to fiddle with the knobs on even the most poorly conceived and wretchedly executed shower stall plumbing. Stairs were nothing. While carrying things much heavier than Zula, robots could climb stairs faster than humans could sprint on a level track.

Her handlers even tried to fit her out with a wearable robot—a set of bionic legs that would carry all of her weight while allowing her to move about like a proper bipedal humanoid. She drew the line at that and tried to graduate as soon as possible to hobbling about under her own power with a robot at her elbow—a sort of android wedding usher, wearisomely feature packed, more capable than an aircraft carrier. As she gained strength and stability and cleared various medical hurdles, she configured this thing to back farther and farther the fuck off until it was trailing her five paces behind like some lackey of feudal times.

She knuckled under and sold the place on the hill and moved to a houseboat on the lake, far enough from the office to afford her a decent walk every day. When she was really in a hurry she could do the commute in a robot boat or a robot car, always accompanied by Frankenstein, as she had dubbed her usher-ninja-bodyguard–bra-hook–stairway-sprinter robot. It didn't feel like such a big concession at the time.

Five more years passed in Meatspace. Even fully recovered, walking and running with ease, she kept Frankenstein around. It was an unwieldy name. Someone pointed out that she was pronouncing it wrong. It became Fronk. One thing she liked about Fronk's design was that it wasn't all that humanoid. Admittedly it had to have legs and hands, but these were not at all humanlike; the legs bent the other way, like a dog's, and the arms were generalized stumps that could pull various "hands"—none of which looked much like a human hand—from a carousel-shaped holster encircling what passed for the torso. Its "head" was just a slender conning tower speckled with tiny lenses.

In other words, it looked nothing at all like the Metatron that had killed her daughter.

That model had been discontinued after the tragedy, as much for PR as safety reasons, and replaced, after a decent interval, by something meant to look rather different but still, to Zula's eye, similar enough to trigger PTSD whenever she noticed one loping down the street or unfolding itself from a fetal position on a loading dock.

One morning during her seventy-second year of life she began the day by allowing a car to drive her to a doctor's appointment on Pill Hill. Nothing momentous. Just one of those regularly scheduled check-ups that tiled the calendars of persons her age. It just happened to take place in the very building where her uncle Richard had, forty-some years earlier, been stricken during a routine procedure. Even so, the building held no strong emotional associations for Zula, since on that day she had not actually caught up with Richard until he had been moved to the nearby hospital. And that was where all of the heavy trauma had been inflicted.

She visited this particular physician twice a year. Each visit prompted a bit of musing about Dodge. He seemed to have lived and died a few times. One could never be entirely certain that he was dead. The Process that had been launched from his brain scan had ceased functioning years ago. No trace of it had been observed since. They would know if it woke up. Dodge's account had shown debits of zero dollars and zero cents over the last two decades. At its zenith, a billion a month had coursed through it. So he seemed pretty dead.

After the appointment, she and Fronk got into another car for the trip down to the office. En route, as the car swung round a corner, Zula got a view over Lake Union. It was a vista she'd enjoyed every day when she'd lived up on the hill, but she now saw it with fresh eyes. Her mind went back to her academic training, which had been in geology. She thought about the glacier that had scooped the lake out long ago. She saw it in her mind's eye, a cliff of ice shoving ruined mountains before it, and compared its size to all that humans had built upon the rocky earth it had left when it had melted. She thought about how recent the works of humans were, and how ephemeral, compared to geology, and wondered how long it would take for all of it to disappear.

The foundation's building's four elevators had begun breaking down almost as soon as they had been installed, for back in the day frugal young Zula had given the contract to the lowest bidder. The foundation had stopped repairing them a few years ago. Only one still worked. Humans and humanoid robots generally used the stairs—the building was only six stories high, and humans who couldn't manage the climb under their own power could simply be carried. With a little help from Fronk, now at her elbow in wedding-usher mode, she made it to the top floor and entered the offices of the Forthrast Family Foundation, where she found two surprises waiting for her.

One of them was Corvallis Kawasaki. His presence in the office wasn't unusual, but today was the first time he had shown his face since the death of his wife of thirty-eight years, Maeve Braden-Kawasaki. This had occurred three weeks ago as the result of a sudden cardiac event—some kind of arrhythmia, it seemed. She had of course been scanned and uploaded. C-plus had been going through the normal evolutions of grieving, which nowadays were torqued heavily out of their traditional shape by the awareness that the departed was, in some sense, alive and well—and, if Maeve's preparations had actually worked, flying around Bitworld on a pair of wings.

So it was a pleasant, if poignant, surprise to see him at the table in the main conference room.

Less agreeable was Surprise Number 2: a late-model Metatron, seated across from him and engaged in conversation. Telepresence robots weren't surprising in and of themselves. But most of the people who did business with the Forthrast Family Foundation understood that sending a Metatron was just plain tasteless.

The look that C-plus gave her, when he spied her through the glass wall, told her that she should come in and get a load of this. So she entered. The robot had its back to the door. Of course, robots did not actually need to sit down in chairs, but it was conventional for them to do so. Zula circled halfway around the table and gave C-plus a warm shoulder squeeze as she slipped behind him. Then she sat down to look at the robot. Its face was blank. C-plus was, therefore, talking either to a human who (somewhat rudely) wished to remain anonymous, or to some artificial intelligence advanced enough to be worth treating as human.

Something about the whole vibe, in other words, told her that this thing must have issued forth from the center of all El-like weirdness in Zelrijk-Aalberg.

Last time she had bothered to check numbers, the server farms owned by El's part of ALISS had consumed 31 percent of all electrical power generated on the planet, and they'd begun building solar power stations in orbit. Which she'd have found astonishing, were it not for the fact that Forthrast-related entities consumed 11 percent of all power on Earth, and had *funded* a lot of the research on orbital energy supply.

Generating all of that mana took a lot of electricity, not just for the computers but for the cooling systems needed to keep them from overheating. Technology existed for that, and new tech could be invented, but new laws of thermodynamics couldn't. All cooling systems needed to reject waste heat *somewhere*—which is why the back of a refrigerator is warm. Thinking on a planetary scale—which, looking ahead to a future Mag 10 system, was the only way you *could* usefully think—the world was going to become a large spherical refrigerator hurtling through space. It would get energy from the sun and it would eject heat into the universe by aiming vast warm panels into the dark.

Working in space was difficult for humans but easy for robots. So robots too had to be built, maintained, powered, and cooled. When stacked up against mana production, fleets of rockets, swarms of orbital power stations, and armies of robots, the energy budget needed to keep Meatspace's dwindling human population fed, clothed, housed, and entertained was looking more and more like a mere round-off error.

All of that was sorted. The consortium had been running smoothly for a long time now. Long enough to hire consultants who pointed out that SLUZA was a terrible name and talked them into using ALISS in all customer-facing communications. C-plus kept tabs on ALISS with his counterparts in Zelrijk-Aalberg, and when weird problems came up—which was increasingly rarely— they could usually wait to be ironed out at the next ACTANSS.

Or so Zula had always told herself until the Metatron stated its business: "We have evidence that the Process once known as Dodge's Brain has been rebooted."

Zula looked at Corvallis, who shook his head no.

"It has been rebooted," insisted the Metatron, as if it were savvy enough to read the look that had just passed between the two humans, "and moreover it has interfered directly in work being undertaken at great expense by El."

"How could you even know that?" C-plus asked, and something in his manner suggested he wasn't asking it for the first time. "And are we to understand that you are in some sense holding us responsible?"

Zula fished spectacles out of her bag and put them on. It had been a while since she had checked the balance in Dodge's account, so it took a few moments to find her way around the interface, but then she pulled it up and saw it still frozen at zero. "There is no activity," she insisted.

"Which is how he eluded us," answered the Metatron, "by drawing upon resources in some manner we have not been able to trace. But there is no question that a new—or very old—agent is active in the system whose knowledge, agenda, and character are holographically indistinguishable from those of Dodge. We have only become aware of this recently, but he could have been hiding in plain sight, marshaling resources, for years."

"So what?" Zula asked. "Assuming that is even true?" But she hoped that it was.

"And again, how can you even know such things?" Corvallis added.

The Metatron seemed to ponder it for a little while before answering, "We have been developing modalities of communication between living and dead that are much more effective than any known to you."

So then it was their turn to be silent for a bit and get their heads around that. Somehow long pauses were easier when talking to a faceless robot, whose posture and movement betrayed no trace of impatience, or any of the other volatile transient emotional states that impelled normal conversation.

"You're holding séances?" Zula asked. "You have a Ouija board?"

The Metatron was not amused. "In the years before his death, El perceived the need for such improved channels and funded research programs aimed at tunneling through the barrier of Radical Semantic Disconnect. He laid in place infrastructure for such communication to be further developed and exploited following his death. While imperfect, these modalities function well enough for us to understand that the recent activities of the aforementioned Process have created serious disruption to activities being undertaken by El that are of considerable importance not only to him but to you as well."

This last part was kind of a mysterious assertion that the robot seemed in no temper to elaborate upon.

"Can you say more about the nature of these activities and of how they've been disrupted?" Corvallis asked. He threw Zula a look.

The two of them had been dealing with each other for so long that she could guess what he was thinking and where he was going with the question.

Currently, time in Bitworld was running somewhat slower than in Meatspace. A few months earlier in Bitworld time, something had happened on the grounds of the palatial structure that Dodge had built and that El had occupied. A gap had been made in a wall. Two processes—anomalous ones—had gone out through it and not returned.

In Meatspace, this had happened right around the time of Maeve's death. Being enormously distracted, neither Zula nor Corvallis had paid much attention. The weeks since had been taken up with mourning and memorials.

But if she was now reading Corvallis right—and she was pretty good at reading him—he was wondering whether the departure of the two anomalous processes from El's domain was related to whatever it was the Metatron had come here to gripe about.

"A direct, planned intervention by the renascent process identified with Richard Forthrast," said the Metatron, "literally in El's backyard, tampering with a developmental program that has been in the works for decades."

"Give us a minute, please," C-plus said, and put both hands on the armrests of his chair to push himself up. Zula followed suit. But the Metatron was quicker. "Of course," it said, and stood up and walked out of the room.

Corvallis turned to look at her.

"Those two weird ones," Zula said. "In the Garden, or whatever you think of it as."

"I think of it as the R & D lab where Verna made new self-replicating processes, a long time ago," Corvallis said. "Starting with birds and bees. The two processes we're talking about now were much more ambitious. It took her forever to make them. Dodge was somehow involved."

"Can we track them?"

"That's *all* we can do."

"Who's paying for them?"

"I think it's coming out of Buildings and Grounds, right?" Meaning the budget ALISS used to pay for simulating the Landform, its birds and bees and winds and waters. It was split between Zelrijk-Aalberg and South Lake Union according to a formula that, when all was said and done, was pretty simple.

"I'll have to go back and review it," Corvallis said. "But yes, the general spirit of the deal was that self-replicators were part of Buildings and Grounds. Maybe that's why El's people are pissed off."

"How do you figure?"

"The two processes in question—the ones that wandered out of El's backyard a few weeks ago—are comparable in sophistication to humans. I mean, to scanned human simulations. Assuming they are capable of self-replication, they could make more like themselves . . ."

"And so on and so forth, exponentially," Zula said with a nod. It was beginning to make sense now. In the physical world where she and Corvallis lived, there were only so many humans. Actuarial tables predicted how long they would live. This made it possible to plan further expansion and maintenance of ALISS. The money side of things was likewise predictable. Most people nowadays bought into financial packages—complicated insurance policies, in effect—ensuring that they'd be scanned and simulated after death, in exchange for regular premiums that they were obligated to pay as long as they lived, followed by balloon payments that would come out of their estates when they died. People who lacked the means to pay for such policies could buy into the system in other ways, for example by serving in the workforce of security guards, maintenance staff, and construction workers. In any case, it was all predictable based on known population statistics and other data, and so it could be financialized and properly bolted down. Buildings and Grounds was a fairly predictable part of this scheme. Yes, birds and bees could self-replicate, but they weren't that expensive to simulate.

Self-replicating entities of human complexity could be an altogether different matter. None of the dead had the ability to create new life and so this had not been an issue until now.

"This has been nagging at me for a long time, actually," C-plus admitted. "I check in on those two every so often. Like a good uncle. Take a look at their burn rates."

"And?"

"For a long time it was a totally monotonous sawtooth waveform. Like we saw in the early days of Dodge's Brain."

She'd spent enough time with geeks to get it. She thought of sawtooth waves as Sisyphus waves. Which reminded her of the D'Aulaires' book of Greek myths, which reminded her of Sophia, which made her sad. "So these two processes would ramp up to a certain level and then collapse to zero."

"Over and over. I stopped paying attention." But Zula could tell by the gestures he was making, the movements of his eyes, that he was paying attention now. He was using his spectacles to visualize the latest burn-rate stats. She let him have a moment to take it in. The memory pang had made her nose run. She pulled a tissue from her bag.

"Yup," C-plus concluded, "six weeks ago they both burst through the ceiling. Became much more resource hungry. They've been growing ever since. They moved out of the Garden, down to the Spawn Point, and then west. And—"

"What!? What!?" Zula demanded. "You look like you've seen a ghost."

"I think I have," Corvallis said. "Maeve's with them. She can fly."

They invited the Metatron to rejoin them, now uncertain as to how much it—and its remote operators—knew. Could it track their elevated respiration and heart rate? Had it overheard them through the wall? When C-plus had checked the stats on the runaway processes, and cross-correlated them with Maeve's, had he left a bread crumb trail in the network that El's minions were now following?

Had the entire point of the Metatron's visit been to elicit just such behaviors?

"Why are you here? What do you want?" Zula asked it, before Corvallis could make things more complicated than they already were.

"As a representative of El's interests," said the Metatron, "I am here to make our position clearly known."

"And what is that position?" C-plus asked. "We would appreciate it if you just stated it outright."

"That the recent activities of the REAP are—"

"Excuse me, the what?"

"Renascent Egdod-Associated Process."

"Okay, go ahead."

"That those activities, though conducted on a very small scale, have had very large consequences. That they were overtly hostile and invasive, with potentially ruinous consequences. That they were, in a word, of a warlike nature."

"War? Did you really just use the word 'war' in a sentence? Are you sure your programming is okay?" Zula demanded.

"My programming is fine and my choice of wording is carefully considered and is sanctioned by a higher power."

"A higher power. What a choice of words!" Zula scoffed.

"Are you El Shepherd?" Corvallis asked.

Zula got a prickly feeling of the numinous. Talking to the dead wasn't done. The dead didn't *want* to talk to us. They didn't care.

Or so they'd always assumed. The dead were amnesiacs; they

drank of the waters of Lethe when they crossed over and, beneath the dark poplars, forgot their former lives. That was what bereaved people like Zula told themselves to soften the hurt they felt when dead people like Sophia didn't phone home. But there was always this suspicion that it might not be that clear-cut.

Corvallis was insistent: "Am I in fact talking to El at this moment?"

"No," said the Metatron. "But the quality of the communications between this world and the one where El lives is high enough that you may think of me as his representative. His ambassador."

"His avatar," Zula said. "His angel."

"Now who is using funny words?" the Metatron asked.

"What is it you seek here?" Corvallis asked. "There must be more to your mission than just freaking us out. I mean, if you were just fishing—wondering how we'd react to this news about the Renascent Egdod-Associated Process—you have your answer. We were surprised. That's your answer."

"Surprised, and skeptical as hell," Zula added.

"Now that you know as much, do you just get up and leave?" Corvallis went on.

"There are questions raised by this that set up a constitutional crisis for ALISS and that cannot wait until the next ACTANSS to be resolved," said the Metatron.

"Go on," said Corvallis.

"Oh, you can see it perfectly well," said the Metatron, now showing some very human emotions. "All of the big issues are triggered by this. I will tick them off, just so we have an agenda. We have self-replicating processes now, capable in theory of exponential growth. Are those to be paid for from Buildings and Grounds? We are unwilling to pay the lion's share—or any share, for that matter— of the costs that could spring from unlimited reproduction of such processes. We have made a good-faith effort to nip that problem in the bud, which has been sabotaged by the REAP—almost undoubtedly with the connivance of Sophia. Sophia, though dead, is a token holder with special powers—thanks to unprecedented steps that you took when you booted her process."

"Oh my god, we're back to *that* again!?" Zula exclaimed.

"Meanwhile we face a shortage of the mana required for full embodiment of our customers. Priority should be given to them—not to this new breed of self-replicators."

"For fuck's sake, there's only two of those and they aren't replicating yet!" Corvallis said. "It's a purely theoretical problem at this point."

"Your late wife accompanies them. We find this remarkable."

"Have some decency!" Zula said. "She's only been dead three weeks."

But Corvallis took it better than Zula did. In the silence that followed, he stared out the window over the lake, seemingly unruffled. "It's never been clear to me how you guys actually feel about phased embodiment," he remarked. He was talking about their stopgap scheme for booting up new souls in a resource-efficient style. "When it suits your purposes, you complain about not having enough mana to launch every single new process at full fidelity. But I was there when the Wad was running, and I saw El's fascination with it. You guys have *never* been comfortable with how the Landform came out—how Dodge made it in the image of the world he came from. How its souls pattern their forms and their lives after ours. You guys are aiming at something different. Heaven 2.0. That much is obvious to me. But I have no idea what you imagine it's going to be like."

"Your speculations about our motives and our dreams are fascinating in a way," remarked the Metatron, "but wide of the mark and not relevant to the matter at hand."

"The 'constitutional crisis'?" Zula said.

"Even the processes we have now are placing insupportable burdens on the Landform," said the Metatron. "They are making mistakes that we have already made in Meatspace. They need direction."

"We need to tell them what to do," Zula said. Not agreeing. Just trying to translate what the Metatron was saying.

"Exactly."

PART 9

45

During the months that they had ranged over the sea of grass, dwelled on the hill, and explored the valley of the wolves, Adam and Eve had from time to time noticed small knots of aura nestled in deep grass or lodged in the forks of trees. They were typically no larger than a fist and could be difficult to see when looked on directly. In the corner of one's eye they could be detected, and their presence confirmed by the gentle thrill that they raised in the flesh when the hand was brought near them. But they could not really be touched, or clearly discerned, being more the absence than the presence of form. Some grew stronger than others and emitted a faint light of their own that could be seen on dark nights as dim soft gleamings. These came and went, and on moonless nights, when observed from the top of the hill, they seemed to drift westward toward the wooded river valley as if drawn toward the red glow in the night sky beyond.

Mab had explained to them that these were new souls but lately come into the world, which were still in need of solid forms. Those that came into the world at the Hive surrounding El's palace were predisposed to fashion themselves into cells and conjoin themselves to those that had got there before. But others, such as Mab herself, began their lives as solitary motes and might drift about the Land for some while before adopting forms. It was the natural way of such nascent souls to be drawn toward the habitations of others who had dwelled longer in the Land, and this was why Adam and Eve could observe the westward drift on dark nights: these new souls had sensed that a city existed to the west.

During the night that they had spent high up in the tree, they had seen no such wandering souls because their vision had been dazzled by the light of the fire they had kindled below to ward off wild beasts. But earlier today, as they had hiked up out of the valley and over the ranges of hills between it and the city, they had many times glimpsed bubbles of aura or sensed them in their toes as they'd happened to plant a foot near one. After Adam and Eve had spied the tower of white stone that topped the ridge above the city, they'd had eyes only for that—and, when it had come into view below them, the city itself with its innumerable roofs, smoking chimneys, and open fires. But as evening had drawn on, Eve had looked back behind them, checking for wolves, and had seen that they were being followed, not by beasts, but by scores of new souls drifting and bumbling along in their wake.

The tower on the hill had evidently been made by piling one stone block atop another until the desired height had been reached. The closer they came to it, the less it truly resembled the Palace, and yet it could not be questioned that those who had piled up the blocks had sought to imitate the stupendous Pinnacle of El. The structure was several times the height of Adam or Eve— comparable to the height of the great nut tree that stood atop their hill. Its lower portion was simple in design, being just a tapering cone with a spiral ramp twining around it, but above a certain point it became square and vertical, with columns and arches modeled after those of the Palace. Three levels of these, narrowing as they went up, were topped by a small flat roof upon which a fire burned. Adam and Eve by now knew enough of fires to understand that they must be fed, and indeed they could see other souls, of a shape similar to their own, ascending the spiral ramp bent under bundles of wood that they had collected from the forest.

"Welcome in El's name to Elkirk!" were the first words spoken to them by a soul who was standing not far from the base of the tower. Like the wood carriers, he was of a size and a general shape similar to that of Adam and of Eve. He was dressed in a long garment that looked as if it was supposed to be white. Or perhaps it had been once, and had become darkened by smoke from the fire. Had it been cleaner it might have resembled the garments worn by some of El's host.

"We did not bring any wood for your fire," said Adam, "only

because we did not understand the need for it until we had reached the place where there was no more to be had."

"That is perfectly all right! El will take no offense!" said the man in the robe. "Particularly as I see you have brought with you a flock of new souls—a gift much more pleasing to him than fuel for his eternal fire."

"They are not ours to give," Eve said. "They merely followed us."

"Such as these come from all around," said the man, "but rarely so many at once. El has blessed you, it would seem, with some power of drawing them forth."

"In the land to the east we sometimes saw them headed this way," Adam said, "but never understood why."

"Well, now understanding is yours!" the man said, with a nod at the tower. "Praise El."

"Is it?" Eve asked. "We see them and we see your tower with its hungry flame but my curiosity remains unsatisfied as to what happens to such new souls once they have reached this place."

"Well then, come and see! Come and see!" said the man, and beckoned them forward. "I am Looks East and I am the first priest here."

Adam and Eve each stated their own name, since apparently this was the done thing when souls met each other. "We don't know the meaning of 'priest' or what would make you first among such," said Eve. She looked around out of habit, expecting to see Mab, who frequently supplied them with explanations, but the sprite was nowhere to be seen.

"It simply means that I carry in my head much knowledge concerning El, and that I make it my business to explain such matters to the other souls who find their way to the kirk." As he spoke that unfamiliar word he nodded toward the white tower, which they had almost reached.

"Do you speak to El frequently then?" asked Adam, and exchanged a look with Eve. Both had the same thought: perhaps this Lookseast had heard their story directly from El or one of his angels.

Lookseast seemed confused by the question. "No, of course not, if you mean the sort of speaking we are doing now. That's not

El's way. Perhaps it was thus in the age before the Trek, but there are few who remember those times."

"We are not familiar with the Trek," said Eve.

"Oh. It is how Elkirk came to be," said Lookseast. "In olden times, all the souls dwelled together in peace and harmony at the base of El's palace. While El was away tending to some other matters, the Usurper took power for a time. He was a cruel sort, of great power, who hurled thunderbolts from the Palace. All the souls who dwelled below dispersed in terror of his rages. Our fore-bears trekked westward across the grassland and crossed the river and settled in the valley you see below, where they were sheltered from the Usurper's wrath. But later El came and flung the Usurper and his minions into the sky and rebuilt the Palace as you see it today. We built the kirk here upon this high place so that El and his angels can look down upon it from their seat in the clouds and know that we revere him."

Adam and Eve followed Lookseast into the chamber that oc-cupied most of the building's lowest story. This was square, plain, and empty save for two effigies made out of stone. One was male and the other female. They had the same general number and arrangement of limbs, extremities, and external organs as Adam and Eve, or, for that matter, El himself.

Adam and Eve were silent for a while as they contemplated these.

"Lo, these are the forms that El in his wisdom ordained for us. New souls are drawn to this place by the light of the fire. Here they contemplate these forms and shape themselves accord-ingly, each choosing the male or the female type as it suits their nature."

Seeing now more clearly as their eyes adjusted to the dimness, Adam and Eve detected many auras in the room, some larger and better formed, others small and indistinct. They were not scattered about the place but instead surrounded the effigies in a broad ring, as if they were all gazing inward. In the moments after Adam and Eve came into the place, it became considerably more crowded as each of the souls following in their wake spread out across the floor seeking its own vantage point. "These new ones will create forms as is proper, some sooner and some later, for El ordained that not all develop at the same pace. But one day they will each attain this perfection." Beaming, Lookseast extended one arm toward the effigies.

Neither of them looked especially perfect to Adam or Eve; they were lumpish, with indistinct features. "I regret to say," said Lookseast, "that it is too late for the both of you."

"What mean you by that?" Adam asked.

Lookseast changed his look and his tone in a manner that reminded them of El when he had needed to disabuse them of some especially childish misconception. "El has so ordained it that once a soul has adopted a particular form, that form does not change very much. Oh, slight adjustments are possible if one strives long and hard. But what I am trying to tell you is that, formed as you were in the wild lands beyond the river, with no models such as *these* to shape and guide you, your mistakes and deformities are, I am sorry to say, *permanent*. You will never achieve the perfection of *these*." Once again he drew their attention to the effigies. Adam and Eve perceived in Lookseast's manner a kind of reverence, such as the angels were wont to direct toward El. And when he turned the other way to gaze upon Adam and Eve, he got a look akin to how they had reacted to the smell of their first shit.

This turn of events left them speechless for some moments. Adam sensed that Eve was becoming quite wrathful, and rested a gentle hand on her shoulder before saying, "I deem it unlikely that forms such as these are really the ones preordained by El for all future souls to emulate. Their imperfections are easily seen. The woman's left breast is disfigured by what appears to be a chisel mark. Her arm has broken off and been reattached by someone apparently working in poor light. The man's face is asymmetrical, with the right eye hanging—" But here Adam stopped, for Eve had reached out and grabbed his forearm and given it a hard squeeze. Her gaze was fixed upon the face of Lookseast. Adam looked and perceived, too late, that the right eye of the First Priest of El was mounted in his head somewhat lower than the left—just like that of the male effigy.

"What El has ordained," said Lookseast, "is not to be questioned by misshapen yokels from the back of beyond." He cast his lopsided gaze over the crop of nascent souls that had followed Adam and Eve into the kirk. "It is fortunate for these new ones that they came upon this place before being too much influenced by the sight of you two."

"We could simply ask him," suggested Eve. Adam knew what she meant: *We could simply ask El.* But now it was his turn to give her a warning. Something in the way this man spoke about El suggested that he had never actually seen, much less spoken to, El or any of his host.

"Forgive my presumption," Adam said. "I was confused by the fact that I do not see, in this room, any souls that have advanced very far toward having definite forms."

"Those move up to the next level," explained Lookseast, and beckoned for them to follow him up a stairway.

The second story contained no statues, but its walls were decorated with paintings that depicted persons—all more or less resembling the effigies below—engaged in various activities such as quarrying stone, tending plants, spearing wolves, cooking, and copulating. Perhaps a dozen souls occupied this space, all of them well advanced toward having complete forms. It seemed that they were all paying keen attention to the pictures and rehearsing the actions depicted. "This is where they learn the ways of the world El has made, so that when they go down into Eltown they may be of some use. Others, larger and better formed than these, go out into the hills or down into the town, accompanied by the other priests of El, to practice and perfect their skills."

"And the third story above us?" Eve asked.

"That is for me and the other priests of El," said Lookseast, "and it is off-limits."

"What then becomes of the new souls?"

"When they are fully formed," said Lookseast, "they go down into Eltown and dwell there in whatever way they choose."

"Who are the bringers of firewood?" Adam asked.

"You ask a great many questions," said Lookseast. Which struck Adam and Eve as a curious sort of observation for the priest to have made. But after an awkward pause, he answered, "Eltown is, as its name suggests, devoted to the service of El. And so it is expected that all who dwell in it will do their part to keep the fire burning and otherwise help the priests carry out El's will."

It now seemed that the conversation was over. There was no place for Adam and Eve to stay here, and nothing for them to do, and so they left Elkirk behind and began to descend a zigzagging path toward the town below. This they could smell better than see. The air did not stir much in the valley, which had filled up with a hazy atmosphere of smoke and humidity that glowed a dim red in the light of the fires burning below. It smelled strongly of wood smoke and faintly of shit. But as they descended the switchbacks they were able to see Eltown spread out beneath them, a network of streets, mostly irregular, as it conformed to the banks of the river that snaked through its middle. The streets were nothing more than the unbuilt strips of ground between houses. Raised in the Garden, Adam and Eve were new to such ideas as streets and houses, but Mab supplied them with explanations during the hike down, and so by the time they verged on Eltown itself they understood the general notions.

"When we were growing up in the Garden," Adam remarked, "we asked many questions of El and his host, which they were pleased to answer. But that Lookseast did not like our questions one bit."

"You are certainly right about Lookseast," Eve returned, "but my recollection of the Garden differs from yours. Yes, when we were younger El was pleased to answer questions about the names of flowers and other such matters, but in the last days before he threw us out he seemed uneasy with what we asked concerning Spring and the other Beta Gods."

"That is very true," admitted Adam. There was a brief pause while they negotiated an awkward turn in the path. "Perhaps it is well that the conversation ended when it did, for I was about to correct Lookseast."

"Correct him as to what?" Eve said. "For so much of what he said wanted correcting."

"As to why you and I are shaped as we are," Adam said. "According to Lookseast, the common form of souls—two legs, two arms, a head and a face, and so on—was ordained by El. But El himself told us that we were created not by him but by Spring, with some help from Egdod. El came along later. The form adopted by you, me, Lookseast, and all the people of Eltown is not El's work at all."

"If it were," said Eve, "it would be more perfect than those crude effigies in the kirk. Say what you will of El, his creations are more symmetrical and elegantly formed than anything in that place."

"To the people down there," Adam reminded her, gesturing to the town below, "they are beautiful and we are crude, and so we may just have to get used to being looked on as Lookseast looked on us."

To see the houses of Eltown was to understand how they had been put together: in some cases by stacking one square rock atop another until nothing further could be added lest it topple over, in other cases by pursuing a similar strategy with the trunks of felled trees. When these things had been raised as high as their tendency to fall over would allow, they were covered over with frameworks of tree-stuff and grass to keep rain and snow from falling into them. Mysterious to Adam and Eve was where the souls of the town had obtained such a quantity of material. But by following the light of the fires they discovered answers: in the center of the town, along the banks of the river, was a place where many felled trees had been stacked. These were fuel for great fires, contained in stone boxes the size of houses. The earth of the riverbank, mixed with water, formed a mud that could be shaped into blocks and burned in the fire houses until it was dry and hard enough to be stacked up into walls. Another sort of earth—black sand from a different stretch of the river—could be burned until it melted and fused into metal, which could be shaped into tools for tree chopping. These furnaces burned all day and all night. The wood that fueled them was brought to the place by the simple expedient of chopping trees down somewhere else and floating them on the river.

During their first hours in Eltown, Adam and Eve took in a vast amount of knowledge about how souls lived together in a town, how they worked together and built things. The fascination

of learning so much caused them to forget their own hunger and tiredness until day had broken and the sun had risen above the white tower of Elkirk looming high above. But then Eve in particular pronounced herself very hungry and tired indeed, resting a hand on the bulge of her belly.

Food was provided to the workers at long tables in an open space among the great ovens. Little of it was familiar to Adam and Eve. The people of Eltown knew how to bake disks of bread in ovens and spread honey on them, and had apples and other sorts of fruit that Adam and Eve recognized from the Garden. All in all they ate better than Adam and Eve were accustomed to; they did not have much game, but they had fish from the river and a wider variety of plant food. They did not begrudge these to the newcomers, for their practice was that all who worked at the kiln and the forge could eat their fill here. Though Adam and Eve were new to such labors, they had quickly understood the nature of the work and had applied themselves to it. They had learned faster than other new souls and they had carried more weight. For it seemed that in mind and body alike they possessed certain advantages over the souls who had been brought up in the kirk and made their way down the mountain. All of which had been less obvious in smoke and firelight than it was now in the light of the morning. Standing tall among the other souls, half-clad in the pelts of small animals, Adam and Eve were conscious of many eyes upon them, staring out of lopsided faces that all more or less resembled the effigies in the kirk. None of the people of Eltown seemed keen on sharing a table with them and so they sat together at one end of a split-log bench and ate their fill. This led to drowsiness, especially on the part of Eve, who had been sleeping more the larger her belly grew.

They had given no thought as to where they would sleep, accustomed as they were to bedding down wherever it struck their fancy. They now looked about in vain for a tree or swath of tall grass where they might rest. The predicament was a common one among newly arrived souls who had not yet built houses for themselves, and a place had been made for them to sleep in rows under a broad roof, pocked here and there with chimneys rising from wide hearths where fires were kept burning to ward off the chill. Adam and Eve curled up together near one of those and slept until late in the day, when hunger, and a need to shit, woke Eve. Thus they learned about the locals' shitting arrangements, which were shared among all and which emptied at length into the river.

It was during their afternoon meal that they were approached by another soul who looked like them.

Like them he was symmetrically framed and taller than the people of Eltown. Nearly imperceptible in the bright light of the afternoon was the wispy form of Mab, flitting about him and darting ahead to lead him in Adam and Eve's direction.

"I am Walks Far," he announced.

"Adam and Eve," said Adam, speaking on behalf of his companion since her mouth was full of bread.

Walksfar sized them up, as if verifying that the newcomers were indeed of a different order of souls than most here. They did likewise. About him was a graveness and solemnity that suggested he had spawned many years ago and had seen much since then. "Have you dwelled in Eltown for very long?" Eve asked him. For though his form was unusual here, he wore clothes of spun fiber like all of the others, and though he drew some notice as he walked about, most of the townspeople seemed to find him unremarkable.

"Since before it was a town," Walksfar affirmed. "I dwelled in the First Town." He looked them both up and down. "As it would seem you did—and yet I do not recognize you from those days, and I knew every soul in the place."

"This is the only town we have ever been to," said Adam, "and we only just got here."

"Where is the First Town?" Eve asked. "If there are more like us there, perhaps we should—"

"It no longer exists," said Walksfar, "and that you do not know as much suggests to me that you must have some very odd tale to tell concerning how you came to be here."

Adam shrugged. "It is not odd to us. But from what we have lately seen up in the kirk and down here along the river, I will readily admit that it would seem odd when told in this company."

"Not in the company I keep," said Walksfar. "Come with me, if you are so inclined, to Camp." And he directed his gaze across the river.

The west bank too was built up with kilns and forges and houses, but not so much as the east; and what was here seemed smaller and worn out. They crossed over to it in a boat that Walksfar drove across the stream with oars or with a long pole, depending on its depth. A short walk up out of the floodplain took them to a hill settled with log dwellings that were plainly much older than the ones on the eastern bank. Some great trees had been suffered to remain standing and so Camp, as Walksfar called the place, gave Adam and Eve the sense of being once again in the forest—but without wolves.

Camp appeared to have started in a flattish area near the top of a hill, with a ring of dwellings that formed a rough oval centered on a hole in the ground whence they could draw water up in buckets. Around this, more such houses had later been built, but the full count of them did not exceed twenty. Most had but a single room with bed, hearth, and table. Walksfar's dwelling was no exception, though he had extended it with a sloping roof supported by stilts made of small tree trunks planted in the earth. On their upper surface, all of the roofs of Camp were so deeply covered with moss and leaf mold, as well as grass and other small plants that had taken root in them, that the whole neighborhood seemed as if it were being absorbed by the hill.

On his porch, as he called the place under the roof before his dwelling, Walksfar had made a small hearth of kiln stones where a few embers still glowed. Adam and Eve could guess that during the hours they had slept Mab must have sought him out and persuaded him to cross the river and meet the newcomers. He now stoked the fire back up and began to heat water in a container that looked to have been hammered out of a thin sheet of reddish metal. As he busied himself, Adam and Eve sat on a bench on the porch and gazed out over the central area of Camp. They knew themselves to be on a hilltop, but the trees and dwellings were so arranged as to block much of the view. Above them in the distance they could see Elkirk, but all views farther east were closed off by the ridge on which it stood. They did not miss seeing, or being seen by, the distant Palace of El. Mostly what they saw was Camp itself, and a few souls coming and going among its dwellings. Most had the general form of Eve, Adam, and Walksfar. "Those too must have come from the place you spoke of—First Town," Eve remarked.

"That they did," Walksfar said. "Some others dwelled here even before First Town existed. For example Cairn, over yonder."

Walksfar seemed to be indicating a column of brownish-gray stone that was standing on the other side of Camp—and that seemed to have been there for a long time, judging from its shaggy pelt of moss. But then it altered its shape, collecting itself into a somewhat taller and narrower figure. It shook off a few days' accumulation of leaves and advanced into the trees in a swaying, stomping gait that reminded Adam and Eve of how their hill had moved when it had strode across the plain to rescue them from the wolves.

"Others here look more like trees or flowers," Walksfar added, "and some go on four legs, though they prefer living in wilder places. But I, and others who spawned at about the same time, looked to Ward or others of the Pantheon for our shapes."

"What stories you must have of that age!" Eve exclaimed.

"Only some of us. Many are forgettish. That woman there, carrying the bucket—she's older than I but remembers less."

"If you are not forgettish, would you tell us the story of First Town and how Camp and Eltown came to be?" Eve asked.

Walksfar by now was well advanced in some complex undertaking of heating water and throwing dried leaves into it, evidently with an eye toward later decanting it into three smaller containers. "Souls came into being as they do. None of this existed."

"Camp?"

He shook his head. "The Land. The entire Land. In those days it was nothing more than a street lined with trees. The number of souls grew and Egdod came down from time to time and caused houses to come into being, where we lived."

"Did you know Egdod well?"

Walksfar shook his head. "By the time of my spawning, he had raised walls about his abode, and, as is implied by his name, Ward was there to prevent the new souls of Town from wandering about the place. Egdod spent much time farther afield, in places we knew not of. We would see his great wings flapping away into the distance until he disappeared over the horizon. From this I conceived the idea that other places might exist, as worth seeing as First Town, and so one day I walked away, and kept walking. This was where I left off roaming. It suited me better than Town, which had become crowded."

"Did the wolves come for you?" Adam asked, at the same time as Eve was saying, "What did you eat?"

"This was before eating, and before wolves," Walksfar said. "All that came later. I came back to Town after a long sojourn to find everyone putting things into their mouths and shitting from the other end, which explained the smell I had noticed on the east wind several days out. I became an eater and a shitter myself. Later Spring made various creatures, including ones that were predisposed to eat us."

"Did you know Spring?" Eve asked.

Walksfar shook his head. "No one did—save by her works. Spring never visited Town. At the time of the Fall, rumor had it that she was working on creating two-legged creatures, such as us. After that, of course, nothing further was heard of the Pantheon."

There was so much curious in what he had just said that Adam and Eve were unable to choose from among a diversity of questions. Walksfar poured hot brown stuff from the larger container into the small ones and indicated that they might partake if they wished. He treated his own serving with caution, as if it might bite him. The fire had put much heat into it.

"The Fall?" Adam asked.

"Of the Old Gods," Walksfar said, and when this did not seem to register, added, "of Egdod and his Pantheon, when El came in glory with his host and threw them into the sky." He eyed them for a few moments and risked a sip. "You two really are from some remote place if you have not heard some telling of that story."

Eve's face reddened. "We are not so ignorant as all that. We know that El resides with his host in the Palace, high in the clouds above the humming soul hive. We know that Egdod and Spring and others of the Pantheon were there first, and were cast out by El, and seek to return."

"Do they, now?" Walksfar exclaimed. "How strange that you can speak with confidence of a thing as momentous as that would be, were it true, and yet of so many other matters you know nothing."

This brought them to an impasse for a time, and they took sips of the hot stuff.

"The Fall," Walksfar said finally, "is a matter of common knowledge, and I'll not withhold what is easily learned. First Town changed into a kind of hive, which grew to rival Egdod's Palace. A bright thunderbolt he flung, and brought it down. The survivors dispersed all over the Land, dividing up by their kind and the manner of their speech. I led a number of them hither, for it was a place I knew from my wanderings. We trekked across the sea of grass and down into the valley, where wolves came for us in the night; we fought them off with the weapons Thingor had taught us to make and we kept going. We ascended the east side of yonder ridge. We stopped for a time, as I had lost my way in those dark days of pursuit and struggle.

"As I stood on the ridge looking west into the valley, I felt warmth on my back and saw the whole territory cast into shadow by a new light brighter than the sun. The others of my party were exclaiming. I turned around and saw in the far distance the brilliant form of El descending upon the top of the Pinnacle where it rose above the rubble of what had once been the Town and the hive. We saw flashes within that brightness as when the sun gleams on the surface of troubled water, and then saw the forms of Egdod and the Pantheon hurtling away into the sky; and they burned as they fell away from the Land that they had made, and did not leave off falling and burning until they struck the hard vault of heaven, and broke it, and set it aflame. It burns still and you can see it when the night sky is clear."

"The Red Web!" Eve exclaimed.

"It goes by many names. That one is as good as any," said

Walksfar. His beverage had cooled sufficiently that he now took a long draught of it. "That was the Fall of the Old Gods. I turned my back upon the brightness of it, which some saw as glory, and descended into this valley with most of my party and here made Camp. But one of us, Honey by name—she had been my lover for a time—was enthralled by the glory of El, and chose to abide on the ridgetop where she could gaze across the sea of grass and adore him. She it was who built Elkirk. Many souls were drawn to it and made their way into the valley after they had forms. We of Camp showed them how to cut trees, build fires, smelt metal, bake bricks, and practice the many other crafts that had passed into our ken from Knotweave and Thingor. Thus Eltown."

His listeners considered it. "We did not encounter Honey at the kirk," Adam said.

Walksfar nodded. "Honey ceded Elkirk to priests whom she had raised and trained to that duty, and went into the east, crossing the sea of grass toward the Hive and the tower of El in the hopes that she could find some destiny there."

"How long ago was the Fall?" Eve asked. "How long has Camp been here—how many winters has it known?"

Walksfar eyed a man who was staggering across Camp with a log balanced on his shoulder. "Ask him and he'll say it was just a few years, for he is forgettish. If you wanted a precise count, you would have to venture into the west and seek out Pestle, an old soul who has written down the chronicle of all that she has seen. I made no effort to count years until many of them had passed. Then I formed the habit of cutting a mark into the wall of my cabin every year when the great tree shed its leaves. I was just getting ready to make another such mark this morning when your companion, Mab, came and interrupted me. You may come inside and count the marks if it will serve as an answer." Walksfar drew a steel knife from his belt as he said this, and tested its edge on his thumbnail. Then he got to his feet and opened the door of his abode and left it open behind him in case Adam and Eve wished to follow him inside.

They did so, and saw little at first, for light came in only through two small openings. The walls were nothing more than the surfaces of the tree trunks that had been stacked up to make them. The logs were silver with age. As their eyes adjusted they saw many small vertical grooves cut into the wood, no farther apart than the width of a finger. Not all of the logs were so marked, but most were grooved from one end to the other. As they watched, Walksfar trailed his fingertip along one of the logs until he sensed the place where the marks left off. There he went to work with his knife. "Another year gone," he remarked.

Walksfar found them an old cabin in Camp where no one was dwelling, and over the next few weeks taught them the crafts of hewing logs and thatching roofs. They made good those parts of the cabin that had succumbed to rain and rot, and made a home of it for the winter. Eve's belly continued to grow. Her appetite knew no bounds, and yet when she had eaten she preferred rest to work, or else would sit in the cabin practicing certain of those arts that Walksfar attributed to the member of the Pantheon called Knotweave. No longer did Adam and Eve go about clad in the pelts of animals but wore fitted and sewn garments of woven cloth. Eve had little contact during the next months with the folk of Eltown or even of Camp. Mab spent much time with her, imparting knowledge of crafts and other matters. Adam crossed and recrossed the river to fetch timbers, bricks, and the goods required by Eve; in exchange he toiled among the kilns and forges on the bank of the river, or joined expeditions that ranged up and down it.

Three rivers joined into one some little distance upstream of the town. All had been explored and their banks logged for as far as a soul might walk in a day. Likewise downstream. In the early days of the town, when many fewer marks had existed on the walls of Walksfar's cabin, getting logs had been much easier.

Adam and Eve, of course, had been fortunate enough to get a dwelling of their own in Camp. But when Adam went back to the riverbank much later, he recognized souls there whom he and Eve had seen on their first day in Eltown, seemingly no closer to having their own dwellings. Some such joined together into parties that would venture down the river or across the western mountains in the hope of finding better places. Of those, some never came back, while others returned some time later, famished and telling tales of other towns where souls practiced outlandish ways and seemed to harbor exceedingly queer notions about El and other such topics.

Adam made it his practice to sit with these when meals were served and to listen to their stories. For he and Eve had not lost sight of the goal that they had first spoken of in the Garden, namely to range across the Land in search of their mother, Spring. The tales told by those who had gone forth and returned gave him little cause for hope that Spring and the other Beta Gods would be easily found.

The middle and the eastern forks of the river came together at the base of a hill, which had long since been logged, save for a single immense tree that now stood alone at its top and could be seen from a great distance. Wisps of rope still encircled the base of its trunk, for loggers of old had used it to anchor the lines that they made use of in their operations, and a long skid mark, gouged slightly deeper with every rain, still ran down from there to the riverfront, where they had bound the logs into rafts. The tree bore some axe scars where an effort to chop it down had been begun and abandoned.

Adam did not work every day, but when he did, he would rise at dawn and walk down to the bank of the river and seek passage on one of the small boats that continually went back and forth across the river. The workers on the opposite bank could see him approaching. He was bigger than they and, once he had learned the art of axe swinging, could cut wood faster than any two of them. By the time he made it to the river's eastern shore he commonly found himself being importuned by several souls who would begin shouting to him across the water as soon as they hoped they might be heard.

One day, though, Adam came down from Camp to discover a boat waiting for him on the near side. It was the boat of a soul named Feller who lived in a wooden house of his own. Not content with that, he craved a larger house of burned bricks, and so went on cutting trees all the time. At great expense and trouble he had recently made this boat, the better to reach far logging sites, and was sometimes gone for days with his crew, which by and large comprised souls that had acquired more skills and had forms better suited for the work.

"Many mornings," said Feller, "I have looked across the river to this shore and seen you idle as you looked for a way across. It occurred to me that I had the means"—and he laid a hand on the gunwale of his boat—"to aid you."

"I thank you for your consideration," said Adam, "though I cannot help noticing that your crew has also gone out of their way." For six other souls were in the boat, axes across their laps.

"No great matter," said Feller, "but if you are as grateful as all that, perhaps you would consider joining us for the day. With my boat and my crew we can achieve more in that time than any of those feeble and forlorn souls over there can do in a week."

Feller's words kindled a new emotion in Adam's breast: pride in the fact that Feller deemed him more worthy than others of having a place in his crew. Feeling their eyes upon him and noting the excellence of the great axes they bore, he agreed and vaulted into the boat.

He found himself seated across from Edger, a soul he had worked with before. This raised less agreeable feelings since Edger had a habit of glaring at Adam, and watching him closely as he worked, which Adam could happily do without. Edger was not unusually big or strong but she had become skilled in the craft of whetting blades, using an assortment of smooth rocks that she carried with her in a bag made of the skin of some dead animal. In consequence she could cut wood faster than most others. Seated next to her was Bluff, who had been the largest and strongest soul in Eltown until the arrival of Adam. Something in how these two related to each other gave Adam the idea that Edger and Bluff were lovers.

Feller's habit was to row upriver to one of the remote camps of the west fork. The current ran faster in that stream than in the other two, so it was more difficult to explore, and good trees could be reached by one such as Feller who had a nimble boat.

They worked their way up past the first splitting of the river, where the lone tree stood on its hill, and then came to the place where the white water of the Western spilled into the slack water of the Middle. They diverted up the former. The stream sought to expel them as if possessed by a soul of its own. "Bluff and Adam," said Feller, "it is time for weaker oarsmen to move aside and let you bend your strong backs to it."

Bluff arose and took the place of a smaller soul on the bench amidships that was reserved for those pulling on oars. He gripped one of the oars in his great hands and looked expectantly at Adam, who understood that he was supposed to do likewise. He was not accustomed to other souls directing his actions, but he could see plainly enough that this was the way of things. He took the seat on the bench next to Bluff and grabbed the other oar. "Pull," said Feller. Bluff did so and the entire boat pivoted around. Adam was conscious of being looked on askance. "Pull!" Feller repeated, and this time Adam tried to do as Bluff did. Still the effect of Bluff's oar was greater, though not as unequal as before. Feller directed Adam to pull alone, so as to straighten the boat's course.

"And put your back into it, big man!" said Edger, in a tone that reminded Adam of why he wished she were not on the boat.

"Sharper tools and a duller tongue is what I desire from you, Edger," responded Feller. "You have work of your own that I would have you attend to." Adam was taken aback by his tone, for he had rarely heard any soul speak this way. But Edger seemed to accept the rebuke. She groped in her bag for a rock and then began to scrape it along the edge of an axe.

The rowing was arduous, but whenever Adam slackened, Bluff seemed to sense it and to pull harder, causing the boat to swing broadside to the current. This only made it more difficult for Adam to straighten it, and as Feller pointed out several times, it caused them to lose time as the river pushed them back. So Adam learned to sense what Bluff was doing and to match him pull for pull. As the morning wore on Bluff seemed to tire and slackened his pace, and Adam did likewise so as to keep the boat straight.

Before noon they arrived at a place where the stump lands gave way to forest, and there they drew the boat up on the bank, climbed out, and went to work with their axes. Or at least that was true of everyone except for Feller. He spent a while walking to and fro on the bank of the river, gazing intently at the ground. "Thunk and his lot have been here," he said, "I see his big footprints."

Adam went to work cutting down a tree that seemed of a good size to him until Feller told him to attack a larger one instead. So into that one Adam began to swing his axe, but found it did not bite as well as it might have. Testing its edge he found that it was dull. Not far away Edger was making much speedier progress cutting down a smaller tree. Adam asked her whether he might have the use of a whetstone from her pouch. She invited him to wander at hazard into the deep forest and be eaten by wolves—a prospect that seemed to amuse her very much. So Adam went down to the bank of the river and found a suitable rock. Feller came over to him and inquired as to why he was not applying himself to his assigned task. Adam explained matters. Feller took the axe and tested its edge and was displeased. "Edger!" he shouted, despite knowing exactly where she was, for she was in plain sight not far away. But he continued to call her name until she had come over to him. Then he rebuked her. Adam was some distance off, whetting the tool with his river rock, and the sound of the rushing water made it difficult for him to understand the words they exchanged. But their tone could not be misunderstood. The discussion went on for some little while before Feller drew his arm across his body and then whipped it back, striking Edger on the cheek with such force that she spun away and fell to the ground.

It was not the first violence that Adam had witnessed, for workers along the river sometimes fell to it. But the violence of Feller seemed of a different nature; like all else that Feller did, it appeared to spring not from passion but from careful forethought. Adam looked up to the edge of the forest and saw Bluff emerging. Seeing how it was, Bluff neither rebuked Feller nor came to Edger's aid, but rather seemed to shrink into himself.

Later in the day, as Adam, weary from many hours of rowing and chopping, stood back from his work to take a moment's rest, he heard the sharp popping and splintering of a tree giving way. He looked up to see a tree falling directly toward him. He stepped clear of it and received a blow from one of its branches, which drew blood from his shoulder but did not hurt him otherwise.

Later in the day Feller let them all know that it was time to cease work and get back into the boat, and so they marked the logs that they had dragged down to the bank and then pushed the boat into the current and climbed aboard. Travel downstream required less of the rowers, and so smaller members of the crew took turns at the oars while Adam and Bluff rested.

Ever since the moment when Feller had struck Edger in the face, and Bluff, witnessing it, had only hung his head and slunk away, Bluff had seemed diminished to Adam. Edger likewise had taken leave of the pride and the haughty manner that she had shown toward Adam earlier in the day. One side of her face was misshapen and discolored; when she dared to meet Adam's eye, she only looked at him sidelong.

Eve asked Adam about the wound on his shoulder when at last he returned to their cabin that night, weary to the bone. He began to relate the story, but seeing its effect on her emotions, changed it in the telling so that it would not cause her so much distress. He knew what was causing her such concern: word had reached them that some who were gravely injured in such accidents ceased to be; their souls took leave of their ruined forms, which dissolved, and the souls either vanished altogether or fled and did not come back. "I shall take the utmost care," Adam assured her, "never to put myself in the way of any harm so great as that." But in the back of his mind he wondered how it might go if one who wished him ill were to place him deliberately in the way of a falling tree. Eve seemed somewhat reassured. But the fact remained that he had been gone all day and was now bloody, dirty, and exhausted. "Why do you toil so when we have all we need here?" she asked. "Stay in Camp and keep me company!"

"You know why," he returned. "Mab has foretold that soon there will be more of us. This old cabin, cozy as it is, does not have enough room."

Eve did not press the argument further that night, for she could see his weariness plainly enough. They had talked about it before, and it was plain to see that Adam derived a kind of pleasure from venturing into wild places to cut trees, and nothing that came out of Eve's mouth could gainsay it.

Adam made it a practice after that to board Feller's boat in the morning. On the second day he rowed harder than Bluff was capable of, so that the boat over and over again slewed around to Bluff's disadvantage and caused Bluff to become the butt of rebukes and mockery from Feller. From this Adam derived a kind of satisfaction that repaid him in a small way for the injury he had suffered the day before. For he was quite certain now that this had been inflicted upon him by Edger or Bluff in a cunning and underhanded way.

In any event no more trees fell toward Adam after that. He and Bluff, without exchanging any words, arrived at an understanding concerning how hard they would row the boat, and thereby made progress that was more steady, even though Feller made remarks intended to provoke more competition between them. For the most part, though, the journeys to and from the logging site were spent in silence or in idle conversation. Feller inquired about the place where Adam and Eve were living in Camp, whether it was quite large enough for their tastes, what sort of condition it was in, and so forth. Adam came to see that no conversation was truly idle for Feller and that his words always had a purpose. In this case, it was to make Adam desire more, so that he would row faster and cut down more trees.

Too—and just as purposefully—he and the others asked about Eve. They had not actually seen Eve since her first day in Eltown, but word had got around about her curious shape. That was mysterious to them, but all understood that, even though Eve was not so great in stature as Adam, still she was bigger and stronger than most souls in Eltown and could outdo them if she chose to work.

From these conversations it was clear to Adam that none of these people had the faintest idea of what was really going on with Eve. The production of new souls was not a thing that ever happened among them. The nature of his dealings with Feller and Edger and Bluff caused him to think better of divulging all that he knew. So he said only that Eve worked in Camp practicing those crafts that brought satisfaction to her and that she would not soon be joining them in the boat.

They cut down many trees, and bound them together in rafts that they floated down the Western fork to its junction with the Middle, and thence to the place where the East fork flowed into it at the foot of the great bare hill where the lone tree stood. Whenever they passed by that, Feller would leave off for a while from his questions and rebukes and all of the other carefully considered words that emerged from his mouth, and he would gaze up at that tree, and all the rest of the crew, not daring to interrupt his silence, would do likewise, and in time it seemed that they had all formed a shared resolve to go up there one day and chop it down.

Then it would pass from view around the last bend of the river and they would pull up on the floodplain where the great fires burned and the logs they had brought down the river would be counted and sorted and stacked into piles. The logs were marked with glyphs hacked into their bark to say who owned which. Adam learned to make his own mark and to recognize it. For the most part, his pile grew. Sometimes, though, when he went to inspect it he would find that logs had been removed while he had been absent. He mentioned this perplexing phenomenon to Feller, who was ready with an explanation: from time to time it was necessary to "dock" the log piles of crew members, as for example when they did not work hard enough.

It all made sense, and yet Adam felt troubled by it somehow. He felt himself diminished. Feller seemed to understand this. He went on to admit that being docked was by no means an agreeable thing, and to say that he regretted having to do it. But such was the way of things now. Eltown had grown crowded and the distance to the edge of the forest kept growing. Some had abandoned the town altogether and lived now in the woods like wild beasts; Thunk, for example, was the leader of a whole band of such wretches, stealing logs from the honest woodcutters of Eltown and assaulting them in the wild places. A conflict was shaping up in which all the people of Eltown must choose whether to stay here and improve the place or disperse into the woods. Feller's boat was the answer. It was already being copied by some who envied his success.

After that conversation Adam went back home across the river. Eve looked upon him with concern, and said that he seemed tired and worn down. Adam tried to put her at ease by explaining that his log pile continued to grow, and that when it reached a certain size he would lash them together into a raft and bring it across the river to Camp so that they could enlarge their cabin.

Walksfar visited Adam, Eve, and Mab in their cabin frequently. As well they became acquainted with other old souls of Camp, but many of them were forgettish. The growth of Eve's belly could not be concealed. Walksfar said that it reminded him strongly of what happened when four-legged beasts spawned more of their kind. After that, Adam and Eve's secrets all came out in a rush, as when an ice dam melts on a river and all that has been pent up is released in one moment. They let Walksfar know that they were in fact the children of Spring and of Egdod, spawned in a different manner from every other soul in the Land; that they were born and bred in the Garden, expelled therefrom by El himself; and that the swelling of Eve's belly was, just as Walksfar had guessed, the spawning of more of their kind.

When Walksfar inquired as to why El had expelled them, they related the story of the worm that had somehow found its way into the Garden and spoken to them of the First Age and given them names that were relics of an even more ancient past, and finally been slain by the lightning sword of Defender of El.

Walksfar was astonished by each of these revelations, most of all the last. And yet he admitted that he had known from their first day in Camp that Adam and Eve and their guardian sprite must be of some altogether different order of creation from any of the other souls that made their way down from the kirk; that they were so peculiar, in fact, that only a tale as strange as the one they had just told him could possibly serve to explain them.

Thus winter passed into the first stirrings of spring. One night Eve went into a great passion that consumed her mind and body to such a degree that Adam feared she might be torn asunder; her aura burned and burgeoned about her like the great fires where steel was made in the forge, and her form below her breasts and above her knees reverted to chaos that writhed about the limbs of those who sought to comfort her. At the moment when they feared she would dissolve altogether, they heard the small cry of a voice not before known in the Land, and then another, and another. Her passion and the chaos that swirled about her lessened with each that came forth, and subsided well enough that they could all see what she had begotten: twelve souls, tiny and yet perfectly formed after the same general pattern as Adam and Eve. They spawned not as indistinct wisps but as embodied souls, clothed in skin and endowed with toes, fingers, and faces. The head of each was robed in an aura that ever darted out and shrank back.

The bringing forth of the twelve little ones was exhausting even for Adam, though he had little to do other than to look for ways to be of comfort to Eve and to carry out such other tasks as were recommended from time to time by Mab. The sprite for example lacked the strength to go and draw fresh water from the well of Camp but had the wit to sense when a drink or a bath would be of most benefit to Eve.

After the twelve had been brought forth they sought closeness with Eve, whose form was returning to the shape it had possessed when she and Adam had dwelled in the Garden. Most of the little ones were of a mind to sleep, as was Eve, and so Adam saw to it that they were covered and that the hearth was stoked, and went outside to the clearing in the middle of Camp to enjoy the fresh cold air. Night had fallen during the passion of Eve and stars shone brilliant and sharp in the firmament. Directly overhead in its slow transit was the Red Web, its distant fires flickering. Adam had the sense of being watched by a great eye. He diverted his gaze from this, much as he did when he was conscious of being looked on by Feller, and noticed the sprite emerging from the cabin and heading his way.

"It has come to pass as you predicted," Adam remarked, "though it is a mystery to me how you can know such things."

"It is a mystery to me as well," Mab returned. "The knowledge does not seem to dwell in my mind as a thing I have learned. And yet when there is a need, I have some faculty for getting it."

"Perhaps you could put it to use as regards forms," Adam said. "This has been on my mind of late because of certain changes I have noticed from day to day among my crew. I have tended to put it out of mind because it troubles and perplexes me. But observing the twelve perfect little ones that Eve has made has brought it now to the forefront."

"What is it you would know?" Mab asked.

"When we were ejected from the Garden I assumed that our forms would never change," Adam said. "And indeed when we came to Elkirk, we were told by Lookseast that once a soul has adopted a mature form, it does not change thereafter. And yet when first I laid eyes on Edger I saw her as haughtier and more beautiful than she seems now, and I saw Bluff as being the biggest and strongest of all the souls of Eltown, nearly my equal. But I do believe that their forms have altered since they began to work every day in the crew of Feller. They have shrunk into themselves, become round-shouldered. Their heads hang and their eyes dart sidelong at things they would once look on squarely. People who have seen both of them say that Bluff seems now smaller than Thunk, who stands upright and springs about the deep forest with a light step."

Mab flickered silently, as was its way when acquiring new knowledge. "You are correct," it said finally. "There is almost no end to the changes a soul's form might undergo, provided that the change from any one day to the next is slight."

Adam shuddered. "One wonders what Bluff and Edger might end up looking like if they work under Feller for many years."

"Or Feller himself, for that matter," Mab remarked. "His form waxes."

Adam nodded. "Indeed, at the beginning I saw him as of typical size. Now he seems bigger."

"Your form changes too," Mab informed him. "And not for the better."

Adam was wounded by the remark but could only nod in agreement. "The first time I entered the porch of Walksfar, I had to duck under the edge of the roof. But I went there yesterday, and either I am of less stature or he has raised it."

"He hasn't," Mab said.

Adam considered this. "Who knows where it could end?" he asked. "In my own case the change was slight and slow enough that I did not notice it, or did not care. But gazing on the perfect forms of the twelve new ones gives me joy mixed with an aching in my heart when I consider how that perfection might be lost in the future if they remain in this place and live as I have been living."

Adam then shifted uncomfortably, for the cold had penetrated his clothing. He turned away from the cabin where he dwelled with his family and looked into the east, for he had noticed a brightening in the sky there and guessed that dawn must be coming on. But the light in the east moved with much greater swiftness than that of the sunrise and seemed to be concentrated in a single place that moved across the firmament. It was coming toward them, arcing high over Elkirk and now plunging into the valley. As it drew closer Adam saw that it was a winged angel of El's host, and as it folded its wings and descended into Camp he recognized it as the one called Messenger of El. Its form was more graceful than that of El's soldiers, and wings on its feet made it more fleet and agile than they. And yet, like them, it carried a flaming thunderbolt on one hip. "Greetings, Adam," it said. "Know that your absence and that of Eve are sorely regretted by all who knew and loved you in the Palace."

"We think back on it often," Adam admitted, "and sometimes long for its comforts. Yet finding our way about the Land has brought wisdom we could not have obtained in the Garden, and taught us new things."

"So it would seem," said Messenger of El, "for information has reached us that twelve souls are today in the Land who yesterday were not."

"Your information is correct," said Adam.

Messenger of El nodded. "I am sent here to visit and look upon them," it announced.

Adam looked toward his cabin. Messenger of El noted this and marked the place.

"Just now Eve is resting after a great labor, and the little ones too are asleep," Adam said. "Your radiance will disturb their rest." By saying this he meant to stop Messenger of El from going into the cabin at all. But the angel's radiance diminished as when a fire is snuffed out. Its wings shrank into its back and enwrapped its body, taking on the appearance of a cloak. Likewise the wings of its feet became as foot wrappings of some dull material. When the transformation was complete, the angel looked like a young man in a cloak of fair cloth, legs and feet wrapped against the cold; and in place of the thunderbolt at its hip was a long slender object dangling from a belt. "I shall not disturb them," he said.

"If your errand is not to disturb them, then it might most easily be accomplished by not entering the cabin in the first place," Adam pointed out.

"My errand is to see them with my own eyes," said the angel. "El has so ordered it."

"What is that on your hip where the thunderbolt once hung?" Adam asked.

The angel made no answer, but took the thing off and leaned it against the trunk of the great tree. Mab shone light on it and Adam perceived that it was very much like a knife, except longer. Useless he judged it for cutting down trees, but at the same time very dangerous and likely to cause grave injury if mishandled.

Messenger of El strode across the clearing to the threshold of their cabin. Seeing the angel push through the door without knocking, Adam felt in his breast some of the same emotions as when Feller docked a log from his pile; but as with Feller, he made no outward sign of feeling so, and knew himself diminished thereby. It occurred to him to wonder what happened, at such moments, to the substance that had been subtracted from his form. Was it added in the same moment to that of Messenger of El, or of El himself? Was Feller growing at Bluff's expense? Could one soul consume another, given enough time?

In any event, Adam followed Messenger of El into the cabin, and Mab followed Adam. They stood and beheld Eve asleep in her bed, half-concealed under the forms of the twelve new little ones. Some of those slept, stirring and sighing from time to time.

Others lay silently awake, their open eyes taking in impressions of the visitors and the other things around them. Two fussed and were comforted by Mab, who darted in to beguile them with her bright form. Messenger of El, bereft of his wings for the time being, walked around the bed, counting the little souls and bending closer to inspect them.

As this went on, Adam came to notice that the visitor was paying special attention to where the legs came together.

"Six male and six female," said Messenger of El finally.

"Yes," Adam said. "I know of no particular reason why their numbers should be equal, save that Spring so preordained matters. Perhaps she had it in mind that the males and females would form pairs as Eve and I have done."

Messenger of El listened carefully and nodded agreement. "And what purpose do you suppose is served by the forming of such pairs?"

Adam shrugged. "Companionship. Striving together as one to do what is beyond the reach of a lone soul."

"The pairing of male and female is not needed for such purposes," Messenger of El pointed out.

"What do you think then?" Adam asked, for it seemed that the angel already had some answer to the riddle he had posed.

One of the little ones awoke and cried out. Mab flitted to it.

So as not to further disturb the sleeping ones, Adam and Messenger of El opened the cabin's door, stepped outside into the cold air, closed it behind them, and continued to talk beneath the starlight. "For many years to come," said the angel, "those little ones shall require your protection and your instruction. It is a task demanding the energies of two souls, and then some! Spring foresaw as much when she so programmed your forms to spawn males and females in equal numbers."

"You are saying that six such pairs might eventually be formed from the twelve just spawned," said Adam.

"Yes, and each of those pairs might in time bring forth more little ones just as you and Eve have done. And indeed Eve still has it in her to spawn new little ones as well, once she has recovered from the labors of this day."

None of these possibilities had previously entered the mind of Adam, who in his astonishment and exhaustion and joy had not had leisure to work it all through. He now felt some embarrassment at having been so slow to grasp the nature of Spring's plan.

His mind went for some reason to the forests where he ranged every day with the woodcutters. For as far as a soul might travel in a week, the mountains were clad in trees, far too numerous to count. And yet according to what they had learned in the Garden, they and all other things that lived had begun as single seeds that had multiplied and spread with the passage of many years. If the six pairs only just spawned by Eve were to spawn more in due course, the number of souls would soon mount to rival the population of Eltown. Only Mab could calculate the numbers, but the vastness of the forest gave Adam a way of thinking about where it could lead: a Land populated with souls too many to count, all formed after the general shape of Adam and Eve. And they would raise and instruct those souls to deal with one another justly, so that none would wax stronger and more perfect at the expense of another.

"Forgive me," said Adam, "for not having seen it until now. Yes, I do believe I understand the nature of Spring's program now."

"Very well," said Messenger of El. "Raised as you were in the Garden by El to wield your powers of intellect, you were bound to sort it out sooner or later, to perceive the error of Spring and to understand the nature of the problem."

"Error? Problem?" Adam repeated.

"Yes," said Messenger of El. "Quite plainly, the Land has not the capacity to support the number of souls that would in time be spawned by the carrying forward of Spring's misbegotten program. The hills for miles around Eltown have already been logged bare by souls who spawn in the usual manner—and more such come down from Elkirk every day. Do not think that El in his Palace is oblivious to this. Similar stories could be told of other towns and cities all over the Land. To add the descendants of Adam and Eve in their thousands and their millions would soon strip the whole Land bare, and make it as dead and disfigured as *that* place." The angel lifted his gaze to the burning crater of the Red Web high above.

Adam knew not what to say, and thought on it for a while. "I cannot deny that I have with my own hands felled many trees of late, out of a desire to build a larger habitation for the little souls being spawned by Eve. Nor that the same actions carried out by thousands of my descendants—"

"Millions," the angel put in.

"—would lay bare much Land that now is pleasantly forested. But to produce so many souls will take many years, and is it not possible we might change our ways in the meantime? We are not blind devourers. Already the souls of Eltown find ways to live comfortably while cutting down fewer trees."

"That will only delay the inevitable," said Messenger of El. "Fortunately, a simple fix, undertaken now, will prevent anything of the kind from ever occurring. It is the easiest thing in the world." And the angel's hand strayed to his right hip, where the pommel of a small knife gleamed as it protruded from a hidden sheath.

"What is the nature of this fix," inquired Adam, "and in what way does it involve that knife?"

"Inborn to each of those twelve is the faculty of spawning more souls," explained Messenger of El. "The males take after you in this respect, and the females take after Eve. The latter have their organs of reproduction deep inside, but you and the boys wear yours externally, where the mistake of Spring can be fixed by the smallest cut of a knife. No parts will be removed. It is merely the severing of an internal connection, quite nearly painless. While they are sleeping I will just see to it." The angel turned back toward the door of the cabin, drawing the knife from its sheath. Its blade was scarcely larger than Adam's fingernail and it gleamed white under the light of the stars.

Adam reached out and clapped a hand upon the other's shoulder. "If it is all so quick and simple as you say," he said, "then do you come back at some later time after Eve and I have had the opportunity to consider your proposal."

"It is no proposal," said the Angel, turning to face him and shrugging off his hand, "but a thing that is to be done, by order of El himself, this very night."

"The writ of El does not run here," said a third voice, and Adam turned to discover Walksfar approaching them across the clearing. "Camp may be small and mean to you who have come lately from the heights of the Palace, but it is old, founded in a place of wild souls by ones such as I who spawned in the age of the Old Gods and who looked upon Egdod himself with our own eyes. We did not invite El to the Land and we do not grant him the authority to send his minions into our dwellings and alter our forms with knives."

Courage overtook Adam upon hearing these words and seeing the confident stride and proud bearing of Walksfar. He advanced toward the entrance of the cabin so as to prevent the angel from drawing any closer.

"Those are brave words from an indolent hermit who has done nothing but sulk in his cabin and drink tea for centuries," said Messenger of El. "But while you were thus occupied, great changes came over the Land. You would be well advised to walk far again, as you did of old, and familiarize yourself with things as they are before insulting El and impeding his messenger."

Walksfar's face clouded and he did not seem ready with an answer, but Adam spoke: "I am well informed, as you know, and am hardly of a mind to insult El. But I will gladly impede his messenger in this case."

It had now come about that Messenger of El was between Adam and Walksfar, for the latter had not slowed in his advance. Looking both ways and finding himself hemmed in, the angel became an angel again. Its garment brightened until it was making light of its own, and unfurled into bright wings, and it sprang into the air, a little higher than a man might jump, so that Adam and Walksfar were looking upon its winged feet. "I am sent to make matters right here," it announced, "not to bandy words!" The angel spread its wings to an immense breadth and beat them once with all of its might. Adam and Walksfar were flung back on the ground with such violence that they both lay dazed for some little while.

Adam was brought to his senses by the cries of small souls in pain, and of Eve in horror and rage. He got up to his feet and ran into the cabin to find the angel bent over a male soul, at work with the little knife. The infant let out a sharp cry and the angel turned away, finished, blood dripping from its hand. At a glance Adam took in the five other boys, all screaming with small ribbons of blood between their legs. Eve was trying to comfort them. They had all been cut while Adam lay dazed.

"Yes," said Messenger of El, turning toward Adam, "it is all finished—except for you, Adam. One more cut and the Land will be forever safe from the errors of Egdod and of Spring."

Adam reached behind the door and found the handle of his axe and drew it forth.

The angel laughed. "You are more naive than I had imagined if you think to oppose the might of one of El's hosts with that."

Something hard and cold pushed Adam aside, and he felt the earthen floor shake under the tread of one who outweighed him by a hundredfold. Cairn had entered, and now directly confronted the angel, who only looked upon the old soul curiously, as if he had never seen or imagined its like. Cairn advanced one more step, as if obliging the angel's curiosity. They stood face-to-face for a moment. Then Cairn clapped his hands, or rather the blunt extremities of his upper limbs.

Messenger of El burst like a ripe fruit struck with a hammer. Gobbets of its aura sprayed the walls, ceiling, and floor. Its head and upper body were gone altogether. The lower parts and the arms and wings lost coherence and drifted apart, settling in various parts of the cabin. The effect was somewhat like how it had been at Elkirk when Adam and Eve had stood in the lower chamber with many new souls, scattered about the place, barely holding themselves together. The stuff that angels were made of was brighter. Yet the fragments of it lacked the coherence even of new souls, so powerfully had the blow dealt by Cairn disrupted Messenger of El's form. Scarce any part of the cabin's interior had gone unspattered, and the whole place was alight with the fizzing and fluctuating shine of the angel's aura. Adam reached out to comfort the six of the infants who had come under the knife, then drew his hand back as he noticed that it had been spattered. As he gazed in fascination at the gobbet of aura on the back of his hand, the stuff spread out and melted into his flesh, which glowed. This presently faded but he could feel something new coursing up his arm and into his chest, whence it spread through his body, making his head swim and his extremities tingle. He reached out again, this time to steady himself on the table where Messenger of El had done the cutting. The little boy lying before him had stopped crying. Patches of angel-stuff were soaking into him, setting most of his body aglow, and Adam could only assume that the boy was experiencing similar sensations.

Eve was up on her feet, gathering handfuls of it from places where it had spattered on the floor or the walls. Much of it had sunk into the earth. Adam fancied that the ground was shifting under his feet, though perhaps this was just the result of Cairn shambling out the door.

Cairn's rough form was silhouetted by a brilliant light, which caused Adam a moment's fear that more angels were coming, but when Cairn stepped aside, revealed was Walksfar, approaching the cabin holding the sword that the angel had left leaning against the tree. This had reverted to its original radiant form. "I did not expect that today was going to end with us in a fight with angels," said Walksfar, "but if that is the case, Thingor would want us to make use of this."

The talk of fighting was more than Adam wished to hear and so he turned his back to see how matters now stood in the cabin. Most of the angel-stuff was gone, for it was too chaotic and volatile to linger for very long in any one place without an organizing soul to keep it collected. But what had not disappeared yet Eve was scooping up and applying to the infants' bodies as if it were a balm. Seeing the way Adam looked on her she said, "The more of it is in us, the less is there for the use of El or any of his minions."

"Do we then owe something to El by having it in us—constituting us?"

"We owe El nothing save retribution," spat Eve.

"I mean, does it give El some power over us that he had not before?" Adam asked.

"I know not. But I am stronger now, more aware, than I was. And behold the little ones."

Adam beheld them and saw that the twelve were not as little as they had been earlier. In form they were still infants, but they now gazed about them curiously instead of sleeping or fussing, and their size was greater than what it had been.

"It would appear that I need to cut down even more trees," he said dryly. He met Eve's eye and they shared an affectionate look. But this was cut short by a flicker of light, which drew their gazes directly to the floor between them. One of the boys had got up on hands and knees and crawled to the place where Messenger of El had been standing when Cairn had crushed him. The angel's knife had there fallen to the floor and now lay shining like a tiny flake of thunderbolt, beguiling the eye. The child was reaching for it.

As one, Adam and Eve flung themselves at him. Adam was closer, and got there first, and clapped his hand over the bloody handle. He and Eve laughed. They had never laughed before.

Fighting did not come that day, or the next, or the next. Angels flew over Camp from time to time but did not alight. Adam did not go down to the river for two days, though he knew that Feller would dock his log pile. The twelve little ones wanted much attention. During the next few days they stayed close about Eve. The auras of the children and their mother were intertwined in a way that confounded Adam, but Eve, noting his amazement, let him know that this was all well and good, and that in this way the little ones drew from her both sustenance for their forms and knowledge that informed their minds. Each of them, she explained, was developing a personality of his or her own. She could with ease tell them apart. Adam was a little slower to discern them.

There were several souls in Camp who, though forgettish and even foolish in some ways, enjoyed the novelty of having small young souls about the place, and came by the cabin at all hours to look in on them. When it seemed that the little ones could be tended to without his being present, Adam resumed his practice of going down to the river at dawn to board Feller's boat. But the nature of his dealings with Feller had changed. Formerly, Adam had respected Feller and wished to please him. Now all such desires were gone from his soul. For Adam had fathered progeny and struggled against an angel and seen that angel destroyed by an animated pile of rock from the First Age. He had absorbed angel-stuff into his own soul and form. These events made all of Feller's doings seem so small and mean that Adam could scarcely be bothered to pay heed to the words coming from the boss's mouth or to care about the petty deeds and squabbles that occupied every waking moment of the likes of Bluff and Edger. The days when Bluff's size and strength had seemed impressive were now long past. And Adam was not the only soul who thought so, for it was now widely agreed in Eltown that Thunk, the free-roving woodcutter who came to town only infrequently, was the biggest and strongest soul in these parts, other than Adam.

In addition to axes, several other kinds of implements rattled in the bottom of Feller's boat. As the days went by, Adam learned the uses of these: mauls and wedges for splitting tree trunks lengthwise, a saw for crosscutting, knives and fids for rope work. Too there were several rods of iron, about as long as a man's forearm, devoid of any features that might hint at their purpose.

One day they arrived at the logging site to be greeted by the sound of axes biting into tree trunks. No other boat was to be seen, but fresh footprints were on the riverbank and some cut trees had been dragged down and marked with a glyph that was not known to Adam. Feller recognized it though, and reacted with disgust that soon flourished into wrath. He bent down and picked up one of the iron rods and handed it to Bluff, saying, "You know what to do," and then went on to distribute more rods to the others. He ran out of them before he got to Adam, but instead fetched him a spare axe handle, saying, "Watch and learn, for there is no hope for you in this fallen world unless you have it in you to fight those who would take from you." And he vaulted out of the boat onto the bank, where the rest of the crew were waiting, hefting their iron rods and swinging them through the air.

"I would stay here at the boat," Adam demurred, out of not so much fear as lack of interest in whatever it was Feller had in mind.

Feller appraised him and he could sense the others likewise giving him hard looks. "And what good will that do you if those murderers strike us, your friends, down with their axes? Then they will come for you, Adam. Will you fight them alone? Then you may forgo all hope of ever again looking upon the face of Eve."

Adam saw that a concern for his own safety, if not loyalty to his crew, dictated that he go into the woods with the others, and so that is what he did.

The ones Feller had called murderers were easily found, as they were not far away, and making no effort to be furtive.

Adam, not as eager as the others, arrived last, and found Feller already rebuking a woodcutter who, from the looks of things, was the leader of the other group; he was taller and broader than the rest, and the head of his axe contained much iron. This was Thunk. Adam had heard much of him but never seen him until now. Feller and Thunk had faced off in a space that was logged clear, into which felled trees had been dragged so that their limbs could be lopped. Feller had poised his iron rod on his shoulder, and Thunk had done likewise with his axe, which was double-edged. They were maintaining a certain distance from each other while maneuvering slowly about, and since each was gazing fixedly at the other's face, they planted their feet with care as they stepped, ever mindful of the stumps, logs, and boughs scattered underfoot. Feller was flanked by Bluff and Edger and the rest of his crew, but Thunk stood alone, as his people seemed generally of a mind to shrink back and seek refuge in the trees. To judge from the sounds made by these souls as they thrashed through the dried leaves, some of them were simply running away as fast as they could. Less obviously, though, others seemed to be moving around to form a circle about the crew of Feller. Adam, arriving late, nearly tripped over one such, surprising a tall woman as she sidestepped along the edge of the clearing, her attention focused toward the center. She nearly sprang into the air when she realized that Adam was right behind her. Then, recovering her poise, she slipped back, eyes seeking and finding the axe handle first. Only when she was safely out of its range did she give Adam the curious head-to-toe examination that he had grown accustomed to. Adam returned it in kind. She was the tallest woman he had seen, with long muscles showing on her limbs. Slung over her shoulder was a pouch that seemed to contain something heavy. Dangling loosely from one hand was a double length of cord with a scrap of netting woven into its middle.

Adam for his part was beginning to see wisdom, or at least cunning, in Feller's suggestion that they ought to stay close together, and so it was with a certain sense of relief that he strode full into the clearing to close ranks with the other members of his crew. Feller noted this in the corner of his eye, and Thunk risked turning his head to give Adam a look.

"So it is true what was rumored," said Thunk, "that you have brought into your service one of the ancient souls of First Town."

"That I have," said Feller. "He is loyal and will do as I say, and if that means bringing harm to you, then the harm will be as great as his shoulders are broad."

"Someday I would hear the sad story of how one of the great souls of the First Age was brought so low," Thunk remarked. It seemed from his aura and from the tone of his voice that he was not merely bandying words but sincerely disappointed to see one such as Adam reduced to so mean an estate.

Having grown used to the cleverly calculated speech that issued at all times from the lips of Feller, Adam was struck hard by the words of Thunk precisely because they were so plainly spoken. His head swam for a moment with shame and he was obliged to shift his footing in order to stay well rooted on the uneven ground.

"Adam is smarter than he looks," retorted Feller, "and will not be swayed by your poisoned words." And he looked briefly Adam's way, as if unsure of this.

Adam was now thoroughly confused, as it had never before entered his mind that his appearance was such as to convey the impression that he was dim-witted; and moreover Thunk's words had struck him as anything but poisoned, and so he was now wondering whether he, Adam, was not smart enough—whatever that might mean—clearly to perceive Thunk's true nature.

With so much clouding his mind, Adam scarcely heard the next part of the conversation. But he was vaguely aware of Feller proclaiming that only he, Feller, had the "right" to cut trees here and of Thunk denying that this was so and asserting that the Old

Gods had put trees in such places just so that any souls who had need of them could come and chop them down.

What finally dislodged Adam from this reverie was the sound of sudden movement in the trees behind him. He turned around just in time to see an axe flying through the air in his direction, its handle spinning wildly around its bright head. It made a thrum in the air as it whipped past him, and traveled several more yards before clattering off a tree stump near Feller and falling to the ground. Both Feller and Thunk watched it fall, and there were a few moments of silence.

Then Feller and Bluff both came for Thunk.

At first Adam thought Thunk in a bad spot, since he was standing with his back to a felled tree that was still being held up off the ground by its boughs, so that its trunk was at the level of Thunk's waist. But Thunk knew just where it was and leapt to the top of it with ease. "It's on!" he shouted, then jumped down to the ground on the other side and ran toward the edge of the clearing, moving away from the river as if meaning to retreat into the deep woods.

Feller and Bluff were delayed in getting over the log, and the distance separating them from Thunk grew large. A shout, followed by a shower of missiles, came from the trees all around. Adam was struck in the back by a rock, which taught him to face the trees and look out for his own welfare. More projectiles came his way, prompting him to back toward the middle of the clearing until he sensed that his fellows were nearby. There were more people in the woods than Adam had suspected. Their earlier retreat had been merely for show; they had quietly doubled back during the argument between Feller and Thunk. The tall woman stepped into the open, moving one hand in a tight circle. Her pieces of cord whirled about her hand so fast that they could be seen only as a blur. Then from the blur a rock flew out, making a hum as it cut through the air, and struck one of Feller's crew with such force that it knocked him off his feet.

Feller, seeing a few axmen come into the open, cried, "Let's get them!" and ran at the foes holding high his iron rod. He was followed closely by Bluff. The rest, including Adam, took up the rear, less out of a desire to "get them" than from fear of being left behind. Reaching the site of the melee, Adam was nearly struck by an iron rod as Bluff swung it back to bring it down upon the head of a smaller woodcutter who was crumpled on the ground with his crushed hands splayed uselessly atop a skull that had gone all misshapen; his head had cracked open and the aura was pouring out of it, reverting to chaos. To strike again seemed unnecessary but Bluff was doing so, his rod dripping with blood and fizzing with aura. Another woodcutter came at Bluff from behind, raising an axe above his head to strike. In his rage he seemed not to notice Adam, who merely extended his axe handle and laid it across that of the attacker, stopping his strike before there was much force in it. Frozen in position with both hands above his head, this man was assailed by Edger, who seemed to punch him in the stomach. But blood spurted out where the punch landed, and when she drew back her hand Adam saw that it was gripping a long knife, as sharp as only Edger could make it.

Adam was nearly as transfixed by this as the man she had stabbed, until another member of the crew called Adam's name.

Following his gaze Adam turned to see a foe rushing at him from behind. Without any thought he extended the axe handle to push this fellow back. It caught him a glancing blow to the face that was enough to spoil his balance. As that man fell, Bluff's rod came down on his head.

Those moments were the crisis of the fight. It then declined into a series of sporadic brawls as they made their way back toward the river. Feller was keen on getting back to the boat, and would have run straight to it, but the projectiles still hurtling their way from all directions obliged them to retreat in a more deliberate style, walking backward much of the way, alert to the hum of the slings that their foes used to hurl rocks.

As they drew closer to the bank of the river and the cries of their attackers diminished, they became conscious of a distant, repetitive sound, growing more distinct: the *thunk, thunk* of an axe biting deep into wood. It was a sound that filled their days and to which they were well accustomed. But this had a hollow booming character to it, different from the sound of a tree being felled. When they came in view of the riverbank, they understood why: Thunk had got there well ahead of them and flipped Feller's boat upside down to expose its belly. He was standing on its hull swinging his sharp axe down into its keel. A distant splintering noise told them that he had broken all the way through it. As Feller sprinted toward him howling like a wild beast, Thunk watched him and coolly struck a few more blows through its thinner hull planking before stepping back and dropping into the river. A few steps took him out into the current, which bore him away. Feller, mounting to the top of his ruined boat, hefted his rod as if making ready to hurl it at Thunk; but then he thought better of doing so.

They turned the ruined boat back over to find that Thunk's crew had pilfered their axes and other goods. They did not even have enough rope to lash the available logs together into a raft that could bear them downstream, and so instead they walked back to Eltown: a journey that would have taken them but an hour rowing downstream but that on foot consumed the remainder of the day. Of Thunk and his crew they saw no more, though at first every shifting tree branch or scurrying beast caused them to twitch about and unlimber their iron rods.

As the day drew on, however, and weariness and cold and hunger overtook them, they all became less concerned about Thunk and more about getting back to the fires of Eltown. The bank of the river seemed endless. In the early part of the day they were traversing country that had been logged but recently. The undergrowth was scant and the going easy enough. But as they advanced into parts that had been denuded of trees longer, they encountered dense thickets of wild brambles, made of thorny shafts that were stiff enough to impede their movement and yet flexible enough that when struck by their iron rods they seemed to dodge the blow and then spring back in counterattack. Steep sections of bank obliged them to climb inland away from the stream, adding miles to the trek.

Roper—the member of the crew who had saved Adam, earlier, by calling out his name—became especially despondent. It had always been in his nature to take a gloomy view of things and to require encouragement from his fellows and chastisement from the boss. "It cannot possibly be so far to Eltown," he moaned. "Surely we have got lost and are going down some other river now, taking us to strange places where people, if there are any, speak in gibberish."

"That makes no sense," Adam pointed out. "There is but one river; we have kept it to our left the whole time and never been out of the hearing of it."

"Do not be so sure," said Bluff.

"Water runs downhill," insisted Adam. "We may have strayed now and then from the bank, but we cannot have crossed over into some other streambed."

"That may be true where you come from," growled Feller, "but you forget that Eltown was founded by cursed souls who came here to escape El's wrath. Honey saw El's light and adored it, building her white tower above, but the others slunk into this dark vale to be out of El's sight, and made their habitation in places they knew to be infested with wild souls who would not even obey Egdod, to say nothing of El. This river may be one such, for all we know. I have always sensed something uncanny about it. It hates us for what we have done to the forests along its banks and it would not surprise me if it had switched its course when we were not looking, so as to lead us into despair and danger."

"That is a mad notion," Adam muttered.

"Still it is easier going down than up, and so down it is," Feller answered. "To wherever this cursed river would have us end."

More such cheerful predictions followed from Roper, until Edger began to mock him. In the blessed silence that followed they soon heard rapids, and hastened toward the sound to the place where the West Fork rushed into the more placid Middle Fork. "Finally we are rid of that cursed river," Feller said, though the fact that it had taken them here seemed to prove it was not cursed at all.

Downstream of that place the water roamed to and fro over a floodplain and the going was somewhat easier, though still impeded by brush. The range of mountains that hemmed in the valley to the west made for an early sunset, and they walked in shadow for some while even though the land across the river was still sunlit. The white tower of Elkirk came into view briefly, then was hidden again for a long while. But they had all seen it and there was no further talk of wicked ancient souls haunting the land.

Or so Adam assumed until they came around a bend and looked far downriver to the place where the East Fork flowed in. Just beyond there was the beginning of Eltown, whose towers of smoke caught the red light of the nearly set sun. And just before it, plainly in view, was the hill that stood above the junction of the rivers. Its denuded, stump-stubbled lower reaches were in shadow, but its crown was still lit, as if by a dying fire, and the great tree's scarred trunk rose up above that, its winter-bare branches raised up into the sky as if grasping at the last traces of the day's light.

"You have mocked me for the last time, old one," said Feller.

It took Adam some few moments to understand that he was addressing the tree.

"If my boat is no more, why then so be it. We shall seek what is nearer to hand. Tonight our iron bars we will reforge into axe heads ready to be made keen by Edger, and tomorrow we will come for you."

46

The plan of Feller was much slower in coming to pass than he had first imagined. His crew were too exhausted to do anything at all the next day, and the day after that they awoke thinking of the complications that would be entailed, not just in cutting down the big tree, but in reducing its carcass to pieces small enough to be got down to the river. Adam had little interest in the plan and correspondingly little knowledge of its particulars, but when he crossed the river a few days later, everyone in Eltown seemed to know about it and to have become somehow involved—or to be claiming, at any rate, that Feller had entrusted them with this or that aspect of the preparations. Axe heads were being forged just as Feller had promised, but as well there was rope to be twisted, splitting wedges to be made, and supplies to be laid in for the encampment that Feller imagined he would bring into being around the tree. The project was seen as requiring a month's work. Feller's ambitions soon grew to include the creation of a new town on the site, and this brought further delays.

It also entailed docking the log piles of Adam and the other members of the crew. Feller did this when no one was present to raise objections, and later explained it as a necessary investment that would be repaid manyfold when the big tree came down.

Not wishing to make any further investments in a plan that troubled him in more than one way, Adam traded some of his remaining logs for cloth and other items that were required by the children, then devoted some days to rafting the remaining ones together and floating them across the river to the shore beneath Camp. This was a large enough task that he had to adopt the ways of Feller, at least for a time, and hire other souls to help him. It seemed a reasonable plan at the outset but became more trouble than it was worth as the members of his crew found every possible way of doing things wrong; and when not doing things wrong, they fell to arguments, which they assumed must be as momentous to Adam as they were to them, and which Adam was somehow responsible for settling; and none was ever pleased with how they were resolved. As little as Adam liked Feller, he came quickly to understand why Feller dealt with his crew as he did.

Adam had worked for Feller in order to get what he needed to make a bigger dwelling for him and Eve and the children, but it almost immediately became obvious that his labors were at once too little and too much. Too little because the children grew so rapidly that Adam could never have cut down trees and expanded the cabin quickly enough to keep pace with them, and too much because they soon were given accommodations in other buildings around Camp. Adam's log pile, when it finally made its way up the hill, dwindled and disappeared in a matter of days as the wood was used to shore up various structures that had fallen into disrepair as their builders wandered away or became forgettish.

Walksfar had spoken of other old souls who had accompanied him on the Trek, Cairn being one such, but for the most part they had not been in evidence. This changed as the twelve little ones grew and word of them somehow spread into the remote places into which those old souls had strayed during the many years that Walksfar had been drinking tea and carving marks on his wall. For the most part those were not as outlandish in their forms as Cairn; most were closer to Walksfar's shape. But one had been dwelling among beasts for so long that he had begun to resemble a bear, and there was another soul that possessed no physical form at all but was embodied solely in movements of the air, made visible by entrained dust. Beast and Dusty seemed to favor each other's company and were frequently seen together, the former sitting naked and hairy on the ground while the latter swirled about him in the form of a dust devil. Such was the community of souls in which the twelve children learned to crawl, then walk and talk. By the time they could go about on two feet they were already half as tall as Adam.

The existence of twelve large new souls could not be hid from the people of Eltown. Adam was glad to have moved his logs and concluded his dealings with those people, for on the occasions when he did cross the river to fetch something, he always found himself at the center of a crowd of excited souls demanding to know just what was going on over in Camp. Some there were who had seen Messenger of El descend into Camp but not depart, and knowledge of that had become widespread and given rise to rumors of such a far-fetched nature that Adam could not believe his ears when they were presented to him—always with a demand for confirmation or denial. The truth of what had happened that night was, of course, not one that he wished to be known. Walksfar went down into the town with Adam, and settled the people down by explaining that Camp had always been a place of queer folk and queer doings and that there was little gain to be had in concerning oneself overmuch about it.

One morning Mab awoke them with the news that, in the forested valley to the east—the place of the wolves that divided Elkirk from the sea of grass—many campfires were alight. Adam crossed the river to Eltown, where later that day word reached them that Honey had at last returned to Elkirk, and that she was in the company of a host of souls, unlike any in Eltown or even in Camp. They had come across the grass from El's Palace, moving at unusual speed because they had learned to bestride large animals: four-legged beasts of a kind not before seen in the Land, perfectly adapted to the task of carrying two-legged souls on their backs while subsisting on the grass itself.

Later in the day, a queue of these creatures became visible picking its way down the long series of switchbacks that connected the kirk to Eltown. Everyone watched them come, fascinated by the sight of the two-legged souls bestriding four-legged beasts, as if the two kinds of creature had been merged into one. The creatures of the riders did their job so well that the new arrivals were able to manage the tricky and tedious descent in half the usual time.

And so just like that the riders were at large in the streets of Eltown. Once they descended from their mounts they were of the same general form as other souls. They were tall and symmetrically formed, like Adam and Eve, Thunk, and Walksfar. Their hair was long and fair, swept back from high brows, and their clothing, though somewhat darkened from travel, was also fair. They carried long poles with sharp tips of iron, which Adam guessed were made to keep wolves at bay, and at their hips they had long blades, like the one that Messenger of El had carried when he had changed over into the guise of a human. In sum, they were obviously patterned after the angels of El's palace, but without wings. Adam had never seen their like when he had dwelled in the Garden with Eve, and so he judged it likely that they were a fresh creation of El's.

As much was soon confirmed by the name that the riders used to set themselves apart from the ordinary people of Eltown. They called themselves Autochthons, which was a word meaning "one who sprang naturally from the Land."

The Autochthon at the head of the column spied Adam from a distance as they rode slowly through the streets of the town, thronged by curious souls who crowded around to behold them and to touch the muscled legs and flanks of the mounts. This soul, who as they would later learn was called Captain, met Adam's gaze with no particular emotion, save perhaps curiosity. He turned back to say something to the one behind him, and as he did he lowered the tip of his lance to point it at Adam. Word spread back down the column, and the Autochthons all looked at him.

"They are here to replace us" was the verdict of Eve, when Adam told her the story later. "We failed in the eyes of El. He said it himself when he threw us out of the Garden; the taint of the Alpha and Beta worlds could not be scoured away from us and so he gave up on ever making us all that he had hoped for. It is obvious what his next step would have been: to fashion altogether new kinds of souls, free of any such taint, in El's own image, and send them out into the world to achieve what we failed at."

Adam was less glum than Eve, but he had to admit that there was something to her words. "I had been wondering," he admitted, "why El did not send out more angels to cut me, as Messenger of El cut our boys. Now I see it. He can make as many of these new souls as he chooses. We, and our offspring, simply do not matter; we may continue to exist in the nooks and crannies of the Land, as Cairn and other old souls do here in Camp, but it is the Autochthons who are meant to prosper and to rule."

It had been a long while since Adam and Eve had copulated, but they did so on the day that the Autochthons came down from Elkirk, and after that made a habit of it.

The Autochthons made camp in the cleared land surrounding Eltown. This had become overgrown with low scrubby vegetation considered inedible and useless. But the mounts of the Autochthons could seemingly subsist on any kind of vegetation that they could get into their mouths, and so it suited them. When their beasts had cleared an area, the Autochthons, rather than allowing the weeds to grow back, would plant it thickly with seeds that they had brought with them in sacks. Concerning these there was much curiosity among the people of Eltown. Adam did not need to wait for them to sprout and grow to know that it would be some manner of new plant invented by El to sustain his people and that it would grow well and feed them more abundantly than the crops traditionally raised, and the wild plants gathered, by the folk of Eltown.

The Autochthons kept coming, a few at a time. According to Mab, who flew far and wide across the sea of grass, they issued from the base of the Hive every day in scores, each score behind a Captain, and formed up in columns that headed off in several directions. Some rode straight for Elkirk, but others strayed off toward parts of the Land of which Mab knew nothing.

Before long, Eltown was surrounded on all sides, save the riverfront, by fields cleared and sown by the Autochthons. This gave fresh impetus to Feller's project. For until then it had been the habit of the people of Eltown to assume that they could go on forever sprawling out into the treeless waste that they had made around them. But the enclosure of the town changed their thinking and made them of a mind to build more on what space was still to be had. The result was a demand for more logs. Feller renewed his planning and preparations, which had languished as his enterprise had grown more ambitious. His promise to build a new town on the site was of interest to those who now felt hemmed in by the Autochthons and their mounts and their farms.

The old souls of Camp had been slow to grasp the nature of these changes, for little had altered in their world since the days of the Trek. They did not think or act at the same pace as others. Cairn, for example, though he had moved rapidly against Messenger of El, had been known to remain motionless for years at a time. Though they were fascinated with and delighted by the twelve children of Adam and Eve, they were unable to keep up with the speed and agility of their play. The best that they could do was to weave a makeshift barrier of branches and vines around the edge of Camp's central clearing and then try to dissuade the little ones from climbing over it.

Returning every so often from his errands in Town, Adam would tell the people of Camp about the settlements being created by the Autochthons and the tools and materials being stockpiled by Feller. Though they listened and seemed to take in his words, they did not seem to grasp the nature of things until one day when Adam insisted that some of them must leave the familiar confines of Camp, even if only for a few hours, and go down to the river with him.

They made arrangements for the twelve little ones to be looked after, entrusting them to souls such as Mab and Dusty who could be relied on not to be outrun or outwitted. Adam walked down the hill in the company of Eve, Walksfar, Beast, and Cairn. When they had emerged from the woods that girded the hill and come out into the open they were able to look across the river into the heart of Eltown.

Formerly this had been partly concealed behind ramparts of logs, but these had become depleted of late and so the flames and smoke of the forges and kilns were directly visible, and around them the camp where newly arrived souls were wont to dwell in the open. Behind that were the buildings of the town, rising higher by the day as timbers were hauled up to their roofs and used to assemble upper stories. Flanking the town to its north and south, and new to those who had not lately stirred from Camp, were belts of open land now bright green with the fresh growth from the seeds sown by the Autochthons. These new fields were crisply delineated by walls that the Autochthons made by heaping up rocks and stumps that they had extracted from the ground with the help of their mounts. Those walls were highest where they faced the town, which made the souls of Eltown seem pent up inside. Their outlet was to the river, and there on the broad flat plain before the fires they had assembled a fleet of rafts and barges laden with rope, canvas, tools, and other supplies that figured into Feller's plan.

Adam, knowing their purpose, could not help sweeping his gaze upstream to the place where the two river valleys came together. Just above their junction rose the bare stubbled hill with the great tree at its top. Its branches had been naked to the winter winds when Feller had vowed to cut it down, but by this time were green with new leaves. Around it, the slopes of the hill were now marked with ropes strung taut between stakes, and little flags, and tents and awnings that had been put up in preparation for Feller's great undertaking.

Despite the fact that Adam had been forewarning them of all these things for weeks, the old souls of Camp were troubled, and surprised to see what was under way. "Many years ago," said Walksfar, "when this valley was nothing but trees, I stood up over yonder where the tower of Elkirk stands now and looked down and had to strain my eyes to pick out the great one. Now it seems lonely indeed. I would go there now and stand before it and—"

"Talk to it?" Adam asked.

"Try to ascertain whether there is anything there that is capable of being talked to, or of talking back," said Walksfar. "For with these wild souls one never knows; they are not like us."

With that errand in mind they went down farther into the settlement of old buildings on their side of the river. Lately many souls had crossed over and crowded shelters into whatever space they could find. Merely getting through to the river had become difficult. As they picked and shouldered their way among the improvised shelters, various souls emerged to stare at them. For there were many whose knowledge of the Land was limited to what they had seen up at Elkirk and down in Eltown, and they had never seen anything like Adam and Eve, to say nothing of Beast or Cairn. By the time they had reached the edge of the river, where Adam had once been in the habit of getting passage on boats, they were surrounded by a crowd of a few score souls who evidently had nothing better to occupy their time than to follow them around.

"Word of your coming preceded you, Adam," said Strongback, the boatman who had most commonly taken him across the river in the past. He seemed to be referring to a fleet-footed soul who had been running ahead of them, alerting everyone.

"I had not known that it was so remarkable an event," Adam said, "for a few residents of Camp to go on a stroll down to the river."

"Times are changing," said Strongback, "and the folk of Camp are not viewed in the same way as they once were. For many years nothing ever changed there. Then you and Eve showed up. Then there was the strange business with the angel who came in the nighttime. Then all of a sudden twelve new souls who seemed to come out of nowhere. Now the Autochthons are among us and around us, bringing new ways of doing things, straight from El, and with them is Honey herself." He cast a glance up toward the white tower of Elkirk. "And Honey brings new teachings directly from El." He looked at the fleet-footed soul who had gone before Adam and the others spreading word of their approach. This had the look of one but lately come from the kirk and not much used to the rigors of life in the town. "Acolyte, say what you know, that all may hear it."

Acolyte spoke in great earnest, as if nothing in his short life had prepared him for the possibility that he might be wrong: "There is to be a new way of things in the Land. It comes to us from the Autochthons, who are sent out by El to remedy all that was wrongly done before." And as if this were not sufficiently obvious he looked searchingly at Adam, Eve, and the others who had come down from Camp.

They listened in the expectation that this Acolyte might say more, but when nothing was forthcoming Walksfar said, "In what way does this concern me and others in Camp? We lived satisfactorily in First Town before El had even come into the Land, and likewise in Camp afterward. I would draw your attention to the fact that we have not asked El for any advice as to how we might improve ourselves."

"Be that as it may," said Acolyte, "the new town that is to be built on yonder hill will not be another like Eltown but will be ordered according to directions from Honey, who has them from the Palace of El."

"It is high time that I went up to the kirk and talked to Honey," said Walksfar. "Not to dispute the plans you speak of, for they are none of my concern, but to renew an old acquaintance and learn more of these doings. And while I am out of Camp I shall also go up onto the hill and learn how matters stand with that old tree. Strongback, I would cross the river one more time if there is room in your boat."

"There isn't," said Strongback.

"There would be," Walksfar demurred, "if you were to shift that coil of rope back a bit and move that keg of nails."

"The management of my boat and its cargo is no concern of yours," Strongback replied. "There is no room to carry you or any of your sort."

Walksfar was taken aback, and Adam saw in his aura shock and confusion. "Well then," he said, "perhaps on some other occasion."

"Perhaps." Strongback turned away and went down to his boat. His crew untied the lines that held it fast and rowed it out into the stream, headed not straight across to Eltown, but rather up in the direction of the new project.

Cairn was not well formed for speech, but he grumbled out a few sounds to the effect that none of this made the least difference to him, who could not get into any boat anyway without crashing directly through its hull planks and sinking it. He stomped down toward the water's edge and kept stomping until he had disappeared, leaving on the surface a trail of bubbles, mud, and loose debris that was soon swept away by the current.

Accustomed as they were to Cairn and other such old and wild souls, Adam and Eve found this less remarkable than did the townspeople who watched it happen. Far from being delighted by it, however, those took it amiss and grumbled among themselves as to just how unnatural and wrong it seemed.

Another, newer boat was being loaded nearby, but its owner held up a hand as if to stop Walksfar from even looking at it. "We have all heard of what became of the boat of Feller," he announced, throwing a dark look at Adam. Which made no sense at all; but in the faces of the people there seemed to be some kind of certainty that because Adam was somehow involved in the story of Feller's boat, he should never be allowed near a boat again. "The Autochthons," said Acolyte, "are as big and as strong as you, Adam, and their mounts stronger yet. You are not needed anymore and so it were better for you to stay in Camp and look after the twelve creatures you have spawned and see to it that they do not get up to any mischief."

At this Adam and Eve were both full of wrath and had to be conducted away from the place by Walksfar and Beast.

Since it seemed they were no longer welcome on boats, the next day Adam and Walksfar struck out northward from Camp, walking parallel to the bank of the river toward a bluff on this, its western bank, whence according to Walksfar they would have a clear view directly across the stream to the hill of the great tree. Along the way they retraced some of the path that Adam had trod on the day that Feller's boat had been destroyed. Adam spied footprints, which looked fresh. Some of them were uncommonly large, and so it was with little surprise that he and Walksfar came in view of Thunk and his band.

They had made a camp atop the very bluff toward which Adam and Walksfar had been heading. So that way was blocked; but, as they soon became aware, members of Thunk's band were behind them as well. Adam was of a mind to steal away. But Walksfar said, "There is little point in pretending that we have not been noticed." On his back he had been carrying a long bundle swathed in old blankets. He swung this down and peeled away the tattered fabric to expose the handle of the weapon that Messenger of El had carried on his hip. Its blade was shrouded in a dark sheath, but when Walksfar drew it out just a finger's width, the light of it dazzled. "Between this," he said, "and the knife on your belt, we can meet them, should they come for us, with weapons forged by Thingor himself, and I do not think that they will have much relish for that fight."

Adam was left somewhat bolstered in his confidence as well as embarrassed by his own naivete; for in the earlier fight with Thunk's band, he had carried the angel's knife in its sheath the entire time. Never had it entered his mind to wield it against the attackers.

Walksfar stepped out into an open space in view of the bluff and waved an arm above his head and hailed Thunk in a clear voice. As he did so, Adam heard movement in the trees nearby and turned around to see a woman coming into view; she had evidently been following them, but so stealthily that they had not known of her presence until now. It was the woman he had noted before the fight at the boat. Dangling from her hand was that doubled length of cord, a smooth stone nestled in its pocket. Having seen her work before, Adam wondered whether Walksfar's sword would really have been of any use had she decided to stand off at a distance and pelt them with stones.

But no such thing occurred. Shortly they found themselves up on the top of the bluff being treated cautiously but hospitably by Thunk and the others. Adam recognized some of these. There were two who seemed of a mind to continue fighting where they had last left off. But seeing this Thunk stepped between them and spoke to them: "Adam came last to that fight, and only defended himself and his comrades; if you look askance at him for that, ask what your opinion of him would be had he stood by and done nothing while we struck them all down."

This seemed to change their thinking and so they altered their posture and stepped back. Thunk greeted the woman, calling her Whirr, and she greeted him back in a very familiar manner.

On the day of the fight, Adam had not had leisure to look closely at Thunk's people, but now that they were standing at ease around a campfire, he saw various types: some old souls; some newer ones, such as Whirr, who appeared to have developed their forms out in wild places where they had no models or effigies upon which to pattern themselves; and others who had clearly been raised in

Elkirk. But even the latter were taller and more erect in their bearings than their counterparts in Eltown, as if merely living in the wild with Thunk and his band caused them to change their forms accordingly.

The vantage point was excellent, affording views both across and down the river. Nodding toward the smudge of the town, now girded in bright green fields, Thunk said, "So those who are pent up yonder now toil to build a new prison for themselves." His gaze tracked upstream. "Pity that tree is in the way."

Hearing this Adam was of a mind to speak up in defense of the tree until he saw Thunk and Walksfar exchanging a look. Then he understood that the former had been making a sort of joke, at the expense of Feller. "If it were only Feller and his crew," said Thunk, glancing at Adam, "I would go and chase them off. But now he comes with an army."

It was a word Adam had not heard before, but as he saw the souls swarming on the hill he understood it to mean something like El's host. Hundreds of souls were on the hill. Most of them were down along the riverfront unloading boats and stacking various types of supplies, but some were roaming about the slopes above driving in stakes with crisp hammer strokes that could be heard clearly across the river, and stretching lines this way and that.

Near the top of the hill, just a little below the trunk of the great tree, was a large open space, devoid of souls, stakes, and ropes, at the center of which stood a stack of rocks about the height of a man. For the moment it was not moving, but Adam could see from the trail of deep footsteps leading up to it that Cairn had simply walked to this place in a straight line across the bottom of the river. En route he seemed to have destroyed some of Feller's preparations by walking through them as if they were not there, but in his wake repairs were already being made.

"Friend of yours?" Whirr asked. Then she laughed. "His trudge up the hill made for enjoyable watching."

"He has dwelled in Camp for a long time, and knew the wild souls hereabouts when the Land was young and it was possible to roam across it for a whole season and never encounter another soul," Walksfar said.

"Too bad for him," said Thunk, "that he found himself in the midst of so many neighbors."

"I blame myself," Walksfar said, "for welcoming new souls to town and allowing them to proliferate and to spread. I assumed that they would acquire wisdom. Instead there seems no end to their straying."

Whirr turned her back to the river and directed her gaze into the north and the west, where high mountains could be seen, white with snow. "There are other places," she said, "where souls could live and be left alone, at least for a good long span of years."

"Sooner or later the same thing would happen as happened here," Thunk demurred, "unless measures were taken to prevent new souls from drifting in willy-nilly and establishing the same habits and practices."

Walksfar nodded. "I should have foreseen as much long ago, but I was too comfortable alone in my cabin to trouble myself with the doings of the new ones."

"What business do you suppose the cairn that walks might have today on the hill?" asked Whirr, now turning back to look that way.

"We had all hoped to go yesterday," said Adam, "and ascertain whether those ancient souls are still of a mind to engage in conversations. But the boatmen refused to take us. Therefore Cairn went alone. I would suppose that he is talking, in his own way, and listening for any answers that might be forthcoming."

"Supposing he makes himself understood," said Thunk, "and conveys the information that the tree is in danger, what of it? If I warn a member of my band that a stone from Whirr's sling is headed for him, he can duck out of the way, and he is not altered by having moved. But once a tree or a hill has created a form for itself and put down roots into everything and dwelled there for many years, can it move out of harm's way? And supposing it could, would it still then be the same tree? Or would the act of moving change it into something else, so that it was as dead as if it had been chopped down?"

"All good questions," said Walksfar, "to which I lack answers at present."

Adam for his part thought back to the fight between Thunk's

and Feller's crews. He remembered in particular the man whom Bluff had so mercilessly beaten with his iron rod, utterly destroying his form so that the aura spilled forth and reverted to chaos. And in the same vein he thought of Messenger of El, likewise splattered, in such a way that he had not been able to form himself again. Could the same fate befall any soul? Even, perhaps, Egdod himself when El had come for him? Did the soul then go away and cease to exist forever, or could it spawn again and begin the slow process of re-forming itself?

Cairn stood there for most of the day, then suddenly went into movement again, shambling back down toward the river in a gait somewhere between a walk and a minor landslide. En route he touched off some secondary disturbances on the unstable slope and picked up a long train of ropes and canvas that got tangled about him. Some of the souls working on preparations seemed offended. Three of them seemed to embolden one another to the point of action, and approached Cairn, and threw rocks at him. The folly of throwing rocks at a pile of rocks seemed never to have entered their minds. Thunk, Whirr, Walksfar, and Adam laughed at them. This—the fact that they had all seen humor in the same thing at the same time—seemed to establish a friendship among them, such that without needing to speak of it they then parted on amicable terms.

Adam and Walksfar hiked back to Camp and found Cairn standing in the middle of it, sporting a few new rocks. Around him played the twelve children of Adam and Eve. These were now almost as tall as many of the souls who dwelled in Eltown.

Adam went and sought out Eve in their cabin. She could see in his aura that some change had come over him and so they went out and walked in the woods together. "Changes are in the offing," Adam said, "and I believe that we must prepare for a journey."

"Camp has been a good place for us," said Eve, "but staying here has not brought us any nearer to our goal of finding our mother, Spring, and so it is time for us to leave."

"There will be hardships," Adam warned her, thinking of what it would be like to travel with the twelve children.

"I know that better than you," Eve returned. Adam looked

away, ashamed. Eve shrugged. "Perhaps some of our new friends will come with us, and ease our burdens."

Later that evening, when the air had gone calm, they heard the distant sound of axes striking into wood, and a cheer went up from the river.

Adam and Eve walked the next day to a vantage point from which they could see the work in progress. A hundred souls were up in the branches of the tree, hacking off its boughs so that the trunk could be brought down more easily; these crashed to earth every so often, each as great as a large tree in its own right. Workers tied ropes to these so that they could be dragged down the slope. Many more ropes had been made fast to the trunk itself; these all pulled in the same direction, being attached at their lower ends to old stumps or to thick stakes driven deep. Hacking away at the base of the trunk was not just a single woodcutter but several teams of them, each gnawing away at a different spot.

As that day, and the day after, went by, their excavations merged into a single notch, large enough that twenty souls could stand upright inside of it and swing axes. By that point the tree was entirely limbless, just a bare pole projecting from the top of the hill, beginning to list in the direction that the ropes were pulling. It seemed for a while that it might not come down in a single moment but rather just lean farther and farther until it came gently to rest. But in the middle of the third day there was a crack, immensely loud, which was heard everywhere and then echoed from all of the surrounding slopes. The trunk toppled slowly. Or so it seemed from a distance. But the frantic scurrying of souls all around it hinted at the true speed and violence of its fall. A spume of aura shot up into the air from its stump, as when the lid is removed from a boiling pot, and dissipated into the sky. From the souls on the hillside a cheer went up.

Then it turned into a scream as the hill shrugged.

That was the extent of its movement, as it seemed from afar: a slow heaving, as when a sleeping beast inhales deeply and then heaves out a great shivering sigh.

A disturbance flowed from the hill's apex downward, like wind blowing over grass, gathering strength rather than dissipating as it propagated down toward the riverfront. On a closer look this consisted of souls, and all the stuff that they had brought with them. Like crumbs being shaken from a cloth they tumbled into the rivers on either side of the hill, cluttering the water for some moments with all sorts of stuff and detritus.

A moment later they were all buried under a second, darker and heavier tide that had been shrugged off of the hill by a stronger convulsion. This was the hillside itself: all the earth that had clothed it and all the stumps that had been rooted in that earth. It fell upon the souls in the river and buried them. And it fell too upon the water of the rivers.

The two rivers burst out from under the avalanche, forming up into white waves. Seen from downriver, these waves—one in each of the two forks—unfurled like angels' wings, spreading across each of the streams and rebounding from the banks opposite, throwing up spumes of dirty foam as the displaced water piled up into a fluid hill. The water acted as if it had a soul of its own, and the soul was confused; but after some moments it determined that the way out was down in the direction of Eltown. There was further confusion as the two mounds of water came together and clashed at the junction, just at the foot of the hill—or what had been the hill a minute ago. Now it had shed its cloak of earth to reveal a skeleton of boulders, resembling a much larger version of Cairn.

Which on any other day would have commanded their full attention. But now they could not stop watching the slow relentless marshaling of the waters. These settled into a step: a clear and straight cliff that stretched from one bank to the other and marched downstream at a pace that looked stately until one compared it to the movements of a few terrified souls running full-tilt along the banks.

The wave spread across Eltown, inundating it all, toppling its buildings and snuffing its fires, the graves of which were thereafter marked by columns of steam. It spread thence over the new walls and across the green fields of the Autochthons, strewing them with flotsam picked up from the ruined structures of the town. The farther it spread, the slower it went, and at the end it

was no more than knee- or ankle-deep on the legs of the Autochthons and their mounts. They seemed only a little inconvenienced
by the flood. Their fields were left speckled with flat puddles and
strewn with wreckage. Damage was much greater in town, where
many structures had been knocked flat and some, paradoxically,
were burning.

Concerned as they were with trying to help souls trapped in
wreckage, or salvaging their belongings, the people of Eltown had
eyes only for what was close to hand. A similar state of affairs
prevailed in the smaller settlement down below Camp, which had
likewise been inundated. But the higher ground of Camp was unaffected. From there Adam and Eve and the other souls were able
to look up the valley to the place where the river forked. Formerly
they would have said "to the hill with the great tree" but those
were both gone now.

Standing there was a pile of boulders, each bigger than a house.
The shape of it changed slowly; it grew taller and narrower. It was
already as tall as the hill and the tree combined. It changed at the
slow but steady pace of shadows shifting across the ground over
the course of an afternoon; looked on directly it did not seem to
move.

"We should go down there and help those people," said Eve,
fetching an axe from a hook above the door. She turned to go
down the hill. Then, noting that Adam showed little inclination
to go with her, she pulled up short and looked at him curiously.

"Yes, we should," Adam said, "and we shall. But we should do
it with one eye toward leaving this place. Possibly in some haste."

"Why?" asked Eve.

"They are going to turn on us," said Adam.

"That would make no sense!"

"I have spent much time among them," said Adam, "and I regret to say that they do things that make no sense more often
than they show wisdom. They are ruled by emotion and rumor.
Even though we had nothing to do with the cutting down of the
great tree, they will look at that"—he stretched out his arm to
indicate the pile of boulders—"and note its likeness to Cairn, and
they will say that all of us, even our twelve children, are of a

shared kind, which is responsible for what has just occurred and for every other imperfection in the world besides. They will come for us and they will try to do to us what Cairn did to Messenger of El and what Feller and his crew just did to the great tree."

Until then Adam had not been known for wisdom and forethought, being more apt to find surprises in the events of each new day. But all came to pass as he had said. He and Eve went down to the riverfront and bent their strong backs to digging out souls trapped in structures that had fallen over, and passing buckets of water to ones that were burning. Many were grateful but others looked on them darkly and spoke to one another in confidence.

Boats began to come across the river from the ruins of Eltown. Some carried refugees. Others brought assistance in the form of Autochthons come to bend their backs. All, during the passage over the river, gazed upstream toward the place where the hill had once stood. The column of boulders now towered over the joining of the rivers and began to look vaguely two-legged, with an especially large boulder at the top.

The same townspeople who glared suspiciously at Adam and Eve, even when receiving their help, adored the Autochthons for rendering just the same sort of assistance. Matters gradually advanced to the point where some of the townspeople were saying that now that the Autochthons were on the scene, Adam and Eve's assistance was neither needed nor wanted. Others were gathered in a ragged ring around the Captain of the Autochthons giving vent to any feelings that crossed their minds, provided that they were feelings of a fearful or vengeful nature. Eve met Adam's eye and they wordlessly agreed it was time to go back to Camp.

They reached it only a few minutes ahead of a crowd of souls who had noted their departure and come up the hill with axes and iron bars. Nothing prevented them from entering Camp and moving freely among the old dwellings half-buried among the trees. They did so now and it became possible to hear cracking and splintering noises as they attacked the cabins, tearing them apart for their logs and their bricks. But around the clearing at the top of the hill, the people of Camp, some months ago, had made a barrier of branches, living and dead, woven together to prevent the twelve little ones from straying. It would not stop the townspeople for long if they came for it with iron and fire, but it did bring them up short, and caused the flood of invaders to divert around it.

The gate was nothing more than a panel of woven sticks. The defenders did not even bother closing it. But Cairn stood nearby, and Walksfar and Adam as well, in a vigilant posture that sufficed to deter the curious.

Thus matters remained at a stand. Captain came up the hill at the head of a score of Autochthons. He rode in through the gate and pulled up in the clearing, for Walksfar had stepped forth to block his path. Adam stood to one side and Cairn to the other. More Autochthons came in and filled the space behind their Captain, and townspeople came in as well, milling around among the riders' mounts.

"We see how it is," said Walksfar, "and we prepare to abandon this place where some of us have dwelled in peace since the end of the First Age."

Captain shrugged. "Ages come and go. Yours has gone."

"It is a lesson you would do well to study," Walksfar remarked. "In the meantime, since the souls of Eltown seem to respect your authority, perhaps you could ask them to withdraw from Camp and leave us in peace while we gather our things and depart in good order. There will be time enough to sack the place after we have gone."

"Depart for where?" asked Captain. "You departed once before, from First Town, and came to this place, and now look what has happened. Now it seems you are of a mind to repeat the same mistakes in some new setting."

"Have you some other recommendation?" asked Walksfar irritably.

"Stay," said Captain, "and submit to the wisdom of El, and shape your lives in accordance with the new way of doing things. I will see to it that Camp is not molested and that the damage done to it is made good."

Hearing those words Adam felt his resolve falter as he thought of how their life would be, were they to submit as Captain was proposing. He and Eve and their children would live peaceably in Camp among their friends, making marks on the wall of their cabin with each fall of the leaves. It would not be so very different from dwelling in the Garden behind El's palace. He sensed Eve's aura as she came up behind him, and felt her hand as she clasped his.

He came to his senses then and remembered the night of the knife. With his free hand he grasped for it, not to draw it out of its sheath but just to confirm that it was there and to remind himself that it had not been a dream. He spoke to Captain, loudly enough that all in Camp could hear his words: "When Messenger of El came here, Eve and I learned just what would be entailed in ordering our lives as you suggest!" Letting go of Eve's hand, he reached around behind her back and drew her to his side. "What Messenger of El did that night, and what was done to him, cannot be undone," he continued. "We will go out into the world and be no worse off than when we were ejected from the Garden." He turned to look at Cairn, Dusty, and the other souls of Camp, and noted that they were being joined by Thunk and Whirr and other members of their band, who were entering into the compound from the direction of the forest. Adam concluded, "I hold no authority over these other souls, many of whom are much older and wiser than me and Eve, and so I leave them to their own counsel."

He supposed that Walksfar or one of the others might now have something to say in return. Instead he was distracted by a sudden movement of Eve, who first shrank against him and then ducked under his arm so as to move back. For a thin tendril of aura had reached out from Captain to grope at Eve's belly, and his gaze was fixed upon her. Seeing that she did not like being probed in this way, Adam sidestepped to interpose himself between her and the Captain, and waved his arm back and forth in an effort to disrupt the aura. But Captain had already learned Eve's secret. "Again you are with child!" he said. "The first time, you made new souls innocently and were blameless. But after the events Adam just spoke of, there can be no doubt in your minds that such doings are in defiance of El's will. This must not be allowed to continue!" Captain made his mount step forward.

But then he and all the others were dazzled by a flare of light, bright as the sun, as Walksfar drew the sword from its dark scabbard.

"Before you utter another word in such a threatening tone," said Walksfar, "I would that you consider this and recall the fate of him from whom we won it."

The Captain's mount reared up on its hind legs and backed away from the sword of Thingor, and for a moment it was all he could do to bring the beast under control. When it had settled down, the Captain spoke wrathfully. "There are more where that came from," he reminded Walksfar, "whole armories of them in the vaults of the Palace."

A whirring noise tore through the air and a stone smashed into the wall not far from the Captain, shattering a dry branch. All turned to see Whirr. Swinging from her hand was the sling she had just used to throw the stone, and she was already reaching into the pouch at her hip to select another. "Bring your swords from on high then," she said to the Captain. "Down here is no lack of rocks."

Adam had turned round to pay heed to Whirr. He was now distracted, though, by something impossible. A slender object, red and wet, was protruding from his chest, almost to the length of his arm. Disbelieving his eyes, he reached for it with one hand, then the other, and found that it was every bit as real as the ground under his feet. Most of it was a smooth wooden pole, but at its tip was a pointed, double-edged blade of forged iron. He grasped this and its honed edges cut deeply into his palm. The pole had transfixed his body from back to front.

He had been stabbed from behind by a spear such as the Autochthons carried to hold wolves at bay.

He felt a powerful twisting followed by pain such as he had never known, which forced him to turn around until he was facing Captain once more. This also brought him in view of Eve. Her form seemed curiously bent out of shape and he perceived that another, smaller woman—Edger—had come up from behind her and put a blade against her throat. Eve had grabbed Edger's wrist with both hands and was holding the weapon at bay, but Edger was gripping Eve's hair with her free hand, and had sunk her teeth into Eve's ear, and so they were locked in stalemate.

This gave Adam a clue as to who was holding the spear. He turned his head to look back and confirmed that it was Bluff. The handle of the spear was long and so Bluff was too far away for Adam to reach him. Bluff himself did not deign to meet Adam's gaze; but had eyes only for Captain. "Behold, Captain! Not all of us who live in Eltown are as disrespectful as these two!" Bluff said.

He seemed to expect that Captain would approve of the actions that he and Edger were taking. But Captain's face was a picture of shock and dismay.

Adam sank to his knees and looked down to see his midsection dissolving into chaos. The spear was coming loose as his form dissolved around it. He toppled forward onto all fours and blood poured out of his mouth. Eve, still locked in struggle with Edger, moved toward him a pace.

The light shifted as Walksfar advanced. This caught the eye of Edger, who stopped biting Eve's ear long enough to exclaim, "Don't come another step!" Eve took advantage of this to try to wriggle free. In the struggle she advanced closer to Adam. Adam pushed himself upright and sat back on his haunches. The spear no longer had power to control the movements of his dissolving body. His impressions were dark and confused but he saw Eve and Edger within arm's length.

With his last strength he drew the knife from his belt and drove it into the side of Edger's body. Then his view of the world came apart into mere chaos.

Edger fell from Eve's back like a garment that has been shrugged off. Her knife fell from her hand. She lay next to Adam and the two of them came apart into chaos and were no more.

Eve dropped to her knees and tried to gather Adam's form back together with her hands, but it was like trying to collect smoke. The only thing that remained was his radiant knife. This she snatched up and beheld, though it stung her eyes. Then a notion of vengeance came into her mind and she looked toward Bluff.

The murderer had dropped the spear and backed away from the menace of Walksfar's sword, only to find himself caught between that and Thunk's band. Eve advanced upon him, knife in hand. Captain rode forth to intercept her, but his mount pulled up short as Cairn moved into its path with a ponderous stride. The other Autochthons thought to advance, but Captain made a gesture to say that they should come no farther.

"This valley has witnessed enough destruction for one day without your proposing more," said Captain. "Adam is no more; Edger is no more; Bluff is disarmed and helpless, and for you to slaughter him now will in no way improve matters."

"He has done murder. We all saw it," said Walksfar.

Captain nodded. "El in his wisdom has seen the need to write laws and has appointed magistrates to enforce them. That is part of the reason for our coming to Eltown. Give Bluff over to us unharmed and we will see to it that El's justice is done."

Walksfar considered it. "He is only one. What of the next Bluff, and the next one after that, who come here seeking to steal and kill?"

Captain said, "We will make an example of Bluff that will give those others much to think about. But El has not granted me power to turn other minds aside from foolish decisions."

Bluff, spying a desperate chance, spun away and tried to run. Dusty was swifter, and enveloped him in a cloud of grit that blinded him. As he faltered he was struck in the back by a sling stone that dropped him to his knees. Two of the Autochthons cantered over to round him up.

Once he was satisfied that Bluff had been made captive, Captain turned his attention back to Walksfar. "And speaking of foolish decisions . . ."

"None of this changes our minds," said Walksfar. "I cannot speak for all these souls. But to watch murder being done, and to hear your talk of laws and magistrates from El, only strengthens my resolve to be rid of this place."

Captain nodded. "We will see to it that you are left alone for a little while. After three days we will make no further efforts to protect Camp from the vengefulness of the dispossessed souls of Eltown; and then you may find that they too know about rocks."

Walksfar sheathed the sword, plunging the clearing back into the normal light of day, which seemed now like twilight.

Captain issued commands to his Autochthons, who went out the gate and rode through those parts of Camp that lay outside the makeshift wall, seeing to it that the souls of Eltown left off sacking the cabins and withdrew to the river.

Captain backed his mount toward the gate, gazing down at Eve, who stood weeping freely between Cairn and Walksfar. It was apparent in Captain's face and in his aura that he was deep in thought. He shook his head. "This state of affairs," he said, "could hardly be more different from how El imagined it when I met with him in the Palace only a few short weeks ago and he sent me forth with my company to bring the affairs of Camp and of Eltown under control." He turned his head to one side and lifted his gaze to the hill-giant in the distance. "And I refer only to the terrible events just witnessed here. *That* creature is a surprise of a whole different order."

Eve had collected herself to a point where she could listen shrewdly. "Of Camp," she repeated. "What said El of Camp, and how it was to be brought under control?"

"That several souls dwelled in it, most of whom were willful and strange, but only two who were of any great concern to him."

"Adam and I," said Eve.

"Yes."

"Because of our ability to spawn more of our kind."

"Indeed."

"And what shall you say to El, when you make your report?" Eve asked.

"That Adam is no more," said Captain.

"And that is all you will say?"

"Yes," said Captain, "but soon enough he will know the truth." He glanced down toward Eve's belly.

"Then I thank you for sparing me, and for holding my secret in confidence," said Eve.

Captain considered it, and shrugged. "It seems right," he said. "It is not precisely what El wanted; but enthroned as he is in his Palace, viewing the Land from a high seat, he does not see its complexity. This Land was made wrong. All of his efforts to make it right only spread the wrongness about in new ways. It is left to souls like me to decide what to do about it; and though I cannot see all the answers, I can guess that adding more wrongness will not help matters." And with that Captain made his mount turn around and rode out through the gate.

Assisted by Thunk and his band, the people of Camp bent their backs taking what useful things as could be removed from the cabins and preparing them to be carried on a long journey. Two days were spent in the preparations, which only seemed to grow more complex and fall farther behind the more effort was put into them; but on the third day they all formed up, staggering under back-loads, and looked to Walksfar for some indication as to which way to start walking. "There are many places we could go," he said, "but I believe our simplest course for now might be to walk in the footsteps of that thing." And he pointed north toward the hill-giant, who in the last day had made a long stride westward out of the river, and seemed to have an intention of climbing up out of the valley to see what lay beyond the mountains.

Down to the river they all went, and found it much wider than it had been yesterday, and brackish with salt from the distant sea.

47

Much of the time, watching Bitworld through the LVU was literally like watching grass grow. Eventually its souls might get around to inventing paint, and then spectators in Meatspace might also have the pleasure of watching it dry. And yet millions watched it anyway because there was just enough crazy to make it interesting.

Sort of like baseball. Corvallis Kawasaki had never been a fan of that sport despite—or perhaps because of—a youthful stint in Little League and efforts on the Japanese side of his family to interest him in it. On the South Asian side they had all been cricket maniacs, and so the young Corvallis had had two vaguely similar sports to choose from, both of which were characterized by long spans of nothing happening with just enough sudden bursts of excitement to keep the fans from wandering off.

That all came in handy during the year or so following Maeve's death and the weird visit of the Metatron with its portentous and vaguely threatening talk of the REAP. Something was most certainly going on that involved the "Adam" and "Eve" processes. They didn't move around much once they had settled down, but they interacted frequently with the Maeve process, and after a while they made babies. Something bizarre immediately happened involving one of Elmo Shepherd's winged minions. There was what could only be described as an altercation between it and an old Mag 1 process that had decided to embody itself as an animated pile of rocks. Weird flows of mana had occurred. Accountants and lawyers from Zelrijk-Aalberg had taken the unusual step of flying to Seattle to yell at their counterparts in person. It was bad enough, they complained, for the "children" of Dodge and Verna to consume resources from Buildings and Grounds. It was worse yet for them to spawn more of their own kind. But now they were some-how absorbing mana directly from servers that the Zelrijk-Aalberg people had, at staggering expense, set up in orbit.

They were cheating. Or, at least, the powers that be in Zelrijk-Aalberg felt cheated. Viewing the aftermath in the LVU, it just looked like raising babies and chopping down trees. Pointing that out did not in any way calm down the bean counters from Flan-ders. On the contrary, they saw it as C-plus's willfully refusing to acknowledge facts obvious to them. They hinted that he was, at some level, smirking. This notion that C-plus was a secret smirker enraged them. Enoch Root had to be brought in to mediate.

During those days the Time Slip Ratio had swung back and forth around approximately one, which was to say that sometimes the denizens of Bitworld appeared to move slowly and other times quickly, but they never just froze up, or dissolved into blurred streaks. On average, Bitworld time, as tallied by day/night cycles, was not far off from that in Meatspace. Fluctuations seemed to be tied not to what was happening in Bitworld—which didn't change much—but rather to the progress of, or setbacks in, huge engineer-ing projects being run out of Flanders, most notably a big habitat that the Zelrijk-Aalberg people were constructing in geosynchro-nous orbit.

That had all stopped being true at the moment of the Grand Slam, as Corvallis thought of it.

It was a baseball analogy. Sometimes in a baseball game a sit-uation would gradually develop, over the course of a long, slow inning, where the bases became loaded, and the batting team was down to its last out, and the count had gone full, the manager had made a couple of trips to the mound, a replacement pitcher was warming up in the bullpen, the batter was fouling off one pitch after another, the crowd was about to piss itself—and then in a moment something happened that changed everything.

Some such thing happened one day in Bitworld. Adam was dead. Eve was on the move, pregnant, following a member of the Ephrata Eleven that had incarnated itself as an enormous human-oid made of boulders and dirt. They were traveling across a chunk of the landform that had snapped off and was drifting out to sea, fragmenting as it went. New souls—apparently spawned from scratch, not based on scans of dead people—were issuing from El's spire in the center of the Landform and taking up residence in strategic locations and, to all appearances, bossing around the souls that had got there in the usual way.

It was all terrifically expensive, mana-wise. The events that triggered it—the chopping down of a tree, the awakening of a giant, the inundation of a town, the murder of "Adam," and most of all the fission of the continent—took place over the course of a few days as experienced by the souls of Bitworld. Simulating all of that, however, ended up taking almost a year in Meatspace. Millions of spectators lost interest in the Landform Visualization Utility. Those who stuck with it had to find new sources of enjoyment, such as zooming in on individual flowers, gazing upon mountain vistas from various angles, going on virtual hikes through frozen landscapes where birds hung nearly motionless in the air.

This intermission, if you wanted to think of it that way (in baseball terms, maybe a seventh-inning stretch), lasted for a couple of Meatspace years. During that time both SLU and Z-A were laying plans for the next phase of Bitworld's expansion: the demographic transition from Mag 6 to Mag 8 (a million souls up to a hundred million); the bringing online, in orbit, of vast new arrays of solar power, computing systems, and thermal radiators to shine dull infrared into the cosmos. So it wasn't a bad time anyway for an intermission. When finally the switches were thrown and the new equipment brought online, the Time Slip Ratio sprang ahead by orders of magnitude, to the point where months would fly by in Bitworld during a single day in Meatspace. Over the course of an afternoon C-plus could, if he so chose, watch bare trees wax soft and green, go red and orange with the colors of the fall, and lose their leaves.

As such it became impossible to really track the stories of individual souls. The audience could no longer follow it like a Mexican soap opera or a Russian novel. Now the fans were all like psychohistorians, seeing history unfold in broad sweeps.

The new race of souls that El had invented in his tower continued to issue forth in waves, and it seemed clear that El had given them the task of making things run smoothly, seeing to it that the customers—the much more numerous souls spawned from scanned biologicals—didn't run rampant. They rarely crossed the widening channel that separated most of the Land from the chunk that had split off. This continued to fragment over time, gradually turning into a close-packed archipelago. Sooner or later most of the Mag 1–3 souls ended up there in various guises. The later children of Eve had sex with each other and made more of their kind.

Centuries passed in Bitworld, years passed in Meatspace. C-plus felt himself undergoing a slow transition from young-old to old-old. He spent less and less time trying to track events in Bitworld, only checking in occasionally on Maeve, Verna, and a few others. Metatrons showed up occasionally to lodge complaints about alleged further activities of the REAP. C-plus heard them out patiently, as one did with a distant relative who has gone off his rocker and begun fulminating about the Illuminati. Dodge was here, Dodge was there, Dodge was everywhere in disguise, something had to be done about Dodge. Eventually they seemed to fix the problem and then they stopped complaining.

He didn't care, because he was flying.

When he had been a child, ninety years ago, Corvallis Kawasaki had dreamed of flying. Not in a daydreamy way, but in really convincing night dreams in which he had spread his arms like wings and taken to the air above the town that was his namesake and banked and wheeled above his school playground, looking down on the other kids on their teeter-totters and jungle gyms. All of which had been just as exhilarating as you would expect.

As with so many other things that seemed, in a child's imagination, like they would be awesome, the reality of flight was more complicated, and how you dealt emotionally with the mismatch between the little-kid dream and the grown-up truth of the matter said a lot about you and basically kind of determined what you were going to do with your life. He had also, for a while, wanted to be a fireman, a ninja, and a private eye. But when he had come to understand what those occupations were really like, he had changed his mind. Being a Roman soldier had been fun for a while too, but past a certain age you couldn't dig those ditches anymore.

When Maeve had passed on, C-plus had already been an old man by some standards. He could tell as much by the way strangers treated him. Young women, no longer seeing him as a threat, were open and friendly. Other old men felt free to address him on the street as if he were a member of the same secret club.

So when he had inherited Maeve's flying apparatus and the somewhat disturbing stockpile of neuroactive pharmaceuticals that went with it, he might have been forgiven for junking it with the explanation that he was too old for this.

But then he had remembered his childhood dream of flying, and resolved that this was *not* to be one of those abandoned dreams. Private eye and ninja might never come to pass. But no matter how difficult, even disappointing, the reality of flying might be compared to his childhood conception of it, in overcoming all of that he would show what he was made of.

And that was just in *this* life. In the next one, perhaps it would enable him to achieve other goals. To right old wrongs and discharge old obligations.

So he had fixed up Maeve's rig. He had loved Maeve in spite of, and even because of, certain aspects of her personality—her basic approach to life—that were manifested in every detail of the flying system she had caused to be built at the circus school. It was whimsical, ad hoc, patched together, willfully perverse, down to the level of the choice of fasteners used to hold it together and the stitching on the harness. This was a sacred artifact, not something he could simply hand off to a minion, and so C-plus had spent a year taking it apart himself, the ostrich plumes and the beadwork, the macramé, the Zuni textiles and jury-rigged intravenous plumbing, and he had put all of that stuff behind glass in a kind of museum or shrine in the corner of the *new* space—an old hangar at Boeing Field, formerly used for maintenance of private jets, now empty most of the time since most of that work was being performed al fresco, or even while in flight, by purpose-built robots.

All of the mechanical stuff he redid from scratch. The new harness was made just for him, with smart pads that would prevent him from getting bedsores even if he lived in it for weeks. The servos that made it zoom and veer about were beefier and yet more responsive. He added big fans that would blow wind over him when he dreamed of going into a steep power dive or soaring on a thermal.

While the engineers worked on all that, he researched the hell out of the pharmaceutical side. A lot had been learned since Maeve had started in on this. Some of the drugs she'd used to soften up her brain now seemed dangerously wrong. Some were merely useless, others had become mainstays. He tried to take enough of the right ones to give the effects he wanted while not losing the parts of his brain he needed to do his job—running a significant part of ALISS.

Not needed for ALISS were parts of his cerebellum involved in motor control and visual processing. This made it more and more awkward, as time passed and he got closer to death, to extricate himself from the device. He slept in it, dreaming of flight, hallucinating the afterlife. In the morning he opened his eyes to photons coming not from the sun, but from a rig that pretty convincingly simulated it.

"Why are you doing this to yourself?" Zula asked him.

She was far below, standing on a patch of grass—a mountain meadow that in reality was a green paint square on the hangar's concrete floor. Her voice was raised over the roar of the fans, currently simulating a thermal. Corvallis banked in the updraft. Which was to say that he thought of trimming his wings in a certain way, and it happened: the thing on his head read his mind, the simulator calculated the effects of the movement and made it so, feeding control signals to the servos that tightened some cables while loosening others, to the fans that made the wind, to the infrared panels that simulated the warmth of sunlight, and to the audiovisual simulation running in his headgear. He wheeled to bring Zula into view, pulled up, dove, flared, perched on a branch (actually a steel pipe mounted above the green paint square). Now he was looking at her sidelong from just a few meters away. The fans shut down, creating a silence in which he could hear his engineers applauding and hooting at how neatly he'd executed the move.

"You have huge fans in both senses of the term," Zula observed.

"That is actually an intentional part of how it all works—it's why Maeve built hers in a circus school," C-plus said. "It is supposed to be convincing on every level, right? Well, what does it mean for a thing to be convincing? Qualia are only part of it. I get those from the visuals, the movement, the air currents. But it turns out that we are wired for intersubjectivity. Our perception of reality is as much social as it is personal. Why are we disturbed by psychotics? Because they see and hear things we don't, and that's just wrong. Why do prisoners in solitary confinement go nuts? Because they don't have others to confirm their perceptions. So when I bust a move in this rig and stick the landing, it's not enough just to simulate it and show *me;* others have to see it, and react. Ratifying the qualia, cross-linking the history into a social matrix."

"Makes me wonder what it must have been like for my uncle, when he was first booted up, all alone, in a world with no qualia at all," Zula remarked. "Was he in hell?"

"I've often thought about the same thing. And did Sophia put him there?"

"Knowingly? Intentionally? Of course not."

"Sure," C-plus said. "But innocently? Inadvertently? I think so. All in the hopes that he wasn't really dead."

"Well, if I hadn't known you for seven decades, I'd say the drugs were going to your head—the wrong part of it, I mean," Zula said. "As it is, it seems more and more like you've found what Dodge wanted for you when he put you in charge of Weird Stuff."

"Thanks. I am. The drugs *are* going to my head, though, and so I hope you won't find it off-putting if I leave this thing on. The visual field stuff gets really problematic if I suddenly take it off."

"I don't mind," Zula said, "though I wish you'd look right at me."

"I actually *am* doing so," C-plus assured her, "it's just that—"

"Crows have eyes in the sides of their heads," she said.

"Do I repeat myself?"

"Yes. For my part, I'd come over and hug you, but—"

"You might crush me. It's a design failing of your exo," C-plus said. "See, you repeat yourself too." He couldn't see it, because the visual simulator shopped it out of the image, but Zula was wearing an exoskeleton—the latest incarnation of Fronk—that handled most of her physical dealings with the material world, and did so in a way that kept the frail nonagenarian body inside it safe from most hazards. "Did you have a nice walk down here?" he asked.

"I ran," Zula corrected him.

"Why the hurry?"

"No hurry. I'm told I need more jarring impact. Helps the bones stay strong. Didn't feel very jarring to me, frankly." But they both knew that the exo had put all sorts of know-how into making the forces on her bones just enough to create beneficial microfractures without posing any real hazard.

"Just coming to say hi to an old man on his deathbed, then?" C-plus asked. "Or does the afterlife need any intervention from me?"

"The before-life, more like," Zula said. "You have visitors. I'll show them in."

"You're not staying?"

"I'm going for a brisk jog around Boeing Field. Thanks anyway."

Corvallis took to the air and went for a spin on some tempting thermals while the visitors were shown in.

Enoch and Solly.

He had known them now for forty years and resigned himself to the fact that their appearance did not change over time. He wheeled around them anyway, peering down on them from all angles.

"Calling a meeting of the Societas Eruditorum?" C-plus asked.

"You're the only member left," Enoch said. "You're a one-person meeting."

"What about you guys?"

"Oh, we're not actually members per se," Enoch said. "More like the advisory board."

"You're not erudite?"

"Nope," said Solly, "just wise."

"Mm. What do I have to do to become wise?"

"Die," said Enoch, "and go to the next place."

"Seems like a stiff price to pay."

"We paid it," Solly said.

"You look alive to me."

"We paid it," Solly insisted, "where *we* came from."

"So, to sum up, here I can only be erudite. To become wise I have to go on to Bitworld, and start a branch of the Societas Eruditorum there?"

"Frankly, we have no idea," said Enoch, who was beginning to sound slightly impatient. "But that seems the most plausible outcome based on our understanding of how we came to be here. Which is flawed. We are cracked vessels."

"All right. Since I'm the only member, I call the meeting to order," C-plus announced. "Is there any new business?"

"As a matter of fact, yes," Enoch said. "Your last hack. Or at least I'm guessing it will be your last hack based on your bio readouts. Who knows, maybe you'll surprise me."

"I haven't written code in a quarter of a century. God, I miss it though."

"This is not a code-writing sort of gig, exactly," Enoch said.

"Well, that's good. I don't think human-written code *exists* anymore. It's code written by code written by code—turtles all the way down."

"Not *all* the way," Solly corrected him.

Corvallis was flying pretty incompetently now, as old and disused parts of his brain were grinding into movement: rust rimes cracking, dust and cobwebs flying into the air. He couldn't do that and, at the same time, with the same neurons, trim his virtual wings in simulated currents of air, so he came in for a crash-landing on his steel perch.

Then he thought about what Solly had just said.

"Well, sure!" he finally answered. "Cruft is forever. If you peel back the layers that have grown on top of other layers, and keep delving, and grep deep enough, you're going to find base code that was written by some Linux geek in the 1980s or something. File system primitives. Memory allocation routines that were made to run on hacked single-core IBM PCs that had never heard of the Internet."

"Old incantations having the arcane force of magic," Enoch said.

"If you say so. I haven't touched anything like that in decades. If it's magic you're after, I know some AIs—"

"You overestimate the difficulty of what we have in mind," Enoch said.

"I'll bite. Though I don't have teeth. What do you have in mind?"

"Copying a file."

"That's *it*!?" he squawked. But he was already feeling a mild sense of unease, wondering whether he could even remember the Unix command line incantation for anything as simple as copying a file. Systems nowadays didn't even *have* files in the old sense. They had abstractions that were so complicated they could almost pass the Turing test on their own, but still with a few old file-like characteristics for backward compatibility.

To cover that unease, he blustered. Not a Corvallis behavior, but he had become part crow. "Why do we need to call a physical meeting for *that*?"

"It's an important file. Both here and . . . where you are going next."

"Is it huge? Complicated? Damaged and in need of repair?"

"It is small as these things go, and perfectly intact," Enoch demurred.

"It's a key," Solly blurted out. "A cryptographic key. With an avatar."

"Should be simple enough, I'd think," Corvallis said. "What does the avatar look like?"

"A great big fucking key, that's what it looks like," Solly said. "Distinctive. One of a kind."

"Until I copy it."

"You know what I mean. Not something you want to leave lying around in the open. Hide it."

"Should I ask how you came into possession of this key?" Corvallis asked, beginning to get the drift.

"No," Enoch said.

"Is it on servers belonging to . . . someone else?"

"It was copied from servers like the ones you're thinking of," Enoch said, "and now needs to be copied once more if it is to pass fully into your control. We think you might be needing it."

"Oh, my god!" C-plus exclaimed. "Is this the One—"

"Don't even say it," Enoch commanded.

"How long has this copy been sitting on whatever bootleg server?"

"Nine years," Solly said.

Which confirmed it. For nine years had now passed since the day when the high sysadmins of Zelrijk-Aalberg had announced that they had at last isolated the security leak that had been allowing the REAP to keep respawning and closed the loophole for good. And, as it were, thrown away the key.

"I'm all ears," said Corvallis Kawasaki.

"You seem all feathers to me," said Solly, "but whatever."

PART 10

48

Six dawns in a row, a new soul glimmered on a branch of the old tree, only to fade in the strong light of the day. Prim, looking out the window in the hour before dawn, could see it there. It looked like a star softened by drifting fog and mist. Even after the light of day had extinguished it she could, by moving about on the grass beneath, make herself see the faint distortion that the soul was creating in the air.

On the seventh morning it seemed to discard all hopes and intentions of ever making light of its own, and darkened and solidified into the form of a black bird. This perched on the branch for some days, seeming dead except that it would shift its footing from time to time when strong winds came down from the mountains. When gusts ruffled its feathers it would open its wings just enough to learn a few things about how they worked, then fold them tight against its body and close its eyes for a while.

Blossoms flourished on a few branches of the ancient tree that were still capable of bearing apples. By the time these had withered and blown away, the black bird was fully formed, and capable of flight—though not very good at it. Prim woke up one morning and looked out her window to find the branch vacant, the bird nowhere to be seen. She felt a pang of loss. But then the still air of dawn was fractured by a clattering of black feathers and a scraping of talons on the stone sill of her window. She leapt back. The bird perched on the window frame and gazed at her curiously. "I am Corvus," it announced, "and I am not like other new souls who come into the Land, though I cannot remember why."

"Oh, of that, there is no doubt," said Prim. For she had never heard tell of a new soul who had adopted a form and acquired the power of speech so readily. Indeed, had Corvus so manifested in other parts of the Land, he'd have been done away with by the superstitious folk who dwelled in such parts. That he had come into being in a tree in the garden of the Calladons was lucky, for the Calladons were queer folk. "My name is Prim," she said. "My family is Calladon. This is Calla."

"What do those words mean? Prim? Calladon?"

"Oh, they are not those kinds of words!" she answered. "You see, some words are very old, and their significance forgotten."

"So Calladons have been here for a long time."

She nodded. "We built this house on the back of a sleeping giant at the dawn of the Third Age, if that helps you."

"It doesn't."

This Corvus seemed quite difficult to please. She shrugged. "That is our garden, and this my bedchamber. I have been watching you."

"I know," said Corvus—not really making it clear how *many* of the assertions just made by Prim had been known to him. No matter. The bird looked her up and down. She was wearing a sleeping gown that fell all the way to the floor. "Are you a girl, or a woman?"

"Girl," Prim told him.

"Of how many falls?"

"It is not what matters," she told him. "Calladons are queer folk. Girls become women, or boys become men, when some occasion requires it. Of late this part of the Land has been quiet and such occasions few."

"I require a small party of women and men to accompany me on a Quest and lend a hand in its culmination," Corvus stated.

"What manner of Quest?"

Corvus seemed not to have considered this seemingly basic question. He pondered it for a few moments, then rearranged his wings in a birdy shrug. "Travel, searching, digging something up. I don't know. Very important. Leave immediately."

"May I have breakfast?" she asked.

When Corvus seemed taken aback, she explained: "Others will be there, who might help. And in any case it would never do for one of my family to enter womanhood and embark on a Quest without at least saying a few words."

Corvus shrugged his wings and said he would wait in the tree. He hopped around to reverse his direction and took to the air with a lot more clattering and whacking than was typical of more experienced birds, and found his way, after some misadventures, back to his old perch. There he bided as various hints and clues emerged from the house: chimney smoke, sounds of dish-utensil collisions, opening and closing of doors and window shutters, and rising and falling murmurs of conversation. The house in some places was made of stones piled atop other stones, in others of wood. In some parts of it the weather was kept out by sheaves of grass cleverly bound together, in others by sheets of gray metal or splits of thin rock. It looked, in other words, as if bits had been added on to other bits over a long span of time without any very clear plan, extending this way and that to enclose little yards such as the one where the apple tree grew. No part of it was especially high or grand, with the possible exception of the one that seemed to be making the greatest amount of smoke and noise during the activity that Prim had denominated "breakfast." This was a hall with a rectangular plan and a lofty peaked roof, with windows just under the eaves, high enough to admit light and air.

After a while, people came out of it, following Prim, who had tied her hair back and put on more clothes. They were all of the same form. Most were taller than Prim, but a few were tiny and some even had to be carried around by larger ones. They passed through a sort of arch that communicated with the yard and formed up in an arc centered on Corvus.

"Let's go," Corvus said, and spread his wings to take flight.

"Just a moment, if you would," said a man with hair growing out of his face and extending down onto his chest. "We Calladons are no strangers to Quests, and in fact if you were to fly into our Hall over yonder you would see pictures on the walls of our ancestors engaged in some, as recently as a hundred falls ago. So it cannot be said that you have come to the wrong place altogether. But before you make off with our Prim, we would like to know one or two things about just what it is you have in mind. Such as: which direction are you going?"

"I had given very little thought to it," said Corvus.

"Well you see, that does concern me a little," said the man. "For some directions are more hazardous than others; and if you should happen to pick the wrong one, why, you will only get farther away from your destination with each beat of your wings."

Corvus meditated upon these words. "Very well," he said, "I'll be back." He began to flap his wings but had some difficulty getting clear of the apple tree's impossibly gnarled branches.

"There is carrion out back of the kitchen," said a younger man with hair on his upper lip. "It might give you greater strength if you ate some."

Standing next to that man was a woman with yellow hair. "And the greater your strength, the farther you can fly . . . from here," she added helpfully.

"If you go south or east," said Prim, "stay high—because of arrows."

"North or west, low—eagles," added the man who had spoken first.

Thus advised, Corvus worked free of the tree's grasp and flew over behind the hall, to a little yard where someone was tossing food out of an open door onto the ground. There it was being fought over by various low-to-the-ground creatures. Wanting no part in their squabbles, Corvus flew in through the door and found a piece of a dead animal lying on a slab of wood. He picked this up in his talons. The woman who had been throwing the food took exception and hurled a metal container at him, but it did not strike him, so he flew into the Hall, carrying the piece of the dead animal, and went up to a high exposed piece of dead tree that seemed to be playing a part in holding the roof up. There he bided for a while, tearing the "carrion" into shreds small enough to swallow. As had been promised, the building's walls, below the windows, were adorned with images. Some were made by the weaving together of colored fiber, others by applying colored stuff to flat things. At first these made little sense to him, but as his stomach filled with carrion, his powers of understanding grew and he saw that all of these were ways of tricking the eye to make it see things that were not actually present. Apparently the figures shown were Calladons. Or at least some of them were. The handsome ones astride four-legged beasts—probably Calladons. The ugly misshapen ones they were depicted as killing—probably something else.

Prim had made passing reference to a giant who was asleep. It could be guessed that the very large biped made of rocks, prominently featured in one of the larger pictures, was the very same—though, during the events shown, most definitely awake.

Stringing all of these pictures together into a story looked to be an all-day project, but Corvus didn't have to go to all that trouble to get the drift: Calladons and other suchlike persons had come here a long time ago as part of an epic adventure featuring not only giants but floods, avalanches, packs of ravening beasts, flying bipeds with bright swords, and diverse other entities that did not look much like them. Strange-looking cities had been visited, caught on fire, fled. This had at some point given way to a more settled way of life in circumstances that were nicer but, on the whole, colder. Crops and orchards had been planted, animals husbanded, babies made, buildings raised. Efforts, apparently successful, had been made to defend all of that through the systematic application of violence. These doings accounted for most of the pictures. But there were a few that did not fit into that general scheme, in which extraordinarily good-looking individuals—at a guess, Calladons—went to outlandish places to fight odd-looking critters and/or collect peculiar objects. Which confirmed in the mind of Corvus that these "queer folk" would make adequate Quest material.

Thus nourished with an agreeable "breakfast" of carrion and historical imagery, Corvus flew out through an open window and soared high into the air above the hill on which the Calladons had built their house. The place was shrouded in mist and cloud; but once he had flown for some distance and ascended to a greater height, he turned into the east, and saw the Land stretched out before him.

He was back a year later. "My notions have firmed up," he announced. "I know roughly where to go, and several ways to get there, and why some of those ways are preferable to others. What your mounts eat and how much it costs, how far arrows fly, why certain kinds of people automatically try to kill you. All this and more is known to me. Let us be on our way."

A lengthy silence ensued. No one got up. The Calladons were seated at a long table out of doors, in a courtyard next to the Hall, whence food and drink were being brought out to them by persons whom Corvus now understood to be servants. Some of them Corvus recognized from a year ago, others were visitors (as could be guessed from the tired mounts and dusty carts scattered about the premises). The man with the beard was seated at one end of the table; Corvus had learned that his name was Brindle Calladon. At the opposite end, facing Brindle, was a woman who seemed to be the most senior and respected of the visitors; she was called Paralonda Bufrect. Along the sides of the table, Calladons and Bufrects were commingled. Corvus had perched on a sort of wrought-iron tree erected in the middle of the table to support many candles. None of these had been lit yet because the sun had not finished going down. Diners seated near it had scooted back as he had come in for a landing, and some had gripped their eating knives in a not altogether welcoming style, reminding Corvus that he had grown into what was probably the largest raven any of them had ever seen.

"That is the largest raven I have ever seen," said one of the visitors.

"I found tremendous size useful," Corvus explained, "when traversing eagle country."

"And it talks," said another. Which to Corvus seemed as if it ought to have been fairly obvious by now. But Corvus was aware of his own limitations. He had roamed over much of the Land and knew more of it than any of these persons possibly could. But he had been to almost no dinner parties and so was ignorant of practices. Perhaps saying incredibly obvious things was customary. "I am an enormous sentient talking raven who has just interrupted your dinner party—"

"And shat on the centerpiece," observed a woman sitting nearby.

"—and my name is—"

"Corvus!" exclaimed a woman seated down at the end near Brindle. It was Prim. Corvus had not recognized her immediately, for her form and dress had altered during his absence. She stood up and clasped her hands together. "As you can see, I am more nearly ready to take part in a Quest now than when you last saw me. I have grown bigger and stronger and learned map reading and riding and archery and other things as well."

Corvus clucked approvingly. But in truth Prim was the least of his concerns, for he had always somehow known that she would turn out fine. He was distracted by the sheer variety of reactions that his arrival had elicited from the guests. A surprisingly large number of them—more so among the visitors than the Calladons—seemed never to have encountered a sentient, talking animal in their whole lives. Those could be divided among:

Those who had considered such a thing impossible

> . . . and who still persisted in thinking so and were therefore doubting the evidence of their senses . . .
> > . . . because of too much drink taken
> > . . . or adulterants in the food
> > > . . . deliberately and maliciously introduced
> > > . . . or put in by accident
> > . . . or because it was all a dream

Those who believed that such creatures had existed long ago but were strictly things of the past, subdivided into

> . . . those doubting the evidence of their senses (as above)
> . . . those who found the sudden arrival of a fairy-tale creature
> > . . . fascinating and charming
> > . . . or evil/loathsome/dire

Those who had known all along that such creatures existed and who were not greatly surprised to encounter one at dinner, divided into

> . . . one who rather liked him (Prim)
> . . . those calmly reserving judgment (e.g., Brindle)
> . . . those who hated him (the yellow-haired woman and the man with the hair on his upper lip)

At any rate the total number of persons at the table was not enormously larger than the number of categories, meaning that nearly everyone present was reacting in an altogether different way, and in most cases doing so rather strongly, leading to a pandemonium of fainting, screaming, knife waving, malicious glaring, furious remonstration, hand-clapping delight, dismay, judicious beard stroking, etc. to say nothing of secondary interactions, as when a knife waver collided with a screamer. Corvus, accustomed to soaring alone, found himself frankly quite overwhelmed and thought it best to fly away. He did not go off to any great remove but, from their point of view, probably vanished into the darkening sky, touching off a resurgence of the doubting-the-evidence-of-their-own-senses crowd.

The dinner seemed to have been terminated. At least half of them went into the hall, many pausing on the threshold to cast suspicious looks over their shoulders. But when it seemed things had settled down, Corvus descended and perched on the back of a chair that had been vacated. Still present were Brindle, Prim, Paralonda (though she had taken advantage of the upset to pick up her goblet and move closer), and half a dozen or so mixed Calladons and Bufrects. The latter seemed generally in the astonished-but-agreeably-fascinated camp, whereas Calladons, being queer folk, seemed more likely to view talking animals as part of the natural order of things.

This was the moment when a human would have apologized for having ruined the dinner party, but one of the liberties that went along with being a raven was never being sorry for anything.

"Can you say anything more about the *nature* of your Quest?" asked Brindle. "You mentioned that you knew which direction to go in, and that is certainly an improvement upon how matters stood a year ago. But what do you expect to find at journey's end, and what do you envision doing once you have found it?"

While Corvus was thinking about this—and to be quite honest, he was thinking about it for the first time ever—the man with the hair on his lip and the woman with the yellow hair emerged from the Hall. They moved with more haste than grace in a straight line for Prim. "Merville," said Brindle. "Felora. Would you care to sit with us? There is no lack of empty chairs." But it seemed that Merville and Felora preferred standing behind Brindle and Prim to sitting just a tiny bit farther away. "What I don't get is this," Merville announced. "This creature is quite obviously capable of flight—which *we* are *not*. It can go anywhere it pleases, any time it chooses. Why then does it not simply go to wherever this Quest is to be—culminated, or whatever—and do whatever needs doing?"

After a short pause, Felora spoke. "*I'll* tell you why not. It must be that the completion of the Quest requires humans. The raven can't get it done without us. And what are humans good at that ravens are not? Well, fighting and all that goes with it in the way of getting hurt and maimed and dying and so on." And she rested a hand on Prim's shoulder. This made Prim twitch, but she did just manage to control an impulse to shrug or slap Felora's hand away.

"Huge talking ravens actually *can* fight," Corvus pointed out, "and I have scars to prove it."

"And this is supposed to reassure us?" asked Merville in an incredulous tone.

"I can't shake the notion that the Quest will somehow involve going underground," Corvus said, "or at any rate into some sort of structure so deep and convoluted that it might as well be underground, and perhaps that is why I have been absolutely certain from the beginning that humans must be part of it."

"Again," said Merville, "if the intent of these statements is to reassure us as to the nature of the planned activities—or, for that matter, whether you have even the vaguest notion as to what those activities are to consist of—then you might wish to fly away again and stay away for a good deal longer and come back with a plan."

"Or better yet, find some other family to pester," put in Felora.

"I have pestered several. Yours is best," said Corvus. "Look, the nature of the Quest far transcends ordinary concerns of day-to-day existence, such as eating, drinking, staying warm, and not getting maimed or whatever. It has to do with the fundamental nature of reality—the Land of whose existence your mind convinces you from one moment to the next whenever you are awake. People who actually bother to think about this—which is, as far as I can tell, not very many of them—come up with various overarching stories about it that seem more or less convincing depending on what strikes one's fancy, story-wise. Just ask anyone you meet what they believe about El, Egdod, and all that. For my own part, I know it to be the case that I came into this world under unusual circumstances and with certain powers, instincts, and predispositions already built in. That cannot be denied even if I lack clear memories as to how it came about. I think it reasonable to assume that I was sent hither on a one-way trip from another plane of existence whose exact nature will forever remain mysterious to us. But the powers of that world know about us and care about us and have plans, or at least hopes, for us, and it is their desire and their intention that we should come into possession of certain knowledge that will give us power to affect the Land for the better. The nature of that knowledge is mysterious, but it awaits us at the end of the Quest. Even if going there and getting it were within the powers of a solitary giant talking raven—which I do not believe to be the case—doing so would be beside the point since the Quest's purpose, as preordained by the mysterious powers in the world from which I was sent, is not just to make everything perfect for one raven but rather to effect a transformation in your souls. We leave at first light."

Rather a lot of arguing and discussion ensued, very little of which seemed to require the presence or participation of Corvus—who, in any case, had already told these people everything he knew. People came and went between this outdoor table and the Hall in greater or lesser states of furor. As they did, Corvus hopped sideways from chair-back to chair-back until he was almost down to the far end. Then he flew off into the night and soon found a comfortable perch on a tree branch near the Hall. From it, he was able to see through open windows to the interior, which was lit up by burning things. He reviewed the tapestries and paintings that he had seen a year ago. These made more sense now that he had actually been to some of the places depicted (albeit not very realistically) and laid eyes on some of the categories of souls shown.

One item had made no sense at all to him when he had first seen it, but now he understood what it was. This was ostensibly a painting of a very large tree, but curiously bedizened with little pictures of people who appeared to be attached to its branches like apples. The pictures were labeled with words. He now knew how to read these, because he had visited the Tower of the Ink Grinders in the fair city of Toravithranax and perched in the window of the high atelier where Pestle herself taught her students the Three Runic and the Eleven Scribal Alphabets as well as two completely different and incompatible systems of writing said to be used by strange people in the Teemings of the far east. Two different alphabets from three discernible epochs were represented among the names on this tree.

Reclining naked against the tree's trunk were a man and a woman labeled in very old script as ADAM and EVE. Below them, shown underground, were roots labeled EGDOD and SPRING. Other queer old names such as "Ward" and "Longregard" were scattered about on other rootlets; Thingor and Knotweave toiled in little subterranean cavelets, making things. Above them, standing on the ground to one side of the tree and bathing everything in white light, was El. Scattered about was an assortment of souls: to El's side of the tree, winged angels and mounted Autochthons and hunched scuttling Beedles. To the other side, bipedal rock piles, animated whirlwinds, and other oddments.

Low down, the trunk of the tree pushed out an ungainly side branch that looked as if it really ought to have been pruned off for starters. Chiseled into its bark in one of the Runic Alphabets were the number 12 and a word that meant something like "Great Ones" or perhaps "Giants." It forked in two; its lower fork had six branches all labeled with names that sounded masculine, and its upper fork six that were more feminine seeming. The former were all dead ends, but the latter produced various subbranches. Meanwhile the tree's main trunk went straight up for a bit, throwing out eight major side boughs. The eight boughs likewise sported an even mix of male and female names, and most of them forked and reforked profusely, so that the total number of little branches, out at the periphery, must have numbered in the hundreds, if not thousands. But unlike a real tree, this one included countless places where twigs from different branches came back together. To Corvus of a year ago this had made no sense, as real tree branches never did this, but he now understood that this was *not a tree*. It was a way of explaining how the descendants of Adam and Eve had recombined to populate the Land. And so in a case where, for example, the second son of Adam and Eve had mated with their third daughter to produce a child, it was necessary for those branches to bend together and merge in a distinctly non-treelike manner. More than two or three generations along, these had become impossible for the artists to keep doing and so beyond that point they had resorted to drawing lines between widely separated branches or simply duplicating names. This did not make the tree any easier to make sense of. Once Corvus got the overall gist of it he began to feel that the more he stared at it, the less he knew. But one good big patch of it was labeled PEOPLE BEYOND THE FIRST SHIVER, and right in the middle of that was CALLADON and not far away was BUFRECT, which Corvus gathered was the family name shared by most of the visitors. In relatively clean, fresh paint, BRINDLE was assigned a leaf of his own, but no one seemed to have got round to filling in any more recent arrivals. Likewise the most recent addition to the Bufrect family was PARALONDA, which was the name of the lady who had been seated at the other end of the table from Brindle.

Corvus was tired and desirous of sleep, but before his eyes closed he devoted some effort to tracing the branches backward from Brindle and Paralonda, working his way down the tree. Finally he traced the connection he was searching for, all the way back to the root, and then traced it back outward again, confirming that it led to the people who had built this Hall. Then his eyes closed and he slept, lulled by the dull roar of arguing Sprung. For in most of the Land, that was the term for souls who were descended from Adam and Eve.

"Quests are a thing that we do; it is a point of pride with us, in fact," Brindle told him a week later.

They had attained the high point of a pass through the mountains. Weather was good for a change; though, on Calla, this only meant that the clouds were higher than the tops of the mountains. So, at the suggestion of Corvus, Brindle had scrambled up to the summit of a nearby peak whence a better view could be had. Much of this Bit (as islands were called in this part of the world) could be surveyed from here. Directly below them was the stopping-place where the other members of the party were resting their legs, drying out their clothes, and making tea over a little fire. Looking to the south they could see the winding valley up which they had been toiling for the last several days; somewhat hazed-over in the greater distance was the rolling green country where the Calladons' house stood. Turning about and looking then to the north, they could see another ridge, and another one after that. Brindle knew from maps, and Corvus knew from actually having been there, that those eventually gave way and dropped into a green valley where the going would be much easier, all the way down to the sea.

Brindle went on: "Some people, however, would have gone around the mountains instead of directly through them. I wonder if your ability to fly might have impaired your judgment as regards route finding."

"There is a road," Corvus pointed out. "We have been following it."

"At its best—when it is traversing a well-drained meadow, for example—it is better described as a path or trail. At its more frequently seen worst, on the other hand—"

"It all connects up. I have followed it from one end of this Bit to the other."

"There is also a road—a true road—that circumvents the mountains on their eastern flank. And the Bufrects have ships that could take us up the western coast. Oh, I'm not complaining, yet. As I said, we are Questing folk, and this feels quite a bit more Questlike than lounging on the deck of some boat. But if you don't mind—"

"How many Quests have you performed?" Corvus asked.

Brindle sighed. "When I was a boy, I sailed across the First Shiver to the mainland, and rode with my father from our house to the ford of the river Thoss, a journey of several days. There I bade him farewell, never to see him again—though of course I did not know that at the time. Then I went home. There were wolves, and a scuffle with some rough characters." He glanced in the direction of a heaving mound of skins and furs with a spear next to it. Somewhere under that was a rough character named Burr.

"And . . . ?"

"That is all."

"No Quests for you, other than that?"

"That is correct."

"So when you say, Brindle, that you are Questing folk—"

"I am saying that it is how we define ourselves. The tales we tell, the pictures we hang on the wall. But it has been a long time since any Calladon has taken part in a Quest worthy of being so called. This has weighed on my mind for many years. I am trying to tell you, Corvus, that I consented to place myself and my friends and family at hazard not so much because I find you convincing, but because the mere fact of going on a Quest is its own reward. And so cutting directly across the mountainous center of Calla, instead of scurrying around the edge, isn't the worst thing in the world. But if you continue to make perverse choices in route finding, and we in consequence run out of food, or get hurt, questions will begin to be raised; and at that point I shall need to have a better answer than 'Oh, going on Quests builds character' and you shall have to have something better than strange talk about the fundamental nature of reality and how you fancy you were sent here from some other plane of existence that you cannot actually remember."

"Well, the way *we* are taught it is *this*," Prim was saying. It could be guessed from the looks on the others' faces, and from subtleties about their posture, that some sort of disagreement had arisen while Brindle and Corvus had been up above. The glance that Prim now threw Brindle's way as much as proved it. He had been enlisted on her side of a dispute he knew nothing of.

The topic seemed to be an old map that had been unrolled and spread flat to dry. They carried their maps in a tube that had got soaked by the rains, and several were scattered about. This particular one purported to show the entire Land. It had been painted, inked, embroidered, and gilded onto the skin of a large animal, and it had quite a lot to say. When she'd been younger, Prim had stared at it for hours. It appeared that one of the Bufrects had somewhat rashly ventured an opinion and that Prim was summoning all of her self-restraint to remain civil while setting him straight. Brindle, having arrived a little too late to finesse the situation, was helpless to do anything but stand by and nod as Prim launched into it, thus: "The Land was shaped *long* before El came into it, and it was shaped by *Egdod*. He started here, in what is now the middle, where El's Palace now stands atop its pillar—perhaps this is why you are confused—and flew generally east."

"Following the great river?"

"Creating it as he went, more like, until it had grown so wide that he felt it ought to empty into something. He marked that place with an enormous rock on the south bank and then began to fly north, keeping the sea to his right and creating the shore to his left. About here"—Prim pulled an arrow from her quiver and used it to point to a broad steady curve that formed the northeastern extremity of the Land—"Egdod thought better of making the Land any more enormous than it already was and swept gradually round until he was flying west. Which he did for a long time. Which is why the generally straight-ish northern coast of the Land, which stretches on for such a vast distance, is known as the Backhaul."

"Oh, hmm," said Mardellian Bufrect. "To me that was always just a word. It never crossed my mind that it was based on anything. *Back-haul*." He cleared his throat and blushed slightly. Then, in what he apparently thought was a more authoritative voice, he added, "Pray continue." He exchanged a glance with his kinsman Anvellyne. "With your *entertaining* tale." Mard and Lyne (as they were generally called) grinned at each other, a detail Prim did not notice, as she was shifting round to the map's northwest corner. Weaver, sitting on a rock nearby going through her damp things, shot her most peevish look at the two young men. Burr still appeared to be sleeping. Corvus was hopping about the place showing his usual complete lack of interest in what the humans were talking about.

If the map was considered the splayed skin of a dead animal, with its butt end pointed due east, then Prim had come round to its right foreleg—the northwest quadrant. "Lacking any means of judging distance," she continued, "Egdod overshot the Palace considerably, which is why as much of the Land lies to the west of it as to the east. The Second Bending, hereabouts, is where he decided to turn south again."

"It doesn't look the least bit like the First Bending," pointed out Lyne, in a tone of voice meant to indicate he was having none of it and just humoring Prim as a sort of private game with Mardellian. "It's just a mess of islands with channels between them."

"That mess of islands—the Bits and Shivers—is *your home,* and Calla is the largest of the Bits!" Prim scolded him. "And it wasn't thus when Egdod made it. It, and the First Bending, used to be as symmetrical as a pair of shoulders!"

Mardellian seized on this pretext to gaze at Prim's shoulders—as if he needed a flesh-and-blood model in order to fully grasp her meaning.

"The whole region west of the river—west of where Secondel-town now sits, here—snapped off."

"Snapped off?"

"Gradually, as big things move slowly," said Prim, sensing a bit of weakness in her own position. "So the big channel here—the First Shiver, which *used* to be a river—is the widest, and you can't see all the way across it except in some places. This whole chunk that broke off just happened to contain most of the wild souls and the giants."

Lyne sighed. "So much talk of giants, in all the old stories—yet I have never seen one."

"You see them all the time."

"You will see one tomorrow," croaked Corvus, "if you will only shut up and accept your fate as a two-footed thing, namely, to walk."

Brindle broke the awkward silence. "A game we used to play, looking at this map, was to think of all of the little islands among the Shivers as if they were shards of a broken pot. Then try to mentally imagine how they could be reassembled."

Anvellyne and Mardellian exchanged a look. They seemed uneasy with Brindle's proposing that any activity so tedious could be categorized as a game.

"If you look at them for long enough, you can see how an indentation in one Bit's coastline matches a protuberance in the coast of the Bit facing it across the Shiver," Brindle insisted.

"Shiver" was the local term for a channel running between Bits—or, in the case of the First Shiver, between the Bits and the mainland.

Meanwhile Prim had skirted around behind Brindle to the southwest—or, the dead animal's left foreleg. This was conveniently occupied by a peninsula that reached for some distance out into the sea. "Before turning inward again, Egdod asked himself how far the ocean might extend, and struck out south and west for some considerable distance until he became bored with it, which is why we call this arm of the Land the Asking, and the prominence at the end of it Cape Boredom."

"Huh!" said Lyne in spite of himself. "Boredom, I never put that together."

"But after satisfying himself that the ocean was quite limitless, and mindful of his responsibilities back in First Town, Egdod turned back and flew east, headed generally back toward the huge rock that he had set up to mark the outlet of the great river. It was a long journey, as you can see. He grew weary of flying in a straight line and began turning this way and that, and ever since this series of gulfs and peninsulas that complicate the Land's southern coastline—so different from the Backhaul—has been known as—"

"The Turnings!" exclaimed Mard. "Another of those funny old words . . ."

"The largest of these Egdod later enlarged into the Central Gulf. But in due course he spied the big rock where his circumnavigation had begun and made his way to it, throwing in lots of picturesque headlands and cliffs here along the southeastern corner, as he sensed it was his last opportunity to use up his best ideas before he got to the end. And that is why the Land has the shape that it does—it's *nothing* to do with El."

"I heard he got a lot wrong, though," said Mard. Lyne shot him a look. "I mean, even people who believe in the old songs and tales say as much." He said that for the benefit of Weaver, who had begun fussing with her harp—an instrument that was nearly impossible to tune even when it was bone-dry. She was older than Prim, and seemed to have devoted most of her years to memorizing stories and ballads. When her harp was in working order, which actually was not that often, she would sing them with enough conviction to make everyone present believe that they were true recitals of the facts.

Sensing that the others were looking her way, Weaver shrugged. Oddly enough, she always seemed a little bewildered when she found herself the center of attention. "It would be a sign of great learning to be able to recite all the tales of Egdod and Pluto. I know only a small portion of them and yet could devote an entire evening to the telling of stories in that vein."

"And she *will*, if we sit still for it," said Lyne.

"It's easy for fault finders to come along thousands of years later and say that Egdod shouldn't have made Pluto's job so difficult," said Prim. "But that's *nothing* like claiming that El made the entire Land. Why, that's just rubbish."

"But the Pinnacle, the Palace, the Hive!" Lyne said. And he made a quick glance over his shoulder, roughly eastward, and bowed slightly at the waist. Even though they were too far away to see the Palace, this was a common gesture among persons who were inclined to take El's side of things. Mard belatedly did the same. The others—Brindle, Prim, and Weaver—glanced east but omitted the bowing part of it. Burr jerked in his sleep. Corvus flapped his wings irritably.

"Those are places, yes, where El changed things dramatically," Brindle admitted. "But even the most fervent priests of El accept the notion that Egdod started it all. It works in their favor, actually, since whenever they notice something about the Land that seems ungainly or cack-handed, they can blame it on Egdod."

"I know," Lyne admitted. "It's just that it all seems a bit made-up."

"What do you mean, made-up?"

"Egdod flying about and putting this here and that there, and Pluto cleaning up after him."

"Make *this* up, stripling!" shouted Corvus in a voice even more strangled and cacophonous than the norm. They all turned toward the boulder where he was perching and saw—a man. A naked man enrobed in long black hair, and a long black beard, with beady black eyes. His skin was ocher and his nails long and yellowed and talonlike. He was sitting on his haunches. His beard dangled down between his legs and concealed the place where one would expect to see a penis. The mountain breeze was whipping his hair around his face, only his eyes burning through the blur.

"Oh. My. Goodness," Brindle said.

"Where did *he* come from?" Lyne asked, looking around for a weapon. "And where's the bird?"

Burr levered himself up to his full height, which was considerable, using his spear. It didn't take long for him to notice the strange naked man on the rock. He took a step in that direction and brought the spear's tip down to bear on the intruder.

"I think he *is* the bird, Lyne!" Mard said.

Weaver had set her harp aside and stood up. She was fascinated. She sidestepped over Burr's way and rested a hand on the socket of his spearhead, just behind the glinting leaf-shaped blade, and pushed it gently aside. "Singing of this and actually seeing it are very different things," she said.

Prim stood still through all of this, gazing into the man's eyes. "It's you," she concluded, "it's still Corvus."

"Now that I have your attention," Corvus announced. But then he gagged, hacked, and spat, as if having some difficulty learning to use the new vocal apparatus. When he had recovered, he went on in a somewhat deeper and more human tone: "There'll be no more wanky chatter about such topics during the Quest." He hocked up a little more and spat it in the general direction of the map. "Now roll that thing up, and don't take it out anymore. What the hell are you doing, wasting your time looking at the map, when the world itself is spread out all around you?"

And with that his glossy black hair and beard wrapped themselves around his body and came together to coat all of his face save his eyes and his nose, and the nose and jaw extended and hardened into a beak. His feet shrank and his toes lengthened into talons. There was a lot of unsightly twitching and spasming and vocalization that caused everyone except Weaver to avert their gaze; Mardellian even clapped his hands over his ears, and Prim had to step lively as the creature voided its bowels in midtransformation. Then it was just Corvus again. He made two experimental hops and then took to the air.

The other six members of the party all looked at one another, just to confirm that this had really happened. Prim was still clutching the arrow she had been using as a pointer. She put it back into its quiver, then dropped to one knee at the eastern edge of the map. Before she began to roll it up again, she took one long last look at it, the way you do at an old friend before you set out on a long journey without them.

Burr had never unpacked; he was already good to go. Turning his broad back on the way they'd come, he gazed down the pass. The convolutions of the valleys below beguiled him for a while. But after a bit he picked out a plausible-seeming direction and indicated it with his spear. Then he looked at Corvus and raised his eyebrows.

"Ugh, more!" Prim blurted as they came round yet another bend in the valley. For she'd been hoping that *this* time it would be different and they would see open country, green pastures, a giantess looking after her beasts. "Is this what it is, or was, like to be Pluto?"

Brindle, who was ahead of her, turned his head in profile, frowning. Then he seemed to understand—or perhaps he was merely humoring her—and he smiled and turned back to the next rock, the next footfall.

"I mean," Prim went on, "is it the case that Egdod said, 'I want a valley here, with mountains at the top, and, at the bottom, a river emptying into the sea,' and then flew on in the satisfaction of a job well done? And then Pluto came along later and shaped each individual rock and thought about where to set it down?" She feigned a yawn. "'Oh, the previous two thousand rocks were all set in place rather firmly, I do believe I'll balance this one just so, to trip up an inattentive traveler who might happen along a few eons from now.'"

She looked back at Burr to make sure he'd noticed the rock in question. As usual he was paying more attention to the heights around them than to the ground in front of the shaggy mukluks that for him served as boots. But he had a third leg in the form of his spear and fell no more often than anyone else. Occasionally he would stop and shush them all, and in the silence they would hear the cry of an animal echoing from the cliffs that hemmed in the valley, or see a little cascade of stones dribbling down from a vantage point.

Anvellyne was ahead of her at the moment. For he and Mardellian tended to grow bored, and dawdle and fall behind, whereupon Burr would grow stormy-looking and Brindle, noting as much, would yell at them, and then they would come racing down pell-mell and run on ahead until Burr and Brindle checked them. Lyne turned half around and said, "According to Weaver's stories, Pluto didn't make all of this anyway!"

Weaver got the hunched, furtive look she always did when someone was trying to draw her into the conversation, and scuttled on ahead, leaving Prim to answer: "Of course he did!"

"What I'm saying," Lyne replied, "is that in those stories this all snapped off and got redone after Pluto and the rest had been flung into the sky and got rid of. So maybe if you don't like the way these rocks are set down you should complain to Edda. When and if we actually see her."

"No soul went to the trouble to shape these rocks one by one, as a baker's hand shapes a loaf," Corvus ruled, banking slowly over their heads on a cool breeze coming up the valley.

"Then how did they come to be here," Prim asked, "with the shapes that they have?"

"Why, when you step wrong, do you fall down?" Corvus replied. "The Land is so constituted that it has laws, which all things heed without the need for souls to observe, think, act, and do other soul-like things. So everything falls. Fall simply *is*. And besides fall there are other such laws and tendencies. Hill-giants maybe are aware of the slow forces that splinter cliffs and shape rocks, but not the likes of us."

"So maybe Edda *will* have something to say about it!" Mard put in. He was only joking, as Prim could tell from the look he threw Lyne. But if Corvus understood it as a jest, he had no patience for it. "If I see one more of you ground-pounders craning your necks and scanning the skyline for a glimpse of her kneecap, I'll croak!" he exclaimed. "Attend to the rocks. It won't be much longer."

But it *was* much longer, and so after a while Prim took up the theme again. She had a hidden motive; these debates made the time go by faster, and kept Lyne and Mard nearer the rest of the group.

Prim required further convincing. "I have not seen the Palace," she began.

"I have," said Corvus.

"But I have seen many depictions of it, and heard it described in the songs of Weaver, and if there is any truth in those, it perches on a spire of rock that is so tall and slender it cannot answer to the same laws that, according to you, govern . . . *this*." And after a brief pause to be sure of her footing she looked up and spread her arms to indicate the cliffs all round them.

"It is an exception, to be sure," Corvus admitted.

"It was so shaped in the Before Times," Weaver assured them, "when there were many such prodigies that could never be brought into being today. It was the last such, and some say that in making it Egdod spent his powers and made himself too weak to overcome . . . *the Usurper*." This last word she spoke quietly, in confidence to Prim, for it was a forbidden word, not safe to say aloud in certain company. But Prim took no note. For as she had raised her gaze just now from the next rock and the next, she had spied, around the next bend in the valley, a patch of blue sky above a field of green.

"You have to understand," Corvus remarked, as the party lengthened its strides into Edda's valley, "that being a giant, or a giantess, is not about being giant—or even large. That's just a common misconception."

Mard and Lyne turned back to gawp at him. They simply could not believe the things Corvus said sometimes.

"People have got impossibly confused," Corvus went on, "because of hill-giants and other wild souls—who actually *are* unbelievably enormous. Edda has a form like ours."

Lyne was beyond exasperated—ready to turn on his heel and walk home, it seemed. "Then why denote her as a giantess?" He threw a look at Weaver, as if it were her fault. "F'relsake, can't we come up with a different term?"

"The First Children of Eve are known by many names, if you only listen with care to the old songs," said Weaver. "Angel Eaters, Adam's Woe, Cairn's Care . . ."

"Fine!" Lyne snapped. "All better names than 'giantess.'"

Burr had stopped a few hundred paces short of a cottage that they had all, without discussing it, been heading for since it had hove into view. Until recently they had been traversing wolfish country, where even the creatures that weren't wolves tended to come equipped with a remarkable array of horns, tusks, and claws. In such places Burr liked to advance to the head of the group. Brindle liked to bring up the rear. Remarks he'd made along the way suggested he was afraid of being attacked from behind by unspecified creatures who—or so it could be guessed—were extraordinarily quiet in their movements and patient in their approach to hunting. But there hadn't been much excitement so far. Everything that had come at them had done so from the front and found itself on the wrong end of Burr's spear. A few times Prim had taken up her bow and nocked an arrow, just in case, but not let any fly.

At no point during even the most thrilling encounters had Burr actually shown signs of excitement, or exhibited the least reluctance to keep forging ahead, and so it was strange that he now stopped, in an open space with no wild beasts of any kind in evidence, and no obstructions. A stone's throw away, off to their left, a couple of mounts were eating grass, bending their necks to crop it from the ground and then bobbing back up to eye them curiously as they chewed.

"No walls, really," Burr pointed out. "No weapons. Livestock out in plain sight, unafraid."

"Yes indeed," Mard said, "it seems very safe."

"*Why?*" Brindle asked. Rhetorically. "That's what Burr is asking himself."

Mardellian hadn't considered that angle. Neither had Prim.

"Well," Mard guessed, "you know, we haven't seen what's inside the cottage yet."

"Bread baking, to judge from the fragrance," Prim said.

"It could be full of armed Autochthons."

"It's not," said Brindle, and nodded at Burr. The man-at-arms, after giving the cottage only a quick look, had turned his back on it and was now surveying the sweep of dark hills that enclosed the valley and the pair of snowcapped peaks at its head, between which they had passed yesterday.

"You see—" Brindle began.

But Lyne, impatient with the lesson, cut him off. "We've been making our way through her defenses ever since we came down the pass and spotted that wolf up on the ridgeline, staring at us."

"We're . . . surrounded?" Mardellian asked.

Burr reversed his grip on the spear so that it became more walking stick than weapon. The party spread out to stroll across the pasture seven abreast: On the left flank, the young men Anvellyne and Mardellian, on loan from the clan Bufrect. Then Weaver, who seemed to be vaguely attached to House Calladon. Brindle, its patriarch, walked in the middle. To his right was Prim. Well off to the right was Burr, who preferred keeping his spear arm free of flesh-and-blood obstructions. In the open space between him and Prim, Corvus hopped along, occasionally flying for short bursts when he fell behind or needed to clear one of the stone walls that divided the pastures.

In spite of Corvus's words, Prim had been holding out for something in a gigantic vein. But as they drew closer to the cottage it became undeniable that it was in no way of unusual size. Not cramped, for certain, and of a somewhat rambling character, as bits had been added on from time to time. One could make out foundation stones of wings that did not exist anymore. These erupted from the ground like rows of teeth from gums. Those must have been relics of ancient sections of the cottage that Edda had built, lived in for a time, and got rid of—or simply allowed to disintegrate with the passage of time.

She wasn't tiny, at least. She opened the door to greet them and was revealed to be about as tall as Burr. Her hair was white, full and long, braided down her back. She wore an apron streaked with flour, which she took this opportunity to give a brisk shake. The breeze caught the loose flour and bore it gently away. The flour caught the light as it drifted, and beguiled Prim's eye, for the shape that it took and the manner of its movement was just like that of clouds in the sky when they drifted overhead on a summer's day. This impression was so strong that it seized her mind entirely for a few moments, during which she could think of nothing save various times in her past life when she had gazed out her window or lain in the grass looking up at clouds.

She did not entirely return to the here and now until she found herself some moments later standing, along with the others, right in the forecourt of the cottage, gazing up at the face of Edda. Or actually not gazing up, since Edda wasn't that tall; yet it *felt* up. Corvus, perched on the roof over the door, was doing the introducing, poking his long beak at each of them in turn and squawking out their name. Edda favored each of them with a look and—not a smile exactly, but an openness about the face that put one at ease somewhat as a pure and unfeigned smile might. "Primula," she said, as if she'd *heard* of Prim.

"How do you do," Prim said back up to her—but again, not really up. She got lost then in the striations in the iris of Edda's left eye. These were immensely complex, and of all colors, having about them the same balance of order and wildness as exposed tree roots, tendrils of smoke in the wind, tongues of wild flame, the swirling of water where rivers came together. Prim wondered if the striations in her own irises were anywhere near as complicated. She guessed that the answer was probably no, and then wondered how such things got shaped in the first place—were you just born with them or did they grow in complexity over time? Or was it different, when you were a giantess? Had Edda consciously worked on hers, or had they just taken form on their own?

"Weaver!" Edda said. Somehow they'd all entered the cottage and found seats around a table. A loaf of warm bread was there. They'd been tearing hunks from it and eating heartily, but there was plenty of bread remaining. Prim had got lost staring into the structure of a bread hunk, somewhat as she'd once sat for hours staring at the map of the Land. There was a lot to this bread, and biting chunks out of it only exposed more. Steam escaped from the tiny round cavities and came together in roiling cloudlets shaped like flowers, men, and monsters—until she began to notice them, whereupon they undid themselves and became invisible currents of scent.

Weaver had been lost in admiration of the tabletop, which was an enormous slab of polished stone, a hand span in thickness, supported at the ends by boulders founded in the earth—the floorboards, unable to bear such weight, had been carefully cut around them. The stone had complex patterns, and you could see some distance into it, as if it were part crystal. Hearing her name spoken, Weaver tore her gaze from this only to get distracted by Edda's braid, which the giantess had flipped to the front so that it trailed down over her bosom. There was a lot more to it than just a simple three-strand braid.

"Yes, my lady?"

"I have not had the pleasure of your company since two hundred and thirty-seven years ago, when you sat just where you are sitting now, and I taught you the Lay of Valeskara and Blair."

Prim remembered that vaguely: two lovers who, as a side effect of a war between a hill-giant and a troop of angels, had found themselves on opposite sides of a freshly made Shiver. Before they could find a way across, Blair had become embroiled in a fight with some Beedles, who had put him in chains and taken him away to a castle or something, where Autochthons put him in a dungeon. Valeskara still walked on the cliff top awaiting his return. So that, at least, was familiar. But Weaver's being at least two and a half centuries old was news to her—and apparently to Brindle.

Evidently it was even news to Weaver. "That may very well be, my lady, but . . ."

"But you have no recollection of it, for you must have passed on at least once since then."

"One would think so!" said Weaver.

Lyne raised his face out of his bread hunk just long enough to gaze across the table at Mard, with a look that said, *No wonder she knows so many fucking songs.*

"Before you leave, I shall teach you more," Edda promised.

"That would be a high honor—"

"Not going to happen," Corvus announced from his perch on the sill of a window that Edda, perhaps unadvisedly, had left wide open. "There's to be no 'leaving.' You're coming with us."

For the first time, Edda smiled. She turned her attention to Brindle and Prim, who were seated next to each other.

"You two are as father and daughter," she observed, "but that is not so?"

Brindle shook his head. "Her mother and father passed on, more than likely. Oh, it happened some time ago—she chose to remain a girl for many years, and I saw no point in rushing her along."

"Wise," Edda said. "Dough given more time to rise makes a finer loaf." Then, to Prim: "You make a fine young woman, which means you chose correctly."

Prim blushed and fell into a reverie, listening to the tones of Edda's voice but not at all following the words. Her voice was as complex as her braid, and its strands were flutes, birdsong, and the lapping of waves on a lakeshore in the still of the evening.

Brindle was squeezing her arm under the table. She looked at him. He inclined his head toward their hostess, whose last sentence rushed into her mind all at once: the giantess had said, "I see from the calluses on your fingers that you like archery; I could teach you what little I know of flint knapping."

"That is most generous," Prim said. "The heads of my arrows are all forged."

"Much more practical," Edda said, "but stone ones have their uses too."

"Learning that will burn *weeks*," Corvus protested. "Think *hours*."

Edda didn't seem to hear the giant talking raven. She turned her attention to the others, each in their turn. She remembered Burr as a warrior who had once passed on gloriously in single combat with an angel. This revelation certainly caused Lyne and Mard to look at the spearman in a new light.

Those two Bufrect boys came in for examination next. Their clan lived round the edges of a steep rocky peninsula projecting from the southern end of Calla. It pointed into a broad, short Shiver that connected straight to the ocean. So they were seagoing folk. They'd joined the Quest on a lark, not without one or two swift kicks in the arse from their matriarch Paralonda. Since then, during wetter, colder, duller moments, they'd made no secret of regretting it. But by the time Edda was done talking to them it was clear there'd be no more second thoughts.

"You make Questing sound grand," Corvus pointed out. "Perhaps setting foot out of this valley every few centuries would do you good!"

Brindle was the only one of the visitors Edda had not chatted with yet, and so it seemed natural he'd be next. But instead he and Edda merely looked at each other, arriving at some wordless understanding.

Food had made them all sleepy and so at Edda's invitation they spread out into various rooms of the cottage. For a small place, it had an extraordinary number of nooks and, as it were, backwaters, always surprising the visitor as she came round a corner. Before long Prim had found the perfect one for her, curled up in it, and fallen asleep. She rose once in the middle of the night to go outside and empty her bladder, and as she went in and out she overheard Edda and Brindle conversing in low tones, but could make out only a single word, which was "Spring." After that she slept very soundly.

She had a dream in which radiant light was shining down from the Palace, and she could not escape its glare, which penetrated even her closed eyelids. She was down on the ground far below, prostrate, but through the earth she could feel, more than hear, a deep grinding, as though the underpinnings of the Land itself were being invisibly reshaped. This was not the pick-and-shovel work of Beedles toiling under the lash, but something that hearkened to the Before Times and the doings of Thingor. Standing up and turning her back to the light, she found herself gazing up into mountains, black at the base, white with snow above that, but hidden at the top behind storm clouds that reached up into the sky as high as El's Pinnacle, wreathed at the top with blue lightning.

She opened her eyes and flung out a hand to brace herself. In her dream she had been standing on a grassy plain but in fact she was lying on her side, back turned to the light of the morning, which was cutting in under the clouds and coming in straight through a window. That had been real, at least. The Pinnacle and the storm had been dream figments but that deep grinding sound was certainly there, pervading the cottage and coming up into her bones through the floor.

She got up. The sound had a directionless quality that made finding its source no easy task. But soon enough she found her way into the kitchen. At the other end, by the door to a pantry that looked bigger than the rest of the house put together, a stone rested atop another stone. Both were round and flat, like thick coins, or slices of a sausage. Their diameter was about the length of a person's arm. The one on top had a hole in its center, which was full of golden grain. Edda was standing next to it, one hand resting on the upper stone, and she was pushing it round and round. Flour trickled from a hole in the lower stone and collected in a bowl on the floor. This was, in other words, a mill like any other, save it lacked the waterwheel or the team of beasts that would normally be required to budge anything so heavy. Edda moved it as easily as if it were a spinning wheel.

"Is there . . . some way I could help?" Prim asked.

"It is about time to empty the bowl," Edda pointed out, and nodded at a large table in the middle of the kitchen, on which a considerable heap of flour already stood. Prim stepped in, picked up the bowl, and carried it to the table, where she dumped it out atop what was already there. Then she paused for a few moments, for the shape of the heap was strikingly like that of the mountain in her dream, and the cloud of loose airborne flour still swirling above it was like the thunderhead that obscured the heights.

But she knew that the flour was spilling out onto the floor by the mill, so she hurried over and reinstated the bowl. While she was there kneeling at Edda's feet, she scooped up loose flour in her hands and transferred it into the bowl. The scent of flour was everywhere, of course, but so was the scent of Edda, which was faint but bottomless.

"Baking more bread?" Prim asked. For it seemed that Edda had baked more than enough of it yesterday.

"Hardtack," Edda corrected her. "To sustain us on the road."

49

Two days' easy walking took them to the place where the river emptied into a broad bend of the Shiver that formed Calla's northeastern coast. From there, across several miles of open water, they could see a solitary mountain guarded by ranges of foothills. It was not evident from here, but Prim knew from maps that this was a separate Bit unto itself, with another Shiver cutting around its backside and separating it from the much larger Bit that lay off to its east. Formerly all three landmasses had been one huge Bit, but the solitary mountain had drawn to itself all the wildest and most fractious old souls that still dwelled in the Land, and the place had become so unmanageable that, like a nail driven into a block of brittle old wood, it had snapped the big island in half and found itself standing alone in the midst of a newly formed Shiver. The waters girding it and the air above were infamously fickle and hazardous. Reaching this harbor, as beautiful and placid as it seemed, was therefore considered too dangerous to be attempted by sea. This did much to explain why Edda had been able to enjoy such isolation in her valley, for one end could only be entered by going over the pass, and the other was, to all intents and purposes, barred to mariners by the wild souls on the Bit opposite. But there was a village at the river's mouth where a few doughty souls lived from fish that they caught along the nearer shore. This was notched with little coves where they could take refuge when air and water were raging. One of these, a man named Robst, agreed to take the party as passengers on his boat, *Firkin,* if they would pull on oars, and perform other tasks, when needed.

It took no time at all to agree on this plan, but Prim was surprised by how long it took to embark and get under way. She was not accustomed to boats and watery doings; she was taken aback by how many lines and knots were involved. Robst had a lot to say on the subject of ballast.

"We traveled too light," Mard explained to her.

"First I've heard of it," Prim replied. "My pack felt heavy to me!"

Mard nodded. "Yes, we all carried as much as we could. But Brindle, you'll recall, said from the very beginning that we mustn't use mounts . . ."

"Because we would only have to abandon them when we reached the water and boarded ship," Prim recalled. "Of course, it's a different story with Edda's."

She nodded at two mounts who were standing on the shore near the dock, taking a very dim view indeed of the crests of incoming waves. Edda had laden them with baggage for the trip down, so that the rest of the party could walk free of their heavy packs. The beasts had now been unloaded, and Edda had let them know that they were free to leave. They didn't seem to like the waves at all, and so kept edging back from the shore. But they liked Edda quite a bit, and were reluctant to part from her.

For all the toil that had gone into transporting them to this place, the bags did indeed look like not very much when they were all piled up on the strand. "*Firkin* is made to carry lots of heavy stuff," Mard said. "Just now the hold is empty, and it is riding very high in the water."

"It is?" Prim asked. To her it just looked like a boat.

"Bobbing like a cork," Mard confirmed. Bufrects, dwelling on the coast, knew more about such things than Calladons in general. In fact Lyne had already boarded the vessel and was clambering around familiarizing himself with how it all worked. "Not safe to sail. Our baggage weighs nothing compared to what that boat could carry, and so Robst is going to have to put more stuff into it just to make it ride lower in the water."

"What kind of stuff?"

"Rocks," Mard said with a shrug.

"Ugh, rocks again!"

Edda pulled her modest bag from the pile and slung it over her shoulder. She went up to each of the mounts in turn for a sweet face-to-face conversation and a goodbye kiss, then turned her back and stepped up onto the pier, which ran out into the harbor on a series of boulders and pounded-in tree trunks. *Firkin* was tied up at its end. When she stepped aboard, it settled much lower in the water, as if tons of rocks had just been deposited in its hold. The mounts turned tail and walked off, following the bank of the river back up in the direction of Edda's cottage.

Robst—who had been engaged in a detailed conversation with Brindle on the topic of rocks—stood still for a long time, gazing at his boat as if he were expecting it to bob back up again. It did not, however, and so after a while he shrugged and walked down the dock to board it and continue his preparations. He struck a deal with two younger kinsmen and a local woman; these would provide him with a skeleton crew so that he could sail *Firkin* home after discharging the passengers. A short while later they were under way.

Using sails when they could and oars when they had to, they proceeded north up the Shiver in a furtive way, hewing close to the near shore until the mountain of the wild souls was well behind them. Then they ventured out into the middle of the channel, which was many miles broad this far north. They passed out of the Eternal Veil of Mist that surrounded Calla and came out into full sunlight. They caught a stiff west wind that was sluicing down another Shiver that delineated the north coast of Calla. This drove them eastward at a good clip. Prim's home island fell away aft. At some point Prim realized that she could not see Calla—or, to be precise, the Eternal Veil—anymore, and wondered when or if she would ever see it again. They were navigating now generally eastward between Bits that seemed on the whole darker, colder, and less welcoming. It was because they were covered mostly in trees—the greenish-black trees of far north and high mountain—with only rare patches of farm and pasture.

Four days' voyaging took them round the south cape of another Bit. As soon as they'd cleared it, they hooked northward into the First Shiver, which in these parts was so broad as to be more of an inland sea than a channel. The coast opposite was not always visible, but they could see hills rising above it. And so this was how

Prim got her first look at the Land proper. From the deck of this boat, it looked no different from another Bit in the distance. But Prim could not help gazing on it and thinking about the fact that once you set foot on it you could reach all the places on the big map: not just the Lake Land, which was the nearest part, but the Knot, the Fastness, the Hive, the Palace, and the teeming lands surrounding the great river as it flowed down to the far eastern sea.

Soon visible off to their left was their destination: West Cloven. This port had a sister city, unsurprisingly known as East Cloven, just opposite on the shore of the mainland. In the old days they had been one town straddling a river that drained part of the Lake Land. Like Eltown and Toravithranax farther south, it had been settled in the time after Egdod had thrown down the first Hive, and the souls who had dwelled in it had dispersed to all corners of the Land.

Their home island of Calla had been settled by souls who had begun their journey around Camp, across from Old Eltown, and made their way north and west, following trails laid down by migrating giants. So the speech of the Calladons and Bufrects was a dialect of what was still spoken around Secondeltown. But different folk altogether had created the town that later became Cloven. Its two halves, East and West, had been separated long enough by the gradually broadening Shiver that a different dialect was spoken in each. At the opposite end of the First Shiver, many days' journey to the south, the people of Toravithranax spoke yet another entirely different language. Of all of these places, Secondeltown, being closest to El's Palace, and indeed having a direct view of the Palace from the vast and magnificent Temple, Basilica, School, and Monastery of Elkirk looming above it, spoke a language thought to be closest to that of First Town in the Before Times. A simple version of that language—Townish—had come into use up and down the length of the First Shiver as the common tongue of mariners and traders. It was close enough to what the Bufrects and Calladons spoke that with a little practice, and by pruning their sentences, they could make themselves understood around the docks in West Cloven. Or so they were assured by Robst as he piloted them safe into the old harbor after a reasonably uneventful journey. It was not the biggest town they'd ever seen—Farth, the capital of Calla, was bigger and certainly nicer to look at—but it was a considerable town. Much larger vessels than theirs were moored all about, unloading cargo from the Lake Land across the First Shiver. In its place the produce of many Bits was transferred into vacated holds: honey, wax, timber, fish, grains, and fibers.

Robst knew where to go, but even still they'd have been lost without Corvus. Yesterday the giant talking raven had flown away without explanation as soon as the back side of this Bit had hove into view. Today he had appeared high above them as they rowed into the harbor. "He'll not perch anywhere that his size will draw attention," Brindle predicted. "Not all folk are as easygoing as we Calladons in the presence of such creatures."

But one other soul had apparently been keeping an eye on Corvus's movements, for when they at last found a mooring place, he was standing on the shore waiting for them. Corvus, apparently satisfied the connection had been made, flapped away toward some nearby cliffs topped with dark trees.

The moorage here was makeshift, with smaller craft simply hauled up on the beach. Robst had everyone pull on the oars for a few moments while aiming *Firkin* at an empty patch of sand, and ran it up just far enough to stick. Lyne scampered up onto the prow and cast a rope down to the soul who was waiting for them. Thus was Edda able to disembark without causing the boat to bob back up in a way that might have attracted notice. For many hereabouts seemed to have a lot of time on their hands, which they whiled away by staring at newcomers. Edda, the moment she touched down, wrapped herself in a long cloak of simple nubby stuff that was nothing to look at—literally nothing, since, once she had pulled it up to cover her, it concealed every bit of the engrossing complexity in her form. Save, of course, the irises. But one had to stand close to see those.

"My name is Ferhuul," said the man on the beach, extending his hand in peace, "and I would be bowing in token of my respect if I did not wish to avoid drawing attention to your arrival, my lady." He averted his gaze, perhaps not wanting to become lost in hers, and clasped her hand briefly. Then he likewise greeted the others, guessing their names correctly, though Mard and Lyne required a little straightening out. He spoke Townish with the accent of Cloven, which was presumably his native tongue. "If you will please follow me," he said, "I know of a place where *all* of us can talk in comfort." He cast a wary look at Burr, but the man-at-arms had had the common sense to leave all of his weapons, save a belt knife, aboard *Firkin,* where Robst and his three crewmates could keep an eye on them. Satisfied of that, Ferhuul led the party on a stroll up streets that were flat and straight at first, winding and even zigzagging later as they climbed up out of the harbor flats.

"Try to act like you have been here before," Brindle told Prim, "or at least to some place like it."

Prim nodded and, for a little while, fixed her gaze on the cobblestones coming and going under her feet.

Practically all of the souls Prim had ever met in her life had been Sprung: descendants of Adam and Eve, which meant that they had come into being within the bodies of mothers who had been impregnated by fathers. As was proved, or at least claimed, by the great family tree on the wall of the Calladons' hall, every such soul could trace his or her ancestry back to Adam and Eve. Though they each looked a little different, all such souls shared a common form that, according to their legends, had been preordained by Spring in the Before Times.

Spawned, on the other hand, had not been born of a woman but had simply appeared here or there, first as inchoate glimmers of near-chaos. From those beginnings they had developed forms. It had been thus in the Before Times, when many such had developed at hazard into wild souls of outlandish shapes and powers. Even in the days of First Town, though, they had tended to shape themselves into two-legged, two-armed, one-headed creatures of a common size. Egdod's casting down of the hive and the destruction of First Town had dispersed such souls to all parts of the Land, where they had clumped together into new communities. There were variants characteristic of certain regions, the best known being Beedles, who spawned in the vicinity of Secondeltown and were shaped to be the servants and soldiers of the Autochthons. And souls who spawned in very remote areas could still take on unusual forms. But for the most part, Spawned were indistinguishable from adult Sprung. The only difference that mattered was that Spawned could not have children.

Spawned were rarely seen in the middle of Calla, where Prim had lived her whole life, but they were all over the place here. Children ran and played in the streets—these were obviously descendants of Eve. But those of finished, adult form might be either Spawned or Sprung. Prim was naturally curious to see whether she could tell them apart; Brindle had noted her gaze lingering too long on strangers' forms and faces and given her a gentle warning. Farth, the only other town of any size she'd spent time in, was a friendlier sort of place where everyone knew each other. Cloven felt altogether chillier and less welcoming.

"Souls of all kinds come here from the Bits, the Lake Land, the whole length of the First Shiver. Even from as far south as the Asking and as far east as the communities lining the Hive-Way," Brindle explained. "So it's not at all like Farth. They don't all speak the same languages or observe the same customs. You might even see the odd Beedle scuttling up out of the hold of a cargo ship from Secondeltown. In places like *that*"—and he nodded at the open door of a tavern, full of souls having a common look and speaking a language Prim had never heard—"they may be warm and sociable, but the streets and wharves are a different matter and you'd do well to bridle your curiosity."

Their destination turned out to be an old stone house at the end of a street where it ran smack into the base of a cliff. A stone wall enclosed the house and its court. The place was heavily worn around the edges but well kept where it mattered. Ferhuul explained that it belonged to a man and woman of his acquaintance who owned more than one vessel and were currently out to sea aboard one such. "The stairs and the ground floor are stone all the way down," he said to Edda. "The upper story—mere wood."

Edda nodded and sat down on the top of the low stone wall that ran along one edge of the courtyard. Prim understood that Ferhuul had been warning the giantess that the floors upstairs might not bear her weight.

Edda let the cloak fall from her head but kept it snug around her body. Others sat on wooden chairs and benches at a table nearby. Weaver had been silent for some days as sea travel did not agree with her, but now tuned her harp and sang a song that Edda had been teaching her, verse by verse. Dusk fell, somewhat concealing the approach of Corvus, who swooped down from the cliff top and perched on a long and extraordinarily massive tree bough stretched out above.

Corvus seemed uncharacteristically content to sit and listen to the song. Prim reflected that the giant talking raven had been in the Land for but one year, and though he had flown far and seen much, he could not have learned but a fraction of the tales known to the likes of Edda and Weaver.

The song was written in a very old poetic style, with many allusions to other songs and myths. But the basic story was familiar to anyone who had grown up around books. So Prim climbed up into the tree—which was easy, even though she had stopped being a girl and turned into a full-grown woman—and sat on the bough next to Corvus and whispered explanations at him so that the story would make better sense.

The story went that Egdod and Spring, who were lovers, found themselves separated after the Fall. She was tied to the Land, which was where all of her creations—soon including Adam and Eve—had their homes. He had been exiled to the Firmament. Again and again Egdod sought to return, beating his great black wings to soar across the void separating Firmament from Land. But again and again his approach, be it never so stealthy, was detected by El's watchful angels, and he was flung back. For El in his wisdom had woven an invisible net about the Land, which could detect Egdod's approach no matter how craftily he disguised himself. The Red Web grew as crater after crater was added. Finally Egdod learned from Sophia—a member of the Pantheon who was privy to mystic lore from another plane of existence—the truth: El's magic would always see through his deceptions and disguises. The only way for him to return to the Land was to give up his very self: to die and to grow again from nothing. Now, Sophia in her way was the most terrible of all the Pantheon, for she held the power of life and death over every soul. Even Egdod. He requested that she sever the thread of his life and she consented. With that Egdod fell dead. But his dying made it possible for him to begin again, as a new soul in the Land. Slowly he returned to life, and, in the chaos beneath the Fastness, he made a form for himself. He went out into the Land, hiding himself in the humble guise of an insect or a worm, and sought out those dear to him. Spring he could not find anywhere, for she roamed at will and in many guises, but Adam and Eve were confined to a garden and easily found. In that garden and other places he made mischief and thereby incurred the wrath of El, who could not fathom how the Old One had slipped through his net. Again and again El in his fury struck down any creature whom he suspected of being Egdod in some new guise. Again and again Egdod returned, patiently creating new forms in which he roamed about the Land: sometimes a cloaked wanderer, sometimes a bird or a wolf or even a gust of wind. Yet always Spring eluded him.

At length El came to understand that it was in the Fastness where Egdod found sanctuary whenever he was struck down, and where each time he wove a new form about his naked soul. It was in the library of that great fortress where he taught himself to read, and learned his own story, and pored over maps, and came to understand who and what he was and what he must do. It was there in Knotweave's spinning room where he would make clothes, and Thingor's forge where he would fashion tools and weapons, that he would not venture out into the Land naked and unarmed. That was when El and certain of his high angels ventured to Toravithranax and went to the high atelier of Pestle and demanded any accounts she might have concerning the Fastness, particularly diagrams of the fortress and maps of the Knot in which it was embedded; but they were frustrated when they came at length to understand that the Knot could not be mapped, for it did not make any kind of sense that could be reduced to ink on a page. So El sent his angels to go and look at the place. But they could not penetrate the storm, and several did not return.

El resolved to journey there afoot, and rediscovered from of old the Shifting Path, which led him to the Broken Bridge. This had been built at the end of the First Age when the minions of El had gone to that place in great numbers to build a wall around the Fastness. Since then the wall had fallen into disrepair and the middle span of the bridge had been struck down into the chasm. El crossed over, and stood before the Fastness, and in his pride fancied that he would tear it down and altogether reduce it to chaos. He summoned then an army of angels. They changed themselves into the form of wingless souls and marched upon the Knot following the convolutions of the Shifting Path until at last they too stood before the very gates of the Fastness.

It was there that El at last found a limit to his power. He was not able to tear down the Fastness as he had hoped, for situated as it was in the heart of the Land where the four mountain ranges were tied together, it bore the same relation to the very fabric of the Land as a keystone to an arch; to destroy it, even if such a thing were within his power, would be to unmake the Land itself, to break it asunder into chaos and make all of its souls homeless.

But there was one thing El *could* do that would rid him of Egdod once and for all, and that was to lock Egdod inside. So El made a great forge out of a volcano that stood not far away, and there caused prodigious amounts of iron to be brought together from all parts of the Land by armies of Beedles. He rebuilt the bridge so that it could be reached from the north. He summoned hill-giants to serve as his smiths and made for them a stone anvil by cutting down a mountain and flattening its stump. On it, the giants forged bands and chains of iron. The bands were as thick as roads and the chain links as big as houses. These they wrapped and bent about the Fastness. The windows they covered with iron plates and the doors with slabs of stone. Over its top they fashioned an iron dome of great curved plates joined together with rivets as thick as tree trunks. El in the meantime was fashioning a lock to fit in the hasp that joined all of the bands and chains together. When every exit—even drains and sewer holes—had been sealed, he locked it up, imprisoning Egdod there forever. El withdrew, and broke the bridge, and dropped its rubble into the Chasm. Then to his Palace El returned. Egdod had never since been seen abroad in the Land.

.   .   .

Weaver trailed her fingers across the strings of the harp and let its tone slowly fade away. The song, it seemed, was at an end.

Lyne was ready for it. "Hang on," he said, "you can't just stop there and not say what El did with the key."

"On his way out, after breaking the bridge, El flung the key in after it," Weaver returned.

"That seems like an incredibly careless way to treat the one object capable of releasing his most feared enemy from his imprisonment," Lyne pointed out.

Weaver wasn't having it. As she knew perfectly well, Lyne had heard versions of this story many times during his young life and was only feigning surprise. "The Chasm is a crack in the world. It has no bottom. The key tumbled into chaos and was unmade. It ceased to exist."

"Still, the sheer carelessness of it—" Lyne sputtered.

"The key was a piece of solid iron the size of an oak a hundred years old," Weaver said. "Taking such a thing to the top of the Pinnacle would have been a stupefying feat unto itself, and all to no purpose. He destroyed it."

"Locks can be picked!"

"Not this one. El saw to that."

"You'll know," Corvus announced, "that across the water, less than a day's sailing, lies East Cloven. Now, many of its people never set foot outside of its wolf walls, but those who do are walking right into the Bewilderment."

The mere utterance of this word caused Mard and Lyne to make that little bow in the general direction of the center of the Land: an invocation of El, just in case El happened to be listening and cared about them.

The term normally used, in polite company, for the region that lay inland of East Cloven, south of the Backhaul and north of the mountains, was the Lake Land, and so this was what everyone had been calling it up to this point. "The Bewilderment" referred to exactly the same place. But it was generally used only in old poetry of a grim temper, or when trying to scare children, or to dissuade loved ones from going to any part of it other than its outermost fringes. If that was their next destination, then, in Prim's opinion, Corvus might have done well to avoid using that term for it.

"A pretty place in some ways," Corvus went on, "but a labyrinth of waterways all hooked up to one another in some pattern not even Pluto could sort out. As a giant talking raven I am in possession of certain advantages, but if I could not fly, I would never venture into it without a knowledgeable guide. Ferhuul here is one such."

"Thank you for going to the trouble of crossing the Shiver, Ferhuul," said Brindle. "I daresay you could have saved yourself the trouble and met us in East Cloven tomorrow!"

Ferhuul acknowledged Brindle's courtesy with a nod, but then glanced away.

"Not all of you will be crossing over, exactly," Corvus announced. "At least, not tomorrow. So this was the only way to get everyone together for a few moments."

Prim could tell that Brindle was angered by this, but he bridled his temper. "Perhaps you might tell us a little more of what you are proposing, then. Since I was under the impression that our quest was taking us over to the mainland."

"That much is true," said Corvus, "but there is one other member of the quest whose services, I am pretty sure, we are going to require. He'll need to be fetched from south of here. An easy enough voyage by sea. But it makes no sense for all of us to go."

Weaver, who hated being on the boat, heaved a great sigh of appreciation. Burr too seemed relieved to hear it; there was little use for him on the water, and he became intolerably restless. "Perhaps on land I could serve some purpose other than ballast," said Edda.

"Your thinking aligns with mine," said Corvus. "Our absent hosts own a ship, a cargo carrier much bigger than the boat of Robst, onto which you could *discreetly* embark without drawing much notice or arousing the superstitions of the crew. Weaver, Burr, and Ferhuul can sail over with you, and once you are on dry land you can begin journeying east—Ferhuul is in command of the specifics—and get a head start on certain aspects of the Quest. Acquiring legendary weapons. Delving into cryptic archives.

Meanwhile, the rest of us can board *Firkin*, if Robst is willing, and fetch the chap from down south."

Prim was somewhat crestfallen to learn that she would not be journeying directly to the mainland (to say nothing of acquiring legendary weapons and delving into cryptic archives!) and so was a few moments putting her feelings in check.

"A minute ago you said 'south of here' and now it's 'down south,' which to me sounds farther," Brindle pointed out. "In plain language, just where is this person?"

"Well, it's impossible to be sure," said Corvus, "but at last report he was pursuing a line of investigation that only makes sense if he is hanging around along the brink of the Newest Shiver."

Brindle could scarcely believe it. "But that runs across the Last Bit!"

"Yes," said Corvus with a nervous sideways hop.

"That is very nearly as far south as Toravithranax!" Prim exclaimed. But whereas Brindle might have said the same words in a stormy tone of voice, Prim couldn't help sounding rather pleased.

"Yes," Corvus allowed, "and really it will be simplest if we just tell Robst that that's where we are going. I'll mention the side trip to the Last Bit once we are under way."

"Well, if we're to sail right under the towers of Secondel . . . ," Brindle began, employing a common abbreviation of "Secondel-town."

"No choice," put in Lyne, "in that small of a boat."

". . . then we had *better* make other arrangements for Edda and Burr!" Brindle concluded.

Prim didn't entirely follow, but it seemed reasonable to guess that it might have something to do with the detail that had come up the other evening about Burr's having terminated one of his past lives by getting into some kind of altercation with an angel. That was the sort of activity that could, among the El-fearing souls of Secondel, certainly put a dent in one's reputation.

Prim had noticed that Edda slept rarely, if at all. She was up at all hours with night owls like Brindle, and yet no matter how early Prim got out of bed, Edda was always awake and engaged in some sort of project. That night, Brindle broke form and went to bed early enough that his breathing kept Prim awake, and so she got up and went to the house's front room, on its ground floor, where they had piled the things they had carried with them up from the boat. Among those was the tube containing the maps. Prim had a thought that she might unroll the big one—her favorite—and refresh her memory. But as she descended the stairs she saw lantern light flickering on the wall, and when she came round the corner into the front room she found Edda seated cross-legged on the floor with the big map spread out on her lap. It had suffered some damage from moisture. The dyes had dissolved into stains and some of the stitched-on bits had been ruined. Prim's instinct would have been to make such small repairs as she might, in the hopes of preserving what information still remained. But Edda, not one for half measures, had simply pulled out all the damaged parts, stripping the map down to bare animal hide, and begun to redo them. The old needle holes in the leather, the stains from the dyes, the pattern of faded and unfaded hide, presumably gave her some reminders as to where the rivers were supposed to flow, where cities and mountains were thought to exist, and so on. But as Prim padded over to watch the darting of Edda's needle, she saw that the giantess was not overly concerned with precisely copying the story that the map had formerly told.

Prim found that shocking in a way, since she had grown up staring at this map, and had always believed it to be a true and correct depiction of the Land. So at first she doubted her own senses, and wondered if this was a trick of the light, or even if she was really still asleep and merely dreaming all of this. But stepping in closer and bending down to watch, she saw beyond doubt that Edda was blithely and confidently altering the courses of rivers and the coastlines of Bits, moving a city to the opposite side of a river, changing deserts to forests. And yet this was not done carelessly. Had such changes been wrought by anyone else, Prim would have felt outrage, but as it was she could only assume that Edda knew better than whoever had originally made the map and that it was better now than it had been. In a half-asleep way she even fancied for a few moments that Edda might be working a kind of magic here and that the people who lived in that city would wake up to-morrow morning astonished to find that the entire thing had been translated across the river while they slept.

The faded and frayed threads Edda had torn out were strewn about on the floor: coarse tufts of weakly colored fiber such as one might use to stuff a pillow. In her needle was a filament so fine that Prim had to drop to her knees and bend close in order to see it; but when she did, it was the color of a new blade of grass when the sun first comes out from behind the clouds after a week of spring rain. Edda was using it to correct a sliver of map that had formerly been depicted as the edge of a desert. Now she was making it into a for-est by using needle and thread to fashion a lot of clever little knots that looked the way trees must have looked to Corvus when he was soaring high above. The movements of her needle were delib-erate, unhurried. Prim, no stranger to embroidery, winced a little whenever Edda's needle plunged into the map, for it was as fine as the green thread and it seemed impossible to shove it through the tough ancient hide without breaking it. But it slipped through as if Edda were sewing in burlap. The smoothness with which the giantess worked was hypnotic to Prim, who passed into a state that somehow combined the most delicious alertness with a lack of moment-to-moment awareness akin to sleep. Time passed at once quickly and slowly. The tying of an individual tree knot, or a series of running stitches marking the course of a river's tributary in bright blue silk, was carried out in carefully considered steps, and yet when Prim tore her gaze away from the detailed operation of the needle and rocked back to gaze at the entire map, she saw that a vast territory had been so depicted. And yet the sun had not yet begun to lighten the sky, and the lanterns had not consumed much oil.

Edda seemed to be working her way around the map accord-ing to whatever whim took her at the moment. She had begun with some corrections to the network of Shivers through which they would have to sail in order to get past Secondel, but then she had jumped down to the Last Bit and done some work with the silvery-blue silk that she favored for drawing the slender arms of the sea where they reached between islands; it was the color of cresting waves and so it warned mariners that here was surf over shallows and stones. Thence she had jumped over to the mainland and brightened the city of Toravithranax with many fine stitches in all colors, then continued eastward across the Land, running generally parallel to, and south of, the long feature known as the Hive-Way. Though Prim had never seen it, she had been told that it was made of the same stuff as the great Hive that buttressed the tall spire upon which El kept his Palace. In the middle of the Land, the Hive-Way fattened to an elongated lozenge enclosing the spire and the Palace, but east and west of there it was as slender as needle and yarn could make it. If one thought of the Hive-Way as a road, then it connected the Land's west coast, at Secondel, to its east coast at Far Teem and North Teem, passing round the Palace in the middle. If one thought of it as a barrier, however, it cut the Land in two, between a north and a south half that were roughly equal in area. In order to get round it, one had to travel by sea—or, if one were Corvus, simply to fly over it.

Prim yawned, and all of a sudden had it in mind that she'd been up with Edda for a long time. She had been assisting the giantess by fetching lengths of colored silk, as requested, from her sewing kit, which was small enough to go in a pocket and yet seemed to contain no end of threads and needles. Threading such fine needles ought to have been nearly impossible in such dim light, but Prim had found that if she gazed fixedly upon the eye of one of Edda's needles, it would seem to open up until it was the size of a doorway.

"Do you ever sleep?" Prim asked.

"I can sleep if I choose," said Edda, "but if I don't, it is fine."

"Why is that, I wonder?" Prim asked.

"You see much in the day that needs to be sorted through, picked over, weeded, made sense of. That happens while you sleep. When you wake up, you remember what was important and you have it all sorted. For me, these things happen in the moment. And I have less need than you of forgetting."

"Does that mean you remember more?"

"I am constituted differently from you. There is simply more to me," said the giantess.

Feeling that the conversation had gone into wild territory, Prim decided to change the subject. "When I first came down here," she said, "I guessed you were only mending the damaged parts of the map. But you have added much."

"Where you are going, Primula," Edda answered, "details matter."

Prim bent closer to look at the web of Shivers in the vicinity of Secondel. "Lyne said that because our boat is small we shall have no choice but to sail right past Secondel. What did he mean by that?"

"As you can see there are only two ways south," said Edda. "One must either go straight down the main channel of the First Shiver—which is well protected from the sea, and safe for even the smallest craft—or else swing wide around the big is-land of Thunkmarch, which because of its situation will bring you straight out into the open water here. Rounding this cape is perilous—wind and waves will fling you against a lee shore unless you sail much farther out into the ocean than is wise for a craft as small as *Firkin*."

Prim nodded. Edda was referring to features of the map that were small and easily overlooked until she drew attention to them and supplied these explanations, but then Prim could visualize the surf hammering the rocky southwest cape of Thunkmarch as if she were there atop the cliff looking down at it.

"Well, I shall hope we slip past Secondel without incident, then," said Prim, turning her attention to the safer inland route. "I look forward to seeing it; but part of me wishes I could simply cross over to East Cloven with you tomorrow."

"Today," Brindle corrected her.

Prim looked up to see him standing in the doorway, framed in pink dawn light. "Have you stayed up all night?" he asked.

"Yes," said Prim, suddenly feeling shy, "but I shall sleep on the boat."

Edda set her needles and silks aside and began to roll up the map, beginning at its eastern limit and working west. Prim understood that this was to a purpose; if they wished to consult it later for information about the western part, where the Bits and Shivers lay, they would only have to unroll the first part of it. Considerable time might pass before Prim could see the whole thing again, so she let her eye roam curiously over the parts that were about to fall under Edda's roll, enjoying the beauty of her handiwork. By and large the old parts of the map that had not been damaged and not been repaired—the parts so familiar to Prim—now seemed as if she were looking at them through a fogged windowpane, from which Edda had wiped away the mist in the areas she had mended. But one region, lying well to the north of the Hive and the Palace, but south of the Bewilderment (as it was frankly labeled here, this being a very old map), stood out from all the others for being very nearly blank. "Why is nothing on the map there?" Prim asked.

She already had notions as to why, but she wished to hear how Edda would choose to answer.

"Some things by their nature cannot be mapped."

A newcomer to watery things, Prim had thought *Firkin* rather pretty when she had first laid eyes on it, but soon came to understand that it was a short, tubby cargo barge, and quite slow, especially compared to the large vessels that did nothing but make the run up and down the First Shiver between Cloven and Secondel. For much of the way, this body of water was more of an inland sea than a channel. Robst liked to stay in the lee of the chain of big Bits that formed its western shore, and so the Land proper, when visible at all, was seen at a distance through obscuring mists and hazes. Larger vessels sailed right down the middle, where they could take the full measure of the wind. Many were the occasions when Prim would notice Mard or Lyne taking a break from nautical duties to gaze wistfully at a bigger ship in full sail, overhauling and blowing by them as if *Firkin* were dragging anchor.

As days went by, Prim began to notice more and more details on the opposite coast and understood that it was drawing nearer. For the great Shiver was narrowing, just as the maps had always told her.

Early on the sixth morning, she felt her hammock rock strangely and knew that they had struck, or been struck by, a current. She went abovedecks to see dawn breaking over mountains on the rim of the Land, now very close. Turning to gaze west at the nearer shore, she saw not the usual scrub-crusted brow of coastal bluffs, but a strange and arresting landform: knuckles of bare, broken stone protruding from barren ground that sloped steeply down and dove into the sea.

So they had reached the southern tip of the Bit known as Chopped Barren. In ancient times the region had been cleared of trees by woodcutters from Eltown. It was still covered mostly in grass and scrub. The broken and tumbled scape now taking the light of the dawn was Feller's Point: the mess that had been left behind when the hill-giant had stood up and walked away, and everything west of the river had broken off from the Land and begun its slow drift into the ocean.

Just on the other side of Feller's Point would be another Shiver, or rather a cauldron where a few of them joined together. The broadside current that had nudged Prim's hammock came from there. Once it had been the junction of two rivers, a few miles above Eltown.

This then was the place where they would have to choose. By doubling back round the point and fighting both the current and the wind, they could make for the western sea. En route they would pass familiar territory where the kinsmen of Mard and Lyne dwelled. Then they would face the passage round the cape that Edda had warned of. The mere mention of that idea made Robst uneasy. On the other hand, if they stayed their southerly course, they would pass down the main channel between Secondel and the large Bit known as Thunkmarch.

Only the most perfect weather and calm winds could have persuaded Robst to take the former course. To Prim's untrained eye, dawn was breaking in a sky clear and calm, but Robst did not like the color of it, and soon claimed to see high rippling clouds that foretold stormy days. So the decision was made. They would sail beneath the watchtowers of Secondel.

They beached the boat on a scrap of rocky shore at the foot

of Feller's Point and spent part of the morning tidying up. The purpose of this was but vaguely explained, but Prim inferred that the Autochthons who held power in Secondel took a dim view of certain types of cargo that Robst might have carried, and certain ports of call where he might have put in, at one time or another. Therefore it was prudent to throw overboard any evidence to that effect. This took a while, as *Firkin* had a lot of crannies, and only Robst knew where to look. Prim passed the time looking up at the waste heap of Feller's Point and trying to picture in her mind's eye where Cairn, at the end of the Second Age, had trudged up out of the river (for it had been a mere river in those days) and gone to the top of the hill to talk to the hill and the tree.

Larger vessels passed them by as they worked. They had nearly finished their tidying up when one of these slackened its sails, put out its oars, and aimed its prow at them. Noting this, Robst squinted under his hand across bright water and gave the ship a good long look. It was of too deep draft to come very close, but presently it dropped a smaller rowboat. Two men climbed down into this and began to approach. The younger man pulling on the oars had his back to them, but the passenger was recognizable to Robst as some old seagoing acquaintance of his from the northern Bits. Soon they drew close enough to greet each other. They began a conversation, shouted back and forth across the water, in the language of Cloven. As far as Prim could make out, this began with the newcomer asking Robst if everything was quite all right, and Robst reassuring him that they had not beached because of any difficulty. Thus put at ease, the two skippers—for this man was pretty clearly the boss of the larger vessel—fell into chitchat, as the boat drew nearer, about where they had come from, where they were going, and what they were carrying. The words of Robst, though polite, seemed clipped and vague. The visitor was more talkative. His eyes kept scanning the length of Robst's vessel, and whenever they did, his gaze seemed to snag and linger on Prim or Brindle. Eventually, despite Robst's forced breeziness, he beached his rowboat nearby, obliging Robst to clamber down and walk over and afford him the courtesy of a handclasp and a few minutes' conversation. In due time the visitors shoved off with a little help from Robst, who walked back to his boat with a bit of a pensive, even stormy, look about him. He invited Brindle to join him in his cabin. Brindle, who seemed to have a better idea than Prim as to what this was all about, insisted that she be part of it. So the three of them convened in Robst's cabin, which, even with the hammock stowed and the little desk folded against the bulkhead, barely fit them.

"Down in Secondel the Autochthons are marking every boat, be it never so small, that tries to pass south. And believe me, there is nothing they cannot see. They seek an older man and a younger woman traveling together, and speaking in the accents of Calla. As well, certain others matching the descriptions of Burr, Weaver, and Edda are being looked for. Our boat will be boarded and it will be searched. If either of you is found . . ."

Robst seemed to think it would be a waste of breath to finish the sentence. Even more annoying, Brindle appeared to take his meaning. "What?" Prim asked. "What will happen?"

"You have heard the stories," Brindle said, "more are true than not. Fortunately Corvus foresaw this eventuality, and gave us a plan."

Two days later, she found herself walking toward Secondel's northern gate alone. She was on the mainland. Robst had dropped her off in a little cove a few miles to the north—as close as he could sail to Secondel without coming in view of one of its watchtowers, or the much higher vantage points of the Temple complex. The day before that, they'd deposited Brindle on Thunkmarch, which was the opposite shore. In ancient times Camp had been situated there, and so that stretch of its coast was still known as Campside.

The plan was simple enough in its general outlines. If Brindle and Prim stayed aboard *Firkin*, the Autochthons would see the boat, search it, and find them. So those two needed to find another way to get past Secondel. As soon as they got just a few miles south, Robst could pick them up again and they could resume their journey down toward the Last Bit. So, they would have to travel on foot. An older man and a younger woman, speaking in the accents of Calla, were just what the Autochthons were looking for, and so it wouldn't do for them to walk together. The way through the city was safe in the sense that it was orderly. Many souls of all descriptions traversed it every day, for it was the only practical route down the west coast of the Land. The city was full of Beedles of course, but they were tame ones, perfectly under the thumb of the Autochthons. Campside, on the other hand, was infamously wild and lawless. Perhaps the powers that be in Secondel preferred it that way, as it prevented the founding of a rival city across the channel. Or perhaps the stories were true and the place had lain under a curse since the day Adam had been murdered there, and Eve and Thunk and Whirr and the others had forsaken it to follow the hill-giant up into what later became the Bits and Shivers. In any case it was where rogue Beedles escaped to when they had disappointed their masters. When they scuttled up onto that shore they found themselves in a maelstrom of Shiver pirates, bandits, wild souls, and even a few Autochthons who had forsaken El and gone over to seek their fortunes. Brindle knew a few people there and seemed to think he could manage a few miles' hike south along Campside's shore. But he thought it wiser for Prim to take a different way, direct through the city, so that no one would ever see the two of them together. The whole thing could be accomplished in a day. Brindle on the west shore and Prim on the east might have to cool their heels for a night as they waited for Robst to collect them, but the distance they had to cover simply was not that great.

So Prim strode south along the coast road, finding it easy going compared to the mountain passes of Calla. She was wrapped in a blanket that was pulled up over her head like a cloak, and carrying a bag slung over her back that contained a few days' simple food, a purse with a few coins in it, and a writing kit: quills, a penknife, and the oddments needed to make ink.

The road followed the coastline, which was not straight. Every so often she, and the other travelers strung out along the road near her, would come round a point and see the city. The place had been protected very early by a seawall—or, in those days, a riverwall—put up to prevent inundations such as the one that had destroyed the first Eltown. Newer buildings, mostly of burnt mud, had later gone up around the outside of the walls and now blurred its lower reaches with a confusion of various rooflines and drifting smoke. But easily discerned was the wall top, running straight from one tower to the next.

The towers were five in number and arranged so as to command interlocking vistas of the First Shiver and, opposite, Campside. Impressive as those might have been, they were dwarfed by what loomed above them. The slopes of the mountain behind the city were grown with trees that, since the death of Adam, had become quite ancient. The trace of a road-cut could be discerned zigzagging up the slope. But at its top, the skyline was a froth of white stuff, like the foamy crest of a wave poised to break over the city. Accustomed to the mountains of Calla, Prim would have pegged it as the thick lip of a glacier had she not known what it really was: Hive. A complex of cells inhabited by souls that were unimaginably different from the sort who walked around on two legs and talked to one another with words, songs, looks, and gestures.

Little could really be known of the Hive save that it surrounded the base of the Pinnacle in the middle of the Land, and spread out from there along the Hive-Way, thin tendrils running east to the Teemings and west to the ridge above Secondel. There, over time, the Hive had filled in the gaps between the great stone temples and basilicas that Beedles had piled up to the glory of El, forming a seamless complex running for a mile along the ridgetop. Few of the souls who dwelled below in the walled city of Secondel ever set foot in the Temple. If they toiled up the switchbacks to the top of the ridge, they might pass through an aperture in the middle that marked the beginning of the great road east. But entry to the Temple itself was an honor conferred only on a few.

"I am bound for Toravithranax," she said. She had rehearsed it a hundred times, learning to say the words in the thick accent of the cold Bits that lay north of Calla. This was the first time she had spoken them directly to a stranger.

"And what is your business there?" inquired the Autochthon.

Prim and a score of other travelers were milling around before the north gate of Secondel, being looked at and interrogated by a few Autochthons who nudged their mounts about, approaching anyone who aroused their curiosity.

She tried to ignore this Autochthon's mount, which was curiously shoving its huge nose into her pack, drawn no doubt by the scent of the apples. Instead she shielded her eyes with her hand—for the sun was very near the Autochthon's head—and looked him in the eye as best she could.

"I have been sent into the south by my family to learn the art of writing from Pestle," Prim said—meaning, as this Autochthon would understand, the Academy that Pestle had founded ages ago.

"Who's to say they'll have you?" asked the Autochthon, looking her up and down.

"If they won't, I shall learn it from one of the lesser scribes who, it is said, have little schools around the verges of the great one."

"And what is writing to your family, that they would send you so far to learn it?"

"We have three ships and much need of keeping records."

The Autochthon still had her at a disadvantage, because of the angle of the sun, but she could only assume he was giving her a close look. "To the narrow gate," he commanded, and then looked up at the top of the wall to be sure he had been understood by those who kept watch there. Prim followed his gaze and saw a row of helmets, strung bows, full quivers. Below were two gates: a wide one bestriding the road and affording passage for even the largest teams and wagons, and another just wide enough for a single soul on foot. The former gave way to the main waterfront street; the latter was merely a doorway into the ground floor of a building that lay inside the wall. How far that building might extend and what might go on in it she had no way of knowing. But several of those helmets were now inclined toward her and she knew she would not get far if she disobeyed. Glancing over her shoulder the way she'd come, she saw that going back was just as likely to draw unwanted notice and arrows between the shoulder blades. Not that she had any thought of doing so. To give up now was to fail in the Quest before it had really got started.

So she walked through it into a sort of antechamber, and then drew up short as she came face-to-face, for the first time in her life, with a Beedle.

She'd seen them depicted in storybooks and tapestries, typically in the background, filling in blank spaces in the artwork, carrying out various none-too-savory tasks under the direction of Autochthons or angels. In one of the rooms in the great hall of Farth there was a Beedle stuffed and mounted. During her brief stopover in West Cloven she had spied them from a distance clambering spiderlike through ships' rigging that needed mending or crablike over hulls that needed scraping, and of course the row of helmeted guards atop this very gatehouse were all Beedles. But here she was staring one in the face. He was posted next to a doorway that led to a larger room sliced into lanes by long plank tables. He had laid his helmet by and leaned his spear against the wall, but still wore armor of stiff hide divided into overlapping plates, and was armed with what was either a very long knife or a very short sword. Prim had been forewarned to expect a distinct lack of symmetry, and was not disappointed. Beedles came in various colorations and ranged in stature from midthigh to shoulder level compared against Prim and her kin; it all depended on how they were used, and where. But they were invariably bigger on the right side than the left. For the story always told of them was that they had sprung up in Eltown of old, and got to work at such simple tasks as woodcutting, mining, brickmaking, and smithing, but had lacked any real purpose or direction until the Autochthons had shown up and begun looking after them. The Autochthons knew what to do and how to do it, but were not very numerous. So the folk of Eltown—or, after that had been destroyed, of Secondeltown—had become the Autochthons' right hands. Strong they had grown, and stocky. Intelligence was of little use to them, and some strains could barely say a word, so their heads were small; their mouths more suited to the chewing and swallowing of rude rations than to speech; their ears large, the better to hear the commands issued by their masters. They grew thick hair on their bodies but little on their heads, and they shed it in warm weather, spinning it into coarse bristling ropes of stuff that they used to fashion nests, where they would sleep together in dense snoring and shifting clusters. They were no longer divided into male and female, as copulation served no use that was of any profit to the Autochthons. Their masters might crop their ears, tattoo them, or make any other such alterations that would display their purpose at a glance. Dangerous work killed them or wore them out. They were replaced by new ones sent down from a place, somewhere in the Temple complex above, where newly spawned souls were gathered in and so given shape.

Prim had been taught manners, and so upon coming face-to-face with this Beedle she had to stifle an impulse to bid him good day and make some offhand remark about the weather. But from one who looked like Prim, no Beedle would expect anything except direct orders or pleas for mercy.

Sure enough, though, he *did* receive an order from someone within, which made no sense to Prim—for it was in a crude sort of speech used only by Autochthons to boss Beedles around. The Beedle smashed his heels together, pivoted, and extended his weak left arm toward the doorway. Prim took that as her cue to pass through into the next room. The purpose of the long plank tables soon became clear as an Autochthon directed her to place her bag on one for inspection.

Indoors, standing on his own two feet, unarmed and unarmored, this Autochthon was not much bigger than Mard or Lyne. Burr would have been more than a match for him. But where Burr's features were rough and bold, the Autochthon was elegant, and Prim felt herself responding to his beauty as he cast his pale eyes and long lashes down at the mean assortment of apples, undergarments, and writing tools that he was pulling from her bag and setting out on the table. He examined one of the apples and gave it a long sniff with his fine-boned nose. It was a variety that grew in the far north; he seemed to know this. More interesting was the wooden box that contained her writing supplies. Rolled up in there were several leaves of paper, made of northern linen, on which Prim had scratched out two different alphabets.

He bade her pack up her things and directed her to another door. This one took her up a curving staircase and past another Beedle into a chamber with a table, two chairs, and a little window through which she could look out into the streets of Secondel. There playing out below her was a curious sort of commerce in which various roles were played, according to their kind, by Beedles, Spawned, Autochthons, and—

"Sprung," said a woman's voice.

Prim turned to see an Autochthon in a long white gown who had entered the room while Prim had been gazing out the window. She had long full yellow hair cast back behind her shoulders, and such was her bearing that it looked as though that hair was going to stay where it had been put. It was hard to guess how long she had been there, but a faint sweet fragrance now making itself welcome in Prim's nostrils hinted that she had only just arrived. "Souls patterned after Spring, and her notions of what people ought to look like," the woman explained. "Sprung. That is our word for them. For you."

"You are—" Prim began.

"Externally similar. The same really. Aesthetics apart." She looked Prim up and down. "The world would be less confusing if Autochthons had a completely different form from Sprung—if we were as different on the outside as we are here." She raised a hand, causing a white sleeve to tumble away from a graceful, pale wrist, and tapped her forehead. "But El in his wisdom had reasons for giving us a like form." She turned slightly toward the east and inclined her head as she said El's name. Prim remembered her manners just in time and did likewise. "It is good in one way, which is that it enables us to converse, as you and I are doing now. Thus do the Sprung serve as an endless source of fascination and bemusement to us."

"Happy to be of service," said Prim. Distracted as she was by all of the curious things that the woman was saying—as well as by her beauty—it was all she could do to remember to speak with the far-north accent she'd been feigning. For this woman was speaking perfectly the language that Sprung spoke on the Bits, and she'd be quick to notice any inconsistency in the visitor's pronunciation.

"Then you may be of further service by writing out a word." The woman was going through Prim's writing box as if she owned it. She chose a fresh leaf of paper and spread it out on the table.

Next to it she set out a quill and a bottle of ink, which she gave a little shake, and unstoppered. "Quercus. Or, in your language, oak-gall," she announced, after giving it a sniff. "Good stuff." She said it in a way that left considerable room for doubt as to whether she was being sarcastic. "You may write your name," she said, and looked Prim in the eye.

"In which alphabet?"

"Does it matter? The purpose of the exercise, quite obviously, is to test the veracity of the story you're telling. Write it as Pestle would. Go ahead."

Prim had written out hundreds of pages of flowing confident script in the old alphabet, the new, and others besides, and understood perfectly well all that had just been explained to her. But to show this would have contradicted her story. So she dipped the quill into the ink and copied "Primula" out with a deliberation that must have been as frustrating to the lady as it was to Prim, making sure that the quill dumped stray puddles of ink here and there. At last she sat back so that her work could be inspected.

"Well," said the lady, "the Academy has its work cut out for it." The Autochthon took the page and examined Prim's work. But her response was curiously delayed, in a way that gave Prim the feeling she had somehow made a poor choice.

"Primula is your name?"

"Prim for short, if you please. May I know your name?"

The Autochthon looked sharply at her, as if this were an exceedingly odd question. "My full name is Sooth of El." She seemed bemused that anyone would not already know this. "In the kind of speech used by Sprung, it is unwieldy, and so you may call me Sooth."

"Thank you," said Prim, a little preoccupied now as she wondered what other kinds of speech the lady might have in mind.

"You are from some far northern Bit."

"Shatterberg."

Sooth gave a little shiver. "No wonder you go about wrapped in a blanket. The language you speak up there must be very queer and old. Primula is what we would refer to, in these parts, as the common daisy."

"Yes, that is so. You call it 'daisy' here."

"Is that a common flower, then, up on Shatterberg?"

"The growing season is short," said Prim. "Only a few simple flowers have time to spring up and grow."

Sooth was gazing at her fixedly. "The name has a . . . complicated history that goes back to very ancient times and that is particularly important to us. If your parents had studied the ancient myths, they might have known as much, and thought better of calling you Daisy. But to them, yes, it would just be the name of a local weed. They wouldn't *mean* anything by bestowing it on a daughter. A daughter they never expected to leave Shatterberg and find herself among cultivated people."

· Prim could feel herself blushing. She well knew the legends of which the lady spoke. Daisy was the last member of the Pantheon of Egdod. According to the old myths, she had appeared suddenly on the very eve of the coming of El, and tried to warn the Pantheon of what was coming, and been cast out along with Egdod and the others.

"Well, Primula, I am calling you Prim when we are in polite company, and hoping that no one else knows it is a synonym for Daisy."

"Polite company?"

"Others like me," Sooth explained.

"I thought that I might simply be on my way," said Prim.

"Why so hasty? The Academy of Pestle has been there since the dawn of this age."

"I was told it is best not to stay in the city after dark," said Prim, trying to cast her best worried-country-bumpkin look out the window, where the shadows were stretching across the street.

"Good advice for a girl on her own," said Sooth. "As my guest, you have nothing to worry about."

"I'm . . . your guest?"

"I believe that is what I just said, Prim."

"Why would you bother? With one such as I?"

"It is a sensible question and I shall give you a plain answer," said the lady. "I am cultivating you. Recruiting you. Even one as backward as you must have heard that El's domain extends here"—she divided the tabletop with a downward slice of her hand—"And no farther. That way"—she gestured toward the waterfront, and by extension all the Shivers and Bits that lay beyond—"is the domain of giants, wild souls. Rumors there are, even, of a giant talking raven who flies about trying to deceive the ignorant Sprung who live in those parts into believing all sorts of claptrap that is an abomination to El. Autochthons we send across the First Shiver are as apt to fall into dark doings as they are to remain faithful. When I meet a young, unspoiled Sprung from those parts, of a decent family, already somewhat literate and wishing to become more so, I consider it my sacred duty to make her welcome in this city. You shall dine well and sleep soundly tonight, and tomorrow I shall see to it that you be conducted up to the Temple, where you may view the glory of El's Palace from afar, and see the magnificence of all that has been built there. Prim, you need not travel one step farther south if your purpose is to learn the art of writing. There is nothing taught in Toravithranax that is not to be learned here; and here you may learn it without all the rubbish that Pestle brought with her in the old days."

Prim had no choice but to thank the lady most kindly and to go where she was taken next: an apartment in one of the watchtowers, guarded and looked after by Beedles, but reserved for Autochthons and their guests. This had a little balcony with a fine view out across the water toward the Campside shore, and it was equipped with certain conveniences, in the way of bath and toilet, the likes of which had never even crossed Prim's mind. The house where she had grown up on Calla was reputed to be a rather good one, and she had never found it lacking in any respect, yet it came off poorly in comparison.

A less blanketlike garment was found for her: a white gown made after the same general pattern as that worn by Sooth. To Prim it seemed markedly impractical until she reflected that dressing in such a way might actually make sense as long as chamber pots were being emptied and other such chores being taken care of by Beedles.

She attended an Autochthons' mess in a hall on the tower's ground floor, where the officers who looked after the waterfront, and a few Sprung guests, sat at long tables and had dishes brought out to them by Beedle waiters in special uniforms. Prim listened carefully to the conversation but understood little. Oh, she understood their speech perfectly well. But the *nature* of what they were talking about—abstractions related to money, law, the management of Beedles, and the day-to-day operations of a city—did not always make sense to her. The unsophisticated Shatterberg girl she was pretending to be would have been able to follow almost none of it. So her role was an easy one to play: she ate, spoke when spoken to, stared at the pictures on the walls. She had been realizing that these depicted some of the same historical events as the tapestries that decorated the Hall of the Calladons; but she had not understood this at first, because the roles of the heroes and the villains had been reversed.

The next day she accompanied Sooth up to the Temple. No Autochthon would dream of making that ascent in any way other than astride a mount. It was possible for a big mount to carry two souls, but Prim expressed a willingness to give riding a try. Sooth said that a mount might be available, which was owned by a friend of hers but available to be borrowed.

Here Prim had to conceal the fact that she knew perfectly well how to handle a mount. She had been riding since she was little. But she had to feign ignorance as the Autochthon who supervised the stables explained things to her. She could not conceal the fact that she was confident and calm in the presence of such beasts. The mount she was borrowing—a very big and impressive black one—sensed as much and behaved so well Sooth expressed surprise. Prim tried to explain it away by claiming that her family back home used a few mounts as draft animals and that it had been her job to groom them.

The ride up the switchbacks looked long from below. Prim dreaded all of the fake conversation she would be obliged to make with her hostess en route. But once Sooth was satisfied that Prim would not fall off her mount, she made no great effort to stay close or to keep up a steady stream of words. And this left Prim alone to think about the unexpected turn that the Quest had taken during the last day.

By any reasonable standard it had gone gravely awry. Yet in a way, this ride through the forest and up the mountain felt less strange to her than the Quest per se. It was not terribly different from what she and her family did on Calla when they were in the mood for an outing.

That feeling came to an end when they topped the ridge and came in view of the Temple of Elkirk, which presented her with so much to see that she reined in the mount and sat there for some time taking it all in.

Almost straight ahead was a squat tower, not much to look at, that Prim guessed from her history lessons must be the original Elkirk. Right next to it, nearly as old, was a gate. She knew that this was the beginning—or, depending on how you looked at it, the end—of the road that stretched all the way to the Far Teeming on the opposite side of the Land. The part of it that she could see was lined with stone buildings that were of similar age and size to much of what constituted Secondel.

All told, these mean old buildings made up but a small fraction of the complex. The story told by the rest of it was that Autochthons had shown up, found a place where Pluto had been so considerate as to leave a sizeable deposit of white rock, domesticated a lot of Beedles, and, for an eon, made them pile stone higher and higher, building ever larger structures: magnificent ones facing east toward the distant Palace, and imposing ones glowering down over Secondel, the First Shiver, and the Bits beyond.

Somewhat later, after they had run out of ideas, stone, or Beedles, the Hive had made contact with this place. This it had done by growing slowly from the base of the Palace, sending a long tendril along the road like a vine growing along a tree branch. Once it had connected to the Temple complex here, it had broadened and ramified, filling gaps between the stone buildings with a foamy lattice of cells. It reminded Prim of what happened when you left bread dough to rise, and forgot about it, and came upon it much too late to find it had expanded right out of its bowl and found other places to go. Yet it seemed to have a kind of commonsensical ability to avoid windows and doors: those still peered out in regular rows and columns through curtains of Hive-stuff that were otherwise bulgy and lacking in any sense of plan or of order as Autochthons or Sprung might think of it.

It occurred to her that she had been sitting still for quite a while, taking this all in, and yet Sooth—who had ridden some distance farther toward the gate—was showing no signs of her usual brisk impatience. Instead she was allowing her mount to crop grass from a broad lawn that stretched along the west front of the Temple complex, and was just sitting there in the saddle, quiet but attentive, as though listening to music. Prim persuaded her own mount to stop tearing at the grass and rode slowly toward Sooth. Yet the Autochthon took no notice but only kept her face turned toward the east, like one who has emerged from a storm wet and cold and now wishes to bask in the warmth of the sun. Which was definitely the sort of look she had on her face when Prim circled round to approach her from that direction. Prim had in the meantime become conscious of a low hum suffusing the air and the ground.

"The Hive," said Sooth. "So much is in it that I shall never fully understand. Yet even in what little comes through, I feel myself connected to it and to El."

They left their mounts to graze near the gate. Sooth showed Prim the old tower of Elkirk, which was no longer used for giving forms to newly spawned souls; but she saw the old statues, looking halfway between Beedle and Sprung, from which in ancient times the souls of Eltown had taken their original shapes. A much larger building now served the same function, and was equipped with statues of various subtypes of Beedles after which new souls were patterning themselves in preparation for service down below. The same building had upper stories that Sooth described as a school where Beedles who had ripened to their final forms learned how to empty chamber pots, chop vegetables, carve stone, or fight.

The fighters, once they had acquired a few skills, seemed to spend most of their time out of doors, drilling in formation on expanses of pounded dirt under the direction and the discipline of mounted Autochthon officers. Those were of various ranks, and they lived in barracks, each with a bed or a private room according to their seniority and their sex. Sooth breezed through the living quarters of males and females alike as if she owned the place, and each Autochthon who saw her afforded her some small gesture of respect before casting a curious glance Prim's way. These barracks had baths in them, and male Autochthons emerging from those steamy places always covered themselves with towels. This raised a question in Prim's mind she had never previously thought to ask. She knew—or at least had been told—that Autochthons did not become pregnant. They were never children. El brought them into being fully formed in the Palace.

"We have the parts that you have," said Sooth, "for sex." They had emerged from the barracks and were skirting a courtyard where twoscore Beedles were being trained to shoot arrows at targets consisting of vaguely humanoid bundles of grass. Not for the first time, Prim knew that Sooth had somehow guessed what she was thinking.

"Our sex does not cause the creation of new souls," Sooth went on. "Spring erred in bestowing that power upon her children. We do not believe she was evil in so doing. Merely unwise—deceived and beguiled by Egdod, who wished to populate the whole Land with his spawn. El makes only as many of us as are needed to hold dominion. Beedles, left to their own whims, would ruin the place, and so it is given to us to regulate them and see to it that their labors are spent in ways that better the Land rather than exhausting it."

They had reached an aperture in a side of the courtyard, which would take them toward larger buildings beyond. Prim, before passing through it, cast a look over her shoulder at the Beedles riddling straw men with arrows. They put the military part of the complex behind them and entered a covered gallery that stretched across a garden, running eastward toward a building whose shape and decorations hinted at a more sacred function. The garden was planted with a variety of plants the likes of which Prim had only read about.

"You see the Beedles at arms, practicing to fight," said Sooth, "and part of you scoffs at me for claiming that they are bettering the Land. But just across the First Shiver are outlaws: runaway Beedles, barbarian Sprung, and wild souls who acquired immense and strange powers during the First Age when there were no limits as to what a soul could do. Confined to the Bits, there is only so much damage that they can inflict—especially if they are at odds with one another. But the price, for us, of keeping things that way is eternal vigilance. You admire this garden. I can see how much you like it, feel the pleasure you are taking in the beauty of each flower. But it is only thus because of the likes of him." And she pointed to a small gnarled Beedle who was down on his knees in a corner, worrying weeds out of the dirt with a metal shiv.

Then they entered a great door carven with too many decorations for Prim to take in, and passed into a vast light-filled space. Long and barrel-shaped, it was oriented toward the east, and the far end of it consisted mostly of windows. Rising up from the middle of the floor to about the height of Prim's head was a stepped platform which blocked their view until they circumvented it. Doing so opened up a full view of the Land to the east: rolling hills and valleys giving way to grassland that stretched away many days' journey. Far away, half obscured by haze, was a white needle projecting straight up into the air, impossibly high.

So this was the first time Prim had seen the Pinnacle and the Palace with her own eyes. It took several moments for her to register them against the many depictions she had seen and descriptions she had read during her education, all of which approximated, but none of which quite approached, the real thing. Few details could be made out at this distance, but that only made the thing seem more enormous. Its upper half was sheer and narrow, but below that it broadened rapidly to a wide base that Prim knew consisted almost entirely of Hive. Prim had eyes mostly for what was on its very top. Gazing at it long and hard, she fancied she could resolve tiny features such as towers and outbuildings. Haze and distance made those evanescent.

Something strange was undoubtedly going on in Prim's mind. For in all honesty there was nothing she could possibly see atop that Pinnacle at such a distance. Yet pictures of it *were* coming into her head. Since they could not have been coming in through her eyes, they might have been figments of her imagination, seeded from storybooks and brought to life by the strange vibrant air of this Temple. Or they might have been memories. They seemed very much like things she had once seen, perhaps in dreams, and forgotten for a long time. If so, those were not altogether happy memories.

"Two visitors. Alike welcome. One familiar, one new to me," said a male voice behind them. "How different their reactions to the sight of El's Palace! One so joyous, the other somehow sad."

Prim had whirled around upon hearing the voice. Sooth was a step behind her, and a little off to one side, still facing the window, and indeed there was no question that her face was alight with happiness.

The voice was emanating from the top of the stepped platform. This was circular, shaped like a stack of coins that got smaller as they went up. The top was a few paces in diameter. Its back portion was rimmed by a low parapet that appeared to be made out of embroidered cushions. Its front was open toward the window wall. Seated atop it, right in the middle, leaning back comfortably, was an Autochthon. He looked as if he would be magnificent were he to stand to his full height. But they had come upon him lounging in a long robe made of some shimmering material. Or perhaps that was just his aura. He actually had one. It was big. To judge from old books, auras had once been common, but Prim had only seen a few in her whole life, and those had been barely discernible layers of shimmer painted over people's heads. This Autochthon's aura occupied most of the platform.

Sooth's smile broadened, and altered in a way that struck Prim as false. She pirouetted to face the platform. "Delegate Elshield," she said, "may we approach the Divan? I would introduce you to my guest."

"You may not only approach but join me up here if you would care to," said Elshield. In his tone was a kind of suggestive familiarity hinting that he and Sooth spent rather a lot of time in each other's company. Sooth cast a glance back at Prim and then began to approach. Following in her wake, Prim was conscious of a rise in the Hive-hum that only grew more intense with each step. Looking up she saw a peculiarity she had missed before: a broad inverted pillar, like a fat stalactite descending from the ceiling, centered directly above the platform. It was made entirely of Hive-stuff, though here it was in a more orderly geometric shape than Hive that grew in the wild. It descended close enough to the top of the Divan that Elshield, if he could have been bothered to stand up, might almost have touched it with an upraised hand. Its under-surface was concave. In the cells exposed on its underside, souls squirmed and glowed to illuminate Elshield in flat, fluctuating light. It must have been they who were the source of the hum, for with each step Prim took toward the lowest tier of the Divan, the sound grew more intense, coming in through not just her ears but her skull, and addling her wits. The sorts of stray dreamlike memories she'd experienced while staring at the Pinnacle were now breaking loose all over and making it impossible for her to see or think clearly. She stopped and backed away to a more comfortable distance. Sooth, untroubled, quickened her pace and ascended the platform steps, all bouncing locks and flouncing skirts, pleasing enough to Prim's eye and more so to Elshield's. He lazily raised a hand. She reached out to grasp it, then spun round and dropped to sit next to him. Both leaned back comfortably against the cushions and seemed to take in the emanations of the Hive for a minute.

"Our young visitor is fascinating. Mysterious," said Elshield, and Prim felt he was not stating his own opinion but that of the Hive. "Will you not step closer, young lady?"

"I prefer not to," said Prim. "I prefer to use plain ordinary words, when sharing my thoughts with strangers."

Sooth smiled. "And when you use words, do you prefer the accent of Shatterberg, or of Calla? It seems you are capable of both."

Prim was ashamed but not surprised that the Autochthon had seen through her. The hints had been many. Her disguise had never been meant to fool anyone save a lowly gatekeeper.

"We shall have ample time to plumb her depths in the months and years to come," said Sooth. "I believe she understands today the nature of the Land in a manner that was hid from her, quite deliberately, by those who sheltered her until now."

Prim's alarm about *months and years to come* had scarcely begun when it was shoved out of the way by that very odd and wrong statement about her having been somehow misled by her own kinfolk.

"Very well," said Elshield, "We may begin immediately, on the ride down to Secondel."

"You are going down to the city now," said Sooth, half statement and half question.

"I have an important meeting—with a barbarian king!" said Delegate Elshield. "One of my more exotic duties."

"Splendid," said Sooth, "let us ride then."

Elshield rose to his full height, which was impressive, as if he had been made to be a lord. Which, come to think of it, he probably had. He descended, arm in arm with Sooth, and made a gesture toward Prim that said, *After you, my dear.* But soon enough the two Autochthons had overtaken her with long sure strides and got her between them. They went out by a different way, passing through a sort of foyer where a Beedle helped Elshield out of his robe and into a long riding cloak made of heavier stuff, all black. First though he slung a wide swath of leather over one of Elshield's shoulders. It fell diagonally across his body to his left hip, where a scabbard hung from it, and into the scabbard went a sword of burnished steel that Elshield took down from a rack.

From there they went out of doors and directly made their way back to the place near the gate where Prim and Sooth had left their mounts. Sooth got up into the saddle and Prim did likewise, leaving Elshield afoot. Given the style in which Elshield lived generally, she assumed that a Beedle would come scurrying up at any moment holding the reins of a mount even larger and more magnificent than the one that she was borrowing. But no such thing happened. The two Autochthons exchanged a look and Prim assumed that private thoughts were passing between them. Then Elshield stepped over to the flank of Prim's mount and in one smooth graceful movement vaulted up onto its back right behind her. The contours of the saddle were such as to press them together quite firmly. She recoiled from the unwanted closeness but he had already reached his arms around her. His right hand closed over hers, which was holding the reins. "There will be no need of those," he said, so close to her ear that she could feel his breath. "Only Beedles use them. We have more refined ways of controlling the animal."

Right on cue, the mount bolted across the grass. Elshield snaked his left arm around Prim's waist and drew her back against him. "The ride will be faster than you are accustomed to, but I shall see to it you do not fall," he explained.

Hearing hoofbeats to the right, Prim turned her head to see Sooth galloping past them. Within moments they had crossed the belt of grass and plunged into the forest that cloaked the mountainside. The pace felt wild to Prim, but the mount and the Autochthon both knew the way and never put a hoof wrong. Prim's fear lessened over the course of the first couple of switchbacks, to the point where she could tear her gaze away from the road ahead and hazard a look down over the First Shiver and the waterfront of Secondel far below.

Two of the Autochthons' military ships—galleys with many oars—were venturing out across the channel, going perpendicular to the general flow of shipping. It looked as though they might be planning a mid-Shiver rendezvous with a vessel that was approaching from the coast of Thunkmarch. Perhaps that one was carrying the barbarian king that Elshield was going down to meet? It was not a particularly kingly looking vessel; but terms like "king" were rarely used out among the Bits.

Tell me more, Elshield wanted. He had not uttered a word. But she knew it was what he desired. She had not said a word either; so if she had "told" him anything, he had somehow worried it out of her mind without her willing it. Disgust followed by panic overwhelmed her good sense and she tried to wriggle away. But Elshield's arm was like a band of wrought iron bent round her body, the saddle itself was an inescapable trap, and even if she had wriggled free it would have been the death of her, as she'd have been dashed against the hurtling road. *I will know what you are, Primula,* Elshield let her know, *not what you claim to be.*

And when she knew that he knew her true name, it broke her, and she fell into a reverie, remembering various things from her life in no clear order, and she knew that it was Elshield, inside of her, ransacking her mind in a way she was helpless to prevent.

Which ought to have satisfied him as much as it disgusted her. But after it had gone on for a while she sensed that he was only becoming more frustrated the more he saw. He was rooting deep, trying to draw up her earliest memories. But he looked on those as false—as lies planted there by someone who had gone to great lengths to deceive her as to her true nature.

By Brindle.

A darkness like sleep had come over her so that she did not know where she was. Impressions seeped into her mind of a gate, city streets, docks, and boats. Memories being looted by Elshield? No, for she had not seen these places before. These were no memories. She was coming back to the here and now, for Elshield had turned his attention away from her and was issuing commands to Beedles. She was conscious of being draped over him like a damp rag. She sat forward, bracing herself on the rim of the saddle. Elshield, knowing that he had her, made no further effort to hold her close.

They rode out onto the top of the wall above the stone quay. By now the two military ships Prim had noticed earlier had completed their rendezvous and returned to within a bow-shot of Secondel's waterfront. Beedles in uniforms were deploying along the rim of the quay, some carrying boathooks or coiling lines, but others armed with lances. The top of the wall was picketed with archers.

Elshield diverted the mount down a ramp that took them to the level of the quay; Sooth elected to look down upon the scene from atop the wall. Still dazed from what had happened during the ride, Prim was only vaguely conscious of many orders being given and a lot of boat-related activity as the vessel carrying the barbarian king drew near and swung about sideways and was coaxed toward the moorage.

She had never seen a king—barbarian or otherwise—before. Curiosity lifted her out of her stupor. Her gaze traveled up and down the length of the boat's deck looking for a royal entourage in all its finery. But all she saw was a solitary man in scruffy traveling clothes, wrists and ankles hobbled with shackles. His hair and beard were matted, and his face masked, with dried blood. A noose had been thrown around his neck like a leash, and the end of the rope was held by the largest and grimmest Beedle she had yet seen.

Elshield swung down out of the saddle and saw to it that the mount's reins were entrusted to a Beedle. He grunted out a command in the Beedle's crude language, throwing a look up at Prim. Clearly the mount was going nowhere. Prim too dismounted.

A wooden gangplank had been dropped into place between the ship and the quay. The big Beedle crossed over it, the shackled man helplessly stumbling along in his wake.

Elshield took the end of the rope and looked at the prisoner. "Welcome, Your Royal Highness," he said to the barbarian king.

The king said nothing, for he had recognized Prim. And she had recognized him.

It was Brindle.

She was a princess, apparently.

"You lied to me," Prim said. "My whole life . . ."

"You must fight your way out now," Brindle said.

"How are we to do any such thing? Look about you!"

"*You* must do it *alone*," Brindle corrected her, raising his hands to show the chains. "You will find it within yourself," he insisted. "Better sooner than later."

"What is that supposed to mean!?"

"I lied to you because I love you," Brindle said. And then, taking advantage of some slack in the rope, he stepped into the gap between the quay and the boat and plunged straight down into the First Shiver.

Elshield's mind-reading ability let him down in this case, for he was holding the end of the rope only loosely, more as a ceremonial gesture than anything else, and it popped loose from his hand. The entire length of it buzzed over the edge of the quay and disappeared into the water in a manner suggesting that the king on the other end of it had been pulled straight to the bottom by the weight of his chains.

In the astonished silence that followed, Prim lunged forward, headed for the point where the rope had last been seen. "Brindle!" she called.

"No!" Elshield commanded.

A moment later, when Prim had shown no sign of heeding him, he called, "*Her* we need! Stop her!"

Prim had dropped to her knees at the edge of the quay, hoping to see the floating end of the rope. But it was entirely submerged. Hearing a heavy footfall nearby, she looked up to see the great grim Beedle coming for her, reaching out with his right hand.

She dove in headfirst. The hem of her long skirt, trailing in her wake, caught on something—or was grabbed by the Beedle's claw. She tried to kick and wriggle free, and felt the garment tearing at her waist. In a moment it came away and she plunged deeper into the water, both arms flailing in a blind search for the rope. Something gripped one of her ankles, and in the same instant she felt, as much as heard, another body plunging into the water. It was the big Beedle, gripping her by the leg, piling in on top of her.

Something grazed the back of her right hand. The water here was too murky to see much but she thought she glimpsed the free rope end undulating just out of her reach. She tried to kick back against the Beedle but his grip was strong. And his arms and armor were heavy, so he was sinking where Prim, left to her own devices, would have floated. The world pivoted around her as her buoyancy raised her head and body while the weight of the Beedle dragged her leg down. Again she tried to kick loose but his grip only tightened, and now his free arm snaked around her other leg and gripped it as if Prim's body were a ladder he could ascend into the air. He was now in a panic as he understood he was going to drown.

Absolute was her certainty that she had been in a situation like this before, though she could not remember it. In her childhood she had never been near a body of water as cold and as deep as this. Like the rope end she had felt but been unable to grasp, the memory eluded her the more she reached for it. It was one of those memories Elshield had tried and failed to extract from her mind during the ride down the mountain.

Still pointlessly trying to climb her body, the Beedle wrapped an arm around her waist. She reached down to push him away and found his face with the palm of her hand, but had nothing like the strength needed. Rough stone skidded along her shoulder: the wall of the quay, along which they were slowly descending. She groped at that with her free hand but could not find purchase.

She knew that the Beedle would not release her until death took him. Would she still be alive? Which of them would drown soonest? She desperately wished that *he* would. That now, while she still had the strength to swim to the surface, he would just die.

Her hand—which had been shoving at his face—felt nothing but water now. The arm was no longer around her waist. She was free, and beginning to float upward. She kicked her legs in case the Beedle had any thoughts of making another grab for her, and felt nothing. Looking down she saw nothing where the Beedle had been save an amorphous bubble of faint light—like the gleaming of a formless soul newly spawned.

A crevice between stones gave her a handhold she used in a panicky ascent. That and a few kicks and arm strokes took her to the surface. She erupted from it head and shoulders, and threw one arm up over the edge of the quay—where it was immediately pinned down by Elshield's knee. It felt like he was putting his full weight on her wrist. She'd have cried out in pain were she not simultaneously coughing up water and whooping in air. She got her other hand out of the water; he caught it in his, then stood up and hauled her full-length into the air and flopped her down on the pavement like a landed fish. "Got her!" he called. "Call off the search!"

"No!" she gurgled. "Brindle! The rope!"

"You weren't listening to what Sooth had to say!" said Elshield, sounding like a disappointed uncle. "We maintain the balance of the Land by seeing to it that the Sprung never get too organized, too powerful, out there on those Bits. Brindle was the best king among them. Having him free was unacceptable. Holding him prisoner would have been better—though not without risk. Having him dead—by his own hand, no less—now, that is the best outcome I could imagine. I think we'll leave him just where he put himself."

Hearing this, Prim became so wrathful that she rolled to her stomach, got up on hands and knees, and staggered up to her feet.

She turned to face Elshield and took a step toward him, wishing she could get her hands around his throat. But then his mind was inside hers again, and he forced her to stand where she was. Controlling her like one of his mounts.

"*You*," Elshield said, "we'll keep around. You'll make a lovely little tame princess to reign over Calla from a high tower."

She knew he could do it, too. He would not even need to put her in chains. The Autochthons, once they had got into your mind, had no need of such crude restraints. The only way to be free of Elshield's power was for him to cease existing.

She wished he were dead.

His black cloak, empty, collapsed into a heap on the pavement. The steel hilt of his sword clattered on stone as it slid half out of its scabbard. Elshield was gone. Gone from the quay and gone from her mind.

Above she heard Sooth give out a shriek. Other than that, the whole place was silent for a few moments. Then it erupted into a welter of voices, mostly in the crude simple version of Townish spoken by Beedles. They all wished to know where Delegate Elshield was. Very few had seen him cease to exist, and so all they knew was that he was nowhere to be seen and that his clothes and weapon lay on the quay as if he had discarded them.

The only possible explanation seemed to be that he had disrobed and jumped into the water in an effort to rescue Brindle, and so a lot of Beedles who had only just climbed out from trying to rescue Prim now jumped back in again. All was wildly confused.

It wasn't merely that no one knew what had happened. The removal of Elshield's mind from the top of the chain of command had left not only the Beedles but the Autochthons uncertain as to what they should do.

Prim, enjoying now the luxury of being completely ignored, became conscious of the fact that from the waist down she was naked except for a pair of dripping-wet drawers, and from there up only had a thin white bodice that was soaked through. Elshield's long black cloak looked comfortable and warm, and no one was using it. She bent down, picked it up by its collar, and twirled it around herself. The sword and strap tumbled loose. It couldn't hurt to have such a thing, and Brindle had given her a few lessons in what to do with a sword, so she picked it up and got the whole rig arranged over her shoulder. It dangled much too low on her thigh, but she could adjust it later.

She did not for one moment, though, imagine that swordplay had been what Brindle had meant, a few minutes ago, when he had said she would find it within herself to fight her way out. No, he'd known from the beginning that she was different. Her whole life, he'd lied to her to protect her from the burden of knowing what she was.

The Beedle to whom Elshield had handed the black mount's reins was just standing there like a flesh-and-blood hitching post, doing his duty as chaos swirled around him. He, at least, had clear orders: hold the horse. He watched her approach. Elshield's cloak was much too long for Prim, so its skirt dragged behind her as she walked. Scurrying Beedles kept stepping on it. In spite of which she presently drew to within arm's length of the mount. She reached out and grasped the reins, above where the Beedle was holding them.

"Let go," she commanded.

"My lord Elshield ordered not let go," the Beedle answered. Eyeing Prim warily, he transferred the reins to his weak left hand so that his strong right hand could find the pommel of a long knife in his belt.

For the third time in her life, Prim wished someone dead, and no sooner did the thought form in her mind than the Beedle ceased to exist. She stooped to pick up his knife, which looked more wieldy than Elshield's sword. Then she put her bare foot in the stirrup and mounted up into the saddle. No one seemed to notice or care save Sooth, who had been seeing all of this from the top of the wall above. "After her! After her!" Sooth screeched as Prim kicked the mount up to a canter.

The gate leading from the quay into the city was wide open. She rode through, turned south on the main street, and made the mount gallop. Behind her she could hear hooves on paving stones and knew that some Autochthons were in pursuit.

Navigation, at least, was simple. There was the one street and it ran direct to the south gate. The one she was supposed to have passed through yesterday, when all had been so different.

As she galloped toward it she saw it being swung closed by a Beedle, who then shoved a massive iron bolt into position to hold it closed. Seeing this, the mount had the good sense to slacken its pace, and came to a stop in the courtyard just on the near side of the gatehouse.

It was there that a squad of four Autochthons caught up with her. They spread out as they entered the yard, surrounding her but maintaining a respectful distance.

"Princess Prim," said the one who was evidently their leader. He certainly looked it. Yet his aquiline good looks were a little discomposed by the strangeness of addressing a barbarian princess who had, somehow, impossibly and unaccountably, stolen the cloak, sword, and mount of the high lord delegate of Secondel. "Dismount, please, and place those weapons on the ground."

"No," she said. "Listen. I have just now become aware of certain peculiarities as to who I am that place you all in grave danger. Get away."

"That's enough of that kind of talk!" exclaimed the Autochthon on her right. His mount moved toward her until it noticed that it was suddenly riderless.

She heard the creak of a bow from atop the gatehouse and looked up to see a Beedle archer pulling an arrow to half draw, still aimed at the ground, gazing at the head Autochthon for orders. Then he ceased to exist. The arrow flew wild and stuck in the ground. The bow clattered down the wall and bounced in the dust of the courtyard.

Prim wheeled her mount and made it walk toward the Beedle who had, a minute ago, shot the bolt. He was still standing there, watching her come on.

She didn't really know the speech of Beedles and so she made it as simple as she could:

"I am Death," she said. "Now, which one of us is going to open the gate?"

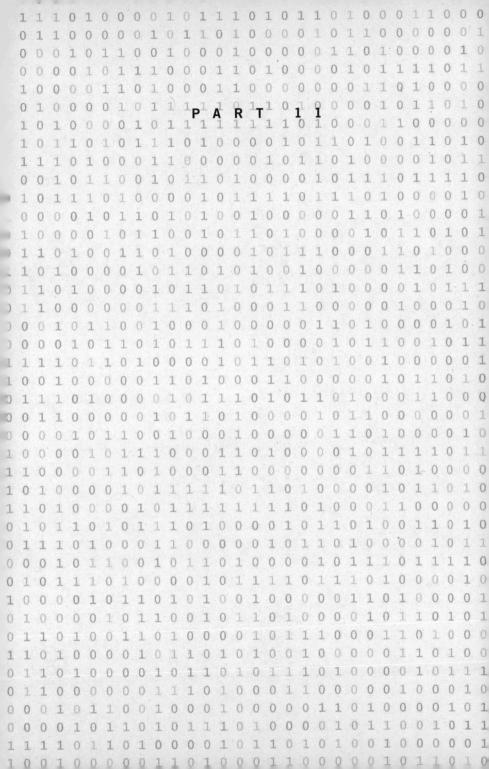

P A R T 1 1

50

While we have this all-too-rare opportunity for a private chat," said Primula—or, in the language of these parts, Daisy—to the giant talking raven perched above her on *Firkin*'s boom, "I thought I might make a few remarks about your management of the Quest thus far."

Corvus shook himself all over. "Have at it," he said, with an affected carelessness. "Just don't get so worked up that you wish me dead."

Prim glanced over to the shore of the Bit off which *Firkin* lay at anchor. Mard and Lyne and the three crewmates of Robst were there, gathering fresh water from a stream and poking around in the mud for edible crustaceans. They were out of earshot. Robst was at the other end of the boat. He was half-deaf. Prim had not shared with them some of the stranger and more surprising particulars about the day she had spent in Secondel; the news that Brindle was dead seemed like quite enough for them to take in. But Corvus obviously knew, and had known all along. "Why can't it work in reverse?" she asked, just thinking out loud. "Why can't I bring Brindle back, by wishing he had not passed on? Because I do so wish it."

"Destroying is just easier than creating," said Corvus, "and that's that. They say it took Spring an eon to summon the power to bring a bug to life."

"I feel that if you had not hid from me certain facts, things might have come out differently in Secondel."

"Some would say the facts were plain enough and you were blind to them," said Corvus. "That Brindle was a king, and you a princess, ought to have been somewhat obvious."

"You never think of yourself that way."

"Spoken like a true princess."

"And of course I knew that the matter of my parentage was a bit muddled. But still!"

"Come on," said Corvus, twitching a wing irritably, "was there *ever* a girl who was a girl for as long as you were? I'll bet that gnarled apple tree outside your window was a *sapling* when you moved in."

"I planted it," Prim said. "But living, as I did, a sheltered life, I thought all of that was normal."

"You were sheltered for a reason."

"And would you care to share that reason with me?"

"It's a bit obvious now, isn't it?"

"Yes, but how did I come to be on Calla, behind the Eternal Veil, being raised as an ordinary girl?"

"An ordinary princess, you mean? I haven't the faintest idea! No doubt if we could communicate with the other plane of existence from which we all seem to have originated, we could get an answer straightaway. As it is, we can only speculate. Your speculations are probably as good as mine, Princess, now that you have seen El's cathedral at Secondeltown and killed a high lord of the Autochthons with your brain and made off with his sword and his horse." He glanced at the former. Prim had taken it out of its sheath to rub oil on the blade, lest salt air rust it. The mount they'd been forced to abandon on the shore, since *Firkin* could not accommodate large beasts. "Whether by dumb luck or perhaps by some volition hidden from the likes of you and me, you have managed to live a long, quiet, and blessedly uneventful life in an out-of-the-way Bit, shrouded by an Eternal Veil, until recently. It was not until you came into womanhood, embarked—willingly I might just point out—on a Quest, passed out of that Veil, and set foot on the Land that all hell broke loose."

"Now, *that* is the part I wish to speak to you about," Prim said. "When we parted ways from Edda and the others in Cloven, you abandoned us."

"I had to abandon *someone*. That's the thing about parting ways."

"Why us? You must have known the dangers of Secondel. We could have used your help."

"Both of you. I abandoned *both* groups, you see. Edda and Burr and Weaver are just as vexed as you are."

"How *could* they be? Brindle is *dead!*"

"His decision to pass on surprised me, I'll grant you that. Had he decided otherwise, we'd have rescued him. Difficult. But well within the scope of a Quest."

"It goes to show how desperate he believed the situation to be. All because of a lack of information—which *you* could have supplied, *had you been there!*"

"I have so much less information than you seem to believe," said Corvus, "and when I am not with you, helpfully imparting such information as I *do* have, I am flying into the dodgiest situations you can imagine trying to get more. To the Island of Wild Souls I have lately been, arguing with tornadoes and temblors incarnate, and the Last Bit, and decidedly unwholesome parts of the Bewilderment, and I have even made an attempt to fly into the Evertempest: the perpetual storm that squats over the Knot. But it turns out I'm no Freewander. I cannot get anywhere near that thing."

"Hmph. Well then," said Prim, looking again at Mard and Lyne, who were pushing *Firkin*'s dinghy out into the channel, headed back to *Firkin* along with the rest of the crew. "All I can do is take you at your word. Do you think they suspect anything?"

"You mean, do they suspect that their traveling companion is a disguised member of Egdod's Pantheon who can kill anyone by wishing them dead? I doubt it; but if you notice young Mardellian Bufrect treating you even *more* courteously than he does already . . ."

Prim blushed, and tried to hide it with a grin. "Maybe that's why?"

"Just maybe." And Corvus took to the air with a cackling squawk that might have been a laugh. He playfully dive-bombed Robst, who was at the other end of the boat mending a sail, and beat up into the air to have a look round.

Prim, wishing she could see what he saw, summoned forth a memory of the map. They were at the place where the First Shiver forked into two equal branches that both ran to the ocean. The one to the left ran southwest to Toravithranax-by-the-Sea. The other ran northwest and was less frequented. Between them lay the spearhead-shaped island named the Burning Bit, so called because, seen from the high places of Toravithranax, it gave off an orange glow by night and reddened the sun with its smoke by day. Venturing around to its seaward edge would be too hazardous for little *Firkin*, but if they went down the inland fork to a certain place, they could hike up across a narrow part of the Bit and scout around on its west side, which was not a single coherent coast but an ever-ramifying web of steaming Shivers "cast into the sea," Edda had told her, pulling silver silk through the map, "like a fisherman's net."

That westerly wind prevailed for another day, but thenceforth it bore smoke, strange mineral odors, and even tiny flecks of grit that speckled *Firkin*'s canvas and crunched beneath their feet on the deck planks. Trimming his sails to it, Robst made good time up the inland coast of the Burner, as he called it. In due course they eased into a sort of dimple in that coast, not really profound enough to be called a proper bay, but enough to give them some shelter. They made camp on the beach in the shadow of a sharp ridge that ran up the spine of the Burner, and built a fire that they used to smoke some fish and oysters that they had collected over the last couple of days. Victualed with that and with some berries and greens gathered along the water's edge, Mard and Lyne and Prim set out early the next morning, seeking the least difficult path over the island's crest. In that they were aided by Corvus, who did not abandon them *this* time. The bird didn't completely understand the travails of ground-pounders and so they could not always trust his judgment, but he did at least warn them off from a few turnings that would have taken them to dead ends. And in the most disheartening moments of the journey it was a comfort to see him soaring overhead and know that, at the very least, they had not got lost.

The Newest Shiver cracked this Bit in twain down toward its southern end. If they followed the coast south, they would find it running directly across their path—they couldn't miss it if they tried. So that is what they did once they had crested the island's spine and gone down to the edge of the sea.

To their right was a drop-off that betokened a very long final few moments for anyone who went over it. Far out to sea were sails of large vessels, showing due respect for the danger posed by the cliffs and the sentinel rocks that stood off from them. Strewn along a thin ribbon of beach far below were wracks of ships that had got it wrong. But when they prudently drew back from the precipice and lifted their gaze to the country ahead, they saw a wall of steam piling up from the ground and blocking their view south. It was pearly white. Silhouetted against it, sometimes standing out crisply and sometimes shrouded in the murk, was a hut that had been built apparently on the very limit of the Last Bit where it gave way to the glowing gorge of the Newest Shiver. Not far from it, from time to time, they could make out the silhouette of a man, pacing back and forth—not in the style of one who was actually tending to any particular business, but more like one lost in thought, or trying to find his hat (it was on his head).

As they drew closer—which did not happen quickly, since the ground near the gorge was broken, upheaved, and punishingly sharp—they saw a somewhat smaller figure who seemed to be trying to keep pace with the first one's restless movements. The big one loped across tilted slabs and leapt between them. The small one moved in a style that it was not unfair to describe as scurrying. Some kind of discourse was taking place between them, the big one pointing at things with an elaborate walking stick and the smaller one looking where he pointed, then writing things down on a tablet. The former had eyes only for the evidently hot and fascinating goings-on down below, but the latter occasionally had moments of leisure while the former stroked his beard or held the stick up to his face. It was during one such moment that she—for by now the visitors had drawn near enough to discern that, notwithstanding a short haircut and boyish clothes, the small one was female—noticed Prim and Mard and Lyne picking their way up the rampart of shrugged-off shards that had accumulated near the brink of this new Shiver. She had seated herself on a slab edge so that she could write on her lap, but now reached up and tugged at the hem of this big one's garment. This was long, and if its purpose was to protect the wearer from flying sparks and cinders, then it had put in long service and perhaps saved his life.

He turned around to face them and repeated the queer gesture of holding the head of his stick up to his face.

"Querc," he said, "it would seem we have visitors."

Querc's response was to glance up. She pointed into the sky, and Prim, following the gesture, saw Corvus wheeling high above, out of range of the glowing rocks that occasionally launched from the gorge. "I told you that was no ordinary crow, Pick!"

"And I pointed out that that much was obvious!"

Querc was already shuffling through loose pages in a sort of wallet slung over her shoulder. "My notes will show that I predicted the giant crow betokened other visitors to come."

"Then don't bother digging them out," Pick said wearily. "They're never wrong; and if they were, I'd have no way of proving it, since my opinion would be contradicted by your bloody notes."

By now the visitors had drawn to within a few yards, near enough that ordinary persons might have greeted them and ventured some remarks in a conversational vein. But Pick and Querc were not ordinary persons. Prim decided to make the first foray. "Hail, denizens of the Last Bit!" she said. "We have come from faraway Calla to gaze upon the far-famed Last Shiver."

"It's twenty miles long," said Pick, and then glanced at Querc as if worried she might pull a sheet from her wallet and contradict him. But she was silent, allowing him to go on: "But you *just happened* to come directly to us. No, it's us you want to see, and not the Newest Shiver."

Prim had no comeback. Querc scrambled to her feet and said, "But as long as you have come so far, you might as well have a look anyway!" She extended an arm toward the brink, only a long pace away from her.

Much in the postures of Mard and Lyne suggested that they were aware that a sweep of Pick's stick would knock them over the edge. He was a big man, and in no way pleased to see them. But the thing in his hand seemed too elaborate and contraption-like to serve as a weapon. Its foot was shod in steel, forged in the shape of a paw with extended claws. Those were worn almost to nubs, and when Prim saw how he planted it on the rock to steady himself, she understood why. At the other end, where a cane might have had a knob or a curved handle, this thing had a sharp pick, forged in the shape of a bird's beak, and it too had been worn down from hard use. The head of the bird sported glass eyes, through which light shone. From that and from Pick's habit of holding it up to his face, she guessed it was a spyglass. Somewhat emboldened, she stepped past Querc and then dropped to one knee, then both knees as she neared the edge. Not to be outdone, Mard dropped into a similar attitude next to her. Prim had imagined a glowing river of lava flowing to the sea, for she had read of such things in books—at least one of which, come to think of it, mentioned this Pick chap by name. But if any such thing existed at the bottom of this gorge, it was obscured by steam and only hinted at by a lambent glow.

A red star hurtled straight up. As it hissed past them, they saw it was about the size of a fist. "Lava bomb!" said Pick.

"Type three," Querc elaborated. "Heads up, strangers!" But the warning was somewhat unnecessary as they were all taking their cues from Pick. He moved his stick sharply upward, using the bird beak to strike the underside of the broad brim of his hat so that it fell back off his head. It was restrained by a thong around his neck. Exposed was a tousled gray head, bald and scarred on top. He gazed intently at the sky, tracking the bomb, somewhat aided by a squawk of alarm from Corvus. Presently it began to fall. It had already darkened as it cooled. Pick took a few long strides and heaved his stick, making it spin about in midair. He caught it just below the bird head, now brandishing it like a sword, and swung it at the falling lava bomb. He caught it just before it struck the ground. It shattered into fragments that sprayed all over the place, not without posing some hazard to the eyes of the onlookers. Lyne flinched and pulled a splinter out of his forearm. "Thus glass," Pick remarked.

"That's him being friendly," Querc said. She said it in a quiet voice. Prim looked around and perceived that she was addressing the remark privately to Lyne.

Fish were eaten. A midden of small bones out back of the hut suggested that this was far from the first time. They had rigged up a system of nets and traps that they could deploy from the cliff top, hauling the fish straight up out of the surf "already cooked," Pick claimed, possibly in jest—it was hard to tell with him.

Querc was of a slightly more talkative disposition. She related her story. She was Sprung. Her family were seekers and traders of gemstones who roamed about the empty southwestern quarter of the Land between Toravithranax and the Central Gulf. From time to time they would make a foray into a city to conduct business, but their dealings had become complicated enough to require, and profitable enough to pay for, training a member of the family to read and write. Querc had been chosen from what sounded like a healthy surplus of children. Off she went to Toravithranax, where she was, after a couple of false starts, accepted into the Academy. She applied herself to the tasks assigned her by the acolytes of Pestle. A year went by, then another, then three more with no word from her family. She spent the money she'd been given and began to sell off, one by one, the gemstones her mother had sewn into hidden pockets in a leather belt. Word finally reached her from a cousin in Chopped Barren that the family had fallen victim to a series of disasters that had led to their surviving remnants being pursued across the wastes by a small army of Beedles, purportedly rogues, in all likelihood supported by local Autochthons. In any event they'd split up. This cousin, having made his way at length to a comparatively safe place in a northern Bit, was writing to Querc—the only member of the clan who had a fixed address—on the assumption that various others would have already had the same idea, and done likewise, and that Querc would simply be able to tell him where they had all found refuge. But she'd heard from none of them.

Accordingly Querc had truncated her education and let it be known that her services as a scribe were available to anyone who might have need of such. This had led to what sounded like an awkward interview with Pick, who had made a rare trip into Toravithranax in the wake of the sudden and unexplained disappearance of his previous amanuensis, "most likely blown off a cliff during a tempest." Despite its evident drawbacks, Querc had been strangely attracted to the position. She had no fondness for the Land, and in a sense you couldn't get farther from the Land than the Last Bit and the Newest Shiver. Oh, other Bits were farther away as the giant talking raven flew, but this felt more removed just because of its newness, the fact that it was on fire, and the fact that no one lived there except Pick. Yet it was close enough to Toravithranax that she could go there a few times a year and check to see if any further news of her family had arrived (though the tone in which Querc said this—wistful, even sheepish—hinted that she now saw that as naive). But the thing that really sold her on the job was its subject matter. Much of what Pick liked to talk about put her strongly in mind of her gem-hunting forebears and the notions they'd handed down as to how different kinds of precious stones came into being and where they might most profitably be sought. Some of which now struck her as eminently reasonable while much was completely demented. Pick had a whole picture in his mind that strung together all of the former while firmly rejecting the latter. So she had gone with him and had never regretted doing so—though, she had to admit, greater variety in food would have been nice.

Thus Querc. Her tale-telling was interrupted several times by complications having to do with the preparation and serving of the meal, and during those interludes Prim looked about the hut curiously. From a distance it had looked far more ramshackle than it really was. That was because its roof was patched together from whatever they could find.

But that was only the roof. Seen from the inside, it was one of the most solid edifices Prim had ever beheld. And this was because it wasn't really built at all, in the normal sense of the word. Most of it was belowground, simply sunk into the living rock. It was a square cavity that went straight down to about the height of Pick's head. That was divided into three rooms by stone walls. But the walls had not been built by piling one rock atop another. They were just *there*. The table on which they ate their fish was a stone mushroom that came right up out of the floor with no scam. Purpose-shaped niches in the walls held candles, cook pots, books. Strangest of all was that there was a drain in the floor. It was a smooth-bored tunnel in the stone floor, and it apparently led away somewhere. No hammer-and-chisel-wielding Beedle could have carved *that*. Yet there it was, and neither Pick nor Querc showed any hesitation about throwing stuff into it. Olfactory evidence suggested that it terminated at length in some place that was very hot. Prim had never seen anything remotely like it. The only analogy she could come up with was that if one were to begin with a block of ice, cut from a frozen lake in the far north, and shape it by plunging in red-hot irons, one might produce forms such as these.

According to the old stories, there *was* a precedent for this in the creation of the Palace, the Pinnacle, and First Town by Egdod and those who came after him. For that matter, the Land itself must have been created *somehow,* and the usual explanation was that Egdod had done it simply by flying around and willing it into existence. If they had come upon a hut such as this one in the middle of the Land, Prim might have explained it by supposing that Egdod or Pluto had made it thus for some long-forgotten reason, and left it there, and Pick had happened upon it. But the Last Bit was supposed to be *new* land.

"Lithoplast" was a word that Prim had heard Corvus use in obscure late-night conversations with both Brindle and Edda. Part of it meant "rock" and part of it had to do with shaping. At the time, she had not been able to make heads nor tails of it. She wondered now if it might be a word for a particular sort of person.

Corvus was almost offensive in his lack of curiosity about Querc. He had got a fish of his own by diving into the ocean and grabbing one and dragging it up here. So, laced all through Querc's narration were rude noises of rending, disemboweling, cracking, and gulping. But he minded his manners and hopped closer when Pick—loosened up, somehow, by Querc's story—began to speak.

"I am not Pluto," he began.

The confused silence that followed was so obvious that even Pick was moved to explain himself. "Sometimes when strangers such as you seek me out in the way you have done, it is because they think I am Pluto."

"Pick, let me set you at ease, as far as that sort of thing is concerned," Corvus said. "We are well informed, even by the extraordinarily high standards of the landed nobility of Calla. In particular

Prim and I have both seen remarkable things. I think that between us we have a clear-eyed view of how matters stand. Let me assure you that none of us would ever make such a gross error as to confuse you with the long-exiled member of the Pantheon known as Pluto."

"I have met him, though," Pick offered, in a mild tone of voice that would not ordinarily be used to deliver such remarkable news.

The next silence was even longer. Apparently not even Corvus could offer a comeback. It was left to Mard—in some ways the most naive, and most content-to-be-naive, member of the party—to respond. "Wow! How'd that work, since Pluto is in exile up in the sky, and you live in the Land? Are you one of the old souls of First Town, who knew the Pantheon before El hurled them out?"

"Not *quite* that old," said Pick. "I did live in First Town for a brief time before Egdod blew it up, and saw the Pantheon from a distance. But by that time they had already grown remote from the doings of common souls such as I, and Pluto of course was ever the least sociable of the Old Gods."

"By process of elimination, then, your claim is that you met Pluto . . . *after* he was exiled? You traveled up to the Red Web?" Lyne was the one to ask this, and he did so in a skeptical tone.

"Yes and no," said Pick. He crossed his arms and looked Corvus straight in the eye.

"That's all I needed to hear," said Corvus. "Let's go."

"We've only just begun to hear Pick's story!" Prim protested. "We can't just walk away from him now."

"They're coming with us," Corvus explained.

"Where do you imagine we will be going in one another's company?" Pick inquired.

"Oh, you know," Corvus answered.

Abandoning the hut, though extraordinary, was apparently not unprecedented, for Pick had procedures. These were unfamiliar to Querc and so it could be guessed that Pick had not abandoned it *recently*. A perfectly circular crack in the floor turned out to encompass a stone disk about a hand's breadth in thickness, which

Mard and Lyne with some difficulty pulled up and rolled out of the way to reveal a cylindrical cavity about half as deep as a person was tall. Like every other feature of the hut not improvised from beach-wrack, this just *was,* and showed no sign of having been chiseled out or built up through any discernible process. Pick took some stuff out of it and put other stuff into it. What he put into it consisted of items likely to be damaged by water or fire: mostly notes in Querc's hand, and blank paper, and old books. What he took out of it consisted of even older books and a thing he denoted the sample case and that Mard, Lyne, Prim, and Querc—who took turns carrying it—soon called That Fucking Box. All of which was still in the future when they replaced the stone disk and sealed it around the edges with mortar that Pick whipped up from water, sand, and various powders taken from sacks and clay urns around the property, one of which was labeled BONES.

Having seen to that, they simply walked away. All of this happened, apparently, as a result of a private side conversation between Pick and the giant talking raven that took no longer than it did for the junior members of the Quest to clear the table and do the washing up. It took place out of earshot, which, around here, with the wind and the surf and the seething and gnashing of the Newest Shiver, wasn't saying much. In short, Corvus did not seem to have lost any of his knack for talking strange persons (supposing Pick was even a person) into going along on the Quest. Thinking back on the case of the late Brindle Calladon—who had agreed to the idea ostensibly just because he thought Quests were the sort of thing Calladons and Bufrects ought to do—Prim guessed that Corvus must have had some way of getting people to see why the Quest was a good thing *for them.* What that might mean in Pick's case she dared not even guess at.

51

Pick was very firmly of the opinion that the Quest's odds would be boosted immeasurably by a little excursion to the Asking— the long peninsula that, south of here, reached far out to the southwest for no discernible reason other than the folkloric one that Egdod, as he flew that way, was asking himself what if anything might lie out in that direction.

Privately, Lyne was of the opinion that this side journey was nothing more than a way for Pick to get even farther away from civilization than he already was. In a somewhat pedantic vein, Prim the map memorizer pointed out that it wasn't even technically a *side* journey, since they would in fact be traveling a great distance directly *away* from their presumed goal.

They made their way back across the island to a little port on the eastern coast that lay across the very southernmost reach of the First Shiver from Toravithranax. There they met *Firkin,* which had come down the Shiver on instructions from Corvus. They took possession of all their maps and other gear and said farewell to Robst and his three crewmates, who sailed back north; they had now traversed the entire length of the First Shiver from West Cloven down to here, and needed to head for home, looking en route for any such trading or shipping opportunities as might profit them.

Across the Shiver came a different sort of vessel altogether, which Corvus had somehow talked into the job. Prim could only suppose that he had flown across to the city, transformed himself into human form, stolen some clothes, and put his powers of persuasion to work. Aboard *Firkin* had been a certain amount of money; perhaps that had now changed hands. The new vessel, *Silverfin,* was a thing called a keelsloop. So Mard and Lyne agreed, and such was the firmness of their agreement that Prim knew better than to ask for an explanation. Querc explained it anyway: these things weren't very capacious—the hulls, though long, were narrow—but something about the part under the water combined with the sail plan made them quite good at sailing close to the wind, which was what you had to do if you wanted to make your way down the Asking.

Fern, the skipper of *Silverfin*, would take a bit of getting used to. Robst had been quiet, sturdy, and more interested in deciding how best to carry forward Corvus's plans than in debating their wisdom or lack thereof. Fern, from the outset, carried herself more as an equal partner. In Prim's experience, ferns had always been small, delicate plants unfurling their lacy leaflets in damp, placid glades. This naturally gave her preconceived notions about the look and disposition of any soul who bore that name. In the case of *this* Fern, those were all wrong. Whoever had named her might have been nearer the mark with something like "Tree-Volcano" or "Whirlwind-Boulder." She was a big woman with dark skin that probably served her well as she sailed about below the southern sun. She was Sprung. When she bared her midsection, which, in this climate, was more often than not, it could be seen that she had a lot of scars, some of which looked to have been inflicted in random misadventures, others symmetrical and/or repeating, therefore deliberate adornments.

Fern had three permanent crew members. In addition, she had brought over two new hires for the purpose of this voyage. But after interrogating Mardellian and Lyne, she decided that those two Calla boys were at least as good as the sailors she had brought with her, and sent the latter back to Toravithranax with a bit of money for their trouble.

Her three permanent crew were Rett, who could run the whole keelsloop by himself; Swab, who cooked, cleaned, mended, organized, and slept with Fern; and a relatively new hire named Scale, who seemed to end up doing things that were chancy or arduous.

As they loaded their stuff onto *Silverfin*, Prim still harbored some hope that the wind would be every bit as impossible as it was cracked up to be; for during the three days they had cooled their heels in the little port, she had spent hours gazing across the Shiver at the high ateliers of Toravithranax, which (consistent with much lyric poetry she had read during her long girlhood) glowed gold, then copper, then coal red in the light of the evening. All it would take was a spell of really terrible weather and *Silverfin* would be driven back to its refuge there, and she would be able to see the place and explore certain gardens and markets that Querc had been telling her about as they had taken turns lugging That Fucking Box across the Burning Bit. But as it turned out, the winds were absolutely perfect, to the degree that the crew of *Silverfin* (according to Querc, who spoke their language) couldn't stop exclaiming about it. So just as soon as they rounded the sharp southern cape of the Burning Bit, they unfurled those special sails to catch a steady wind coming at them from a little ahead of starboard, and the keelsloop took off like an arrow launched from a bow, and Toravithranax sank into their wake as Prim sat in the stern pining for it. Off into the southwest they sailed, traveling as fast as it was possible to travel in the wrong direction.

Fern was Rett's equal when it came to the actual sailing of the ship, but she seemed to have more of a head for business. In a way this made her somewhat troublesome, since, by the time they met her, all of the business arrangements had been settled. So there was nothing for Fern's mind to work on save the larger picture of what they were actually doing. And this was poorly understood by all—even, apparently, Corvus. Fern's wish to know more—even to shape the Quest's direction—was clearly exasperating to Corvus. And yet if Fern had not been driven by that sort of curiosity, she would never have agreed in the first place to go on the Quest. You could not have one without the other; Quest-goer-onners were not ordinary souls, and so Quest leaders had, as Prim now understood, to devote a great deal of attention to contending with all of that want of ordinariness.

The peninsula marked on the map as the Asking was said to have all of the shortcomings of the desert to its east, where climate, vegetation, etc., were concerned. But since, unlike said desert, it did not lie between two more interesting and hospitable places, there was really no reason to go there at all. It just reached far out into the ocean and trailed off. If it were literally true that the peninsula had been formed by Egdod's asking himself "What lies out this way?," then the answer was nothing.

This topic was quite literally on the table in the sense that Prim had taken advantage of the spotlessly clear weather to unroll the big map. The table, like everything else that mattered aboard *Silverfin*, was bolted in place. She and Querc had been looking at it and Corvus was looking at them. They were up at the front end. Abaft, where the tiller was, Fern was meeting with her crew, including Mard and Lyne.

The map, as improved by Edda's needle and thread, agreed with what they could see off to port: a place along the sere coast of the peninsula where a stream flowed out from its stony guts and limped all the way to the ocean without drying up. Or so it might be guessed from the color of the surrounding landscape, which was a somewhat greener shade of brown than what stretched to either side of it. Straddling the outlet was an orderly arrangement of low buildings, and a single high watchtower, made of sun-dried mud bricks. A stone mole protected a moorage, above which several bare masts protruded. Between them and it, a galley was crawling like a many-legged insect across a simmering pan of water. All of it was military, for there was no settlement and no commerce here. The galley was going through the motions of trying to intercept *Silverfin* so that it could be boarded and inspected. It would fail. The entire point of keelsloops was that they could go faster than such galleys, provided there was wind. And along this coast that was almost always the case. Yesterday they had outrun two such, and Fern said that tomorrow they would have to outrun one, maybe two more. Beyond that they would be so far out on the Asking that the Autochthons didn't bother maintaining such outposts.

"It seems—I don't know—*expensive*," Prim remarked. "I may be just a barbarian princess, but even I can see that it doesn't add up."

Corvus performed his bird shrug, a small gesture magnified by huge wings. "Each of those outposts has only a few expensive-to-maintain Autochthons. There's plenty of fish. As to other necessities, they are resupplied by ships out of Secondel. Almost all of the souls are Beedles, purpose-grown to live in such places and to row boats. They grub in the muck for clams and seaweed. It's worth it, even if you do no more than take seriously the reason they claim."

"What reason is that?" Querc asked.

Prim knew. "To keep Sprung out." She rested her hand on the part of the map that showed the Bits and Shivers. "We mostly live up here." She tripped over the "we" since, as she had to keep reminding herself, she wasn't actually Sprung.

She swept her hand a short distance south and a little to the west. It now lay on the north coast of the Asking—the same coast they could see over the boat's port rail. "If you don't mind sailing out of sight of land for a few days and trusting to the mercy of the sea, you can make that voyage easily, far out of sight of the watch-towers of Secondel and Toravithranax. Fetching up on the shore of the Asking, you'd perish of thirst in a few days—"

Querc nodded. "Unless you landed where a river reached the sea—but that is where the Autochthons have made their watch-posts."

"They have to guard the river mouths," Prim concluded, "lest Sprung settle there, and once again get a foothold on the Land and begin to populate it."

Seeing someone in the corner of her eye she turned and met the eye of Mard, who, having been dismissed by Fern, had come round to listen. He blushed, averted his gaze, and slunk away like a man who had murdered his own father. She could not for the life of her work out why, until she later saw Lyne flirting with Querc. Then she understood it was because she had uttered the word "popu-late," which implied having babies.

Apparently, the upshot of the meeting that Fern had just convened and concluded was that Mard and Lyne were off duty for a bit. Accordingly, they began to swordfight. Mard was swinging the sword that Prim had acquired by killing Delegate Elshield on the quay at Secondel. Rusting away in a storage locker belowdecks were a number of other weapons, mostly shorter cutlasses, much less glorious than Elshield's but wieldy enough to be used against it in practice. Part of Prim wanted to resent the way that the young men—and particularly Mard—were assuming a kind of ownership over the sword. If circumstances had been different, she might have laid claim to it more forcefully. But be it never so magnificent, it could never be anything more than a token for Prim. Knowing she had another way to kill, she could never be as fascinated by it as Mard and Lyne were, and was happy to let them get good at using it. Querc, who was obviously quite taken with Lyne, went to watch them play.

Fern came forward for a look at the map. She spent as much time staring at this thing as Prim. This had been a little disconcerting at first given that Fern was supposed to know where she was going. She shouldered her way into the position most advantageous for peering at the part that depicted the Asking. She did not quite shove Prim out of the way but just kept sidling closer and closer, so that it seemed easiest for Prim to move. As Fern gazed at the map, Prim gazed at Fern, taking in the ridges and whorls of her scars. The skipper was quite unbothered to be looked at in this way.

Prim wondered if that was part of the point of having such adornments. People were going to look at you anyway. Might as well give their eyes something to do.

What then did Fern see in the map? She seemed to be looking not at the coastline of the Asking itself, but at the open sea to its south. Prim had never paid much notice to that part of the map; it was just a featureless expanse of animal hide that had been dyed blue.

Or was it? Fern was gazing at it much longer and more intently than made sense for a featureless expanse.

"What do you see?"

Fern reached out with a scarred, weathered hand, dripping with rings, and brushed a part of the map where the dye had set unevenly. "Just the ghost of a memory, perhaps," she said. "I was of a big family. The youngest. From here." She indicated a river delta on the south coast. "We booked passage on a vessel bound for Toravithranax."

"All the way around the Asking?"

Fern looked at her. "Yes, for the family was too large to attempt the crossing of the desert." She glanced at Querc as if to hint at why: people like Querc's family might have attacked them? Then she shifted her attention back to the map. She kept stroking, with the tip of her index finger, that irregularity in the dye, as if she could bring it to life; or maybe it *was* alive to her. "Somewhere around here it took all of my family."

"*What* took all of your family?" Prim asked. "Why, that's awful!"

Fern just tickled the map as if it could yield up an answer.

"A storm?" But Fern's language had hinted at something with a will. "Or . . . a big fish? A . . . sea creature?" She'd been about to say "monster" but didn't want to sound stupid.

"You're thinking wrong," Fern said. "Trying to make it out to be a normal thing of this world."

"Oh."

"That's not what it was at all," said Fern. She was firm on that, but in her mood was a quiet hopelessness that Prim—or anyone— would understand. "You see, I have sailed these seas for many hundreds of falls and seen many storms and many big fish. This was not of the normal order of things, this one that took my family."

"Is it possible—" Prim began.

"That my seeing of it was wrong because done through a child's eyes? That is what everyone says."

"I'm sorry."

"'Storm,' 'maelstrom,' 'beast,' 'monster' . . . those words are not wrong, though. Provided you use them only as poets say 'my lover's lips are a flower' or some such."

"But this was more—a thing unto its own kind," Prim said.

"Yes."

"You've been looking for it ever since."

"Yes."

"I believe you," said Prim. "From a distance once I saw the Island of Wild Souls."

"And you were raised on the back of a sleeping giant."

"Corvus told you?"

"Yes."

"That's why you agreed to join the Quest. Not for the money."

"The only purpose of the money," said Fern, "is to do away with any need of making awkward explanations to my crew."

"Swab would follow you anywhere, I'll bet."

"Yes," said Fern, "but even Swab needs to eat."

The wind faltered, and shifted round in a way that was less favorable. Fern diverted farther from shore lest the next galley catch them becalmed. This got them into "a bit of weather" that seemed to the landlubbers nothing short of apocalyptic. How terrible, Prim wondered, must the thing that killed Fern's family have been if this was but a poetic figure of it? Parts of *Silverfin* that seemed quite material had to be dismantled and remade. The thing might have gone badly had Corvus not been able to fly up high and supply information about where they were, and how best to bend their course back to shore while remaining out of sight of the last outpost that the Autochthons had bothered to construct. Thus when the Asking next hove into view, they were looking at a part of it deemed so remote and inhospitable that El didn't really care whether Sprung went and attempted to live there.

In the next day they spied only two things that looked like river mouths, but there was very little greenery around them; they looked instead like avalanche scars.

None of these drawbacks seemed to make much of an impression on Pick. And for reasons that could only be guessed at, Corvus had all but ceded the leadership of the Quest to him. So they dropped anchor into a cove, deep enough to accommodate *Silverfin*'s keel, sheltered enough to prevent its being flung against the rocky shore by wind or wave. They let their little longboat into the water. Mard and Lyne, deeply tired of being hot, stripped off their shirts, thinking to dive in and swim to shore, an easy stone's throw away, but Swab told them not to, on the grounds that she had better things to do with her time than go over every square inch of the swimmers' exposed flesh with red-hot tweezers.

Rett and Scale produced kegs of fresh water from down in the hold and took them ashore so that they could be decanted into canteens and skins. They also had hammocks, and nets to go over them, and curious funnel-shaped tin collars to tie round each hammock rope to prevent unspecified creatures from crawling down them in the nighttime. Mard and Lyne, already thwarted from swimming, had fancied that they would hike practically naked, but Pick, after a vigorous half hour of roaming about the beach killing things with his stick, let it be known that the lads would be worse than useless unless they wrapped heavy canvas around their legs all the way up to the groin, reinforced below the knees with gaiters of the thickest sort of leather.

None of them were, as a rule, complainers. They had, after all, agreed of their own free will to go on a Quest. Unlike Brindle, they were still alive. And unlike Querc, they hadn't suffered much hardship—just moved around quite a bit. Nevertheless, the next morning, having all spent a sleepless night listening to airborne things whining and ground-based things gnawing, they were in a low mood as they sat round the cook-fire. And they had not ventured more than a few yards from the shore.

"I do sometimes wonder what Spring was thinking when she created certain types of things," Prim said, scratching at a red swelling on her arm that she hoped was nothing more than an insect bite.

"This is nothing," Pick scoffed. "Your ancestors Adam and Eve were pursued by wolves—and they were the very *children* of Spring!"

"Granted," Mard said, "but I'm not sure how that answers Prim's question."

"It's more like you have only reasked it in a more pointed way," Querc put in. She was more bedraggled than had been expected by Prim, who'd hoped and assumed that the scribe would perk up and flourish in her native desert environment. That she *hadn't* did not seem to bode well for those who were new to it.

"It has to suck this badly," said Corvus, "in order for everything to make sense."

"What do you mean, 'make sense'?" Fern demanded. She had slept on the boat—a good idea—but come ashore for breakfast. "Nothing makes sense." And she looked out toward the ocean.

"Oh, but it does. You might not *like* it. And this might lead you to question things, even to say, 'This is senseless!' But whenever I think that, I take a closer look, and lo, it *does* make sense, from end to end and top to bottom. Because it *must*. Because if it didn't, the whole thing would split open and fall to pieces in an instant."

"What whole thing?" Lyne asked. "What are you even talking about?"

"The Land. All of it."

"You'll see," Pick said, "you'll see."

"I look forward to it," said Corvus. "Now, let's get going before the sun gets any higher."

Back at home, Prim had been on many hikes in the interior of Calla where the going had seemed slow, even difficult at times, and yet when you reached a high place from which you could turn round and look back, you were astonished by how far you had come.

This was not like that at all. Half a day's strenuous scrambling had left them exhausted and bloody. In some pitches they had to leave That Fucking Box behind and haul it up on a rope later. When they at last crawled up out of the long crack to a place where they could look down, they saw *Silverfin* at anchor in the blue pool directly below them, seemingly so close that they could throw stones and hit its deck. Which they were tempted to do, since Fern—who had decided not to join them on the climb—and her crew were comfortably dozing under the shade of stretched tarpaulins. But the effort of throwing rocks would have made them hotter than they already were and so instead they scuttled across an open ramp of hot stone to a place where they could shelter from the afternoon sun in the shade of a cliff. Pitching a tarpaulin of their own, they made themselves as comfortable as they could and tried to catch up on some of the sleep they had failed to get last night. When the sun got low and the air finally began to cool, they broke camp and hiked until it was full dark, coming at last to a site that Corvus had picked out from above. They ate their rations and then found it impossible to sleep.

The night sky in these parts seemed to hold ten stars for every one that they could see in Calla. Lying out under them one had the feeling of trying to sleep on the stage of an amphitheater while a thousand eyes watched.

The red constellation that some called Egdod's Eye was wheeling over them, higher in the sky than they ever saw it at home. It was the first time Prim had got a really good look at it since certain facts had been brought to her attention in Secondel. As a girl she had seen it as a place of myths and legends: where Egdod and the rest of the Old Gods were said to be building a counterpart to the Land from which they had been exiled. Not wishing to pursue such work in view of El, they had drawn a veil of smoke over it.

So much for the myths. But if it really was true that Prim was one and the same as Daisy, or Sophia, then it meant that she had actually been there in a previous life. Felt its hard blackness in her bones as she had impacted upon its surface, digging a crater that burned and glowed even now, one of an irregular constellation of flickering flame-colored stars, like so many distant campfires on a darkling plain—

"What do you see?" It was Mard, also craning his neck to look up at the sky. "I see Knotweave's Loom." It was a well-known constellation. So familiar that to point it out seemed a childish gambit for starting a conversation. She hadn't heard him coming, but now that his voice and his presence—he took a seat on the ground quite close to her—had brought her back to the here and now, she heard a giggle—a giggle!—from Querc on the other side of some low scrubby bushes, and Lyne's low voice saying something indistinct that made Querc giggle again.

So if Mard was being a little clumsy, it was because having a chat about stars wasn't really why he was here. He scooted even closer—so close that unless Prim moved away, any shift in her position would bring them into contact.

The last thing he was expecting was probably an answer to his question. "The Firmament," she said.

It took him a moment to place the reference. According to old books of myths—stuff read only by young children and elderly scholars—that was the shell of black adamant that formed the vault of heaven, pocked with god craters and veiled from the Land. It was usual to speak of the Red Web, Egdod's Eye, the Fire Nebula, the Crimson Veil, but not of the theoretical abstraction that lay behind it. But with a moment's reflection Mard got the idea. "It is awfully high in the sky here," he said. He reached up and, somewhat theatrically, squeezed the back of his neck. "Gives me a crick in the neck just looking at it. Easier to lie down." He did so, somehow in the process managing to shift even closer to Prim. "The rock is still warm," he remarked, brushing it next to him with his hand.

Prim wondered if Mardellian Bufrect had the faintest idea how badly she wanted to lie down alongside him and stop looking at—and having this inane conversation about—the sky. But a question had come up that needed answering. "Now that you are warm and comfortable—"

"Not as much as I *could* be."

"—what do you see when you look at the Red Web from this most excellent of vantage points and most convenient of positions? Surely in your whole life you have never viewed it with so many advantages."

"I see . . . the Red Web!" Mard answered. He was not precisely frustrated yet, but perhaps a little dismayed that his lame opening about Knotweave's Loom seemed to be developing into an actual conversation about astronomy. *That'll teach you,* Prim thought.

"Describe what it looks like. I have a crick in my neck, I can't look right at it."

"Well, you know, it's like a campfire when a kettle is boiling on it on a cold night, a proper full rolling boil, making a great cloud of steam that obscures your view. It glows from the light of the flames that you know are beneath it, and from time to time as the steam swirls and dances you may get a glimpse of a red-hot coal or a lick of fire—but then it's hidden again and you wonder if you really saw it."

"Well described," she said. "I can almost see in my mind's eye what you are seeing."

"If you make yourself comfortable here," he suggested, patting the ground next to him, and considerately flicking a pebble away, "you can just look at it. I might even be able to help you with that crick in your neck. I'm good at—"

"My neck is fine," she admitted. "Would you like to know what I see?"

"Sure," he said, not really sounding all that sure.

"The sharpest, clearest sparks of red fire. Not the flickering of something that burns but the steady glow of lava. A big one in the middle where Egdod fell. Scattered about it, smaller ones where the rest of—" She was about to say "us" but substituted, "—the Pantheon landed. Hundreds of scintillas—the lesser souls who Fell in Egdod's wake. But then in the dark places between, crevices like fiery roads—like the Newest Shiver, you might say—and along them palaces, houses, fortresses of black adamant gleaming by firelight."

"Wow," Mard said. "It sounds like you fell asleep and dreamed it."

"You're the one who dreams. I'm the one who sees."

Mard sat up and shifted away. He didn't seem to know what to do with his arms, so he crossed them in front of his body.

"Chilly?" she asked.

"Maybe a bit."

He needed an out. She provided one. "You know, Querc over there has been alone with her grief for years. I'm just getting acquainted with mine. I was reflecting yesterday how little time has really passed since Brindle sacrificed himself for the Quest. A fortnight at most?"

"It's true," Mard exclaimed, a bit hastily. "No question about it."

"If I see weird things in the sky, maybe it's because I'm looking through tears."

"Oh, I'm so sorry, Prim!"

"Don't be," she said, "but do be patient."

After dawn, a brief walk over comparatively level ground brought them to an arresting rock formation. The steepness of the rocks they'd climbed yesterday had hid it from the sea. Only Corvus could have directed them here. Prim already knew what it was called, because she'd heard Corvus and Pick talking about it: the Overstrike. As she saw the actual thing, the name made perfect sense. It was probably just the upper reach of the crack they had climbed up yesterday—a fault that, she was beginning to understand, might run all the way from the north to the south coast of the Asking. As had been obvious yesterday, it was not an active, moving Shiver but a thing that had occurred a very long time ago and then become still and dead. Consequently its lower reaches were so full of rubble, gravel, soil, and opportunistic plants that it required some squinting and head-cocking and use of the imagination to understand its nature. Up here, however, it could not have been more obvious. The crack was not vertical but heeled over at an angle about halfway between vertical and horizontal. The width of it—the gap between the two opposing faces—might have been twenty paces. They approached it on its lower side, and the nearer they came to the edge of the actual split, the more its opposite face loomed above them. They passed into its shadow, which in this climate was always a welcome relief. But it made them aware that the opposite face was now jutting out *above* them, so that any loose stone that might be dislodged from the sharp brink would fall on their heads.

A smooth and featureless ramp of stone descended into darkness. It was strewn here and there with loose pebbles and maculated with patches of white shit from colonies of birds that had built hivelike nest complexes on the under-surface of the crack's overhanging face. Which—as they saw, when their eyes adjusted—was absolutely featureless. Other than those hanging birds' nests, nothing was up there for their eyes to gain purchase on. It was as if the under-surface of the Overstrike did not even exist; it was a night sky without stars.

"Adamant. It is what everything was at the dawn of the First Age," said Pick, after he had given them a good long time to behold it, "after Egdod had conferred on the Land a general shape, and lit stars on the Firmament, before Pluto had come along to look after the particulars. He told me once, long ago, that there were parts of the Land unchanged since Egdod's First Pass. Pluto knew those must be seen to eventually. But he had left them untended to in places that were so remote and unfrequented that he did not think it would matter. More important was to make good those parts of the Land that were seen and trodden and worked by souls every day."

"And there are other such unfinished places in the Land?" Prim asked.

"Many. All of them as difficult to reach as this one," said Pick.

"Otherwise Pluto would have done them up," Lyne guessed, "so that ordinary souls would never see such strange holdovers of the Before Times."

"Just so," said Pick.

"Why have we then come here?" asked Mard, letting the sample case down onto the ground with a gentleness that in no way reflected his true feelings toward it.

"To be elsewhere," said Corvus. "Look, I am a bird and I do not love having rock over my head. So I'm going to get out from under the Overstrike and do what birds do."

"Eat worms?" Querc asked.

"Shit all over everything?" said Lyne.

"That's the spirit! Now shut up and keep Pick from killing himself down there," said Corvus, and after a few hops back down the way they had come, took off squawking into the sunlight.

"You're going . . . down there?" Lyne asked Pick.

Pick unlocked the front of the sample case, which hinged down to form a table, variously burned and stained. Revealed were numerous niches and drawers, labeled in very old script such as Pestle had, according to legend, learned from the Old Gods in First Town. Prim, who knew how to read it, saw words like PRIMORDIAL ADAMANT—FROM THE LARGEST ROCK and AURIC CHAOS—PARTIALLY SENTIENT and other terms that made considerably less sense even than those.

The general plan of action was to anchor ropes up here that Pick could use to secure himself as he descended the ramplike surface of the crack face. Up here it was strewn with stuff that had fallen on it over the centuries, but once he descended to a depth "profound enough to be worth visiting," it would be as clean and featureless as the opposite, overhanging face, and he would begin to slide.

"You can't just stop there," Mard objected.

"What do you mean?" Pick asked. He was uncoiling, and inspecting, a very long rope.

"'Begin to slide.' Then what?"

"Keep sliding?" Lyne guessed.

"At increasing velocity?" Querc offered.

"But, to where?" Mard demanded. "Where would you stop?"

"Better to ask *whether*," Pick said. "Careless as he was, I see no reason to assume that Egdod bothered to supply every hole in the ground with a bottom. Tedious work, that. Not his way."

This left the younger members of the expedition in silence as they went about their work—though the vision of Pick's falling into a bottomless chasm did have the salutary effect of making them very keen about sound knot-work and proper anchoring of rope ends. They more and more avoided the lip of the fault.

At some length Pick approached the sample case and opened a drawer labeled PURE CHAOS, which had been noticed and remarked on by the others but which perhaps understandably they had been reluctant to open. They crowded around to look. It was full of a nothing that made the upper face of the Overstrike, featureless as that was, seem like something. The drawer itself was not dovetailed wooden planks but hewn from black stone—the primordial rock that Pick referred to as adamant. Its outer surface was barely visible; when he pulled it open, its inner surfaces could not be seen at all. With very close attention they could see fluctuations of light and dark, and hear a dull hiss. It reminded Prim somewhat of aura she had seen around Delegate Elshield and in the cells of the Hive. But that had been radiant and had moved in ways that, though unpredictable, bespoke a kind of sense. This stuff was to that as a rotting corpse was to a living animal.

Aura reached out from Pick's head like a beetle's pincers, converged on the drawer, and pinched off a bit of the chaos about the size of a nut. He closed the adamant drawer. The sample of chaos moved with him, suspended in front of his face at arm's length, enveloped in a swirling pattern of aura. He moved now with the gliding, cautious gait of a servant who is carrying a brimful glass of rare wine on a slippery tray. He made his way to the brink, where Querc passed the rope around his body in a very particular manner, enclosing him in a kind of sliding hitch that would enable him to control his descent with a single hand. In his other, no surprise, he held his pick. He backed slowly away from them over the brink of the fault, moving with care as he planted each foot—he had taken his boots off—on the surface below and behind him. In this manner he gradually receded from their view, his form growing smaller and less distinct, until all they could see was the glow of his aura. That too became small and faint. The only way they could be sure he was still in and of the Land was the rope, ever tense, but twitching, and occasionally traversing from side to side.

He was down there for a long time, which might have made the day tedious had Corvus not come flying in with dire tidings: "Beedles! A whole galley-load. I must warn Fern."

"Should we extract Pick?" Mard asked.

Corvus was already beating his wings hard, building speed out into the open sky. "No point!" he squawked.

Prim ran down into the open and retraced the path they'd taken earlier today until she could get a clear view down to the cove where *Silverfin* had anchored. No Beedles were in sight, but the keelsloop, apparently having been warned by Corvus, had weighed anchor and struck the sunshades. Canvas was beginning to unfurl from mast and boom, but mostly what was moving the boat at this point was oar power.

"Not much of a breeze today," Mard remarked. He had been only a few paces behind.

Prim and Mard stood there and watched for a time. *Silverfin* inched her way out into the open sea and unfurled all the canvas at her disposal. She steered into a northwesterly course, away from land. Prim understood that this was not an attempt to go anywhere in particular, but to harvest as much speed as they could from the wind available.

Then at last they saw what Corvus had seen much earlier: a galley, a small one with a single bank of oars on each side. Probably two dozen oars all told. From this high vantage point they could just barely make out the forms of the Beedles pulling on those oars. Above them, running right up the vessel's centerline, was a catwalk connecting a poop deck at the stern to a foredeck at the bow, and those were populated by others, armed and ready for war—or so they could guess from the flashes of light that gleamed from their midst.

Mard let out a long breath. "Impossible," he said.

"What do you mean?"

"There is no way *Silverfin* can escape from this."

They watched the pursuit a while longer. It was obvious that Mard was right.

"That galley must have followed us," he said.

"Keelsloops don't normally just *stop* and wait to be caught up with," Prim guessed.

"Why would they?" Mard agreed. "But we did. And somehow they knew. They got wind of the fact that we were here to be caught."

"The water!" Prim explained, as the thought came to her. "The fresh water, and the other stuff we left on shore—"

"We have to go get it, while there's time!" Mard agreed. And without any further discussion they were off, descending yesterday's climb in skidding, sliding, pell-mell style.

Meanwhile the pursuit of *Silverfin* unfolded slowly. Though the disparity in speed between the two vessels was obvious, *Silverfin* had been given a decent head start by Corvus's warning, and even Beedles could only row for so long at top speed. Mard and Prim frequently lost view of one or both vessels as their descent took them into various gullies and chutes. The two of them descended faster, and the pursuit at sea went slower, than they had feared. Presently they found themselves on a ledge just above the cove. There they stopped for a few minutes to watch the culmination of the chase. From here details could not be made out. But Mard had explained how galleys were equipped with grappling hooks and spiked, hinged bridges that could be dropped onto the decks of vessels they wished to board. They clearly saw the two ships come together and merge into a single dark knot on the water, some miles out. From that point forward, they could do little more than imagine what might be happening to Fern and her crew as armed Beedles poured across those boarding ramps. Invisible at this distance, but presumably there, must have been Corvus, high enough to be out of the range of Beedles' arrows. Perhaps later they would hear the melancholy tale from him. In the meantime it behooved them to fetch the casks of drinking water and other valuables they had left on the shore, and move those inland. For if those Beedles had gone to the trouble of following them this far, it stood to reason they might come ashore and hunt around for any stragglers.

That was what they were now. Stragglers. Prim remembered some of the grimmer parts of Querc's story. She hoped Querc was still down beneath the Overstrike, not seeing any of this.

"A sail. It is definitely a sail!" Mard announced, just as Prim was turning her attention to the last phase of the descent. He'd mentioned it previously, but with less confidence. Prim looked out and thought she could see a white triangle bobbing up and down on swells.

"Do you know what they did?" Mard asked. It seemed a rhetorical question and so Prim just waited. "Fern saw it was hopeless and so gave *Silverfin* up as a decoy. The Beedles boarded the keelsloop, yes. But Fern's in the longboat. They've raised sail. They are putting some distance between them and the galley."

"Don't the Beedles have a longboat of their own?"

"Maybe, maybe not. But it would have no advantage in speed. In a sailing contest, my money's on Fern."

"Could the galley not just disentangle itself from *Silverfin* and swoop down on them?" Prim hated to keep asking questions in such a negative vein, but she was having some difficulty understanding why Mard was so very pleased by this turn of events. She began to descend the last few hundred yards toward the cove. After a bit, he followed her. "I suppose it depends on which they want more: the vessel, or the crew," he answered.

Prim chose not to answer out loud: *They have both. They can simply camp out on the shore and wait for us to run out of drinking water. And when Fern and her crew join us, that will only happen all the sooner.*

She was too optimistic, as it turned out. The Beedles were not content merely to wait on the shore. They sent hunting parties inland.

The way it went the rest of that day was that Mardellian and Prim, after a brief water break on the shore, began moving the casks of water, and such weapons as they had, inland—which meant uphill. Lyne showed up and helped. He let them know that Querc was still looking after the rope beneath the Overstrike and that Pick was still doing whatever he had gone down there to do.

Silverfin's longboat sailed into the cove and ran up on the beach. In it were Fern, Swab, and Scale. Rett had died en route from an arrow wound. Scale had suffered a crushing injury to one leg when it had got pinched between *Silverfin* and the galley as they rolled together. He could not climb. They left him down below while they worked on carrying supplies uphill. They had intended to go back down and fetch him later, but at some point they noticed that he had put out to sea again in the longboat—presumably in the hope that he might sail it up the coast to some safe harbor.

They worked all night carrying the goods up to the high camp near the Overstrike. When dawn broke they were not surprised to see the Beedles' galley anchored in the cove below, and a column of smoke rising from the sea in the distance where they had scuttled *Silverfin*.

Their hopes—if that was the right term for a prospect so dismal—that they would simply be left alone while they ran out of water were dashed when Swab staggered into camp with an arrow in her back. A lot of squawking and screaming not far distant was suggestive of a Beedle-vs.-giant-talking-raven fight, and soon they had a blind Beedle on their hands—Corvus had seen him shoot Swab, and taken his eyes out.

The Beedle died because he would not stop screaming and Prim wanted him dead. That she had killed him was not obvious to the others, who found it puzzling when he ceased to exist. Yesterday she had tried to use her power on the Beedles in the distant galley, but it hadn't worked—she couldn't just kill a whole ship full of anonymous victims miles away; it seemed to be more of a face-to-face transaction.

Everyone in the camp was now going armed. Mard had belted the great sword of Elshield around his waist. Lyne had taken out a sword of his own: a family heirloom that he had brought from home and kept packed in his baggage until now. It was not much less magnificent than the one Mard carried. Given the circumstances, however, he was paying more attention to his bow and arrows. Fern was strapped with a cutlass and a dagger. Prim, like Lyne, had a bow strung and a quiver at her hip. But only because it would seem odd *not* to. She could kill all of the Beedles, she knew, one by one, and they could simply take the Beedles' galley. But none of her companions, save Corvus, was aware of that. And so, once they had made sure no additional Beedle snipers were any-where nearby, they turned their attention to the arrow lodged in Swab's body. This had gone in her back, up high between spine and shoulder blade, and passed most of the way through her body. It had broad, vicious barbs, so deeply embedded that Fern ended up deciding that the only way to get it out was to push it all the way through and out the other side. And this she did after giv-ing Swab a potion from her medical kit that in theory would dull the pain. To judge from the way Swab reacted, it didn't work very well. Watching the operation from Swab's front, Prim saw the flesh begin to bulge outward beneath the collarbone. Then the highest part of the bulge lost its form. A lesion appeared on the skin, and it was made of chaos. The point of the arrowhead erupted from its center and then the whole thing came through easily. Once the barbed head had been removed, Fern was able to pull the shaft out of Swab's back. Blood came from the wound. They bound it up as best they could.

Intent as she was on looking after Swab, Prim paid little note when Corvus flew in from one of his reconnaissance sweeps and summoned Mard. But when they finally knotted the bandages round Swab's wounds and made sure she had all the water she desired—and she had become very thirsty—Prim looked round and saw that Mard and Corvus were both absent.

They took turns carrying Swab the rest of the way to the Over-strike. Whoever wasn't carrying her carried water or other sup-plies. The hike seemed to last an eternity, but the sight of Corvus circling overhead gave them some comfort that all was well at their destination and that they were not being hotly pursued.

They found Mard sitting bareheaded out in the open sun before the dark grin of the Overstrike. His sword was across his knees. On the ground next to him was a rag stained with fresh blood, which he'd apparently been wiping from the blade—for that was glittering clean. But he seemed to have finished with that task and was now just staring out over the distant sea. A short ways before him, just downslope, was a great deal of blood, painting the slope with a ramifying pattern as it discovered paths between stones. Lying unclaimed on the ground, considerably farther away, was a cutlass whose blade—as Lyne verified by picking it up and turning it this way and that in the sun—bore no trace of gore. "Mard must have kicked it away," he explained.

As they came closer, giving the blood lake a wide berth, they saw that Mard was shivering violently. Prim went to him and knelt down. Lyne, out of a nervous habit, turned and looked back. But from here they had a clear view of the ground below for at least a bow-shot, and Corvus was still patrolling farther out. Fern kept trudging up the slope, breathing heavily and sweating freely with Swab on her back, trying to get her into the shade of the Overstrike.

"I know that swordfights are part of what one signs up for," Mard remarked, in a low voice, "but that was so different from everything I trained for as to be another thing altogether."

"But it—your training—worked, did it not?" she asked. "Lyne said you kicked his sword away. How did it end up on the ground in the first place?"

"I would like to be able to say that I executed a clever disarm as I was taught, but really I have no idea. And it's as likely *he* kicked it by accident as that I did on purpose."

"Let's get into the shade," she suggested. She stood up and extended her hand. After a few more moments of gazing out at nothing in particular, he met her gaze—but only for an instant—and reached up and took her hand. She gave him a tug—mostly symbolic, for he was quite capable of standing up by himself. He let go of her hand and wiped his on his pant leg as if worried it still had blood on it. Side by side they walked up the slope until they passed into the shade of the Overstrike, whereupon they had to wait for a few moments as their eyes adjusted.

Lyne had gone up before them and was squatting there, bow across his knees, gazing outward. Farther in, Fern had lain Swab down on the flattest place she could find and was trying once again to satisfy her thirst. Querc was tearing about the place full of nervous energy. It was obvious that something had upset her, so Prim got her to stop moving by firmly embracing her and hanging on for a spell.

"I came up to get something for Pick, and he was just *there,* looking at the sample case."

"The Beedle?"

"Yes. All I could think of was my family, and all the Beedle fights they used to talk about. I tried for the longest time to scream for help, but I was just frozen—he hadn't seen me yet. Then he noticed me, and took a step in my direction, and I pulled this out." She patted the hilt of a long knife sheathed at her hip. "That made him pause for a minute. If he'd come after me I don't know what I'd have done. But then Mard came running in. He stopped at the edge of the dark and drew his sword. That spooked the Beedle. He drew out his sword and ran at Mard. Mard backed out into the light and they fought each other."

52

Pick, as the sole member of the Quest who did not seem injured, shocked, or distracted, had taken it upon himself to come up with a plan. They all collected near where Swab lay so that they could talk about it. Everything about the manner in which Pick spoke of this plan seemed to indicate that he thought highly of it, "given the circumstances." But no one could understand what he was proposing.

"Given the circumstances," Lyne repeated. "Given the circumstances. We are trapped in a waterless, foodless hellhole at the arse end of the world, being hunted by Beedles, and there is no one to help us. So, what you're saying is that, given *those* circumstances, this is a better plan than just dying of thirst or being murdered."

"If you have some other suggestion," said Corvus, "now's the time to pipe up."

After some moments went by without anyone's piping up, Corvus said, "Right! Settled."

"The most excellent plan I can think of," said Lyne, "is not to get talked into Quests by mysterious giant talking ravens." He shared this with Fern, Mard, and Prim after Corvus had flown away to reconnoiter and Pick and Querc had taken turns going down the rope into the huge mysterious crack. Swab had been quiet of late. Fern was sitting by her side, holding her hand, perhaps trying to ascertain whether she was alive or dead. Prim looked at them, trying not to be obvious, and saw that Fern had begun to unwind the bandage. It was no longer doing service. Swab had stopped bleeding, for the place where the arrow had gone in was now dissolving into chaos and no longer supplied with blood. Fern had, however, been following the conversation, and now spoke.

"As I understand matters," she said, "I have lost more than any of you. My keelsloop is gone. Of my three crew, Rett is dead. Two are wounded, and one of those absconded with my longboat. If you don't mind, I'll be the judge of whether going on this Quest was worth it. And I'm all in still."

"How *can* you be?" Prim asked, in a tone of gentle curiosity. Of course she knew from her reading of old Quest stories that there was fighting and blood. But to observe the consequences of a single arrow fired into a single body had forever changed the way she would think about such adventures. Fern had seen worse in the last day, and various clues about her, her ship, and her crew had suggested that this was far from her first scrap.

"This happens all the time anyway," Fern said, her voice quiet but severe. She flicked her eyes down at her suffering partner. "Perhaps not to those of you who live in castles on Calla. But I have seen it all before. I have *not* before—not in a thousand falls of sailing the sea—seen a giant talking raven who can transform himself into a man and hold forth with authority on the Before Times. To be called into such doings is a gift that has never been given to me before and will not come again. I have seen wonders already that no one to my knowledge—and I have lived long and journeyed far—has ever seen or spoken of. Young as you are and living on a veiled island where magical beings are apparently of little note, you do not understand this. You must think," Fern said, rising to her feet, "of the arrow that Swab took for us, and how, having taken it, and understanding its barbed nature, she agreed that it was better to shove it all the way through than to reverse its direction. That is where we are all poised now in respect of this Quest. To surrender is to pull out the arrow backward: no better and probably worse than to push through."

Fern bent close, cocking her ear toward the lips of Swab, and listened to words that no one else could hear. After some time she nodded her head, then turned her face to Swab, brushed back her hair, and kissed her. Fern then got up on one knee and pulled Swab's good arm up across her shoulders. With a great effort she stood up. As Swab felt herself being lifted, her legs stirred and she got her feet on the ground, taking some small portion of her weight. On the side that had been struck by the arrow, the entirety of the shoulder and the arm attached to it had dissolved into chaos, and most of that no longer clung to her body, nor did it make any pretense of hewing to the form of a normal soul, but was dispersing like smoke.

Fern trudged with slow heavy footfalls up the last few yards of slope to the brink of the fault. She crested the slope and descended a few paces, planting her feet with caution that became more evident as the adamant sloped away beneath her and the surface became cleaner and slicker. When she had gone as far as she dared, she bent her knees and her back, and carefully let Swab down so that she was sitting on the smooth adamant, using her remaining arm to prop herself upright. For a little while then they stayed together, Fern squatting next to her stricken partner and embracing her as if her heavy arms could hold in the chaos that had once been Swab but was now escaping from her form. Finally, before it was too late, Swab shoved off with her good hand, and began sliding into the fault. Unable to remain upright, she flopped sideways, rolled lazily over, slid, picked up some speed, rolled over twice more, and was gone.

Prim watched it all from a respectful distance. Long after she had lost sight of Swab, she saw a faint flare of chaos down in the abyss, and knew for certain that Pick was correct in suggesting that neither Egdod nor Pluto nor El had bothered with putting a bottom on this thing. The Land was built upon mere chaos, and in places you could reach it.

Another Beedle sniper came up to reconnoiter, but his approach was almost offensively obvious. Lyne shot him and he fell wounded. His companions—for others could be heard, and occasionally seen, farther down the slope—let him lie where he had fallen. Insects came out of nowhere and feasted on his blood.

Night fell. They lit no fire, lest it dazzle their vision. There was almost nothing to be burned in any case. Prim had worried that the Beedles might come in the night, but the air was so dry and thin in these parts that moon-and-star-light let them see, and shoot at, anything out there in the no-man's-land below them.

In Secondel, Beedles had always been under the command of Autochthons. But none were in evidence here. Fern ventured the opinion that a larger flagship would probably be not far off, commanded by an Autochthon, and carrying Beedle marines who would prove more formidable opponents than the scouts and mere galley slaves who had them bottled up at the moment. And indeed when day broke Corvus flew in from scouting and reported that just such a galley had entered the cove, and that reinforcements were climbing the hill, led by an Autochthon.

"Don't kill him," Corvus suggested, when he got a chance for a private word with Prim. "Or anyone, unless you do it like a normal person, by putting an arrow through them or something."

"We may have no other choice. We have a day's water and no food to speak of. Pick's preparations are taking *forever*."

"Pick and Querc are doing good work," Corvus said. "Almost ready."

"Then why not just get out while we can?"

"I would like to know what this Autochthon knows."

And then, for the second time that Prim had seen, Corvus transformed himself into the shape of a man.

"Ugh!" he hawked, when the thing was done. "I hate this. It's why I have *you* people. But where we go next, wings are worse than useless." He borrowed clothes from Mard and Lyne, and put a dagger on his belt for appearances' sake. But for the most part he had no idea what to do with his arms, to say nothing of his hands, and so he strutted about with his thumbs jammed in his belt, just to prevent his upper limbs from flailing.

The new contingent of Beedles made no effort to be subtle about their approach. Quite the opposite, as it was their habit to intone marching chants ("songs" was not quite the right word) to keep in step on the trail. If their purpose was also to intimidate, then it worked. By the time they drew up along the edge of the no-man's-land, just out of the range where archery would be of much use, it was perfectly obvious to all the members of the Quest that they could with ease simply run up the slope, protecting themselves with shields, and take the camp with few if any casualties.

After allowing a few minutes to pass, the sole Autochthon stepped forward, flanked by a couple of shield-bearing Beedles. He had the same fair, fine looks as the officers Prim had met at

Secondel. He came up the slope boldly until Lyne and Prim both nocked arrows. Then he stopped, smiled, and displayed empty hands. "I just hate shouting," he explained.

"We can hear you," said Fern. They'd agreed she would speak for them.

"Thirsty? We have tons of water. Literally tons."

"We are fine, thank you."

"You'd be the smuggler. Fern."

"You may certainly address me as Fern," she allowed.

"I am Harrier. Where's the big crow? He going to peck my eyes out?"

"Taking his ease in the delicious shade, Harrier."

"Is it nice up there? I'm told that if you go too far in, there's a nasty surprise."

"We have used it to bury our dead."

"You've noticed, then, that El's military is taking all of this more seriously than the many voyages you have made along this coast in the past," Harrier said.

"It had not escaped me."

"Perhaps you're associating with the wrong sorts," said Harrier. "I've admired you from a distance—a frustratingly enormous distance—for years. Our futile pursuits of *Silverfin* have been a fine training exercise for our crews. No better way to find out which Beedles still have strength to draw oars and which are ready to be . . . reassigned. This time it's different though."

"Why is it different?"

"Because of the young lady. Presumably the one to your left, glaring at me like a true princess, arrow nocked."

"What of her?"

"No idea. You're not familiar with how the military works, are you? The way it works is that they don't tell me such things unless I need to know. I'm to bring her in. It has been made clear that I am to do so with the utmost politeness and consideration for her feelings and her personal safety—which is why I'm standing out in the hot sun talking to you instead of simply marching up there behind a shield wall. *Nothing* was said to me about *you*, Fern, and so I will be more than happy to convey you, and the young Bufrects for that matter, back to civilization in a cool cabin with a lot of fresh drinking water. Or, you could all die here."

"You keep mentioning water, as if it will wash away our resolve," said Fern. "Since you have so much of it, do you go back to your camp and drink it or bathe in it or pour it over your head or whatever it is you do with such an abundance thereof, and leave us alone to consider matters."

"Very well. We march up this hill at nightfall," said Harrier. "If you make it difficult for us, you'll be the first one into the crack." He turned on his heel and walked away, followed by his two Beedles, who scuttled backward, shields high and eyes sharp.

Pick went through the sample case one drawer at a time, removing tools and instruments, or bits of strange rock, from some drawers and finding ways to secrete them on his person or on Querc's. Other constituents he wistfully left in their assigned places. Then he closed it up and, with visible effort, turned his back on it. "Go ahead," he said to Mard and Lyne, "I know you want to."

The young men dutifully picked it up between them, carried it up to the brink, and one-two-threed it out into the blackness.

Then they took turns descending the rope into the fault. The slope became steeper the farther you went down. They went down to the point where it became a nearly vertical cliff. The waning light of the day, filtering down from above, was of little use at such depth. Pick had rocks that glowed in the dark, but their light seemed to penetrate little more than a hand's breadth.

Their gathering place was a ledge, about a foot wide, that was not visible until you found it with your feet. They all had to wait there until the last of them—Corvus, still in human form—had descended the rope. The final length of this had been doubled over a peg that Pick had driven into the rock some distance above. When Corvus let go of one end of the rope he was able to pull the whole thing around and off the peg.

"*That* should give Harrier some trouble should he decide to follow us!" Pick chortled.

No one bothered pointing out the even greater difficulties it would pose for *them*, should they ever be of a mind to go back. But going back would not have ended well. So they went forward—which meant following the ledge in a direction that took them generally away from the sea. They would all have fallen off the ledge and into the crack in a very short time had Pick not provided a hand rope, fixed to the rock with iron pegs.

Above, Harrier must have suspected something. Or perhaps he simply grew impatient and broke his promise. For they heard the marching chant of the marines, punctuated by clashing of cutlasses on shields, echoing from the ceiling of the Overstrike even as the faint light of dusk still shone on its dangling skeins of birds' nests. It was not possible for them to see up to the brink, which was to their advantage, but they heard the march of the Beedles grow very loud and then falter as a demand for silence made its way up and down the line. After that, nothing but indistinct talking, and the occasional tock-tock-tumble of a stone being projected experimentally over the brink.

"Can they follow us?" Prim—who was second from the rear—asked Corvus, who was behind her. For during her tour of Elkirk she had seen all the different varieties of Beedles that the Autochthons were capable of producing, and she knew that there were many who spent their whole lives down in mines.

By way of an answer, Corvus leaned back, trusting the hand rope, and shone the faint light of his glow-rock at the ledge behind him.

There *was* no ledge behind him.

Prim's feet had been upon it only moments before, but now the surface was featureless. Likewise when Corvus passed the next of those iron rope-pegs he was able to draw it out of the stone as if it were thrust into sand. He handed it to Prim, who passed it on up the line. Some time later they went by the same peg again, fixed firmly into the stone. But ahead of them were no sounds of drilling or hammering. Pick, the Lithoplast, was shaping the adamant fore and aft.

Things in the rear became noisy for a time as Harrier's marines apparently carried many rocks up and rolled them over the brink to kill anyone they supposed to be clinging to the face of the crack below them.

They collected as close together as they could and pressed themselves against the face of the stone, extinguished or hid their lights, and waited. They could hear dimly the Beedles talking far above, and they could distinctly hear boulders rolling and bounding down the slope, picking up terrific velocity before hurtling by. Some seemed to approach directly, as if they would score a direct hit, but those caromed from some kind of overhanging brow that apparently jutted from the cliff directly above them. This held, and made the stones leap far out into the darkness. Prim did not for a moment suppose that it was a natural feature. Pick had prepared it as a refuge. They used it as such until hours had passed since the last hint of light, sound, or falling rocks from above. Then they risked making some noise and lighting some candles.

They moved on into the night for many hours, using the ledge-and-rope scheme. Erasing the ledge behind them apparently required some effort on Pick's part, and so after it seemed they'd put a safe distance between themselves and the Beedles, he gave up on that and just left it there.

So they were going now toward the interior of the Asking, both in the sense of getting farther from the coast *and*, as gradually became impossible to ignore, in the sense of getting deeper belowground. Their movement seemed mostly on the level, but the mountains were ramping higher and higher above them as they moved away from the coast.

Which raised the question of what, if anything, might be coming up from below to meet them. They knew that the fault had not been equipped with a bottom; that once you descended, or fell, beyond a certain depth you entered into the nothingness of chaos. But where was that depth? Was chaos like water, which had everywhere a constant level?

That topic of water was much on Prim's mind, and she knew the others had to be thinking of it as well. They had only brought so much of it with them, and none was to be had on the surface of the Asking. So the only way in which this journey could not lead to their all dying of thirst was if Pick was leading them toward some subterranean spring.

Prim began imagining a hidden cavern, deep belowground,

whose floor was a lake of delicious fresh water, gathered slowly over thousands of years. She wanted it so badly she could smell it. More than that, she could feel its humidity in her nostrils, which had become so accustomed to dry air. And she could hear the teeming of the water—like waves brushing a shore, or rain falling on a lake—condensation, perhaps, dripping down from the cavern's roof? And some kind of faint luminescence emanating from the water itself?

"I see light," Corvus said. "Put out the candle!"

Querc, ahead of them, was carrying it in a lantern. She did not snuff it out but closed the lantern's shutter to make nearly perfect darkness. They rested in silence for a time. Pick let out a long sigh. He must have needed rest more badly than any of them. Prim had no idea how Lithoplasty worked but it obviously required effort.

As their eyes got used to the darkness, there was no question but that they were seeing *something*. But it was diffuse and indistinct, and as usual, opinions varied.

"It is the light of day, far above us," opined Lyne.

"It can't be day yet," Mard objected.

"Time is tricky down here."

"There is no light. It is a trick of the mind," said Fern.

"I'm inclined to agree," said Prim, "since a minute ago my mind was tricking me into dreaming of a lake where waters glowed faintly in a dark cavern."

"That was not just a dream," said Fern, "there is no question I have smelled fresh water. Not all the time. Whiffs of it here and there."

Prim was becoming concerned about Corvus. He had never spent so long in his human form. He had spoken many times of how much he disliked being in confined spaces. He did not like being in the dark or unable to see for a distance. He had now been suffering all of those for a long while. In quiet tones that only Prim could hear, he kept insisting that he saw a light ahead of them—either showing them the way or beguiling them into a trap. She was more and more certain that Corvus was not in his right mind. But she kept smelling lake water where quite obviously it was not possible for a lake to exist, so who was she to judge?

All of these considerations became moot when they traversed

round a bend and came in view of an expanse of frank open chaos that after those hours in total darkness seemed as big and bright to them as the night sky above the desert, and as loud as a waterfall. But it was more brilliant and more lively than the dim and almost imperceptible stuff that Pick had kept in his adamant drawer. Light shone from this, or rather shone through it, here and there at different times. It would flare in one place and draw their gaze, and it would seem for a moment that they could almost perceive forms in it. Then the light would flee as if it knew it was being looked at. At all times this was happening not only in one place but in several, more often than not in the corner of one's eye.

"There is a floor beneath it!" Pick affirmed. In the patches of light beaming out of the chaos they could see him wading out away from the wall of the fault. "Pluto caused it to be here, for this place was important to him and he passed through it often."

"Passed . . . *through* it?" Lyne asked. He was cautiously following Querc, who was following Pick. The rest of the party did likewise. Prim understood how the conception had entered her mind of a luminescent, hissing lake in the darkness. The chaos was below as well as above them, so it was as if they were wading into a pool whose bottom could not be seen, but only felt by groping with the feet.

"There she is! Showing us the way!" Corvus exclaimed.

"She?" Prim asked. She had become distracted by a distinct whiff of pine forest.

"The light that moves!" Corvus said. His voice was changing midsentence—less human, more birdlike.

"Does anyone smell wood smoke?" Mard asked.

Corvus was now a giant talking raven again. Which seemed most impractical. "You don't understand," he said. "To get out of here we must have a guide star!"

Prim was now pretty sure she saw what he was seeing—and it was no star. It was indistinct, but female, with wings.

"Get me a rope end!" Corvus commanded. "And hold on for dear life!"

As it happened, ropes were practically the only thing they had left. Mard heaved a coil off of his shoulder, groped for its end, and held it up. Corvus snatched it in one talon as he flew by, then veered off in pursuit of the glowing will-o'-the-wisp. "Hurry! And stay together! All hands on the rope no matter what!"

As it turned out, the only one of those commands that Prim, for her part, was able to obey was the last. Keeping both hands on the rope was the only thing she could hold in her head during what came next. The notion of *hurry* meant nothing when time and distance had ceased to make sense, which became the case immediately when she tried to go where Corvus had gone. Staying together meant nothing at all. Not only did she not know where the others were, she did not even remember their names. All became pure chaos more than once. Sometimes there was nothing at all save the rope in her hand, and she had no way of guessing whether those times might have spanned centuries or mere heartbeats.

The first clear and steady sensation that came to her senses was that smell of lake water she'd caught whiffs of earlier. That, and the rope still in her hand. Light obtruded itself next, and it was steady light always in the same place. Hard ground was then under her feet. This had a natural unevenness, unlike the flat ledge made by Pick. Dark shapes interrupted the light: the silhouettes of a person and of a large bird.

All of those became constant enough that she was fairly certain of walking along a cave, headed toward its exit—which was the source of the light. And of the fragrance: the sharp scents of pine trees and burning wood, underlain by the heavier and more subtle aroma of lake water and of something that powerfully brought her in mind of Calla: leaves that had but lately fallen from trees and were lying damp and red on the earth.

All that surrounded her had now grown solid and real. There was no trace of chaos save the fog that was still beclouding her mind. But some of that was simple confusion as to where she was. The stony ground had many small ups and downs, but on the whole it ran gently downhill.

The cave broadened as they went along. The light that blazed into its entrance was as bright as the midday sun on the Asking, but far more inconstant; one moment it would shine directly into their faces, forcing them to fling up hands or arms to shield their eyes, the next it would be a darkness like the one they had just emerged from—yet with rays and glints stabbing and hurtling out of its midst. Prim noticed that the rope had gone limp in her hand. In a moment when a beam of light swept across the cavern's floor, she saw it lying on the ground. Pick had dropped it. He had slowed. The others had piled up behind him and formed a crowd. Their silhouettes fractured the unruly light. They had stopped some yards short of the cave's mouth. Beyond it, Prim could see between the others' legs a flat wrinkled surface that glittered when light flashed upon it. Recent events caused her to think at first that it might be another pool of chaos, but then the sun seemed to come out for a moment. Stepping into a space between Mard and Querc she got her first good look at what lay beyond the mouth of the cave and understood with perfect clarity that it was a lake. Its near shore washed the floor of this cave directly before them.

In the middle distance, a bow-shot away, a sandbar extended across the water from their left, evidently connecting an unseen part of the lakeshore to a rocky islet that rose out of the water to a height of a few yards. It supported a few mature trees whose seeds had been carried to it by birds or wind. One of them was fully engulfed in flame. Another had been snapped off at about the height of a man's shoulder; its upper part, still attached to the shattered stump by tortured splinters as thick as a man's arm, was bent over and down into the water.

The light of the burning tree was weak and pale by comparison with what shone nearby. The sky beyond and above was dark, with stars visible here and there, and a faint pink glow off to their right; the dawn was coming.

She heard the din of clashing arms, and a shout. A radiant bolt swung round, leaving a meteor trail across her vision, and veered downward, only to be stopped in its course by a darker obstacle that somehow withstood the impact and whipped away from the collision as if it had drawn power from it and was now pursuing intentions of its own. The light was eclipsed for a time by a silhouette; this had arms and legs like an ordinary soul, but it also had wings.

Pick's reason for going no farther was clear enough now; they had stumbled upon a fight, and at least one of the combatants was an angel. The prudent course was to stay well back. Prim shouldered past him, though, and strode on. She could hear, between clashes of weapons, Mard calling to her, but she paid him no heed. Her view of things improved as she neared the cave's mouth and she saw that the angel's opponent was Burr. He was armed not with a sword but with a long spear, which he whirled about him to block the angel's attacks; when an opportunity presented itself he would seek to punch the angel with the spear's heavy iron butt or slash with its sharp head.

She came full out on the lakeshore and felt the cold water soaking her boots. To her right a formation of gray stone ramped up to terminate one side of the lake in a sheer cliff. More caves were in it. To her left the stone gave way to a flat beach that not far away curved back to make the sandbar. Prim went that way, striding across the sand at first and then breaking into a run as the grunts and cries of Burr made her fear that he could not much longer hold out against the angel's onslaughts.

Before she could get onto the sandbar, though, she drew up short in the face of a new kind of soul who had darted in to block her way. This gave off light too, though nothing like the radiance of the angel's sword. The whole creature stood about a foot high, though she would have stood a few inches higher had her legs not terminated as stumps below the knees. What she lacked in that way she more than made up for with a set of wings that she used to dart and flicker through the air with far greater skill than Corvus could ever seem to manage. This was, in other words, the soul that had found them in the dark fault beneath the Asking and showed them the way here—wherever *here* might be. "Do not," she implored Prim. "Do not exercise that power that is yours, here and now, for then El will know that you have entered into the Land, and his bright angels will descend upon us in their thousands."

Part of Prim wanted to ask what was the point of owning such a power if it was never to be used, but she was distracted, now that she was standing still, by a curious sensation transmitted into the soles of her feet from the ground.

In a way it was but a faint reverberation, and yet it came over and over again, with quickening pace, and the fact that it was shaking the ground itself bespoke some great power behind it. The fight on the islet had bated for a few moments as the combatants, drawn apart to a safe distance, caught their breath. The angel's sword was making a fiery road across the lake between him and Prim, as when the sun sets across a great water. Within it she could see ripples that coincided with the thuds she felt in her legs.

The sprite lacked that connection to the ground and so was slower to sense it. Perhaps she was now alerted by those ripples, or by the snapping of thick branches that could be heard in the forest spreading away from the shore of the lake. She beat her wings several times and shot directly upward to a great height as if to survey the area, then dove toward the forest. She pulled up before getting involved in the trees and veered back toward the place where the sandbar was rooted to the beach. Her light grew brighter. Prim got the idea that she was both lighting the way and acting as a guide star for whatever was coming through the woods and shaking the ground with those heavy footfalls.

A sudden shifting of the light told her that the angel had brandished his sword. Turning to look at the islet, Prim saw that the angel had risen from kneeling and partly unfurled his wings. He had felt what Prim had felt and was looking toward the shore of the lake.

A small tree fell over near the shore; this was clearly visible in the illumination cast by the sprite.

A moment later Edda emerged from the woods. She was not quite running, but striding briskly, and each footfall shook the ground and discomposed the water. She crossed the beach in a few strides and started walking up the sandbar toward the islet.

Prim, for her part, had been expecting something like a hill-giant, or at least one of the enormous wild beasts with which Spring had populated the forests of the north. That it was Edda made sense to her, of course; but she could not help looking at the angel to see *his* reaction. Did it make sense to *him*? Did angels *know* about giantesses and wild souls and talking ravens and sprites? Were they taught about such things in some kind of angel academy? Were they omniscient? Or did El prevent them from knowing about such prodigies, so as to better control them?

Halfway along the sandbar, a young tree got in Edda's way. She put her shoulder into it and it went down. Its entire root ball emerged from the loose ground and she kicked it into the lake. This did not go unwatched by the angel, who now spread his wings wider and bent his knees, preparing to spring into the air.

Burr had other plans. With a great swing of his spear he severed the angel's right wing from his shoulder. It fell to the ground gushing aura. A moment later the other joined it.

Staggered and unbalanced by the loss of those appendages, the angel was barely able to raise his sword by the time Edda strode onto the islet. In spite of the fact that there was a foe to his side who had just inflicted grievous damage upon him, the angel chose to face, and to brandish his sword at, the unarmed woman coming directly for him. He raised it on high above his head, poised to bring down a killing blow.

Burr rang down one of his own, severing both of the angel's arms between wrists and elbows. The sword fell back onto the stone and clattered and scraped its way down into the waters of the lake, which did not extinguish it but now glowed from within.

Edda spread her arms wide. She wore a long cloak that hung from them like dark wings. Without slowing her pace she met the angel with the full front of her body and embraced him, shrouding his form in her garment.

By the time Prim had run up the sandbar to the islet, all trace of the angel's form was gone. Edda was there, looking like Edda.

"Welcome to Lost Lake," she said. "You'll be thirsty."

Burr was squatting on his heels, elbows on his knees, face in his hands, too tired to move or to speak. Lying on the ground next to him, barely visible in the rose glow of the northern dawn, was his spear, and its shaft was made of smoke.

"*You* seem to have found it," Lyne objected, when Edda told him the name of the place.

Ferhuul did not care for Lyne's wit. "And *you* seem to have popped out of a magic hole in the ground. Easy, was it?"

Footsteps, terminated by a crunching thud, signaled the return of Burr, who had come out of the woods bent under a bundle of firewood. It was all fallen dead timber, collected in silence with no use of axe or maul.

"No," Lyne admitted, "it was not easy."

"One day," said Weaver, "if we all get out of this, I will combine your story of the Asking with ours of the Bewilderment, and sing it as one epic song, and I daresay that the two parts of it might contain a like number of verses."

The East Cloven contingent had somehow managed to recruit a magical sprite, whom they addressed by the name Mab. Such a being figured into certain tellings of the tale of Adam and Eve, so if this was the same Mab, then seeking her out and persuading her to join the Quest might have been every bit as strange and perilous as what the *Firkin* group had got up to. Somewhere along the line they had furthermore acquired a magical spear with a shaft that appeared to be literally made out of black smoke and that was impervious to blows from angel swords. Where had *that* come from?

Moreover these people had crossed the entirety of the Lake Lands from East Cloven to Lost Lake. All that Prim really knew of the Bewilderment was that going there was inadvisable, because many who went in did not come out. Survivors who did straggle out to one of the chilly seaports along the Backhaul spoke not of wild beasts or lawless brigands—though those certainly existed—but of an endless maze of lakes connected to other lakes by flat streams meandering through mushy land where one could neither walk nor paddle. *Bewilderment.* Fish and game were plentiful, fresh water everywhere, and so a person with a few skills could live there indefinitely—they just couldn't leave.

"Most people who come here only wish to get out," Ferhuul said. "*These* lot are the only ones I have ever met who wanted to go deeper in, ever deeper, and that has presented challenges I did not come well prepared for." He cast a look toward Edda, then glanced significantly at the place on the beach at the mouth of the cave where they had beached their canoes. It was out of the question that Edda could set foot in anything so small and frail. She must have walked, finding an overland route that somehow kept abreast of the movements of the canoes—and that had got her to Lost Lake just in time.

"Did you get any help from Mab?" Prim asked. "She was of great help to us in finding *our* way."

"We only just met her," Ferhuul said. "She haunts this place."

He looked back over his shoulder across Lost Lake. The sun had risen an hour ago and they had taken the risk of kindling this fire. They had done so in the mouth of the cave. This afforded them some shelter as well as giving them a place into which they could retreat should they once again come under attack.

Fern had recovered the angel's sword from the bottom of the lake by stripping off her clothes and diving deep for it. It had plunged like a dart and half-embedded itself in the stony bottom. Blinded by its brilliance, she had swum back to the surface with her eyes closed and carefully handed it hilt-first to Mard, who had found its dark scabbard discarded on the ground near the scene of the fight. Thus shrouded, the weapon was now leaning against a boulder nearby. Fern, still shivering, was squatting against the cavern wall near it, wrapped in blankets and drinking from a mug of soup Edda had given her. Absent was the usual Fernish brusqueness, the impatience that sometimes seemed like outright disdain. The passage through chaos, the angel fight, the intervention of sprite and giantess, the spear of smoke, and the sword forged by Thingor: these were the sorts of prodigies she had been fruitlessly questing after since one such had revealed itself in the sea and taken her family from her. She had flirted with twelve kinds of death and found satisfaction.

"That angel was extraordinarily brave, or reckless, or ill informed," Edda said. "This is a place of terror to the servants of El."

This naturally made Prim's scalp prickle. "Why?" she asked. She turned to Weaver. "What is to be found in this place that is so dangerous to them?"

"You," Weaver said.

. . .

None of the members of the *Firkin* contingent was in a mood to climb mountains. But after they had rested in the entrance of the cave, slaked their thirst with sweet lake water, and eaten of the provisions that Ferhuul and the others had brought in their canoes, they did venture out onto the beach and climb for a little distance up onto the formation of gray rock from which they had emerged and that formed the abrupt southern shore of Lost Lake. The forest was a mixture of dark evergreens such as they had seen from *Firkin* while sailing between far northern Bits, and deciduous trees familiar to those who had spent many falls on Calla. The latter were still mostly green but touched with flame in their upper branches. Enough red and orange leaves had already fallen to cover the ground with a patchy smear of color, like paint scraped over bone. The smell of those fallen leaves spoke more powerfully to Prim than any book or song.

Before their tired muscles and sore joints could put up too much of a fuss, they emerged into an open space near the top of the cliffs above the lake. To the north they had a clear view across Lost Lake and the Bewilderment, which, according to the map, extended all the way to the distant northern rim of the Land. This was pretty enough with its colorful trees sprinkled across rolling hills, and blue water pooling in the bottomlands, but they had already heard enough about it that they did not gaze on it longer than it took to take some pleasure in the prospect. Then they turned their backs on the Bewilderment and looked south.

For some while it was impossible for them to look at or care about anything other than the storm that, seen from here, constituted most of the southern sky. In that quarter of the world there was no horizon, since the boundary between the sky and the Land was hidden behind gray curtains and skirts of rain, wreathed in mist and bejeweled with silent flashes and twisting whips of lightning. The under-surface of the Evertempest was flat, though here and there, whirling convolutions above resolved into spinning formations below that extended, slowly and inexorably, until they punched into the ground. Those would scour the surface of the Land for a while, rooting around like pigs in the dark, then grow narrow and frail before dissolving. The main body of the storm was a stacked, churning architecture of wind-driven cloud, black and silver, riven with long horizontal bolts of lightning that could not but remind them of the angel's sword. At its top—which according to legend was of equal height with the Palace of El, hundreds of miles to its south—the storm extended a long sharp horn like that of an anvil. Cloudbursts heavy enough to inundate any city in the Land fell from high shelves of cloud only to be swallowed by lower parts of the storm before they could get within miles of the ground.

The Calla people, as well as Querc and Fern, had been reading or hearing of this thing their whole lives but had never seen it. So there was nothing to be done for a while but let them drink it in, much as they had earlier sated themselves with lake water. Then, however, they began to lower their gaze to examine the territory ahead.

If the tangle of mountains that lay beneath the storm were a tree, and the tree had thrown out roots of an ancient gnarled character, and those roots were made of stone, and reached greater or lesser distances from the trunk, then the farthest flung of them all, at least on this northern side, was the one that finally plunged into the ground at the shore of this lake. They were standing on its utmost tendril. It was at least partly hollow. And though Pick had not yet gone to the trouble of coming right out and saying as much, all who had descended into the fault in the Asking, only to emerge here, understood that Pluto had, in the waning years of the First Age, explored these deeps and connected them with roads of chaos so that he might more easily make his way from one part of the Land to another without having to trudge across all of the intervening ground. To follow those roads without going astray and losing oneself in unknown realms was subtle and dangerous, but Pick knew how to find their beginnings and Mab knew how to trace them to safe ends.

The canoes were laden with goods and victuals that they now unloaded on the shore of the lake. A lot of the cargo consisted of clothing; lacking very much of it, the *Firkin* contingent simply put that on. The remainder they distributed among packs that they could carry on their backs or suspend from poles that two could carry between them on their shoulders.

Pick was of a mind to explore the several other cave entrances that could easily be seen from here, but Corvus literally bristled at that suggestion. "It would take forever," he said. "Mab assures us they do not lead where we wish to go. Now that you know how to find this place you can come back here later, after we have saved the world, and do all of that."

"If our purpose is to save the world," said Ferhuul, "this is the first I have been made aware of it."

"Yes," said Lyne, "you might have mentioned it earlier."

"Oh, come on!" said Fern. "It's perfectly obvious. Has been all along."

"Sometimes I must express myself in few words," said Corvus, "so that these Quest councils don't go on forever. If 'save the world' is objectionable I can expand on it. Doing so wouldn't help. Things are wrongly set up in the Land now, as anyone who has seen what we have lately seen would agree. Even if you can't quite put your finger on it, I think you'd have to admit it's not how a proper god would compose a world. It is not going to fix itself. That is probably why I came here from the other plane of existence. Things were set in motion there that it is my purpose to see through here. Stop arguing."

"What does seeing them through *mean*, exactly?" Lyne inquired, in a most polite and agreeable tone, to emphasize that he was not arguing.

"I don't know," Corvus admitted, "but I think we are all going to be glad that Ferhuul had the presence of mind to bring warm dry clothing. Our road runs south into the Stormland."

"You're saying," said Prim, "that we are going to the Fastness. You want to penetrate the storm and break into the Fastness."

"It has just been sitting there since the Fall of the Old Gods," said Corvus in an almost defensive tone.

"Just the other day," Lyne pointed out, "we sat and listened— very patiently, I might add—to a song from Weaver explaining that it's locked up behind magical chains and such."

"Anyway, no one can get anywhere near that thing," Weaver

objected. "The Expedition of Lord Stranath couldn't even get within *sight* of it."

"According to that one survivor, sure!" Corvus said. "But he turned tail and ran home when the Lightning Bears sprang their ambush. Not even halfway to the Precipice, which according to the Dark Codex is the first vantage point from which it's possible to even glimpse the inmost convolutions of the Knot."

"The Dark Codex blinds any person who reads it," Weaver scoffed.

"You have to set it up in a mirror and read it backward," Edda put in.

"Oh."

"And I'm not exactly a person," Corvus added. "Look, we have to go there—it is the entire point of the Quest—and we have many advantages compared to Lord Stranath. We will not be tackling the Lightning Bears, and the Vortex Wraiths are overrated."

"I've never heard of *them*," said Weaver. Behind her back, Mard and Lyne exchanged satisfied looks.

"Then the less said, the better. Coming to the Fastness? Our way lies south, on the surface for now. Abandoning the Quest? There are some perfectly serviceable canoes awaiting you just there."

"And the whole Bewilderment to cross," cracked Lyne to Mard.

"I can cross it," Ferhuul pointed out, "as I have just demonstrated. And cross it again is what I am going to do now. Any of you is welcome to come with me."

They all looked at him. After a few moments, he shrugged. "The only reason people like Weaver know enough of Lord Stranath to sing songs about him is because one of his company 'turned tail and ran home' when that struck him as intelligent. Such a moment has now arrived for me. You are all mad. I have seen all I care to see of angels and such. Farewell, and please look me up in East Cloven if you make it out, and sing your songs."

No one else showed interest in the Bewilderment. So once they had helped Ferhuul go on his way, paddling north in the stern of his canoe, they began the journey south. From here all was mountain and storm; but, for now, they knew which way to go.

53

When El came in glory and flung Egdod, and the Pantheon, and the old souls loyal to them, into the outer darkness, they kindled red fires on the blackness of the Firmament where they struck it," said Weaver. "Not wishing that El and all the other souls of the Land should gaze upon their humiliation every night when the Red Web rose in the eastern sky, Egdod drew a veil of smoke and steam across its face. What goes on behind that veil is ever a mystery to us."

The campfire had burned down to red coals, glowing clear and sharp in the night. Weaver was attempting to draw a poetic contrast between them and the Red Web, which was putting in an appearance above the eastern horizon just as she said. It was going to be a fleeting appearance, since its arc would soon take it behind the eternal storm looming to the south.

Querc, Mard, and Lyne were looking back and forth between the embers of the fire and the constellation as if Weaver's point made all kinds of sense to them, but to Prim the two did not look much different: both were clear and crisp as the lightning bolts that occasionally fractured the thunderheads. She saw no benefit in pointing this out.

Mard, perhaps remembering their uneasy conversation on the Asking, glanced at her. When she pretended not to notice, he gave her a more searching look. Then a huge bolt illuminated the whole camp for a moment with sharp blue-white light. She looked back at him and he glanced away.

Querc rose to the bait. "Growing up in the southern desert I heard songs and tales of these parts," she said, "but many scoffed that they were superstitions of frostbitten northerners."

"You are about to walk into one of those superstitions," said Weaver. "Some call it the Madness of Spring."

"I saw the phrase once, in an old book I was copying," said Querc, "and remembered it because of its strangeness. But that is all I know of it."

"Strange indeed," said Weaver. "I shall say more of it tomorrow, as we are marching into it."

"I think we're already there," Mard said. "When I was gathering firewood, I'm fairly certain a tree tried to kill me—and a squirrel put him up to it."

"Singing that song would wake everyone up," said Weaver, showing what some members of the Quest might have considered uncharacteristic consideration for those of her traveling companions who were fond of peace and quiet. "Tomorrow. The point is, be careful of anything that is alive."

"This is one of those songs that begins right in the middle," said Weaver the next morning, after they had got under way and found a solid marching rhythm. Or, in the cases of those who didn't march, settled into a flight pattern apparently meant to scan the path ahead of them while keeping an eye peeled for airborne threats. Corvus was of the view that no force in the Land short of a battalion of angels would dare take them on; but he was nervous anyway, and would be until they got beneath the Evertempest, after which he would be nervous for different reasons.

At some point between Cloven and Lost Lake, Weaver had modified her kit. During the journey's first phase, from the Hall of the Calladons to West Cloven, she'd been carrying a couple of flutes and a harp that required so much tuning that it was useless. Those were gone now, and in their place she had an instrument called a Road Organ. Though to refer to it as a single instrument was to understate its ambition, for it comprised several devices that looked to have been crafted in different historical epochs by artisans with clashing views as to what the point was.

The preparations involved in grappling this thing to Weaver just after breakfast and checking out its various systems had led to a lot of foreboding and dreadful glances between Mard and Lyne.

Even Prim, who enjoyed Weaver's singing, set forth on the day's journey with a certain amount of trepidation as to the scale and duration of the planned entertainments. But when Weaver began to play some little marching ditties on the Road Organ, Prim thought that they blended so naturally into the mood of the place that it wasn't at all like enduring a performance.

They were hiking very slightly uphill, and as they gained altitude, dark evergreens supplanted leafy sorts of trees. The latter were now in the full brilliant color of the fall, just at the point when enough leaves were on the ground to paint it with reds, purples, yellows, and oranges that had not yet faded. Yet enough were still clinging to the trees that the branches did not look bare. Walking all day through such gaudy color would have inured them to it. But as they went on, dark stands of evergreens were more and more frequently interspersed with the deciduous trees, so that when they would top a ridge or traverse round the flank of a hill and suddenly come in view of a deciduous stand, they had it in them to be surprised and delighted all over again by its glory. The leaves called to Prim in a way she did not understand, and she kept picking individual ones off the ground and gazing at length into the subtle and tiny variegations in their color and the repeating patterns in their veins, shot like branched lightning through the flesh of a cloud. Weaver's improvisations on the Road Organ were in harmony with this hypnotic condition of mind. To the point where Prim was somewhat discomposed—almost offended—when Weaver began to talk.

"Now, if you were one of the sorts of souls to whom this was originally sung, you'd already know the first part. Namely that the vast scope of work entailed in converting the Fastness into an ironbound prison for Egdod reverberated all through the Land, as Beedles went here and there to mine in places where Pluto had deemed it good to situate ore, and Autochthons ventured into remote and wild places to recruit hill-giants and make them into blacksmiths, or to round up and enslave great beasts of burden. It didn't last for long—perhaps three falls—but it touched all parts of the Land. And so at last Spring came to know of it. She did not know at first the nature of the undertaking, but she could see well enough that it was affecting her creations. Trees that she had planted were being toppled to build ore wagons, and beasts she had created with the intention that they should roam free upon the Land were being yoked together under the whips of Beedle teamsters. Starting from a very remote place in the Asking—where she had been trying to create plants and animals more capable of dwelling in that harsh place—she began to make her way in toward the center, following wheel ruts of ore caravans, footprints of migrating giants, carpets of tree stumps.

"By the time she at last came under the Evertempest, El had finished his work and pitched the key off the Precipice. He and his angels and the Autochthons were already long gone. Beedles were marching away in long columns, headed back to the places whence they had been mustered. Hill-giants, released from bondage, were stomping about aimlessly. Beasts of burden, no longer needed for anything, had simply been turned loose in harsh country where forage was scarce. Spring by then had come to understand that Egdod had returned to the Land, not just once but many times, and had roamed up and down it in diverse guises looking for her to no avail."

The ground shook beneath their feet, and not just with the footfalls of Edda, to which they had grown accustomed. Because of the nature of Weaver's narration, more than a few of them were predisposed to interpret it as the approach of something really bad. Mab flinched and fluttered. But then a long chortling rumble reached their ears and they understood that they were now close enough to the Evertempest that they could hear its thunder as well as see its lightning. Burr, who had put a second hand on the smoky haft of his weird spear, let go and went back to using it as a walking stick.

"Get used to *that*," Corvus suggested.

Lyne, once he had got over the brief fright occasioned by the thunderclap, was back on the topic of Weaver's story. "No wonder the Asking is still such a shithole," he said.

"You could almost say god-forsaken," Mard responded.

"*Gods*, plural," said Querc, with a glance toward Pick. "Remember Pluto ditched out on it too."

"We may yet come to wish that Spring had been as careless of these parts," said Edda. Not in a notably fearful way. More of an observation.

Prim caught Corvus looking at her. "Yes," he said, "get ready to kill things." Burr, Mard, and Lyne each fondled their weapons. Burr had claimed the angel's sword but did not risk his companions' eyesight by drawing it even a finger's breadth from its scabbard. He contented himself with patting its hilt. But Prim knew that Corvus had been talking to her.

Fern well knew where her cutlass and dagger were to be found, and so kept her arms crossed in front of her. She was eyeing a tree, not far off, that stood dead and black at the top of a rise. Lightning had carved a charred spiral from its top to its roots and blown its bark off.

"We're there already, aren't we?" Fern asked. When no one answered, she glanced at Edda and Weaver and saw that it was true. For the rest of them, she explained: "In the Stormland. Oh, I know it isn't raining, that the wind is light and that patches of clear sky are to be seen. But that is always how it is when you are in the midst of a wild tempest. It's not wild all the time. Moments like this one come and go."

"We have been in it all day," Corvus confirmed, "and merely been lucky so far."

Lightning flashed behind a veil of cloud. Prim noticed that Mab disappeared altogether; she was a thing of light, who in brighter light was shown to have no solidity whatsoever.

Weaver had begun flapping her arms as if she too wished to take flight. But she stayed earthbound. She was operating bellows. Air hissed from leaks in the Road Organ's plumbing. A rosined wheel whirred as it spun up. Weaver opened a valve that conducted air to a low drone pipe, and made a small adjustment to a string that caused the rosin-covered wheel to saw at it and emit another, higher tone that harmonized with the drone. Whether by accident or craft, this was timed so that the peal of thunder rolled in just a moment later, creating the impression that Weaver was making use of the Evertempest as a percussion instrument. She began to sing in the somewhat outlandish haunting tonalities that Prim associated with the seagoing bards of the northern Bits.

O'er the high fells of the Knot-lands she strayed
In search of the home that her lover had made
Though battered by thunder and lashed by the rain
Lured on by the hope she might see him again.
"Egdod, my only, first god of the Land,
Fly to me, darling, reach for my hand,
Roam with me, lover, o'er the hills that you made,
Where forests I've planted and green meadows laid."
Birds and bees were her family, wild lands her home,
And so aimlessly, over the Land she had roamed,
For thousands of Falls; but lately she'd learned
That her dear one, long lost, to the Land had returned.
"Lord of the Firmament, answer my call!
Heal the sundering rift of the Fall!
Together we'll bide in this world of our making,
All cares of the Palace and strangers forsaking."
Southward across the Bewilderment strode,
Its riddles to her as plain as a road.
Ravening beasts came friendly and meek
To sniff at Spring's hand and to lick at her cheek.
As nothing to her was the rage of the storm.
Much as she'd rather be cozy and warm,
She knew that ahead of her, deep in the Knot,
Was a place she'd once visited, never forgot,
And doubtless be welcome in: Egdod's retreat,
Where soon enough she could repair, drink, and eat.
Hearth to dry out her hair and to warm up her face,
Then a long night wrapped up in her lover's embrace.
Thus the fond fancy that beckoned Spring on,
Blind to the traces of those who had gone
Earlier there, in vast force arrayed,
The Knot mutilated, the Fastness remade.
The path shifted beneath her, the Precipice yawned,
But was nothing to Spring, who pressed quicker on.
Came at last to where roots grew together
Of mountain-chains, ancient and scarred by the weather.
Whence a lightning-flash brighter than day

Lit up a vista that to Spring's dismay
Was not what she'd hoped for. A fell prison
In place of the Fastness had risen.
Like a proud warrior, who, taken in fight,
Swarmed under by foes and reduced to the plight
Of a captive, with collar and chain,
His courage and beauty made perfectly vain,
The Fastness of Egdod, bright ornament there
In the deeps of the Knot and the turbulent air
Had been ruined. Not by breaking it down,
But despoiling its nature, lashing it round
With crude shackles. Bright airy Towers
Now lidded with iron, 'neath which gardens of flowers
Spring had once put there to make a fair park
Must be dead, brown petals, seeking light, finding dark.
Heavy upon the grim prison's front gate
Sign of El's victory and seal 'pon the fate
Of him captive, depended a lock
There to stay. There to mock
Any who came to this pass armed with hope.
There to mock Spring, if she thought she could open
That door. In old times El's captive, when Adam and Eve
Were growing inside her, then suffered to leave
Without her two children, Spring understood better
Than anyone how strict were those fetters.
How fell the enchantments such that only one key,
Precious trophy of El, could ever set Egdod free.
Horror drove Spring from that place once so fair,
Now so abominable. Sparks pervaded her hair
As she recklessly fled, borne on storm's wings,
Her only thought vengeance against the bright King
And to peel from the Usurper's dead hand
The key that would set Egdod free in the land.
Halfway down, though, Spring encountered a bard
The Autochthons had sent off riding toward
Parts of the Land where descendants of Eve
Therefore of Spring herself, given leave

To exist round the Land's wild rim,
Egdod remembered, still hoped for him
One day to return, the Fall to undo,
El to throw down, rulership true
To establish, peace with all folk
If they wanted it, once free from El's yoke.
The grim charge of this minstrel being to spread
In such reaches the news that, though he was not dead,
Egdod might just as well be. News she told first
To Spring, when, telling the tale, she saved worst
For last: that Lord El in his spite
Had hurled the one key down into the night
Deep and eternal of chaos, from which fate
Naught returned. Spring was too late.
Too feeble for Spring's grief were tears.
She went mad, and stayed mad for years.
Raged over the Knot-lands and country around,
To pinnacles lofty and chasms profound.
Spurned likewise that body in which she had dwelled
And roamed everywhere. It would never be held
In the arms of her lover, so could not please
Her, hadn't in it her anguish to ease.
Shaped herself after, came one with the Storm,
Whose energies can't be confined to one form,
But rampantly lash out and whirl and stray
As they burgeon and propagate every which way.
When air, Spring was lightning, making night into day
As her bright tendrils out from her aura would stray.
When water, a cataract, sundering hills
And emptying rivers that Pluto had filled.
When earth, Spring was adamant, throwing up walls
Traps and hazards, El's troops to appall.
When fire, a forge, smelting stones into steel
To arm vengeant legions that in time she'd reveal.
For the greatest by far of all of Spring's powers
Was to make life: not just birds, bees, and flowers,
But as well dreadful beasts armed with talon and horn

Who, when they mated, could make more to be born
And so on and so forth: which explained why El hated
Her, and all of her progeny, and never abated
His strife against Adam and Eve, and all of the Sprung
In so many battles of which stories are sung.
The task that Spring set herself, mad though she was,
Was to retake the Land and kill El. And because
El had warriors, she needed ones stronger,
More vicious, more swift, standing tall, marching longer.
And so in the depths of the wilderness fort
Spring set to work making beasts of a sort
So terrible . . .

"Hang on," said Lyne. "Have you, Weaver, given any consideration to the effect that you are having on morale?"

"It's okay," said Weaver. "Eve shows up. Calms Spring down before things go too far. You'll see." And she drew breath to continue the stanza, but then she was interrupted again, this time by Pick.

"Are you that bard, Weaver?" he asked. "The one who encountered Spring in the wilderness and gave her the news that drove her mad?"

"I believe so," said Weaver, and looked to Edda, who nodded to confirm it. "Since then I have passed on several times, and in my mind the distinction is not always perfectly clear between what I saw with my own eyes and what I later heard of from other bards. But the Madness of Spring I know well. For it is a rare song in which the storyteller is part of the story."

A few minutes later, Weaver was struck by a lightning bolt and vaporized. The surviving members of the party scarce had time to become shocked by this turn of events before the sky turned nearly black. At first some of them looked to Fern, as one who had survived a lot of strange weather, but she was too fascinated by what was going on in the sky to be of much use. Corvus was busy changing himself into human form, maybe reckoning wings and feathers would only get torn off by whatever was going to occur next. Mab seemed unconcerned; Prim had a clue as to why, which was that she might not have a body at all. But she was in some form of communication with Edda that no one else was privy to. Edda thus became the leader of the Quest, at least for now. She conducted them down a slope that they normally might not have descended in such haste. A knuckle of bedrock protruded from the soil; they barely glimpsed it before a plank of wind struck them from behind and they all fell down, went blind, and became thoroughly drenched in a few moments' time. Completely unaffected were Edda and Mab. The latter showed the way while Edda helped the others into a niche beneath that outcropping of stone. This afforded but a little shelter, however it grew larger as Pick sculpted it and the others dug into the earth and flung it out to be snatched from the air and sluiced away by the rain.

By the time they had thereby gained some small measure of comfort and begun to feel a bit of satisfaction, the storm abated—not in the sense of slowly dying away. It just stopped, and the sky turned green. Not a muddy pea-soup green but the green of thick moss on a wet rock when a beam of sunlight strikes it. This was extraordinarily beautiful, but peculiar enough that it did not make anyone especially keen on venturing out from cover. Which was good, because when their ears adjusted—which took a little while because of the recent detonation, at close range, of Weaver—they heard something that sounded very dangerous and large.

"What is that crackling?" Querc shouted. She referred to an element of the sound that put them in mind of a pig chewing up dry acorns.

"Tree trunks snapping," Edda said. Then, noting the effect on the others' faces: "Oh, it is much too big to be a Vortex Wraith. This is just a tornado."

In a way, though, this set them at ease, since if all of those snapping noises really were tree trunks, then the thing snapping them had to be terrifically enormous and hence far away.

The storm later hit one more time, as bad as the first, with an aftershock following that. Finding no lack of downed tree branches they kindled a large fire—really more of a wall of flame—just downslope of the shelter rock, and dried things out. No one was feeling proud of the distance they had covered from last night's camp, but it was clear that they were done for the day; even if the storm had not occurred, a decent respect for the memory of their bard would have dictated a stop. As Corvus pointed out, after changing back into a giant talking raven, they needed to get used to a new set of hazards. Angels were not going to come here. Egdod himself had made the Evertempest to prevent winged souls from pestering him, and according to legend only he and Freewander could traverse these skies. Autochthons and Beedles were unlikely to pursue them into a wilderness that mad Spring had populated with creatures whose purpose was to kill Autochthons and Beedles. So the Quest could move in the open, and they could light all the huge fires they pleased, and fear other things.

"Could someone please say more about the Lightning Bears?" Querc pleaded, as it got dark—not because of a storm but because the sun went down—and the fire was raked into a more compact shape and dried clothes repacked. "Because they were mentioned in passing the other day. I know nothing of them but the name causes me a certain amount of trepidation." To judge from the look on her face, she was forcing herself to understate, as much as she could, the force of her emotions on this topic. Prim, who sometimes found Querc annoying, and who was frankly jealous of the intimacy the girl shared with Lyne, suddenly felt empathy for her. In Querc's mind, the Quest might have been done and dusted when they had performed the prodigious feat of descending into a fault in one part of the Land and popping out of a cave somewhere else to watch a giantess kill an angel. And really, what sane soul *wouldn't* be satisfied, after all of that, with going home and living a quiet life?

No one had really explained anything about the remainder of the Quest, to which the epic proceedings heretofore were, as she was now seeing, just minor preliminaries.

"Bears get bigger and lighter in color as you go to colder places," Corvus said, as if speaking to a child. "In the far north they are white, and really huge. In the mountains of the Knot they are made out of lightning, and correspondingly huger. We will come nowhere near any Lightning Bears. They live on the glaciated heights where the Shifting Path leads—for some definition of 'leads'—to the Precipice. We are going to avoid all of that thanks to your boss and mentor."

Mab hurled herself at Corvus, passed all the way through his head, and came out the other side. En route she must have inflicted some punishment, for "And Mab" Corvus added in haste.

"How about the Vortex Wraiths?" Querc asked. "Are we going to avoid them as well? And what the hell are they?"

Edda's fall of white hair shifted in the firelight as she turned her unfathomable eyes on the young scribe. Prim had learned the knack of not gazing directly on Edda unless she had the time and the desire to get lost in what she saw. She knew that Edda's hair right now was a mountain waterfall lit by the orange rays of a stormy dawn. All well and good, but not to the point at this particular moment. "An attempt that Spring made, while she was completely out of her mind, to imbue parts of the Evertempest with some level of intelligence by combining them with souls," Edda explained. "It didn't work. It's like combining oil and water—the two always separate before long."

"But are they still around? Thousands of years later?"

"The souls who became involved in this experiment of Spring's were changed by it. It turns out that they rather enjoyed being incarnated as disturbances of the wind. That is the only form they are desirous of having—even if they can only have it for a few minutes at a time. So they haunt the Stormland, formless and very nearly invisible, and they wait."

"For *what*?" Querc asked. "Victims? Those must come along rarely."

"Opportunities to take forms," said Edda. "Typically when a great whirlwind descends out of the Evertempest and they can draw strength from it."

"So there might be some around now? Because that just happened, did it not?"

"Yes," said Edda, "but there aren't. Not this time. We'd know."

"What would you suggest we do," Mard inquired, "should a Vortex Wraith come along on a future occasion?"

"Lie flat and cover your head. I'll take care of it," said Edda.

"Can anything kill you, Edda? Are you afraid of anything?"

Querc asked. It seemed that Edda's matter-of-fact answers were calming her down.

Prim now made the mistake of looking at the giantess, and toppled into her. For Edda was looking Prim's way. One eye was obscured by the cataract of her hair, but the other's pupil was the eye of a mile-wide tornado into which Prim plummeted as if she'd been dropped into it by a god. She heard Edda's voice as if it came not from her lips but from the earth all round. "Yes. Most certainly."

And then Prim came to, and it was obvious that she was just sitting around the campfire with other members of the Quest. Several of those were looking at her strangely and she had the sense she'd lost the thread of the conversation.

"Time for bed," she said.

The next day they walked across the stretch of country where the tornado yesterday had snapped off all those trees. The disaster had raised a question in the mind of Pick, who had been debating it with Mard and Lyne: if tempests like that were a frequent occurrence round here, how could there be any forests left standing? Why wasn't the whole region nothing more than an Asking-like stretch of bare rock?

Before their theories and speculations on the matter could advance very far, they got to where they could see answers—or at least hints that would point them to answers—with their own eyes. Trees that had fallen yesterday were already dissolving into the wet earth, and green shoots coming up. If it was in the nature of Spring's creation for living things to die, and for their dead forms to give up the stuff of which they'd been made for the use of new things that were growing, why then Spring had so ordained it that, here, it all happened faster.

"I wouldn't say *faster*," Pick eventually said, watching as a slender green vine spiraled up the shaft of his stick like a snake ascending a tree. This sort of thing had been fascinating ten minutes ago and was well on its way to becoming a nuisance.

"Really? How can you say that's not fast?" Lyne demanded.

"It's as fast as it needs to be," Pick explained. "If all of the vines were behaving thus all of the time, why, every tree standing would

FALL; OR, DODGE IN HELL | 815

be overwhelmed by them in no time. Once the forest has reestablished itself, it settles down."

They were interrupted by a squawk from Corvus. Rare for him, he sounded surprised—even alarmed. He had perched on a broken-off side branch projecting from what was left of a big old tree. This bare snag, and the perch, which was about twice a man's height off the ground, had probably looked safe from above. But in the few moments that Corvus had been resting there, ivy had grown over his talons and lashed his feet in place. He was flapping his wings to no avail. The green tendrils stretched and tore, but the few that didn't snap drew thickness from those broken, which thinned and withered like twists of smoke from a snuffed candle. They were well on their way to becoming barked branches by the time Burr climbed to a lower bough from which he was able to reach up carefully with his spear and use its edged head to chop through the sturdiest branches. Corvus then burst free, vegetation still flailing from his feet, and flapped about in an ill temper until the clinging vines had withered and he had shaken them off. Burr climbed down in a decisive way as the ivy had become interested in him.

This was all quite entertaining after a fashion, while it was in process, but when Burr kicked his way free, bringing the performance to an end, and they all glanced down to see new growth spiraling up their legs, they all had in their minds a common daydream of where it might have gone, had things come out slightly differently: Corvus and Burr both lashed to the tree, smothered and strangled by vines that had hardened into wood, asphyxiated, and now food for nourishment of fresh growth.

Within a very few moments, they were all simply running.

The leaden sky afforded no clues as to where the sun might be and so they had no sense of direction, and might have run in circles were it not for Corvus and Mab, who knew the way to go. Just as important, they warned of dead ends and stretches of difficult going where they might have faltered long enough for the plants to make a meal out of them. Fallen branches, scattered everywhere, impeded them enough to make things interesting even where the going was level.

Before they utterly exhausted themselves, they crested a rise and spied below them a blaze of red-orange: the channel of a small river running across their path. The shape of the land had sheltered this from the whirlwind, so it was still covered with mature deciduous trees that were all the colors of flame. They ran down into it and thereby passed out of the swath carved through the wilderness by yesterday's storm. They kept running anyway, just to be sure, and sloshed across the river and finally stopped in a small clearing. Every one of them stared fixedly at their feet for some while. Or to be precise at the ground around their feet. They were waiting for thin green vines to erupt. When this did not happen, they needed no discussion to agree it was time to put down their burdens and rest.

They had lost one of the big packs that they carried on a pole; Mard and Lyne had set it down for a breather and, at the moment when all had decided to run away, found the pole rotted half through and the pack lashed in place by vines. But Fern had been insisting all along that important supplies be distributed evenly among all of the baggage. Thanks to that, the loss was not so damaging to the Quest's prospects as it might have been.

They ate a meal, since the day was only half through. A storm moved across higher land a mile away. This made Pick nervous and he insisted they cut their rest short and move on. By the time they had grudgingly repacked and got to their feet, the stream they had easily forded had risen to a torrent that would have swept all but Edda away, had they dared set foot in it.

They made for higher ground. For a little while it seemed that they were being pursued by the river. They could have made themselves perfectly safe from rising water by scrambling a little distance up one of the low ridges that divided its tributary creeks, but above a certain level they began to notice a lot of lightning-blasted snags that reminded them of the one they had been gawking at shortly before Weaver had been killed. Mard and Lyne—who, free of their big pack, had resumed their old habit of scrambling ahead—made a hasty descent from one such ridge and reported that something strange had happened to them as they approached its top: their hair had stood on end, their fingers had tingled, and—

"A glowing fringe could be seen around the branches of trees," Fern said.

"Yes!" the Bufrect lads said in unison.

Fern had adopted the mildly stunned expression that came over her when she was dumbfounded by the foolishness of landlubbers. "It is Thingor's Aura and it is known to mariners," she announced. "You were wise to descend."

Fortunately they did not have to choose between escaping the river's rise and tangling with Thingor's Aura. They found a place in between where Pick could squat on his haunches and watch the torrent until he was certain it was beginning to recede. But another day was spent.

The next morning they moved along the slope of a ridge that was getting in their way until the sky brightened and Corvus descended from it and said he judged it safe to cross over the high ground, provided they stayed well apart and avoided clearings. So they devoted an hour to doing just that. Prim, walking alone as per instructions, took the small risk of going a little higher than she needed to and looking around. Far ahead of them, the ground surged up out of a plateau of dark evergreen forest. It rose like a rampart, and as it did, it shouldered off the cover of the trees and was nothing but brown rock for a while until that was glazed, then frosted, then, above a certain altitude, completely buried in snow. This continued up into the storm's lower reaches, which obscured its heights. It looked impossible. But map and myth agreed that the Fastness could only be approached along the route that she was surveying now.

Corvus came flying in from the north. He must have spied Prim on her high perch, for his broad wings narrowed to blades as he banked toward her. "Don't dillydally," he said, "this break in the weather won't last." He touched down and skipped to a stop on open ground near her.

"Who's dillydallying?" she retorted. "I thought you would be scouting the way ahead."

This stopped him for a few moments. "It is also wise," he said finally, "to be mindful of what might be behind. Come on, let's get moving!" And he took to the air and went careering back and forth along the Quest's line of advance, flapping and squawking at any stragglers.

That day neither sky nor forest nor river attempted to kill them. But they had now left the bright colors of the deciduous fall behind and entered into that more elevated stretch of evergreen-forested territory. In some places the trees stood well apart, shooting arrow-straight from a fragrant carpet of needles that was soft beneath sore feet.

They had come to a pass where because of victuals consumed, victuals spoiled by damp, and victuals abandoned while running away, they needed more victuals, and so a day was set aside for hunting and, should the hunt succeed, butchering and dressing of meat. Prim was pressed into service as an archer, and played along despite knowing that if any beast were within range of her skills as a bow-woman, it would be close enough for her to kill it by wishing it were dead.

It proceeded like any other hunt, with a lot of dull waiting and framing of over-elaborate plans that detonated into chaos at the first contact with reality. A big thing with horns—clearly descended from beasts of burden that had been brought here to tow ore carts and since altered form and personality to live wild—was struck by a shot from Lyne, and in its flight chanced to come near Prim. She drew an arrow and took aim. Then, taking pity on it, she did the thing in her mind that cut off its life. A wolf emerged from the undergrowth, having scented blood and given chase to the wounded beast. Prim thought that one to death straightaway as it was sniffing at the downed prey.

It seemed worthy of note, and quite likely a sign of larger trouble, that even a single wolf had turned up right in the middle of what had been drawn up, with sticks in dirt, as an orderly perimeter of alert hunters. Prim tried calling out the others' names: Mard, Lyne, Burr. Another wolf came in from the same general direction as the first. She made it die. She could do that all day; she was Death afoot; nothing alive could hurt her unless she suffered it to.

Camp she could find, and people might need help there, and so that was where she went, breaking into a run as she became certain she was on the right track.

She was relieved to find that all was well here. Edda was pacing round the campfire in a wide circle. Querc was stoking it to make it blaze up. Pick was limbering up his stick technique to one side and on the other Fern was standing with dagger and cutlass drawn, the dagger in a reversed grip, blade tucked along the bone of the forearm, ready to raise up and stab down. She had not joined the party; to her, hunting was an uncouth procedure carried out in pointless wastelands by half-savage souls whose purpose in the grand scheme of things was to offer meat for sale in waterside markets.

Burr came into view, backing toward camp one carefully measured pace at a time, wielding his spear with both arms, butt high above his head and blade low, whipping round in great brushcutting arcs but sometimes vaulting across the top to strike downward. He approached a tree, and Prim gasped in a breath to warn him that it was going to block his spear. The warning would have come too late. And it would have been unnecessary, as it turned out. His hands went on turning and the blade of the spear kept moving in its gyre and the column of smoke that was the spear's shaft passed through the tree trunk, or perhaps it was the other way round. Neither spear nor tree, at any rate, seemed to take any note of the other's existence. But when the spearhead intercepted the face of a wolf on Burr's other side, the results were very material. It had to be a trick of her vision, Prim thought; but a moment later it happened again. "Where are the lads?" asked Fern, who was striding past Prim toward where Burr was embroiled.

Prim thought she glimpsed a giant raven wheeling above the crowns of the trees. "Watch my back!" she called to Pick, who shouted back "Good idea!" and took after her in a wading and flailing gait.

Mard and Lyne were not as far off as she had feared. Mard was dragging one leg and wielding the sword of Elshield with one hand. Lyne had a short hunting lance that he used in more of a thrust-and-stab style. They were a bit downslope of Prim. She descended to a clear vantage point, drew an arrow, and shot. She missed, but not by much. Lyne saw the arrow's fletching and glanced up at her. "This way!" Prim called. Noting another wolf off to one flank, she caused it to stop living, then drew another arrow and managed to shoot one that had chosen to crouch, cringe, and snarl in a location where she could get off a clear shot.

The sub-pack that had taken after Mard and Lyne was dwindling in numbers and faltering in resolve. Lyne stabbed another, which ran off yelping horribly. Two others turned tail and followed it. Pick came up behind Prim and reported all clear. She dropped her bow, ran down the little slope, and helped Lyne drag Mard up, both his good and his hurt leg simply trailing behind him on the ground. But he seemed to be bleeding much more heavily from his left arm.

In a short while, all the party had gathered round the fire, which Querc had made so enormous they could hardly come near it. The woods all round were ringing with the cries of wolves. Prim did not speak their language but she guessed its import: "Invaders have come!"

"It would seem more efficient," Lyne pointed out, "if we could somehow get Spring's various creations to understand that we are on Spring's side and trying to bring about changes that Spring herself would probably approve of."

Edda was somewhat preoccupied sewing Mard's arm up. But she was often at her most conversational while busy with needle and thread.

"Is it going to make her angry," Prim asked, "perhaps to the point of going mad again, that we are going to have to fight and hack our way through?"

"Spring isn't troubled by death," said Edda. "On the contrary."

"Where *is* she?" Querc inquired. "Did she ever take settled form again? Is she roaming around somewhere?"

"Probably the Eye of the Storm," said Edda. "A place in these parts where she went with Eve, when Eve found her, and turned her away from the path of madness."

Prim had avoided this until now, but finally forced herself to go and look at Mard's arm. She had to know how bad it was. She expected wolf bites. Which indeed she saw; but the big wound that Edda was sewing up had been inflicted by a blade.

"It is a self-inflicted wound," Mard admitted. "I pivoted round, thinking to help Lyne, and judged poorly the timing of it, and my arm came into the way of my sword already descending."

At this news Prim was silent.

"You know not what to say," Edda observed. "For such mishaps—though they happen all the time—are never recorded in legends and songs. The hero who falls because of a cramp in his hamstring is not sung of."

More might have been said in that vein had Corvus not flown in and let them know that it would now be necessary to abandon nearly everything they had been carrying and run away.

They had been aware for some time that the howling of the wolves had been noted by other, larger, more solitary beasts; but they were not afraid of those. Several members of the expedition appeared to know that Prim could kill anything. Even if she elected for some reason to withhold that power, it was difficult to imagine anything standing up to Burr. So Prim was inclined for a moment to suppose it was only Corvus's sense of humor at work. But only for a moment. His startling pronouncement had caused everyone to go still. And in that stillness they sensed the approach of something that seemed to come on like rain, in that it affected the whole of the forest instead of being in any one place. Supposing it was even alive, it must have been too numerous and spread out for even Death to be of much use against it.

"Mard can't exactly run," Lyne objected. For his kinsman had suffered bites to his legs as well as the cut to his arm. But Edda was already knotting a bandage over her unfinished seam. She slung Mard over her back as if he weighed approximately as much as a chicken, and in a few long strides vanished into the forest south-bound.

The threat consisted of insects. From any distance greater than a stone's throw—not that stones would have been any use—they simply looked like smoke. As Prim saw when they were overtaken by a lobe of that "smoke," they could take to the air in an ungainly combination of leaping and fluttering, and the wind was their friend. As she learned when one landed on her arm, they could bite off freckle-sized scoops of flesh.

Corvus had insisted that they carry nothing but weapons (useless now, important later?) and firebrands, and that they run upwind. They did not have to run for more than an hour before they encountered a rising slope where going was difficult because of undergrowth and low branches. There the insects caught up with them and did damage and made going very disagreeable indeed with their propensity for attacking eyes, ears, noses, and mouths. But before panic consumed them they got deep enough in that Corvus deemed it time to set fires. Those spread downwind with great speed. But upwind the flames advanced slowly enough that outrunning them was possible. That was the good news. The bad news was that they had to run more. This time, at least, they were not inhaling bugs. At length they passed into more open territory that had evidently been burned in the past, so that the flames could not follow in their wake. There they stopped and were rained on all through the night as the storm, having apparently replenished its energies, returned at full strength.

"Fuck this," Corvus shouted, when it became light enough to see. "Enough of orderly and well-planned Questing. There's nothing for it now but to make a run for the cave."

"Which cave would that be?" Lyne asked.

"The one we're heading for," Corvus said vaguely. Which would have led to further questions had they not just spent the whole night exposed to the storm.

They had crawled under a fallen tree whose branches were stiff-arming it just high enough above the ground that they could wriggle under it. This sheltered them from direct laceration by rain and hail but did nothing to keep them dry. If any one thing had saved them it had been the giantess, who made more warmth than all the others put together. Curled up next to Edda during the long hours of the night, Prim had gone into another of those strange dreams in which it seemed to her that Edda was as tall as a tree, and Prim a thing like a squirrel, nestled in the crook of a bough, wet but warm.

Now, in the light of the morning, Edda was plainly a woman of normal size. Prim feared, though, that she was diminished; she squatted on her haunches to keep off the soaked ground, and wrapped herself in her cloak, and remained still, eyes closed, for a long time as Burr tried vainly to light a fire. Prim was remembering Edda's cottage on Calla, and her sheep and horses, and the flour she would grind to bake bread. How long had it been since she had taken such nourishment? Did absorbing the whole form of an angel give her some power that she could call upon at times such as last night?

"We are in no condition to run anywhere," Burr pointed out. "We could march."

"We need food," said Pick. "Other than this, I mean." He waved in front of him a fleck of jerky, his portion of all the food they now had remaining.

"None is here," Corvus pointed out, "but if we march, as Burr suggests, Mab and I can keep an eye out for things that might be eaten."

So that was how it went. For much of the morning it rained, but this was plain old ordinary rain, which compared to the storm seemed like no rain at all. Perhaps the sound of it covered the noise they made walking and enabled them to get within sight of another of those horned creatures. They spied it across a clearing. It fell dead. Burr's response was to flatten himself against the ground. "Get down!" he whispered. "Someone else is hunting here!"

Prim did not get down. She kept walking until she had reached the beast, which was lying there as if asleep. Burr, still convinced of danger, caught up with her a few moments later, spear at the ready. When the rest of the party caught up with Burr, he was rolling the dead beast over, looking for some sign of the arrow that had slain it. But of course there was none.

He stepped back from it. "I saw a similar thing during the wolf fight. I did not believe it."

"We saw something like it too," Mard said. "A wolf simply died."

"Some fell presence stalks these woods, and slays what it will by magic."

"I am the fell presence," Prim said. "Let's eat."

This time, no wolf pack came. Neither were they molested by larger beasts or clouds of insects. Not even when they lit a fire and the aroma of roasting meat spread on the breeze. The rain stopped while they were cooking. They were on the edge of a meadow that sloped up out of the country they had covered during the last day. Below them in the distance they could hear wolves raising the same alarm they had heard yesterday: "Invaders have come!" This seemed to arouse the curiosity of Corvus, who had already supped on raw flesh. He flapped into the air and then beat his wings powerfully to gain altitude, heading back north.

"The raven thinks we are being followed," said Burr.

None of the others seemed to think that this was news. Fern paid no note at all. She had been inspecting Prim since the latter had revealed her nature. Tiring of the attention, Prim met her eye.

"I *wondered*," Fern said. "Just being a princess isn't enough to get you invited on something like this."

Prim was doubly offended. She hadn't even thought of herself as a princess at the beginning; she'd taken Brindle at his word when he'd said that Quests were just a thing that Calladons did. A sort of birthright. But she was too tired and hungry to enter into a dispute with Fern just now.

"Could you kill any soul in the Land?"

"According to the legends, I killed Egdod," Prim reminded her. "I have to be close to what I'm killing, though."

"Could you kill El?"

"I don't know. The opportunity has not presented itself. He might have ways of killing me sooner."

"Spring made a creature for that purpose," said Querc. "Or so Weaver told me, the night before she died. It is made of chaos and adamant. It is called the Chasmian, and it waits under the Broken Bridge for any who makes it that far."

"And did Weaver have anything to say about what additional hazards we must pass through in order to be in a position to be menaced by the Chasmian?" Lyne asked.

"First, the army of Beedles that Spring ensnared and converted to her services," said Querc. "They'll be dug in on yonder slope." She stood up and drew their attention to the rampart of rocky ground that rose up out of the forest south of them. This had become visible as the weather cleared. It was markedly closer now than when Prim had looked on it yesterday. It seemed much higher and steeper than her earlier view of it had led her to expect. Details could now be made out that hinted at its being inhabited. Not in the sense that structures had been built atop its surface. No, this had been burrowed into. If there was any truth to the old myths, the Beedles that Spring had brought into her service were miners. They must have been very accomplished miners now. Mile-wide fans of spoil spread away from pinhole-sized orifices in the slope. Every one of those stones had been hacked out of the bowels of the earth by one of those Dug—as the converted Beedles were called. For they had dug and dug and dug until Dug was all they were.

"And second? Third? Fourth?" Lyne prompted Querc.

"Between the Dug and the Chasmian—which is to say, along the Shifting Path that goes across the top of the glacier—nothing except for, well, you know, Lightning Bears."

"Good to know," Lyne said.

"But I don't think we are going that way," Querc added. "Corvus said something about a cave." She looked toward Edda. "Is that where we are going, my lady?"

"It is where we are *headed*," Edda corrected her. She did not meet Querc's gaze, or anyone's. She was standing a little apart from the others, who were clustered round the fire in the hopes of drying out their clothes. She seemed content to gaze upon the vista opening up to the south as the weather continued to clear off. Some of the high mountains leading into the Knot were now revealing themselves. They were the grandest thing Prim had ever beheld. But Edda's gaze was fixed low, toward a green plateau that was difficult to resolve distinctly, as clouds and rain still swirled close about it. It was a small shelf that looked to have been cut into the eastern extremity of the Dug-infested rampart that blocked their way. Indeed its shape and situation were so convenient that one could easily imagine it had been purpose-built by Dug with picks and shovels. High and remote though it was, yet it seemed to exist at the bottom of a well of golden light, the overabundance of which made the swirling veil of mist into a blurry glow that dazzled and befogged the vision.

"Is that the Eye of the Storm then?" Querc asked.

"Yes," said Edda, "that is the Eye of the Storm." And not until she pronounced it thus did Prim's childhood memory produce in her mind an illustration from a storybook she'd enjoyed many times on Brindle's knee. It depicted just such a place, a green and golden glen nestled in mountains where Spring dwelled with Eve and certain of her favorite creations, and flowers bloomed and sweet fruit hung ripe from trees all year round. That explained why Edda gazed at it so. Her mother and grandmother were there.

No flowers or fruit were *here,* and so they tore into the meat as soon as it was warm and slurped fat off the bones before it would be wasted by melting into the fire. Corvus returned and declined to say very much about what, if anything, could be following them. But he seemed to think that moving faster would be better, and so they wrapped up more meat for later and continued on their way.

Mard had walked in the morning, slowly and stiffly and with his face screwed up in pain. He carried on thus now. When the going became difficult, someone would put a shoulder under his good arm and help him along for a few paces. His injured arm he kept beneath his cloak, folded against his belly.

Meadows became more frequent, and larger. Burr pointed to signs that fires had been set to burn back encroaching forest and leave open land where grass could grow and edible beasts fatten themselves on it. They found skeletal remains of two such beasts, and Burr showed them marks that had been left by knives, and even a rusted iron arrowhead stuck too deep in a pelvis to be worth prying out. "Dug," Burr said, as if there could have been any doubt. "The forest yields all the food they need, provided they keep it clear of wolves and other such beasts. Beware traps." By which Prim assumed he must mean ambushes that the Dug might lay for invading souls such as them. But not a quarter of an hour later they came upon a cunning snare that had been baited with meat.

They avoided the meadows from then on, and stayed in the deepest woods that Mab and Corvus could steer them to. Thus without further incident they came to a place where the ground ramped sharply upward. The soft earth of the forest gave way to a rubble of sharp stones that had quite obviously tumbled down here from the bare high ground above. Fat drops of icy rain began to thud down. From off to their right the sun was slicing in under the storm and lighting up the whole face of the rampart, all the way from where they stood—near its western extremity—down to its eastern end, many miles away, where it sank like an axe into the buttresses of a mountain range. The Eye of the Storm was there, but could no longer be seen save as a vague column of iron-gray weather round which the whole rest of the Evertempest turned like the millstone in Edda's kitchen.

"Stop and have a good look at it then," Corvus said, as quietly as it was possible for a giant talking raven to form words. "We go up under cover of dark, and we go *there*."

"Where?" Lyne asked, for all of them.

"*There*. I'm pointing right at it."

"You have no way of pointing."

"I am pointing with my *beak*."

"Never mind, I see it," said Pick. He had dropped to one knee and planted the foot of his stick on a rock, the better to peer through its lenses. Between that and the direction of Corvus's beak the rest of the party were able to see what was being looked at: the tiniest black pore in the surface of the rampart. It was directly above them, for Corvus had led them right to it. Unlike the various entrances made by the Dug, this did *not* have an enormous fan of spoil pointing right at it.

"Is that the famous cave?" Querc asked.

"Famous to this little band. To the Dug, more *infamous,* and rarely entered."

"Strikes me as odd," Pick remarked.

"Yes," said Lyne. "Why wouldn't they go into a conveniently situated natural cave?"

"I don't like where this is going," Mard said.

"Terror" was the answer of Corvus. "Fear of what becomes of any who strays more than a few yards beyond the entrance." Continuing in the same level tone, he added, "Memorize landmarks that may be useful in the dark."

"Why not go up now?" Querc asked. "The storm is brewing up again."

"Dug patrols on the heights."

"They've seen us?"

A raven shrug. "If not, they *will*. It's their purpose for existing."

The heavy slugs of half-frozen water developed into a steady fall of ice-rain, which prompted them to retreat just a few yards down to a marginally more sheltered place. The light had dimmed, footing was slick, and Mard's injured legs weren't moving well. He toppled forward and reflexively threw out both arms to avoid planting his face right on the stones. But only one hand—his good one—made effective contact with the ground. The injured one gave way, so that he twisted at the moment of impact and struck with his shoulder. Momentum then rolled him onto his back, where he lay for a few moments, grimacing with agony.

His injured arm was missing. Or rather, beyond the point where he had cut himself with the sword of Elshield, a forearm, wrist, and hand still existed. But they were made of aura. The fingers were wispy ghosts. Prim could see right through the palm of his hand. She came very close to crying out. What stilled her was not the fear of being heard by Dug. It was the way Mard looked into her eyes: altogether steady and calm. He had known, of course, and had been hiding it under his cloak.

She naturally had a great many questions as to the prognosis, but hiding from Dug patrols during a mountain hailstorm was not a good situation for that kind of talk. They huddled together as they had done at other such times. But on this occasion Prim chose to lie next to Mard so that the two of them could share the warmth of their bodies with each other.

They waited until it was full dark and then began to ascend. "I shall go last," Edda offered, "as I may touch off avalanches."

Despite their earlier efforts at memorizing landmarks, had it not been for Mab they'd have been hopelessly lost. Corvus had adopted his human shape again. The occasional lightning bolt lit up the entire mountainside as bright as day, but not long enough for the eye to seek out and fix the location of the cave's entrance. They learned to cringe and tense themselves in anticipation of the thunderclap that would always follow a fraction of a second later.

"Thingor's Aura!" Fern called, after it seemed they had been blundering around for an hour. Prim, who had been staring fixedly at the ground in an effort to make out where she ought to plant her feet, looked about to see that the rocks around her were limned in green fire. Before she could feel any sense of wonder or awe at this, Fern followed up with, "Lie flat!" So she tried to do so and learned that the very idea of lying down had no clear meaning on ground as stony as this. A bolt struck very close, the light and the sound penetrating her skull at the same instant. Querc screamed. Prim craned her neck to gaze up the slope. Pulsing rivers of the green fire ran up and down it as fast as thought. Something extraordinarily brilliant could be seen high above, as if suspended in the sky; it had the dazzling brilliance of a lightning bolt, but it persisted, like the sword Burr had taken from the angel. And yet it moved about like a thing alive, sometimes down on all fours and other times rearing up to stand on its hind legs.

It was a bear. A Lightning Bear. It was on the top of the ridge high above them, far beyond where they had any thought of going; but it had seen them and it was not happy that they were coming up its mountain.

It was a short while later that rocks began to tumble down out of the darkness. One came straight for Prim, moving so fast she could not possibly dodge it; but it caromed off another and brushed past her.

It was just like being down beneath the Overstrike with Beedles up above rolling rocks down onto them. But this time, she felt certain, it was Dug who had been alerted to their presence, perhaps by the vigilant bears.

The sun came out, illuminating the whole slope above. She could see all: In the near ground, boulders tumbling toward them. Above that, less than a bow-shot distant, the entrance to the cave. And on the higher ground above that, pale figures with the squat asymmetrical forms of Beedles. Perhaps a dozen of them. The sudden light had caught them in the act of prying rocks loose from the slope. Their work stopped as they were blinded by it: the light of the angel sword, which Burr had drawn full out of its scabbard. Seeing now the way and the enemy, Burr sprang forward with a roar. The rest followed as best they could. Prim shielded her eyes from the glare so that she could take advantage of the light in picking her way up. She turned back to look once or twice and got fragmented glimpses of other members of the Quest, arms flailing for balance on shifting and ice-covered ground. Fern and Lyne were coming up fast with weapons drawn. The light of the angel sword flashed and swept. Lightning struck. A furious roaring came down from on high: bears. The ground leveled. A dark hole was before her. She stumbled into it, carried more by momentum than any plan or desire. Others piled in behind her, blocking the way out. She had a mind to go back out of the cave and be of help in the fighting, but before she could do so, the mountain was plunged back into darkness. The sword had gone back into its sheath. Rocks scrabbled and chattered as they slid down from above. Lightning flashed and outlined the silhouettes of Burr, Fern, and Lyne. They stepped into the cave.

With that the Quest concluded its traversal of the Stormland, and entered into the underpinnings of the Knot.

54

C ome on," Corvus said. "Pick, we need to seal the entrance."

"I thought you said the Dug would not follow us in here," Lyne said.

"*They* won't," Corvus answered vaguely. "Pick? Sound off! Can we have more light?"

Mab brightened. They had gathered a few strides in from the cave's entrance. Burr had stationed himself nearest it, spear at the ready, and Fern and Lyne were still backing him up. Next was Edda, standing still as a mountain in her cloak, which glistened with ice. Querc was crumpled near the giantess, weeping. Mard, Prim, and Corvus had advanced deepest into the cave, but Corvus was now stalking back toward the entrance as Mab flitted to and fro in the style of one who has lost something. "Where is Pick?" Corvus asked. "We need to send out a search party!" He seemed of a mind to go and look down the slope.

Edda brought him up short by withdrawing from her cloak a small gleaming object. Its nature wasn't clear until Mab cast greater light on it. Then it could be seen that this was the bird-shaped head of Pick's stick, somewhat deformed, as if it had partly melted. The eyes were now blind sockets, as the lenses were missing. A blackened shard of wood still dangled from the hole where the shaft had been affixed.

It was the rare moment when Corvus was not well ahead of everyone else. That combined with the fact that he was in his human form, and closely illuminated by Mab, made it possible to see emotions in his face that Prim—who had known him since he was a new soul in the Land—had never seen there before. He was completely astonished. It was that kind of surprise so total that one's first reflex, be it never so out of place, is to laugh. Which he did in a faltering and nervous way. Then he became serious and thoughtful.

Querc's grief was total, as was her shock at what she had witnessed. Prim remembered the scream Querc had made after a certain close lightning strike and knew it was true. Corvus knew it too: Pick was gone.

"Well!" he said. "That certainly changes a few things about the Quest. We can't do this without a Lithoplast."

There was a brief silence as this sank in, and then everyone looked at Querc.

They went deeper in, just to put more distance between them and any Dug who might have the audacity to come in after them. Sealing the entrance through Lithoplasty, which had been Corvus's original plan, was no longer possible. But as this was a natural cave, it had twists and bottlenecks that they were able to chock up behind them with rocks. Edda had the strength to shift boulders, and Burr's angel sword could cut stone. So they were able to make going difficult for any who might pursue them into the depths of the Knot.

Or for themselves, should they try to get back out. But it was obvious that this cave was another of those that Pluto had salted about the Land to make going from place to place easier, and that they would be emerging somewhere else.

This mere activity—the going in deeper, clambering up and down the cave's convolutions, helping one another through tight places—had a calming effect on Querc as the scene of that horror fell away behind them.

The descent became treacherous, and Corvus grew cautious, then irritable, then impossibly annoying as he insisted that all be careful of their footing. Echoes from ahead of them—which was to say, below them—suggested that this narrow shaft was about to open up into something much larger. Light—not from Mab— began to gleam from smooth, damp cavern walls. Prim knew what to expect, and soon saw it.

The shaft broadened suddenly into a vast cavity whose floor was chaos. The shape of the space was something like a melon poised on end. They had angled down into a location that was neither high up in the dome of its ceiling nor down low in its wall but somewhere in between. The reason for Corvus's irritability became clear; anyone who lost their footing during the descent of the shaft would have gained speed falling down it and been projected out helplessly into the cavity, then fallen down into the lake of chaos. But by making a controlled descent, the party was able to stop on a bit of a ledge that some Lithoplast—perhaps Pluto himself—had sculpted at the outlet of the tunnel. It could not accommodate all of them. Corvus, Prim, Querc, and Mard spread out along it while Edda, Lyne, Fern, and Burr remained backed up in the tunnel, shifting about to peer over one another's shoulders. Mab soared free, exulting in the vastness of the space, her light illuminating diverse veins and layers in the rock. To watch her was intoxicating but dangerous; Prim had to avert her eyes when she sensed she might lose her balance.

Mab settled into a looping flight pattern, remaining more or less on a level about halfway between them and the surface of the chaos below. The surface was not of uniform brightness but dappled, and the dapples came and went. Sometimes they were big and slow, as if something huge was trying to shoulder its way up out of the deep, and other times they flickered so rapidly that by the time the eye had darted to them they had vanished. Over and over Prim had the maddening sense that she was just on the verge of making something out for what it was, as when a name is on the tip of your tongue or a sneeze pent up in your nose. Mab seemed to be looking at the same. Perhaps she had some faculty Prim lacked of collecting the scattered fragments of imagery into a definite vision.

Something shifted in the chaos. Mab whipped round in a tight circle and then shot vertically up to their level, blazing bright enough to illuminate the walls of the whole cavern. "Now! Follow me!" she cried, then wheeled about so she was head down, and dove.

Corvus put his shoulder into Prim, who fell into Querc, who fell into Mard, who with his bad arm had no way of stopping. They all fell off the ledge and tumbled helplessly into chaos.

Somewhere in it, down became up and they began to fall slower and slower instead of faster and faster. Snow, mottled with patches of rock, was skimming below them. Prim put out her hands defensively. The surface came up to meet her. She skidded, then plunged into deep snow that brought her to a stop without breaking anything. When she tried to stand up, she sank to midthigh.

A bright moon was out. A brighter light banked past her, then went back the way they'd come from. Prim watched Mab descend toward a river of chaos that ran through a gorge a short distance beneath them. The sprite hunted back and forth along it for a minute, then plunged back in.

Not far away Prim could hear the uncouth gagging noises that she had come to associate with Corvus's changing back into his bird form. There was no better place to be a bird. They were very high up in mountains. Half the sky was clear. The other half was stone. Below them chaos filled the lower reaches of a deep straight-sided canyon. Its opposite bank was a sheer cliff topped with a glacier. Beyond that the land dropped away into dark forest.

Her brain put it all together from maps. The cliff on the opposite, or north, side of the canyon was the Precipice. The plateau atop it was the domain where the Shifting Path threaded among hidden crevasses across territory patrolled by Lightning Bears.

They had simply skipped over, or tunneled through, that whole portion of the journey. They would not need to cross the Chasm; they had just put it behind them. They had reached—they were standing on—the Knot. The Fastness must have been nearby.

Four dark forms hurtled up out of the Chasm and tumbled and skidded through the snow around her. Edda took longer to stop than the others, carving a deep gouge in the snow and finally coming to a stop a bow-shot higher up the slope. She was laughing. Her laughter was music, bells, and birdsong. She got to her feet. Looking a little beyond Edda, higher up the slope, Prim perceived that the snow became patchier and soon petered out altogether, giving way to bare rock. Which stood to reason since it was more and more sheltered by the overhanging brow of stone that blotted out half the sky: a place Prim had heard about but never seen depicted on any map, since it could not be. Instead, bards tried analogies:

thick ropes knotted together or folds in heavy blankets, except bigger, and made of mountains.

They climbed. It was slow going and exceptionally hard work. That might have been a blessing in disguise since it was very cold indeed, and only the most strenuous effort was going to keep them warm. For a while it seemed like her wading and staggering in the deep powder was making no difference at all, but finally she got to a place where it improved noticeably with each step, and soon after that she joined several of the others who were huddled together for warmth on bare rocky ground. They were all tending to look in the same direction: back the way they had come and down the slope. So once Prim got up there and made sure of her footing, she turned around and looked at what they were looking at.

Seeing what mattered took a moment because it was a graceful and slender thing in a world of slabs and chasms, silver and sharp in snow-reflected moonlight.

"The Broken Bridge!" she exclaimed. "I never thought I would actually see it!"

The place where it was anchored to the opposite wall of the canyon was plain to see. A heavy buttress gripped the rim of the precipice. One foot of an arch was jammed against the canyon wall below. That and the bridge's deck reached only part of the way across the Chasm before they were terminated by a little tower, arching over a gate to nowhere. Reaching toward it on this side would be its twin. Prim could complete the bridge in her imagination and get an idea of where it must have connected on this side. But the folds and convolutions of the Knot got in the way, so they couldn't see their end of it. It would be a couple of miles from here.

They began to walk in that direction. Or so it seemed at the beginning. But Corvus wanted them to go in ways that did not make obvious sense to ground-pounders. Everyone in this party understood that the usual rules of getting from one place to another would be worse than useless in the Knot. The fact that they were, on the whole, getting deeper in, where the wind left them alone and the air was less frigid, helped.

So they arrived at the Cube.

It stood in a little side fold of the mountain, sheltered from weather. You'd have to have known it was there in order to find it. Which raised the question of how Corvus had known that the Cube was here.

There was no question whatsoever as to what the Cube ought to be called. You could not conceivably call it anything else. In height, breadth, and depth it was about twice Burr's arm span. It was made of adamant, a substance of which most of them had seen more than a lifetime's worth in the fault. But it was something of a novelty to Burr, who ran a hand across one face of it and down one of its vertical edges. Then he drew back with a curse and showed them a bloody fingertip. The Cube's edge was so crisp it had cut him.

So the Cube it was, without a doubt. But Prim had never heard of the Cube. She looked at Querc, but Querc could do nothing but shake her head and turn up her palms.

Edda must have known about the Cube! They looked to the giantess.

"Corvus," she said, "you have me at a disadvantage. What is this thing? Other than a cube of adamant sitting in the Knot for no apparent reason."

"Proof," Corvus said (he was perched, naturally, on top of the Cube), "of the reality of the other plane of existence of which I have spoken repeatedly in the past." Then, because he couldn't resist rubbing it in, "Oh, I have seen you roll your eyes when I speak of the other plane of existence. I know you think—"

"It's not that anyone thinks you're crazy," Prim said. "It's just that the other plane of existence is just a lot of made-up stories until you can present some kind of, uh . . ."

"Proof," Corvus said. "Behold."

"This doesn't prove it," Lyne said. "Seems like something Pluto might have put here to amuse himself."

Prim braced herself for a retort in a bitter or vindictive tone from the giant talking raven. Instead he gave a bird shrug. "Fair," he said. "You'll be singing a different tune, though, when Querc melts away the adamant to reveal what is embedded in this thing."

"You've known this was waiting for us all along," Prim surmised, while Querc was busy clapping her hands over her face and shaking her head in dismay.

"It was put here long ago by an entity on the other plane of existence. Hidden away where no one would find it unless they knew exactly where to look. Sealed in adamant so that only a Lithoplast, guided by an incorporeal sprite, would know what to do."

"My sword could cut it," Burr pointed out in a mildly offended tone. He was gazing at Querc, who still seemed notably lacking in self-confidence. Lyne had put his arm around her shoulders and was mumbling some kind of presumably encouraging words into the side of her head.

"It may come to that," said Corvus, "but I don't wish to damage what is inside."

"It's not just a matter of knowing what to do, and how to do it," Querc explained. "Certain things are needed."

"Can you be a little more specific?" Mard inquired politely.

"Well—going back to the very beginning—according to Pick, chaos came first. When it began to take on those patterns that embodied or enacted thought, it became what we call aura."

Mard shouldered his cloak back and looked down at his aura hand. "So aura is chaos, but . . ."

"*Patterned* chaos," Querc said. "Like a wave moving across the water, which is water *plus* something: a shape that retains its character even while it propagates through the stuff of which it's made."

"How does aura become form, then?" Mard asked. To him it was a very personal question at the moment.

Prim, not wishing to stare, glanced away. But this only brought Mab into view. And what was Mab if not an extraordinarily focused bit of aura? As if to make that very point, Mab flew into the cube and popped out the other side a moment later.

"The very first of all solid things was adamant," said Querc. "Which seems quite different from chaos. But really it is just one configuration of chaos that happens to be stable. Egdod found it very early, and made the Land out of it, and as long as the Land—and later the Firmament—remained nothing more complicated than adamant, they could be reshaped—"

"Through Lithoplasty. I understand," said Mard. Leaving unspoken the fact that he was really trying to find out how he might get his hand back.

Hand, and arm. For he used his good hand now to pull his sleeve back, well above his elbow. Flesh had retreated and aura had advanced well above the place where the sword of Elshield had cut into him.

Querc sighed. "It is old magic, not understood or practiced much since the First Age. Pick knew it. We of this age are confined for the most part to fixed forms, bounded by our own skins. In the Before Times, forms were more fluid and many had auras that reached beyond their forms."

"I saw it among the high Autochthons of Secondel," said Prim.

"And Pick could do it," said Lyne. "We saw his aura reach out from his head beneath the Overstrike."

"I, unfortunately, cannot," said Querc. "Which is where Mard might come into the picture. But first, there is another thing. In Pick's sample case were bits of chaos and so on that he had collected from various locations such as the Chasm we just crossed."

"I have no other purpose here," Lyne offered.

"Nor I," said Fern. "We can go to the brink of the Chasm if Mab leads the way."

"*I'll* lead the way," said Corvus. He was swinging his beak side to side, watching with his beady black eyes as Mab flew back and forth through the Cube. "Mab is more useful here."

With a short, slow movement of his blinding sword, Burr sliced a corner from the top of the Cube, since Mab had flown through it and reported nothing there. He used the tip of the sword to hollow out the surface, making a nut-sized depression. He repeated the procedure with another corner. The two pieces, clapped together, now made a container that crudely approximated one of the carven adamant drawers from Pick's old sample case. Lyne and Fern borrowed as many warm clothes as the others could spare and set out with Corvus, carrying this makeshift sample holder with them. On one side of the Cube, Burr began to carve off more bits where Mab told him it was safe to do so.

On the opposite side, where the light of the angel sword would not be such an annoyance, Querc talked at length to Mard, recounting what she had learned during her years with Pick. Mard began to experiment with reaching into the Cube with the hand that was no longer material. That inability to come to grips with solid objects had seemed an important deficiency when he was trying to button his cloak or break his fall. But here and now it was enabling him to perform what for lack of a better term one would have to call magic. "Can you feel anything?" Querc was asking him. "Are there sensations in that hand?" Mard insisted it was altogether numb, as if it weren't there at all. "But you can open and close it, can you not?" Querc asked.

Mard withdrew his hand from the stone and made it clench into a fist, then opened it again. So there was the answer. "No sensation, though," he insisted. "Just tingling."

"Tingling is a sensation," Querc pointed out.

Some hours passed. Prim, having nothing to do at the moment, found a hollow in the rock where she could curl up and pull her cloak up over her head to block most of the light from the sword. This flared and flashed unpredictably as Burr wielded it against the Cube. Edda had boosted him onto its flat top. He was carving off bits under the direction of Mab, who seemed to have a very clear notion of where it was and was not safe to remove material. From time to time a chunk of adamant would break free, slide off, and bang into the ground, startling Prim. So this was far from the most restful nap she had ever taken.

She must, against all odds, have gone to sleep, though, because at some point she woke up. A deep boom, transmitted through the bedrock of the Knot, had been felt in her ribs and was already just a memory. It was not accompanied by a crash of severed stone from the nearby Cube. This had nothing to do with that. It was bigger, from farther away. Yesterday she might have identified it as a thunderclap. Indeed they were still within the Evertempest, the entire purpose of which was to protect this place. But this didn't rumble and reverberate like thunder. And no sound was reaching her ears. She peeled the hood back from her head and squinted in the light as chill dry air bathed her face. The others were still at work, much as before. The shoulders and sides of the Cube had been cut down quite a bit; Burr was now standing on a pedestal just wide enough to support him. Around that the stone sloped roughly down where he had chopped it away, and the crisp base of the Cube was obscured by shards that had sloughed off. Prim shaded her eyes with one hand and lay still for a while, maintaining firm contact between her body and the living rock of the Knot. Then she felt another of those shocks. She took her hand from her eyes, raised her head, and looked at the others. None of them seemed to have noticed. Burr and Mab were intent upon their work, as Querc and Mard were upon theirs.

Where was Edda? Prim stood up, more than a little stiff, and found the giantess off to one side, sitting on a natural bench in the rock. She was leaning a little to one side, gazing down as if the stone were a window, resting the palm of one hand upon it like a mother checking the pulse of a child's heart.

So Prim wasn't just imagining things. Which did not answer the question of what was shaking the foundations of the Knot so.

It seemed a natural topic of conversation. But before Prim could go and take it up with Edda, she heard voices approaching, one of which had the distinctive harsh timbre of a giant talking raven. Corvus came into view first, and not far behind him were Fern and Lyne. The latter was bearing in his hands a heavy thing all wrapped up in cloth.

"Easier than expected," he announced, dropping to one knee and setting his burden down near what a few hours ago had been a cube. He began carefully to unwrap it.

"We found a stair," Fern explained, "that some Lithoplast, I suppose, had made in the face of the cliff that descends into the Chasm. It took us right down to where the Land gives way to chaos."

Lyne had exposed the two fragments of adamant that Burr had earlier cut off and whittled into a makeshift container. These were clapped together, but when Lyne carefully shifted the top one, they could all see chaos within. "Scooped it up like water into a ladle," he said. After he had handed the sample to Querc, Prim went to him and Fern—who seemed great friends now that they had been on an adventure together—and asked, "Did you see, or hear or feel, anything moving—perhaps just beginning to move—in the depths of the Chasm?"

"You've seen chaos," Lyne answered. "When is it ever not moving?"

"I mean not its usual fluctuation but something coherent and purposeful. With a mind," Prim explained.

"No," Lyne said, and his sincerity was plain.

Prim's gaze shifted to Fern. "Nothing small," she said. "What I am asking about would be like the thing that took your family in the southern ocean."

Fern froze up in the way Prim had sometimes seen men do when they were getting ready to lose their temper. But no such outburst came. "I understand," she said, after swallowing a bite of food. "You're saying it might be too big to notice."

"Something like that, yes."

Fern was now gazing off at nothing in particular. Lyne, either bored or uneasy, ambled off toward Mard and Querc. Edda by this point had boosted them to the top of what had been the Cube and was gradually becoming more of an irregular obelisk as Burr cut away at it.

"I understand the nature of your question," Fern said. But that was all she said for now.

Something in chaos was infectious and could break down adamant or other solid forms. Normally adamant was proof against it. That was the whole point. It was why Egdod had brought it into being: so that he could make something permanent in the ocean of chaos. But Egdod had done so when he had been a formless swirl of aura. What he had done could be undone. Chaos could infect adamant, or anything solid, when directed to that purpose by the will of a soul. If that soul were embodied in a solid form, it would suffer the same fate even as it was performing the work. This was why Pick had used his aura, not his hands or any physical tool, when going about such tasks.

Destroying was a thousand times easier than building up. For Mard the neophyte to convert chaos to adamant—to say nothing of more complex things—would not have been possible. But melting adamant into chaos was a simple trick easily learned.

And so what transpired over the next few hours was that Mard and Querc, working together with her knowledge and his aura, and beginning with the sample that Fern and Lyne had fetched to them, melted away the adamant. Mab told them which parts of it to remove. It became chaos and dissipated like smoke, and what was left of the Cube seemed to dissolve like a chunk of ice left in the sun.

What began to emerge from it was a thing made out of iron. The first part to be exposed was a sort of handle, ornately carved with symbols that put Prim in mind of the decorations on the Temple complex of Elkirk. Below that for some distance was nothing but a shaft, thick as Burr's thigh, oriented vertically within the Cube. Below a certain level this broadened and ramified into an extraordinarily complex tracery, the very look of which made them all glad that Burr's sword had not come anywhere near it. Even the most talented sculptors of the faraway Teemings, working with their finest chisels, could not have freed this thing from the stone in which it had been embedded without damaging its finer convolutions, some of which were no bigger than hairs.

"It is plainly enough a key," Edda said to Corvus, as the work proceeded. "Which means it must purport to be *the* key. You brought me here because only I can carry something that heavy. This all makes sense, to a point. But it is perfectly well-known to all learned persons that El destroyed the key to the Fastness. As Lyne was pointing out the other day, for El to have done otherwise would have been utmost folly. The merest glance at the complexity of that object makes it obvious that no copy or counterfeit is possible. So there is something to this whole matter that reaches beyond my understanding. I who was born in Camp to Eve, and saw Cairn kill Messenger of El, and drank the angel's stuff into my form, and have dwelled in the Land ever since and been all over it, have no ken of what goes on here."

"I myself am somewhat amazed, and cannot give sure answers," said Corvus. "But I have known that Cube and key were here for longer than you, and so I have had a little more time to ponder such questions. Suppose that the other plane of existence is real, and that it was preexisting. Which is to say that the Land was born out of it, much as you were born out of Eve. It follows that in that other plane are powers or faculties of creation that somehow account for the whole story of the Land's coming into being, and underlie every aspect of what we take to be real. Moreover that plane is populated by souls who know of us and our doings, and who from time to time may for reasons we cannot even speculate on choose to effect changes to the Land—but to do so without violating what makes the Land coherent. If you accept those premises, can you not accept that an object that once existed in the Land, having been crafted to a purpose by El, and used and then utterly destroyed by El, might be brought into existence again? Not by any craft of any soul who dwells here, but by one on the other plane of existence, wielding powers the nature of which we cannot begin to understand? The only way that I can explain the existence of this key is to suppose that all of those things are the case. And moreover that my purpose in crossing over from that plane into this one is to see that key being turned in the lock on the Fastness."

At a certain point the key simply toppled over, forcing Mard and Querc to jump out of the way. It was entirely free now of the matrix of rock in which it had been embedded. Some of its crannies were still plugged up with adamant, but Mard, having got the hang of this, could melt that away easily enough. Edda walked to it, bent down, hooked both arms under the shaft of the key, and tried to move it in an exploratory way, getting a sense of its balance. At Mard's request she rolled it over to expose a part of it that needed his attention. One by one, though, he polished off those lingering traces. A few clots of adamant clung to the decorative work of the key's handle, where presumably it wouldn't make a difference. But the part that was meant to go into the lock seemed perfectly clean. It was the most complicated object any of them had ever seen, like a hundred mazes made out of smaller mazes, wrought in solid iron and brazed together. Encircling the delicate and complicated parts was a protective shroud of thicker metal— this explained why nothing important had been damaged when the key had fallen over. The shroud would have served its purpose perfectly well had it been square or cylindrical in cross-section, but of course it had innumerable grooves and protrusions, clearly meant to go one way, and only one way, into a matching keyhole.

Mab flew in and out of it for a while, inspecting parts so deep in its convolutions that they could not even be seen by anyone else. She directed Mard where he needed to reach with his aura hand in order to dissolve the last few clinging bits of rock. When she pronounced the work finished, Mard and Querc backed well clear of the thing as Edda stepped forward, bent her knees, got an arm under the key's shaft, and heaved it up onto her shoulder.

Then for the first time since meeting the giantess at her home on Calla, Prim saw in her face signs of distress. Edda was feeling what ordinary souls felt when they shouldered a burden so heavy as to raise the fear that their strength was not equal to it. "Let us be on our way, crow," she said. "In the soles of my feet I sense things moving it would be well for us to avoid."

They walked for perhaps an hour. Not because the distance was so great but because Edda needed to plant each foot with deliberation. Sometimes she went the long way round when footing was uncertain.

The air began to move in ways suggesting that they were leaving behind the sheltered convolutions of the Knot and approaching a more open area. All of them, seeing how Edda labored under her burden, felt a natural impulse to go to her and lend a hand, as anyone would if they saw their mother bent under the weight of a log, and in danger of losing her footing. But those considerate feelings were useless here; none of them had strength to help the giantess, and by going to her they could only get in her way and risk grave injury. So instead they scampered ahead, scouting for shortcuts or for places where loose gravel might put her at hazard.

It was on one of those scouting-ahead runs that Prim surmounted a fold in the bedrock and felt icy wind in her face and saw, revealed all at once below her, the entirety of the Broken Bridge. As well she could see much of the open space on the near side of it, which on maps was called the Anvil Plain. Formerly, according to the most ancient legends, it had been the Front Yard of the Fastness. It was beginning to collect light now from the eastern sky, which had brightened to the point where stars were dissolving into it. Turning her head to the west, she saw the Red Web a hand's breadth above the horizon, and wondered if the eyes of the Pantheon might be upon her at this moment.

She could from this perch have drawn an arrow, aimed north, let it fly, and watched it arc down several long moments later at the place where the bridge gripped the bedrock of the Knot. From there it reached far out across the Chasm to the nearer of the two gatehouses. The opposite—which she had seen earlier from another vantage point—resumed on the far side of the break and led to the top of the glacier. This was alive with silent distant lightning, as if the whole fury of the Evertempest had been poured down upon one small target. The light shattered her vision and obliged her to instead look down at closer things. "This way!" she called to those coming up behind her. "But you'll need to find another path round." It was out of the question for Edda to climb what she had climbed.

The Chasm was not a straight ditch; it forked and curved like a canyon. Beyond the near terminus of the Broken Bridge, a branch of it split off and curved aside toward the Knot. Running parallel to that was a road, meandering somewhat, but on the whole cutting south across the Anvil Plain. Its first few paces were exposed to the sky and buried in snow, but beyond that it cut through an old rampart of stones and ducked under the shelter of the mountain range and so ran over bare ground. It was too cold here for any plants to grow. Instead of vegetation the road ran among scraps of iron, slag heaps, unfinished chain links, rusted and broken-down wagons, and mounds of coal next to forges that eons ago had gone cold and dark. For El's legions clearly had not seen any point in tidying up after themselves when they had completed their great work and retreated across the bridge. Notable was a huge curving plate, roughly triangular but evidently forged as one segment of a dome. This was simply leaning up against a cliff as if some giant had propped it up there to cool off and forgotten about it. Not far beyond it, the road, and the Chasm's side fork, ran out of view. She had to move sideways a little distance in order to see what gave the Anvil Plain its name: the truncated stump of what had once been a stone crag. El himself had cut it down and flattened its top to make a surface against which his giant smiths could beat out metal. Lying next to it were a hammer and tongs, sized to match.

She felt a bit of a letdown that she could not actually view the Fastness from right here. But the enormous works and discarded pieces of iron that she *could* see were proof that it could not be much farther away, once they got to the Anvil Plain.

She could have scampered down to that in a few moments. Finding a path suitable for Edda might take a little longer. Turning her head she saw Lyne, Mard, Fern, and Querc exploring a possible route under the illumination of Mab. From habit she knew to look for Burr either ahead of or behind the main group—wherever he judged danger to be greatest. Indeed she now picked him out clambering over the rubble wall below, ghostly in predawn skylight. He would soon reach the bridge. Meanwhile Prim could feel each of Edda's footfalls as she made her way. She soon would turn right, toward the Fastness, where Burr had gone left toward the bridge.

But as well she sensed other, deeper disturbances, like the one that had awakened her earlier. Those had first begun when Lyne and Fern had descended to the Chasm and scooped up their sample of chaos. Since then they had come irregularly. But now a series of them came all at once in rapid succession, causing loose stones to skitter down from the slope below her.

A great being was on the move down there. It could only be one of the wild souls left over from the very beginning of the Land.

A thing like a grappling hook reached up from below and caught on the bridge just where it was anchored to the rim. A succession of booms ensued, and then the Chasmian—it could only be the Chasmian—got a second hook-hand planted on the cliff edge. Head, then shoulders appeared, and then the whole thing came up out of the deep at once. It must have planted a foot on the bridge's arch and used that to vault up. First one knee, then the other, came down like thunder on the snowy ground of the Chasm's rim. It was on all fours. Then it rose up, got its feet under it, and stood.

Prim had never actually laid eyes on a hill-giant, unless you counted the sleeping one upon whose back the Calladons had, according to legend, constructed their estate. She had read enough books and seen enough depictions to know that the Chasmian was something made after the same general pattern. Perhaps Spring during her madness had rounded up one such who had been enslaved by El and made to do blacksmith's work. Indeed once the Chasmian had drawn himself up to his full height he stepped over the rampart with a single stride and went on an aimless stroll among the dark forges, and reached down with one of his claws to touch the flat top of the great stone anvil.

But hill-giants were put together out of ordinary stones. Between those was earth. Soil covered them like flesh when they stopped moving for more than a few falls, and in the soil grew grass and flowers and trees. If the Chasmian had been that kind of hill-giant at the beginning, one could guess that his vegetation had been burned off by the heat of the forge as he toiled for El, or frozen by the cold of the Knot when he was allowed to rest. When El had broken the bridge and abandoned it here, the giant must have been nothing more than boulders mortared together by sand and clay, clothed in ice.

In that estate Spring would have found him wandering upon the Anvil Plain, alone and without purpose. Since then his boulders had been replaced, one by one, with chunks of adamant shaped to their purposes: long ones in the limbs, clusters of lumps at joints. Instead of earth, what held him together now was chaos, flowing and surging between the stone bones as they moved. Prim thought for some reason of watching Edda knead dough in her kitchen, how her strong hands made the soft stuff surge out from beneath them and escape through the spaces between her fingers. The chaos did something like that as the Chasmian's adamant skeleton pushed it this way and that. Whenever it seemed it was about to escape and dissipate, it would turn back inward, proving that it was under the power of an animating soul.

Another thing said of hill-giants was that they didn't have discernible heads—at least, not the kind that swiveled on necks and had faces on them. But this Chasmian had ordered itself differently. Above the shoulders, a never-ending avalanche of smaller chunks of adamant was turning itself inside out, driven by an inner core of turbulent aura that could only be glimpsed through ephemeral gaps opening and closing between the storm of black stone. Stared at closely, this looked a little like a whorl of dry leaves caught in a pocket of wind, save that the wind was a soul and the leaves were chunks of primordial rock. But if one tore one's gaze from it—which required some willpower—and looked at it sidelong, in the overall scheme of the Chasmian's form it answered to the posture and movements of a head.

Which meant that it could turn this way and that, and look at things. During its first moments on the Anvil Plain, it looked mostly at the ruins of the works where it had once toiled. But then its attention—as well as Prim's—was drawn to a brilliant light that had exposed itself.

Burr had drawn his sword.

The Chasmian saw it, and knew it. Something in the way it moved made it clear that it recognized the weapon; feared it; and hated it. El's angels must have used such things to drive the Chasmian, as Beedles drove beasts with sticks and whips.

"Burr, no!" Prim called. She was already on her way down to him. As she descended she cut across the path that Edda was soon to tread with measured steps toward the Fastness. Burr's plan was clear: he would draw the Chasmian back toward the bridge, distracting its gaze and leaving the way clear for the rest of the party to cut behind it and get to the Fastness.

"Stay well back, Princess!" Burr shouted to her. Indeed she had slowed as she got nearer to him, for the brilliance of the sword made it difficult for her to see the path ahead, and the footing was difficult. "This is a task for me."

"It is a task for *me!*" Prim insisted. "I see that now. It is why I was brought here." Shading her eyes with one arm, she looked about for Corvus. Corvus had foreseen all of this. He had known that only Prim could slay the Chasmian. With a word, Corvus could cause Burr to sheathe the sword. But she did not see the giant talking raven anywhere. Only the Chasmian. Its rage had overcome its fear and it was advancing toward Burr with a fixed regard and a steady pace.

Edda emerged into the open ground of the Anvil Plain, following Lyne, who was showing her the way and kicking loose pebbles out of her path. The Chasmian either did not see her or did not care. Burr ran laterally, brandishing his sword, both movements calculated to draw the giant's attention away from Edda. Edda looked ancient and bent under her burden but seemed to find it in her now to lengthen her stride a bit and cover ground faster.

So that was all to the good. Prim went the way Burr was going. She might not have been able to talk Burr out of his mad scheme, but once the Chasmian drew close enough, she could kill it. Provided that she went where it was going. Which was wherever Burr was waving that sword about.

"It's working!" she informed Burr, when she thought she had advanced within range of his hearing. "The others are cutting around behind. But you do not have to fight this thing! Run away!"

"Look about. We have our backs to the cliff edge. The bridge is broken. What choice is there but to fight it?"

"You know perfectly well."

"Oh, no, Princess! You must not!"

"Why not, Burr!?"

"This thing is the only being that has the power to stop him who pursues us!" And Burr—normally a stand-square-to-the-enemy type—took the unusual measure of turning his back on the Chasmian for a moment and pointing with his sword to the opposite side of the gorge.

"Burr! Look out!" Prim shouted. But instead of taking the time to look, Burr dove sideways and rolled to his feet. In the place where he had been standing a moment earlier, an adamant claw had sunk into the snow and broken the rock. It was the extremity of a writhing snake of stone and aura that reached all the way back to the Chasmian's shoulder. Both Burr and Prim had assumed the foe to be far out of range; but they now knew it could fling its arms out to a distance many times their apparent length. The claw began to drag backward across the ground, then sprang into the air as its owner retracted it.

While the Chasmian was reassembling itself, Prim spared a moment to look the way Burr had pointed. The last time she had paid any attention to the top of the glacier, she'd seen nothing but a lightning storm, strangely focused on one place. As if all of the Lightning Bears had come together for a purpose. Now, though, there was nothing to see opposite save an individual soul. He was walking along the path toward the far end of the Broken Bridge. He was barefoot, and lightly dressed for the weather in a white robe. In form he was like an angel, but he did not have wings. Circling high above him, like a crow harrying an eagle, was Corvus.

So this, it seemed, was the soul who had followed the Quest all the way across the Stormland. Instead of passing through the cave as they had done, he had simply strolled barefoot along the Shifting Path over the glacier. No wonder the Lightning Bears had been so furious. But they had not stopped him.

Once again the Chasmian lashed out from a distance, forcing Burr to dodge and roll clear of a meteoric claw.

"Sing of me that I fought this," he said to Prim as he came to his feet. Then he leaned forward and took off running toward the giant, hoping perhaps that in the time it would take the foe to collect itself he could get close enough to attack its legs. "No!" Prim cried, and took off running on a parallel track.

The next blow came sooner than expected, but Burr was in a position to dodge cleverly behind a mound of slag, and so barely broke stride before he was able to resume his headlong attack. Prim could not match the warrior's pace. But she thought she was close enough now. She fixed her gaze on the storm of stone that served as the Chasmian's head—

—and found herself skidding across the ground with snow in her mouth. Something had knocked her down. Not the Chasmian, or she'd have been dead. She rolled onto her back and looked up to see Corvus wheeling back around toward her. "You must not do it," he said. "The Chasmian is the only thing that can buy us the time we need. Spring made it for the purpose it must carry out next, and for long ages it has collected its strength in the deep, preparing for this day. Do not seek to deprive this one of his destiny."

The light of the angel sword flashed. Prim got to her feet and looked to the Chasmian. Burr had got close enough to have a go at its ankles. Any part of the creature above its shins was out of his reach. The warrior was able to close in and land a few strikes.

Even that sword could do little more than cleave off shards of the adamant boulders that served the Chasmian as feet. Preoccupied as he was with avoiding kicks and stomps that the Chasmian aimed his way, Burr was blind to what came from above: a long downward sweep of the arm that caught him full along the side of his body and launched him into the air. Somewhere in midflight the sword fell from his nerveless hand and sank blade-first into the frozen earth, casting the plain into darkness. Burr tumbled and rolled for some distance when he came down again. Some of those movements recalled those of a living soul. But when he stopped, he stopped for good.

"Nothing could have survived that," Corvus said. "Burr did his job! Now do yours and get after the others!"

The Chasmian had turned his head to look curiously toward Prim. She put her back to the bridge and began running. The giant took a step toward her, perhaps thinking to bar the way, but then Corvus was in its face, distracting it for long enough that Prim was able to dodge behind an abandoned ore wagon that was larger than some people's houses. From there she identified another hiding place a short distance away, in the form of a mound of coal beside a forge, and from there another and another until she had put a good distance between herself and the Chasmian without ever having to spend too much time in the open.

She reached the shadow of the stone anvil. Risking a look behind her, she saw that the danger was past. The Chasmian had lost interest in her. It stood with its back to her now, facing north toward the bridge.

Curiosity now overtook her good sense. She trotted up a set of rude stair steps that led to the anvil's flat top. There she had a look round. First she looked south, thinking only to glance at the rest of the party and make a note of where they were. Which she did; but then, gazing a little farther down the road, where it led deeper beneath the overhang, she spied something that demanded a longer look.

She had imagined for some reason that the Fastness would be farther away and more deeply embedded in the Knot. But there it stood. It was right before them. And sweeping her gaze quickly from side to side, she took in the whole scene and understood how it was that the four great mountain ranges of the Land came together in this place, each with its own kind of rock, and were involved with one another in a manner that explained why it was called the Knot and why it could not be undone without breaking the Land asunder. Looking up at the Overhang, she could see snow and loose stones resting upon surfaces where by rights they ought to have fallen down on her head. She sensed that, had the Quest approached from some other direction, they might have been standing there right now and looking "up" at where Prim stood and wondering why she did not fall off the anvil.

But if you approached it from the north, as they had done, why, then when you reached this place the Fastness stood upright as a proper castle ought to and the road led straight to its front door. It was not surrounded with a moat or other fortification, like some castles down in the Land, for it was guarded by the Evertempest and all the terrain the party had put behind them during the last few days. Its walls rose sheer from the black bedrock to a great height. For Egdod had raised it with the power of his soul, the same that had made the entirety of the Land, and observed no ordinary limits as to where building stones might be quarried or how high they might be stacked up. He had done it, according to legend, to prove to himself that he still had that power, at least when he could work in a solitary place without the eyes of other souls upon him. So its bastions and towers borrowed some of their general shapes from fortifications of a more practical nature, but were fantastical and strangely wrought according to Egdod's whim. The front of it was symmetrical, perhaps as a way to discourage curious visitors, but farther back along its sides Egdod had experimented with more fanciful inventions in the way of high towers and oriels, some of which were still connected to the living rock of the Knot that enfolded the whole structure. The road led straight to its front gate, and the side fork of the Chasm tunneled beneath.

But those parts Prim had to guess at and see in her mind's eye, for, as Weaver had sung, the whole top of it was surmounted by an iron dome of curving plates riveted together, rough and ready like the battle helms that Beedle smiths hammered out in their forges and issued to Beedle sergeants. From the rim of it, chains and straps of iron depended and lower down were connected in a haphazard improvised style to more ironmongery that encircled the walls, clasping plates over windows and doorways. From this distance it put her in mind of how it looked when a carter piled a lot of assorted cargo on a wagon and then threw loops of rope around it every which way, tying a knot here, bending a rope through another rope there and hauling it tight, not caring whether the web had any order or symmetry about it provided it served its purpose. She almost wondered whether its very crudeness had been intended to mock the beauty of what it enclosed.

Beneath her feet the anvil shook. She whirled about to see that the Chasmian had turned about and was now headed her way! But during the few moments that she stood paralyzed with shock, it diverted to one side and stepped over toward the huge curved plate of iron she had noticed earlier, leaning against a cliff. She had assumed it was a portion of the great dome that for some long-forgotten reason had never been used. And perhaps it was; but the Chasmian intended to use it now. The giant gripped the plate between its claws and rotated it to show its concave side. This had a length of chain riveted in place like the straps on the back of a warrior's shield. The Chasmian slung it over its shoulder.

While it was thus occupied Prim had a clear view north up the road to the bridge. The white figure had by now advanced from the far side of the Chasm all the way up the bridge to the first gatehouse. Calmly he raised his hands, and the bridge began to grow ahead of him. He strolled forward, planting his bare feet on newly made bridge deck that had not existed moments earlier. Beneath that, the supporting arch mounted at a pace to match. The near stump of the bridge had become tinged with chaos, like Mard's arm where it had been cut. It began to extend itself north, reaching across the gorge to join up with its other half.

The Chasmian picked up a chain link that had been lying discarded on the ground for millennia. It had been made by taking a rod of iron as thick as the body of a full-grown man and looping it round. The giant reared back and slung it directly at El. For the white figure on the bridge could only be El himself. El saw it coming and with a casual flick of the arm made it falter in its flight and crash down upon the bridge. There it did damage. But El had the means to repair it and so this did not much slow him. The Chasmian threw other things, with similar results; the bridge, on the whole, continued to heal itself. The gap narrowed. El advanced.

The dawn had progressed to the point where the whole scene was well lit. Prim could see Corvus silhouetted, wheeling about the Chasmian and apparently trying to offer suggestions. And somehow he must have got through to whatever passed for its mind, for suddenly it unfixed its gaze from El and looked straight up. Then directly it hove up its shield, just in time to deflect a rock the size of a house that had dropped straight down out of the sky. The sound that it made when it caromed from the iron plate was sickening.

Prim looked up and saw a rock falling directly toward *her*. It, and more, were coming from the Overhang. El, through some conjury, was reversing the direction of gravity up there. She ran across the flat of the anvil and dove over its edge just before the boulder smashed into the place where she had been standing. The stairway caught her fall. Immediately she rolled onto her back and gazed up, expecting more. El's strategy was clear. He knew that he faced Death. He must keep Death at bay.

That being the case, she did not wish to endanger her comrades by coming too close to them. They were struggling up a long stair that led to the front gate of the Fastness, where the great lock hung askew in its web of chains. They were most of the way there. Prim could see a mote of light orbiting round the lock, darting into its keyhole and out again. Lyne was up there, moving on a chain like a spider on silk. Querc and Marc had already got to the lock. Mard was reaching into it with his auric hand, perhaps cleaning out thousands of years' piled snow and dirt. Fern was pacing Edda on her slow and labored ascent of the stairs, turning to face her. Prim knew what she was doing: talking to the giantess, who now looked like nothing other than a poor hag bent under a burden far too heavy to bear. Yet there was nothing Fern could do to help her other than to offer words of encouragement. With each step Edda surmounted, Fern celebrated and praised her and urged her to the next.

Battle had been joined at the bridgehead, and part of Prim regretted she was not there to witness it and perhaps write it in a song, or, one day in the future, describe it to a weaver who could make of it a tapestry. She looked up to see if any more boulders were falling but saw none. Perhaps El had his hands full for the moment fighting the Chasmian. One would certainly think so! There had to be limits even to El's power. If not, why did he fear Egdod so? Why had he not, in El's absence, altogether remade the Land as he wished to see it?

And he feared Prim. He feared the power that was hers enough that he had tried to kill her once already.

Did El know—could he know—that they had a key to the Fastness? It must have lodged in that cube of stone for a long time. Had El known of its existence, he'd have destroyed it. They had only got it free of the Cube this morning. But El had been following them across the Stormland for *days*. So it could not be the case that the knowledge of the key had drawn him here.

Sophia had drawn him here. Even at the Quest's outset, El had somehow known that a person of interest would be passing through Secondel and had alerted Elshield. The death of Elshield and of several others must have confirmed what he had perhaps suspected, or feared: that Sophia was abroad in the Land and knew her power. He had made a second attempt to catch her at the Asking, but she had vanished. And at almost the same instant, one of his angels had died at Lost Lake. El must have known of Pluto's system of chaos tunnels and must have guessed that Sophia had made use of one. He had gone to Lost Lake and followed their trail. Now he was here, raining boulders against the Chasmian's shield while advancing one step at a time across the remade bridge. The Chasmian was giving almost as good as he got, lashing out with his claw to attack while shouldering his shield to defend. His weapon did not seem able to penetrate the sphere of aura that surrounded El.

As Prim watched, its claw faltered in midstrike and fell like an amputated hand into the gorge. The Chasmian was soon able to replace it with a discarded piece of ironmongery, a huge tong that must have been used once to hoist a crucible. But while he was doing so, El advanced, at last putting the bridge behind him and setting foot on the near side of the Chasm. Prim had the presence of mind to guess that El might now take advantage of his foe's disordered state to aim more attacks at her, and she was correct; looking up she saw several more rocks fall loose from the Overhang and come her way. Seen, they were easily avoided.

She was more worried about the party on the front steps of the Fastness. Preoccupied as they were with the key and the lock, they wouldn't know that El had crossed over and would not be looking for incoming rocks. But El did not seem to be sending any their way. Which confirmed in her mind that El might not even have known about the key. He might have been asking himself why Sophia had gone to such trouble to come here, where her one power was of no use; but his only thought was to get to her and kill her.

So she ascended the stair again, all the way to the flat top of the stone anvil, and put her back to the Fastness and walked north to the very edge, making sure that El could see her. She could actually feel his gaze upon her when he had a moment to take his eyes away from the Chasmian. She felt almost close enough to look him in the eye and kill him. But he knew her power and would keep his distance. By standing here and merely staying alive, she could keep him at bay. She could keep El from reaching, or even knowing about, the ones behind her with the key. So there she stood, observing the fight and standing sentinel for anything El might throw her way.

He was finding more opportunities to do so. From time to time he would absorb a blow from the Chasmian that would nearly reduce him to formless aura, but he had the power to regenerate before his foe could wind up to deliver another. The Chasmian took somewhat longer to reorganize its form when El had disrupted it. Balancing this was the fact that the Chasmian had an infinite reserve handy of the two things of which it was made: rocks and chaos. At one point a flying boulder laid it out flat on the brink of the gorge, right next to the bridge, so that Prim feared it would slide off and sink into the chaos below; but instead the chaos came to it, and replenished what it had lost, and the boulder that had struck it down became part of its form. Thus the battle raged back and forth, and Prim dared not go back to the other edge of the anvil to see how Edda was getting along. But she did notice a conflagration of Lightning Bears up on the glacier, seemingly headed toward the bridge; and in their midst was a darker form that she took at first for an Autochthon, since it was riding a mount.

But the bears would have annihilated any such. They were not there to fight the rider. They were escorting it. Escorting *her*.

El seemed aware of this. Prim could very nearly read his mind. He wanted no part of fighting the Chasmian while being trapped between Death and this personage on the galloping mount. He made himself larger, and in a few moments' time delivered such a barrage upon the Chasmian, from all directions, as to derange it completely. It collapsed to a disordered pile of rocks and chaos, most of which avalanched down into the gorge. Prim sensed it was not dead. It would always come back. But in the time it would take for it to reorganize itself, El could attend to other matters. He glanced toward Sophia for a few moments, then turned his back to her; faced the bridge; and brought it down with a gesture.

Prim had learned to look up when El might be in a position to attack her. She did so now, and saw nothing. But she did get dizzy, as sometimes happened when looking up, and this time it was enough to drop her to her knees. She felt a pain in her breast and tried to put her hand to the spot, but it was interrupted by something hard.

She looked down to see that she had been transfixed by a black arrow. It had gone straight into her chest. It had come, she understood, from El; he had conjured it into being and launched it at her during that brief glance. Its shaft was already enshrouded in her aura as her body began to dissolve around it.

She fell over on her side. With her eyes half-open she could see the rider gallop down to the bridgehead and rein in her horse at the bridge that was now again broken. Behind her a pack of Lightning Bears was coming in off the glacier.

It now seemed for a little while that the world consisted entirely of noise. She had heard many loud noises of late, what with all of the Evertempest's thunder and the clamorous boulder duel between El and the Chasmian. Those were but clicks and whispers compared to the sound that came now from the direction of the Fastness. It was so loud that it startled El, and the rider across the gorge, and her Lightning Bears. Prim, before her vision dissolved into chaos, had at least the satisfaction of seeing El turn around, and astonishment come over him. It was such a distinct reaction that she had to turn her head and see what he was seeing: the Fastness unbound, its iron dome rocking from side to side where it had been shrugged off, and chains and hasps still avalanching down all round it. Perched on the top of the castle was a figure nearly as great as the Chasmian, but of human form.

Or so it seemed until it spread its wings.

Egdod saw at once that the tempest he had laid over the Knot in ancient times had served its purpose and was no longer of use to him, and so with a wave of his hand he stilled it. In the calm air that followed he spread his wings and took flight, but glided only a short distance to the top of the stone anvil, where Sophia lay dying. He took her dissolving form up into his arms as a mother takes up a baby, and gathered her into his chest.

"Once again our time together is all too brief," said Sophia to Egdod, though she had lost the power of forming words and could only speak through the connection of their auras.

"The sweeter for that," Egdod returned. "Know that your sacrifice was not in vain. The Quest is complete."

"Edda will need rest," she said, her aura growing very faint.

"She has come to a good place for resting," said Egdod, "as have you."

Then the thread of her life was severed.

The sun had now erupted through the broken wall of clouds. It was not the only source of light. El had stood astonished for some while at the sight of the lock opened, the Fastness unbound, and Egdod free in the Land. Now he forsook the form of an ordinary soul walking. He rose into the air and made himself as large as Egdod, that the two of them might converse as beings of equal stature. He grew as well in brilliance, shining with a golden light as that of the sun. Egdod for his part seemed content with the form he had taken at the time of the Fall, which was as dark as the Firmament into which he and the other members of the Pantheon had been projected. For some while neither he nor El spoke. Both were marshaling their forces. Behind El, opposing sides of the Chasm had gone into movement, thickening and bending toward each other. When those two sides touched they would form an arch a hundred times broader than the old bridge. Waiting on its opposite side were Spring upon her mount, and her escort of bears; and behind them marching in a long file down the Shifting Path were legions of Dug she had summoned to arms.

Seeing this El laughed in Egdod's face. "Shall you and I trifle further about the bridge? You can build it up and I can throw it down for the next thousand years."

Egdod responded, "I am taking no action in the matter. The changes you see are the work of another who has an interest in such things." And he looked back toward the Fastness. Atop its highest tower a hooded figure stood, extending his arms and sending forth his power. Besides Pluto, others could be seen now too: Love below on the steps, tending to Edda, who lay spent next to the open lock. Freewander darting high and Thingor limping along the battlements, directing the work of other souls who seemed to be emerging in force from the depths of it, and War marshaling formations of armed and armored souls pouring forth out of chaos from the Firmament, moving in synchrony with wild musics emanating from Pan and an orchestra of music-making souls that Pan had drawn up along a high parapet.

"It is of no account whether your hand or Pluto's shapes the bridge," El said. "Even when I walked over the Stormland in the guise of an ordinary soul, alone and unarmed, I swept away Dug like so many insects, and the worst assaults of the Lightning Bears were mere diversions to me. The Chasmian that Spring made to greet me at your front door was a greater foe, I will admit; but it lies broken at the bottom of yonder gorge, and when it climbs out I shall break it again. Only Sophia had power against me; and I can see that she is no more."

Egdod held out his right hand. Cupped in it was a tiny knot of aura. "That is saying too much," he answered.

"We may also trifle over words," said El, "but to put it plainly, your plan has failed."

"My plan," said Egdod, "is still unfolding. Pent up for so long in the Fastness, I have learned patience. It is a faculty you have lost, ruling the Land from your high Palace where all things come quickly, and you confuse delay with failure."

Their sparring lapsed for some time as many things were happening all round. Above the glacier opposite, a giant raven could be seen wheeling over the vanguard of the Dug army, showing them the way. The farther they advanced, the broader their front became, as they found that the narrow path had swelled to a broad road. Pluto was healing the cracked glacier beneath their feet, mending the crevasses that since ancient times had always threatened to swallow unwary travelers. Their swiftest scouts were even now reaching the bridgehead. This was developing a green tinge as plants of various kinds erupted from what had long been barren ground. The two sides of the Chasm had extended to where they nearly touched above the center of the gorge. Vines and roots had already reached across the gap.

But El had legions of his own. His angels, long held at bay by the Evertempest, must have issued forth from the Palace at the moment the key had entered the lock and undone the gate of the Fastness. On swift wings they had covered the distance from Pinnacle to Knot as Sophia had expired and Pluto had reshaped the Land and Thingor had begun his works upon the battlements. Now they were beginning to appear, in ones and twos and soon enough in echelons, in the clear sky above. Their bright swords they kept sheathed for now. The only unsheathed weapon in the whole scene was in the hand of winged War, who had emerged from the Fastness after Egdod, and drawn Burr's angel sword out of the earth where it had stuck. He looked a match for any ten angels. But above were already more than ten, and soon there would be hundreds.

Horns were blowing and hooves beating the earth to the north and west. A battle flag appeared over the crest of a ridge on the other side of the Chasm. Next came a row of lances whose sharp edges gleamed in the light of the sun. It was a regiment of Autochthon cavalry on their mounts, and at its head was a woman whose long yellow hair streamed like a pennant from beneath her bright helm: Sooth of El. They must have been summoned days ago through the weird emanations of the Hive, and ridden to this place.

In this way did the armies of El converge toward the Fastness, and it had to be admitted that in their speed, their number, and their beauty they made the opposition seem feeble and disarrayed. It was only the towering form of Egdod himself, standing upon the stone anvil with the tiny ball of aura cupped in his hand, that could give any hope whatever to those who rejoiced at his return.

The hoofbeats of a solitary mount traversed the Anvil Plain from the direction of the bridge. War flourished his sword in salute and bowed low to Spring as she galloped past him. Egdod gazed down on her approach with a face that showed sorrow and joy. But knowing that the eyes of El and many others were upon him he spoke brusquely, and not to Spring but to Freewander, who was dipping and wheeling about him: "Show her where to form up."

And so for a time the Anvil Plain was alive with preparations for battle as Freewander led Spring to a position where the advance of the Autochthons could be blocked, or at least slowed, should it come to a clash of arms. The Lightning Bears followed her and the Dug followed them. Behind the old rampart they formed up, facing north toward the bridge. War strode to and fro along their lines mustering them into battle array. The blasts of Pan's trumpets brought order; the booming of Pan's war drums made their blood boil.

"None of this matters," said El. "You can make whatever preparations you please on the ground. The air is filled with my angels."

Sooth's cavalry came in force over the bridge to the Anvil Plain. They arrayed themselves facing the Dug. Spring was amusing herself by causing thick sweet grass to grow in the place between, and Sooth's mounts, seeing and smelling it, were causing no end of trouble for their riders. They must have been galloping for days from Secondel and they must have been ravenous.

"Summon your angels to war then," said Egdod, and suddenly beat his wings and launched himself into the air. A few angels who had made bold to swoop low got well clear of him. He flew back to the Fastness and landed upon a high battlement from which he could see all and all could see him. Below, the gate boomed shut. Edda and the other members of the Quest had been made guests within.

Defender of El led the charge, an echelon of warrior angels behind him. They wheeled down out of the blue sky in a wedge and came straight for Egdod.

"Fire," said Egdod.

And there was fire: bolts of it stabbing from the tops of the Fastness's walls and from embrasures farther down. It came from dark tubes of metal, each of which had a crew of souls to feed it, and as soon as all of them had been discharged, they set to work preparing them to fire again.

All of which was a detail little noticed since Defender of El and many of his angels had fallen to the ground and were lying dead or broken on the plain between the anvil and the Fastness.

Another rank of angels wheeled into position above, ready to renew the attack. Defender of El lay dead. All eyes turned to El, who hovered a little distance above the ground at the opposite end of the battlefield, near the wide bridge already carpeted in green and growing things.

"At your command, Lord El!" shouted an angel who seemed to have assumed command.

The same words were echoed a moment later by Sooth below. She had raised her sword as if to signal a charge.

El hesitated.

The ground was shaking, but El did not know it because his feet were not in contact with the Land.

The Chasmian vaulted out of the gorge behind him. No longer impeded by its massive shield, it lashed out with both arms and wrapped them around El's form from behind. In an effort to escape the bear hug, El became mostly a thing of aura. The two forms became intermingled as they struggled and writhed at the brink; then, with the slowness of a great tree that has been cut through at the root, they toppled into the Chasm and disappeared.

"Hold your fire," Egdod commanded, and took to the air again, flying in a broad circuit over the battlefield. Which was now merely a field, since it was suddenly clear to all present that no battle would be taking place on the Anvil Plain this day. To Sooth he spoke: "Your task has been accomplished. Not the one El had in mind for you, which was false. But the one I ordained, which was to see what you just saw. You may complete it by grazing your mounts on the sweet grass and then riding home to tell everyone you see—Autochthons, Beedles, Sprung, and wild souls of all shapes—what has here occurred."

He then beat his wings powerfully and mounted up into the air, where the surviving angels were arrayed in their echelons. Many were too bright to look upon, but they dimmed when Egdod commanded them to sheathe their swords and they did so. "Your weapons were stolen from Thingor," Egdod said. "He will collect them below. If you regret giving them up, console yourselves with the knowledge that they are useless against what Thingor has conjured up in the ages since. Go out into the Land and do useful things. One day I shall come back to my Palace to inspect it; I expect that everything will be in good order there."

Swooping down low over the Fastness he spoke to all within and around it: "I have business in the Firmament. Before long I shall return. You know what to do." And pulling up high, he made a pivot in midair, folded his wings, and dove headfirst into the center of the Fastness. Those standing outside, who saw him plunge out of view and who did not know that place's secrets, might have expected to hear a crash as he plummeted headfirst into the ground. But those within saw him fall into the chaos upon which the building had been founded.

The door of the Fastness opened. A frail old lady emerged, supported to either side by younger souls. She tottered down the long stair, pausing more than once to rest. The ground before her was strewn with fallen angels dissolving. The stuff of which they had been made began to converge upon the old lady, and she began to gain weight and strength from it as she drew it into her form.

55

Zula had fallen out of the habit of watching Bitworld, because, by and large, it happened too fast to be really intelligible. She wondered if she was senile—or if she seemed that way. She had a memory of a Thanksgiving, more than a hundred years ago, when she and some of her cousins had been hanging out in the TV room of the Forthrast farmhouse in Iowa, passing the time with a video game, and she had looked up at some point to see Uncle Claude, spry and curious at eighty-three, standing in the doorway looking at the big screen perfectly aghast. It was hard to tell how long he'd been standing there trying to make sense of it all. But there was clearly a feeling that some combination of age and culture shock had shifted Uncle Claude into a lower gear than all the other people in the room, that his clock was ticking at a slower rate than everyone else's.

When Zula—or anyone else in Meatspace—watched Bitworld, that was, of course, literally true. The Time Slip Ratio had veered all over the place during the century that Zula had been doing this job. But in the last couple of decades, since ALISS had gone orbital, the trend had been toward greater speed. Freed from earthbound limitations on how much power could be generated, how much heat dissipated, how much fiber laid, and how many resources quarried out of the ground (for they built everything out of asteroids now), they'd kept pace with demand and then some. Consequently time in Bitworld had, on the whole, sped up. It was no longer like watching a human drama acted out in real time. More like an ant colony.

So she had stopped looking at it. Oh, she could see it perfectly well. Presbyopia had given way to cataracts, organic lenses replaced with artificial ones. The retinas she'd been born with had been swapped out for new ones, grown in a lab, hooked up to her optic nerve by a microscopic robot surgeon. For a while, her brain's visual cortex hadn't known what to make of the new and improved signals coming in on that channel, and so she had had to learn how to see again—a difficult thing for one of her age, but made easier by neuroplasticity medication derived from the stuff Maeve had experimented with ages ago.

So now Zula could see every bit as well as she had been able to when she had been seven years old. It was just that she would rather use that faculty to look at things in the real world. When gazing into the land of the dead, she felt that same bafflement, the same disconnect, as Uncle Claude.

Uncle Claude had stood there anyway and gamely tried to bend his old mind around it because he had known that the youngsters in that room were his kin and that this stuff was important to them. Likewise Zula was aware that during recent days (as time was measured in Meatspace) momentous things had been going on in Bitworld involving the processes that had been booted up there to simulate the consciousnesses of her daughter, Sophia; her friends Corvallis and Maeve; and perhaps others as well. They had been moving around the Landform rather a lot, and interacting with one another, and Sophia had terminated a few other processes. Zula was aware that this was all being watched with great interest by the dwindling population of living humans who still existed on planet Earth.

So she walked down to the office one lovely fall evening to see what all the fuss was about. She could walk—or run, for that matter—all day if she wanted. Of course, it was Fronk whose feet actually contacted the ground, whose joints took her weight, whose sensors and algorithms saw to it she didn't keel over. She had been wearing Fronk for decades now and would die pretty quickly if she doffed it. She could not have walked, or even stood up, without it. She wore it to bed. It *was* her bed.

South Lake Union had held its own as a place where biological humans physically came together to work on things. Nowadays, mostly what they worked on was the high-level management of ALISS. Of course, the bulk of the *actual* work was performed by robots in space. None of those was even remotely humanoid. Their AIs were tuned to analyze space rocks and to solve conundrums relating to scheduling of tasks, logistical coordination, and resource allocation. You couldn't talk to them, and if you could, it would have been like having a conversation with a shovel. The humans working below on the surface of Earth were just keeping an eye on things, looking way down the road, making sure that the robots could go on finding more space rocks and fashioning them into more robots until they ran out of space rocks. Then, if they needed to, they could begin busting up unused moons and planets, or go out to the asteroid belt between Mars and Jupiter, where there were many more rocks. The end state of all this would be a Dyson sphere: a hollow shell of rock and metal that would capture all of the sun's power, spend it in computation, and radiate the waste heat into the cosmos as dull infrared light. But it would take a long, long time to get to that point. Long enough for every human now living to die of natural causes, even if they all used as many life-extension technologies as Zula. Earth, or at least a patch of Earthlike ecosystem, would be preserved as a kind of park, and bio-humans could live on it, if that was what they were into.

Nowadays the building looked as it had in the very beginning, when the steelworkers and the concrete pumpers had roughed in the structure but the framers had not yet shown up with studs and drywall. The floor-to-ceiling windows still looked exactly like windows, but were now actually complicated robots in their own right, making all kinds of moment-to-moment decisions about which wavelengths, and how much of them, to let in or out of the building.

When she walked in, the place was *crowded,* more so than she'd seen it in years. The windows had figured out, or been told, that people wanted it pretty dark so that they could watch Bitworld. Of course, everyone had glasses that would show them whatever they felt like seeing. But at times like this there was a lot to be said for shared communal viewing, so they had fired up a larger and more powerful appliance, a stationary holographic projector that could pump out a lot of photons. So everyone was looking at its output with naked eyes, sharing the experience.

"You got here just in time!" someone exclaimed. It was Eva, a younger staff member whose mere presence and energy always made Zula feel very much like Uncle Claude. But she was a lovely person and Zula really didn't mind.

"Just in time for what?" Zula asked. Her voice cracked and rasped; she didn't use it much nowadays. She was maneuvering sideways trying to get a better angle; Fronk was respecting her overall dictates but doing so in a way that didn't violate any safety heuristics. Zula, left to her own devices, would have used her little-old-lady prerogatives to elbow her way through the crowd. So progress was safe, polite, and slow.

She was piecing together glimpses. The display had been zoomed and panned to a part of the Landform that was not immediately familiar to her. She had a strong Uncle Claude feeling of not being able to make sense of what she was looking at. Then she spied a detail that helped her understand that this was the vicinity of the region once dubbed Escherville, exactly because it did not, in fact, make sense. It was a zone where notoriously the Landform Visualization Utility had never been able to pull together a coherent geometry. For decades, Ph.D. students and postdocs had tried to debug it. They had concluded that there was no bug; the LVU was working perfectly; the Landform hereabouts actually did not make any sense and so it just had to be shown in a suggestive and unstable way.

So Zula was looking at Escherville: the baroque castle-like structure that Dodge had built in the middle of it, the unsightly additions that El had made to it later. Not far away, the verdant zone where Verna tended to hang out with one of the new processes she had spawned—the one that looked female—inevitably, Eve. Probably, come to think of it, the namesake of the young woman at Zula's elbow.

"What's been going on?" Zula asked.

"Time Slip Ratio has been dropping—big processes using a lot of mana, loading the heck out of the systems," said Eva. "It is actually approaching one now. That's the lowest—"

"Lowest it has been in decades," said Zula.

"But earlier today—in Meatspace time, that is—Sophia and the people she's with *teleported* from the extreme southwest to an area north of here. Later they teleported a second time—not as far."

Eva was so freaked out by that that Zula felt obliged to let her know, "Pluto used to teleport, way back when. We haven't seen much of it since he moved to Landform Two."

"Well anyway, they've been on the move southward ever since."

"They?"

"Sophia and a group of other processes—including Corvallis and Maeve! And guess who has been hot on their trail?"

"I don't need to guess," said Zula. She had finally maneuvered to a position where she could clearly see El himself striding south across high territory toward Escherville. "All of this just happened in the last few hours?"

"Meatspace time? Yes."

Zula glanced at a chronograph on Fronk's arm. It was now eight o'clock in the evening. "How long is that in Bitworld?"

"Three days have passed there. But as you can see," Eva went on, "it is slowing way down. And look! Now Verna is on the move!" Her attention had been drawn by exclamations from other viewers positioned farther to the east. Indeed it was possible to see a female form astride a horse, galloping as if to intercept El. The movement was too fast for the horse's gait to look quite natural. But as Eva had pointed out, the Time Slip Ratio was dropping fast. So it got slower and more normal-looking as Verna drew closer.

"What is *that* woman carrying? It looks heavy!" Zula asked, pointing to a figure who seemed to be bent under a heavy load.

"We've been trying to categorize it. Grepping through ancient datasets. It seems to be the avatar of a cryptographic key. El made it a long time ago. Then he destroyed it. But not before Corvallis did something sneaky—used his privs to make a copy."

"So, that's the copy?"

"Apparently."

One reason for the slowdown was obvious: the Landform was changing its shape. El was causing a bridge to grow across the gap separating him from Escherville, where Sophia and Maeve and several others were up to something at the approaches to the abandoned castle.

"I get it," Zula said, in a bold assertion of non–Uncle Claude-ness. "He's burning a lot of mana. Actually reshaping the Land-form in real time. But just making a bridge isn't expensive enough to slow things down that much."

"True that," said a young man nearby. Inevitably, Zula couldn't remember his name, but she basically liked him, which was all that mattered. "Most of the slowdown is actually being caused by mana use from processes over in Landform Two. Old-school Pan-theon gangstas. Including the notorious REAP."

True That, as Zula had decided to call him, had been mostly hanging around in a corner of the big room with a smaller cluster of people who were looking at visualizations related to Landform 2: the separate chunk of Bitworld where the Pantheon seemed to hang out. Because it was all veiled in weird crypto over there, no one could really tell what it looked like, and so they were looking at abstractions: moving charts, fluctuating surfaces of data, rivers of text.

"And how do you know it is a Renascent Egdod-Associated Pro-cess?" Zula asked.

True That got an awkward look on his face. She could tell she'd committed a sort of faux pas. If she'd been a twenty-year-old in-tern he'd have confidently mansplained it to her. Because she was who she was, he couldn't see a way forward.

She had to find it for him. "Never mind," she said. "You can just tell. You have heuristics. REAPs just give off a certain holographic vibe. When one pops up, alarms go off."

"Something like that, ma'am," he answered with a nod so deep it almost became a bow. Behind him, she could see the thing they were looking at over there: one of those 3-D data visualizations you had to have a math degree to make sense of.

A notion occurred to her and she tossed it out, just to be mis-chievous: "Has anyone actually *looked* at it recently?"

"At what?"

"Landform Two. You know, my uncle's neighborhood."

"Well . . . you can't see anything there, it's . . . scrambled."

She shrugged. "Just curious. You definitely can't see if you don't look."

True That seemed to take her point. He raised a hand in a way indicative of working with some kind of interface. But Zula's across-the-room conversation with him had become impossible as the larger group in the middle of the room had become very noisy. Not so much like professionals in a meeting. More in the manner of fans at a boxing match.

So Zula, along with everyone else, watched it happen. The Time Slip Ratio was definitely less than one, and so things happened slowly, on a time scale that reminded her of grand opera, where a twenty-minute aria might stand in for what normal people would cover in a quick exchange of text messages. Some kind of epic slugfest was taking place between El and a rock monster. All kinds of other things were going on too and were being excitedly noticed and pointed to by various onlookers. A lot of El's custom-made humanoids were galloping toward Escherville. Other humanoids, and things that moved like bears, were on the move with Verna, crossing a bridge luxuriant with flowered vines, forming a defensive perimeter.

Her growing sense of Uncle Claude–like confusion was—mercifully—broken by a touch on her elbow. It was True That. "Something you should see, ma'am."

"More so than all of *this*?" she exclaimed, gesturing at the melee in Escherville.

"I think so. Oh, and would you like a snack? It's after midnight." He proffered an energy bar or something, a gnarled confection of chocolate and granola. She accepted it gratefully, and chomped into it with artificial teeth.

She followed True That into the corner where he and his claque had been hanging out for the last few hours. They had extinguished their inscrutable data-viz-ware and replaced it with a rendering of a city.

It was a city she had never seen before. As she walked closer to it, she assumed it was somewhere in Europe. As she got closer, she began to think China. Some older burg, low lying, built on broken terrain, with an irregular medieval-style street pattern and the odd ancient castle. But it had been modernized with newer high-rises. One in particular rose above it all: a dark tower that somehow managed to combine features of a modern skyscraper and an ancient fortification.

The only thing that made it *not* look like a realistic rendering of a city on Earth was a huge figure poised atop that tower. It had wings. Leathery, not feathery. It was gazing downward in a brooding way at a big lake below the tower. The lake was almost perfectly circular.

"What is that?" Zula asked.

"Landform Two," True That said. "Uncloaked. This is the first time we've ever actually seen what it looks like. As you know. Ma'am."

"And the figure on the top of the tower is—"

He nodded. "The REAP."

It was about then that the whole room came apart into pandemonium as, apparently, very dramatic and exciting things happened in Escherville. Zula didn't know what to look at. The REAP spread his wings and sprang into the air. He was diving into the lake. But he did so in slow motion.

A few minutes after disappearing beneath the surface of the round lake, he popped up in Escherville, on top of the castle that he had built there long ago. The stuff El had bolted around it had all fallen off. She couldn't make out where her daughter was. This distressed her as a mother.

Much as she wanted to stare at Landform 2, nothing was going on there. All of the Pantheon had followed Dodge (there was no point in calling him anything else now) through the portal that apparently connected the lake to the unshackled castle. So she made her way back to the place where everyone was watching that. Some kind of slow-motion melee played out. The rock monster made another appearance and bear-hugged El into a canyon. People screamed, not so much in horror as in sheer astonishment.

Long ago in the early days of the Pantheon, Zula had got in the habit—which she knew at some level was lazy and wrongheaded—of identifying certain of its members with classical deities of antiquity. Dodge was some combination of Zeus and God. Pluto was, well, Pluto. One of them had always struck her as very Mercury-like in the way he moved about. Another she saw as a kind of Mars. Not that there were a lot of wars to fight in those days, but he was big and seemed to serve as a kind of bouncer. Since they spent all their time in Landform 2, it had been decades since she had seen them.

But there they were, embroiled in this melee around Escherville. Two of them—"Mars" and "Mercury"—took flight, headed south. Whoever was controlling the display made it zoom out so that the spectators could keep those two in view. They were winging southward, soaring over snowcapped mountains, and pretty obviously headed for the palace on the pinnacle. Time was speeding up again as things stabilized. Even so, covering that distance took them a little while. Spectators went out for bathroom breaks or snacks, leaving Zula largely alone. She stood there for a long time watching Dodge, who was tending to something very small and faint that he had cupped in his hand.

Mars and Mercury landed atop the palace without opposition. Meanwhile, back in Escherville, Dodge flew to the top of his castle, then dove into the crack that ran beneath it. Zula, getting the hang of it, swiveled her head toward the Landform 2 display. Sure enough, Dodge emerged a bit later from the round lake in the middle of the city. He beat his wings to gain altitude, then spread them wide to come in for a landing on the top of his dark tower.

At the same moment, in a strikingly symmetrical way, back over in the middle of Landform 1, Mercury rose up into the air above the white tower. In one hand he was holding a thing that looked like a horn. He raised this to his lips, and blew.

They could not hear the sound of it, but they could *see* it spreading outward like a shock wave. Above, this dissipated into the sky like one of those ice halos sometimes visible around the sun on a cold day. But below, as it propagated downward along the sheer shaft of the pinnacle, it seemed to touch off a disturbance in the hivelike cellular structure that had grown around the rock. This was a little like seeing a trail of gunpowder flash into smoke. Or one of those things atomic scientists used to see the trails of subatomic particles through vapor. A cloud chamber. But too it put her in mind of buds unfurling in time-lapse.

It propagated quickly down the skinny part of the pinnacle where the hive was thin but slowed dramatically as it reached the lower stretch where it broadened to include many more cells.

And at some point, the display simply froze up. She turned toward Landform 2 and saw it frozen as well. She heard a man, an older chap, making a joke about needing to reboot the projector—a reference that meant nothing to most of the people in the room.

"It's not actually frozen," someone explained. "The Time Slip Ratio has dropped to *ten to the minus three*. And still dropping." Meaning that a thousand or more seconds had to elapse in Meatspace to simulate one second of time in Bitworld.

"I see it changing though!" Eva exclaimed. She sounded so convinced of this that Zula maneuvered closer to where she was standing, trying to see it. Eva was gazing at "Mercury," suspended above the palace with wings spread wide, horn pressed to his lips. And something about him created the most extraordinary impression in Zula's mind. He was not moving. And yet he was changing all the time. Changing for the better. His wings, his hair, the expression on his face: the display simply couldn't update itself fast enough to capture all the detail.

Zula was remembering her early days working for Dodge's video game company, when the graphics cards that drew the pixels on your screen sometimes just didn't have the oomph to get the job done and so you would have to turn down the resolution, slow the frame rate, get rid of the fancy textures, just so you could play the game at full speed. It made everything look bad, but sometimes you just had to do it. When you turned that stuff back on, it was striking how beautiful, how real, the graphics could look.

What was now clear to her was that all her seeing of the Landform up until now had been with the graphics turned down to the fast-but-crappy setting. It had to be that way, for the LVU to keep up with the pace of events in Bitworld.

"Ten to the minus four," someone intoned. "Just unbelievable."

Ten thousand seconds—about three hours—now had to go by to simulate one second of time in Bitworld. The system was overwhelmed.

"But everything's still basically *working*, right?" Eva asked.

"Perfectly." Meaning that the processes who inhabited Bit-world were not experiencing it any differently than they had been before this slowdown. The flow of time, the qualia they experienced, were all the same.

And what qualia! Zula stepped in even closer. Every hair on Mercury's head was now being rendered by graphics algorithms that suddenly had a lot of time on their hands and that had been turned up to eleven. The sun was not only bouncing off of but refracting through every shaft of hair, making it both gleam and glow. The lenses of his eyes glistened with moisture, and she could see that he was just about to begin weeping. But the tear in the corner of his eye had not yet broken loose. She could see the world reflected in it.

He was beautiful. The whole place was beautiful.

"Makes you want to go there, doesn't it?" asked a man's voice, just next to her.

She turned to see that older chap who had made the joke earlier, and recognized him as Enoch Root.

"Did you really just ask me if I want to die?" she shot back.

He just got a wry look and said nothing. As if she had caught him out in some mischief.

"Why don't *you* have a go," she suggested, "and send me a message back from the next world?"

"I still have responsibilities in the previous one," he answered.

"So this has happened before?" she asked. She began strolling over toward the visualization of Landform 2, where Dodge—Egdod—the REAP—whatever you wanted to call him—was poised, wings spread, above the top of his dark tower.

"Perhaps not *this,*" said Enoch, walking by her side, "but—"

"You know what I mean."

"Yes," he confirmed.

"Ten to the minus five!" called True That. He was speaking a little distractedly, as he was fascinated by the appearance of Dodge.

"It's all because of what is going on in the hive," confirmed Eva. She'd been checking out some stats, evidently. "The processes in those cells are breaking loose—emerging into the world—like larvae coming out of their cocoons. Seeing the Landform for the first time, thinking, interacting. It's like we're uploading thousands of new processes every second. And it's only going to get more so."

"Ten to the minus six."

"What are we going to do with all our free time?" someone joked.

"Look at basically freeze-frames," Eva guessed. "Like illustrations in an old paper book, sort of."

Zula had now drawn close enough to confirm that Dodge's graphics had also been turned up to eleven. His face was not exactly that of Richard Forthrast, but his expressions matched what she remembered of her uncle. His gaze was intent upon the cupped palm of his hand, where nestled a tiny burst of finely structured light. In its complexity she imagined she could see the beginnings of a human form.

"I understand the speed of light!" she blurted.

Faces turned toward her, gawped, then turned away. A hundred years ago, someone would have taken her up on the gambit. Now people were too intimidated—or perhaps they assumed she was finally losing it.

Except for Enoch. "Explain it," he urged her. "I've always wanted to understand."

"Ever since I was a child, I've been hearing physicists insist that nothing can travel faster than light. That it would break the universe somehow. Something to do with causality."

"You can't have an effect until the cause has arrived," Enoch said, nodding. "And causes can only travel so fast."

"Never completely made sense to me when it was explained that way. Seemed arbitrary. Like a rule that had been imposed from outside the system."

Enoch was nodding and smiling.

Zula went on, "But it's what *we* are doing *at this very moment* to Bitworld! We are saying that according to the rules of the simulation, everything, everywhere, has to march forward in lockstep. As much as we might like to see how it all comes out—whether that tear is going to break loose from Mercury's eye, for example—we *may not*. We can't throw more mana at it and fast-forward that one part of the simulation, because then it would be out of sync with all the other parts. It would break the world."

"And we can't have that, can we?"

"No! We can't have that, Enoch."

Enoch looked over at the frozen god. "This is not going to change for a very long time," he said, "for the reason that you just mentioned. There are young people here who may spend the next ten years of their lives managing the systems in orbit above us that will generate the next few moments of time in Bitworld. But you know what?"

"No. What?"

Enoch pivoted so that he was standing beside her, and bent his arm in what Zula recognized as a very old-fashioned courtly sort of gesture. She reached out with some caution, not wanting to poke him with her exoskeleton, and took it. "Outside," Enoch said in a quiet voice just for her, "the sun is about to come up on the other side of the hill."

"We've been here all night!?"

"We've been here all night," he confirmed, "and I don't know about you but I could use some fresh air and a leg stretch."

Without really talking about it, they walked in the general direction of the place where she had been living for the last few years, on the top of Capitol Hill. She had moved back up there after she'd become bored of the houseboat on the lake. The whole point of the boat had been to provide her with a flat walk to work, after her knees had gone bust. But the modern Fronk had no difficulty with hills and she had felt like getting a place with more of a view. So she had moved to a huge old mansion up on the crest of the hill, a thing built in the early 1900s for a ten-child family with a full complement of servants. It had been sitting empty for a while. She had acquired similar properties to either side of it, knocked the houses down, and converted their lots to gardens. It had amused her to populate these with small creatures, and so they now supported a carefully tended fake ecosystem of chickens, peacocks, goats, alpacas, and a pair of big mellow dogs. It was being looked after by a couple of young people who had been staying in her house for the last few months. She had forgotten their names. Having children was now an eccentric activity, so it was a good bet that their parents were what they had used to call hippies, or at least artists. Anyway they liked animals and enjoyed looking after them and had nothing else to do.

As they ascended, she fancied for a moment that something had gone awry with her vision system, for everything began to look soft, and she couldn't see as far. She drew air into her lungs. One of those was the original, the other had gone on the blink some while ago and been replaced with a brand-new printed substitute. Anyway, when she drew the cool air into her new and her old lung, she sensed it was heavy and humid. Then she understood that up on the heights where the air was cold, it was foggy. Or, to put it another way, she and Enoch had, in a quite literal and technical sense, ascended into the clouds.

The time of year was late fall. Some leaves were still on the trees, and many more on the ground, but the color had gone from them, unless you considered dark brown to be a color. The lack of foliage drew attention to the trees themselves. These had become rampant. Planted along the streets two hundred years ago, they must have been mere saplings when the neighborhoods were new. By the time young Zula had moved to town, they had become problems. Their roots heaved up sidewalks and made great ripples across old red-brick streets. Their limbs fell off in windstorms. Their branches interfered with utility lines. Taxpayers paid for crews of arborists to roam about cutting weird rectangular vacancies in them for wires to run through. Paving crews did what they could about root damage.

Those days were over, and had been for a long time. Modern vehicles were as likely to move about on legs as wheels, so no one really cared about bumps in pavement. Modern utilities ran underground. Even had those things not been the case, the tax base wasn't there to support all those arborists and pavers. So the trees—all of them deciduous imports from the East Coast or Europe—had been doing as they pleased for decades. And what pleased them was apparently getting drunk on sky-high levels of atmospheric CO_2 and flinging out roots and limbs as wide as they possibly could. Capitol Hill was becoming a forest straight out of Northern European high-fantasy literature. The fog was now becoming tinged with pink and gold light as the rising sun shone on it, and the boughs of the trees cast shadows through that.

They reached her neighborhood, where the trees were hugest, and linked by nearly as ancient hedges of laurel and holly. A soft glow pervaded everything and tinged solid objects with iridescence. Beyond that, there was nothing. No sky, no neighboring houses, no trees, no mountains. The fog had clamped it all off. It muffled sound too. Not that there was much of that in a half-abandoned city where vehicles were a thing of the past. She and Enoch were existing in a bubble of space maybe a hundred paces across. Beyond it, as she knew perfectly well, was a whole world. But one of the delicious qualia that emerged from certain kinds of weather—snowfall was another of them—was the childish illusion that the world really was small and simple enough to be comprehended within a glance. And that she, the one doing the glancing, was always at its center.

She wondered if it had been thus for Dodge in the beginning, when he had been alone in Bitworld and the Landform had begun to take shape around him.

"This is where I leave you," said the voice of Enoch.

"Where on earth are you going?" Zula asked, looking about for him. But she had lost him in the radiant fog.

His voice was clear, though. It was the only sound in the world.

"I'm not entirely sure," he admitted. "But I'm done *here*. I did what I was sent to do."

The golden light grew until it was all she could see, and his voice was heard no more.

56

D odge became conscious.

He had slept well despite dreaming long elaborate dreams about the other plane of existence. The sun had awakened him, rising above the rim of the distant Land and flooding the Firmament with light.

He had slept, as he did most nights, on the open lid of a tower that rose high above the streets of the city. For many years the lid had been an open and featureless disk of stone, but more recently he had raised a ring of pillars around its edge, and between the pillars Spring had caused vines to grow and interweave to make a low barrier. It came only to midthigh on Dodge, but it was high enough to prevent a little soul from toppling over the edge.

Spring had not slept with him last night, though. When Dodge got to his feet and strolled over to the western side of his tower he could look across several miles of city to the park. For long ages that had been a mound of rubble that the souls of the Firmament had carried there, one back-load at a time, and piled up as they had patiently excavated and reshaped the cratered landscape where they had come to rest on the day of the Fall. Thus they had built the city with its black streets lit by fire. But the rubble pile had not become a park until Spring had gone to it and begun to adorn it with her creations.

He spread his wings and beat up into the air. His destination would be the park, but, as was his habit, he took a brief excursion around the city first. Its buildings tended to be of regular shapes with straight sides and edges, framed of stone and faced with glass to afford views and admit light. But they were built along streets that since the beginning of the Second Age had veered round diverse hazards and obstructions. Most prominent of all such was the crater that Egdod had made when he had smashed into the Firmament and broken it. This was now a circular pond of chaos round whose shores many buildings had been erected out of the ring of rubble that had once surrounded it. Dodge flew over that, as he always did, and gazed down into it. In its depths he saw the Fastness. He could tell at a glance that all was well there. In its towers and courtyards would be many souls whose work it was to look after those realms of the Land where Egdod held sway. No doubt many of them would have news to relate and questions to ask. But there was nothing that required his attention this morning.

Satisfied of that, he banked round over the district between the crater and the park. In the midst of that, a new building had gone up of late. Pick's Cube, they called it. It was sheathed in adamant and styled after the Cube from which the members of the Quest had retrieved the key. They had named it after the soul who had fallen just short of that goal. On its roof, well back from the edges so that it could not be seen from the streets, was a perch surrounded by bones, and on the perch was a giant talking raven.

Though it was early in the day, Dodge could see Querc approaching its front door. She divided her time between Land and Firmament. While she was here, she worked in Pick's Cube with Thingor and Corvus and Knotweave and other curious souls who were skilled at plumbing the deep nature of things. They strove to divine the hidden secrets of the other plane of existence and to fashion ever tinier and more sophisticated machines.

Spring could force a tree to grow tall in an hour if that was what she wanted, but she preferred to let them take their time. Only a few years had passed since the Fastness had been unchained. She had begun coming here to look after the park, and so most of what grew here was flowers and vines and grasses. In one place Dodge had caused stone arches to curve out of the rubble and enclose a little place where he had set an adamant bench and a low table. Spring had made flowering vines grow exuberantly on the arches, covering the stone altogether to make a vaulted bower of blossoms just now opening their petals and turning toward the sun.

The girl was waiting on the bench just as she did every morning. She was paging quietly through one of the picture books strewn about the table. Egdod sat next to her. "You've lost our place!" he exclaimed in mock dismay. "How are we going to pick up the story now?"

Sophia knew perfectly well that her uncle was only teasing her. "We were almost at the end!" she chided him. "I went back to look at the picture of the lady with the yellow hair. In the white temple. She's pretty! But mean. She was cruel to poor Prim."

"Yes, she was."

"I wish she was dead!"

"You should *never*," Dodge said, "wish that of anyone. Just imagine: what if your wish came true?"

But Sophia had already lost interest in the picture of the lady with the yellow hair and paged forward to very near the end of the book. "We were here," she said, showing him a two-page illustration crowded with small figures. It was a map of the Land, drawn in a childlike style with oversized buildings and other features here and there: the Palace in the middle atop its Pinnacle, the Fastness to its north amid snow-covered mountains, cities along the western coast, and various castles and legendary beasts scattered among the Bits and in the ocean beyond.

"Right!" Dodge said. "Where were we?"

Sophia reminded him by putting her fingertip on a depiction of a boat sailing in the western ocean. Aboard was a dark-skinned woman, decorated with jewels and markings on her skin.

"Fern had finally seen what she had been searching for ever since the sea monster had taken her family when she was a little girl," Dodge said. "Having seen it, she was satisfied, and wanted only to live a seafaring life. And since her new friends the Bufrects were famous mariners, she went with Mard and Lyne to Calla, and there built a boat and called it *Swab*."

Sophia's finger had already strayed to the island of Calla (she had heard this story a hundred times) and come to rest on a castle rising from the top of a green hill. "Hello, giant!" she said. "I see you!" For the artist had cleverly drawn the hill so that if you looked at it the right way you could see it as a hill-giant curled up on the ground sleeping.

"Ssh, you'll wake it up!"

"That's not what it says in the book!"

"All right. After King Brindle gave his life for the Quest, Paralonda Bufrect was the rightful queen of Calla. But she had no desire to rule and so she passed the crown to Prince Anvellyne."

"His friends called him Lyne," Sophia informed him gravely.

"And King Anvellyne ruled wisely over Calla with Mardellian as his closest friend, adviser, and . . ."

"Magician!"

"Mard the One-Handed became a wizard, yes. Together they saw to it that . . ."

Sophia's finger had already strayed north to a cottage surrounded by livestock. A white-haired woman was shown carrying a bushel of wheat on her hip. "Edda!"

". . . that Edda the Giantess was made to feel welcome whenever she chose to stay alone in her cottage. But she loved to wander back and forth between there and . . ."

Sophia's finger made a huge swipe eastward across Bits and Shivers and Bewilderment to a golden glen in the mountains not far from a towering black fortress.

"Yes," said Dodge, "the glen where she loved to spend time with her mother and her grandmother."

A wild look came into Sophia's eyes and she looked up into Dodge's face. "How tall *is* a giantess, Uncle Dodge?" she asked, as if she did not ask the same question every single day.

"As tall as she wants to be," said Dodge.